P9-CEG-440

"A REMARKABLE LITERARY ACHIEVEMENT . . . A WORK OF IMAGINATION, BRILLIANTLY WRITTEN AND INCREDIBLY TEXTURED . . . WINGROVE IS A CRAFTSMAN WHO HAS CREATED A MEMORABLE WORK OF FICTION."—*The Chattanooga Times*

Critical raves for
**DAVID WINGROVE**
and his magnificent saga of the future
**CHUNG KUO**

"WINGROVE HAS CONCEIVED AND EXECUTED A WORK ON AN UNPARALLELED SCALE!" —*Booklist*

"David Wingrove is one of the best writers in the field today and someone to watch for in the future."—*The Bookwatch*

"COMPELLING . . . Wingrove has fashioned his own literary shell. A nonexisting world that comes fully to life."—*Fort Worth Star-Telegram*

"PLENTY OF ACTION, meticulous wordbuilding and very respectable characterization."—*Chicago Sun-Times*

*Please turn the page for more extraordinary acclaim. . . .*

"AN INSTANT CLASSIC, EQUALING OR EVEN EXCEEDING ITS PRECURSORS—ISAAC ASIMOV'S FOUNDATION SERIES, JEAN AUEL'S EARTH CHILDREN BOOKS, AND ABOVE ALL, FRANK HERBERT'S MUCH-BELOVED DUNE SERIES."—*Fort Lauderdale Sun-Sentinel*

"SKILLFULLY WRITTEN descriptions of sexy sex, quick violence, and a generation-spanning struggle between good and evil."—*The Philadelphia Inquirer*

"GRAND, MAJESTIC . . . AN UNPARALLELED MASTERPIECE!"—*Daily News* (Woodland Hills, California)

"Wingrove is a powerful storyteller!"—*The Denver Post*

"MESMERIZING . . . A VAST, DETAILED FRESCO . . . WE'RE COMPLETELY IMMERSED IN A STRANGE NEW WORLD AS IT UNRAVELS, PAGE BY PAGE, BEFORE OUR EYES."—*The Milwaukee Journal*

"The achievement of a master world-builder."—*Omni*

"COMPLEX, EXOTIC, ENTICING—A RICH TAPESTRY OF INTRIGUE AND ACTION."—*The Providence Journal-Bulletin*

"EXOTIC, INTRIGUING . . . an imaginative, fast-paced exploration of the future."—*Library Journal*

"STUNNING, EVOCATIVE, FUN TO READ. . . . Let your imagination carry you for a fascinating ride."—*The Neshoba Democrat* (Mississippi)

"Cleverly conceived plots enhance the unusual premise of David Wingrove's epic creation."—*Pasadena Star-News*

"The reader is plunged into a world of sights, smells, and imagery vivid enough to sustain interest throughout."—*Salisbury Times* (Maryland)

# CHUNG | KUO

## BY | DAVID WINGROVE

### BOOK 7:
### DAYS OF
### BITTER STRENGTH

A DELL TRADE PAPERBACK

*For John and Ruth Murry*
*with love and affection, and in*
*remembrance of days in the Golden Valley*

A DELL TRADE PAPERBACK

Published by
Dell Publishing
a division of
Bantam Doubleday Dell Publishing Group, Inc.
1540 Broadway
New York, New York 10036

If you purchased this book without a cover you should be aware
that this book is stolen property. It was reported as "unsold and
destroyed" to the publisher and neither the author nor the
publisher has received any payment for this "stripped book."

Copyright © 1997 by David Wingrove

All rights reserved. No part of this book may be reproduced or
transmitted in any form or by any means, electronic or
mechanical, including photocopying, recording, or by any
information storage and retrieval system, without the written
permission of the Publisher, except where permitted by law.

The trademark Dell® is registered in the U.S. Patent and
Trademark Office.

Library of Congress Cataloging in Publication Data
Wingrove, David.
Days of bitter strength / by David Wingrove.
p.    cm.—(Chung Kuo; bk. 7)
ISBN 0-440-50794-4
I. Title.   II. Series: Wingrove, David. Chung Kuo; bk. 7.
PR6073.I545C5   1990   Vol. 7
823'.914—dc21                  96-47793
CIP

Printed in the United States of America

Published simultaneously in Canada

August 1997

10   9   8   7   6   5   4   3   2   1

BVG

When the oak at last had fallen,
And the evil tree was leveled,
Once again the sun shone brightly,
And the pleasant moonlight glimmered,
And the clouds extended widely,
And the rainbow spanned the heavens,
O'er the cloud-encompassed headland,
And the island's hazy summit.

—*The Kalevala*

# CONTENTS

## BOOK 7
# Days of
# Bitter Strength

# MAJOR CHARACTERS

*Ascher*, Emily——Trained as an economist, she was once a member of the *Ping Tiao* revolutionary party. After their demise she fled to North America, where, under the alias of Mary Jennings, she got a job with the giant ImmVac corporation, working for Old Man Lever and his son, Michael, whom she finally married. When America fell she fled with Michael to Europe, but tiring of that high-level social world she went back down the levels and became a terrorist again. It was while undertaking a terrorist mission that she was attacked and badly wounded. Lin Shang, a simple "mender," found her there and nursed her back to health. Now, almost two decades on, she is still with him—his constant companion.

*DeVore*, Howard——A onetime Major in the T'ang's Security forces, he has become the leading figure in the struggle against the Seven. A highly intelligent and coldly logical man, he is the puppet master behind the scenes as the great War of the Two Directions takes a new turn. Defeated first on Chung Kuo and then on Mars, he fled outward, to the tenth planet, Pluto, and its twin, Charon. From there he launched a new, massive attack on Chung Kuo, which was only defeated at great cost to Li Yuan and his allies. Now, after a dozen years away, he is set to return.

*Ebert*, Hans——Son of Klaus Ebert and heir to the vast GenSyn Corporation, he was promoted to General in Li Yuan's Security forces, and was admired and trusted by his superiors. Secretly, however, he was allied to DeVore, and was subsequently implicated in the murder of his father. Having fled Chung Kuo, he was declared a traitor in his absence. After suffering exile he found himself again, among the lost African tribe, the Osu, among the desert sands of Mars, where he became their spiritual leader, the "Walker in the Darkness." Returning to Chung Kuo, he played a major part in helping Li Yuan defeat DeVore and was pardoned for it. Now he lives with the Osu in their new homelands in Africa.

*Karr,* Gregor——Marshal of the European Security forces, he was recruited by General Tolonen from the Net. In his youth he was a "blood"—a to-the-death combat fighter. A huge man physically, he is also one of Li Yuan's "most-trusted men." As a respected pillar of society and the father of four growing daughters, he has risen beyond all early expectations and is now a pivotal figure in the politics of City Europe.

*Li Yuan*——T'ang of Europe and one of the Seven, as second son of Li Shai Tung, he inherited after the deaths of his brother and father. Considered old before his time, he nonetheless has a passionate side to his nature, as demonstrated in his brief marriage to his brother's wife, the beautiful Fei Yen. His subsequent remarriages ended in tragedy when his three wives were assassinated. Despite his subsequent remarriage to Pei K'ung, his real concern is for his son, Kuei Jen.

*Pei K'ung*——Fifth wife of Li Yuan, she is eighteen years his elder and a plain, straightforward woman from a Minor Family background. Ten years ago she was handed the reins of domestic government by Li Yuan and that experience has changed her profoundly, as has her belated discovery of sex in all its forms.

*Shepherd,* Ben——Great-great-grandson of City Earth's architect, Shepherd was brought up in the Domain, an idyllic valley in the southwest of England, where he pursues his artistic calling, developing a new art form, the "Shell": a machine that mimics the experience of life. In his middle years, however, he has become far more involved in politics and—against all expectations—is now Li Yuan's closest adviser.

*Ward,* Jelka——Daughter of Marshal Tolonen, Jelka was brought up in a very masculine environment, lacking in a mother's love and influence. Yet her attempts to recreate herself—to find a balance in her life—have only brought her into conflict, first with a young soldier, and then with her father, who—to prevent her having a relationship with Kim Ward—dispatched her on a tour of the Colony Planets. Returned, she married Kim and is now his inseparable helpmeet and mother of his two children, Sampsa and Mileja.

*Ward,* Kim——Born in the Clay, that dark wasteland beneath the great City's foundations, Kim has survived various personal crises to become Chung Kuo's leading experimental scientist. Hired by the massive SimFic Corporation as a commodity-slave on a seven-year contract, he finally achieved his ambition of marrying the Marshal's daughter. Now, as head of NorTek Europe, he is one of City Europe's richest and most powerful men.

# LIST OF CHARACTERS

## THE SEVEN AND THE FAMILIES

Hsiang Lu Yeh—Minor Family Prince

Hsun Chu-lo—Minor Family Princess and first daughter of Hsun Teh

Hsun Lung hsin—"Dragon Heart"; Minor Family Princess and second daughter of Hsun Teh

Hsun Teh—Head of the Hsun Family (one of the Twenty-Nine Minor Families)

Li Kuei Jen—son of Li Yuan and heir to City Europe

Li Pei K'ung—wife of Li Yuan

Li Yuan—T'ang of City Europe

Yin Fei Yen—"Flying Swallow"; Minor Family Princess and divorced wife of Li Yuan

## FRIENDS AND RETAINERS OF THE SEVEN

Adler—General in Security, City Europe

Bell—Colonel in charge of Security, Bremen spaceport

Bujold—General in Security, City Europe

Carl—security guard at Karr's mansion

Chang Li—Senior Surgeon at the San Chang

Chao Chung—Senior Warden of Edingen Prison

Cheng Nai shan—assistant to Ming Ai

Chu Po—lover of Pei K'ung

Chu Te—Commissioner for Mainz

Dawes, Richard—Security Captain reporting to I Ye

Ebert, Pauli—bastard son of Hans Ebert and Golden Heart and Head of the GenSyn Corporation

Edmonds—Captain of Security

Egan, Josiah—Head of NorTek America and grandfather of Mark Egan

Egan, Mark—grandson of Old Man Egan

Farren—General; Commander of City Europe's Second Banner

Fen Chun—First Secretary to Heng Yu

Haavikko, Axel—Colonel in Security

Hagenau, Horst—Major in Security, working for Karr

Haller—Security operative

Hart—General in Security, City Europe

Heng Yu—Chancellor of City Europe

Holzman, Daniel—palace guard

I Ye—Colonel, Chief of Security in the San Chang

Jia Shu—Steward in Li Yuan's palace

Kan—*Wei*, or Security Captain, of Kuang Hua *Hsien*

Karr, Gregor—Marshal of Security, City Europe

Kung Chia—*Wei*, or Security Captain, of Weisenau *Hsien*

Lai Wu—secretary to Cheng Nai shan

Lauther—Security Captain at Edingen Prison

Lo Wen—Master of *Wushu* and tutor to Li Kuei Jen

Ming Ai—Personal secretary to Pei K'ung

Nan Fa-hsien—Master of the Inner Chambers and eldest son of Nan Ho

Shepherd, Ben—"Shell artist" and Chief Adviser to Li Yuan

Steen—Captain of shuttle craft

Su Ping—*Hsien L'ing*, or District Magistrate, of Weisenau *Hsien*, and twin brother of Su Chun

Tanner, Charles—General in Security, City Europe

Tsui Ku—*Tai Shih lung*, or Court Astrologer, in the San Chang

Wang—*Hsien L'ing,* or District Magistrate, of Kuang Hua *Hsien*

Ward, Jelka—wife of Kim Ward; daughter of Knut Tolonen

Ward, Kim—Clayborn scientist; owner of the NorTek Corporation of Europe

Wen—Steward in the San Chang

Wiley—Captain of Security, Edingen Prison

Yun—Third Cook on the imperial barge

### OTHER CHARACTERS

Ai Lin—Sampsa Ward's girlfriend and twin to Lu Yi

Ascher, Emily—real name of Emily Lin

Calder, Alan—Mashhad-born terrorist

Calder, Eva—sister of Alan Calder and maid to Warlord Hu

Chan Sang—maid to Michael Lever

Chao Ta-nien—"Slow Chao," Red Pole to the Iron Fist Triad

Cho Yao—*Lu Nan Jen,* or "Oven Man"

Chou—third-year schoolboy at the Seventh District School

Chuang Kuan Ts'ai—"Coffin-filler," adopted daughter of Cho Yao

Chung—"Ice Man" Chung, Big Boss of the Iron Fist Triad

Costas—friend of Alan Calder

Curval, Andrew—Head of Research, NorTek Europe

Dogu—infant son of Catherine Shepherd

Eduard—guard in Marshal Karr's employ

Fang Sheng-chih—neighbor of Emily Ascher and Lin Shang

Hamsun, Torve—Captain of the *Luoyang*

Hannah—anglicized name of Shang Han A

Harris, Joseph—young host at the *Ch'a Hao T'ai,* the "Directory"

Hei Fong—merchant

Ho—"Madam Ho," owner of a brothel in Hattersheim *Hsien*

Ho Ko—"Harmonious Song"; singsong girl on the flower boats

Ho Tse-tsu—Third Secretary to Su Ping

Horacek, Bara—Mother of Josef Horacek

Horacek, Josef—son of Vilem and Bara Horacek

Horacek, Vilem—Father of Josef Horacek

Hu Feng-lo—second son of Warlord Hu

Hu Wang-chih—Warlord of the Mashhad Region

Ishida, Ikuro—Japanese asteroid miner

Ishida, Kano—eldest brother of Ikuro Ishida

Ishida, Shukaku—eighth brother of Ikuro Ishida

Kao Chen—ex-Major in Security; plantation worker

Kao Jyan—eldest son of Kao Chen

James—friend of Alan Calder

Ji Wang—First Minister to Warlord Hu

Johnson, Daniel—Personal Assistant to Michael Lever

Judd—boy in the tunnels

Jung—madman

Jung Wang—the madman's wife

Karr, Beth—youngest daughter of Gregor and Marie Karr

Karr, Hannah—daughter of Gregor and Marie Karr

Karr, Lily—daughter of Gregor and Marie Karr

Karr, Marie—wife of Gregor Karr

Karr, May—eldest daughter of Gregor and Marie Karr

Lever, Michael—Head of the ImmVac pharmaceutical corporation

Lin Chao—eldest adopted son of Lin Shang and Emily Ascher

Lin Chia—adopted son of Lin Shang and Emily Ascher

Lin, Emily—partner of Lin Shang; real name Emily Ascher

Lin Han Ye—adopted son of Lin Shang and Emily Ascher

Tu Fan—triad runner

Tung Po-jen—club owner in Bockenheim *Hsien*

Tung Wei—merchant in Weisenau *Hsien*

Tybor—one of DeVore's new morphs, his
    *Inheritors*

Wang Ti—wife of Kao Chen

Ward, Mileja—infant daughter of Jelka and Kim Ward

Ward, Sampsa—son of Jelka and Kim Ward

Wei Yu—First Steward to Michael Lever

Wen—"Big Wen," butcher in Weisenau
    marketplace

Wen—"Old Wen," boatman for the flower boats

Wen Ch'ang—assistant to Kim Ward; also known as
    Tuan Wen-ch'ang

Yang Chung—trivee actor; hero in *Moving the Mountain*

Yang Wei—"Old Wang"; hardware-store owner

## THE OSU

Dogo—one of the "eight"

Echewa, Aluko—Headman and one of the "eight"

Efulefu—"Worthless Man"; chosen name of Hans
    Ebert among the Osu

Nza—"Tiny bird," an Osu child, adopted by
    Hans Ebert, and one of the "eight"

## THE DEAD

Althaus, Kurt—General of Security, North America

An Hsi—Minor Family Prince and fifth son of An
    Sheng

An Liang-chou—Minor Family Prince

An Mo Shan—Minor Family Prince and third son of
    An Sheng

An Sheng—head of the An Family (one of the
    Twenty-Nine Minor Families)

Anderson, Leonid—Director of the Recruitment Project

Anna—helper to Mary Lever

Anne—Yu assassin

Ashman—henchman of Pasek

Barrett—GenSyn "sport"; brothel-keeper in the Clay

Barrow, Chao—Secretary of the House at Weimar

Barycz, Jiri—scientist on the Wiring Project

Bates—leading figure in the Federation of Free Men, Mars

Beinlich—ex-Security lieutenant, working for Von Pasenow

Bercott, Andrei—Representative at Weimar

Berdichev, Soren—head of SimFic and later leader of the Dispersionist faction

Berdichev, Ylva—wife of Soren Berdichev

Berrenson—Company Head

Bess—helper to Mary Lever

Blaskic—henchman of Pasek

Blofeld—agent of special security forces

Blonegek—"Greasy"; Clayman civilized by Ben Shepherd

Brock—security guard in the Domain

Brookes, Thomas—Port Captain, Tien Men K'ou, Mars

Cao Chang—Financial Strategist to Stefan Lehmann

Chang Hong—Minister of Production, City Europe

Chang Te Li—"Old Chang," *Wu*, or Diviner

Chen So—Clerk of the Inner Chambers at Tongjiang

Ch'en Li—associate of Governor Schenck

Cheng Lu—Lehmann's ambassador to Fu Chiang's court

Cherkassky, Stefan—ex-Security assassin and friend of DeVore

Chi Hu Wei—T'ang of the Australias; father of Chi Hsing

Chih Huang Hui—second wife of Shang Mu and stepmother of Shang Han A

Ch'in Shih Huang Ti—the first emperor of China; ruled 221–
              210 B.C.
Cho Hsiang—Hong Cao's subordinate
Chou Te-hsing—Head of the Black Hand terrorists
Chu Heng—"*kwai,*" or hired knife; a hireling of
              DeVore's
Chu Shi-ch'e—*Pi-shu chien,* or Inspector of the Imperial
              Library at Tongjiang
Chuang Ko—private secretary to Tsu Ma
Chuang Tzu—ancient Han sage and Taoist philosopher
              from the sixth century B.C.
Chun Wu-chi—head of the Chun family (one of the
              Twenty-Nine Minor Families)
Chung Hsin—"Loyalty"; bondservant to Li Shai Tung
Clarac, Armand—Director of the "New Hope" Project
Coates—security guard in the Domain
Cook—duty guard in the Domain
Cornwell, James—director of the AutoMek corporation
Crefter—"Strong"; Clayman civilized by Ben
              Shepherd
Cui—Steward of Marshal Tolonen's household
Cutler, Richard—leader of the "America" movement
Dawson—associate of Governor Schenck
Deio—Clayborn friend of Kim Ward from
              "Rehabilitation"
Deng Liang—Minor Family Prince; fifth son of Deng
              Shang; Dispersionist
Dieter, Wilhelm—Black Hand cell leader
Donna—Yu assassin
Douglas, John—Company head; Dispersionist
Duchek, Albert—Administrator of Lodz
Ebert, Berta—wife of Klaus Ebert; mother of Hans
              Ebert
Ebert, Klaus—head of the GenSyn Corporation; father
              of Hans Ebert
Ebert, Lutz—half brother of Klaus Ebert
Ecker, Michael—Company head; Dispersionist
Edsel—agent of special security forces

Egan—head of NorTek

Ellis, Michael—assistant to Director Spatz on the Wiring Project

Endacott—associate of Governor Schenck

Endfors, Pietr—friend of Knut Tolonen and father of Jenny, Tolonen's wife

Erkki—guard to Jelka Tolonen

Eva—friend of Mary Lever

Eyre—henchman of Pasek

Fairbank, John—head of AmLab

Fan—fifth brother to the *I Lung*

Fen Cho-hsien—Chancellor of North America

Feng Chung—Big Boss of the Kuei Chuan (Black Dog) Triad

Feng Lu-ma—lensman

Feng Shang-pao—"General Feng"; Big Boss of the 14K Triad

Fest, Edgar—Captain in Security

Fox—Company Head

Franke, Rutger—Vice President of SimFic; Dispersionist

Fu Chiang—"The Priest," Big Boss of the Red Flower Triad of North Africa

Fu Ti Chang—third wife of Li Yuan

Fung—*Wu*, or Diviner, to Yin Fei Yen

Gesell, Bent—leader of the *Ping Tiao*—"Leveler"— terrorist movement

Golden Heart—concubine to Hans Ebert and mother of Pauli Ebert

Grant—henchman of Pasek

Green, Clive—head of RadMed

Griffin, James B.—last president of the American empire

Haavikko, Vesa—sister of Axel Haavikko

Hama—Osu wife of Hans Ebert

Hammond, Joel—Senior Technician on the Wiring Project

Hart, Alex—Representative at Weimar, Dispersionist and ally of Stefan Lehmann

Hastings, Thomas—physicist; Dispersionist

Henderson, Daniel—pro-tem Governor of Mars

Heng Chi-po—Li Shai Tung's Minister of Transportation

Henssa, Eero—Captain of the Guard aboard the floating palace Yangjing

Herrick—illegal transplant specialist

Ho Chang—merchant friend of Lin Shang and Emily Ascher, and onetime landlord to them

Ho Chin—"Three-Finger Ho"; Big Boss of the Yellow Banners Triad

Hoffmann—Major in Security

Hong Cao—middleman for Pietr Lehmann

Hooper—senior engineer aboard DeVore's craft

Hou Ti—T'ang of South America; father of Hou Tung-po

Hou Tung-po—T'ang of South America

Hsiang K'ai Fan—Minor Family Prince

Hsiang Shao-erh—head of the Hsiang family (one of the Twenty-Nine Minor Families)

Hsiang Wang—Minor Family Prince

Hsueh Chi—Big Boss of the Thousand Spears Triad of Southern Africa

Hsueh Nan—Warlord of Southern Africa and brother of Hsueh Chi

Hua Shang—lieutenant to Wong Yi-sun

Huang Peng—Steward at the Ebert Mansion

Hui Tsin—"Red Pole" (426, or Executioner) to the United Bamboo Triad

Hung Mien-lo—Chancellor of Africa

Hwa—Master "blood," or hand-to-hand fighter, below the Net

Hwa Kuei—Chief Steward of the Bedchamber to Tsu Ma

I Lung—"First Dragon," the head of the "Thousand Eyes," the Ministry

Jackson—freelance go-between, employed by Fairbank

Jeng Lo—Security Pilot, Rift Veteran

Jill—principal helper to Mary Lever

Joan—Yu assassin

Kan Jiang—Martian settler and poet

K'ang A-yin—gang boss of the Tu Sun tong

K'ang Yeh-su—nephew of K'ang A-yin

Kao Jyan—assassin; friend of Kao Chen

Kavanagh—Representative at Weimar and Leader of the House

Kemp, Johannes—director of ImmVac

Kennedy, Jean—wife of Joseph Kennedy

Kennedy, Joseph—head of the New Republican and Evolutionist Party and Representative at Weimar

Kennedy, Robert—elder son of Joseph Kennedy

Kennedy, William—younger son of Joseph Kennedy

Kennedy, William—great-great-grandfather of Joseph Kennedy

Krenek, Henryk—Senior Representative of the Martian Colonies

Krenek, Irina—wife of Henryk Krenek

Krenek, Josef—Company head

Krenek, Maria—wife of Josef Krenek

Kriz—senior Yu operative

Kubinyi—lieutenant to DeVore

Kung Wen-fa—Senior Advocate from Mars

K'ung Fu Tzu—Confucius (551–479 B.C.)

Kustow, Bryn—American; friend of Michael Lever

Kygek—"Fat"; Clayman civilized by Ben Shepherd

Lai Shi—second wife of Li Yuan

Lao Jen—Junior Minister to Lwo Kang

Lao Kang—Chancellor of West Asia

Lasker—Captain, Decontamination, Ansbach *Hsien*

Lehmann, Pietr—Under-Secretary of the House of Representatives and first leader of the Dispersionist faction; father of Stefan Lehmann

Lehmann, Stefan—"The White T'ang"; Big Boss of the European Triads and onetime ally of DeVore

Lever, Charles—head of the giant ImmVac Corporation of North America; father of Michael Lever

Lever, Margaret—wife of Charles Lever and mother of Michael Lever

Li Chin—"Li the Lidless"; Big Boss of the Wo Shih Wo Triad

Li Ch'ing—T'ang of Europe; grandfather of Li Yuan

Li Han Ch'in—first son of Li Shai Tung and once heir to City Europe; brother of Li Yuan

Li Hang Ch'i—T'ang of Europe; great-great-grandfather of Li Yuan

Li Ho-nien—servant at the Ebert Mansion

Li Kou-lung—T'ang of Europe; great-grandfather of Li Yuan

Li Pai Shung—nephew of Li Chin; heir to the Wo Shih Wo Triad

Li Shai Tung—T'ang of Europe; father of Li Yuan

Lin Pan—Uncle Pan; adopted uncle of Lin Shang

Lin Yuan—first wife of Li Shai Tung; mother of Li Han Ch'in and Li Yuan

Ling—"Old Mother Ling," worker on the Kosaya Gora Plantation

Ling Hen—henchman for Herrick

Liu Chang—brothel keeper/pimp

Liu Tong—lieutenant to Li Chin

Lo Chang—Steward at the Ebert Mansion

Lo Han—tong boss

Lu—surgeon at Tongjiang

Lu Ming-shao—"Whiskers Lu"; Big Boss of the Kuei Chuan Triad

Luke—Clayborn friend of Kim Ward from "Rehabilitation"

Lwo Kang—Li Shai Tung's Minister of the Edict

Ma Ching—servant at the Ebert Mansion

Maitland, Idris—mother of Stefan Lehmann

Man Hsi—tong boss

Mao Liang—Minor Family Princess and member of the *Ping Tiao* "Council of Five"

Mao Tse Tung—first Ko Ming emperor (ruled A.D. 1948–1976)

Matyas—Clayborn boy in Recruitment Project

Melfi, Alexandra—wife of Amos Shepherd and real mother of the Shepherd boys

Meng K'ai—friend and adviser to Governor Schenck

Meng Te—lieutenant to Lu Ming-shao

Mien Shan—first wife of Li Yuan; mother of Li Kuei Jen

Milne, Michael—private investigator

Ming Huang—sixth T'ang emperor (ruled A.D. 713–755)

Mo Nan-ling—"The Little Emperor"; Big Boss of the Nine Emperors Triad of Central Africa

Mo Yu—Security lieutenant in the Domain

Moore, John—Company head; Dispersionist

Morel—The "Myghtern," King under the City

Mu Chua—Madam of the House of the Ninth Ecstasy

Mu Li—"Iron Mu," Boss of the Big Circle Triad

Nan Ho—Chancellor of City Europe

Nan Tsing—first wife of Nan Ho

Needham—Captain of *Shen T'se* elite security squad

Nolen, William—Public Relations Executive; Dispersionist

Pao En-fu—Master of the Inner Chambers to Wu Shih

Parr, Charles—Company head; Dispersionist

Pavel—young man on Plantation

Peck—lieutenant to K'ang A-yin (a *ying tzu*, or "shadow")

Pei Ro-hen—Head of the Pei Family (one of the Twenty-Nine Minor Families) and father of Pei K'ung

Peng—Madam Peng; matchmaker

Si Wu Ya—"Silk Raven," wife of Supervisor Sung

Song Wei—sweeper

Soucek, Jiri—lieutenant to Stefan Lehmann

Spatz, Gustav—Director of the Wiring Project

Spence, Leena—"Immortal," and onetime lover of Charles Lever

Ssu Lu Shan—official of the Ministry

Steiger—Director of the Shen Chang Fang of Milan

Steiner—Manager at ImmVac's Alexandria facility

Sun Li Hua—Wang Hsien's Master of the Inner Chambers

Sung—Supervisor on Plantation

Tak—the Myghtern's lieutenant

Tan Sui—White Paper Fan of the Red Flower Triad of North Africa

Tan Wei—Chief Eunuch at Tsu Ma's palace in Astrakhan

Tarrant—Company head

Teng Fu—plantation guard

Tewl—"Darkness"; chief of the raft people

Thorn—Security operative

Ting Ju-ch'ang—Warlord of Tunis

Todlich—giant morph

Tolonen, Hanna—aunt of Knut Tolonen

Tolonen, Helga—wife of Jon Tolonen; aunt of Jelka Tolonen

Tolonen, Jenny—wife of Knut Tolonen, and daughter of Pietr Endfors

Tolonen, Jon—brother of Marshal Knut Tolonen

Tolonen, Knut—Marshal of Security, Acting Head of the GenSyn Corporation; father of Jelka Tolonen

Tong Chu—assassin and "kwai" (hired knife)

Tsao Ch'un—tyrannical founder of Chung Kuo

Ts'ao Wu—cell leader in the Black Hand

Tsu Kung-chih—nephew of Tsu Ma

Tsu Ma—T'ang of West Asia; son of Tsu Tiao

Tsu Tiao—T'ang of West Asia; father of Tsu Ma

Tsu Tao Chu—nephew of Tsu Ma

Tu Ch'en-shih—friend and adviser to Governor Schenck

Tu Fu Wei—private secretary to Tsu Ma

Tu Mai—security guard in the Domain

Tung Cai—low-level rioter

Tung Chung-shu—MedFac's senior arts reviewer

Tynan, Edward—Above businessman and Representative
at Weimar; Dispersionist

Vesa—Yu assassin

Vierheller, Jane—Black Hand member

Virtanen, Per—Major in Li Yuan's Security forces

Visak—lieutenant to Lu Ming-shao

Von Pasenow—ex-Security Major

Wang—Steward at Astrakhan palace

Wang Chang Ye—first son of Wang Hsien

Wang Hsien—T'ang of Africa; father of Wang Sau-
leyan

Wang Lieh Tsu—second son of Wang Hsien

Wang Sau-leyan—T'ang of Africa

Wang Ta-hung—third son of Wang Hsien; elder brother
of Wang Sau-leyan

Wang Tu—leader of the Martian Radical Alliance

Wei Chan Yin—T'ang of East Asia

Wei Feng—T'ang of East Asia; father of Wei Chan
Yin and Wei Tseng-li

Wei Hsi Wang—second brother of Wei Chan Yin and
heir to City East Asia

Wei Tseng-li—T'ang of East Asia; younger brother of
Wei Chan Yin

Weis, Anton—banker; Dispersionist

Wells—Captain in Security, North America

Wen Ti—"First Ancestor" of City Earth/Chung
Kuo, otherwise known as Liu Heng;
ruled China 180–157 B.C.

Wiegand, Max—lieutenant to DeVore

Will—Clayborn friend of Kim Ward from
"Rehabilitation"

Wilson, Stephen—Captain in Security under Kao Chen

Wong Yi-sun—"Fat Wong"; Big Boss of the United Bamboo Triad

Wu Shih—T'ang of North America

Wu Wei-kou—first wife of Wu Shih

Wyatt, Edmund—Company head; Dispersionist

Yang—"Old Yang"; Deck Magistrate, employee of Lehmann

Yang Chih-wen—"The Bear," Big Boss of the Golden Ox Triad of West Africa

Yang Lai—Junior Minister to Lwo Kang

Yang Shao-fu—Minister of Health, City Europe

Ye—Senior Steward at Tongjiang

Yi Ching—Colonel of Internal Security to Tsu Ma at Astrakhan

Yi Shan-ch'i—Minor Family Prince

Yin Chan—Minor Family Prince and second son of Yin Tsu

Yin Shu—Junior Minister in the "Thousand Eyes," the Ministry

Yin Tsu—head of the Yin Family (one of the "Twenty-Nine" Minor Families) and father of Fei Yen

Ying Chai—assistant to Sun Li Hua

Ying Fu—assistant to Sun Li Hua

Yu I—proprietor of the Blue Pagoda teahouse

Yue Chun—"Red Pole" (426, or Executioner) to the Wo Shih Wo Triad

Yun Ch'o—lieutenant to Shen Lu Chua

Yun Yueh-hui—"Dead Man Yun"; Big Boss of the Red Gang Triad

Yung Chen—eunuch from the women's quarters in Tsu Ma's palace at Astrakhan

Ywe Hao—"Fine Moon"; female Yu terrorist

Ywe Kai-chang—father to Ywe Hao

# OF GIFTS AND STONES

Where did it all begin? When was the first step taken on that downward path that led to Armageddon? Perhaps it was on that fateful June day in 2043 when President James B. Griffin, last of the sixty-two presidents of the United States of America, was assassinated while attending a baseball game at Chicago's Comiskey Park.

The collapse of the sixty-nine States of the American Empire that followed and the subsequent disintegration of the allied Western economies brought a decade of chaos. What had begun as the "Pacific Century" was quickly renamed the "Century of Blood"—a period in which the only stability was to be found within the borders of China. It was from there—from the great landlocked province of Sichuan—that a young Han named Tsao Ch'un emerged.

Tsao Ch'un had a simple—some say brutal—cast of mind. He wanted to create a Utopia, a rigidly stable society that would last ten thousand years. But the price was high. In 2062 Japan, China's chief rival in the East, was the first victim of Tsao Ch'un's idiosyncratic approach to realpolitik when, without warning—following Japanese complaints about Chinese incursions in Korea—the Han leader bombed Honshu, concentrating his nuclear devices on the major population centers of Tokyo and Kyoto. When the dust cleared, three great Han armies swept the smaller islands of Kyushu and Shikoku, killing every Japanese they found, while the rest of Japan was blockaded by sea and air. Over the next twenty years they would do the same with the islands of Honshu and Hokkaido, turning the "islands of the gods" into a wasteland while the crumbling Western nation states looked away.

The eradication of Japan taught Tsao Ch'un many lessons. In future he sought "not to destroy but to exclude"—though his definition of *exclusion* often made it a synonym for destruction. As he built his great City—huge, mile-high spiderlike machines moving slowly outward from Pei Ch'ing, secreting vast, tomb-white hexagonal living sections, three hundred levels high and a kilometer to a side—so he peopled it, choosing carefully who was to live within its walls. As the City grew, so his servants went out among the indigenous populations he had conquered, searching among them for those who were free from physical disability, political dissidence, or religious bigotry. And where he encountered organized opposition he enlisted the aid of groups sympathetic to his aims to carry out his policies. In Southern Africa and North America, in Europe and the People's Democracy of Russia, huge movements grew up, supporting Tsao Ch'un and welcoming his "stability" after decades of chaos and suffering, only too pleased to share in his crusade of intolerance—his "Policy of Purity."

Only the Middle East proved problematic. There a great Jihad was launched against the Han—Moslems and Jews casting off centuries of enmity to fight against a common threat. Tsao Ch'un answered them as he had answered Japan. The Middle East and large parts of the Indian subcontinent were reduced to a radioactive wilderness. But it was in Africa that his policies were most nakedly displayed. There the native peoples were moved on before the encroaching City, and, like cattle, starved or died from exhaustion, driven on by the brutal Han armies. Following historical precedent City Africa was reseeded with Han settlers.

In terms of human suffering Tsao Ch'un's pacification of the globe was unprecedented. Contemporary estimates put the cost in human lives at well over three billion. But Tsao Ch'un was not content merely to eradicate all opposition, he wanted to destroy all knowledge of the Western-dominated past. Like the First Emperor, Ch'in Shih Huang Ti, twenty-four centuries before, he decided to rewrite the history books. Tsao Ch'un had his officials collect all books, all tapes, all recordings, allowing nothing that was not Han to enter his great City. Most of what they collected was simply burned, but not all. Some was adapted.

One group of Tsao Ch'un's advisers—a group of Scholar-Politicians who termed themselves the "Thousand Eyes"—persuaded their Master that it would not be enough simply to create a gap. That, they knew, would attract curiosity. What they proposed was more subtle and, in the long term, far more persuasive. With Tsao

Ch'un's blessing they set about reconstructing the history of the world, placing China at the center of everything—back in its rightful place, as they saw it. It was a lie, of course, yet a lie to which everyone subscribed . . . on pain of death.

But the lie was complex and powerful, and people soon forgot. New generations arose who knew nothing of the real past and to whom the whispers and rumors seemed mere fantasy in the face of the solid reality they saw all about them. The media fed them the illusion daily, until the illusion became, even for those who worked in the Ministry responsible, quite *real* and the documents they dealt with some strange aberration—a mass hallucination, almost a disease that had struck the Western peoples of the great Han Empire in its latter years. The officials at the Ministry even coined a term for it—*racial compensation*—laughing among themselves whenever they came across some clearly fantastic reference in an old book about quaint religious practices or races of black—think of it, *black!*—people.

Tsao Ch'un killed the old world. He buried it deep beneath his glacial City. But eventually his brutality and tyranny proved too much even for those who had helped him carry out his scheme. In 2087 his Council of Seven Ministers rose up against him, using North European mercenaries, and overthrew him, setting up a new government. They divided the world—Chung Kuo—among themselves, each calling himself T'ang, "King." But the new government was far stronger than the old, for the Seven made it so that no single one of them could act on any major issue without the consensus of his fellow T'ang. Adopting the morality of New Confucianism, they set about consolidating a "peace of ten thousand years." The keystone of this peace was the Edict of Technological Control, which regulated and, in effect, prevented change. Change had been the disease of the old, Western-dominated world. Change had brought its rapid and total collapse. But Change was alien to the Han. They would do away with Change for all time. Their borders were secured, the world was theirs—why should they not have peace and stability until the end of time? But the population grew and grew, filling the vast City, and, buried deep in the collective psyche of the European races, something began to stir—some long-buried memory of rapid evolutionary growth. Change was needed. Change was wanted. But the Seven were against Change.

For more than a century they succeeded and their great world-spanning City thrived. If a man worked hard he could climb the levels into a world of space and luxury, if he failed in business or committed a crime he would be demoted—down toward the crowded, stinking Lowers. Each man knew his place in the great scheme of things and obeyed the dictates of the Seven. Yet the pressures placed upon the system were great, and as the population climbed toward the forty-billion mark something had to give.

It began with the assassination of the Li Shai Tung's Minister, Lwo Kang, in 2196, the poor man blown into the next world along with his Junior Ministers while basking in the imperial solarium. The Seven—the great Lords and rulers of Chung Kuo—hit back at once, arresting Edmund Wyatt, one of the leading figures of the Dispersionist faction responsible for the Minister's death. But it was not to end there. Within days of the public execution of Wyatt in 2198, the Dispersionists—a coalition of high-powered merchants and politicians—struck another deadly blow, killing Li Han Ch'in, son of the T'ang, Li Shai Tung, and heir to City Europe, on the day of his wedding to the beautiful Fei Yen.

It might have ended there, with the decision of the Seven to take no action in reprisal for Prince Han's death—to adopt a policy of peaceful nonaction, *wuwei*—but for one man such a course of action could not be borne. Taking matters into his own hands, Li Shai Tung's General, Knut Tolonen, marched into the House of Representatives in Weimar and killed the leader of the Dispersionists, Under-Secretary Lehmann. It was an act almost guaranteed to tumble Chung Kuo into a bloody civil war unless the anger of the Dispersionists could be assuaged and concessions made.

Concessions were made, an uneasy peace maintained, but the divisions between rulers and ruled remained, their conflicting desires—the Seven for Stasis, the Dispersionists for Change—unresolved. Among those concessions the Seven had permitted the Dispersionists to build a starship, the *New Hope*. As the ship approached readiness, the Dispersionists pushed things even farther at Weimar, impeaching the *tai*—the Representatives of the Seven in the House—and effectively declaring their independence. In response the Seven destroyed the *New Hope*. War was declared.

The five-year "War-That-Wasn't-a-War" left the Dispersionists broken, their leaders dead, their Companies confiscated. The great push for Change had been crushed and peace returned to Chung Kuo. But the war had woken older, far stronger, currents of dissent. In the depths of the City new movements began to arise, seeking not merely to change the system, but to revolutionize it altogether. One of these factions, the *Ping Tiao*, or "Levelers," wanted to pull down the great City of three hundred levels and destroy the Empire of the Han.

Among the ruling council of the *Ping Tiao* was a young *Hung Mao*, or "European," woman, Emily Ascher. Driven by a desire for social justice, Emily orchestrated a campaign of attacks on corrupt officials designed to destabilize City Europe. But her fellows on the council were not satisfied with such piecemeal and "unambitious" methods and when the new Dispersionist leader, DeVore, offered them an alliance, they grabbed it against her advice.

Once a Major in Li Shai Tung's Security service, Howard DeVore had been instrumental in both the assassination of Li Han Ch'in and the "War" that followed. Based on Mars, he sent in autonomous copies of himself to do his bidding, using any means possible to destroy the Seven and their City. The House of Representatives, the Dispersionists, the *Ping Tiao*—each in turn was used, then discarded, by him, cynically and without thought for the harm done to individuals. Aided by a network of young Security officers he had recruited over the years, he fought a savage guerrilla war against his former Masters, his only aim, it seemed, a wholly nihilistic one.

Yet the Seven were not helpless in the face of such assaults. Tolonen, promoted to Marshal of the Council of Generals, recruited a giant of a man, Gregor Karr, a "blood," or to-the-death fighter, from the lowest levels of the City—the "Net"—to act as his foil against DeVore and the Dispersionists. Karr was joined by another low-level fighter named Kao Chen—one of the two assassins responsible for the attack on the imperial solarium that had begun the struggle.

For a time the status quo was maintained, but three of the most senior T'ang died during the War with the Dispersionists, leaving the Council of Seven weaker and more inexperienced than they'd been in all the long years of their rule. When Wang Sau-leyan, the youngest son of Wang Hsien, ruler of City Africa, became T'ang after his father's suspect death, things looked ominous, particularly as the young man seemed to delight in creating turmoil among the Seven. But Li Yuan, inheriting from his father, formed effective alliances with his fellow T'ang, Wu Shih of North America, Tsu Ma of West Asia, and Wei Feng of East Asia to block Wang in Council, outvoting him four to three.

Even so, as Chung Kuo's population continued to grow, further concessions had to be made. The great Edict of Technological Control—the means by which the Seven had kept change at bay for more than a century—was to be relaxed, the House of Representatives at Weimar reopened, in return for guarantees of population controls.

For the first time in fifty years the Seven began to tackle the problems of their world, facing up to the necessity for limited change; but was it too late? Were the great tides of unrest unleashed by earlier wars about to overwhelm them?

It certainly seemed so. And when DeVore managed to persuade Li Yuan's newly appointed General, Hans Ebert, to secretly ally with him, the writing seemed on the wall.

Hans Ebert had it all; handsome, strong, intelligent, he was heir to the genetics and pharmaceuticals Company, GenSyn—Chung Kuo's largest manufacturing concern—but he was also a vain, amoral young man, a cold-blooded "hero" with the secret ambition of deposing the Seven and becoming "King of the World," an ambition DeVore assiduously fed. While Ebert turned a blind eye, DeVore began to construct a chain of fortresses in the Alpine wilderness at the heart of City Europe, preparing for the day when he might bring it all crashing down. But that was not to be. Karr and Kao Chen, aided by a young lieutenant, Haavikko, uncovered the plot and revealed it to Marshal Tolonen, whose own daughter, Jelka, was betrothed to Hans Ebert. Tolonen, childhood companion of Ebert's father, Klaus, went straight to his lifelong friend and told him of his son's betrayal, allowing him twenty-four hours to deal with the matter personally.

Hans, meanwhile, had been instructed by Li Yuan to destroy the network of fortresses. His hands tied, he did so, then returned to face his father. Klaus would have killed his only son, but Hans's goatlike helper—a creation of his father's genetic laboratories—killed the old man. Hans fled the planet and was condemned to death in his absence.

Li Yuan, it would seem, was saved. Yet the seed of destruction had been sown elsewhere, in the infatuation of his cousin Tsu Ma for Li Yuan's beautiful wife, Fei Yen. Their brief, clandestine affair was ended by Tsu Ma, but not before the damage was done. Fei Yen fell pregnant. Li Yuan was at first delighted, but then, when Fei Yen defied him and, late in her pregnancy, went riding, he destroyed her horses. She left him, returning to her father's house. There, alone with her husband, she told him that the child she was carrying was not his. Devastated, he returned home and, after his father's death, divorced Fei Yen, thus preventing her son—born two days after his coronation—from inheriting. The rift, it seemed, was final. He married again that day, taking three wives, determined to put the past behind him.

But the past casts long shadows. Just as the brutal pattern of the tyrant Tsao Ch'un's thinking was imprinted in the restrictive levels of his great world-spanning City, so the blight of those twin betrayals—by his wife and by his most trusted man, his General, Hans Ebert—was imprinted deep in Li Yuan's psyche. A darkness settled within the young T'ang, leading him to pursue new and quite radical solutions to his City's problems—solutions like the Wiring Project.

As civil unrest proliferated and control gradually slipped from the Seven, as the lower levels of their great Cities slowly fell into the hands of the Triads and the false Messiahs, so the temptation to control the civilization by other means grew. For Li Yuan there had long been only one solution. All of his citizens would be "wired"—a controlling device placed in every adult's head so they might be tracked and, if necessary, destroyed. It was a vile solution, but no viler, perhaps, than the alternative—to see the great Cities melt away and the rule of the Seven at an end.

As if to emphasize that necessity, new opposition groups sprang up one after another—the violently terrorist *Yu*, the North American–based Sons of Benjamin Franklin, the Black Hand, and many more, each wishing to destroy what was and replace it with their own vision of what a society should be. The demand for Change became a mad scramble for power. Yet still the Seven maintained control . . . of a kind.

In the summer of 2208 Wu Shih, T'ang of North America, decided to draw the dragon's teeth, arresting the Sons and incarcerating them, refusing to give them up to their powerful fathers until a guarantee of good behavior was signed and sealed. He got his way, but in doing so sealed his own fate, for it was now only a matter of time before his City would fall. In seeking to stem the Revolution, he had merely fed its flames. When the Sons emerged from their fifteen-month imprisonment they had been hardened by the experience. Under the leadership of Joseph Kennedy, the latest scion in that long and prestigious line, they formed the New Republican Party, determined to bring about a political sea-change and to wrest power from the hands of the Seven.

Within the Seven the internecine fighting had worsened, and when the T'ang of Africa, Wang Sau-leyan, attacked Li Yuan's floating palace and killed his wives, war between them seemed inevitable. But lack of proof and fear of even greater chaos held Li Yuan's hand. The Seven were divided as never before, yet still the Cities stood. Even so, the experience had once again scarred Li Yuan deeply and served to throw him ever closer to his fellow T'ang, Wu Shih and Tsu Ma. Among the three of them, perhaps, they might yet rule strongly and wisely. The unthinkable—the destruction of the age-old rule of Seven and its replacement by a strong triumvirate—was now openly discussed.

But Li Yuan's greater schemes had once again to be set aside in the face of trouble in his own City. The death of DeVore's earthbound copy—pursued and finally killed by the giant Karr—left a power vacuum in the lower levels, a vacuum soon to be filled by one of DeVore's erstwhile allies, the albino Stefan Lehmann.

Lehmann, estranged son of the onetime Dispersionist leader, fled to the icy Alpine wastes after the fall of DeVore's fortresses. It was from there he returned in the spring of 2209, hardened by the experience, and set about making a name for himself in the Lowers of City Europe, infiltrating the cutthroat world of criminal activity and ruthlessly climbing the ranks of the Triad brotherhoods until, in a massive campaign in the summer of 2209, he defeated the combined forces of the five great Triad lords and became the White T'ang, Li Min—"Brave Carp"—sole ruler of the European underworld.

At that single instant Li Yuan might have acted to crush Lehmann, for the albino's power was weak after his efforts. But Li Yuan—emotionally shattered by the death of his wives and the depth of division that had been revealed among the Seven—failed to take advantage of the situation. Li Min, the "Brave Carp," survived and began to consolidate his dark and brutal empire in the lowest levels of Li Yuan's City.

On Mars the real DeVore, learning from the failures of his first "embassy" to Chung Kuo, was planning a new assault upon the Seven—preparing a new range of genetic copies, subtler and more deadly than the last. Yet even there, among the nineteen cities of the Martian Plains, unrest had reached fever pitch and needed only a single incident to trigger violent revolution. And when it came, it was from an unexpected direction.

Hans Ebert, much changed after his great fall from power, had found himself on Mars, in DeVore's employ as a humble sweeper in one of his huge genetic factories. Wearing a prosthetic mask to conceal his features, Ebert had slowly refashioned himself, motivated by a deep aversion for the creature he had once been. However, pushed beyond his limits, he killed a man, placing himself once more in DeVore's power. Fastening on the opportunity, DeVore planned to use him in a scheme to destroy Marshal Tolonen emotionally by kidnapping Tolonen's daughter, Jelka—on Mars on her way back to Chung Kuo—and marrying her to Ebert. But Ebert refused to take part in DeVore's schemes and, aided by a lost race of Africans, the Osu—descendants of the early settlers of Mars—helped release Jelka even as the cities of Mars burned.

As the cities of the Martian Plain had fallen, so, too, might those of Earth—of Chung Kuo, the great Han Empire, for there, too, it needed but a single incident to trigger violent change. And of the seven great Cities of Chung Kuo, the most powerful—North America—was also the most vulnerable. Rumors of a lost American Empire—thrown over by the Han—were rife, and old and young alike had begun to clamor for a return to past glories. Wu Shih, T'ang of North America, saw this and, much concerned, strove to control the leaders of the new movements—particularly Joseph Kennedy, who seemed to embody the spirit of the age. But for all his power Wu Shih did not have it all his own way.

One of those facing him in North America, and standing in stark contrast, was Emily Ascher. Smuggled out of City Europe when the *Ping Tiao* movement disintegrated and given a new iden-tity—as Mary Jennings—she met one of the Sons, Michael Lever, and became his wife. That marriage made her rich beyond all dreams, yet riches of themselves meant nothing to her. She was still driven by a vision of Change, and now began to pursue it by other means, playing Conscience to the great North American City and taking on the role of "Elder Sister," determined to allevi-ate the suffering in the lower levels of her adopted City. Ranged against her, however, were other forces with different agendas: the Old Men—Michael Lever's father, Charles, foremost among them—with their insane pursuit of Immortality; Wu Shih with his desire for stability at any cost; and Joseph Kennedy, whose crusad-ing zeal had been effectively neutered by Wu Shih. All in all it was a recipe for disaster, and disaster eventually overtook them in the winter of 2212—though not from any of these sources.

Wu Shih might have survived Emily's "Elder Sister" campaign; he might even have survived Joseph Kennedy's on-air suicide; but when one of the orbital factories—its systems' refurbishments long overdue—fell from the sky into the midst of his City, he could not ride out the storm that followed. Wu Shih died, attacked in his own imperial craft, while his great City burned.

Many got out—Michael and Emily among them—but billions perished when North America fell, and the dark shadow of that fall etched itself deep in the minds of those that remained. Tsao Ch'un's dream of stability—of a Utopia that would last ten thou-sand years—once so solid and unchallengeable, was coming to an end.

For some time the actions of the young T'ang of Africa, Wang Sau-leyan, had created divisions among the Seven, particularly in Council, where all important decisions were made. In the autumn of 2213, however, division tipped over into open warfare. Wang's direct assault on his fellow rulers at one of their ceremonial gatherings—an attempt that almost succeeded, with two of his cousins killed and another badly wounded—brought a swift reprisal. Li Yuan's dream of a ruling triumvirate finally came about—though in darker circumstances than he had envisaged—when he, Tsu Ma, and Wei Tseng-li, the new T'ang of East Asia, sent their armies into Africa to destroy Wang Sau-leyan's power.

The death of the odious Wang closed one chapter of Chung Kuo's history, yet it could not stem the headlong tide of Change. In the seventeen years since Li Shai Tung's Minister, Lwo Kang, had been assassinated in the imperial solarium, all respect for the Seven had drained away. Li Yuan sought to reverse this tendency by giving the people greater representation in government and—in the war against Wang Sau-leyan—by creating people's armies, but it was not enough. The great House of Representatives at Weimar spoke only for those with money and power and then only on a limited range of matters, for real power remained firmly in the hands of the Seven. And all the while a number of other factors— the corruption of officials, the constant nepotism, the vast disparity in wealth between those at the top of the City (First Level) and those in the Lowers, the ever-increasing population—only served to stoke the great engine of popular discontent.

To be honest, these were not problems that had begun with the City—such things were millennia-old long before the first milehigh segment of Tsao Ch'un's world-spanning megapolis was eased onto its supporting pillars—but conditions within the City exacerbated them, and while the rich continued to prosper, the poor grew daily poorer and more hungry. Something had to give.

Indeed, something *would* give. Yet behind the struggle for power—that age-old battle between the haves and have-nots—was another, far greater struggle for the imagination, and for the very *soul* of Mankind: the "War of the Two Directions," a war that would ultimately center upon a pair of individuals who, in their work and lives, would embody entirely different approaches to existence.

Those two were Ben Shepherd and Kim Ward, the former the most talented artist of his time, the latter the most gifted scientist. Growing up during these years of dramatic change, their work came to represent a level of creative life that, for more than a century, had been harshly suppressed by the Seven. The world into which they were born was culturally sterile: its science was at a standstill, filling in gaps in old research and perfecting machines developed centuries before; its art even worse, having returned to principles more than 1,500 years old. Its scientists were technicians, its artists artisans. Coming into this climate of creative atrophy—a climate carefully nurtured by the Edict and the "Rules of Art"—Ben and Kim could not help but be revolutionary.

Ben Shepherd, the great-great grandson of the City's architect, was born in the Domain, an unspoiled valley in England's West Country. There, in those idyllic surroundings, was nurtured his fascination with mimicry, darkness, and "the other side" which was to culminate eventually in his development of a wholly new art form, the Shell. Over the years he would shamelessly draw upon his own life—the death by cancer of his father, the lost love of a young woman named Catherine, and his complex sexual relationship with his sister, Meg—weaving these elements together to create a powerful tale.

Kim Ward, on the other hand, was a product of the Clay, that dark land beneath the City's foundations. Rescued from that savage hell, he spent the formative years of his early youth in State institutions, surviving that brutal regime through an astonishing quickness of mind and a matching physical agility. His innate talents recognized by Berdichev, Head of the great SimFic Corporation and a leading Dispersionist, Kim was bought and then, almost as casually, discarded when Kim's darker side—rooted in his experiences in the Clay—emerged after one particularly provocative incident when he badly hurt another boy.

Fortunately Berdichev was not the only one to recognize Kim's unique intellectual talents and he found an unexpected benefactor in Li Yuan, who, when Ward emerged from a long period of character reconstruction, gave him both his freedom and the wherewithal to begin his own Company in North America. But that was not to be. The Old Men, seeing in Kim the means of achieving their dream of Immortality, deliberately set about destroying his business venture, hoping to force his hand. But Ward would not serve them.

Kim had other dreams, among them the dream of marrying the Marshal's beautiful daughter, Jelka. But Tolonen would not permit the match and sent his daughter away on a tour of the colony planets. Kim, devastated, swore to wait until she came of age and signed a seven-year contract as a Commodity slave with the SimFic Corporation in a deal that would make him fantastically rich. And while he waited he would pursue his other dream—his vision of a great Web, first glimpsed in the dark wilderness of the Clay.

Shepherd and Ward, Shell and Web—the two are antithetical, representing in many ways those very things over which Li Yuan and DeVore had fought for so long—the "Two Directions" facing Mankind in the future.

Ben's Shell is the image of inwardness, a body-sized sensory-deprivation unit designed to replace objective reality with a subjective experience that is more powerful than real life. Unlike reality, however, its very perfection is as seductive and consequently as addictive as the most lethal drug, its perfection a form of death by separation—a withdrawal from the world.

The Web, on the other hand, is the very symbol of outwardness, a vision of an all-connecting light: quite literally so, for Kim's Web was conceived as a means of linking the very stars themselves.

The safety of the past or the uncertainty of the future? Inwardness or outwardness? Connection or Separation? These choices, like the perpetual Yin and Yang of the ancient Tao itself, would determine Chung Kuo's future. Yet the shadows cast by past events would also play their part.

Back in the summer of 2203 Li Shai Tung called together his relatives, his advisers, and his closest friends to celebrate the betrothal of his son, Li Yuan, to the Princess Fei Yen. But while outwardly he smiled and laughed, secretly the old T'ang had misgivings about the match. Fei Yen had been his murdered elder son's wife, and though the marriage had never been consummated, it felt wrong—an affront against tradition—to let his younger son, now heir, step into his dead brother's shoes so blatantly.

That same day his son received two special gifts. The first was from Li Shai Tung's archenemy, DeVore. It was a *wei chi* set, a hardwood board and two wooden pots of rounded stones. Such a gift was not unusual, yet whereas in a normal *wei chi* set there would be one hundred and eighty-one black stones and one hundred and eighty white, DeVore had sent three hundred and sixty-one white stones. Stones carved from human bone.

Symbolically the board was Chung Kuo, the stones its people. And white . . . white was traditionally the Han color of death. DeVore was telling Li Shai Tung that he would fill the world with death.

But there was a second gift, this time from the Marshal's daughter, Jelka. Her betrothal present to Li Yuan was a set of miniature carved figures: eight tiny warriors—the eight heroes of Chinese legend, their faces blacked to represent their honor.

Shocked by the symbolic message of the first gift, Li Shai Tung was delighted by the second. A bad omen had been overturned. There would be death, certainly, yet there would also be heroes to fight against its final triumph.

Yes. It was written. When the board was filled with white, then, finally, would the eight black heroes come.

And so it transpired. When DeVore finally returned, at the head of a vast army of copy selves, it was Hans Ebert and the Osu—eight black heroes—who faced him and, aided by the Machine, a benign Artificial Intelligence, defeated the great archenemy. The mile-high city was destroyed, the rule of the Seven effectively ended. Li Yuan, for once totally indebted to his servants and allies, was forced to promise to build a new world, different and more humane than the old. But that was ten years back. . . .

## *Abandoned in Whiteness*

The cold night drum. Its arrow points to dawn.
In the clean mirror I see my haggard face.
Outside the window, wind startles the bamboo.
I open the door. Snow covers the whole mountain.
The sky of falling flakes quiets the paths
and the big courtyard is abandoned in whiteness.
I wonder whether you're like old Yuan An in his house,
locked away inside, and calm?

> —WANG WEI, "Winter Night, Facing the Snow,
> Thinking of the Lay Buddhist Hu"
> *Eighth Century* A.D.

I T W A S *Ta Hsueh, the Time of Great Snow, and in the
hutong of Kuang Hua Hsien paper lanterns hung outside
every house. Among the dim-lit, crowded thoroughfares people were preparing for the festival. Charms had been pasted to
doorways beside small strips of red and gilt paper bearing the character
fu—"happiness." People stopped to talk or called cheerfully to each
other as they passed, "Ni hao?" and "Tsai chien!"*

*Waddling along the narrow passageways, Bara Horacek could feel the
weight of the child in her swollen belly pressing down against her bladder.
If she wasn't home soon she would piss herself. Breathless, she paused,
leaning heavily against the greasy wall, nodding as two of her neighbors
hurried by. She winced as a pain stabbed through her lower abdomen. It
would be just her luck if her waters broke, with Vilem gone to his
mother's and the boys staying with friends. She should never have let
Vilem talk her into having another child, not at her age, but with the
new legislation going through he had argued that there might never be
another chance, and so . . .*

*The pain grew. For a moment Bara closed her eyes and gritted her
teeth, trying not to groan, not to cry out. It wasn't due. The baby
wasn't due. . . . Not for six weeks yet. But she knew that feeling.
Home—she had to get home.*

*As the pain faded she walked on, each step jolting her stomach as if
she'd been kicked there. Oh, gods, she thought, feeling the sticky wet-*

3

ness on her thighs and trying to keep calm. What if it's a miscarriage? What if . . .

She pushed the thought from her, concentrating on the simple business of getting back to the house. How far was it now? A hundred?—a hundred and fifty paces? But each step now seemed a gargantuan effort, the space between each step a small eternity. Eight steps. Nine. A tenth. And then time slowed as the pain returned, enlarged, fiercer than before.

She cried out and almost fell. Two men from a nearby stall hurried to her aid, holding her up, their Han faces pushed close, anxious for her.

"Is it coming?" one of them asked. "Can you feel the baby coming?"

Bara nodded, uncertain. Too old, she thought. I told Vilem I was too old. . . .

"Fetch a blanket," one of her neighbors, an old Han woman, shouted, taking charge of things. "Get her on her back. The child will be here any moment."

Bara let herself be laid onto a blanket between the stalls. There was a crowd of fifty or sixty gathered about her now, a small sea of curious faces, mainly Han, but she was beyond caring.

"Tell Vilem. . . ." she said weakly, trying to talk over the babble of voices. "Tell him. . . ." And then the pain came again, like a huge black wave, taking her breath.

It's dead, she thought, despair gripping her. My child is dead.

Someone had removed her sodden panties, exposing her, but it didn't matter. All that mattered now was the pain and those small brief moments between the pain. Someone was gripping her hands from behind, someone else holding her knees up, her legs apart, but she was scarcely aware of it, all she could feel, all she knew, was the urgency inside her, the burning, tearing desire of the dead thing within her to get out into the world.

She groaned as if she'd been impaled, the shock of the breaching making her nerves sing in agony.

"Come on," someone said encouragingly. "You're almost there."

Sweat blinded her, distorted what she saw. Faces swam before her—goggle-eyed, staring faces filled with horror, as if what she were pushing from her was deformed, a hideous monstrosity. She imagined it, a slick, black scaly thing with burning eyes, and whimpered with fear. No, she thought. Don't let it come out. Don't . . .

"Push," the old Han woman whispered at her ear. "Come on now, Bara. One last push and it's there."

She tried to hold back, but it was impossible. Her muscles pushed. There was a scream—her own, she realized—and then an easing of the pain, a sense of absence. There was a babble of voices and then, above them all, the cry of a child—a robust and healthy sound.

"It's a boy," the old Han woman said, bundling it up and thrusting it at her. "A fine, healthy boy. The gods have smiled on you, Bara Horacek."

Bara tried to shake her head, to say she didn't want it, but the child was in her arms, its clear blue eyes staring up at her as if it knew already what she was thinking.

Dead, she thought. You're dead. But the child stared back at her, its very existence a denial, its strange perfection sending a chill through her. Behind it, like a white hole in the blackness of the sky, the unfamiliar moon shone down.

Dead, am I? those eyes seemed to say, mocking her. We'll see how dead I am.

---

*HALF A WORLD AWAY*, in a tiny room close to the southern wall of Li Yuan's great European city, an old man stood over the dead body of his teenage wife, his shoulders hunched, his face in his hands, weeping. There was the sound of a child crying somewhere in the cold and ill-furnished apartment, an awful, insistent sound that had not stopped for an hour. The old man shuddered and half turned his face, a flash of anger, of bitterness, making his lip curl. He would silence the child. Would kill it for what it had done.

He went through, then stood there over the cot, staring down at the naked, kicking form. A girl. . . . As if the gods hadn't mocked him enough! If it had been a boy . . . but no, his wife had suffered and died merely to bring a girl into the world. And what use was a girl? Would she sweep his grave after his death? Would she carry on his father's line? No. Well, he would have none of it. He would say she was stillborn.

He lifted the pillow and placed it firmly over the child's face, closing his eyes and pressing down, anger giving him the strength to overcome any misgivings he had. The sudden silence was like a relief and as the child ceased struggling he eased the pressure, then slowly lifted his hands and backed away.

The pillow . . .

He stood there, unable to move; then, with a tiny shudder of aversion, he went to the cot and removed the pillow. The child lay still, almost peaceful, it seemed, and for the briefest moment, looking down into her still and tiny face, he felt a pang of regret. She was so like her. So like his darling Tian. Turning away, pushing that brief flicker of pity from his heart, he went through to tend to his dead wife.

━━━━━

*WHEN THE REGISTRY OFFICIAL* came an hour later the old man was still sitting there, staring blankly at the wall, his wife's hand cold and stiff within his own. The official looked about him, taking it all in at a glance. With a nod to the man, he stepped through the bead curtain into the bedroom.

The child was dead, he could see that at once. And a good thing, too, he thought, writing a brief note on his report. What good was a newborn daughter without a mother to look after her? This way, at least, the old man was free of all burdens. He could buy a new wife, have sons, and no worries about the new birth quotas. No, it was for the best, all things considered.

He went back and stood over the seated man. "Did you give the child a name, lao jen?"

The old man looked up at him, expressionless. "Chuang Kuan Ts'ai," he answered tonelessly. *Coffin-filler.*

The official swallowed, then left the appropriate box on his form blank. There were procedures for cases like this. They would allocate a number back at the office—something for the Oven Man's records. All that remained was for someone to come and remove the bodies.

"I'll leave you now, lao jen," he said, bowing respectfully. "If there's anything I can do . . ."

But the old man wasn't listening. He was staring down into the pale and vacant face of his young bride, his deeply lined cheeks wet with tears.

Too bad, he thought, unclipping the form and placing it at the bottom of the pile, checking to see where his next call was. It was usually the husbands who snuffed it first, and rare was the young bride who missed the old bastard. But this . . .

He shrugged and turned away. It was as they said: Life was cheap, flesh plentiful. The old man would get over his loss. Why, with a new young wife in his bed he would have forgotten all about this one in three months!

He closed the door, nodding to himself, thinking of the evening ahead. Shit, maybe he'd call and tell his wife he was working late. Maybe he'd go see that woman down on Chang Lin Avenue who had been so good to him last week after her husband had passed on. A woman had her needs, after all, and his wife . . .

He snorted, then walked on. His wife could hang herself for all the good she was. Her and her two good-for-nothing brothers. Why, if it wasn't for him, they'd all be eating air!

Families . . . they were nothing but trouble. He saw plenty in his line of work—why, he made twenty, often as many as thirty calls a day, and always it was the same: those who survived either loved too much or too little. The lucky ones were the dead. They, at least, could sleep easy.

At the corner of the alleyway he tore off the completed slips and, walking on a bit, posted them through the Oven Man's door, then carried on toward the crossway. That, too, could be said for the dead—they helped keep the living lit and warm. He chuckled, amused by the thought, elbowing his way through the crowd by the transit station, then stepped inside.

Here's to the dead, he thought, giving an imaginary toast as the doors of the northbound transit hissed shut and the carriage began to slide along the rails. And to young Chang Kuan Ts'ai, he added soberly, for being no bother to anyone. . . .

———

VILEM STOOD BY THE DOOR, cradling his son, a proud paternal grin lighting his features. Bara stared at him from where she lay in her bed, trying to share his happiness, but there was nothing. She kept trying to find something in herself—some trace of the love, the deep-rooted affection, she had felt for her first two sons—but there was nothing, only that strange coldness, that sense of wrongness bordering upon aversion that gripped her every time she looked at her newborn son.

"We'll call him Josef," Vilem said, nodding decisively. "Jo-sef . . . like his great-grandfather. Josef Horacek. It's a good name, neh? A strong name for a strong little boy!"

She nodded, but all she felt was a numbness. A name . . . why, she'd not even considered a name. . . .

"You want to hold him again?" Vilem asked, offering the child to her.

"No . . . no . . . you hold him a while longer. Get him to sleep for me, won't you?"

She rolled over, onto her side, uncomfortable to be lying like that, but not wanting to see Vilem with the child. Not wanting to see him smile the way he did when he looked at the boy, or hear him laugh the way he laughed.

Why couldn't he have died? she found herself thinking, and felt guilt slice through her.

Maybe it would pass. Maybe it was just the circumstances—the shock of giving birth there in the alleyway between the stalls. Yes, maybe that was it. Maybe if she slept it would all be all right.

There was a noise, a gentle snuffling, from the child, like the inarticulate mumbling of a drunk. At the sound of it she felt a shiver flash down her spine; felt her whole body go cold, her nerves tingle with aversion.

I hate him, she realized with a shock. My own son . . .

She could hear Vilem pacing back and forth, cooing softly to the child.

What was wrong with her? What in the gods' names was wrong with her? Was she ill? Was that it? She closed her eyes, trying to shut it all out, to forget and start anew, but it wouldn't go away.

Josef . . . Josef Horacek. It was a good name—as Vilem said, a strong name—yet for some reason the mere thought of it made her shudder convulsively and curl up tightly into a ball, hugging her empty stomach.

Dead. He should have been born dead.

Maybe. But it was too late now. He had escaped. He had kicked and fought his way out into the world. And no one—neither she nor all the gods—could put him back inside.

———

THE CRATES WERE STACKED to one side of the courtyard where the two deliverymen had left them. Beside them, on a trestle table by the gate, were the blue undercopies of the delivery notes. There were fourteen of them this morning—nine adults and five children. It was less than usual; even so, it would still take him a good forty to forty-five minutes to burn them all, and there were two more lots to come before the day was out.

The Oven Man slurped down the remains of his soup, set the bowl aside, then stood, yawning and stretching his arms. He might as well get these done now, then he could log them in the book and get a few hours of shuteye before the next delivery.

He was a big, severe-looking man in his forties, his chest broad, his upper arms heavily muscled from years of doing what he did. His name was Yao, like that of the legendary monarch—Cho Yao, in full—but so few called him that these days that he had almost forgotten it himself. Those who didn't shun him—those who, through their calling, had to deal with him—called him Lu Nan Jen, "Oven Man." The rest . . . well, the rest had little to say. They merely stared at him sightlessly, grinning their eternal grins.

He went across and began, hauling the first of the crates from the top of the nearest stack. The crates were shaped like narrow baths, with two long ridges molded into the base so that they could be slid onto the runners. They were made of semiopaque ice—the same lightweight superplastic from which the great City itself had once been made—back before the war with the White T'ang. A thin seal of toughened plastic covered the top of each, allowing a clear view of the occupant.

The first was an old woman, Mu Tao according to the printed label. Her body was shriveled and tiny like a child's, her face puckered into an expression of surprise, as if Death had crept up on her from behind. He set her down before the oven door, then took the gloves from the hook on the side and slipped them on.

As he pulled back the heavy door, light spilled into the room. He had stacked and lit the furnace an hour earlier and the heat from it was fierce. With a practiced ease he lifted the crate and swung it onto the parallel tracks, giving it a gentle, almost tender shove. There was a brief darkening of the light and then a sudden flare. He shouldered close the door and, wiping his brow, turned to get another crate.

Turned . . . and stopped. There was a sound. A whimpering. He frowned, certain he'd made a mistake, then heard it again, clear and unmistakable.

"Kuan Yin . . ." he muttered, then hurried across, beginning to search through the crates.

It took only a few moments to find where the noise had come from. It was a child, a newborn. He shook his head, astonished. In all his years . . .

He looked about him, then went through to the kitchen, emerging a moment later with a knife. He wouldn't be able to cut through the toughened ice itself, but it was just possible that he might prize it loose along the edge where it had been heat-bonded. He slid the knife back and forth, then felt the plastic give with a sigh, wrinkling back as if it were consumed by flames, leaving only the label.

He shivered and threw the knife down, then reached inside. As he did the child opened its eyes and put its arms up to him.

"Gods . . ." he whispered, cradling it awkwardly against his chest, amazed by the living warmth of it. "Kuan Yin preserve us. . . ."

There was no printing on the label, only three handwritten characters—Chuang Kuan Ts'ai—"filling up the coffin."

He frowned, angry suddenly, wanting to go at once and confront the Registry Official, to curse him for his carelessness . . . then he stopped, pondering the situation.

The child was dead. Officially dead. The forms were signed, the paperwork filled out. If it had not cried out just then, he would have fed the crate into the Oven's mouth.

"Dead," he said, surprised by the strangeness of the word in his mouth, then held the child out, away from him, studying it. It was a pretty little thing, a faint wisp of dark hair covering its scalp. If it had been his . . .

He took a long breath. No one knew. No one but him. He could kill the child or save it. And if he saved it?

Slowly he drew the child back toward him, cradling it gently, tenderly, against his chest, then looked down into its face, conscious of its dark eyes staring back at him.

"Well, little Chuang," he said softly, a smile lighting features that had never before that moment smiled. "Now, what are we to do with you?"

# China on the Rhine

Orchids in spring and chrysanthemums in autumn:
So it shall go on until the end of time.

—*Honoring the Dead*, Li Hun, *Second Century* B.C.

Under conditions of peace the warlike man attacks himself.

—*Beyond Good and Evil*, Friedrich Nietzsche, 1886

# CHAPTER ONE

# Days of Ease

**T**OM STOOD AT the prow of the imperial barge, one hand shielding his eyes against the sun's glare, the other gripping the rail as he looked south. It was stiflingly hot and traffic on the Rhine was heavy, but all gave way before the golden barge and the great banner that hung limply in the air above him.

He gazed up at it. Once, so his father said, the *Ywe Lung* would have flown, the great wheel of seven dragons circling snout to tail, their eyes forming a seven-starred hub at the center, but those days were long past. For ten years now this new flag had flown throughout the great northern city—a red dragon, emblazoned across a full white moon, like a bloodied eye staring out from the starless black.

Tomorrow, for the first time, he would meet the owner of that dragon, the great T'ang, Li Yuan himself. Tomorrow, when they docked at Mannheim, on the marbled shore before the San Chang, the imperial palaces, he would step down and ritually embrace his father's oldest friend.

A heavily laden junk was passing thirty yards to port, its sails furled, its engine chugging softly. Its dozen or so crew members—shaven-headed Han—stared curiously, almost insolently, back at him, knowing from his *Hung Mao* face that he was not one of the imperial family.

He looked beyond them. Crowds packed the embankment everywhere he looked, drawn by the passing of the T'ang's own vessel: young and old, male and female, their bare-arsed children—round faced and endlessly identical—propped up before them on the long stone wall. The people, the unending masses of the people.

Tom frowned. He had lived all his life on the river, on the shore of the peaceful Dart, but this was different. This huge, winding waterway could swallow up a thousand Darts. Nothing in his sixteen years could have prepared him for this. No, not for the masses that packed its banks for hundreds of miles to either side, nor for the endless rows of identical one-story houses with their high gray walls and their orange-red terra-cotta tiled roofs.

He closed his eyes, searching—for that brief moment searching in his mind—for Sampsa, but for once there was no second presence in his head. He sighed and glanced down at his hands where they gripped the rail. It was as his mother said: he had grown too insular, too self-enclosed.

He half turned, looking to where his father's women sat on the upper deck, ensconced in huge, cushioned chairs, a pale silk awning shading them. Catherine, wearing a dark green dress that matched her eyes, stared languidly into space, as if in trance, her flame-red hair let down despite the heat. Beside her his mother slowly fanned herself, her own dark, lustrous hair gathered in a tight bun at her neck. As he watched, a steward brought iced drinks, then, bowing, backed away.

He studied them, surprised once again by the strength of feeling—that strange bond of familiarity—which linked him to them. They had had the worst of it these past six months while his father had been away. Not that life was hard in the Domain—far from it—yet he had seen how much they missed his father's presence. As if the place were empty without him.

*Empty* . . . The idea made him realize just how fortunate they were to have the Domain; how tranquil his existence was. In their slow progress upriver they had passed through the crowded *hutong* of the northern city and he had glimpsed something of the people who inhabited that endless systems of canals and narrow alleyways. So different those lives were, so circumscribed. Alone in his head, watching them, he had begun to reflect upon his own existence.

Had he been born within that sprawl, his life might well have been one of endless misery, endless struggle. He would have been but another mute, another face to be fed. As it was he had a name. Useless as his tongue was, he was still a Shepherd, and that counted for something in this world. Yet what was he to do with it? Was he to follow his father's example? Or was there something better for him to do? Something linked, perhaps, to what he'd newly seen?

He sighed, his thoughts grown vague, and turned back, staring out at the crowded shore again. Here, half a day's sail from Mannheim and the San Chang—the imperial palaces—the river's banks were dominated by the factories of the four great Companies— SimFic, GenSyn, MedFac, and NorTek—each massive complex surrounded by sprawling warrens of cramped workers' houses, all of it constructed in the traditional Han style his father had first envisaged a dozen years ago.

The thought made him smile, for this was his father's world, grown from his head, just as surely as the old world had been the dream of Old Amos Shepherd, two centuries before. This was Ben Shepherd's world: his dream of China on the Rhine.

Tom laughed silently, wondering if anyone else thought that strange, or whether he alone understood just how deeply—how profoundly—his father had changed, had *subverted*, history. The fiction—that sensory network of lies his father had presented to the world as *The Familiar*—had now become reality.

But so it was. It was the way of men to make their dreams into realities. Heaven or Hell, it did not matter. Such was the species's glory . . . and its curse.

Tom stared at the weblike shape of the great NorTek complex and sighed, wondering what Sampsa was doing at that moment, wishing he could see through his eyes. Even now Ward, Sampsa's father, was up there in space somewhere, preparing to test-fire his lasers. And if they worked . . .

*If they work, then another dream begins.*

For a moment he wondered about Ward. He had seen the man so often—working, playing, and at rest—but still he did not fully understand what drove the Clayborn, no more than he understood his own father. SimFic had bought the ailing European arm of the great NorTek Corporation and given the gutted company to Ward. And it had proved a wise move. These days the city was full of Ward's subtle inventions, put out under SimFic's license. It was hard to think of a single aspect of modern life that was untouched by his clever mind. Yet what Tom knew—knew because he had *seen*, through Sampsa's eyes—was that Ward himself thought such innovations trivial, a waste of time and talent.

What Ward wanted, that he knew. Ward wanted to link the stars—to lay a great web of light between those distant burning points. But why he wanted that—what dream had spawned that mad desire—he did not know.

*And my father?*

He tapped the rail softly with his fingers, then turned, making his way across to join the women.

What did his father want? What drove him in the way that Ward was driven?

*Darkness*, came the answer. *My father is in love with the darkness.*

Opposite poles they were, Kim and Ben. Like twin planets, circling, orbiting each other, the force of attraction and repulsion between them balanced perfectly.

*Like Sampsa and me*, he thought, and briefly he pictured meeting Sampsa, physically touching him. How would that feel? To touch someone who for so long had been a presence in your head, a window through which you'd seen so many things.

In two days he would know. On Wednesday evening, at the banquet, they would finally come together.

———

EMILY STOOD BY the embankment wall, holding Ji up so he could see, staring out past the child's shaven head as the great barge slid by in the middle of the river. It was a huge boat, its broad gold-painted hull splendidly adorned with dragons and other mythical beasts, its antique superstructure like a miniature palace. As it sailed by, a ripple of awe passed through the watching crowd. This was Majesty. This was evidence of power—power beyond their wildest dreams. Emily watched the young man turn from the rail and felt a momentary twinge of regret for the life she had chosen to abandon. But such regret was brief; was more for the man she'd left—for Michael Lever, her once-husband—than for the luxuries she'd chosen to renounce.

She turned her head, taking in the marveling faces of the two older boys, and smiled warmly. No, given the choice again she would change nothing. Given the choice she would be right here, right now, despite the heat, the flies, despite the smell of unwashed bodies, the ever-present stench of decay. Here at least she had a role to play. Here she could do something real.

She spoke softly to the older boys: "Pei, Lao, fetch the cart. We'd best be getting back."

With obedient nods the two boys turned from the spectacle of the barge and scampered barefoot to where the loaded cart was parked against the wall and, one pushing, one pulling, turned it so they could maneuver it down the narrow alleyway.

She helped Ji down, then went across, taking over from Lao, who put a hand out for young Ji to take.

"Master Lin will wonder where we've got to," she said cheerfully, looking about her at the boys who were watching her closely. "He'll be pacing the compound asking himself why we are so late."

Ji frowned, his big eyes troubled. "Will he be angry, Mama Em?"

She laughed gently. "Is Master Lin ever angry? No. But he will worry until we are home. You know how he always worries."

It was no more than the truth—a truth she often reminded the boys of—yet for once she realized what that meant and understood at the same time just how fortunate she was. Someone to care for you: that was all you ever needed in this life. Someone who worried when you were not back on time.

And these boys . . . they understood that too. For they had once been lost, abandoned by the greater world. They knew what it was like to have no one care; to have no one worry whether they lived or died, let alone were late.

She smiled and began to push the heavily loaded cart, Pei straining beside her to match her efforts, ignoring the buzz of insects in the afternoon heat. And as she pushed, she looked at what they had collected. Broken things. That's all they ever brought Lin. Broken, discarded things. And he would mend them. She could see him now, sorting through the spread contents of the cart and

stooping to pick up this and examine that, his mind already calculating how to make them good again.

Like the boys.

It had been her idea originally. There had been so many of
them, after all. Thousands of them, lost or abandoned after the
great city's fall. A thousand million orphans, it had seemed, and no
one to care. She had seen little Chao crying hopelessly in the ruins
and had taken him home to Lin. That was the start of it. Now they
had eight of them. Boys who were cared for. Boys who would now
make something of themselves in this world, thanks to herself and
Lin.

*And that, surely, is true richness,* she mused, thinking of the
golden barge and all it represented. *Against that even the most lofty
T'ang ought to count himself the lowest pauper.*

Only now did she understand. Only now, in her fiftieth year,
gray hairs among the black, had she finally made sense of things.

"We did well today, didn't we?" Lao said, beaming at her.

She smiled back at the ten-year-old. "We did, Lao Chan. Master
Lin will be very pleased. It would not surprise me if there were
seconds tonight."

*"Really?"* Young Ji's eyes lit up like lanterns. "And will there be
cake, Mama Em?"

She laughed, brushing away a persistent fly. "Maybe not cake,
young Ji, but we'll see, eh?"

They went on, laughing, happy, talking all the while, making
their way through the bustling market square, then cutting through
the crowded back-alleys. As ever, friends and well-wishers called to
them as they passed. Emily returned their greetings warmly, the
certainty of knowing she belonged here filling her, taking away the
tiredness in her limbs.

It had been a long day.

As they came into Ch'in Shao Street, the lamps at the far end of
the road were being lit. Stalls were being packed away, while others—food stalls mainly—were being set up for the evening ahead.
Their compound was halfway up on the right, the doors open as
ever, the span of the low brick arch broken by Lin's hand-painted
sign reading TSO TSO CHIA—"Make Do House." Seeing it, she

smiled. It was Lin's idea of a joke, yet it was also his philosophy. Making do—it was what they did best.

Sending young Ji ahead to pull the doors right back, they maneuvered the cart across, bumping it over the raised stone step and into the outer yard.

At once they were surrounded by the rest of the boys.

"Mama Em! Mama Em!" they cried, beaming at her, their hands reaching out to touch her.

"Chao . . . Han Ye . . . let us through now!" she cried, mock stern, her laughing eyes giving her away. "Haven't you boys work to do?"

"We've finished it, Mama Em," the eleven-year-old Chao said, coming alongside her. "We were waiting for you, Mama Em. We—"

"Pei, get the doors!" she said, gesturing toward them, then looked back at Chao. "You what, Chao?"

"We got a letter, Mama Em," Chao said, excitement shining from his eyes. "From the Big House."

"The Big House? You mean from the Merchant, Tung Wei?"

Chao nodded. "From his First Steward, Liu Yeh. He says he has something for us. He says you must call. Tonight."

"Tonight?" She frowned, then heaved the cart into motion again as the inner doors swung open. Beside her half a dozen of the boys strained to help her push it across the cobbles. "And what does Papa Lin say?"

A figure appeared in the opening ahead, tall and gray haired, his face disfigured on one side. "Papa Lin says where have you been, Mama Em? The boys are hungry."

She looked up from the cart and smiled. "And you can't cook?"

"Oh, I can cook, all right," Lin answered, stepping back as they squeezed the cart through the narrow space, "but then how could I mend? And mending's what I'm best at."

"Then we must teach the boys to cook, Papa Lin."

He considered that, then nodded. "A good idea, Mama Em. And who knows, maybe some of them will find positions in one of the big houses."

"Who knows?" she said, looking up at him and smiling as she pulled the cart to a halt.

"So what have we?" he said, poking through the pile, picking out things and setting them aside. Behind him, she saw, the two workbenches had been cleared in preparation.

"Bits and bobs," she said, uttering the words she always uttered.

He looked up at her and smiled, then continued with his work. "I take it you went to see the imperial barge."

"How did you know?"

"Oh, I know you, Mama Em," he said, not looking up from where his hands were busy working through the pile. "Besides, young Ji has been talking about nothing else for days now, and I knew you'd not disappoint him."

She looked down at the child at her side and smiled, resting her hand on his head. "I guess not."

"So, Ji," Lin said, taking a chipped blue-and-white *chung* from the left of the pile and frowning at it, "what was it like?"

Ji glanced at Emily, then answered his adopted father. "It was wonderful, Papa Lin. Solid gold, it was."

"Solid gold, eh?" Lin looked back at Ji and nodded gravely, as if awed, then looked past him at Emily and winked. "And yet it floated. That is a miracle, neh?"

"A miracle," Ji agreed, his eyes widening as he took in what Lin had said. "And there was a prince—a *Hung Mao* prince—standing at the very front of the boat, holding on to the neck of the dragon. He had long black hair and a nose like a great hunting bird."

"Like a bird, eh?" Lin said, nodding once more. "That must have been Shepherd's son."

"Sheh-pud?" Ji frowned, not recognizing the name.

Lin looked to Emily once more. "Something big is happening, Mama Em. They say people are coming to Mannheim from all over. The spaceport has been closed to normal traffic and there's talk that ships have been coming in from Africa and America."

"America?" She stared at him, astonished. "But I thought . . ."

"The times are changing," he said, setting the *chung* aside and stepping across. "Fan Sheng-chih was here earlier and he was saying that the word from the palace is that the prince is about to take a bride."

"What would Old Fan know?" she said dismissively. "Why, if one were to believe one tenth of what he says!"

"Maybe. But for once I think he might be right. Rumors are buzzing about like flies on a corpse right now, and that would not be so were there not *something* behind it all. Besides . . . you saw the barge."

She nodded. She had indeed seen the barge. And as for the rumors—well, she'd heard enough to convince her that *something* was happening.

Lin turned back to the cart and began to sort through it once more, setting down items on the table at his side. "Old Fan says the garrisons upriver are on alert."

"Uh-huh?" But this time she didn't query it. No, for she'd heard the same, from one of her friends whose son was in the Schwetz-ingen barracks.

"So what do you think, Mama Em?" Lin said, lifting a thread-bare doll from the pile. "Is it a bride for the prince, or is it some-thing else?"

~~~~~~

"MASTER THOMAS?"

The voice came from outside in the corridor. Tom sat up, then turned slowly on the narrow bunk, staring across the cabin toward the part-opened doorway.

"It me, Master Thomas. It Yun."

A face poked round the door—the face of the young Third Cook, the left side of his face pocked like gritted stone. It was an unashamedly ugly face, but the almond eyes were bright.

Tom raised an eyebrow in mute query.

Yun stepped inside and, closing the door behind him, turned, holding out his hand.

Tom edged forward. It was a tiny black cassette, no bigger than an old-fashioned snuffbox—a Stim. He reached out and took it, turning it in his hand, studying the embossed logo—the symbol *kuei*, "casket," enclosed within a hexagon—then made to give it back.

"No," Yun said. "It for you. You must try. You like. I guarantee."

Tom looked at him dubiously. Only one thing was certain where Yun was concerned—whatever it was, it was illicit and it was prob-ably trouble. If there were any scams on board, Yun was at the center of them. He might only be seventeen—less than a year older than Tom—yet he seemed ancient in the ways of the world.

Tom stared at the Stim a moment, then shrugged and put it on the bedside table.

Yun smiled, satisfied. "What you do tonight?"

Tom shrugged. *Nothing. He was doing nothing, as ever.*

"You come with me? Meet my family?"

Tom stared at him, surprised, then nodded.

"Good. After we dock. You wait hour, then meet. At stern gangplank. My friend Chan on duty. He no see us slip past, neh?"

Tom almost smiled at that. Fine, but he would have to find some excuse; feign illness, perhaps.

Yun beamed, showing uneven, yellowed teeth. "I see you then. In meantime you be good boy, eh, Tom? Very good boy."

He sat there after Yun had gone, staring at the cassette. He knew what it was—at least, he *thought* he knew—but did he really want to *know?* For a moment longer he hesitated, then jumped down and rummaged through his trunk, searching for the special trimline headset his mother had bought him for his last birthday. Maybe it wasn't a PornStim, after all. Maybe it was a SportStim or an EduStim and Yun was just teasing him. But what if it was?

His hand closed on the headset's casing. He swallowed, then went across and drew the latch on the door. Back on his bed, he pulled on the headset and lay back.

*If it is . . .*

With trembling fingers he fed the Stim into the slot. There was a soft accepting hum and then the visor slid down, molding itself over his eyes and cheeks like a mask.

Suddenly, vividly, he was there.

She was tall and willowy, her skin pale, her long black hair flowing loosely down her naked back. At first she was standing with her back to him, but as she turned he saw she was *Hung Mao;* saw—with a small ripple of surprise—that her breasts were full, her nipples stiffly erect.

He shivered, his mouth suddenly dry.

"Hello," she mouthed, smiling at him, her dark, hazel eyes seeming to recognize him. "It's been a long time since you came to see me. Where have you been, you naughty boy?"

*Nowhere,* he wanted to say, *I've been nowhere,* but she was speaking again, moving toward him as she did, leaning over him so that he could smell her lightly perfumed skin.

"You should come and see your Aunt Lucy more often, you know. It's very"—he felt her brush against him, soft as silk, and shuddered, conscious of the growing stiffness at his groin—"unfilial of you."

Part of his mind wondered what was unfilial about not visiting this woman whom he did not know, but mainly he was conscious of the sudden, overwhelming warmth of her as she eased herself onto his lap, her legs wrapped about him.

*So real she felt. And if he were to place his hands on her . . .*

He moved his hands, even as, in the Stim, ghost hands reached out to cup her firm, warm buttocks and draw her down onto him, groin to groin. For a moment the doubleness confused him. The trick, they said, was to relax and let the Stim do all the work. He let his real hands fall back onto the bed, his ghost hands stroking the soft, firm flesh of the woman's back, his lips moving to her breast to lick and kiss the firm bud of her nipple.

And even as he did, he felt something give beneath the insistent stiffness of his penis and he was inside her, her softness breached.

He groaned silently, his whole body going into spasm, and still the Stim went on, her movements against him seeming to milk him, to draw him up out of himself into a darkness he had never known.

For the briefest instant his mind went outward, searching for connection . . . for Sampsa. Then, feeling a great wash of shame, of self-loathing, he reached up and ripped the mask from his face, throwing it aside.

There was a familiar patch of wetness at his groin. Sitting up, he took a long, slow breath.

Ashamed, yes, but part of him had wanted it; had longed for it to continue.

For a long time he sat there, his chin pressed against the balls of his clenched hands, staring at the discarded Stim. It was still running. So what was she doing now? What was *he* doing to her?

*No,* he said silently, but the instinct of curiosity was strong. He wanted to know.

He climbed down and picked the headset up, examining it, then sat again on the edge of the bed, closing his eyes, feeling the soft reverberation of the unit against his palms.

*What was she doing now? What was he doing to her?*

He lifted it and put it on again. Suddenly, vividly, he was back there with her.

She was crouched now on the floor, head down, her arms spread, her buttocks exposed to him, and he was pressed against her, thrusting into her from behind, each movement agonizingly slow, the stiffness of his ghost penis coaxing his real one back to life.

He could smell the animal musk of her and hear the soft, wicked grunt she made with every thrust of his. That smell, those noises—somehow they triggered something in him: something dark and primeval. Unconsciously he mimicked the movements of the Stim, moving his groin slowly, sensuously, as if she were really there in the empty air before him.

"Yes," she was saying now. "Yes, my naughty boy. That's it. Oh, gods, that's it!"

His movements quickened, more urgent suddenly as she pressed back against him.

"Yes," she was saying. "Fuck me. Come on, now. Fuck me hard. Yes . . . that's it. Harder now. Harder . . ."

He seemed close, very close, then suddenly he was aware of another presence in the Stim. Somewhere nearby a door had opened and someone had stepped into the room. There was a tingling presence somewhere at the back of his head.

Someone was standing right behind him—a big man in a black, full-length cloak. He stood there, glowering, his left hand holding a vicious-looking bullwhip.

"*Aiya!*" the woman cried, moving away, her flesh suddenly, disappointingly separate from his. "The gods help us, it's your uncle!"

"What's going on here?" the man asked, his voice heavy with threat. "Is *this* what you get up to when I'm away?"

*No*, he wanted to answer, fear making his heart hammer, *this is the first time*. But the man didn't want an answer. He leaned close, glowering, his face muscles twitching with anger.

"You've been bad, both of you. Very bad. And you know what happens to bad people, don't you?"

He took a step toward them and cracked the whip. Tom could feel its passage in the air close by his face then jumped as it connected with the soft flesh of the woman's haunches.

Her cry was one of fear, but also pleasure.

The man threw off his cloak. Beneath it he was naked, his penis stiff and long.

"Very bad," he said again, but this time he smiled. He stroked the whip slowly along the length of her spine, then, stepping closer, reached down and, gripping her brutally beneath the chin, lifted her face until it was level with his groin.

It went on, darker and yet darker until, toward the end, Tom threw the headset off once more, sickened and shaken, unable to believe that one human could treat another in that manner. And he . . . he, too, had been a part of it, aiding and abetting, hurting the woman, using her, some small dark part of him *enjoying* it.

He was sheened in sweat, his thin clothes clinging to him damply. Twice more he had come, the stickiness at his groin reminding him of his compliance with the illusion.

*So that's it,* he thought, glad that Sampsa was not there to share his guilty shame. *So that's how things are in this world. That's what happens in the darkness of their rooms.*

And was that his fate? To share in that wickedness?

He stood, looking about him, as if uncertain that he really was back among real things, for it seemed that everything was suddenly doubled—that behind each and every thing he saw lay a darker, unseen presence.

*Maybe that's what my father sees. Maybe that's what he's after.*

And if it was?

Tom shivered violently. Then, not knowing what else to do, he went to the washroom and, throwing off his clothes, stepped beneath the shower, keeping his hand on the control pad until the flow fell icy cold.

THE PUBLIC BATHHOUSE dominated the small square just off the main marketplace of Weisenau *Hsien*. Like most district bathhouses it was a big square building with a two-tier, red tile roof pitched steeply in the northern style. An eight-*ch'i*-high wall surrounded it unbroken on three sides, while at the front broad steps ran the length of its porticoed and impressive front. Like many of the buildings in Weisenau it looked old, its gray-white surface weathered as if by age, yet like much else here the appearance of antiquity was false. Nothing in the northern city was older than a dozen years.

As twilight fell and the sky darkened, so a stoop-backed servant stepped from the inner shadows carrying a flickering taper and, slotting it into the end of a long-handled stave, set about lighting the six oil-filled lamps that stood on tall poles in front of the building.

Earlier the bathhouse had been filled with noise; with the slap of the masseur's palms against oiled flesh, the hiss of water poured on hot coals, with voices, loud and soft, echoing back from the vaulted ceilings, with the soft pad of naked feet on tiles and the dull splash and indrawn gasp as one or other moved from the heat into cooler water. Now, however, the baths were almost empty.

Almost.

At the far end of the great bath, beneath the dim, mist-shrouded illumination of a hovering glow globe, were four figures. Three of them luxuriated on the broad, shelflike steps, their naked bodies half-submerged, the fourth sat on the edge of the bath, his feet dangling idly in the heated pool.

Just now the eldest of the four—Su Ping, the *Hsien L'ing*, or District Magistrate, of Weisenau, a solid-looking Han in his sixties with gray hair and a neatly-trimmed beard—was talking.

". . . what I *don't* want is to find us in the grasp of some avaricious Junior Minister, lining *his* pockets while our brother here"—he indicated the young man seated close by—"is kept waiting outside the door."

"My elder brother speaks wisely," Su Chun said from beside him, languidly wiping a hand across his sweat-beaded brow. "Yet there are ways we might ensure Su Yen receives fair treatment, neh?"

Su Ping stared at his twin—younger than he by a mere eight minutes—and narrowed his eyes. "I want no violence, brother. The risks—"

"Are negligible," Chun said quietly, laying his hand on his brother's arm. "You worry too much, Eldest Brother."

"And rightly so. Am I not *Hsien L'ing?* If word got back to my masters . . ."

"No trail will lead to your door, brother, I promise you. Besides, if we choose our man correctly—"

Ping sat forward, suddenly alert. "You know such a one?"

Chun looked about him, his smile quietly confident. "Do you trust me, Eldest Brother?"

The faintest flicker of uncertainty passed across Ping's face. He hesitated a moment, then nodded.

"Good. Then leave this matter with me, neh? What you do not know will not harm you."

"If you say so, brother." Yet Su Ping remained uneasy. As well he might, for though they were twins, the brothers' lives had followed very different paths.

Their mother had been a singsong girl, a common *men hu,* who, finding she had suddenly not one but two mouths to feed, had chosen to give one of her children up for adoption. They had been pretty babies and it had not been difficult for her contacts to find a childless couple from the Mids. They had chosen Ping and taken him uplevel. Chun, identical in every way, had stayed behind, to grow up in the brothel with his mother. So the fates had decided.

It might have ended there, but eight years ago Su Chun, passing through the district on his way to deliver a package to a "friend" in Mainz, had stopped for a bite in the marketplace of Weisenau and—to his astonishment—had glimpsed, seated in splendor in an official sedan, his double. After making his delivery he had come back and, once he'd established without doubt that this *was* the twin his mother had so often talked to him about, had returned a week later with his half-brother, Su Yen.

That day had been a great one for the Su family, and the celebrations had gone on long into the second week of their reunion. But Su Ping was a cautious man, and though family feeling was strong in him, he had his twin checked out—discreetly, of course, making sure no word of it got back to Su Chun.

What he discovered worried Su Ping greatly. He had always tried to be a good and honest man, and his official record was, if undistinguished, also unblemished. His brother, in contrast, had been in and out of trouble all his life, and while no *definite* proof existed, word was that he was linked at the highest levels to the great brotherhoods, the Triads, which organized almost all of the major criminal activity in the city.

Put briefly, Su Ping had been faced with a dilemma. Should he carry out his official duties and expose his brother for what he was—a minor *tong* boss, stealing and killing to his masters' orders? Or should family obligation override such considerations?

The fact that Su Chun was, in almost every sense, a stranger to him, made it curiously worse. If he had known Chun all his life, if he had shared his twin brother's fortunes and been made to face the same harsh choices, would he still have been the same good man he was? Or would adversity have shaped him just as it had shaped Chun?

In the end he decided to do nothing; to simply watch and wait and try to do his duty to both government and family. And thus far he had succeeded. But now there was this other matter—this matter of Su Chun's political ambitions for their half-brother Yen.

Su Ping pulled himself up, half out of the water, onto the top step, then turned and gestured with his hand. At once a servant hurried up and handed him a towel. Su Ping pulled it about his shoulders, then stood, looking down at the fourth of them there.

"Will you share a *chung* of *ch'a* with me before you retire, Kung Chia?"

Kung Chia turned his close-shaven head slowly and looked up at the *Hsien L'ing,* a lazy smile on his face.

"Forgive me, but not tonight, Su Ping. I have other things to do."

"Ah . . ." Su Ping stared a moment at his *Wei*—his Captain of Security—then shrugged. "As you wish. Su Chun . . . Su Yen. Good night."

"Good night, brother," Su Chun answered softly, his half-lidded eyes studying Kung Chia thoughtfully.

As the doors at the far end slammed shut, Su Chun lifted himself a step and leaned forward. His words, like the faint light from the glow lamp, shrouded in secrecy.

"Thank the gods the old fool's gone. Now listen, and listen carefully. . . ."

TOM FORCED HIS WAY through the packed crowd in the narrow street and grabbed Yun's arm, pulling him back.

The young Han turned, surprised. To either side of them people pressed close, the noise, the physical presence of them overwhelming, the strong scent of exotic spices spilling from the shops to either side, filling the warm night air.

"S'okay," Yun said, answering Tom's unspoken query. "We almost there."

*Yes,* thought Tom, for once frustrated by his inability to speak, *but where is "there"?*

They had walked for almost an hour, through busy thoroughfares and narrow *hutong* where whole families crouched before cheap trivees, past long rows of food stalls and soup kitchens, past endless hawkers with their trays of wares, and cripples—some blind, some lame—who'd call to him from where they lay, rattling their cups and moaning piteously. And always there were the children, the endless unwashed, unwanted children. He had seen sights and smelled scents he had never experienced before, but now he was tired. Tired, and just a little apprehensive.

*Where are we?* he wondered, wishing Sampsa were there in his head to reassure him. *Where in the gods' names are we?*

"Come on," Yun urged. "Two minutes and we there."

Tom sighed, then walked on, following close, knowing now that he should never have agreed to come.

The back street opened out into a square. Beyond it, beneath an ornate arch decorated with coiled dragons, was a park. Tom looked about him, frowning, trying to place himself, but it was impossible. Even with his perfect memory it was hard to know precisely how far he'd come or what directions he had taken. If he had studied a map of the district beforehand it might have been different, but he'd never thought . . .

Again he sighed, more heavily this time. How close was the river? How far was he from the barge?

*And how much danger am I in?*

He slowed, looking up at the arch as he passed beneath it. Yun had walked on—was disappearing into the darkness beyond. Tom hurried to catch up, then slowed, catching his breath.

*Why, it's beautiful. . . .*

Just ahead, beyond the courting couples and the old men strolling along the milk-white gravel path, the land fell away—the grass slope silver-black beneath the moon—to a canal.

Yun turned to him and called. "Come on! We here!"

Tom walked slowly down the path, between the whispering willow trees in the moonlit evening's warmth, entranced. Directly ahead of him the path ended in a curved white bridge. The lamps on the bridge shone brightly, reflected in the water. But his eyes were drawn beyond that, to the right. There, less than fifty *ch'i* from the bridge, drawn up in ranks of two against the far bank, a line of old-fashioned junks was moored, their decks lit with brightly colored lanterns.

He walked down onto the bridge, stopping beside Yun, who was leaning on the polished balustrade, watching as a tiny rowboat crossed the space between them and the moored lantern-boats.

As the craft came closer, Yun hailed it.

*"Lao* Wen!"

The rower—an old Han, gray-bearded and bent like an ancient tree—glanced up. He gave a single, decisive nod, then, digging his right oar deep into the water, slowly turned the boat toward the shore.

"Quickly," Yun said, turning to Tom and taking his arm. "We go meet him."

They went down to the bank, and while Yun held the gunwale, Tom climbed in, clambering behind the old Han as Yun pushed off and jumped into the swaying boat.

Tom sat, staring at the back of the old man's shaven head. Was this where Yun's family lived? And the old man . . . was he an uncle? If so, did all of Yun's family smell as bad? Tom looked past him to Yun, hoping to take some cue from his face, but Yun was turned away, looking back at the retreating bridge.

Slowly the boat came about until they were heading directly for the first of the lantern boats. As they slid past into the shimmering, colored water-passage between the two lines of boats, Tom could hear voices—high-pitched female voices—and, from within one of the cabins, the sound of a Chinese lute, a *p'i p'a*. There was laughter and the sweet scent of perfume.

He leaned past the old man, seeking Yun's eyes. This time Yun beamed back at him.

"You like?"

Tom grinned and nodded. *He liked.*

Suddenly Old Wen lifted both oars, letting the rowboat slide smoothly between the high-sided lantern-boats. As it slowed to a halt, he dug the right-hand oar deep into the flow and turned the boat about, bringing it close in against the side of one of the outer boats, then reached up to grasp a securing rope. A short rope-ladder led up. Yun pointed, indicating that Tom should climb it, and stepped past Old Wen, placing something in his palm, then held the bottom of the ladder taut as Tom climbed.

As Tom poked his head up over the side, it was to be met with an unexpected sight. There, playing cards at a silk-covered table on the deck, were four young Han women. Seeing Tom emerge, they set their cards down and leaned in toward each other, giggling. There was a brief exchange—too low for Tom to catch—and then one of them came over, even as Yun climbed up alongside him.

"You, boy!" she said, facing him arrogantly, the faintest smile on her lips. "You want fuck?"

He looked to Yun, bewildered, but Yun was laughing—looking past him at the young girl and laughing quietly.

"Tie Ning!" he said, scolding her. "You must treat our guest much better, okay? Tom here is *ch'un tzu*. Great man."

He extended his arms as if to describe a huge figure of a man, then reached out to touch Tom's arm.

"Choose one, Tom. Go on."

Tom stared at the girl, then back at Yun, not understanding.

"What matter with your friend?" Tie Ning said, a petulant expression settling on her face. "He dumb or something?"

Yun stepped past Tom, taking the young girl's arm and placing his head close to hers to whisper.

Freed from her fixed stare, Tom was able to see her properly for the first time.

Her clothes were curiously old fashioned, like something from a trivee costume drama, the full-length dress made of a cheap ersilk that was brightly colored and diaphanous in places. Her long, black hair was done up in a bun, fixed with ribbons and wires, while behind her right ear she wore a salmon-pink paper chrysanthemum. In the colored lantern-light her face seemed pale, almost ghostlike, the bones fine, the eyes large. A pretty face, but worn, mistrustful.

He looked about him, taking in details, noticing for the first time how it all connected. And slowly, very slowly, it dawned on him. *Laochu* they were. Singsong girls. And the boat—the boat was one of the "flower boats" he'd read of in his father's books—a floating brothel. He looked down, blushing fiercely.

There was a sudden waft of perfume, then he felt the girl's fingers brush against his arm.

"Forgive me, Master Thomas," she said softly, giving a small curtsy, her head lowered, demure suddenly, all arrogance gone from her—like an actress changing roles. "If I had known . . ."

She could not help herself. Placing a hand to her mouth, she giggled. Behind her, at the table, the others joined in. Tom looked up, seeing how she was watching him, sympathetic suddenly and curious. Unable to prevent himself, Tom smiled.

"That better, neh?" she said, letting her hand rest gently on his shoulder. "You okay. Yun vouch for you. He say you nice boy."

She turned, clicking her fingers, then looked back at him. "We find you nice girl, neh?"

Some part of him, remembering the Stim—the awful, degrading feel of it—wanted to draw back, to refuse what was being offered here, but the sheer proximity of her, the warmth, the perfumed smell of her, was like a trigger, freeing him from restraint.

For the briefest moment he was confused, uncertain. He looked to Yun.

"It okay," Yun said, as if he sensed Tom's hesitation. "This one on me, neh? You choose which girl you like. She do whatever you wish. Suck your cock all night, if make you happy!"

The spell dissolved. Tom looked about him, seeing it all for what it was; seeing how cheap the girls' silks were, how the shabbiness of the boat was masked by the colored light from the lanterns. It was a web, a sticky web, there to rob him of his senses. He shook his head, *No*, he thought. *Not like this. I want—*

From one of the nearby boats he heard, once more, the music of the *p'i p'a*. He turned, looking toward the sound, listening.

It was a song he knew—the nostalgic "Like Waves Against Sand." For a moment he held himself perfectly still, enchanted by the music, his eyes half-lidded, in a trance, then felt a touch upon his arm.

Yun was standing next to him. He leaned close, speaking to Tom's ear. "You want meet her, Tom? You want meet girl who make music?"

Tom hesitated, then gave a single nod.

Yun laughed, relieved. "Okay. You follow me. As I say, all paid for. Anything goes. You hear me, Tom? Anything goes."

But Tom could hear nothing. Nothing but the clear notes of the ancient lute, carrying across the water from the nearby boat, like waves lapping against the shore of his consciousness.

━━━━━

THE DAY WAS DONE, the boys were all asleep, the insect nets pulled across the open fronts of the stalls. Standing there in the cobbled outer courtyard, in the faint light cast by the lamp above the compound gate, Emily looked about her, listening to the soft snores of her boys, conscious of the unfamiliar vastness of the open sky above.

She looked up. The moon was bright and almost full, the sable sky dusted with stars.

It was beautiful. So peaceful. And this place . . . She smiled to herself. She had never thought she could feel so content, so *satisfied* with life. To want nothing but this—to need nothing *beyond* this—that surely was fulfillment.

It hadn't always been so. More had died in the first few years after the city's fall than in all the wars that had gone before; maybe nine tenths of the population, from disease and starvation. DeVore had indeed unleashed the Four Horsemen, and when they were done a great mountain of bones had filled the southern lands. Here in the north things had been better, but only just.

Emily remembered those times vividly. She had only to smell the sickly-sweet scent of slightly rotting meat and it all came back to her with a nightmare clarity. The rotting corpses, the big-wheeled death carts stacked high with lifeless bodies, the sight of hundreds, thousands, driven mad by despair; the awful sense they'd all had that this was somehow the judgment of the gods. And maybe that was why they'd made a go of it these past ten years— because of that memory: a memory etched deep within the consciousness of those who had survived. The city was a far better place to live these days. There were exceptions, of course—mainly the great urban centers like Frankfurt and Berlin, where the Triads had reestablished themselves—but in the suburbs, among the genteel poor, life was good. There was crime, certainly—such things were universals, after all—but it was mainly petty stuff, the exception rather than the rule, and generally one could trust one's neighbor.

The paranoia of that great World of Levels had been ended, washed away in a great tidal wave of blood and suffering.

And now, without doubt, they had a new chance; and not just for some, but for everyone. There was room enough, food enough, work enough, for all. Each passing month saw an improvement in their lot. Her boys were fed and educated. If they were sick, there was enough to pay for a doctor to call, if a doctor was needed. Times were good. The best she'd known them.

The thought made her feel . . . No, there was no word for it. This little island of being, this *sanctuary*, had become the focus, the epicenter, of her life. Having this, she wanted nothing else— neither riches nor revenge. For her, time had ended, the circle had closed. She could live her life like this and be content, knowing that in dying she had fulfilled her destiny, her fate.

Before this she had been restless, discontented. She had sought constantly to fill the raging void within her—that same void that had been inside them all when they were yet prisoners of the World of Levels. But now that world had gone, vanished like some evil dream conjured from the dark. Now they were free to begin again, to live as they'd been meant to live, with their feet on solid earth, their faces open to the sky.

A long way she had traveled to be standing here, by many and diverse paths. She had been a terrorist, a ruthless political killer with a price on her head, and then—in another life, it seemed— the wife of a great Company head; a Great Lady with a mansion and a thousand servants. Yet here she was, rooted, finally rooted in this place they had made their home.

Home. The very word seemed strange. For she had never had a home before, only a succession of places she had stayed.

She looked about her, smiling, knowing how lucky they had been to get this place. At first they had been forced to rent rooms in shared apartments in Mainz, making do in cramped, unsatisfactory conditions, but then one of the local merchants—a nice old man named Ho Chang—had heard of their circumstances and offered them this compound. They'd not thought they could afford it, but the rent he'd asked for was ridiculously low, and so they had moved here. That had been three years back, and though the old man was dead now, his daughter let them stay under the terms they had agreed with her father.

"Emily?"

She turned, surprised to find Lin at her shoulder. "Yes?"

"I thought you'd gone."

Emily laughed softly. She had been on her way out to the merchant's house, but that had been ten, fifteen minutes ago. "I was thinking."

"Thinking?" He came around and stood before her, his disfigured face revealed in the lamp's soft light. She studied it, then reached out to touch his right cheek. Lin looked back at her unselfconsciously, letting her fingers trace his skull's deformity. It had never worried him. Unlike most others she had met, he seemed to have no sense of self, only a feeling for those he might help. It was why she loved him. Why she had stayed with him all these years.

"It's enough, don't you think?" she said quietly, letting her hand fall away. "All this. . . ."

Lin nodded, his eyes half-smiling, then answered her softly, using the words of the ancient sage Lao Tzu.

"The nameless uncarved block is but freedom from desire. And if I cease to desire and remain still, the empire will be at peace of its own accord."

She sighed. "Would that it were so simple, neh?"

"But it *is*, Mama Em. Men have but to realize it, that is all. They struggle so. They . . ." He shook his head, then laughed softly. "But you must go now. Steward Liu will be waiting for you."

"Then I will not keep him waiting any longer." She touched his arm. "Take care of my boys, neh, Papa Lin?"

"I will. You know I will."

Tung Wei's Mansion was fifteen minutes' walk, on the far side of the district. Tenth bell was sounding as she stood before the massive gates, waiting to be admitted.

Steward Liu had given them many things in the past, broken household things that would otherwise have been simply trashed, but it was rare for him to send for her.

As the smaller door within the gate creaked open she stepped forward, expecting Steward Liu's clean-shaven head to duck out beneath the lintel, but it was not Liu Yeh. The man who faced her was much younger than Liu, with a full head of black hair and the number six embroidered on the ersilk patch he wore at the center of his chest; moreover, he was scowling.

"What do you want, old woman?"

"I . . ." Disconcerted by his manner, she fumbled in her jacket for the letter Liu Yeh had sent, then realized she had left it on the table in the inner courtyard. "Forgive me, I—"

Abruptly, he stepped forward and shoved her, sending her off-balance. "Be off with you! Now! Before I call the guard!"

She stared at him, shocked. Behind her a small crowd of passersby had begun to gather. "But Liu Yeh said—"

Eyes glaring, he shoved her again, sending her sprawling. "Begone! We'll have no beggars here!"

There was a murmuring from the crowd. A single voice called, "Leave her be!"

In answer the servant made a gesture, as if he were going to cuff each one of them in turn with the back of his hand. "On your way, you rabble! Clear the street, or I'll turn the hose on you!"

He turned, looking to where Emily lay on her back looking up at him, then hawked up a gobbet of phlegm and spat into the dust beside her.

"Beggars. . . ." he muttered, a sneer of distaste on his face, then turned and, slamming the door behind him, went inside.

Slowly Emily got to her feet, hands reaching to help her and brush her down.

"Who the fuck does he think he is?" one of them—an old fellow she recognized as a stallholder from Lung Chi Lane—said, handing her a cloth to wipe her hands.

She turned, nodding her gratitude, and, biting back her anger, smiled at him. "Why, surely you know, *lao jen?* Our friend is Number Six. He is a *big* man in Tung Wei's mansion."

They laughed at that, but their laughter was uneasy, for all there remembered how it had been back in the World of Levels. There was not one there who did not recall the constant petty slights and humiliations heaped on them by their supposed "betters."

Looking about her, Emily felt a shadow fall on her. At core these people were still afraid. Fear lay at the back of their newfound freedom: a deep-rooted fear that this was but a dream—a brief dream of open skies and happiness—and that soon they would wake, to find this new world vanished like the old. And then?

She sniffed, then wiped her hands and handed back the cloth. "Thank you," she said softly, smiling at him again, and looking about her. "Thank you all."

There were nods, looks of understanding and sympathy, and then, unwillingly it seemed, the crowd began to disperse.

Emily turned, staring at the door, wondering for a moment if the young man had been carrying out Liu Yeh's orders, whether this were some subtle ploy to remind her of her relationship to Liu Yeh's master. With a shrug she moved away, making her way back to the compound, the full moon shining brightly high above.

━━━━━━

THE MUSIC HAD STOPPED. Tom stood there on the plank bridge between the boats, staring down at the surface of the water a dozen *ch'i* below. To his right, where the lantern light fell, it seemed both strange and magical, a shimmering, ever-changing mask, yet here between the boats it was simply dark. He could see oil in the water, the floating detritus of the town washed up against the grimy hull.

*So it is,* he thought, feeling a sudden disenchantment. Yet the music still intrigued him: intrigued because it was so unexpected, here in this setting.

"Tom?"

He looked up, meeting Yun's eyes, then, realizing he had been there some while, moved quickly on, jumping down onto the deck. As he did a young man—a *liumang,* or "punk," by the look of him—stepped out from the cabin farther down the deck. He approached them slowly, like a lizard, his eyes the merest slits in his face, his knife drawn. For a moment it seemed as though the situation would get ugly, but a brief, murmured exchange between Yun and the punk seemed to settle things. The *liumang* stepped aside. Slipping the knife back into his belt, he waved them along. Yun went quickly through, yet as Tom passed the *liumang* leaned close, sniffing him suspiciously, like a dog getting the scent of an intruder.

Questions. Suddenly he was full of questions. And no Sampsa to answer them. No Ben.

Tom ducked beneath the lintel, pulling the small, glass-paneled door to behind him, then turned, looking into the room, conscious at once of the heavy scent of perfume in the musty air.

It was a long, low-ceilinged room, two small lanterns, hung from a beam to his left, casting a sickly pink glow over everything. To his right a couch rested beneath a long window, over which cane blinds had been drawn. Beside it was a low table, on which were placed a silver cigarette box and a folded lady's fan. A patched silk curtain—was it blue, green? the lamplight made it hard to tell—concealed the far end of the room. From behind it came the faintest rustling, silk upon silk.

He looked to Yun, a query in his eyes. His companion smiled and beckoned him on.

*She there,* Yun mouthed. *You wait. I go.*

He wanted to stop him; wanted, despite his burning curiosity, to back out of there and return to the barge. But it was too late. He heard the door creak open, then close behind him.

Slowly he crossed the room, conscious of the noise each footfall made. The bare planks had been swept, but here, at the center, a colorful rug had been spread. He stared down at it, noticing how stained and threadbare it was. Like all else here, it had the air of fallen elegance.

Again the faintest rustling came from behind the screen.

For an instant he felt the urge to step across and tear the curtain aside, but the memory of the music stayed his hand. He looked around, wondering briefly if it hadn't perhaps been a trick, after all; if that beautiful music hadn't been artificially produced. There was no sign of any instrument. Besides, this place . . .

He laughed inwardly. What had he been imagining? That he would find some pearl, some jewel of a girl, in a place like this? No. For there were only whores here. Pleasure girls. Girls who would do anything if the price were right.

He turned away, meaning to leave, then stopped, hearing the curtain move on its runners.

"You want to go, mister?"

He stood there a moment, undecided. The voice was not as common as he'd expected.

"Well? Don't you want to look at me before you make up your mind? I'm a nice girl. I'll treat you well."

Words formed in his mind. *I want . . .*

*What do you want?* he asked himself suddenly, as if it were Sampsa in his head and not himself.

*I want to know where that music came from?*

He turned, not knowing what to expect, telling himself, even before he saw her, that he would go once he had seen her face.

He looked. For a long time he stood there, studying her, drinking in the sight of her, surprised—beyond all imagining surprised—by just how beautiful she was. And young too. Younger, perhaps, than himself.

"Well?" she asked finally, the faintest smile on her glistening red lips. "You like me? You want to stay all night?"

*I want . . .*

Slowly he raised his right hand and, placing his forefinger to the tip of his tongue, shook his head.

"You're dumb? Is *that* what you're trying to say?"

Tom nodded.

She stepped closer, taking his hands in hers. "I'm sorry. I'd have liked to know all about you. What you do. Where you come from. I like to know such things. But we can be friends anyway, neh? You come and sit with me. I'll talk, you listen. Okay?"

*Okay,* he answered in his head, the sweet, jasmine scent of her intoxicating now that she was so close, the feel of her tiny hands in his making him feel strange, unreal.

He looked down at where their hands were linked and thought-lessly began to caress the backs of her fingers with his thumbs. For the briefest moment he waited for the doubled sensation of the Stim, for that abrupt transition as the guide track switched in to control his muscles, but there was nothing this time—only the singular response of his own nerve ends.

"That's nice," she said, a new softness in her voice. "You're very gentle."

He looked up, meeting her eyes, seeing how openly they smiled back at him, surprised by that.

*You're real*, he thought, strangely awed by that; yet even as he thought it he knew how ridiculous it was. Of course she was real. Cut her and she would bleed, kiss her and—

"Well?" she said for the third time. "Shall we sit down? Or do you want to fuck me right away?"

The straightforward manner in which she said it took his breath. But why should he be surprised? It was as he'd told himself only a moment earlier: however beautiful she seemed in this half-light, however "different," the girl was still a whore, a singsong girl. Any-one could have her, no matter how fat or ugly, old or foul of mind they were. What he was as a man meant nothing here, only the money he brought. No, he was not to fool himself: this was not romance, this was *trade*.

He looked away, troubled.

Removing her hands from his, she reached up and turned his face gently, her fingers warm on his cheek and neck, making him look at her again.

"What's the matter?" she asked, her eyes trying to read him. "Don't you like the way I talk?"

He sighed, then shrugged.

"Would you like me to play for you, perhaps?"

She saw how his eyes lit at that and smiled. "You'd like that, yes? Maybe you heard the music on the other boat and you thought, *Who is that girl playing the* p'i p'a? And maybe you thought you'd like to see that girl, neh?"

He nodded.

"Good." She seemed excited now that she understood. "You sit down there while I get ready, okay?"

She made her way across, then turned, a new look—of curiosity—in her eyes.

"You have a name?" She gestured to her hands. "You spell it with your fingers, maybe?"

He signed for her, straight forefinger to forefinger, forefinger and thumb looped, then the V of thumb and forefinger linked to forefinger and middle finger.

"Tom? You're called Tom, right?"

He nodded.

She smiled. "That's a nice name. Tom suits you. I'm glad now you have a name. I'll not have to call you 'mister' all night."

For the first time since he'd stepped into the room he smiled. *All night . . .* The words took on a whole new meaning, a whole new sense of promise.

He watched her cross the room, conscious suddenly of the scent of her—not of her perfume, but of *her*—and of each silken, whispering sound her body made within its clothes. Suddenly, unexpectedly, he was alive to her. It was like waking.

As she disappeared behind the curtain, he looked about him once again, seeing this time a dozen tiny details he had passed over the first time he had looked—things he had seen but not seen. Reaching out he lifted the fan and unfolded it, studying the picture cut into the scented wood.

It was a town, an ancient Chinese town, with boats on the river and a bridge. He smiled and replaced it, then sat back, waiting, looking about him, his eyes—like his father's eyes—recording everything, unable to forget.

The curtain twitched back, the girl stepped out, carrying the lute as if it were a child.

He could see at a glance that it was an ancient instrument—a real collector's piece—and wondered how she, a young whore on a flower boat, had managed to afford it.

It was beautiful, its pear-shaped sound-box tapering delicately into the long neck, the ivory tuning pegs jutting out like the display feathers of some strange and elegant bird. Its four strings—tuned A-D-E-A—were of the finest gut. Looking at it, he had no doubt that it was from this instrument that the sounds he'd heard had come.

She sat, facing him on the sofa, crossing her legs, the *p'i p'a* held upright against her, her right hand curled about the sound box, the fingers of her left resting loosely against the upper frets. For a moment she seemed almost to doze, her head tilted, resting against the neck of the instrument, then she looked up at him again and smiled.

"What do you want me to play? 'High Mountain, Flowing Streams'? 'Crescent Moon at Dawn'?"

He shrugged. For once it did not matter. He just wanted to see her play. She smiled as if she understood, then, wordlessly, she began, the notes spilling clear and pure into the air.

He watched her, entranced. As she played so she seemed to caress the instrument like a lover, her whole being lost in the ancient melody, her fingers moving expertly, the bright red nails plucking the strings with faultless ease. He looked to her face, conscious that for that moment he did not exist for her. Her mouth had fallen moistly open, her eyes stared distantly away, as if she was somewhere else, lapsed out, beyond this mundane world of deals and betrayals.

He shivered violently then reached out to touch her. . . .

The tune died. Slowly she looked to him, her dark eyes vague, part of her still there in that timeless realm. She gave a little shudder as if loath to return; then, her eyes focusing again, she smiled.

"Well?"

He smiled and nodded. Reaching out, he took her hand. She laid the lute down carefully and, never once relinquishing his hand, moved closer, kneeling by his side.

He caressed her cheek, her hair, then leaned closer to inhale a long, deep breath of her. That made her laugh; made her look up at him.

"You like that smell?"

Again he nodded.

Slowly her face changed, became more serious. She tilted her head, her lips falling open once again, and as if compelled, he put his mouth to hers, sinking down into the warmth, the sensual darkness of her kiss.

He felt her hands move softly to his neck, caressing his skin, sensed the growing stiffness at his groin, but for that instant it seemed he was entirely detached from that, his whole self *focused* into the meeting of their lips, the whole of him poured like molten metal into that single point of contact. Such gentle, moist surrender it was; such shivering, sensational delight. The wires of his nerves sang, as if a massive sensory superhighway had suddenly opened up between the surface of his lips and the deeper levels of his brain.

He pressed hungrily at her, his face forcing hers back, a sudden, animal savagery taking him. His hands tore at her clothes, ripping them from her back as he pushed her down. But his urgency was matched by hers. She grunted, her face mirroring the lust he felt, encouraging him. As he lifted her skirt, her hands tore at his clothes, freeing him. For a brief moment she held him back with her left hand, the fingers pressed against his inner thigh, while with the other she gently traced the length of his swollen penis.

He groaned, wanting at that instant to thrust right through her, to pin her to the floor and stab at her time and time and time again, but still her left hand held him while her fingers stroked and caressed his shaft, his balls—those same long fingers that had coaxed the ancient melody from the air.

She was smiling now; a lascivious, animal smile of lust. "You like that, Tom? You *like* that?"

Again he groaned. It was unbearable, utterly, hideously unbearable. His penis hurt it was so hard, the skin so tight it seemed that at any moment it would burst. He pushed at her, trying to reach her, but still she held him, her strength matching his own.

She whispered, her breath hot against his neck.

"That's the secret, Tom. Don't you understand that? It's like the music. You have to want it. Want it beyond anything you've ever wanted. Only then is it any good. Only then. . . ."

He groaned again, then suddenly, unbelievably, he was inside her, his hardness breaching her softness, her body pressing up against his, the hot wetness of her, the sensation of her flesh against his own exploding like a dark star in his head, blinding his senses. Mindlessly he thrust at her, again and again and again until, with a broken cry that was half sheer agony and half pure bliss, his body arched.

"Yes!" she said breathlessly. "Yes! *Yes*, my love, that's *it!*"

The spasm made him jerk like a corpse, his face grimacing in unseeing agony above hers, his arms locked stiff either side of her head, his teeth gritted as, with one final violent thrust he buried his pulsing seed deep within her.

"*Jeee-eee-arghh!*"

The sound—savage and inchoate—came from deep within, from a part of him that wasn't chained to silence.

Slowly, very slowly, he relaxed.

"That's it. . . ." she said softly, gently stroking his back, caressing his tensed and naked buttocks. "That's it, my darling boy. You see? You see now what I meant?"

───◆◆◆───

AT THIS LATE HOUR the massive hangarlike building that was Mashhad fast-track terminus was echoing empty. The crowds that had packed the station earlier had dispersed, some home to their quarters in the Warlord's sprawling mountain capital, others to their various destinations in distant East Asia and the neighboring West Asian states. One name alone remained now on the destination board: Krasnovodsk.

In five minutes that, too, would be gone and the station would be closed, its gates locked. Even now the guards were checking their timers, the last few late travelers boarding hastily, hauling their luggage up onto the narrow walkway that ran alongside the carriages.

As the three-minute warning hooter sounded, Eva gripped her brother tightly, then, giving him a brave smile, urged him on board. They had said their good-byes earlier, though whether they were temporary or final neither knew.

"Take care, Alan," she said, steeling herself not to cry, not to let him down at the final moment. "And if you hit trouble, remember—save yourself, not the shipment."

He sniffed deeply, then nodded. "I shall, my darling Eva. Be assured I shall."

He turned to go, yet as the one-minute hooter sounded, he stepped back and hugged her one last time. Then, quickly, he climbed up onto the running board and hauled himself inside. And not a moment too soon. With a loud hiss the doors slid shut, the bolts falling into place with a soft double-clunk. Pressing his face to the window, he began to wave.

Slowly, very slowly, the fast-track pulled away, accelerating all the while, heading north toward the Gonbad Gap, then on to Ashkhabad. There it would stop to pick up passengers before traveling on northwest to Krasnovodsk on the southeastern shore of the Caspian.

"The gods protect you," she said softly, as she waved him out of sight. "And pray we'll meet again, sweet brother."

———————

IT WAS AFTER two when she returned to her quarters in the palace, surprised to find the main lights on, guards everywhere. Arriving at her rooms, she found a young lieutenant going through her shelves and cupboards.

"What is it?" she asked him, suspecting the worst, but he was apologetic.

"Forgive me, *Nu Shi* Calder," he said, turning and bowing to her, "but I have my orders. We have been told to search the grounds thoroughly. It seems a few things have gone missing from the Warlord's collection. Important things."

Eva swallowed but said nothing, gesturing that he should carry on. Besides, he would find nothing now.

"What has gone missing?" she asked after a moment.

He glanced at her. "I'm afraid that's confidential. But there's a hell of a stink about it. It seems security was breached at the highest level. Hu Wang-chih was livid when he heard."

"Yes. . . ." She could imagine. Her heart was pounding now. She hadn't gambled on them finding out so soon.

"Do they know who it was?"

The young officer shrugged, then carried on his work, pulling things down from the shelf and shaking them, then putting them back in a desultory fashion. "No one can say for sure. It seems the security cameras were broken. But I'd put good money on it being one of the guards."

"Ah . . ." She hesitated, controlling herself again, then asked. "Why's that?"

"Because they had access."

"Ah," she said again. Yet others had had access, too, herself among them. But then, Hu Wang-chih trusted her implicitly. After all, it was she who fed him, shaved him, bathed him, even—from time to time—slept with him.

She shivered, then, hearing the click of booted footsteps in the corridor outside, turned.

"Lieutenant Stocken?"

The young officer turned, then straightened up, facing the newcomer. "Yes, Sergeant?"

"Are you finished here, sir?"

Stocken looked about him then nodded.

"Then you are to report to the Main Courtyard." The sergeant turned, looking to Eva. "You, too, *Nu Shi* Calder. Warlord Hu has summoned the whole household to attend."

"Attend? What for?"

The sergeant smiled grimly. "For the executions."

"Ah . . ." And now the full significance of what she'd done tonight hit her. And, as she followed the two young soldiers out and down the corridor, heading for the Main Courtyard, her mind went out to her brother. He'd be in Ashkhabad by now. Unless something had happened. Unless they'd stopped and searched the train.

---

THE FOUR GUARDS had been shaven and beaten. Dressed only in their loincloths, their hands bound behind them, the livid marks of the lash striping the pale flesh of their backs, they knelt beneath the arc lights of the Main Courtyard as the palace household slowly gathered.

The local Warlord, Hu Wang-chih, stood close by, his chest bare, glistening in the light, the leather whip in his right hand, a spiked glove on his left. He had administered the beatings himself, and though none of the four had confessed, there was little doubt that one of them was guilty.

As the last few people arrived, Hu looked about him and, raising his voice, began to speak.

"You all know why we're here, so I won't waste words. Simply this. If you work for me, here in the palace, I must be able to trust you. I must be able to count on you absolutely. These men"—he gestured with the whip, not deigning to look at the kneeling men—"these *insects*, rather, betrayed that trust. They *stole* from me, and I will not tolerate that kind of behavior in my household, understand me?"

There was nodding from all around, a faint murmur of agreement.

"Good. Then bear witness. For if I find any of you—*any* of you—behaving similarly, this will be your fate."

He turned and nodded to his Chief Executioner, who smoothed a gloved hand over his masked face, then stepped forward, hefting his ax.

Watching from thirty *ch'i* away, just to the right of Warlord Hu, Eva felt a shiver of fear run through her. Not for the poor guards, but for herself; for her immortal soul. For she knew they were innocent. Knew for a certainty that they had done nothing wrong.

Not that that meant a thing now. As the ax swung back then fell, she heard herself cry out. But she was not alone. All about her others looked on with fear in their eyes.

Yes, and that was why she'd had to act. To end this.

*Maybe,* she told herself, forcing herself to watch—to fix it in her memory. But she would have to live with this, knowing that she had killed these men, as surely as if she'd swung the ax herself.

The blade glinted and fell, glinted, fell.

As the last blow fell, a shuddering sigh passed through the watching crowd. For a moment no one moved. Then, at some unseen, ungiven signal, they began to disperse, back to their rooms, their stations, in the palace.

She sighed, and looked across. Warlord Hu stood there, breathing deeply, staring at the headless corpses where they lay toppled, ungainly in death. Then, as if waking from a trance, he turned and, seeing her, smiled, beckoning her across.

"Eva!" he called, a strange note of excitement in his voice. "Come, see to me!"

TOM WOKE TO FIND the room in moonlit darkness, the girl beside him in the bed, asleep, her naked body turned from his, facing the window. For a moment he lay there, perfectly at peace, remembering.

After that first time she had taken his hand and led him to her bed. There she had made him stretch out on his front while she massaged his back and sang to him in a soft, lilting voice; old songs in her native dialect—songs he did not recognize. Then, when he was aroused once more, she had made love to him a second time, on top of him in the half-dark, her every movement silken, like a warm wind on a summer's day, or like the gentle flow of water through a sunlit meadow. Again she played him, like an instrument, coaxing him, rousing him, slowing him when his passion grew too much, her hands, the smallest motion of her body, seeming to control him, until their sweating bodies seemed to melt into a single force, driving on and on, the pleasure mounting until, with a single cry, they merged in blissful darkness.

They slept and woke much later. For an eternity, it seemed, they had lain there face to face, toying with each other, fingers on flesh, mouths meeting in the merest brushing touch, their eyes locked gaze to gaze, as if to look away would break that sensual spell.

Remembering that—remembering the sheer intensity with which he had stared into her eyes—Tom shuddered. He had never guessed. Nothing he had read or seen or experienced had prepared him for this night. Nothing. It was like being born again. Like . . .

No, there were no likes for this. This was itself—unique and incomparable. And the girl . . .

He exhaled a shivering breath. He was in love. Unbelievably—inexcusably, perhaps, for what could come of it?—he was in love. In love with a singsong girl, a whore, whom any man could have.

A girl whose name he didn't even know.

He turned his head slightly, looking at her, seeing the way the silvered light lay softly on her back, picking out in chiaroscuro the ridged bones of her spine, the curve of her naked buttocks, the sweet fold and flow of her legs.

He close his eyes, his peace disturbed. *Sampsa?* he called, but his head was empty. It would be another day at least before he could talk to his friend.

Okay. So what was he to do?

*Nothing*, he answered, playing Sampsa's part. *You can do nothing, for she's a whore and you—you are a Shepherd.*

Maybe. Yet his father had defied convention more than once. Two wives he had, one stolen and one his sister. So maybe—just *maybe*—he could buy the girl. Or marry her.

He could almost hear his mother's laughter. *How old are you, Tom?* she'd ask, staring at him as if he'd lost his senses. *Sixteen? Just sixteen? And you seriously think you know what's best for you?*

No, even to contemplate it was a kind of madness. Yet to think of not seeing her again—to think of leaving her here and living out his life, knowing she existed in the world—filled him with despair.

It had been so sweet.

He stretched out his hand, meaning to touch her, to wake her and make her somehow understand, then drew his fingers back.

No. It was impossible. Impossible.

He turned and, slipping from the bed, careful not to wake her, bent down, searching in the darkness for his tunic. Finding it, he pulled it over his shoulders, then went to the cabin door.

He climbed up onto the roof of the boat, expecting to find Yun there, maybe, or the punk, but there was no one. All was quiet, the lanterns dark. Only the moon shone down, huge and pale in the night sky. Tom stared at the great white circle for a time, wondering where exactly Sampsa was in relation to it.

And what would Sampsa say when he knew? What would he think? For this would surely change things between them: would make things . . . *different.*

He went to the front edge of the cabin's roof and sat, hunched into himself. The night was warm. A soft breeze blew in from the darkness, tickling his chest. In the distance, beyond the darkened urban sprawl, lay the high-rise towers of Frankfurt *Hsien*, warning lights winking from their upper stories. He watched them absently a moment, then looked away.

He ought to leave. Now, before she woke and found him gone. He ought to chalk this up to experience and move on. But he was loath to move on. Something special had happened here tonight. Something unexpected. And the girl, she had known that too. He had seen it in her eyes that final time, felt it in the gentle kiss she'd planted on his brow before she turned from him to sleep.

No matter that she was a whore, she was a person, too, with needs and the desire for love. If he took her from here . . .

He drew back, trying to see it clear, to think it through the way Sampsa would have thought it through.

*Why now?* he called to him across the emptiness. *Why did you have to go away from me now?*

Yet if he hadn't, if Sampsa had been in his head throughout, seeing it all, sharing it, would he ever have fallen? Would he have even taken the first step?

No. He knew that for a fact. Sampsa's absence from his head may have made him vulnerable, yet it had also made him free.

*Nothing will ever be the same again,* he thought, letting a sigh escape him. *Nothing.*

There was a noise; the creaking of a board. Tom turned sharply. It was Yun. The young Han smiled apologetically then came across, crouching beside Tom.

"So, Tom, how did it go? You fuck her good, eh? You give her what for?"

Tom reached out and took Yun's arm, then pulled at it sharply. There was a startled yelp, a splash. A moment later a slick head broke the surface of the water, gasping.

"What the fuck?"

Tom stood and turned. It was time to go.

———————

*CHUANG KUAN TS'AI stood in the Oven Man's garden, beyond the shadow of the high brick walls, her round hazel eyes wide as she watched the flickering patch of crimson dancing in the sunlight. So red it was—so vividly, startlingly red.*

*"Hu t'ieh," she murmured beneath her breath, the habit of silence strong in her. "Hu t'ieh . . ."*

*She took a slow, careful step, like a cat closing on its prey. Yet she had no thought of capturing the tiny, dancing creature. No. Let it go free. Let it fly to another garden and delight some other child the way it had delighted her.*

*Slowly, like a flower opening, her seven-year-old face budded in a* smile. Hu t'ieh . . . like in the story Uncle Cho had told her, about the old man who had dreamed he was a butterfly—hu t'ieh—and when he woke could not say whether he had been a man dreaming he was a butterfly, or was now a butterfly dreaming he was a man.

She watched it settle on a leaf, red against green, resting in the midday heat, seeming to soak in the brilliant sunlight, as if recharging itself.

Another step, and another; then, crouching, her eyes on a level with the leaf, she stretched out a finger, slowly, careful not to startle it. Surprisingly it did not fly off, but alighted on her finger, soft, light, ticklingly light.

A tiny shiver of delight passed up her spine as it slowly closed and opened its wings. She drew her hand back until the tiny creature rested only inches from her face, its compound eyes staring back at her as if understanding the sudden awe in her eyes.

"Hu t'ieh," she whispered, naming it again, her breath making its gossamer wings shimmer. "Hu t'ieh."

Slowly she turned it, trying to make out the mirrored design on its wings, then caught her breath in surprise, recognizing the logo from the trivee ads she had seen. A capital G with a smaller S inside.

GenSyn. The butterfly was GenSyn.

For a moment longer it rested there, barely moving, its wings stretched open, the tiny solar panels soaking up the sunlight; then, with a lifting, fluttering movement that perfectly mimicked the flight of a butterfly, it launched itself into the sunlight, climbing up out of the Oven Man's garden, its camera eyes sending back a constant stream of images.

Young Chuang watched, feeling a sudden, overpowering sense of disappointment. Then, conscious that Uncle Cho would soon be home, she went back inside to set the table and begin to make the tea.

———

JOSEF HAD SEEN it there two days ago; had seen the lao jen take the heavy plastic container and set it down beside another at the back of the shop, the distinctive marking—the bright yellow casing with its skull-and-crossbones warning sign in black—catching his eye. Even then he had known he would be back. It was just a question of time. Of time and careful planning.

For a whole afternoon he had sat on the bank opposite the quayside shop, watching the comings and goings, his feet dangling idly in the water while he thought it through. Now, as his head broke the water's surface and his hands sought the slick stone steps that led up into the back of the shop, he knew exactly what to do.

The front of the shop was closed, the security shutters pulled down, the lao jen at his lunch. For an hour the coast was clear. He had only to keep from being seen.

He crouched low in the water, keeping to the deep shadow by the wall. Out on the river the heat beat down. It was the hottest part of the day and the whole world seemed to doze. On passing boats the sailors lounged or listlessly went about their duties. No one had eyes for the boy crouched in the water by the wall.

The back door was locked, of course, but that was no problem. Josef was good at picking locks. He had been doing it since he was four. Besides, there was always the ventilation hatch above. He was small enough and lithe enough to climb through there if need be.

It proved unnecessary. The lock gave easily and he was in, the door closed to a tiny crack behind him. Inside it was dark, the scent of herbal preparations strong. All around him he could sense the shadowy shapes of the great cupboards, their tiny drawers—row after row of them—reaching up right to the ceiling.

Feeling his way along, he found the counter and climbed up, perching himself beside the till. For a moment he rested, getting his breath, looking about him as his eyes grew accustomed to the dark. He had no interest in the money—at least, not in this money—yet it was necessary to take it. To make it seem that there had been a proper robbery.

Smiling, he took a sealed plastic packet from inside his sodden shirt and popped the neck, spilling its contents onto the counter. It held four things: two gloves, a small clear plastic storage jar with a screw-on top, and a badge—a school badge from the Seventh District School.

Quickly he slipped on the gloves and, ringing up a sale, opened the ancient till, taking out all of the high-value notes and chips. These he placed inside the packet. He patted the boxlike note-tracer beside the till fondly, then climbed down, going over to where the two containers sat side by side against the wall. He tried the right one first. It was heavy, clearly full, the seal unbroken. He set it down and lifted the other. It was much lighter. He put it down, then reached in his pocket and set the storage jar down beside it, unscrewing the top. Taking great care, he lifted the container once again and tilted it slowly, pouring the smallest amount into the jar.

Satisfied, he sealed the top again and put it back beside its fellow. No one would know. They would think money the motive for this burglary. He popped the top back on the jar, making certain it was secure, then went across and slipped it into the packet, along with the money.

And now the badge. He looked about him, seeing it as the investigating officer would see it, and dropped it on the floor beside the till.

Four minutes had passed, no more, as he removed his shirt and, holding the resealed packet in one hand, mopped behind him with the sodden rag, removing the print of his feet on the erwood floor.

At the back door he waited, listening, hearing a laden barge chug by, then slowly, very slowly, opened the door a fraction, widening the crack until he could see the far bank clearly. No one.

Quickly he slipped out and onto the steps. In an instant the lock was sprung, the door secure again, and he was in the shadows by the wall, neck deep in the oily water.

As he rested there, getting his breath again, a rat swam by. He smiled. What he had in the jar would have killed the little bastard and a few dozen more besides, but it wasn't rats he was after.

No, and as he pushed out into the river's sluggish flow he chuckled to himself, thinking through the next stage of his plan.

# CHAPTER TWO

# Butterfly Vision

I YE, PEI K'UNG'S Chief of Security, rested one gloved hand lightly on the operative's shoulder, then leaned across him, studying the picture on the screen.

"She's a pretty young thing," he said softly, pointing to the screen, watching as the child's eyes slowly widened in realization of what she held. "What sector is that?"

"Hochheim," the operative answered, a faint, apprehensive quaver in his voice. "Approximately two *li* from the river."

"Ah," I Ye said, nodding to himself, then watched the image break up momentarily as the bug-cam lifted from the girl's hand. For a moment he saw her standing there in the center of the walled garden, her face turned up to him as she followed the butterfly's erratic flight, then she was gone.

"I can give you a precise position, if you want, Colonel," the operative said, his fingers hovering, waiting to punch in a superimposed map-grid.

"No," I Ye said, straightening. "I was curious, that's all."

They had "bugs" all over the Northern City now, the tiny, mimic life-forms programmed to carry out overlapping search patterns. It wasn't perfect—the losses from birds and other scavengers alone had proved extremely costly—but it was better than using men. This way, at least, their enemies remained unalerted. This way, perhaps, they had a chance of finding what they were looking for.

He moved on, looking from screen to screen along the row, seeing a dozen snapshot images. As he came to the end he heard the guard at the door snap to attention with a crisp click of his boots and turned to meet the eyes of the Chancellor, Heng Yu.

"Well?" Heng Yu asked, without preliminaries. "Have we got him yet?"

"Nothing," I Ye said, taking a step toward the Chancellor and bowing low, acknowledging his superior status. "We know he's here, though. Our man in Mashhad said he left there yesterday evening."

Heng glanced at the screen nearest him, then met I Ye's eyes again. "What if he's been delayed?"

"Then we'll keep looking, Master Heng, even if it takes five, ten days. My men will not stand down until they've found him."

A faint smile flickered on Heng Yu's face. He nodded. "Good, Colonel I. Our Mistress would expect no less of you."

Mention of Pei K'ung brought an instinctive response from I Ye. He snapped to attention and lowered his head. "You may tell our Mistress that I shall inform her the moment there is any news."

Heng Yu stared at the Chief of Security as if at an unwanted cockroach in the palace kitchens. "No, Colonel I. You will inform *me*. You understand? Our Mistress is not to be disturbed right now. She is very busy."

*Yes, and we all know what she's busy at,* I Ye thought, keeping his face a blank. *Fucking young serving boys two at a time!*

"As you wish, Master Heng," he answered unctuously. But again Heng Yu was quick to correct him.

"No, Colonel I. As I instruct."

OUTSIDE THE OPERATIONS ROOM, Heng Yu paused, then turned, snapping his fingers to summon his First Secretary.

The young man hurried across, head bowed. "Master?"

"Has our man been dispatched?"

"Yes, Master."

"Good. If we hear from him, I want you to let me know at once, *whatever* I am doing."

"Master?"

"You heard me, Fen Chun. Now go and see to the arrangements. I have an audience with the Empress."

"Master."

As the young man hurried away, Heng Yu let out a long breath. So much was happening just now that this other matter threatened to be . . . how had Shepherd put it? Ah, yes, the straw that broke the camel's back.

He hurried on down the broad, high-ceilinged corridor, heading for the Empress's palace, ignoring the guards who abased themselves at his approach, lost in his thoughts.

It had been pleasant having Shepherd here these past few months. Pleasant and enlightening, for there were few men who knew as much, few who saw so clearly or thought so deeply, as Ben Shepherd. Indeed, the more time he spent in Shepherd's company, the greater the esteem he held him in. If any man in Chung Kuo was fit to be Emperor, Shepherd was that man. Or so he held in the privacy of his thoughts, for to utter such a thing aloud would be clearly treasonous, however much it echoed his Master's own oft-expressed sentiment.

The greater world saw Shepherd merely as an artist—a great one, admittedly, but still an artist, with an artist's disdain for worldly matters—but he knew better. If the great Yellow Emperor had been reborn in the form of a man, then Ben Shepherd would have been that man, for he saw men and their doings with a god-like clarity that stripped them to the bone. Not only that, but he could formulate policy better than any councillor, yes, and penetrate the motives behind each courtly twist and turn.

Most important of all, in the twelve weeks he had been here, he had managed to bring Li Yuan out of his shell.

*Out of it, yes, and straight into another,* Heng Yu thought, both amused and faintly disturbed by the insight.

But what was good for Li Yuan wasn't necessarily good for Pei K'ung. The Empress, after all, was a proud woman and had grown used to her husband giving her a free rein in internal affairs. Since Shepherd had been here, however, Li Yuan had taken greater in-

terest in events, and she had been forced to put up with his constant queries. Not that he had changed a word of any document
she had put before him, just that . . . well, to put it mildly, Pei
K'ung did not take kindly to being questioned about her motives,
not even by her husband.

Coming to the end of the corridor, Heng swept through the
great doors and down the broad stone steps into the Central Gardens. On the far side of a narrow lawn, beyond a stand of ancient-
looking willows, lay Pei K'ung's palace—a low sprawl of gray stone
buildings, their steep-pitched red tile roofs gleaming in the late
morning sunlight, the whole surrounded by a high stone wall studded with guard towers. Approaching the West Gate, Heng Yu
slowed, rehearsing what he was going to say.

*Unfortunately* . . .

No. Start again. Pei K'ung did not believe in misfortune, only in
failure and incompetence.

*It is with regret* . . .

Better, but still too apologetic. He could imagine the tightening
of her neck muscles, the sudden hardening of her face.

*Forgive me, Mistress, but it seems the bastard has fucked up.* . . .

Yes, that was it. Blame another. Deflect her anger with his own.
Let some other poor sod catch the fallout.

Maybe so. But this once he was far from happy with the tactic,
for this once the poor sod who had "fucked up" was a good friend
of his. Yes, and a loyal ally, come to that. And such men were rare
in life; rarer yet in the hostile, backbiting atmosphere of court.

*True,* Heng thought, *but what choice have I? If I take the blame for
this, she'll have my balls. Or worse, my job.*

And if she had his job, then *all* of his friends would suffer, not
just one. All in all it was a devil's bargain, but he ought to have
been used to that: his life these days was, after all, a spiderweb of
deceit and ill-wrought compromises.

Above the gate a camera swiveled, focusing on him. Two guards,
clutching lantern guns and wearing the emerald-green of the Empress's own force, stepped back, waving him through, their bowed
heads acknowledging his status, yet from here on his high rank
meant nothing. Within these walls Pei Kung's word alone was law.

He crossed the enclosed courtyard, then stepped inside, into the comparative darkness of the West Corridor. Halfway along, where a smaller corridor intersected it, stood Pei K'ung's Private Secretary, Ming Ai, waiting between two torch bearers, his five assistants at his back like shaven-headed gargoyles.

The sight of them made Heng Yu's stomach tighten with a mixture of aversion and apprehension. Eunuchs, they were, with all the spite and petty jealousy of their kind; all the suppressed anger and resentment. It had been Pei K'ung's idea to resurrect the ancient practice, and it had not been long before Ming Ai and his shadows had secured their icy grip upon the Empress's Court. Just as Heng Yu was within Li Yuan's palace, so Ming Ai was here. But whereas he could roam the empire as he wished, Ming Ai was confined within these walls, imprisoned, as it were; a half-man ruling only the microcosm of an empire. Such certain knowledge of one's limitations could and surely did warp a man's soul. It was with that thought in mind that Heng Yu stopped before Pei K'ung's Secretary and, bowing his head, greeted him.

"Ming Ai . . ."

"Master Heng," Ming answered, no tone in his surprisingly deep voice, no warmth to his expression. "My Mistress is awaiting you."

As Ming Ai turned, so his assistants parted before him, forming up behind Heng Yu as they made their way down the corridor that led to the Great Hall, the flickering torchlight on their jet-black cloaks, the sickly-sweet stench of their perfume making Heng Yu feel as if he were within some dark and nasty dream.

*How many have come this way in fear of their lives?* he wondered, forcing himself to ignore the nausea he felt, keeping his eyes directed straight ahead lest he glimpse one of them smirking at him.

It was a place of shadows. Both within and without.

Ahead a locked double door barred their way. Stepping up to it, Ming Ai took a thick black iron rod from within his cloak and hammered on the upper panel. From inside a female voice—distinct and clear—answered.

"Enter!"

As the doors eased back, Heng Yu knelt and lowered his head, touching his brow to the floor three times. He crawled forward into the doorway and repeated the ritual, then walked across the stone floor of the massive room, bent almost double, until he was before the massive desk. There he prostrated himself again, completing the *k'ou t'ou*. Behind him Ming Ai and his shadows remained on their feet, unbowed before their Mistress.

*A mistake,* he thought, not for the first time, *for to exempt such scoundrels from showing their respect surely gives them a sense of self-importance they ought not to possess. And from such tiny seeds grow great oaks of ambition. All should bow low or none. It is the only way.*

As Heng Yu straightened, he glanced at the Empress where she sat behind the desk, ink brush in hand, writing busily. She had aged this past year. What had been plain in her had now grown ugly. Her long nose had thickened coarsely; her mouth, once pleasant, was now thin lipped and drawn, and her chin, never the most pleasing of her features, now seemed absurdly blunt and angular, as if something forged of iron moved beneath that thin covering of flesh.

Ugly, yes, but that outward show was not the worst of it, for she had grown mean and vindictive these past twelve months. She had grown old not in wisdom, as the sages supposedly did, but in bitterness. That was not to say she was a stupid woman, far from it, for if a single person could be said to have held the Empire together these past ten years it was Pei K'ung. But what had once been political virtues—her stubbornness, her ruthlessness, her desire to succeed at any cost—had, in the last few months, become liabilities. In short, she had become a monster.

What was worse, she had come to despise her husband; to consider him a weak man, incapable of action. Not that she said as much—not openly, anyway, for who could tell what might get back to Li Yuan—but Heng could read between the lines of what *was* said. She thought this new society a sham, the promises Li Yuan had made to Ebert after the war unnecessary compromises. She thought they had given too much away; that they were pampering their citizens. What *she* wanted was the old ways back again; the old certainties of levels and hierarchies. Indeed, if the truth were told, she was driven by a far greater desire: the desire to take back what was lost—to reunite Chung Kuo under a single ruler. This, he was certain, was her life's goal, the very pinnacle of her ambitions.

A monster.

Heng lowered his eyes, lest she look up suddenly and read his thoughts there in the wrinkled tablet of his face. The question was, did she know? Had she the slightest inkling of what she had become?

*No,* he answered silently. *For true monsters do not analyze themselves.* What self-knowledge his Mistress had once possessed had slowly atrophied, like an unused limb, and now it hung, limp and ignored, against her back.

Behind him Ming Ai cleared his throat.

*Yes,* Heng thought, *and there's another sign. For those who rule are not like other men and women. One should judge them not by their own actions but by the actions of those that surround them—those whom they choose to carry out their will.*

Men like Ming Ai and I Ye and the odious Chu Po.

He shuddered inwardly at the thought. That, at least, was a small mercy—that Pei K'ung's favorite was not here this morning. Only last week he had felt like striking the young rogue for his impertinence. Why Pei K'ung allowed him such free rein with his tongue the gods only knew, for she had many other lovers besides him. Or maybe that was Chu's role—to be a goad to such as he.

"Well, Heng?" Pei K'ung asked, setting down her pen and looking across at him, her eyes like dark beads in her long, pale face. "Have we found him yet?"

Heng Yu remained kneeling, knowing he had not been told to stand. "Not yet, Mistress. But Colonel I is scouring the city for him. His men will stay on shift until they have located the man."

*If his own man did not find him first. . . .*

"Ah . . ." Pei K'ung stood and came around from behind her desk, standing over him, the flowing folds of her dark green, almost black, silk robes whispering against the stone flags of the floor. Her voice, so unyielding before, now softened. "And the other matter?"

Heng Yu swallowed. "Forgive me, Mistress, but the bastard has fucked up!"

Unexpectedly she laughed.

He looked up at her, astonished. *"Mistress?"*

She stared back at him, her long, heavily lined face giving nothing away, then gestured for him to rise. He stood, wrong footed and confused by her lack of anger, watching as she crossed the room to a table where a number of scrolls were laid out.

"Come here, Master Heng," she said, studying one of the scrolls. "I think you'll find this interesting."

As he came close, she turned and handed him the scroll. Her eyes were strangely amused.

Bowing low, he took the scroll and unfolded it.

"I wondered how you would break the news, Master Heng."

He nodded distractedly, then looked up, startled. "But this is—"

"Jia Shu's confession," she said tonelessly, taking the scroll back from him.

"But if you knew . . ."

Her smile faded like winter sunlight. "A little test, that's all."

He lowered his head, chilled by the abrupt change in her mood. She was not normally so volatile.

Pei K'ung stared at the scroll thoughtfully, then looked to Heng once more. "So what are we to do?"

"Do, Mistress?"

"*Do,*" she repeated emphatically. "My husband is planning something and I want to know what it is. You assured me that your friend Jia was in a position to find out for me, but it seems Jia was careless. Now my husband has been alerted and it will prove even more difficult to discover what he's up to. So . . . what do you *suggest?*"

The cold tone of threat in her voice was unmistakable. Heng Yu met her eyes briefly, then glanced to the side where Ming Ai stood with his arms folded across his chest, smiling at his rival's discomfort.

For a moment Heng's mind was a blank. What *could* he do? He had tried everything! Then, from nowhere, he had his answer.

"I shall ask him, Mistress."

"*Ask* him?" she laughed scornfully. "And you think Li Yuan would tell *you?*"

Heng lowered his eyes. It wasn't quite what he'd meant, but if that was what she thought . . . He shrugged. "I am, after all, the T'ang's First Minister. If he cannot trust me—"

"Can *I* trust you?"

"Mistress!" He fell to his knees, his forehead touching the cold stone floor beside her long silk shoes. "You have my undying devotion. As the gods are my witnesses—"

"Pah!" She turned away, her every movement stiff, expressive of a barely controlled frustration. Seeing it, Heng Yu smiled inwardly. She was a dangerous woman, there was no doubting it—a veritable viper of a woman—and yet she was also, in this single matter, deeply vulnerable. For almost a decade now she had ruled the San Chang—the three imperial palaces—at Mannheim with an iron grip. For ten long years she had been the all-seeing, all-knowing presence behind it all. But now her husband had woken like a dragon from his slumber and was planning something—something neither she, nor he, the T'ang's First Minister, knew anything about.

*It's Shepherd's doing,* Heng thought, convinced that no one else could have pulled off such a thing right under the Empress's nose. But what was he up to? What could possibly warrant such secrecy?

He heard his own words echo in his skull. *I shall ask him, Mistress.* Of course! He would go to Shepherd's quarters later on and ask him.

*And if he won't tell me?*

Then he would have discharged his duty. For if Pei K'ung's spies could not unearth this secret, then what chance had he, except, perhaps, by such directness?

He lifted his head; saw she was watching him, a faint scowl on her lips, her hazel eyes half-lidded, cold as a corpse's.

"There is another matter, Master Heng."

"Mistress?"

"Here," she said, handing him a second paper. He got up slowly, and unfolded the document. For a time he was silent, reading, then he looked to her again. *"Taxes,* Mistress?"

"Why so surprised, Master Heng? We have discussed the matter often enough, surely?"

"But, Mistress . . ." He tried to collect his thoughts, to muster arguments against what he knew she was about to say, but she raised a hand. Immediately he fell silent.

"You know how often my husband has argued for this. How it is his dream to reunite the lands his ancestors once ruled. Well, it is time to begin the realization of that dream. To give it substance."

He stared back at her, seeing the steel in her, the hard, unyield-ing core that lay behind the aging flesh, and knew no argument would shift her. So she had decided at last—made up her mind to raise an army and retake the East. Well, he was not surprised. It was merely the timing of the thing. If they imposed taxes now, before the hardship of the winter . . .

"You have something to say, Master Heng?"

Heng Yu shook his head. "Not at all, Mistress. If you feel the time is right."

"I do. So please take that to my husband and have him place his signature to it."

He stared at the document a moment, then folded it and slipped it into the inside pocket of his cloak. "I shall do so at once, Mis-tress."

"Good. Then you may go."

"Mistress!"

━━━━━⌁⌁⌁⌁━━━━━

L I  Y U A N had dried himself and was pulling on his shirt when his Master of the Inner Chambers, Nan Fa-hsien, appeared in the doorway. Seeing his old friend's son, Yuan smiled.

"What is it, Master Nan?"

Nan Fa-hsien lowered his head respectfully. "You have a visitor, *Chieh Hsia*. Master Heng is at the door, requesting audience."

"Master Heng . . ." Li Yuan gave a single nod, surprised. Heng was not due to see him for another two hours. "Has something happened?"

"I do not know, *Chieh Hsia*. He seems . . . troubled."

"I see." Li Yuan turned, studying himself in the full-length mir-ror, drawing a lock of dark hair aside with his fingers. Satisfied, he turned back, facing his young servant. "Tell Master Heng I shall see him in a moment. Oh, and Fa-hsien . . ."

"Yes, *Chieh Hsia?*"

"See if you can't find out what's been happening with the royal barge. I understand there's been trouble of some kind."

"At once, *Chieh Hsia!*"

As Nan Fa-hsien hurried away, Li Yuan looked about him, checking he had not forgotten anything. For ten years now he had attended to himself within these rooms, letting no servant bathe or dress him, living more simply than he'd once lived, taking the time to read and think and write. Now, after long preparation, he was ready to take the reins up once again; to take what he'd learned these past ten years and use it. To refashion his kingdom in the same way he had refashioned himself.

Pulling on a thin silk cloak of imperial yellow, he went through the anteroom and into his study. There, on the far side of the room, Heng Yu was waiting, his head lowered patiently. Yuan glanced at him, then sat behind his desk.

"Well, Master Heng?" he asked. "What brings you here so early in the day?"

Heng came across and, bowing once, laid the scroll on the table before him. "It is from the Empress, *Chieh Hsia*. I promised her I would deliver it at once."

"I see." He smiled back at Heng Yu, ignoring the scroll. "And how *is* my wife?"

"She is in good health, *Chieh Hsia*. She sends her best wishes."

"And that little band of thieves and ruffians she calls her servants?"

A smile flickered briefly on Heng Yu's lips, then was gone. "They thrive, *Chieh Hsia*."

"Yes," Li Yuan said acidly, "as cockroaches thrive after some great disaster." He stared at Heng a long moment. "And the banquet, Master Heng? Are the preparations proceeding well?"

"Very well, *Chieh Hsia*. Everything is being done to the letter of your instructions."

"Good. Then you may leave me, Heng Yu."

Heng Yu looked up, meeting his eyes. "But I thought"—he gestured toward the scroll—"I thought you might wish to read it, *Chieh Hsia*."

"And so I shall, Master Heng. Tomorrow. Now . . . is there anything else?"

"No, *Chieh Hsia*."

"Then go. I have much to do."

Heng Yu bowed and backed away. When he had gone, Li Yuan let out a long breath. He was not usually so abrupt with his Chancellor, but this morning he had other things on his mind.

Picking up the scroll, he tucked it into his pocket, then left the room, hurrying down the corridor toward the guest suite where Shepherd had set up his workshop.

As he paused before the massive double doors, he could hear the sound of Shepherd singing to himself within. Waving the guards aside, he pushed back the door and looked inside.

Ben was sitting at a piano on the far side of the room, making shapes with his hands on the keyboard as he sang, but from the piano itself came no sound.

Li Yuan closed the door, then turned.

Ben smiled, beckoning him closer. "You want to hear?"

He nodded. At once strange chords filled the room—an awful, hollow sound, like the sound of eternal suffering.

He winced and looked down at Ben's hands, noting that all the keys were black.

"It's a symphony," Ben said, his fingers stopping suddenly, the final chord freezing, echoing in the air, chill as the north wind itself. "A symphony for the dead."

*Of course,* Li Yuan thought. *What else could it be?*

He turned, looking about him, realizing suddenly just how tidy the workroom was. In the corner the shiny black casing of the Shell was covered by a dustcloth.

"What's up?" he asked, puzzled. "I thought—"

"I've finished," Ben said, standing and pushing the keyboard aside.

"Finished?"

"The demonstration tape. It's done."

Li Yuan felt his mouth turn dry, his heart begin to hammer in his chest. "Done?" he said, so quietly he hardly heard himself.

"Yes. You want to experience it?"

He hesitated. Now that the moment had come—now that the thing was finally done—he wasn't sure. If this was as real, as powerful, as Ben claimed, then . . .

*Then what?* he asked himself, conscious of Ben's eyes upon him. *Am I so weak a man that a mere illusion—however powerful—could sway me from my senses? Hasn't that been the point of all my studies— of these long years of meditation—to make myself a stronger, more self-reliant man?*

*Yes*, he answered, hearing the word sound clearly in his skull. *Yet what if he failed this test?*

Steeling himself, he nodded.

"Good," Ben said, taking his arm and leading him across to the Shell. "Strip off. I'll help connect you."

———————

THE  OPERATOR  SAT  BACK, rubbing his eyes, tired—bone tired—despite the drugs he'd taken to keep himself awake. On the screen before him images danced as the bug-cam fluttered through the air, then focused again as it settled. He reached out, meaning to take a swig from the lukewarm *chung* of *ch'a* beside his console, then froze, suddenly alert.

*"Sir!"*

The urgent tone in his voice made the Captain turn from where he was talking to his lieutenant and hurry down the line of operatives until he stood behind him.

"What is it, Haller?"

"There, sir. Look!"

The Captain leaned past him, studying the frame. The bug-cam had settled on a roof overlooking a narrow, dusty alleyway, its high, yellow-brown walls marked here and there with bright red graffiti. Halfway along, alone in the midmorning sunlight, was a man—a *Hung Mao* in his early twenties with neat-cut ash-blond hair. He wore the simple brown *pau* and slip-ons of a common laborer, and a casual observer might have thought him just that, but his refined features and the sophisticated cut of his hair gave him away, as did the slim black case he carried beneath his right arm. In the frozen frame he was glancing up, giving them a clear view of his face.

The Captain grunted. "Enhance."

At once a square formed about the man's face and that section was enlarged to fill the screen. The Captain studied it a moment, then nodded. "Run a retinal scan. Let's see if it matches."

The operative punched in the instruction, then sat back. A moment later two sets of figures came up left and right on the screen, overlaying the enhanced image of the face. Both sets of figures were identical.

The Captain turned, calling to his lieutenant. "Thomas. Go and wake the Colonel . . . *now!*"

"Sir . . ."

But he had barely turned when I Ye appeared in the doorway, pulling on his jacket.

"Have we got him?"

The Captain snapped to attention. "It's him, all right. He's in Bockenheim, sir, three *li* west of Frankfurt Central."

"Good . . ." I Ye grinned, showing uneven teeth, then nodded savagely. "Okay. Let's get the bastard!"

CALDER SET THE case down on the table and clicked open the twin catches, then turned it about, so that the obscenely fat Han behind the desk—the club's owner, Tung Po-jen—could see its contents.

"Is this genuine?" Tung asked, reaching out to take the tiny yellow-gold cassette.

"If it isn't, it's as good a fake as you'll find anywhere."

The Han grunted, then ran his fingers over the *Ywe Lung*—the Moon Dragon—embossed into the face of the case. "So what does your Master want for this?"

"Two hundred and fifty thousand."

Tung laughed coldly. "Too much. A hundred and no more."

Calder reached out and took the cassette back. "Then it's no deal."

The fat man leaned across the desk angrily. "And if I were to tell Security?"

Calder smiled politely. "Then my Master will have lost a loyal messenger and you—well, you will have lost the chance to get very—and I mean *very*—rich."

Tung sat back slowly, his eyes narrowed, staring out the open window at the busy street below. Two hundred and fifty was a lot, twenty times more than he'd ever paid for a single cassette, and he would have to borrow heavily to finance it. But maybe it was worth it this once—that was, if this really was what his contact claimed it was.

"It'll take time. I mean, to get the funding together."

"What can you give me now?"

Tung pulled open a drawer to his left and rummaged through, then tossed a pouch down onto the table. The messenger set the cassette down and picked up the pouch. Untying its neck, he spilled twelve ten-thousand-*yuan* chips out onto the table. Taking a tiny black machine from his pocket—the CoinMak logo prominent on its slimline casing—he slipped one of the chips inside to check its authenticity. At once the machine's display glowed green. Satisfied, he gathered up the chips and pocketed them, leaving the pouch where it lay.

"Okay . . . for now. But I want the balance in two days."

"And if my customers like this?"

The young man smiled. "Then we get you more. Lots more." He reached out and stroked the yellow-gold casing fondly. "Just as many as you want."

———————

TUNG PO-JEN sat there after Calder had gone, staring at the cassette, tracing the embossed imperial logo on its casing with his fingertips, his heart pounding with an excitement he hadn't felt in years.

This was it! This was the break he'd been waiting for! And this—if it was real—was his passport to a life of unimaginable riches.

But he would have to be clever, very clever indeed, if he was not to end up dead. For though the rewards were phenomenal, the dangers were just as great. The mere possession of this was, after all, a treasonable offense. And then there were his trading rivals to consider, the brotherhoods to mollify, officials to pay off. No, he had a long way to go before he could relax and enjoy the benefits, yet to have come this far was something. *More* than something.

A smile came slowly to his lips, creasing the folds of his flesh, splitting his face until, throwing his head back, he laughed, long and loud.

He could see now how he'd do it. Knew, instinctively, whom he should contact, who to involve in this, sharing the risks—financial and personal—that accompanied the venture.

He knew, for instance, just how important it was to disseminate this as widely—and as anonymously—as possible: to spread it so widely and so quickly that it would be impossible for the authorities either to stop its circulation or trace its origin. Only that way would he be safe. Only that way could he make it a financial success.

And, as fortune would have it, one of those he would need was here right now, downstairs in the main gaming room.

Grinning fiercely Tung Po-jen snatched up the cassette, hauled himself up out of his chair and through the door behind him, squeezing his way down the narrow back stairs and along the dimly lit corridor, pushing roughly past the two minders stationed there.

"Lock the outer doors!" he shouted back at them as he disappeared through the bead curtain. "And make sure you let no one in unless I say!"

On the other side of the curtain was a small room, as poorly lit as the corridor outside, its four baize tables empty of customers. As Tung Po-jen crossed the room, the barman, to his left, looked up at him, then lowered his eyes quickly, busying himself cleaning glasses.

Tung glanced at the man suspiciously, then pushed through the door that led to the main gaming room. As he stepped into the room heads turned at nearby tables. There was a lull in the conversation.

"Master Tung!" someone called from a table to his right. "Come! Join us!"

Tung Po-jen went across, squeezing between the tables. Stopping before one of the tables, he bowed low—or as low as his massive girth would allow—then straightened, grinning down at the three men—well-built, middle-aged Han with the muscle tone of fighters—who sat about the table casually, young, scantily clad house girls in their laps.

"*Ch'un tzu . . .*" Tung said, his pleasure at seeing them for once quite genuine. "I am honored that you have chosen to frequent my humble establishment. Our fare is of the very simplest, I'm afraid, but if there is anything—*anything*—I can do for you?"

The two men seated either side of the table stared back at him with a cold suspicion, saying nothing, but the man at the center— a high-ranking Triad member named Chao Ta-nien and known to all as "Slow Chao" because of his legendary quickness with a knife—eased the girl from his lap and sat forward, smiling back at him.

"That is most kind, Master Tung. But we have been made most welcome already. Most welcome indeed."

Tung nodded nervously. "Good. That is . . . good." He licked his lips, unsure quite how to broach this subject. It had seemed so simple, sitting there upstairs, but now that the moment was upon him he hesitated, his courage suddenly failing him. What if he was wrong? What if he couldn't trust Slow Chao? What if Chao's bosses thought this too good a deal to share with anyone else?

Then again, only he, Tung Po-jen, knew where these came from. Only he had the contacts. And if he played this right—if he could involve not just one but several of the brotherhoods—then maybe this would work.

Maybe. For a moment longer he hesitated, watching Chao's face, noting how the other waited, as if he knew Tung had something to offer him. Then, finally, knowing that if he did not take this first step he would have wasted all his money on something he could not use, he forced himself to speak.

He leaned toward Chao Ta-nien, his voice a whisper. "I . . . have something to show you, Master Chao. In private."

Slow Chao raised an eyebrow, amused. "Something . . . *interesting?*"

Tung Po-jen could feel the tension in his neck muscles and his back and straightened up, forcing himself to relax. He nodded, then stood back. "If you would come through into the viewing room?"

He saw how the other two looked to Chao Ta-nien, saw the look he gave them, the slight crinkling around the eyes, like the delicate touch an experienced horseman gives his mount to still it, and felt a tiny ripple of fear pass through him. He walked a deadly tightrope here.

"Lead on, Master Tung," Chao said, standing, his smile serene, almost urbane, as he stepped around the table.

Inside the soundproofed viewing room he made sure Chao was seated comfortably, then locked the door and, seating himself behind the projector, slid the cassette into the machine.

For a moment there was nothing. For an instant Tung Po-jen found himself wondering if he'd been duped; if even now Calder was heading back to Mashhad, laughing quietly to himself, twelve ten-thou chips the richer for having delivered a blank tape to a greedy fat man who hadn't even had the sense to check the goods before he'd paid for them!

Risks . . . While he'd been thinking of all the other risks, the most obvious of all had slipped his mind.

Then, with a startling vividness, the screen lit up.

Tung caught his breath. It was *her!* It really was her. Or so like her it made no difference. There, glimpsed through a delicate silk hanging, on sheets of bright red satin, was Li Yuan's first wife, the young Fei Yen. She lay on her side, her sleeping silks rucked up about her legs, one hand curled beneath her face, one covering her breasts.

Tung stared and sighed, affected by the beauty of her, something about her—the innocence of her supine figure, perhaps; the lack of artifice—breaching his jaded shell.

Chao Ta-nien, just below him in the darkness, was sitting forward now, watching the screen intently.

As the camera panned back, Tung took in the sight of the imperial bedroom. The bed, at the center of the room, was huge, its scrolled lion's feet embedded in the floor, its four ornate posts adorned with carved dragon and phoenix motifs inlaid with gold leaf. On two of the walls hung expensive silks depicting scenes of imperial splendor. The floor was white marble, the walls paneled with dark wood. Through an open lattice window could be glimpsed the lush green of the palace gardens at Tongjiang. A faint breeze moved the fine lace curtain gently.

There was a sound, the opening of a door below the camera viewpoint. Fei Yen stirred and, turning slightly, opened her eyes.

"Yuan? Is that you?"

The camera turned, focusing on the doorway.

Tung shivered, his mouth fallen open. Despite himself he was awed—awed that he, a mere trader, should be given this glimpse of how a Son of Heaven lived. His mouth had gone dry, his hands were trembling now.

*Aiya!* he thought, as Li Yuan came into view; not the Li Yuan of the regular mediacasts but a much younger, gaucher-looking man, not yet nineteen. *The gods protect me for what I'm doing here!*

Li Yuan crossed the room, the camera trailing him, then stopped, the back of his head just below the camera. He was wearing a satin sleeping robe, golden cranes—symbolizing immortality—embroidered into the pale blue material.

"Fei Yen," he said softly, "I thought you were asleep."

Tung watched, his heart in his mouth, as the young prince sat beside her on the bed, his hand resting gently on her ankle. Unbidden, Tung's penis rose within his silks and pressed hard against the cloth. He shivered, then reached down to hold himself, unable to tear his eyes from the unfolding images.

As Fei Yen raised herself on one elbow, her silks fell back, revealing her perfect, unblemished breasts, their nipples stiffly erect.

Tung groaned softly, his hand moving slowly against the cloth.

"I missed you, Yuan," she said. "I didn't think you'd come."

"I've been busy," he answered, his hand moving gently up her leg beneath the silk, his face moving toward her until their lips met in a kiss.

As they broke from it she moved back, staring at him, then took his hand and placed it on her breast.

"No more words," she said, shrugging the silk from her shoulders. "Show me how much you missed me. Show me. . . ."

She gave a little gasping sigh as his fingers touched her intimately, her lips opening to show clenched, pearllike teeth. There was a faintest flush at her neck now and as his fingers continued to caress her, she let a tiny groan of pleasure escape her.

"Gods . . ." Tung said, close suddenly to orgasm. He had never seen a woman so beautiful, so . . . *desirable.* And as she lay back, exposing herself to her husband almost wantonly, the soft dark mound of her pubis coming into view, Tung came, his huge frame shuddering, making the projector tremble faintly, the image blur, even as, on the screen, the young prince slipped from his silks and, naked as a babe, climbed between those silken, inviting legs.

BEN REACHED ACROSS Li Yuan's naked figure, releasing the last of the pressure pads from the side of his head. Free at last, Li

Yuan sat up, scratching distractedly at his chest and neck, where a faint red stippling showed where the attachments had been made. He shivered, as if the air in the room were cold, then turned his head slowly, looking up at Ben. His eyes seemed vague, unfocused.

"Well?" Ben asked, resting both hands on the side of the Shell.

"It's powerful," Li Yuan said, meeting Ben's eyes—something resembling clarity returning to them. "Like . . . well, like sorcery."

Ben laughed. "And Fei Yen?"

"Was different," Li Yuan said, frowning. "More . . ."

"Welcoming?"

"Yes." Li Yuan swallowed, pained, then looked down. "It's how it should have been. How . . ." He fell silent, then shook his head. "Destroy it," he said.

Ben studied him a moment, then leaned across and pressed ERASE.

Li Yuan stared at him, surprised. He had just wiped out the best part of four months' work.

Ben smiled. "I have it here," he said, tapping his forehead. "So if *you* don't want it . . ."

Li Yuan shook his head, then, letting Ben take his arm to help him, hauled himself up out of the Shell. Taking a silk wrap from the side, he drew it about him, and turned to face Ben again.

"Do you recall the first time we met? At the betrothal ceremony?"

"The sketch?" Ben nodded. He walked across and, picking up a sketchpad from the table at the side, came back and rested it against the edge of the Shell. Taking a charcoal stick from his shirt pocket, he began to draw, each stroke, each blurring motion of the thumb, mimicking to perfection what he had done on that day thirty years before.

"Uncanny," Li Yuan said at last, clearly awed by this exhibition of Ben's eidetic memory. "I have the original still, on the wall in my study."

"Then here's its twin." And, smiling, Ben handed it to him. "Do you remember what was said?"

Li Yuan nodded. "I remember thinking that you were some kind of magician. You seemed to conjure the image from the air, as if you merely traced over what was already there."

"And so I did." Ben laughed, then grew serious again. "You could call it my curse, I guess—to be forever giving form to what already exists up here." Again he tapped his forehead.

Li Yuan watched him, understanding coming slowly to his eyes. "Yes, and you were right, too, that day."

"About the Lord Yi?"

Li Yuan smiled. The picture Ben had drawn for him that day— the same picture that he was even now looking at—was of the great archer Shen Yi and his battle with the ten birds in the *fu sang* tree. In the legend the ten birds represented the ten suns that threatened Mankind with their intense heat. The Lord Yi, by shooting nine of them from the Heavens, had saved Mankind. But the Lord Yi was also a usurper, who stole many men's wives. Not only that, but his own wife, Chang-E, had stolen the herb of immortality and had fled to the Moon, where, for her sins, she had been turned into a toad whose dark shadow could be seen against the full moon's milky whiteness.

It took no *Wu*—no wise diviner—to make the parallel between himself and the Lord Yi, nor between Fei Yen and Chang-E. Any tavern philosopher might do the same over a bulb of sour beer.

"You knew my marriage to Fei Yen would fail, didn't you?"

Ben shrugged. "I knew."

"I should never have married her."

"You had no choice. You were obsessed."

"Yes. . . ." Li Yuan nodded again, then laughed. "Yes, it's strange, isn't it? How little choice we have in such matters. It's as if we're . . . well, *programmed* somehow. The merest scent of her, the way she'd turn her head . . ."

He stopped. Ben was watching him, capturing him, like a camera that missed nothing; that saw both what was external and what was deep within.

"I've changed."

"I can see," Ben said, smiling, offering—for once—no criticism.

Li Yuan looked down, for that one brief moment uncertain, then looked back again. Ben was still watching him, those dark green eyes no less intent than when he'd first looked into them thirty years before.

"You know what I want, then?"

Ben nodded.

"And the rest of them?"

"Will do exactly as you say. Even Pei K'ung." Ben's smile reappeared momentarily. "Every shadow needs something between it and the sun."

Li Yuan frowned. "You think there'll be trouble with Pei K'ung?"

Ben leaned forward and plucked the unsigned edict from Yuan's pocket and unfurled it.

"Pei K'ung *is* trouble. But she can be harnessed."

Li Yuan stared at Ben expectantly, making no attempt to take the document back. "Do you think she knows what we're up to?"

Ben, studying the document, shook his head. He flicked through it quickly, then, with a faint moue of amusement, handed it back.

"Games," he said. "Distractions."

"Maybe," Li Yuan answered, "but they'll serve their purpose, don't you think?"

"They'll serve the Oven Man, certainly. But purpose . . ." Ben shrugged, then went to the window, looking out across the gardens. "What do you think our purpose *is*, Yuan?"

Li Yuan shrugged. "To have children. To—"

Ben turned, suddenly impatient. "No. That's not what I mean.. What's our *purpose*. Our chemical, physical, spiritual purpose? To put it as succinctly as possible—why the fuck are we here? What Great Test are we a part of? And whose?"

Li Yuan was quiet a moment. Ben's outburst had taken him aback. "I didn't think you believed in gods."

"Gods, no. Divine Chemists, yes." His smile now was impish. "This universe of ours was devised by someone with a Chemist's mind, a Chemist's obsessive care for detail. The human side . . . well, Chemists aren't interested in all that, are they? That's why that side of things is such a mess."

Ben laughed. "That's why you're still hung up on your dead brother's wife after all these years. Why I'm still fucking my sister!"

Li Yuan made a small noise of surprise, then, despite himself, began to giggle.

"Perverse, isn't it?" he said, after a moment.

"No more than the usual run of things," Ben answered, coming across to him and holding his arm briefly. "Did you know my son's a mute?"

Li Yuan nodded, embarrassed by the conversation's turn.

" 'God's Judgment,' Meg calls it. As if God—if he existed—could be bothered with such pettiness."

"And you?" Li Yuan asked. "What do you think?"

"Me? I think Tom's happy. I think . . . well, as far as the greater world's concerned, I think it's a blessing that one of us Shepherds can't speak!"

---

TOM SHADED HIS EYES with his hand, staring down the street, trying to make out what was happening up ahead. He knew where he was now. The river was straight ahead, just there where the taller buildings began, and the barge—if it was still where it had been moored the night before—was no more than ten minutes away by foot. But something was going on. At the end of the street they had set up security barriers. Armed soldiers in full riot gear were stopping people from going through.

He wondered what it was. A gang killing? A political assassination? Anything, it seemed, was possible here. Now that he had seen it with his own eyes he understood his father's fascination with it—understood why Ben spent so much time away from home.

*And the girl?* He sighed. The girl was like a dream. Amid all this—all of the bustle and strangeness of the great Han city—she seemed . . . well, *impossible*.

He patted his jacket pocket. His ID was still there. Yes, and the tiny present she had given him. He smiled, remembering, then began to walk toward the barrier.

---

THE TAPE ENDED. Slowly the lights came up again. Tung Po-jen shivered, aware of the warm stickiness at his groin. Chao Ta-nien was sitting forward in his seat, half in trance, his chin resting on one hand. Then he sat up and turned to look back at Tung.

"Was that real?"

Tung nodded. "From the imperial library itself."

Chao raised an eyebrow. "From Tongjiang? I thought the palace was burned down."

Tung shrugged. He knew nothing of such matters. "Here," he said, handing Chao the cover, then watching as the Red Pole studied the embossed imperial symbol, his fingertips tracing the great wheel of dragons.

He looked to Tung again.

"And is this it? Or can you get more of these?"

Tung felt his pulse begin to race. "How many do you want?"

"Ah . . ." Chao stood, then came across, leaning past Tung to eject the tiny tape from the machine. "My Master will be pleased with this gift."

*"Gift?"* Tung stared at Chao Ta-nien open mouthed. This was a turn he had not anticipated. "But I thought—"

"You think my Master's friendship is lightly bought, Tung Po-jen?"

Tung swallowed, then shook his head.

Chao touched his arm, smiling, then proceeded to slip the tape into the case and pocket it. "My Master will be delighted he has such a good friend, Tung Po-jen. He will no doubt wish to *help* you, neh?"

Slowly Tung relaxed. It wasn't what he'd planned, but maybe it wasn't so bad. After all, Chao's Master, Ice Man Chung, was reputedly a fair man.

Chao stared at the box thoughtfully, then shook his head. "It's powerful, don't you think, Tung Po-jen? Men would pay a great deal to set their eyes on this." He looked to Tung, his eyes narrowed. "How much did you have to pay?"

"Two fifty," he said, beginning to sweat.

"Two hundred and fifty thousand . . ." Chao considered that, then nodded. "That must have left you short, Tung Po-jen."

"I . . ." Tung swallowed, then nodded.

"That's a shame. Perhaps we can arrange a loan."

"A loan?" Tung stared at Chao, his heart sinking, all of the excitement—the joy—he had been feeling earlier drained from him in an instant. So it was to be like this. He would borrow Triad money, at Triad rates, to finance the venture, and the Triads would take the profits. Which left him what? The risk. And maybe enough to live on.

"I had hoped . . ."

"Hoped?" Chao Ta-nien laughed. "Hoped for what, Tung Po-jen? Did you think a thing like this could be kept in the hands of one man . . . even so *big* a man as yourself?" Chao took the tape from his pocket and shook it at Tung. "No, Tung Po-jen, this is bigger than either of us. This . . . why, this is like a bomb waiting to be detonated, a virus waiting to be spread. We shall make money, certainly, and my Master will make sure you have your share, but do not look beyond that, my well-fleshed friend. Some men are born to be riders, other"—he looked at Tung scathingly— "others to be grooms."

He slipped the tape away once more. "Be content, Tung Po-jen. And be reassured. You did well to think of me first. I shall not forget it. Nor will my Master."

After Chao had gone, Tung sat there, staring at the empty screen. "Shit!" he said finally, slamming one huge, well-padded hand down onto the machine's casing. "Shit! Shit! Shit!"

He had played it totally wrong. He had been far too hasty. He should have seen the tape, had it copied, put the original somewhere safe. Then he should have got in three, maybe four different parties. As it was . . .

Tung huffed in exasperation. Gifts, loans . . . and all that shit about riders and grooms. Well, fuck them! He felt like packing up and getting out—to Africa maybe. That would teach Chao Ta-nien to be such a prick. Yes, and serve his Boss, Ice Man Chung, a lesson too.

Maybe, but they would find him eventually. And when they did . . .

Tung let out a long, frustrated breath. No. They had him by the ballocks and they knew it. He'd take the risks and they'd make the profits. Just as they always did.

Unless . . .

There was a sudden, urgent rapping on the door. Tung heaved himself up out of the chair as the door crashed open. It was one of his bodyguards. "Master Tung," he began, alarmed, "they're—"

There was a shot, a second shot. The man grimaced and then

slumped across the row of seats beside him. From the darkness beyond him a soldier stepped into view, in full riot gear, his visor raised, his gun pointing in at Tung.

"Okay, fat man, raise your hands where I can see them. And don't even *think* of trying anything."

—————

TUNG PO-JEN opened his eyes with a start.

"What happened?"

"You died."

"Died?" Slowly Tung focused his eyes. The stranger—I Ye? was that his name?—was staring down at him, his thin lips twisted in amusement.

"We almost lost you. Your heart gave up on you. Not surprising, neh? Being so fat must have put a great strain on it. But we brought you back."

Tung tried to move. He couldn't. He just felt numb. Then, like the tide rushing in across a vast, empty beach, he felt the pain return. He groaned.

"It hurts, doesn't it, Tung Po-jen? But that's only the beginning. We like to make things easy for you . . . at first."

A second face appeared beside I Ye's—a doctor's by the look of it. Tung saw the glint of a hypodermic gun as it was passed from one to the other.

"You see this?" I Ye said, holding the hypodermic closer so he could see it clearly. "It's something new. Something they developed in America. It could extend your life by fifty years." The smile broadened, became a grimace. "Just think of it, Tung Po-jen. All that time stretching away in front of you, and every second of it you would be in pain. Such pain as you could not imagine."

Tung closed his eyes. *I died*, he thought. *The gods help me, I died and this bastard brought me back.*

"What do you want?" Tung whined, despair flooding him, knowing that he'd said this once before; certain now that nothing he could tell this cunt would ever satisfy him. "You know all I know. I've told you everything."

"Everything?"

"Everything."

It was true. The pain had loosed his tongue as expertly as it had loosened his bowels. All the shit had come out—every last bit— even that part about him fucking his infant sister.

"Again," I Ye said, bringing his face closer, his stinking breath in Tung's face, his fingers gently caressing Tung's balls, then slowly closing on them like a vice.

Tung screamed.

"Good," I Ye said, as if some hurdle had been successfully nego- tiated. "From the beginning. From when you were first contacted by the messenger."

Tung lay there, sheened in sweat, his limbs trembling uncontrol- lably, wishing he were dead again, that voice—that awful, insistent voice—echoing inside his skull.

"But you know—"

This time the pain was excruciating. He blacked out. A moment later he opened his eyes with a start.

"What . . . ?"

But he knew what had happened. He hadn't died. He had lived. And now an eternity of pain stretched out before him. He was one of the eternally damned, chained to the rock of punishment, in Hell, never to be released, never to be allowed surcease. And what had he done to deserve this?

*I gazed upon the Son of Heaven making love to his brother's wife. I saw him plant his seed in her. Saw his buttocks shudder, the movement in her face.*

He had glimpsed Heaven, and for that he was condemned to Hell. He groaned once more; a deep, despairing groan.

"Again," I Ye said, smiling sweetly down at him as he pressed the hypodermic to Tung's upper arm. "Again."

***

HENG YU was hurrying toward his next appointment, taking a shortcut through an untenanted part of the Eastern Palace. He was late. He was always late these days. If he had been twins he would still have had too much to do, and as it was—

"Master!"

He turned, surprised. A guard—a member of Pei K'ung's own elite—had stepped from the shadows and now stood there, head bowed. Heng took a step back, away from the man, noting from his chest patch that he was a Captain. He sensed something wrong—something very wrong—but tried to keep his voice calm. Beneath his cloak his right hand slid onto the handle of his dagger.

"What is it, Captain?"

"Forgive me, Chancellor," the man began, keeping his distance, aware, it seemed, of the threat he posed, here in this silent corridor. "I mean you no harm."

"You are a long way from your Mistress's palace," Heng said, still tense, not yet certain whether he could trust the man.

The Captain nodded. "I was greatly torn, Excellency. My orders . . ."

Heng frowned. "Go on."

"It is about the prisoner, Excellency."

"Prisoner? What prisoner?"

"The man we took. In the raid. I had orders to report at once to Marshal Karr."

Heng Yu stared at him, not understanding. "Forgive *me*, Captain, but what has any of this to do with me?

The Captain swallowed, then bowed his head. "It's just that Colonel I has given countermanding orders. And as the Colonel is my immediate commanding officer . . ."

Some small glimmer of light began to dawn in Heng's mind. "And this prisoner . . . was he taken in connection to the matter of the missing imperial tapes?"

The Captain snapped to attention, his boot heels clicking smartly together. "Excellency!"

"Ah . . ." Now he understood. "I see." He sniffed, then gave a single decisive nod. "Okay. You go now, Captain. Say nothing of your meeting with me. I will see to the matter personally. And, Captain . . ."

"Excellency?"

"Your action today will not be forgotten. The T'ang has great need of loyal friends, neh?"

"Excellency!" The Captain bobbed his head, then turned, disappearing into the shadows.

Heng Yu took a long breath. He was sweating. For a moment he had thought it was an assassination attempt. But this—this could prove equally important. If Colonel I was countermanding orders, then it gave him the opportunity to break the man—to demote him and humiliate him. *If* he had countermanded orders.

He was still late—more than twenty minutes late now—but his appointment would have to wait. This was far more urgent.

Smiling to himself for the first time that day, Heng Yu turned and, half walking, half running, retraced his steps, heading back to Pei K'ung's palace.

I YE'S GUARDS had tried to stop or delay him. Several of Ming Ai's eunuchs had also interceded, trying to keep him from the cells, but his threats had seen to them. Pushing the last of them aside, Heng Yu grasped the iron handle and swung the door back.

The cell was small and stank of shit and burned flesh. Instinctively, Heng put the cuff of his cloak to his face, covering his mouth and nose.

A single lamp illuminated the manacled body on the table. A single glance told Heng Yu that he was too late. The man was dead, slit open from chin to balls, his entrails scooped out and placed into a large enamel bowl that stood on the floor to one side. At a sink in the corner I Ye stood washing, scrubbing the blood off his hands and arms.

"Ah, Chancellor," he said, smiling into the mirror. "I was on my way to see you."

Heng shivered. How such a man had ever risen to power was a mystery to him. "Is it true?" he asked, lowering his cuff, the stench making him grimace with distaste. "Did you countermand Marshal Karr's orders?"

I Ye turned, the water from his arms dripping red, his face expressing puzzlement. "Countermand the Marshal's orders? I am afraid I do not follow you, Master Heng."

Heng coughed, then straightened up, trying to act as dignified as possible in the circumstances. "You knew the orders, Colonel I. The Marshal was to be informed at once."

"And so he was. I sent my equerry to see him in his office. Unfortunately, he was not there."

"Not there?"

"It seems he was at home with his family. However, a sealed note was delivered to his office. I am sure he will receive it when he returns."

Heng Yu stared at I Ye for a full thirty seconds, seeing how the man's smile became fixed, then shook his head. "You are an ambitious man, Colonel I."

I Ye bowed, as if he had been complimented, then turned, reaching for a towel.

"So what did you find out?"

I Ye turned back, wiping himself, the white cloth of the towel smeared red. "Nothing we did not know already."

"And the tape?"

"Was lost, unfortunately. We cast the net too late, it seems. Either that or one of those we captured managed to hide it."

"Is that possible?"

"If it was, we'll soon find out. These birds sing sweetly when they're caged."

"And this one here?" Heng pointed without looking at the corpse of the fat man.

"Was only a contact. He knew very little."

"So we're no farther on."

I Ye pulled on his tunic, then came across. "On the contrary, Master Heng. We now know several things we didn't before today. We know, for instance, that the tapes are genuine. That they're from the imperial library at Tongjiang. We know for certain where the messenger was coming from and where he went. We know also that he is due to return to get his second payment. All we have to do now is wait."

"And if he doesn't show?"

"Then we'll watch the ports."

"And if he doesn't leave? What if he knows we're looking for him and goes to ground?"

"Then we'll be patient. When he doesn't return, someone will get anxious. Someone will be sent. And when that someone comes . . ."

Heng considered that. Personally he didn't think they had made much progress, but then, it wasn't for him to make that judgment.

"Does *she* know?"

Heng saw the movement in I Ye's face, the momentary uncertainty.

"Not yet."

"You know what she'll do if you fail?"

"I know." I Ye considered that a moment, then laughed. "But if I *succeed . . .*"

"*If* you succeed." Heng forced himself to smile, as if I Ye's ambition were commendable, but he understood now what I Ye wanted, understood—as he hadn't before that moment—what currently motivated him. He wanted Karr's job. He wanted to be Marshal in Karr's place. And so he worked, patiently and with an exact care, to undermine Karr even as he kept within the letter of his orders.

Heng turned, giving the corpse one final glance. "You'll send me a copy of the report, I hope."

"Of course," I Ye answered urbanely. "It will be on your desk before the day is out."

"Good. Very good." Heng made to turn away, but I Ye called him back.

"Master Heng?"

"Yes, Colonel I?"

"Was it my Captain, Dawes, who told you where I was?"

———

IT WAS AFTER SIX when Heng Yu finally returned to his rooms. He had missed three appointments—important appointments with senior officials on matters of great urgency—and even though his secretaries had dealt with things efficiently in his absence, he felt, perhaps for the first time since he had become Chancellor, that the responsibilities of office were getting to be too much for him.

*It is out of control,* he thought, recalling the mad, vain glint in his Mistress's eyes, the distraction in his Master's. *The great experiment has failed.*

Li Yuan's great vision of a new and healthier state had foundered almost at its inception—foundered because he had personally withdrawn from the task of its creation, leaving it to other, less enthusiastic hands. It might have worked—indeed, it *ought* to have worked—but the ship of State had wrecked itself on the rock of Pei

K'ung's vanity, on her obsession with control. In giving her power Li Yuan had effectively destroyed any last chance the new state once possessed. After the City's fall there had been a moment— one brief, deceptive, shining moment—when it might have happened: when the terms of Li Yuan's promise to Hans Ebert could have been fulfilled and a new, more equitable, *saner* society could have been established. But old patterns of behavior quickly reestablished themselves. People forgot the reasons for that Fall. Greed, corruption, fraud, nepotism, addiction, mindless violence, murder, theft, and a thousand other shades of bad behavior . . . the darkness had seeped back, swamping the bright ideal, until, this very day, he had helped promote the document that would douse that light completely.

*Ah, yes, but he hasn't signed it yet,* Heng thought, the faintest glimmer of hope holding out against experience. *And until he does, until he agrees to her insane war, her debilitating taxes, then the vision is still alive.*

But the possibility of that happening was frail. In ten years Li Yuan had not failed to sign a single one of Pei K'ung's edicts.

Heng sat down heavily in his high-backed chair, staring across the huge, empty room sightlessly, a sense of futility gripping him. He had tried to be a good man, to conduct himself as honestly and openly as possible, but it had been hard. In truth the politics of the San Chang were the politics of the snake pit. It was bite or be bitten.

*The gods help us,* he thought. *Soon the sadists and the madmen will take over completely. Ming Ai and his stunted half-men will rule the roost!*

The buzzer sounded on his desk. He stared at it, as if it lay a thousand *li* from where he sat. Then, wearily, he leaned forward and placed his palm against the contact pad.

"What is it, Fen Chun?"

"Master Heng?"

He sat bolt upright, suddenly alert. *"Chieh Hsia?"*

"Come to my rooms at once."

"At once, *Chieh Hsia,*" he answered, instinctively bowing his head, but he was speaking to himself. Li Yuan had already cut contact.

He sat back and closed his eyes. What now? It was but four hours since he had last seen his Master.

The answer came to him at once. The unmarked craft that had arrived an hour back. Perhaps Li Yuan was about to let him in on what was going on.

If so it would bring matters to a head. For a long time now he had sought to serve both his Master and his Mistress equally. Now, however, if Li Yuan insisted on his secrecy, he would have to disappoint Pei K'ung. And that, he realized, was not something he looked forward to. No, he had seen what had happened to those who betrayed the Empress.

The thought of it made him turn pale. Li Yuan might well be the head, but Pei K'ung, without doubt, was the hands. Cross her and he might as well take the knife and use it on himself.

He stood. His legs felt weak and there was a sudden pounding at his temple. *I am ill*, he told himself. But he knew it wasn't any common illness. This was a sickness of the soul.

Li Yuan was waiting for him at the door to his study. Ushering him inside, the T'ang closed the door himself; then, unexpectedly taking Heng's arm, he drew him across to the window.

"Do you see?" he asked, pointing out into the gardens.

Heng looked. There, in the late afternoon sunlight, two young men stood beneath a blossoming cherry tree.

"The Prince!" Heng turned, surprised, looking to his Master. "But I thought he wasn't due back until tomorrow."

"He came back yesterday. We sneaked him in on one of the regular security patrols. The young man with him is an American. Mark Egan is his name. He is one of the New Colonists."

*"Chieh Hsia?"*

"I'll explain tomorrow. Right now I want you to go and see Pei K'ung."

*"Chieh Hsia?"*

Li Yuan smiled, then, going to the desk, rummaged among his papers until he found something. He brought it back across. "Here, Master Heng. Give her this. I know I promised you my answer tomorrow, but I had an hour to kill earlier this afternoon." He held out a large white parchment letter, sealed with his imperial stamp.

"It is my answer to the document the Empress sent me this morning."

Heng took the letter and stared at it a moment, open mouthed, unable to believe that his Master had at last stood up to Pei K'ung. Again this was Shepherd's doing, he was sure.

He looked up, unable to keep the smile from his face. "Forgive me if I seem impertinent, *Chieh Hsia*, but might I ask your reasons for not signing the edict?"

"Not signing?" Li Yuan gave him a puzzled look. "Did I *say* I was not signing? No, Master Heng. You have it wrong. I shall sign her document, and gladly, but I want changes to it first."

"Changes?" Heng Yu asked, the smile fading, the last flicker of hope guttering in his chest.

"Of course. The main thrust of her policy is sound, but her strategy . . . Well, you will see my proposals for yourself. They are . . . refinements."

"Refinements," Heng repeated, knowing for certain now that all was lost, that it would be war, endless war, for years to come.

"And the Prince?" he asked, looking out into the gardens once again and wondering if Kuei Jen's return had to do with this insane plan to reconquer Asia and make Chung Kuo whole again. "Am I to mention that he's back?"

Li Yuan's tight smile gave nothing away. "Not yet, Master Heng. You know how it is between them. They only bicker. Let her think, for the time being, that he is to return tomorrow, in time for the banquet. Besides, I think the letter you are carrying will more than fill her thoughts, neh, Master Heng?"

"Why, yes, *Chieh Hsia*."

Li Yuan laughed. "Then go and let her know my thoughts. Oh, and Heng Yu . . ."

"Yes, *Chieh Hsia*?"

"Cheer up a little. You would think the world had ended by that face of yours."

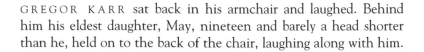

GREGOR KARR sat back in his armchair and laughed. Behind him his eldest daughter, May, nineteen and barely a head shorter than he, held on to the back of the chair, laughing along with him.

On the far side of the room, framed in the doorway, stood Karr's youngest, his five-year-old, Beth, her arms extended at full stretch, her father's white Marshal's tunic draped like a tent about her.

"Gregor?" Marie came from the kitchen, then, seeing what was up, began to giggle. "Beth . . . come now. You know Daddy has to wear that at the banquet tomorrow night. If you get it dirty—"

"Leave her," Karr said good-humoredly, sitting forward and holding out his arms to the child. "I can always get it cleaned."

Marie looked at him fondly as he lifted Beth up onto his knee and cuddled her. "You spoil her, Gregor. She'll become a little Empress."

His look—of mock horror—made her smile. Each knew, without it needing to be said, what the other thought of Pei K'ung.

She looked to May. "Sweetheart, will you chase those two out of the bathroom? It's time I got Beth bathed and into bed."

"Okay," May said, hurrying off.

"They're good girls," Gregor said, smiling at to his wife. "I'm looking forward to tomorrow night. It's not often in a man's life that he can present five such fine-looking women to his T'ang."

She smiled and came across, laying a hand on his shoulder. "You want to see their dresses, Gregor?"

"What, now? But I thought—"

Beth grabbed his chin with both of her tiny hands and turned it, so that he had to look at her. *"Please, Daddy."*

"Okay. But what about that bath? You stink, you little monkey!"

"Oh, I'll bathe her in a while. But they'd like that, Gregor. You know how they always want to show off."

He grinned. "Okay, then. But I'm back on duty in an hour."

She squeezed his shoulder. "It'll take five minutes at most. Come on, you. . . ." And, reaching across Gregor, she lifted Beth and twirled her around. "We'll show Daddy just what a little angel you can be!"

He watched them go, then sat back, enjoying the peacefulness of his own living room, the sound of his girls—his wife and his four darling daughters—moving and talking in the rooms about him. It was rare that he had the chance to relax this way. Most of the time he was in barracks at Bremen, among his men. He smiled, thinking of it. Though he enjoyed it, he had to admit that it was a hard, unashamedly masculine world. It looked and smelled of men. Of leather and sweat. Here it was different. This here was his place of softness—a yin world of perfumed comfort and loving-kindness. Here he could indulge that other, more feminine side of his nature; a side that only those he loved best—only his girls—knew existed.

And his men?

Karr looked down thoughtfully. In the days to come he would learn just how well his men loved him, for there were rumors that the Empress was planning a campaign—unconfirmed stories that she had been holding consultations and commissioning reports. It was hard to know the truth, of course, especially where that viper I Ye was concerned, but Karr had heard enough—and from enough different sources—to know there was some substance to the talk. And if it was true . . .

Karr sighed heavily. He was a soldier, a fighter—bred from the cradle to be a fighter—yet these past ten years had given him a taste for peace. He had seen his family grow and had been glad not to be away from them any more than was necessary. In the past he had spent months, often years at a stretch, away from them, fighting for his T'ang. When he thought of doing that again . . .

"Achh," he said quietly, speaking to himself. "What is the madwoman doing! Why can't she leave things be?"

But he knew the reasons why. It was because what she had was no longer enough for her. She had grown tired of ruling such a tiny piece of land. Like endless kings and queens before her she wanted more, as much as she could grab, and to hell with the consequences. It was of no concern to her how many died in the achievement.

Power, it seemed, was an addiction. It ate one from within. And Pei K'ung had been hollowed. One had only to look at her.

He heard footfalls in the corridor outside and looked up.

"Daddy?"

"But I thought . . ." He sat forward, then laughed and clapped his hands in delight as the four of them trooped into the room, their silk and satin dresses swishing against the walls and the polished wooden floor. "Why, they're beautiful, my darlings! I'll be the proudest father ever when I lead you out between the pillars in the T'ang's Great Hall tomorrow night."

He stood, admiring them. It was true. They looked quite stunning. And though their powder-blue satin dresses reminded him a little of the groups of officials he saw waiting in the T'ang's reception rooms from time to time, no official had ever looked so radiant, so beautiful, as the four of them looked at that moment.

"Hannah, Lily . . . what have you done to your hair, you two?"

"You like it?" Hannah, the second eldest, answered, rushing across to him. "Lily did it for me. It's the latest fashion at Court," she said. "All the great ladies wear their hair like this."

He smiled and reached out to touch it. "It's very nice. *Very* adult."

"Why, thank you, kind sir," she said, and bobbed a curtsy. Behind her the other three did the same.

He laughed again, enjoying himself. "And you know what to say when I present you, I hope."

Marie, standing just behind them, laughed. "They've practiced it endlessly, Gregor. Why, if I hear it one more time!" ·

Little Beth made to open her mouth, but Hannah, seeing it, placed a hand over it.

"Hey!" Beth said, struggling, then gave her elder sister a thump.

"Now, you two!" Marie said, moving between them to break it up. "Best behavior, or the T'ang will be cross with you!"

"Well, *she* started it," Beth said, glowering up at her sister.

Karr sighed. Even their squabbles were a delight to him. "Here," he said, putting out an arm to Beth once more. Yet even as he did, the door chime sounded.

"Are you expecting anyone?" he asked, looking to Marie.

She shook her head. "You want me to get it?"

"No, I'll go." He stood and, patting Beth's head, moved between them. "You look wonderful," he said, smiling at each in turn. "You really do."

The front door to their apartment was half wood, half glass, in the new style. Through the colored glass panels he could see the shadow of a figure. Upright, soldierly.

*What now?* he wondered, slipping the latch and pulling the door open wide.

"Marshal!" The soldier—a Captain of I Ye's elite force, his uniform the bottle-green of the West Palace—snapped to attention and bowed his head smartly.

He looked out past the man, noting at a glance that his own guards were still at their positions in the hallway, then looked back at the waiting officer.

"Well, Captain? This had better be good. If your Colonel wanted me, he should have sent you to my office, not my home."

"Forgive me, Marshal," the Captain said, keeping his head bowed, daunted as much by Karr's sheer size as by his rank. "I— I . . ."

Unexpectedly, Karr laughed. "Damn it, man. Spit it out! I've four young women in there want my attention!"

The Captain's head came up, surprised.

"My daughters," Karr explained, and noted how the man's face changed. He had clearly misunderstood what his Marshal had meant. "Now get on with it."

"Sir!" The Captain fumbled in his tunic, then produced a sealed letter. Coming to attention again, he presented it stiffly, a color now at his neck. Despite himself Karr found he rather liked the man. At least he wasn't the usual arrogant asshole one found doing I Ye's bidding. Karr took the letter and, breaking the seal with his thumbnail, flipped it open.

It was from Pei K'ung. He was to go to her at once. Karr looked up at the young officer.

"Have I time to dress?"

"I . . ." The color at his neck deepened. "Of course, Marshal. I am instructed by Colonel I to accompany you."

"Very well. Wait there. I'll be but a minute."

Karr returned inside, closing the door behind him. Marie was standing at the end of the hall, staring at him.

"What is it?" she asked, as if she already understood.

"I have been summoned," he said quietly, knowing that there could be only one reason why Pei K'ung would summon him so urgently. "I am to see the Empress straightaway."

PEI K'UNG came directly to the point.

"I have a job for you, Marshal Karr—a very *important* job. I want you to be my envoy."

"Mistress?" His eyes went to I Ye and Ming Ai, who stood to the right just behind the Empress, but there was no sign in either of their faces. If anything, both looked a touch unhappy.

"It has been decided that there is to be a campaign," she continued. "A campaign to reunify the hereditary lands. You, as Marshal, shall of course be given the command of that campaign. However, in the present circumstances matters are far from simple. We cannot simply send out an army. There must be careful planning. Yes, and negotiations."

"Negotiations, Mistress?"

The smile she gave him was not because she liked him—Karr knew better than to think she had changed overnight in that regard—but for some intellectual puzzle she had solved. "Negotiations," she repeated. "With Hu Wang-chih and Mao-tun."

He stared at her, astonished. "But, Mistress, those men are bandits!"

"Warlords," she said, giving the word a degree of dignity she did not normally accord it. "And two of the most important Warlords in West Asia. If we can convince them to become our allies—"

She stopped, staring at him harshly. "Have you a problem, Marshal Karr?"

He lowered his head, then, steeling himself to speak, nodded. "I have indeed, Mistress. For several years I have been instructed to undermine these men, to weaken them and take every opportunity to strike at them. Now, overnight, it seems, we are to embrace them and call them our friends. Can I ask why?"

She spoke to him as she might to a small child who did not understand a simple truth. "Because, Marshal Karr, it will make things easier for us. Word is that there is a defensive alliance between the nine Western Warlords—that should we attack any single Warlord, the rest would come to his aid. If that is so—and there is no reason to doubt that it is so—then we might find ourselves getting bogged down in a long and expensive campaign. Any short-term benefits would dissolve. There would be trouble here in the City—discontent, maybe even revolution—and we cannot afford to risk that, can we, Marshal Karr?"

"Maybe not," he admitted grudgingly. "Yet why should Hu Wang-chih and Mao-tun join us? I would say they had every possible incentive *not* to ally with us. We killed Hu's son, burned down Mao's palace."

Pei K'ung stepped closer, looking up into Karr's face, her own as hard as iron. "Because, Marshal Karr, you will offer Hu Wang-chih and Mao-tun the rank of Minor Prince. The Twenty-Nine will be extended to include their families, and they will be allowed to rule their present territories as vassals of the T'ang. In return they will help us against their neighbors."

Karr made a noise of disbelief, stunned by the enormity of what had been decided. "And the Minor Families . . . have they been consulted on this matter?"

Again she smiled. "No. Nor shall they be. For I have no intention of honoring the agreement."

He stared back into her eyes, alarmed. *"Mistress?"*

"You heard me, Marshal. You don't seriously think we could let such rabble—such *bandits* as you so rightly termed them—become Lords, do you? No. Nor shall we. As soon as the other Warlords have been destroyed and their forces dissipated, we shall turn on Hu and Mao and crush them without mercy."

She smiled—a light, almost pleasant smile—then turned from him. "But you will keep that to yourself."

He saw her look to Ming Ai, saw the eunuch smile as if he shared the joke. "And when am I to go?"

"The day after tomorrow," she said, going to her desk and sitting. "You will travel to Mashhad to meet with Hu Wang-chih. I shall prepare whatever documents you'll need and will brief you fully before you go."

"I am to go alone, then, Mistress?"

She looked up at him, then reached across the desk to take a brush and ink it. "Is that a problem, Marshal Karr?"

He shook his head. But the more he heard, the worse he felt about this mission.

"May I ask one final thing, Mistress?"

Her brush, which had begun to sketch out pictograms on the

blank paper, paused. She looked up at him again, her eyes cold, no love for him in them. "Yes, Marshal Karr?"

"Why are you sending *me?*"

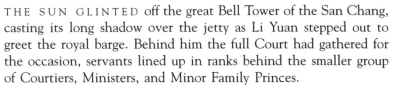

T H E   S U N   G L I N T E D  off the great Bell Tower of the San Chang, casting its long shadow over the jetty as Li Yuan stepped out to greet the royal barge. Behind him the full Court had gathered for the occasion, servants lined up in ranks behind the smaller group of Courtiers, Ministers, and Minor Family Princes.

As the two women stepped down, Li Yuan lowered his head, acknowledging with that gesture the high regard in which the Shepherd family were held—a special status enshrined in the laws of Chung Kuo. Just beyond the women, hanging back at the rail, was Shepherd's son, so like his father that he could have been a younger version.

"Welcome," Li Yuan said, smiling first at Shepherd's dark-haired sister, Meg, then at his wife, the red-haired Catherine. "I am delighted you have come."

"It was very kind of you to invite us," Meg answered, looking beyond him, clearly disappointed that Ben wasn't there to greet them. "My brother?" she said quietly.

Li Yuan moved closer, conscious as he did of the discreetly perfumed scent of the two women, answering Meg in a whisper. "He will meet us inside. He thought it . . . better."

Meg nodded, as if she understood. Catherine, however, seemed less concerned. She stared past him, studying the walls of the palace.

"Your journey was good, I hope?" Li Yuan asked her.

Catherine turned her head and met his smile, her green eyes twinkling momentarily, making Li Yuan understand just why Ben had married the woman. "It was certainly eventful," she said. "It's fortunate young Tom has a good sense of direction, otherwise we'd be looking for him still."

"Ah . . ." Li Yuan looked past her. Tom had moved from the rail and was coming down the gangway. A moment later he stood before the T'ang.

*Astonishing,* he thought, recollecting once again the first time he had met the mold from which this copy had been cast. He took the boy's hand and, instead of shaking it, turned it in his own, as if studying it. It was a gesture so like one Ben would use that Tom looked up and smiled.

"I am very pleased to meet you, Thomas. You are so *very* like your father," he said. "And your mother, of course," he added quickly, looking to Meg, anxious not to offend.

She smiled, and as she did he saw that it was Tom's smile, Ben's smile, as if the three had been cloned from the same DNA.

*Not surprising,* he thought, recalling what Ben had told him of the genetic "program" set up by his great-great-great-grandfather, Amos. For the Shepherds were not a "normal" family—not in any respect.

"Anyway," he said, collecting his thoughts, "come through into the palace. We've nothing formal arranged for tonight, but it will give you a chance to meet a few people. Some you will know. Others . . ." He stopped, realizing he was in danger of rambling; realizing also that it was an age since he had last done this—since he had last taken part in the official, ritual life of his Court.

"It's a beautiful place," Catherine said, as they began to walk toward the palace, Tom bringing up the rear of their party. "I thought it would be more . . . German, I guess."

Li Yuan laughed. "It is the thing about us Han. Wherever we travel, we are never far from home. If one must live in exile, then it is best to surround oneself with such . . . reminders, neh?"

Her answering smile suggested that, if she did not disagree with him, she did not entirely agree either. Again it made him reevaluate her. To be Ben's mate—to keep his interest—that would be some task for a single woman.

Then again, she wasn't a single woman. After all, there was also Meg, sharing Ben's life, his bed.

Li Yuan looked down, remembering in that instant the three wives he had once had; recalling their differences, the special traits he had liked about each.

Dead they were. Gone. Murdered by his enemies.

Yes, but then his enemies were also dead. Murdered in turn. Killed by *his* servants, to *his* order. An eye for an eye, as Ben so often said.

*Such is the world,* he thought, looking straight ahead, smiling fixedly as they made their way through the bowing group of Courtiers and Ministers, his emotions at that moment a mixture of bitterness and sadness. *Try as one might, one cannot change it.*

And he had tried. The gods knew he had tried.

"Are the Osu here?" Catherine asked, the faintest waft of her perfume reaching him as she leaned toward him.

"The Osu? Why, yes. You're interested in their history?"

She laughed, then leaning even closer, spoke to his ear. "Bugger their history! Ben's promised me I can sleep with one!"

---

*THERE WAS A heavy knocking on the outer gate, impatient and aggressive. Chuang Kuan Ts'ai, who was standing on a chair at the sink, her arms elbow deep in the washing-up bowl, turned abruptly, looking to her adopted father, the Oven Man, where he sat at a table cradling his ch'a bowl.*

*"Are you expecting someone, Uncle Cho?"*

*He looked back at her and shrugged, then, setting the bowl down softly, stood, his actions weary. It had been a long, hard day and it was late. Almost tenth bell.*

*She watched him go out, heard his footsteps on the stone floor of the hallway; heard the latch slide back, his footsteps on the cobbles of the courtyard.*

*The hammering came again.*

*"Okay . . . okay, I'm coming!"*

*She could picture him looking through the spyhole in the gate. A moment later she heard the rattle of the chain, the grating of the top bolt as he slid it back.*

*"It's late," he said. "I closed an hour back."*

*"We've urgent business," someone answered gruffly.*

*"Can't it wait?"*

*"No," came the answer. "We've five bodies need storing overnight, till you can burn them."*

*Chuang jumped down from the chair and hurried to the door, peering out across the unlit courtyard. On the far side, framed by the light from the yard's single lamp, she could see Uncle Cho, his face looking around the gate, one massive hand holding it half-closed against them. In the* gap, backlit, was a stranger, a tall, shaven-headed Han dressed in the bottle-green of Pei K'ung's elite. In one hand he cupped an ID badge. Beyond him there were others. How many she couldn't tell.

"Okay," Uncle Cho said, stepping out and beginning to pull the gate open. "But make it quick, now. I've had a long day."

Chuang pulled the door to, so that she wouldn't be seen, then placed her ear to it, listening. There was the metallic click of boots against the cobbles of the yard, the creak of the outer gate, and then the sound of a cart being wheeled in.

For a moment there was silence, then came the sound of a heavy cloth being pulled back.

Cho made a noise of surprise. "Aiya," he said softly but distinctly. "What happened to them?"

"Never you mind. Just store them and burn them. And say nothing, understand? This is your clearance."

In her mind Chuang saw the officer hand across a document; saw her uncle open and study it before he grunted his assent.

"I can't argue with this," he said finally, a hint of resignation in his voice, "but I don't like it."

"You aren't asked to like it," another voice, more sophisticated than the first, said sharply. "Just do what you're paid for, Oven Man, and hold your tongue."

There were more noises—the shuffling of feet, booted footsteps, the creak of the outer gate—then silence.

She waited a moment then, slipping the catch, went out to him.

He was standing on the far side of the yard, half crouched over the cart. Hearing her he made to cover it over, but she stayed his hand.

"Let me see," she said, stepping past him, then walking around the cart, taking it all in.

She had seen many corpses—many more dead than living, if she thought about it—but few that were as grotesque, as badly damaged, as these. There was no doubt about it—they showed the signs of torture. Not only that but they had been strangled. The cords were still tight about their necks, their tongues poking black from their open mouths.

"Who were they?" she asked, looking to him.

He shrugged, unable to keep from looking at them, his eyes, which had seen so much, appalled by this. She leaned across and pulled the rough cloth over them once more.

"Lock the gate," she said, seeing how he was, mother to him at that moment.

He nodded and went across.

"Good," she said, watching him. "Then move the cart into the shed. We'll deal with this in the morning."

Again he nodded, as if in a trance.

She let a long breath hiss between her teeth, then turned, looking at the covered cart. In the dim light of the lamp she saw how blood had dripped onto the wheels and pooled beneath the cart. No doubt a tiny trail of blood led to their door.

Fresh killed, she thought. Or else the blood would have congealed.

She shuddered. They had been touched tonight. Touched by the evil that emanated from that woman's palace. The shadows that flittered here and there about the City had tonight landed in their yard.

She looked up at the sky, remembering the butterfly. GenSyn it had been. A camera eye.

The cart creaked. She looked down in time to see the cart disappear inside the shed. A moment later the Oven Man emerged, closing the double doors behind him.

"Come, Uncle," she said, putting out a tiny hand for him to take, conscious suddenly of how small she was compared to him, how frail, and yet in this much stronger. "Let's get some sleep."

---

IT WAS EASY TO DO. Every house on Teng Sung Lane had a water barrel out in the front, facing the alleyway, where the water bringer could fill them up each morning from his cart. There were filters, naturally, but they were intended to cope with dust and insects and the like, not with the malice of a willful boy. It was simple to remove a filter and replace it afterward. The poison was a white powder, tasteless and odorless—deliberately so, for rats had far more sensitive and discerning palates than humans—and it needed little to achieve its intended end.

From where he squatted on a first-floor balcony at the far end of the alley, hidden from curious eyes behind the carved lattice, Josef watched the dawn come up and saw the water bringer make his rounds. One house in particular—the house with the green doors halfway along the wall that ran the alley's length—interested him more than the others. It *was there he'd laid his bait. He watched the water bringer park his shining metal cart beside it and lift the water barrel's lid to fill it, unaware.*

People came and went. An hour passed. Slowly the City woke, the alley filling with locals, shaking out rugs and greeting each other, stopping a moment to talk. There was the clatter of cooking utensils from within a dozen households, the sound of a baby crying. Below that there was the noise from a dozen screens, voices, an angry shout. Ordinary sounds. Sounds that one might hear throughout the width and breadth of the great city.

The green doors were the last to open. Josef leaned forward, suddenly intent, watching as the mother of the house—a tall Han in her forties—came out and filled a jug from the water barrel. For a moment she stood there in the morning sunlight, her head thrown back, one hand on her hip as she talked to a neighbor, then she returned inside, the doors pulled shut behind her.

He waited, tensed now, expectant, imagining her actions. First she would boil water, then she would add it to the pot to make the breakfast ch'a. Yes, he could see the filled and steaming chung resting there in the middle of the kitchen table, innocuous yet deadly.

For a time nothing, then, distinct above the other normal sounds, a groan—a groan so deep, so filled with pain, that he knew without doubt it had begun. It came again, louder, longer, than before. There was a shout, then the sound of someone retching. Josef pushed himself up, his tiny hands gripping the smooth edge of the lattice.

There was a fumbling at the latch and then the green doors burst open. A young man, naked from the waist up, staggered out into the alley and collapsed, his hands at his throat, as if he were choking himself to death. From inside there came the sound of screaming.

Josef watched, his eyes taking in everything, seeing how neighbors rushed to help. But there was nothing they could do. The poison was deadly and efficient. Whoever had drunk the ch'a would be dead by now.

As the young man shuddered and lay still, Josef turned and slipped away over the rooftops, picking his way barefoot across the tiles with the deftness of a cat.

Dropping into his yard, he heard his mother's voice at once, chiding his long-suffering father for not keeping a better eye on him.

"He's out of control, that child . . . you know it and I know it. If
you don't do something . . ."

"Do something? What can I do? He's a law unto himself, that one.
Seven and you'd think he was seventy. He was born old, that one.
Sometimes I think . . ."

"What?" Josef could almost see her turn upon his father, her eyes
glaring. "What do you almost think?"

"Nothing," he said bitterly. "I think nothing."

Josef slipped into the kitchen like a shadow, taking a cake from the
tray as he passed. Then, silently, unseen by the two figures who stood
confronting each other in the cramped front room, he climbed the stairs
and went into his room.

It was a tiny room, under the sloping roof, but big enough for him.
Crossing it quickly he went to the shelves beside the bed and reached
behind a stack of tape books, his fingers closing on the storage jar.

So far so good, he thought, recalling the choking noise the young man
had made, the screams of the mother from within. But there was one
further thing to do before his scheme could be brought to fruition. One
final, necessary stage.

Downstairs they were arguing again, their voices carrying through the
floor to where he stood.

Tucking the jar into the band of his trousers, Josef went to the window
and undid the catch, then stepped out onto the roof. It would take but
an hour. Then he could come back here and sleep. Yes, and dream,
perhaps, of what was yet to be.

# CHAPTER THREE

# Proclamation

**K**UNG CHIA, *Wei*, Chief of Security for Weisenau *Hsien*, stood before the gates of the Magistrate's *yamen*, his feet spread, as he unfurled the proclamation. His men were formed up in a line in front of him, their visors down, their guns held threateningly across their chests.

Kung looked about him at the crowd of locals packed into the square, then, clearing his throat, began to read, his words echoing back to him from the speakers on the far side of the square. When he had finished there was a moment's shocked silence; then a great murmur swept through the crowd.

Turning his back on the mob, Kung Chia took a long black nail from his pocket and, pinning the top of the proclamation to the gate, hammered it into the erwood with the pommel of his dagger. Taking a second nail from his pocket, he pinned it to the foot of the thick paper, then knocked it in, feeling the door judder beneath the heavy blows.

He sheathed his dagger, then stood back, feeling a sense of profound satisfaction. It was about time Li Yuan did something. About time these miserable bastards paid for something other than their food. He looked about him at the shocked and angry faces and grinned. Let the fucking ingrates moan and argue, the thing was done—*T'ieh pi pu kai*, as it said at the foot of the edict—"The iron pen changes not." Yes, and if any of them thought they *could* change it, then he, Kung Chia, would make sure they changed their minds! The three new water cannons had been delivered only a week back. They sat in the courtyard of the *yamen* even now, their crews ready for action.

With a gruff laugh Kung Chia pushed the gate open and marched back inside the walled enclosure, his men falling in at his back. He was still laughing as the big doors slammed shut behind him.

Outside, in Wen Ti Square, the crowd surged in, clamoring to read the edict for themselves, cries of dismay and anger piercing the morning air. Taxes! For the first time in Chung Kuo's history a T'ang had levied taxes on the common people!

———

EMILY HAD BEEN standing at the very back of the crowd, beside a row of stalls, young Ji up on her shoulders so he could see. Like everyone there she had heard what the *Wei* had said and had no doubt that he had read the proclamation word for word, but still people crowded at the door, keen to read it for themselves, to see with their own eyes what had been decided from on high.

She sighed and, bending, handed Ji down.

"What is it, Mama Em?" the four-year-old asked, staring up at her with his big hazel eyes.

"Trouble," she said, hugging him briefly, then stood and took his hand.

They hurried home. The boys were at school, the outer yard empty, but Lin was at his table in the inner yard, the ledgers stacked beside him, the latest of them open to the last few weeks' figures.

"You've heard, then," she said.

"I've heard," he answered, not looking up, his finger moving patiently across the lines of figures, as if deciphering some ancient language. "Old Wen was here. He said there are to be taxes. Ten *fen* in every *yuan* we earn."

"So it is. Beginning at *Hsiao Man.*"

"So soon?"

*Hsiao Man*—"Small Fullness"—was the week of May twenty-second. It was now a week past *Li Hsia*—"Summer Commences." The new tax would be introduced a mere nine days hence.

She went and stood beside him. "So, Papa Lin . . . what are we to do?"

He half turned, looking up at her, his twisted face unchanged, an inexhaustible patience in his dark Han eyes. "We must work harder, Mama Em, that's what. And Chao . . . Chao will have to find a job."

"But . . ."

She fell silent, seeing the determination in his face. He was right. Chao would have to get a job. It was the only way.

"It cannot be helped," Lin said after a moment, shutting up the ledger and pushing it aside. "Besides, Chao will understand. I'll talk to him. Help him in the evenings. He does not have to give up his studies, only the lessons."

She nodded, yet her heart sank at the thought of telling Chao. Chao was their eldest—the one they'd had the longest—and he had set his heart on graduating from the State College. This news would come as a great blow to him.

She sighed, then leaned heavily against the table's edge, suddenly tired. "Why now? Why *now*, when things are finally okay?"

The patient shrug epitomized Lin Shang. "We will make do. You know that, Mama Em. It is our way, after all. This here is our island, no? And we take care of those we love. As for the bigger world . . . well, how can we change the minds of kings? You tried that once and where did it get you?"

She laughed. It wasn't often Lin referred to her past life, yet when he did, as now, it was to emphasize the futility of action. At least, of the kind of action—terrorism and political activity—that she had once engaged in. For Lin Shang, *wuwei*—inaction—was the key to life.

He gave a faint smile, the way he always did when he quoted the sages. "When the great storm comes the big oaks try to stand against the wind and so fall, whereas the weaker reeds lie flat and, when the wind has died, raise up their heads once more. So it is. So it has always been."

She nodded, but at the back of her mind was the memory of the last great storm that had struck Chung Kuo a decade back, and of the billions of common people—reeds, every last one of them—who had died in it. Whereas the big oaks—Li Yuan, Ebert, Shepherd, and the like—had come through unscathed. It was a fact that seemed to make a mockery of Lin Shang's philosophy.

Ji, standing at her side, had said nothing all this while. Now he yawned loudly. Emily looked down at him and smiled.

"Are you hungry, Ji?"

Ji returned her smile, then nodded.

"Good. Then come and help me make Papa Lin some lunch."

Ji hesitated, his face slowly forming a frown. "And the paper, Mama Em? The paper that the *Wei* nailed onto the *Hsien L'ing*'s door . . . Does it mean there'll be no more food, after today?"

"No more food . . ." Emily laughed, then knelt, holding Ji to her. "No, Ji. There'll be food. Maybe not as much as before, but we'll make do, neh? We always do."

---

TOM STOOD ON the balcony of his father's rooms, looking out across the palace gardens toward a sheltered bower, where, part hidden by the leaves of an ancient willow, three serving maids walked slowly back and forth, giggling among themselves, their heads pressed close together. He watched them, fascinated, reminded by their laughter of the girl, and wondered what she was doing at that moment; whether she, too, would stop at moments and look up, thinking of him.

It was ridiculous. He knew it was ridiculous, but could not help himself. Everywhere he looked he seemed to see her face. When the wind blew, he heard her whispering. When a door creaked open, he would turn, thinking it was her. And nothing he could do—nothing—could take his mind from her.

"Tom?"

He turned as his father came out and joined him at the rail. Ben was silent awhile, his eyes taking in the scene.

"You like it here, Tom?"

Tom shrugged. He hadn't even thought about it. From the bower a peal of laughter, high pitched and melodious, rang out, and as it did he felt a shiver ripple through him, making the hairs on his neck stand up.

"You want to see what I'm doing?"

He met his father's eyes, then nodded. What did it matter after all?

"Come, then."

He followed his father inside. While Ben prepared things at the far end of the workroom, Tom sat in the tall-backed chair beside the window, the sunlight through the glass making him feel drowsy. Ben, by comparison, moved quickly and energetically about, his helmet—a cross between an exoskeletal skull and a surgeon's cap, the delicate metallic frame studded with swivel-mounted lenses—set momentarily on a workbench at the side as he switched on this and tampered with that, then paused to sketch out an "external" for his assistant.

Scaf stood just behind his Master, watching patiently and nodding whenever Ben asked him if he understood. It was Scaf's job to make the roughs—the first-stage 3-D landscapes within which Ben would set his drama. As Ben finished, the ancient Clayman grunted his approval.

"It's like the painting," he said in his gruff Clay voice, taking the sketch from Ben and holding it up to study it.

"Precisely," Ben said. "But only *like*. We must make literal what was allegorical in the painting."

The Clayman's head turned slowly, his eyes—night-dark, the skin about them heavily lined—meeting his Master's briefly, as if registering understanding. Again he nodded.

"Good." Ben laid a hand gently on Scaf's shoulder and smiled. "You get on with that. I'll be setting down the opening viewpoint."

As Scaf disappeared through the end door, Ben looked across at his son, as if noticing him for the first time, though Tom had sat there for the best part of ten minutes.

"So?" he said, mentioning it for the first time. "How *was* the journey?"

Tom shrugged. Behind him, from the garden, came the sound of laughter. He shivered, then moved his hands. *It was . . . eventful.*

"Ah . . ." Ben went to the bench and picked up the helmet, staring at it as he spoke. "I can't stop you having adventures, Tom. To be frank, I wouldn't want to. But you should spare a thought for your mother. You worried her, you know." He looked up, meeting

Tom's eyes, trying to make some kind of contact. "After all, this isn't the Domain. It can be very dangerous out there."

Tom moved his hands in his lap. *I know.* But inside he felt a tremendous restlessness. What was he doing sitting here? What in God's name was he doing? Why wasn't he back there in the cabin with her? Why was he *here?*

Ben set the helmet down and came across. He stood there, just to Tom's right, barely an arm's length from him, staring out into the garden. For a moment the silence was complete. Then Ben looked down at him.

"So what *did* happen out there?"

Tom took a long, calming breath. *Nothing,* he signed.

"I see." Ben made a small gesture, as if it didn't matter. "So you had an eventful journey in which nothing happened, do I understand that correctly?"

Tom almost smiled. Almost. Yet suddenly, frighteningly, he felt close to tears. There was a silence in his head, and his heart. . . .

"Was it a girl?" Ben asked, crouching, facing him now, his eyes staring into Tom's face. "Is that it? Did you *meet* someone?"

He closed his eyes against that searchlight stare, wanting but not wanting to tell his father everything. But so it was. So it had always been. He wanted so much to share it all with Ben—wanted it almost as much as he wanted the girl—yet he was afraid. Afraid that his father would use it, as he used everything. Afraid that Ben would transform his life into a confection—a thing for others to chew upon and spit out. And maybe he had always feared that. Maybe that was why he was silent, for the doctors said there was no physiological reason for his dumbness.

He shook his head, his eyes squeezed tightly shut now, so tight they seemed to bleed.

"Tears?" Ben said, a tone of genuine surprise in his voice. "You want to talk about it?"

The irony of that made him laugh inwardly. His eyes opened to see his father's face a hand's width distant, studying the look of him; scanning his features like a probe above a planet's surface.

*Yes, and I, too, am like that. That much I got from him,* Tom thought, recalling the girl's face—seeing it so clearly that it might have been her crouching there only inches from him.

*I'll tell you*, he signed. *I'll tell you everything. But not now.*

"Okay," Ben said, his eyes releasing him, his hand resting briefly on Tom's knee before he stood. "But if you need help . . . if you need advice . . . well, you know where to come."

Tom stared at him as he walked back to the bench, surprised. Now, *that* was a first. His father had never offered him advice before, let alone help.

Surprised, yes, but also suspicious.

He stood, hesitating a moment in case there was something else, but his father had done with him, it seemed. Already he was working again, the helmet perched on top of his head, the leather strap undone, a notebook open on the bench before him.

*Nothing changes*, Tom thought, taking in the scene. *As long as I have known him he has been thus. Like a machine. A machine that sucks in life and turns out art.*

The thought of it chilled him as it had never chilled him before. And maybe that, too, was the girl's doing. Maybe she had woken more than the response of love in him. If love it was and not some strange illness spawned by need and nurtured by physical infatuation.

After all, how could one love a woman one did not know?

And yet he did.

He turned, leaving his father's workroom, glad to be gone from there, but for once there was no sense of release. It was as if what had been wild in him—the freedom he had felt playing in the fields and secret hiding places of the Domain—was suddenly no longer there. As he paused, staring about him at the lushness of the palace corridor, he felt that there was nowhere to turn, no place for him to go. Something strange, something *irreversible*, had happened to him and there was no way back from it.

*Sampsa!* he called, the crying echoing loudly in the hollow of his skull. *Sampsa, where are you?*

But there was no answer. Only the silence in his head. Only that and the sound of the maids' shrill laughter in the garden.

SAMPSA TURNED, feeling a vague sensation at the back of his head, a gentle tickling reverberation, as if something very small were crawling about inside his skull. He knew that feeling; knew that Tom was trying to talk to him. For a moment he closed his eyes, straining to catch that faint susurration, but it was too faint, too far away.

*What is it, Tom? What are you doing at this moment?*

But no answer came. He shivered and turned back, looking across the platform at his father. Kim stood at the very edge of the platform beside the squat, spiderlike transmitters, his face visible through the lit visor of his helmet as he stared out into the void, as if listening. Beyond him the blackness was dusted with stars. Below him was a million miles of nothingness.

"It's too much," Kim said, as if speaking to himself. "The rate of decay is far too great." He turned, gesturing to Jelka to come across to him. "No," he said, answering the radio signal in his head as Sampsa's mother, her tall shape clothed in a tight-fitting outworlder suit, joined him beside the transmitters. "We need to boost it somehow, to keep the pulse strong. . . . No! It's just not good enough! It has to be much stronger. At least two hundred times stronger. As it is, the beam won't even get a quarter of the way there. We might as well shine a fucking flashlight into the darkness!"

Sampsa watched, surprised. It wasn't often that he saw his father angry.

"What is it?" Jelka asked.

In answer Kim punched out a figure on the display panel on his left arm and showed it to her.

"That much?" she said, shaking her head.

He nodded.

"Shit!"

That, too, was strange; hearing his mother swear. The test results must have been really bad. He looked to his right. There, by the glowing control board, his baby sister, Mileja, was amusing herself doing somersaults in the zero-gravity conditions, the umbilical that tethered her to the platform stretching and coiling, forever pulling her back.

He smiled. It was just wonderful up here. How wonderful he hadn't guessed until now. No wonder his mother and father spent so much time out here. Below him, to his left, so close it seemed he could almost reach out and touch it, was the Moon. Farther down—directly down, that was—sitting there like a blue-green hole in the blackness, was Chung Kuo.

If he wanted he could leap from the platform's edge and fall toward that tiny circle, like a diver falling toward a distant pool. And how long would he take to fall? Weeks, months, perhaps, though he would probably starve long before he ever breached the surface of *that* pool.

He turned back. His father was shaking his head now and tutting to himself. The lenses he wore—saucer glasses designed to enhance his view of the stars—made him seem even more alien than he naturally was with his huge head and tiny frame. And though he had something of each of his parents within his own ungainly frame, he thought once more just how ill matched a pair they looked.

Ill matched yet complementary. Like a double star system, they orbited each other endlessly.

"Sampsa?"

He went across. "Yes, Father?"

"Is the shuttle coming?"

He looked down at the timer at his wrist and whistled, surprised. Was it that time already? "I'll check," he said.

He drifted over to the board.

"I can do doubles," Mileja said, tapping the top of his helmet as she floated past him. "Watch!"

He watched a moment, humoring her, clapping her, his thickly gloved hands making almost no sound. Then, knowing his father would want an answer quickly, he studied the figures on the board's display screen.

"It's on its way," he said, looking to his mother, who was watching him fondly. "ETA eighteen minutes."

"Good," Kim said, his concentration unbroken. "At least one thing's going according to plan!"

Sampsa heard the bitterness in his father's voice, the disappointment, and looked down. Kim had been sure he'd cracked it this time; certain that the rate of decay—the rate at which the beamed laser signal broke up—had been reduced substantially. And so it had. But not enough, it seemed. Nothing like enough.

"Shit!" Kim said, sighing deeply and moving from the platform's edge. "Shit! Shit! Shit!"

Mileja, in midloop, gave a giggle. "Shit!" she said.

"Hey," Jelka said, coming across to her. "That's quite enough, young lady!"

"But Daddy said—"

*"Enough!"*

Again Mileja giggled, so that even Kim broke into a smile.

"Is it that bad?" Sampsa asked.

"Bad?" Kim came and touched his arm. "Oh, far worse than bad. I'd say I've been barking up the wrong tree, if that image made any sense at all out here."

"Mining the wrong asteroid?" Jelka suggested.

"Terraforming the wrong planet?" Sampsa added, joining in the family game.

Kim grinned, his eyes like ostrich eggs behind their lenses, then he gave another sigh. "Whatever . . . it looks like I'll have to start from scratch. Find some other way to tackle the problem. It's not the lasers—they're powerful enough—it's the interstellar dust. There's not much of it, but over the distances we're talking of, the signal just gets eaten by it. *Absorbed.* You might just as well try to send a signal through a mile of steel."

"You'll find a way," Jelka said, putting an arm around him. "You always do."

"Not this time," he said, a hint of despair in the words. "It's just too far."

"No," she began, but he shook his head.

"I'm deadly serious, my love. For once I might just have over-reached myself. I mean, linking the stars, it's a *crazy* idea, don't you think? Building a massive cat's cradle between them. Who but a madman would think of doing that?"

"Or a genius?" Jelka said quietly.

"No." He shook his head again. "No."

"Spiders," Sampsa said. "Think spiders."

"What?" Kim looked to his son, a sudden intensity in his eyes.

"Krakatoa . . . remember? You told me the story once. About how all the wildlife on the island of Krakatoa was utterly destroyed by the volcano. And how a spider was the first creature to return to the island."

Kim's smile grew slowly. "I remember. It was too far from land for it to get there by normal means, so it sailed there on the wind, spinning a thin silk thread as it went."

Sampsa nodded.

"And you think we could use something similar? To sail on solar winds, perhaps. Out into the darkness between the stars, until it comes to land . . ."

"Spinning a thread," Sampsa said. "And boosting the signal as it went."

Kim laughed. "Brilliant!" he said, clapping Sampsa's back. "I think that's brilliant!"

"You think it'll work, then?"

Kim shrugged. "The gods alone know if it'll work. But we'll try, eh? We'll sure as hell try!"

---

CHAO STOOD BEFORE his adopted father where he sat at his desk, the young man's head bowed, listening as Lin Shang spoke of what had happened and what it meant for them all. Chao had heard much of it already, of course, for there was no one in the City who was unaffected. Taxes would hit them all. But for Chao it meant more than most. For Chao it could well change his entire future.

Emily stood to one side looking on, her chest tight with anxiety. If Ji, the youngest, was her favorite, Chao, the eldest, was the one upon whom all her hopes rested. Brighter than the rest and quicker of mind, he had taken to his studies like a fish to water, but who knew what this setback would do to him.

". . . so you understand," Lin said, finally coming to it, "that this will mean sacrifices for us all. We shall all have to work harder. Not only that, but we shall have to do without many things we have previously taken for granted—"

"Papa Lin?"

Lin Shang looked up, surprised that Chao had interrupted him. He straightened his shoulders, a slight tick momentarily making the right hand side of his face jump. "Yes, Lin Chao?"

The boy kept his eyes averted, yet there was something in his face—an earnestness beyond his years—that she had not noticed before.

"Would it help if you did not have to pay for my studies, Papa Lin?"

Lin Shang swallowed, disconcerted by this turn of events. It was clear he had braced himself to break the news to Chao—to be hard, if necessary—but he had not been prepared for Chao's offer.

"It would."

"Then I should be glad to give them up. If it would help."

Lin's face twitched once more, then, abruptly, he bowed his head. It was done.

Emily stared at Chao, impressed by his self-control, by the maturity he had shown—yes, and the unselfishness. She wanted to go to him and hug him tightly, to tell him what a brave young man he was, but knew that would be wrong. From the tension in Chao's neck muscles she could see that his self-control was hard won. Chao, ever quick of mind, had seen for himself what the new taxes would mean and had resolved to make the best of it. Even so, it was a grand gesture.

"Papa Lin?"

Lin looked up again, meeting his son's eyes, a new respect in his own. "Yes, Lin Chao?"

"I thought I would apply for a job. At the big house."

Again Lin swallowed. Again he gave a single nod of his head. Yet as Chao made to turn away, he spoke out.

"Chao . . . Do not give up hope. Your studies . . . You must keep them up, neh?"

Chao glanced at his adopted father, then averted his eyes once more.

"I shall help you," Lin said, his eyes trying to make some connection with the boy. "An hour a night we'll spend, you and I, going through your books. We will make do, neh, Lin Chao? And when things are better . . ."

Chao shuddered, suddenly close to tears. Emily, watching, steeled herself. She had promised Lin she would say nothing, do nothing. She had given her word. But young Ji had made no such promises. As if he read what was in her heart, Ji ran across and, throwing himself at Chao, held on tightly to his leg, wanting to comfort him in his disappointment. Chao looked down, smiling, then knelt and picked Ji up, cuddling him tightly, almost fiercely, then turned and went silently from the inner yard.

As the doors clinked shut she looked to Lin, meaning to say something, but stopped, seeing the first tear run slowly down Lin Shang's cheek.

"Papa Lin," she said, making to go to him, but he raised a hand as if to fend her off.

"Chao sets an example for us all," he said, after a moment. "We must all be strong from now on. And we must make do. Just as First Son Chao makes do."

She looked back at him and nodded, smiling, but her smile was laced with regret. Oh, Lin would keep his promise. He always did. But an hour a night . . . what was an hour a night? Besides, if Chao *did* get a job at the big house, he would be tired when he came home . . . that was, if he did come home and did not stay there in the big house with his new Masters. No, both Lin Shang and Chao knew what this meant. It meant the end of Chao's dream of a College place. The end of any hopes he had of bettering his life.

"Well . . ." Lin began, stirring himself. "I think we ought—"

There was a sudden, violent hammering at the outer gates. From the outer courtyard came the alarmed shouts of her boys, then the sound of one of the big doors splintering beneath a heavy blow.

She had turned the moment she had heard the sound. Now she made to go through, but Lin was behind her, holding her arm.

Emily turned, almost glaring at him in her anxiety to go through.

"No violence," Lin said, his hand gripping her arm tightly. "Promise me no violence. It will not help us."

"Lin Shang . . ." She made to tear her arm away, but he would not let go.

"No violence. *Promise me!*"

*Damn you, Lin Shang!* she thought, then, knowing he would not budge, she nodded. "Okay. I promise. Now let go!"

He let go.

She stiff-palmed the door open, crouching as she came through, ready for anything, but what she saw made her freeze, horrified.

"*Aiya!*"

Chao had set Ji down and now knelt, his head down, a butcher's cleaver, the edge razor sharp, pressed flat against the nape of his neck. The punk who held it stared across at Emily defiantly, an awful, mocking smile on his face. Beside him, standing there looking about them casually, were four others. They were *liu mang*—street punks—but they were also more than ordinary punks. From the bright red bands they wore about their foreheads she knew they were also "runners"—Triad members.

Her boys were scattered about the outer courtyard, some seated in their cubicles, others standing near the shattered door. They looked to her, afraid. Ji, she could see, was staring hard at the floor, trying not to cry.

Knowing how important it was, she steeled herself, keeping the fear she felt from her face, her voice. Taking a deep breath, she stepped forward, confronting the runners.

"What do you want?"

The biggest of them—their leader; a tall Han with a sallow complexion that spoke of a bad diet—turned toward her, taking her measure, then glanced to the side, looking to his friends, a sneer of a smile on his lips.

"We want money, old woman," he said bluntly. "Fifty *yuan* or we smash the place up."

For a moment she felt old instincts call to her—felt the urge to step and kick, breaking the bastard's jaw—but she could see Chao out of the corner of her eyes and knew she'd not be quick enough to save him if she tried to fight them. Besides, she'd promised Lin.

"We can't pay you. We haven't even twenty *yuan*, let alone fifty!"

He came close, so close that she could smell the sweat on him, the sun-heated leather of his belt, and something else—something in his sweat.

She recognized that smell. Knew it from way back. Briefly she met his eyes and saw the telltale signs, that faint gold speckling about the enlarged pupil. The man was an addict, and his addiction was the most deadly drug there was—"Golden Dreams."

Silently she stored the knowledge, knowing from past experience that such things could be used.

"You give me what you have," he said quietly, threateningly, "and maybe no one will get hurt. Okay?"

She hesitated, the instinct to hit him—to hurt him badly—welling up in her again, then nodded. She turned, meaning to look to Lin, to signal to him, but he had already gone inside. A moment later he returned, holding the old "ice" box that held all their money. Coming closer, he held it out, offering it. "Twenty-four eighty," Lin said, his voice small.

The *liu mang* took it with a marked disdain and, without looking at what was inside, handed it back to one of his companions, his eyes never leaving Emily's face.

"You nice old woman," he said, looking her up and down. "We go inside, maybe? Work off what you owe me?"

There was laughter from the punks behind him, but his eyes were cold. Looking at him she could almost read his thoughts—she knew exactly what he had in mind.

"No," she said. "We pay you later. *Okay?*"

His eyes widened slightly, noting the sudden, uncompromising toughness in her voice. Even so, she was at least thirty years older than he. Not only that, she was a woman. How much of a threat could she possibly be? Slowly the smile returned to his face, a fixed and ugly smile, like something painted on a theatrical mask.

"I fuck you now, maybe. Right here."

She laughed, no humor in it. "That would be a very stupid thing to do, my friend."

"Stupid?" He bared his teeth angrily.

"You touch me and Lin Shang there will try to kill you."

The punk looked at Lin Shang and gave a dismissive laugh. "The *lao jen?* I break him like a rotten twig!"

She stepped closer, standing face to face with him.

"You don't see it, do you? Oh, you'd swat Lin Shang as if he were a fly. I know that. Even he knows that. But he would keep coming back, keep on trying to kill you, until you had no choice but to kill him. And if you killed him there would be no one to pay the fifty *yuan*. And if no one paid the fifty *yuan*, what would your Master, the Mountain Lord, say?"

Emily lifted her chin in a tight gesture of challenge. "He'd skin you alive, I'd say."

He stared back at her, taking in what she'd said, then nodded, as if accepting it. But he wasn't done yet. Pushing her aside, he stepped past her, facing Lin Shang.

"She your wife, *lao jen*? You love her? You fuck her every night?"

Emily had begun to relax; now she felt herself tense again. There was no need for this. No need to talk like this in front of her boys. She clenched her fist, angry suddenly, then slowly unclenched it, knowing Lin was right. Violence was not an option here.

Lin's eyes went to her, then returned to the punk who stood before him. She saw him wet his lips with his tongue, saw his damaged face twitch once, a second time. Then, with a casual brutality, the *liu mang* brought his knee up into Lin's stomach.

There was a shocked silence, then the sound of Lin Shang retching.

On the far side of the courtyard Ji, who had been watching everything, began to cry.

"Be quiet, Lin Ji!" she barked, glaring at him, fighting her natural instinct to comfort him; knowing that, this once, it was necessary to be hard—for *his* sake. She knew how they thought; knew they were like sharks, scenting for blood, ready to prey upon the slightest weakness. For her to have been kind to Ji—to sympathize with him—was the worst thing she could have done.

She turned back.

The punk was watching her, his knife drawn, a self-satisfied smile on his narrow lips.

"You want to fight me, old woman?"

Behind him Lin was on his knees, hunched into himself, looking up at her as he struggled for breath, his eyes reminding her of the promise she had made. Besides, there was still Chao to think of.

She let the tension drain from her. "No," she said quietly.

But the frustration she felt at that moment was unbearable. She wanted to punch the little bastard until his face was a bloodied mess, to break every last bone in his body, for what he'd done.

He smiled at her, a nasty, hideous smile, then reached out and stroked her cheek. "You pay, old woman. Tomorrow, when we come back. Or else. You understand?"

"I understand."

"Good." He turned, looking to Lin. "And you, *lao jen*. You make sure you pay, neh? Or your wife she fuck us all."

There was laughter; an awful, braying laughter at that. Emily turned, looking from face to face, imprinting them in memory, then looked down.

*I'll fuck you all, all right,* she thought, something hard—something she had almost forgotten until that moment—waking in her. *I'll fuck you all good and proper, you can count on it!*

The punk turned away, signaling to his fellows. From the corner of her eye she saw the one who'd been holding Chao lift the cleaver from his neck, then kick out, sending Chao spawling.

There was laughter—a mocking laughter—then they were gone.

From the open doorway a crowd of curious neighbors looked in, jostling with each other in their eagerness to see what had happened.

Emily glared at them, the anger in her threatening momentarily to spill over and find a release—a target—in them. Then, with a shudder, she turned away. There was mending to be done.

"Ji . . ." she said softly. "Lin Ji . . ."

Ji stiffened then turned his head away.

She went across to him and knelt, laying her hand gently on his shoulder. "I'm sorry, Ji. I never meant—"

He pulled himself away, his face hard, his whole body set against her. She felt a shadow fall across her. It was Chao.

"Ji?" Chao said gently, as though what had happened to him had been of no importance. "Mama Em wasn't angry with you, Ji. She was angry with the men. Mama Em . . . well, Mama Em loves you. You know that, don't you?"

Ji hesitated a moment, then gave a tiny nod.

"If she spoke harshly, it was only to protect you."

Again Ji nodded.

"Then you must forgive her, neh?"

Chao turned, looking up at Emily, then moving back, gestured that she should approach the child.

"I'm sorry, Ji," she said, kneeling beside him again. "Chao was right. I was angry with the men, not you."

For a long moment he was silent, staring away from her, as if struggling with something inside himself, then he turned, looking at her, tears welling in his eyes.

"Who were they, Mama Em? Who were they?"

She reached out, holding him tightly as his tiny body began to shake and the tears roll down his cheeks.

"Trouble," she said, hugging him fiercely, conscious that it was the second time she had answered him thus that day. "Nothing but trouble."

PEI K'UNG stood at the balcony, one hand gripping the iron rail, the other shading her eyes as she looked out across the gardens at the center of the San Chang, trying to make out what was happening in her husband's palace. Ten minutes back a second unmarked craft had landed in the Eastern Palace hangar. Now she waited, impatient for news, as her spies sought to find out who had come.

"Mistress?"

She whirled about. I Ye stood in the doorway, head bowed, an obsequious smile on his lips.

"Well, Colonel I? Do we know who's come?"

Even before he answered her she knew. Knew from his hesitation; from the way his eyes shifted in their orbits as his mind sought to find the right words to excuse his failure.

"Forgive me, Mistress, but it seems no one knows who was in the craft. Four mutes carried a sealed sedan from the craft and took it directly into the Northern Palace."

"I see. . . ." She let out a long breath, calming herself, and as I Ye raised his head, seeking her eyes, she smiled. "You will find out what is going on or you will find yourself demoted to lieutenant before the evening's out, *you understand?*"

I Ye bowed low. "Mistress!" Then he was gone.

She went back to the railing, straining to see. There was a great deal of activity over there in the previously untenanted Northern Palace. Servants hurried back and forth behind the windows. Guards took up new posts. But as to who they were serving, who defending, not a word came out.

She gave a little cry of frustration, then rushed inside. Heng Yu was waiting there, precisely where she'd left him, standing beside her desk, his head bowed, the Great Ledger, wherein the State's accounts were kept, balanced between his hands.

"*Someone* must know!" she said, pacing back and forth. "It just isn't possible he could have kept *this* a secret."

And yet he had. She turned abruptly, her skirts swishing against the stone-tiled floor.

"Who is it, Master Heng? Who could possibly be so important, he would fly them in here secretly?"

Heng Yu glanced up at her. "One of the Warlords, Mistress?"

"A Warlord?" She stopped dead, considering that, pleased, it seemed, by the explanation. Then, suddenly, she frowned. "Then why keep it a secret? Yuan has always been careful to consult me at every turn. One of the Warlords? No, it makes no sense, Master Heng!"

Heng shrugged. He agreed, it made no sense. But what other reason could there be? Unless . . .

"Unless he wishes to *surprise* you, Mistress?"

She turned, staring at him. "Surprise me? No, that's absurd!"

"Not so, Mistress," he answered, setting the heavy ledger down on the edge of the desk, then stepping across to her. "It is, after all, your birthday in two weeks' time. Perhaps he has decided to use the ten-year banquet as the occasion for a dual celebration."

"My birthday?" Puzzlement slowly turned to pleasure in her face. "And you think . . . ?"

Heng Yu, watching her, felt a wave of relief flood through him, at the same time cursing himself for not having thought of it earlier. "It can be the only explanation, Mistress. As you said, your husband has always been scrupulous about consulting you on matters of State. And if this is not a matter of State, then what else *could* it be? No. I'll warrant this is a special treat he has arranged specially for your birthday. A gift. . . ."

He had lowered his head as he delivered his little speech; now he raised his eyes and almost laughed.

Pei K'ung was grinning—grinning like a lovesick girl.

"Why, the sweet man . . . Of course! And there was I thinking . . ."

She let out a little sigh. "A gift. . . ." Then, clapping her hands together, she went around her desk and sat, suddenly businesslike again, gesturing toward the thick, leather-bound ledger.

"So, Master Heng, where were we?"

JELKA SAT BACK, relaxing as the shuttle took them back to the orbital. It would be their last night up here for some while, and the thought of going earthside again—of the banquet and the endless social whirl that would accompany it—depressed her spirits.

As the years went by, so she felt more and more distanced from that great world down below. More and more she came to see this up here—the sable darkness and the cold, clean stars—as her natural habitat, and that below as some strange, diseased anomaly. And so it was with Kim. Oh, he still persisted with that world—gave it his money and attention, trying to ease its suffering—but he, too, was at home out here.

It was all a question of origins. Down there he was forever Clay, looked down upon by lesser men, no matter his achievements. They were polite to his face, of course, for her husband was a powerful man, rich beyond their dreams, and he could make or break them if he chose, but she had heard their whispered comments often enough to know that no matter what he did they would always consider themselves superior.

Up here none of that mattered. Up here he was a king, with a king's powers, a king's natural elegance of mind and behavior. Up here it did not matter how big one was physically, how straight, only what one did, what one *was*. And what Kim *was* was worth a dozen other men. A hundred, possibly.

She smiled, watching him at work across from her. Already he was taking Sampsa's basic idea of the light-spider and playing with it. On the pad before him were a dozen tiny sketches, a number of mathematical formulae scrawled beside them. As she looked he frowned and scratched his head, then looked across. Seeing her, he smiled.

"What is it?"

"Nothing," she said, returning his smile.

"It won't be for long," he said, as if he read her thoughts. "Two weeks. Three at most. Then we can come back."

"We ought to transfer it all out here. The laboratories. The factories. You could automate it all. It'd be cheaper."

"Maybe. But then I'd have to let workers go. Families would
suffer. No, Jelka. Let's keep things as they are. Besides, what about
the island? What about Kalevala?"

She smiled and leaned forward, covering his hand with her own.
"We could go there once a year, on our anniversay. Or maybe you
could have it shipped up here, brick by brick. . . ."

"And tree by tree?" He laughed. "I'd miss the sea, the wind—"

"You could simulate all that. You know you could."

He laughed, then shook his head. "It wouldn't be the same. The
unpredictability of it . . . that's what I treasure about the island.
The storms. The lightning flashes."

Jelka shivered. It was true. However much she hated all the rest
of it, there was always the island—always Kalevala. For a moment
she had a glimpse of him, there on the island, walking naked
among the trees in the moonlight, stalking her.

She leaned closer, putting her face almost to his, and lowered
her voice so only he could hear. "Just wait till we're back in our
room. I'll give you lightning flashes, Kim Ward. You see if I
don't. . . ."

---

EMILY KNELT BESIDE the narrow bunk, tucking in the blanket. Young Ji was asleep already, his tiny body turned from her, his
right arm curled about his head, four pudgy fingers splayed against
the jet-black of his hair, the thumb hidden in the cave of his palm.

She stood, looking down at him, and smiling to herself, as if he
were her own. That, she'd come to realize, was her only regret: that
she hadn't had children—that she had never *understood,* not until
it was far too late, just how important it was. She sighed, and,
edging around the foot of the bunk, drew the blind.

She stepped out, into the courtyard. It was quiet now that the
boys had settled for the night. The dark curtains to the stalls were
drawn, the lights within doused. The gentle sound of snoring came
from all sides. She looked about her thoughtfully, remembering
what had happened only hours before, then went through, into the
inner courtyard.

Lin was at his desk, his busy hands making a fresh start on the unceasing work of repairing what had been broken. Behind him, stacked floor to ceiling on every shelf, were broken things awaiting his attention. He looked up at her and smiled wearily.

"How are they?"

She placed her hands on his shoulders and leaned across him to kiss the bald spot on his crown. "They're fine. They've been through worse."

"Maybe so. But that was a while back. You forget how young they are, Mama Em. You and I . . . we've seen such things before, neh? But for them . . ." He sighed deeply. "Who were they, do you think?"

She shrugged. To be honest, she didn't know. The headbands they had worn gave little clue. Yet from their arrogance she guessed they were from one of the Frankfurt brotherhoods. If so, it was the first time they had come this far west—the first time they had crossed the river.

"So can we pay them?"

He met her eyes clearly. "If it's a one-off. Otherwise . . ."

She understood. On top of the new taxes a further fifty *yuan* a week would break them. Lin and the boys could not work enough hours repairing things to make that kind of money. And then there was food to buy and clothes, the rent for the compound.

She sighed heavily. "So what do we do?"

His hands stopped, then slowly started up again, as if they had a life of their own.

"What *can* we do? Pay what we can, work harder, eat less."

She gave a bitter laugh. "Eat any less and we'll starve. We need to eat to work. Besides . . ."

His look—a look of profound patience and understanding— made her fall silent.

"We endure," he said after a moment. "If necessary we 'eat bitter.' That is our fate, neh, Mama Em? Perhaps it has always been our fate."

Maybe so, but it irked her that after all they'd done—after all those years of hard and patient work—one edict and a group of airhead punks could destroy it in a day.

"I wanted to hurt him," she said, remembering what the punk had done to Lin. "I wanted to beat him to a pulp."

"I know. And I was proud of you."

"Proud?"

"Yes. For showing such restraint. Our boys will take heart having seen you display such inner strength.

She stared at him, uncertain. "And Ji? You think *Ji* understood?"

Lin nodded. "Even Ji. He was confused, true, but Chao *made* him understand."

*Understand what?* she thought. *How weak we are? How little we can protect our own? Is that any lesson for a young boy?* But she said nothing. For Lin Shang there was but one way—the way of nonviolence. "Avoid Trouble," he would say, "and Trouble will avoid you." Well, maybe so. Maybe that was true in normal times, but what when Trouble came looking for you—what did you do when it picked you out among the many and targeted you? Was it wise, under such circumstances, to simply acquiesce? Or was there a better way?

For now, however, she left it. For now she let him have his way. She smiled at him. "You fancy some soup?"

His hands were already back at work, moving like busy spiders among the pile of broken things. He looked to her, and nodded.

She went through and, warming the stove, flipped open a container of soup.

*We'll cope with this,* she told herself. *We'll come through. We always do. Why, when the world tore itself apart, even then it could not harm us. This . . . why, this is just a little local difficulty.*

The thought calmed her; made her feel that perhaps he was right after all and she wrong. Pouring the soup into a metal pot, she began to sing, softly at first; an old song she had forgotten that she knew—a song from her childhood, from before her family's fall. Briefly the memory disturbed her, made the tune falter on her lips; then she began to sing once more, letting her voice lift clear and high in the tiny kitchen.

After a moment she heard the door creak open.

"What is that?" Lin asked, stepping up beside her.

"This?" She gestured toward the bubbling pot.

"No . . . what you were singing just then. I've never heard you sing before."

She smiled. "No. . . ."

Switching off the stove, she took down two plain earthenware bowls and began to pour.

"Well?"

She looked at him and gave a grunt of laughter. "I don't know. I . . . something from my childhood."

"Ah . . ." He took the bowl she offered and stared at it a moment, then looked at her again. "We . . . well, we've never talked about that. About the time before, I mean. I . . . ."

He stopped, embarrassed.

She spoke softly. "You want to know, Lin Shang? Is that it?"

"I . . ." He hesitated, then shook his head. "It's just . . . well, I'd have liked to have seen you as a child. You must have been very pretty."

She stared at him, suddenly understanding why she'd stayed with him all these years—she who could have had kings and billionaires. There was no more honest man in Chung Kuo than Lin Shang . . . no, nor a kinder one.

"I was a tomboy," she said, smiling at the memory. "I wore boy's clothes and had my hair cut short. My mother despaired. And my father . . ."

She fell silent, pained by the thought. He'd been such a good man. So upright. So trusting. She swallowed back the bile she felt at what had happened to him—at what the system had done to him—then looked up again, meeting Lin's sympathetic eyes.

"Best not, huh?"

He nodded, understanding. "Let's eat our soup while it's hot. And afterward . . . well, Steward Liu sent a messenger. He said to come."

She stared at him. "At this hour?"

"I said I would. He said he had something for us. He said to come tonight."

"After what happened last time?" Emily shook her head. "No. You stay here, Papa Lin. Keep those hands of yours busy. I'll go and see the Steward."

He stared at her, trying to make out why she'd offered, then shrugged. "Okay. But take care, Mama Em. And hurry back."

━━━━━━

THE LANES WERE quieter now and cooler, the streetlamps lit, most of the shopfront shutters pulled down; but people were still out in numbers and Emily was greeted often as she walked along.

At the corner of Nan Yueh Street and Fu Lao Lane she paused, looking up at the big screen that, twenty-four hours a day, showed the latest news from throughout the city. As ever, dozens of people crouched idly beneath it, squatting on their heels in the way the Han had done for over two thousand years, their rounded faces turned up to its light. For a moment she stood there, watching the great golden barge move upriver once again, and looked back in mind to that afternoon, remembering how she had held Ji up to see the splendid sight. She sighed. How soon things changed. How quickly happiness transmuted into fear.

She hurried on. The great bell in Yan Jin Place was sounding nine as she knocked on the twelve-foot doors of the Shi Mang Mansion. Head bowed, her hands folded before her, she waited. Above her a wall-mounted security camera whirred gently as it focused on her. A moment later a smaller door within the great doors opened and a shaven-headed man in bright green silks stepped out, holding a large, plainly wrapped parcel between his hands.

"Steward Liu," she began. "Forgive the lateness of the hour, I—"

"I understand," he said, interrupting her. "You had trouble."

She met his eyes, surprised. "You heard?"

He nodded, then, moving closer, lowered his voice. "We have all had trouble, neh?"

"Ah . . ." She understood at once. It wasn't only she and Lin who had been shaken down that day; the big houses, too, had suffered a similar fate. Indeed, when she thought of it, it was surprising only that they hadn't been targeted long ago, for they were the biggest plums of all.

"It seems I must also apologize to you, Mama Em."

"Apologize?" She looked down, all humility.

"I understand one of the servants treated you badly last time you were here."

"It is of no importance, Steward Liu—" she began, but he shook his head.

"On the contrary, it is of the greatest importance. It was I who asked you here, and though, through circumstances, I was not here to greet you at the time, my staff ought to have treated you with the same civility that I would have done. You can be assured that the servant responsible has been duly punished for his insolence."

She looked up, astonished. "Punished?"

"Oh, it need not concern you. But I was worried lest you thought . . . well, lest you thought me less than a friend." He smiled. "Here," he said, handing her the parcel. "And tell Papa Lin that if there's any way I can help . . ."

She smiled, deeply moved by his offer. She had always known the man was sympathetic—knew because he had regularly given her boys scraps from his kitchen—but how good a friend she had not realized until now.

"Thank you, Steward Liu."

He smiled. "Broken things . . . what good are they to the rich?" Then, with a bow, he went back inside.

She turned, making her way toward the *yamen*—the government offices—in Hsiang Yu Street. If she hurried she could be there in five minutes, and if the *Hsien L'ing* saw her, she might just be back before ten.

*If he would see her . . .*

She had never been to the *yamen*; had been careful, in fact, to avoid it at all costs, in case some file remained from before the Fall—something that might incriminate her. Or worse . . . something that might alert Michael—that might cause him to come and take her back from Lin.

She shivered at the thought and hurried on. As she came into Hsiang Yu Street she saw the *yamen*'s outer gates were open and felt a mixture of relief and aversion.

*You have to do this. You can't back out. Not now.*

Yet every step was made reluctantly. This, she reminded herself, was for her boys. To guarantee their future.

Inside the gates was the guard post. As she went to pass it she was called back.

"Where the fuck do you think *you're* going?"

She retraced her steps. The guard was a bored-looking thug with a stubble haircut and missing teeth. She noted he had put down a porno comic to attend to her. Conquering her instant, instinctive dislike of the man, she answered with a false brightness.

"I've come to see the *Hsien L'ing.*"

His eyes studied her coldly, then dismissed her. Extending a hand, he stared past her. "Show me your papers. . . ."

Putting down the parcel, she fished the ID card from her jacket pocket and handed it to him. He flipped it open, stared at it a moment, then handed it back.

*"Papers!"*

"But . . ." Then she understood. Searching in her back pocket she found a one-*yuan* note and folded it into the card, then handed it back. This time he nodded and handed back the empty card, waving her on. But she had taken only two steps when he called her back again.

"You can't take that in there! Leave it here!"

She stared at him, then understood. He was talking about the parcel. She came back and placed it against the wall, then turned and quickly crossed the darkness of the yard, afraid lest he call her back again.

Inside, in the echoing entrance hall, behind a narrow desk, sat an official. A small globe lamp, hovering just above him, part masked, part revealed his pinched, ungenerous features. A printed sign on the desk in front of him informed her that he was the *Hsien L'ing*'s Second Secretary. Seeing her, he leaned forward, glowering, instantly hostile.

"We're closed."

"But I—"

"You heard me, woman. Now go. Before you get in trouble."

She took a step backward, lowering her head, the instincts of the past twenty years shaping the gesture. Then a spark of her old indignation lit in her. This, after all, was for her boys.

She looked up again. "But I *have* to see him. It's very important."

He stood, his hands resting flatly on the desk. "You hear me, shit-for-brains? *Go*, or I'll call the guard!"

She stared back at him, getting his measure, then bowed her head. "Thank you," she said brightly, and, as she turned away, added beneath her breath, *"May your bowels be twisted and your children loathe you."*

The thought consoled her, but she also felt a sense of failure. She had steeled herself to come; had fought off her reluctance, but now—

*"Pssst!"*

The sound came from the darkness to her right. She stopped, peering into the shadows. Vaguely she could make out a figure, standing in an open doorway, beckoning to her. She glanced around, noting that neither the official nor the guard could see her from where they sat, then hurried over.

A hand reached out and took her arm firmly. "You mending lady, right?"

"Right," she answered, matching the old woman's whisper.

"You want *Hsien L'ing*, right?"

"Yes," she answered. "You know where he is?"

"Maybe. . . ." The old woman leaned closer, the smell of cabbage strong on her breath. "Some nights he go baths. He meet *Wei* there. Much talk. Other things too."

"Ah." She wasn't sure she wanted to know about the other things, but this was useful. If she could see him there—

*"You!"*

She turned. The guard was leaning from his post, looking across.

"Thank you," she whispered, squeezing the old woman's hands, then hurried to him.

As she came closer, the guard pointed at her. "What the fuck you up to, eh?"

"It was my aunt," she said, acting more confidently than she felt. "She was asking after my husband."

She bent down and retrieved the parcel, then looked back at the guard, but it seemed her explanation had been satisfactory. His nose was already buried in the porno comic.

*Asshole,* she thought as she went through the gate and out into the street. *I hope your cock drops off!*

She stopped dead, the simple violence of her thoughts surprising her. Maybe Lin was right. Maybe it *was* best not to fight this. But something drove her on. Ten minutes later she stood in the busy central square, beneath the steps of the bathhouse, staring up past the great stone pillars, trying to make out if there were lights on inside or whether she was just imagining it.

As she began to climb the steps, a figure stepped from the shadows, barring her way.

"Stop right there."

She smiled at the young guard, noting from his blue silks that he at least had been trained to the job.

"Well?" he asked.

"I wish to see the *Hsien L'ing.*"

"Then make an appointment with his Secretary in the morning. Office hours are over."

"But this is urgent."

"Everything is urgent. Now go home. My Master is *not* to be disturbed."

His manner was pleasant enough—far more pleasant than the bastard at the *yamen*—yet there was something about him that told her he was not to be argued with. Bowing low, she backed away.

At the far side of the square she turned, looking back. The steps were empty once again, the guard returned to the shadows. For the briefest moment she wondered idly whether she should sneak around the back of the bathhouse and force her way into the *Hsien L'ing*'s presence, but knew that such a course would only damage her chances. No, the young guard was right; she would have to go back in the morning and face the Second Secretary again.

As she made to turn away, the smell of the nearby food carts caught her attention, reminding her that she had promised Ji cakes.

She went across to the nearest stall and, setting the parcel down, studied what was for sale.

"How much are they?" she asked the old woman, pointing to a small tray of oatmeal cakes.

"Twenty-five for two. Fifteen for one."

Emily fished in her pocket and removed a twenty-five-*fen* coin. Her last. "Here," she said. "Wrap two for me."

As the old woman wrapped the yet-warm cakes in greased paper, Emily looked about her, conscious of the bustle in the square. Nothing looked any different from how it had been the evening before. The sights, the sounds, the smells—all of those outward things remained unchanged. Yet the world had subtly shifted. Once again the darkness was descending on them all.

The old woman nudged her arm. "Here!"

She took the wrapped cakes, returning the old woman's tooth-less smile, then, lifting the parcel once again, began to make her way back, the sky clear and dark above her, the stars burning down like a thousand eyes, watching her as she went.

~~~~~

WITHOUT  PAUSING  TO  KNOCK, Su Ping burst into his brother's changing room, anger making him raise his voice above its normal ice-calm level.

"What in the gods' names are you up to, brother? I've spent the whole day dealing with complaints—"

He stopped dead as Su Chun threw off the flimsy sheet and climbed from the massage bed to confront him. He had a glimpse of a naked girl—a pretty young thing with snow-white curves and jet-black hair—and then a door slammed to his right, making him jump.

Chun came over and poked him in the chest.

"And what in the Lord Fuck's name do you think *you're* doing, brother? You sure as hell know how to pick your times! It's taken a week to get that one into my bed, and now you've gone and fright-ened her away!"

Su Ping swallowed. He glanced down briefly, surprised to find that his twin still sported an erection, then averted his eyes.

"I—I . . ." he stammered, then, remembering why he'd come, he took control of himself again. "I want you to stop your men harassing my citizens."

"Harassing . . ." Su Chun laughed, then laid a hand on Su Ping's shoulder and squeezed it. "Why, that's rather strong, wouldn't you say?"

"Strong? Why, if I were to say what I *really* felt—"

"No, no, brother," Su Chun said reassuringly. "Please calm your-self. If my men were a little *heavy handed,* I'll correct that."

Su Ping removed his brother's hand. His voice was hard now. "You'll do more than that. You'll move them out at once, *under-stand?* I'll not have your men threatening my citizens."

But Su Chun seemed unperturbed. He pulled on a silken robe, then turned back, shrugging. "I'm afraid I can't do that, brother. My Masters . . . well, they have to pay their taxes, too, neh? Be-sides, it will solve our other problem, neh?"

"Our other problem?" Su Ping stared at his brother suspiciously.

"I'm talking about your youngest brother, Su Yen. With the ex-tra we make, we could finance Su Yen's rise quite comfortably."

Slowly, very slowly, Su Ping began to shake his head. "You're serious, aren't you? You really mean to move in on me."

"No, brother. Not at all. I shall keep it all . . . within limits, let's say. But our Masters . . . well, you must serve yours, I mine." He smiled broadly. "And as long as our Masters are happy . . ."

Su Ping stared at that broad, smug face, realizing for the first time just how much he hated it. Without a further word he turned and left the room.

Downstairs, in the great high-ceilinged hallway of the Baths, Kung Chia, his *Wei,* was waiting.

"You sent for me, Excellency?" he began, but Su Ping cut him short, his voice echoing loudly in that huge, open space.

"I want you to rein that bastard in. I want you to make sure his punks are kept in check. If they even spit in the wrong place I want them arrested. And if they dare go near any of the big houses again, I want to know about it immediately. I will *not* have my people threatened, you understand me, Kung?"

Kung Chia, surprised, bowed his head. "I understand, *Hsien L'ing.*"

"Then go. And make sure you serve me well."

Kung looked up sharply. "You doubt me, Excellency?"

"No . . . no, Kung. It's just . . ."

The *Wei* smiled and bowed a second time. "I understand. It's been a hard day, neh?"

Su Ping met his Security Captain's eyes and smiled weakly.

Then, looking tired beyond his years, he shuffled past, heading for his bed.

Kung Chia watched the *Hsien L'ing* go, then turning on his heel, made for the stairs, hurrying now, anxious to speak to his real Master, Su Chun.

EMILY, STEPPING INSIDE the enclosure, pulled the gate to behind her, reaching up to slide the bolt slowly, quietly across.

She turned. Lin was standing on the far side of the outer court-yard, watching her.

"So what did he send us?"

She stared at the parcel, then went across and handed it to him.

He sat down, began to unwrap the parcel, and looked up at her, astonished. "Kuan Yin!"

"It looks new," she said, reaching out to touch the smooth, black, shiny surface of the HeadStim.

"It *is*," he said, awed by the machine. "State of the art. It's . . ." He shook it and it rattled. "It looks like it's been dropped."

"Even so . . ." she said, anticipating his next words.

She hadn't realized. When Steward Liu had said he had some-thing to give them, she had never thought it would be anything like this. Why, even broken, the components would be worth a hundred, maybe two hundred *yuan!* And mended . . . She whis-tled softly. This gift—this *broken* thing—gave them a breathing space, a few weeks free of worry.

Lin looked to her, his eyes troubled. "Are you sure he meant to give us this?"

She nodded. "It seems they were shaken down too. He said—he said whatever help . . ."

She found she could not finish the sentence. Found that this simple human offer of help had choked her up.

*Aiya!* she thought. *I'm getting soft in my old age!*

"That's kind," Lin said, staring at the HeadStim thoughtfully, already considering how best to set about the task of repairing it. "Steward Liu is a good man. Why, I recall—"

He stopped, staring at the door behind her. Emily turned. It was

Ji. He stood there, clutching his blanket, his face pinched, confused by tiredness.

"Mama Em . . ."

"Come on," she said, going to him and picking him up, joggling him gently. "If you don't get your sleep—"

"Mama Em?"

She drew her face back slightly so she could see him properly. "Yes, Ji?"

"Did you . . . remember?"

She smiled and, reaching into her pocket, took out the greased paper that contained the cakes.

"Here," she said. "But not now. In the morning, okay, young Ji?"

There was a tired smile, a clutching of the tiny package to his chest, then he snuggled into her again, content, his tiny body fitting the contours of her own perfectly as she carried him through to his bunk.

She shuddered, part from tiredness, part from the strange mix of emotions she was feeling, then set him down. She tucked him in again, and, for a moment, knelt there, listening to his breathing, making sure he'd settled. Only then did she get up, pausing a moment to look down at him, smiling as she saw the way he still clutched the wrapped cakes to his chest.

*It'll be okay*, she told herself. *We shall come through.*

But the morning would be difficult, and in the days ahead . . .

She sighed deeply, the brief flash of optimism guttering in her. Turning away, she stepped out into the cobbled yard and stood there, looking about her at the shadowed stalls, sniffing the warm night air and listening to the snoring of the boys, as if to fix it all clearly in her mind.

LI YUAN crossed the moonlit gardens swiftly, silently, keeping to the cover of the trees. He climbed the steps, slipping like a shadow into the unlit entrance of the Northern Palace, where his Master of the Inner Chambers, Nan Fa-hsien, awaited him.

"Are they ready?" he asked.

"Almost," Nan Fa-hsien answered. He bowed low, then led Li

Yuan along a broad corridor lit by flickering cresset lamps to a pair of massive lacquered doors.

Li Yuan stepped inside, into brightness and elegance. The room was warm after the coolness of the corridor, making Li Yuan shiver involuntarily. The double doors to the guest suite were directly ahead. To his right a group of high-backed official's chairs surrounded a low jade-topped table, to his left a massive mirror filled the wall. He walked across and stood before it, studying himself, pulling gently at his tightly buttoned collar, then froze.

She had got up from one of the chairs and now stood, looking across at him. As he met her eyes she smiled and lowered her head demurely.

Li Yuan turned, flustered, not merely by her presence there but by the look on her—by her youth; her fresh, untainted beauty.

"Forgive me, *Chieh Hsia* . . ." she began, but he shook his head.

"Who are you? I thought I was alone."

"I know," she said and, raising her fan, flipped it open, concealing the smile that had come to her face.

"So?" he said, after what seemed a lengthy silence.

"Forgive me, *Chieh Hsia?*" she said, lowering her fan slightly, giving him a fresh view of her delicate, almost porcelain features. Her flesh was so white, it seemed to gleam.

"Your name," he said, staring at her open mouthed now.

"Ah . . ." The fan fluttered a moment, and then she answered him. "My name, *Chieh Hsia*, is Hsun Lung hsin."

"Dragon Heart . . ." He laughed softly. "Did your father name you thus, or your mother?"

Her smile delighted him. "I do not know, *Chieh Hsia*. I never thought to ask."

"And your sister?"

"Is inside, *Chieh Hsia*, with my father, preparing themselves to meet you."

"Ah . . ." But suddenly he found that, though it was why he had come, he was no longer interested in meeting her sister. He wanted to know more about *her*. For a moment he was at a loss, not knowing what to say, then he noticed the book lying on the table close to her.

"You were reading?"

"Yes, *Chieh Hsia.*"

He took a step toward her. "Might I see?"

She folded up her fan and tucked it into her sleeve, then, with what was almost a curtsy, picked up the book and held it out to him.

"History?" He raised his eyes from the page, surprised to find hers watching him. Keen, intelligent eyes.

"I was reading about the great T'ang Emperor Ming Huang and his love for the concubine Lady Yang. You know the story, of course."

He did, every schoolboy did, but at that moment he wanted to hear her speak, to watch her mouth and see her dark eyes sparkle.

"Tell me," he said, taking a seat, the book resting in his lap.

"Where to begin?" she said with a rhetorical flourish, then smiled, giving a tiny nod, as if she suddenly knew.

"Ming Huang was, perhaps, the greatest of the great T'ang emperors. In the early years of his reign the arts flourished and the Empire was strong, expanding deep into the heart of Asia. But Ming Huang had a weakness, he worshiped beauty, and most beautiful of all was the Lady Yang Yu-huan, wife of Ming Huang's son, the young Prince Shou. In the thirty-second year of his reign Ming Huang took Lady Yang into his palace, where, bewitched by her, he divorced her from his son and, taking her as his own consort, gave her power beyond her dreams. Beyond them, I say, for the Lady Yang was of humble birth, the daughter of a mere *Hsien L'ing* from Sichuan Province."

He listened, interested to hear her particular slant on the ancient tale, fascinated by the movement of her tiny hands as she spoke.

"How old are you?" he asked suddenly.

She stopped, looking at him thoughtfully. "Fifteen, *Chieh Hsia.*"

It was the age Lady Yang had been when first she'd come to court at ancient Chang-An.

"Continue," he said, telling himself not to draw too close a parallel. After all, Ming Huang had been all of sixty years old when he had first met his little swallow, whereas he was a mere forty-two.

And this girl—this charming, delightful girl—was of noblest birth, her father Head of one of the great Minor Families.

Besides which, it was her sister who was coming to his court, not she.

He watched, bewitched by her.

"They had ten good years. Ten years in which her power in the Emperor's court grew and grew as she promoted relatives and sisters to positions of the highest rank. The arts still flourished, the empire was still stable and powerful. However"—she looked at him directly, her stare seeming to cross the centuries and draw him with it—"the seeds of tragedy were already sown. Ming Huang, infatuated by the beautiful Lady Yang, neglected his duties, leaving it to others to care for his great State. Not only that, but his consort had in the meantime adopted one of his generals, a commoner named An Lu Shan, a gross and hideous man, to be her son."

He shuddered, caught up in her vision, hanging on her words.

"The vengeance of Heaven was swift. Droughts and earthquakes, floods, fires, and invasion followed one upon another. 'The gods have spoken,' people said, and talked openly of the Mandate being broken. A mere ten years after he had first brought her to his court, Ming Huang was faced with open rebellion—a rebellion led by the Lady Yang's own adopted son, General An Lu Shan. The Emperor fled his capital. His advisers told him there was but one course, to execute the Lady Yang's son and her along with him. Only thus, they argued, would the Empire be saved. Bitterly, he agreed. Yet before his beloved Lady Yang could be executed, he lent her a silken rope so she might hang herself."

For a moment the room was silent. Li Yuan looked down at the leather-bound book in his lap and sighed. "And you, Hsun Lung hsin . . . do *you* think it was the vengeance of Heaven?"

He looked up into her face, awaiting her answer.

"So it is written, *Chieh Hsia.*"

"I know that. But you . . . what do you think?"

She shrugged, then smiled, a sad, pensive smile. "I think that love can rob a man of his wits. I think also that, when it happens, it must be like a great tide, sweeping one away."

He nodded. "So it is. I had three wives—"

"Five, surely, *Chieh Hsia*—" She stopped, realizing her mistake, and lowered her head, but his smile was tolerant, his voice soft, no trace of blame or anger in it.

"I mean, I lost three wives, Dragon Heart. Had them taken from me. That hurt me. Hurt more than I ever imagined anything *could* hurt. But do you know what I did, that day after I had lost them?"

She met his eyes again, curious now. "No, *Chieh Hsia.*"

"I went to her . . . to my first wife, Yin Fei Yen. I went to her and asked her to return."

She stared at him, unable to believe what she'd just heard. "But surely—"

"Don't you see? It was like what you were saying. Like a tide, an obsession. It always was with her. One look at her and I was swept away."

He stopped, and stood up abruptly, realizing he had said far more than he had meant to say. Yet there was something about her: something that coaxed confessions from him. He looked at her again. "You understand?" he asked softly.

"I"—Dragon Heart shook her head, her expression apologetic— "I am afraid not, *Chieh Hsia.* That kind of feeling . . . I have read about it, certainly, but the reality—"

On impulse he took a step toward her, holding the book between them. "Would you mind if I kept this awhile?"

"Why no, *Chieh Hsia.* Let it be a gift—"

"No." He raised a hand as if commanding a servant, then let it fall, realizing what he had done. "I . . . only want to read a little from it. I will return it, naturally, when I am done."

The deference with which he said it made her narrow her eyes. "As you wish, *Chieh Hsia,*" she said, puzzled by his behavior. "And as for what you said . . . it shall be our secret, neh?"

He smiled, then, hearing the doors begin to open, turned to face the emerging Prince Hsun Teh and his daughter, Princess Hsun Chu-lo, the young woman his son, Kuei Jen, would be marrying before the week was out.

*CHUANG KUAN TS'AI pegged the last of the washing on the line, then, wiping her hands on her skirts, went quickly back inside. The Oven Man was out doing his rounds, and now that she had finished her*

tasks there was time at last to do what she'd been thinking of all morning.

Pulling the footstool out from beneath the sink, she took it across and set it against the wall, then climbed up, her right arm at full stretch as she dislodged the heavy bunch of keys from the hook. They fell with a rattle against the stone floor.

She jumped down and picked them up, then made her way through, out into the courtyard.

The outer gates were closed, the yard empty. Facing her, the double doors to the cold store were locked. She walked over and stood before them, knowing he would be angry with her if he knew, yet feeling compelled to look once more. One final time before he burned them.

Selecting the key from the bunch, she slipped it into the lock and turned it. Leaving the bunch dangling from the lock, she put both hands to the door and heaved. Slowly the door eased back, the cold of the interior greeting her.

She slipped inside, her fingers reaching for the light pad. At once the room was lit by a cool blue light that seemed to her the very color of death.

How many times had she been inside this room? A hundred? A thousand? However many it was, she had never entered there without experiencing a sense of disconnection—as if, stepping over the threshold of this room, she were stepping into another realm entirely: a realm untouched by simple human warmth.

Slowly she walked around the slabs, studying the bodies. He had washed them and, with a mortician's art, given them the semblance of healthy life. There was color now to their cheeks; even so, a single touch revealed how hollow that illusion was. Their coldness was the cold of the abyss between being and nonbeing, and the knowledge of that abyss—a certainty she had lived with from her first conscious moment—colored her view of them.

Another might have queried why the Oven Man had done this—why, when all he had to do was consign them to the flames, he had bothered to clean them and prepare them for the afterlife—but Chuang Kuan Ts'ai knew and understood, for though she was not Cho's daughter, she was much like him. She understood the need for dignity; for someone—even a stranger—to show some degree of respect at the end. To mark the passing of an individual life.

*Necessary it was, else none of it made any sense.*

She looked, undaunted by their hideous aspect. Now that they had been cleaned, she could see the signs of torture on them clearly and, as she had the evening they'd been brought there, began to wonder how and why they had come to this fate.

Yes, and who they were, for they had come naked on the cart, clothed only in their blood.

She stopped, leaning in closer. Behind the ear of one of them, partly hidden beneath the hair, was a mark. She reached out, lifting the stiff black hair delicately with one finger. It was a number—a serial number—imprinted in the skin.

She stared a long while, memorizing it, thinking of a dozen ways to fix the number in her head, then drew her fingers back.

"Chuang?"

She looked up. Her Uncle Cho was standing in the doorway, looking in at her, surprised—clearly surprised—to find her there. She waited, expecting him to ask what she was doing there, to chastise her, perhaps, for disobeying him, but he said nothing.

He merely turned and, taking his heavy apron from the peg on the wall, slipped it on. Coming over to the slabs, he lifted the first of the corpses and, hefting it over his shoulder, went out into the yard, heading for the Ovens.

She followed him, standing there, watching while he piled the six bodies to one side, then prepared and lit the burners. So many times she'd seen him do this, yet still it held a morbid fascination.

Her eyes went up, tracing the narrow shape of the chimney in the air, noting how the air above it seemed to melt and distort, as if the souls of the departed danced there briefly before traveling on.

"Go inside," he said, turning to look at her, a strange anger in his eyes. "Go in and start the meal."

Yet even as she made to turn away, she knew it was not her he was angry with.

The thought troubled her, for she had never seen her uncle quite so ill at ease. Looking at his eyes she knew that this matter ate at him. It made him feel used; part not of some natural process—for death was nothing if not natural—but of some evil outpouring emanating from the imperial palace. When men could be killed and dumped and burned and no trace of the event remain, what then did life—death's obverse—mean?

*The number. It had to mean something. It had to be a clue. But to what? And how did she find out?*

*She returned inside and, taking a pan down from the shelf, poured water from the jug and set it on the stove to boil, then turned, looking back down the hallway, seeing clearly in her mind the mark behind the dead man's ear.*

*It had to mean something. . . .*

*"'HAVE YOU GOT IT?'"*

*Josef stared up at the boy whose fingers dug into his neck and nodded. Fumbling in his pocket he took out the crumpled five-*yuan *notes and handed them over.*

*"Good," his tormentor said, releasing him, then cuffed him for good measure. "And I want the same next week, understand, little scab? Right here. Same time next week."*

*Josef nodded.* Yes, *he thought,* but you'll not be here to collect it, not if you try to spend what you've just taken from me.

*He scuttled away, one hand shielding his face as if he were crying, but in reality he was smiling. The notes were among those he had taken from the apothecary two days back and could be traced. He knew that because he had seen the* lao jen *painstakingly putting each note he handled through the note tracer beside the till. It was a simple device, but effective, and Security relied on it heavily to cut down the number of petty burglaries.*

*Well, this time they would find more than they had bargained for.*

*Stopping behind a turn in the wall, he counted ten, then poked his head around, looking back. His tormentor was standing with two of his friends, laughing, the notes he'd taken held up triumphantly.*

*Josef watched him turn and walk away, and felt a flood of satisfaction wash through him.*

*The boy's name was Chou and he was a third year at the Seventh District school. A week ago he had ambushed Josef on his way back from the shops and taken money from him. In the brief scuffle the boy had lost his badge—the same badge that now lay in a sealed plastic bag in a security locker at the local* yamen.

*Josef smiled, thinking how easy it had been. The robbery was nothing,*

the poisoning a trifle. Any fool could have done either. But to incriminate another in them, that was a trick that took imagination.

When Chou went to spend his blackmail money the notes would show
up on the shop's tracer as stolen and he would be detained. Before long
Security would discover he was a pupil at Seventh District school and
would remember the badge . . . his badge.

But it did not end there, for yesterday evening, while no one was in
the building, Josef had gone to the Seventh District school and, climbing
in through a skylight, had located Chou's locker. Making sure they were
"well hidden" beneath a pile of Chou's sportswear, he had stashed away
the remainder of the money—over seven hundred yuan—and the storage
jar.

And now, finally, he laughed, picturing the look of astonishment on
Chou's face as he watched the security guard pull out the incriminating
items. The boy would swear blind he was innocent, of course, but the
evidence was overwhelming. The badge, the stolen poison, the money in
his locker, and the notes he had tried to pass. No court in the entire city
would fail to find him guilty.

And guilty meant dead. For murder was a capital offense, even for a
thirteen-year-old.

You bit off more than you could chew, he thought, hurrying now,
eager to get back home. Eager to await the evening MedFac news and
word that a youth had been detained in connection with the poisoning of
the family in Teng Sung Lane.

# CHAPTER FOUR

# Into the Black

I YE SAT BACK, letting the tension ease from him. The tape had ended and once more the room was silent but for his own ragged breathing. Behind him the door to the soundproofed cell was locked. In one corner a boy lay bound and gagged upon a bench, a tightened cord about his neck, blood smearing his legs and back.

I Ye's own hands were also smeared with blood. He stared at them a moment, then went across and began to wash himself at the sink, studying his own face in the mirror as he did.

He was an ugly man, he knew that, even without the scars he'd picked up in his travels, but ugliness was no bar to advancement, not in Pei K'ung's court. Besides, he was useful to her. Very useful.

I Ye laughed, recalling what he'd seen. To be frank he was surprised. Surprised not merely by the beauty of the legendary Fei Yen, but by the young T'ang's stamina. That was some performance, one he would have been personally proud of.

Yes, and Fei Yen had been a far from passive partner. The way she had snarled at Li Yuan and raked his back with her nails! He shivered, recalling it, seeing clearly in his mind that savage, almost feral look as she goaded the young T'ang on.

He looked down at his own flaccid manhood and nodded. Men, women, he did not care who he fucked. No, nor how. Yet some, he knew, were *particular*. Li Yuan, for instance. From what he'd heard, the T'ang liked but a single type: young women barely out of puberty. Salacious innocents, like the maids who'd first seduced him in his early teens. In another man that could have been a problem, but for a T'ang it was merely a matter of recruitment.

Again he laughed, wondering if the old dog was still as lusty, still as passionate, as he'd been in those early days, or whether he'd grown jaded with the years. Did the young maids he took now to his bed merely keep him warm? It would be interesting to know.

I Ye sluiced himself down, then turned from the mirror and reached out for a towel, looking across at the dead boy as he dried himself.

A thousand routes led to the Isle of Pleasure, and he was determined to take every one of them. He smiled. Yes, he would even fuck the old hag herself if she asked him. But Fei Yen . . . he felt his penis stiffen at the thought . . . that route he'd never travel, and for that—and that alone—he envied his Master.

He pulled on his uniform, then went to the projector and removed the cassette. For a moment he stared at it thoughtfully, wondering how he might use this without endangering himself. Maybe he could incriminate Karr somehow? But how? Plant it on him? No. That was too crude. But there had to be a way.

He took the cassette across and locked it in the safe, then went to the door and, throwing back the bolts, summoned his Captain.

"Sir!" the man said, coming to attention in the doorway, his eyes going briefly to the corpse before he lowered them.

"Get rid of it!" I Ye said brusquely, moving past him. "Then come to my office. I've a job for you, Captain Dawes. Something to keep you out of trouble."

THE IMAGE on the screen intensified—each individual color glowing vividly—then faded slowly to black.

"I'm guessing," Ben said, turning to Li Yuan.

"Guessing?"

"About how it is, at the end. There has to be a moment, just before the heart stops pumping and the brain stops sending messages, when the senses fire one last time. A dying flare of consciousness. And then?"

Li Yuan waited, expecting Ben to say more, then shrugged.

"Exactly!" Ben said, beginning to dismantle the equipment. "All the great prophets and philosophers . . . they were just guessing, like me. But if one *knew*."

"If one knew one would be dead."

"Or *someone* would. There has to be a way."

"A way?"

"To record it. To follow the path past that final moment of intensity and into the black."

"The black?"

"Death. That's my next project. To try to track down death."

Li Yuan stared at Ben. Was he serious, or was this another of his jokes? After all . . . *death*.

"I brought you something," he said, offering Ben the tiny book-sized case.

"A gift?" Ben took the case and flipped it open, then looked up, his eyes wide with surprise. "But these—"

"Are the vials from the Melfi Clinic, the last remnants of Amos Shepherd's experiment." Li Yuan smiled. "I've sent the files on to the Domain already."

Ben set the case down on top of the control desk, then prized one of the tiny glass tubes from its velvet niche. On the frosted glass was etched a tiny acorn, symbol of the experiment his great-great-great-grandfather had carried out across six generations. Inside the tube, locked in suspended animation, was the fertilized egg of Alexandra Melfi, his great-great-great-grandmother.

"Why?" Ben said, setting the vial back carefully.

"Because," Li Yuan answered, having no better answer. It had been no more than a whim, after all.

"I'm grateful," Ben said. "It was kind of you, Yuan. But there's something else I want."

"Name it."

"I want access to one of your prisons. I want to work with the condemned prisoners. To tape their memories."

"You mean their deaths."

Ben nodded.

It wasn't what he'd expected, but he had promised. "Okay, I'll arrange something. But, Ben . . . ?"

"Yes?"

"Be discreet. If Pei K'ung finds out what you're up to, she'll use it against you. She doesn't like you. You know that, don't you?"

Ben smiled. "I know. The feeling's mutual. But fine, I'll invent some reason for what I'm doing. Pretend I'm after something else."

"It'll be a waste of time."

"You think so?"

"Death's death."

"So you say. But I'd like to be sure. I'd like to *know*."

———————

THE AIR IN THE GARDEN seemed fresh and wholesome after the stuffiness of Ben's workroom. It had recently rained and the leaves shone wetly in the morning sunlight. Standing there beneath the open sky, Li Yuan realized just how little time he spent outside, how much a hermit he had become these past ten years. It was almost three years since he had last left the palace grounds, ten since he'd been outside his own City. In that time he had shed his youth. Now, at the start of middle age, he felt compelled to make changes—to shake things up and see what would happen.

Recklessness, his father would have called it. A sign of immaturity. After all, what sane ruler would consciously seek change? Yet, undeniably, he felt compelled. He had let things run unchecked too long. Now it was time to take back the reins. Time to take risks.

He looked up. His feet had brought him to the boundary of the Northern Palace. Before him stood a gate. And inside . . .

He pushed it open, wondering as he did how much he was in control of his actions and how much compulsion drove him.

*Like Ben with death*, he thought, though he himself had had enough of death. Life was what drove him; life and the instinct toward . . .

He stopped dead. *Toward what?* Toward what lay between a young girl's legs? Was that it? Was that *all* this was—lust, pure and simple? If so, he might as well turn straight about, for lust was a destructive urge, as he knew well enough from his past. It had destroyed many a good man, the great Ming Huang among them.

The thought made him shiver. Was that what he'd become? An

old goat, dribbling helplessly before a young girl's open legs, doomed endlessly to let his baser instincts foul his higher aspirations?

Or did he fool himself to think he could be other than he was?

He walked on, slowly now, pensively, as if he were walking within one of Ben Shepherd's Shells, following the guide track, his path predestined, his sense of free will merely an illusion preprogrammed by the appropriate chemicals.

*I have to see her again. I have to.*

Because if he didn't, if he left this, then he would never know if what he'd felt last night, facing her, listening to her talk, had been real or simply another damned illusion.

Because . . . well, because he hadn't felt this way in years.

He stopped again, looking up at the latticed windows just above him. She was inside, within her rooms, perhaps, or in the guest suite with her family. He hoped it was the former. He hoped she was alone, because what he wanted to say to her was not something he could utter in the presence of her father. What he wanted . . .

He began to pace, back and forth, trying to comprehend just what was going on inside him.

*You are being ridiculous*, he told himself. *It's bad enough that you take young maids into your bed each night. But to contemplate this. To upset all your carefully laid plans merely to follow a whim. . . .*

But this was no whim. It was not like giving the vials back to Shepherd. This was important.

*Important?* He could hear Pei K'ung's voice query that, the mocking laughter that would follow, as night followed day. No. He could not let his wife know how he felt, for if she did . . .

He said the words aloud, softly, so he could hear them in the air. "If she found out she would use it, just as she uses everything."

"*Chieh Hsia?*"

Yuan turned, surprised to find her standing there, not ten paces from where he stood, watching him.

"Dragon Heart?"

She bowed her head. "Forgive me, *Chieh Hsia*, I did not mean to startle you."

"But . . ." He stared at her, then beckoned her to him. "You should not be out here. Her spies . . ."

She frowned. *"Chieh Hsia?"*

"My wife, the Empress . . . If she were to discover you were here . . ."

"But I thought . . ."

He went to her and took her arm, leading her inside. Closing the door he turned on her. "Did no one tell you?"

She shook her head.

*"Aiya . . ."* He let out a great huff of exasperation. Then, seeing how she stared at him, amazed, as if he'd lost his mind, he laughed. "Do I seem like a madman, Dragon Heart?"

She looked down, flustered. "Why, no, *Chieh Hsia*. I . . ."

He reached out, taking her hands, then drew her close. She did not resist, yet when he made to kiss her, she drew her face back.

*"Chieh Hsia*, forgive me. . . ."

"Forgive you?" He stared at her, not understanding.

"Forgive me, Great Lord, but I am betrothed."

*Betrothed.* The word sank like a stone into his consciousness. But of course. She was a Minor Family Princess, and Minor Family Princesses were always betrothed, just as her sister had been secretly betrothed to his son these past ten years. What had he thought? Even so, the urge to kiss her was overwhelming. Placing his hand gently against her neck, he drew her face to his.

*"Chieh Hsia,"* she said, as their faces drew apart again, her voice a husky whisper. "We shouldn't. You know we shouldn't." But her hands were on his neck and as their faces met again she seemed to yield to him, the urgency with which she pressed her lips to his letting him know that he'd not been mistaken.

THE MARKETPLACE was buzzing with the news. Big Wen, the butcher, had defied the punks and chased them off with a cleaver. There was talk among them of forming a defense committee, but Emily, listening in, wondered how long such talk would last when the runners got really nasty. She knew how they thought, how they acted, and she felt sorry for Big Wen, for today's heroes tended to be tomorrow's victims when you were dealing with the brother-hoods.

She hurried on, meaning to go home, when a commotion broke out on the far side of the square. Like the others about her she went up on her toes, craning her neck to see what was happening. There were shouts, screams, and then a stall went over.

*Aiya*, she thought, *it's begun already.*

As the crowd began to scatter, she found herself pressing for-ward, drawn toward the fracas, unable to stop herself. Suddenly she found herself in open space, the toppled stall in front of her, smashed bowls of uncooked meat littering the cobbles. As she watched, two of the punks dragged Big Wen away by his hair, blood streaming down his face, while another tossed a lighted torch onto the stall. As it burst into flame, she looked up, meeting the young punk's eyes.

"You like?" he said, his gap-toothed mouth laughing. "You fuck-ing like?"

She looked about her, trying to find something to put it out, but there was nothing. Besides, the animal fats had caught and there was little she could have done.

There was an awful stench now, the smell of burning offal. Slowly, knowing she could do nothing, she backed away. They would take Big Wen away and beat him badly, as an example to the others. And so it would go on.

She swallowed bitterly, her instinct to fight them unassuaged. But she was a single woman and they would target her, the way they had targeted Big Wen, and she could not afford that. She had the boys to think of, after all.

*The Hsien L'ing*, she thought. *I must go and petition the Hsien L'ing.*

Sleeping on the matter overnight, she had decided not to; had argued herself into believing it would make no difference. But now she had no option. It was the only way.

And if that failed?

Then the brotherhoods would win and the nightmare—she sighed heavily—the nightmare would begin again.

SU PING set down his brush and, sighing deeply, combed his fingers through his neat gray hair.

*If yesterday was bad, today is worse,* he thought, conscious of the queue of complainants seated in the anteroom outside his office. His half-brother had stirred up a veritable hornets' nest, and he was the one who would have to calm things down.

*Fuck you, Su Chun,* he thought, surprised by the anger he felt. *Before you came I was a happy man, contented, liked by my citizens and trusted. And now?*

Now word had gone out that his men stood by while his brother's men smashed stalls and beat up citizens.

He let a breath hiss between his teeth. Where was his *Wei?* Where *was* Kung Chia when he was needed?

He turned in his chair, hearing the door open behind him, then relaxed. It was only the old woman. She set down a bowl of *ch'a* at his elbow then, with a little nod, backed away.

Again he sighed. What were things coming to? First the taxes and now this! The gods knew he could do without such trials!

He reached out for his *ch'a*, meaning to drink it before it grew cold, then paused, noticing something tucked beneath the bowl.

It was a note. Unfolding it he read: "Do not trust your Third Secretary." Beside the English words was a sketch of a coiled snake lying in the grass, three Mandarin pictograms—spelling the man's name, Ho Tse-tsu—drawn in the space between the coils.

He frowned, folded the note, and slipped it into the pocket of his gown.

The clock on the wall read eleven thirty-seven. He stared at it a moment, then looked to his clerk, giving a nod to indicate he should send in the next complainant.

It was a woman, a *Hung Mao*, in her late forties, early fifties.

"Name," he said, tearing a fresh incident form from the pad and reaching for his brush.

"Lin," she said. "Emily Lin."

"And the reason for your visit?"

He looked up at her and knew, before she said it, what was to come. He listened, taking notes, then sat back.

"I shall do what I can, *Mu Ch'in* Lin, I promise you. This matter concerns me greatly and I shall be taking strong action. Now go. My door is always open. . . ."

He saw a movement in her eyes at that and leaned toward her. "You doubt my word, *Mu Ch'in Lin?*"

She hesitated, then shook her head. "No, *Hsien L'ing*, it's just that I came last night," she said. "I tried to see you."

"It was after office hours," he said, smiling politely at her. "I was at the baths. But one of my officials was here—"

"I know," she said, speaking through him. "I tried to speak to him, but he sent me away. He spoke very harshly to me, *Hsien L'ing.*"

"I see." He looked to his clerk. "Who was on duty last night, Chang?"

"Ho Tse-tsu, Master."

"Ah . . ." His hand went to his pocket, feeling the note there. "I see," he said again. Then, taking control of the situation, he stood. "Well, leave the matter with me, *Mu Ch'in.* I shall do what I can."

When she had gone he signaled to his clerk to close the door, then went through to the back office where the surveillance tapes were kept. He sorted through them until he found the one that covered the *yamen.* Returning to his desk, he fed it into the scanner. At once a screen lifted from the desk. For a time he sat there, skimming through the tape, searching, then froze the image.

There! That was her. He let it run—saw, for the first time, how his staff behaved when he was absent.

*I didn't know*, he thought. *I truly didn't know.*

But it was his fault, anyway. His fault for not checking before now. For *permitting* it to happen.

He paused the tape, then reached across the desk and pulled the Callers Book toward him, turning it to the entries for the evening before. A quick check confirmed what he'd suspected: there were no entries. According to this no one had called at the *yamen.* Closing the book, he drew the note from his pocket, unfolded it, and spread it on the desk before him.

"Send Ho Tse-tsu in at once," he said, looking to his clerk.

He sat back, composing himself. A moment later Ho Tse-tsu appeared at the door.

"Close it," he said quietly. "Then sit down. I want to talk to you."

"Master?" Ho sat, politely attentive.

"You understand your duties, Ho Tse-tsu?" he asked, keeping his tone innocuous.

"Master?" The man seemed genuinely puzzled.

"You know my stated policy. My door is always open. If someone calls you see them, and if you judge the matter urgent, then you contact me, whether I am on duty or otherwise."

Ho bowed his head. "Master!"

"And if someone calls, you log it in the Callers Book, neh?"

"Naturally, Master."

He turned the screen to face Ho Tse-tsu, then leaned toward him. "Then why did you not log the woman caller last night? Did you *forget?*"

"Master?"

Su Ping shook his head, snorting with disgust. "Just go! You are dismissed!"

Ho Tse-tsu stared at Su Ping, astonished. Throwing the chair aside, he turned and left the room, mumbling obscenities as he went.

Su Ping let his breath escape him, then looked to his clerk, who stood in the open doorway. "Send in Fourth Secretary Mao. I have a vacancy to fill."

He looked back at the screen. That face . . . it might be simply that he'd looked at it so long, but something nagged him about it. He frowned, then enhanced the picture, closing in on the woman's eye. For a moment he stared at it, conscious of how strong, how beautiful, that eye was, then looked down at the keyboard and pressed SEARCH.

PEI K'UNG finished signing the final draft of the document. Handing it to her Chief Eunuch, Ming Ai, she looked up.

"You have news, Colonel I?"

I Ye bowed his head. "I have, Mistress. It seems your husband has visited the Northern Palace twice in the past twelve hours."

"And do we know what he did there?"

"Not yet, Mistress. But it seems a number of the rooms have been opened up and prepared for guests. More than fifty, so I am advised."

Her eyes lingered on his hatchet face a moment, then looked away dismissively. "And this is news? Where else would my husband put up the guests? In my palace? In *his*? Or maybe he planned to farm them out, some here, some there, about the locality?"

The tone with which she said the last was indicative of her acute displeasure. I Ye braced himself for a blast.

"Besides," she said, beginning in a calm monotone, "there's still the matter of the missing cassette. Whatever happened to *that*, Colonel I?"

"My men—"

"Are investigating it, I know. And the messenger? You've found him, I take it?"

"No, Mistress."

"And my husband's plans? You've unearthed them?"

"No, Mistress."

"Then a fat fucking lot of good you are, Colonel I!" she yelled, standing, her hands deathly white where they pressed down against the desk, her face red, distorted with anger. "Your job is to give me answers, not excuses! And while you're at it, send Chu Po to me. I want to talk to him."

I Ye swallowed. "He is not here, Mistress."

"I know that. I have eyes. Now send him to me."

I Ye lowered his head even further, almost wincing as he spoke the words. "I mean, he is not in the palace, Mistress."

"*What?*" Her bellow made everyone in that room tuck his head into his chest. In such a mood she had been known to order men stripped and tortured on the spot. "Then where the fuck *is* he?"

I Ye briefly thought of saying the words that had come into his head—*I do not know*—but decided that that was not a wise option in the circumstances. Besides, he had a good suspicion where the no-good lowlife was.

"Would you like me to fetch him, Mistress?"

Her eyes went to him again. "You *know* where he is?"

"Of course, Mistress," he answered confidently, hoping to all the gods he was right.

"Then bring him."

"At once, Mistress!" And I Ye turned, glad for the chance that took him from that office.

Ming Ai waited for I Ye to go then stepped forward. "Mistress? Might I have a word?"

"You have my ear, Ming Ai."

"I meant in private."

She looked at him, measuring him, then nodded. "Leave us!" she ordered.

In a moment the room was cleared. Only Ming Ai remained, facing her across her massive desk.

"So?" she asked. "What is it, Ming Ai?"

He knelt and bowed his head low. "I want to ask a favor, Mistress."

"A favor?" She stood and came around the desk. "What kind of favor? Is this about another of your relatives? Because if it is . . ."

"No, Mistress," he said hastily, glancing up at her. "This is for myself." He took a breath. "I have served you well, great Mistress. Whatever you have asked, I have done. And never, never have I questioned you. But . . ."

He hesitated, his tongue making one quick sweep of his lips, then spoke again. "I feel you are in danger of making a grave mistake, Mistress."

She stared at him coldly. "A mistake?"

"In sending Karr alone to meet with Warlord Hu."

She made to speak, but checked herself, changing her mind. "Go on."

"Marshal Karr is your husband's man. Loyal to him. Intensely loyal. If something were to happen—if some condition were to be raised, perhaps, that concerned you—then Karr would be certain to look after his Master's interests before your own."

"A good point. So you think I should send Colonel I instead?"

"Gods, no, Mistress! I Ye is a vain and selfish man, self-centered and ambitious. To send him . . . well, it would give him ideas above his station. He would want to be Marshal next, and we both know that that is impossible!"

She nodded. It was true. "Then what do you suggest?"

He reached out and took her right hand, kissing the iron ring on the second finger. "Send me with Karr, Mistress. To be your eyes and ears. To ensure your interests are safeguarded in the negotiations."

*"You?"* She laughed. "But your place is here, Master Ming, running my palace."

"Mistress . . . hear me out. There are two or three good men who might keep things running smoothly in my absence—my assistant, Cheng Nai shan, for instance. But who else is there you can trust implicitly?"

She turned from Ming Ai, considering the matter, while he watched her from his knees, his eyes following her anxiously, trying to gauge from the physical look of her—the way she hunched her shoulders or bit a nail—just what her answer would be.

And if it was no? Then Heng Yu would go with Karr. Or so the rumor had it. A rumor he had kept from her, knowing that it would end all possibility of him going.

And he had to go. To get out of this stifling place, before he died here. Besides which, he wanted more than the running of a palace. Much more. He wanted what Heng Yu had: the freedom to move *where* he wanted *when* he wanted—yes, and an Empire to run.

This, if she granted it, would be the first step, for it would set a precedent. Other journeys would follow, other tasks would suggest themselves, until he'd find a way to unseat that weasel Heng and make himself Chancellor.

That was, if she let him go.

Pei K'ung turned, her eyes part hooded as she stared at him, like some great bird of prey examining her next victim.

"All right," she said softly. "You can go."

He gave a tight, exaggerated bow of the head. "I shall not let you down, Mistress!" he said soberly, with all the dignity he could muster. But inside him the elation was like a great warm flood, filling every cell, making him want to whoop.

"No," she said, offering him her hand once more, the ring finger extended. "Make certain you do not, Ming Ai. Make good and certain."

THE FOUR SHIPS landed in a tight formation, their heavy Martian design very different from the other, sleeker craft that were already parked upon the pad. As their huge twin engines whined down, Li Yuan stepped out onto the pad and made toward the lead ship, his guards hurrying to keep up with him.

Ebert was first down the ramp. He had changed little over the years, yet there was a stoutness to him now, a slight touch of gray in his neatly cut hair, that made him look even more like his long-dead father. Two tiny camera-eyes hovered above his head, his own eyes empty sockets.

"Hans," Li Yuan said, unceremoniously offering his hand.

Ebert took it, then drew Li Yuan close in an embrace.

"It's good to see you, Yuan," he said, moving back, showing his perfect teeth as he smiled. "But what's this I hear of taxes and campaigns?"

"We'll talk," Li Yuan said soberly, then smiled, genuinely delighted to see his onetime General again. "But not now. Now you must tell me all that's been happening in the New Colonies."

"Have your spies not kept you informed, Yuan?"

"Spies?" Li Yuan laughed. "You think the Osu would not notice any spies of mine?" As he spoke his eyes went to the tall, dark-faced figures that were stepping down from the other ships.

Ebert smiled brightly a moment. "I guess they would. . . ." Then, unexpectedly, a shadow crossed his face. "To tell the truth, things have been hard, especially this last year. There was a drought, and then one of our neighbors thought they'd take advantage of our temporary weakness."

Li Yuan was shocked. "I did not know. You should have contacted me."

Ebert shook his head. "We coped. It is our way."

"And your neighbors?"

"They will know better next time. Still, enough of this. We have traveled far. It would be nice to refresh ourselves after our journey."

"Of course. . . ." Li Yuan stepped back, meaning to lead Ebert through, then stopped, his mouth fallen open. "The gods preserve us," he said quietly, "who is that?"

The camera eyes swiveled above Ebert. "This," he said, beckoning the young man across, "is an old friend. Li Yuan, meet Nza, our little bird."

The Osu who bowed, then extended a hand to take Li Yuan's was a giant of a man—six *ch'i* at the very least, and broad of shoulder.

"I see you have your very own Karr," he said, nodding to the young man admiringly. "It would be good to see them wrestle, neh?"

"Forgive me, *Chieh Hsia*," Nza said, a tone of genuine deference in his voice, "but I am not a fighter."

"But I thought—"

"Oh, I have fought in the past, but now I am a priest."

Li Yuan looked to Ebert, surprised, but Ebert was grinning. "Do you find it *so* strange, Yuan? I, too, after all, am a priest."

"Not strange so much as"—he laughed again—"*unlikely*."

"As unlikely as a black skin on a human form, perhaps, *Chieh Hsia?*" Nza said, grinning now.

Behind him a dozen of the Osu had formed up, representatives of the new "tribes" that had settled the old lands of Western Africa Li Yuan had granted them. They were an impressive group of men and women whose inner strength seemed to emanate from their physical selves. The very way they held themselves was different.

Osu they were. Martians. Followers of Efulefu, "the Worthless One," the Walker in the Darkness. Li Yuan looked from face to face, then returned his gaze to meet the blind eyes of the Walker himself, Hans Ebert, once his General, heir to the great GenSyn corporation, traitor to the Seven and now High Priest of the Osu.

"You have come far," Li Yuan said, lowering his head in a mark of respect he granted few men.

"The journey has but begun," Ebert answered him solemnly, the words almost ritualistic. "The way ahead is long and hard, neh, brothers?"

There was a low murmur of assent.

"Then come," Li Yuan said, ushering them through into the Northern Palace. "We have much to talk about."

THE STREETS OF Frankfurt Central were narrow and dark, overshadowed by the massive high-rises that surrounded the ancient town center. To the east the snakelike glass-and-silver shape of a hover-rail flashed brightly along its guide rails as it crossed the river, heading south to Darmstadt. I Ye stopped a moment, watching it, then led the hand-picked squad down a cut-through and out into the broad avenue of Berliner Street, at the heart of the area known locally as the *Yinmao*.

Here some of the old pre-City buildings had survived and had been rebuilt, their dry brick shells shored up with steel and plastic. It was between two of these, in a basement club, that I Ye knew he'd find Chu Po.

Posting two men at the door, he took the rest—eight of his most trusted men—down the narrow stairs. A bouncer was stationed at the bottom of the steps, at the end of a short corridor. He was a big man, well used to trouble, but seeing the bottle-green of Pei K'ung's elite, he flattened himself against the wall, his hands raised and open.

I Ye ignored him, sending two of his squad ahead to kick the door down. As it splintered and fell, I Ye stepped through into the darkly lit reception area. There were shouts of surprise from inside, the rustle of frantic movement. Faces appeared at curtained doorways—male faces poking from unclothed bodies—then quickly disappeared again. A guard stepped out at the far end of the main hallway, his gun drawn, and was shot where he stood.

"Find him!" I Ye barked as his men slipped past him. But they needed no word. They knew their tasks and went about them silently, efficiently. There was another shot and I Ye turned, but it was one of his own men, dealing with the guard at the door.

He relaxed, beginning to enjoy himself, as, one by one, the male prostitutes and their clients were brought out from the cubicles and lined up—some half-clothed, most completely naked—against the wall of the reception area.

The whole place stank of sweat and semen.

"Well, well!" he said, as Chu Po was brought struggling into the room, his hands bound. "It seems we've caught a big fish in our tiny net!"

"You'll pay for this, you fucker!" Chu Po said, his handsome, clean-shaven face screwed up with anger, the muscles at his neck tensed like hawsers.

I Ye stared at him briefly, then slapped him hard across the face.

Chu Po stepped back, clearly shaken, his eyes reappraising the situation.

"I could kill you right now," I Ye said quietly. "I could put a torch to this place and leave you to burn alive. And no one would ever know. No one would ever question me about it."

Chu Po swallowed, then, some of his bravado, his natural arrogance, returning to him, he answered I Ye.

"So why don't you? Why don't you end it *right now?* I know you hate me. Or is it just the torturer in you speaking? The sadist that likes to get its kicks from bullying others?"

I Ye shrugged, as if it was of no moment what Chu Po thought of him, but he was conscious of his men standing there at his back, listening, and swore to himself that he would kill Chu Po—would get him in a room and play with him—the moment Pei K'ung tired of him.

"You think you're a big man, don't you, Chu Po?"

Chu Po laughed and nodded toward his penis, which hung, long and flaccid, between his legs. "At least I have a cock. A real cock, that is. Not like that little corkscrew I hear you have between your legs!"

I Ye felt himself tense, but kept from hitting Chu Po. To hit him would be to admit the potency of the insult, and that he could not do.

"You think what you will," he said, more nonchalantly than he felt, stepping right up to Chu Po, so that he was face to face with him, "but she will tire of you. And when she does . . . that day you will be mine."

"Not if you're mine first," Chu Po answered and, moving forward quickly, planted a kiss on I Ye's lips.

I Ye stepped back, spitting, furious.

"Oh, I know you've a taste for it," Chu Po went on. "I'm told you used to come here yourself, back in the old days, when you were just a young lieutenant."

I Ye stiffened. "I would be careful what you say, Chu Po. To slander an officer of the State—"

"Oh, ballocks!" Chu Po said. "Why, I could produce a dozen men who've had you, I Ye, and you know it!"

This time he could not help himself. His blow knocked Chu Po from his feet and split his lip.

"Get up!" he said. "Get up before I forget my orders and kill you!"

Chu Po looked up from where he knelt, touching his bound hands to his mouth, a look of triumph in his eyes. "I was right, wasn't I?" He laughed, then grimaced with pain. "I was only guessing, but now I know."

"Lies," I Ye said, a cold feeling gripping him. Before Chu Po could say another word, he turned and pointed to his sergeant. "Sedate him and get him out of here."

"And the rest, sir?"

"Burn them!" he said, walking toward the door, a cold, clear fury burning in him. "Torch the whole fucking place!"

---

NAN FA-HSIEN stood looking on as the T'ang's *she t'ou*—his official taster—completed his sampling of the dishes, then, at his signal, clapped his hands. At once a dozen stewards gathered up the silver dishes and fell in behind him.

He led them through the imperial kitchens and on along the broad corridor that led to the Hall of Earthly Tranquillity. Ahead of him guards, wearing the purple uniforms of Li Yuan's elite *shen t'se*, hurried to push back the twenty-*ch'i*-high doors, straining, four to a door. Inside, the Hall was lit by blazing torches, twenty-nine carved stone pillars forming a circle around a huge open space, at the center of which was a huge, dark wooden table.

They crossed the echoing stone floor, over a vast mosaic that depicted the world as it had once been, when the Seven had ruled the entire globe, stopping a dozen *ch'i* from the table.

Li Yuan sat at the head of the table in a high-backed chair. To his right sat his son, Kuei Jen, while on his left sat his Chief Adviser, Ben Shepherd. Shepherd's son, Tom, was there also, and two of Kuei Jen's companions—the young "Prince" Egan one of them—but it was to the guests on this side of the table that Nan Fa-hsien's eyes were drawn.

Black men; white eyed, broad nosed, heavy lipped . . . magnificently formed. The sight of them still fascinated him. No less, indeed, than the sight of the onetime traitor, Hans Ebert, seated at his Master's table, facing Li Yuan, hollow eyed yet all seeing.

Nan Fa-hsien bowed low. Behind him his stewards bowed as one, copying the gesture perfectly. Then, at Li Yuan's signal, he stood back, letting his stewards serve the opening course.

There would be fifteen courses tonight. Ten fewer than at an official banquet. This first, however, was a specialty, one the great T'ang himself had insisted on—boiled snake in its skin.

"Is this what I *think* it is?" asked the eldest of the Osu, looking to Ebert for guidance.

"It is a rare delicacy, Aluko," Ebert answered, then gave a tiny bow of his head to Li Yuan, clearly appreciating the significance of the dish. "Snake liver is good for sexual potency, while the meat is good for the eyes."

"That is so," Kuei Jen offered, "though snake fat is said to be bad for the penis. I am told that if one were to eat the fat one's penis would shrivel up."

"Then let us hope these are *lean* snakes," Ben Shepherd offered, bringing laughter from all sides of the table.

As it subsided, Kuei Jen leaned forward once again, looking to the Osu—Aluko Echewa—who had first spoken. "It is also said that one should keep the skin, for it will bring you riches."

"You believe that?" Ebert asked.

The Prince shrugged. "I know only what is said. That a dream in which a snake chases you will bring good luck, while a dream in which the snake coils about you is said to presage change in one's life."

"So many dreams," Li Yuan said, picking up his chopsticks and signaling that they should begin. "Yet what I like the most is the taste, the texture, of the snake."

"Delicious!" one of the other Osu—Dogo—said, after a mouthful. "But not enough of it!"

There was laughter once again, even from Li Yuan himself.

"You would like more, friend Dogo?" he asked.

"I'm sure Dogo would eat a python, if you let him," Ebert said, before the Osu could answer. "But let us not spoil his appetite for other fare."

"No, indeed," Li Yuan said, gesturing to Nan to bring the second course, "yet the gift of a compliment should not go unrewarded. I will give you a basket of snakes to take back with you to Africa, friend Dogo, and servants to teach you how to breed and how to cook them."

Dogo straightened and bowed his head. "You are most generous, *Chieh Hsia.*"

"Not at all," Li Yuan said, dabbing at his mouth with a cloth. "It is not every day I have the opportunity to repay such worthy friends." He looked to Nan Fa-hsien, who, aware of the turn of the conversation, had sent the stewards on and hovered, awaiting his master's instructions. "See to it, Master Nan."

"It shall be done, *Chieh Hsia!*"

He bowed, then slowly backed away, their conversation following him out through the door and into the corridor beyond.

"Are there no snakes in Africa?" Kuei Jen asked.

"Snakes aplenty," Ebert answered him. "But none you could cook and eat."

━━━━━━━

*"WELL?"* Pei K'ung asked impatiently, crouching over the man, trying to see just what he could see that made him stare so intently.

The old man mumbled something incomprehensible, then put his face yet closer to the steaming pile of entrails, so that the longest wisps of his ash-white beard brushed against their bloodied surface.

Moments passed. Finally he turned his head and looked up at her at an odd angle, smiling his toothless smile.

"Auspicious omens, Mistress," he said, his voice almost comically high pitched.

She straightened up, resting her hands on her haunches. "Auspicious? *How* auspicious? In what *way* auspicious?"

His grin widened. "The path ahead is clear. Purposeful action will bring its own rewards."

She felt herself tense, wanting to slap the man, to get him to speak more directly, but she knew it would be no use.

"Well?" she said, when it seemed he would never speak again. "Tell me more."

The *T'ai Shih Lung* shrugged. He had been Court Astrologer these past five years, ever since Ming Ai had recommended him to her, and he had proved useful in the past, but right now she felt like lopping off his head. What good was the old bastard if he only spoke in riddles?

"What path?" she insisted. "What action?"

The old man reached for the bright red cloth he'd brought the entrails in and threw it over the mess. He turned, smiling at her again.

"There is a mystery, neh?"

She nodded.

"Then take the path that leads directly to it. That path is clear. Purposeful action—"

"—will bring its own rewards." She stared thoughtfully at him a moment longer, then straightened up.

*The path is clear. . . .*

She smiled, knowing suddenly what was meant. Li Yuan was entertaining. His rooms were therefore empty, his study unattended. It would be hours before he returned there.

*The path is clear. . . .*

She looked down at the *T'ai Shih Lung* and smiled, then, reaching in her pocket, took out a thousand-*yuan* chip and threw it to him. He caught it like a man a fifth his age, the chip disappearing into his cloak like a stone into a pond.

Purposeful action, eh? Well, there was no one in the kingdom who knew how to be more purposeful.

━━━◆◆◆◆━━━

THREE HOURS had passed, and as the wine flowed and the men about the table grew more relaxed in each other's company, so their talk had moved from the trivial toward the great matters of the day: to where the world was headed and how they, its custodians, might affect its future.

"So you really think the Americans will come to an agreement, Kuei Jen? You really believe they'll make Li Yuan their T'ang?"

Kuei Jen set his wine cup down and looked to Ebert, who had posed the question.

"I do," he said bluntly. "And I'll tell you why. I think the Old Men have had enough of wars; enough of their electrified walls and the need for vigilance. At first, it's true, they rather liked their isolation, the sense that they and they alone were impervious to the chaos that was tearing their great continent apart. It made them feel strong, a true elite. But as year piled on year they grew weary of the struggle and began to long for simple peace. But where was such a peace to come from? From an agreement with their enemies? No. Too much blood had been spilled, too much bitterness stored up between the two sides. What they needed was an intermediary."

"An intermediary, certainly, but a T'ang?" Ebert shook his head, then looked to Li Yuan, who had kept quiet throughout the exchange. "I mean no disrespect to you, Li Yuan, but I can hardly see how making you their ruler will solve their quarrels."

"On the contrary," Ben Shepherd chipped in, "I'd say it was the only solution both sides could possibly agree on. To have a Master more powerful than either—a Master who might *enforce* such a peace."

Ebert's hollow eyes remained on Li Yuan's face. "You mean to send an army, then, Li Yuan?"

"Not at all," Li Yuan answered, almost as if he had little interest in the matter. "It is the threat of force, not force itself, that creates a lasting peace."

"So I was wrong earlier?"

"Wrong?" Kuei Jen asked, looking from Ebert to his father.

"Your father means to wage war against the Warlords," Ebert explained. "Or so the rumor has it. Why, only yesterday he issued an edict raising taxes."

"Taxes?" Kuei Jen stared at his father, astonished by the news. "Is this true, Father?"

"It is true, Kuei Jen," Li Yuan said, noting how silent young Egan was, sitting by his son's side, "and we shall discuss it in the morning. But to answer your point, Hans. Yes, I mean to wage war against the Warlords. A swift, decisive war to bring peace to the troubled Asian continent. Our people there have suffered far too long. It is time to let them know that they have not been forgotten."

"And if you fail?" Ebert asked.

Li Yuan smiled tightly. "We shall discuss this matter at a different juncture, perhaps?" Then, as if that were all to be said on the matter, he turned to Nan Fa-hsien and clicked his fingers. "Bring more wine, Master Nan. My guests' cups are empty."

TOM, sitting to Li Yuan's right, watched the T'ang a moment, then looked down, thinking how strange it was to be there in such company, amid such talk of war and peace and how the world would one day be. All night he had looked on, listening attentively, intrigued by this talk of far lands and foreign places, fascinated by these men who, it seemed, had traveled farther and lived more interesting lives than he himself could ever have conceived.

He reached out, meaning to drain his glass, then stopped, a shiver rippling down his spine. He had felt that faint, familiar tickling at the back of his head all evening, but now it seemed to flood his skull.

*Tom? Tom? . . . can you hear me?*

He felt Sampsa slip into his mind, felt the shock of it as if it were the very first time, then felt himself convulse, the wine cup falling from his hand, shattering on the stone floor.

There was silence all around the table. All eyes were on him. His father's hand closed on his arm. "Are you all right?"

Tom shook his head, hunching into himself, as if wracked by sudden pains, then, pushing his chair back, he stood abruptly and hurried from the hall.

*WHAT'S HAPPENED, TOM? WHY ARE YOU FIGHTING ME?*

Tom groaned inwardly, shaking his head. He was sitting on the edge of the bath, his head in his hands, the strain of keeping Sampsa from his mind giving him the mother of all headaches.

*Tom? Are you in trouble?*

The voice was clear—clearer than it had ever been. It was as if Sampsa were sitting next to him, not hundreds of thousands of miles away, strapped into his seat on the shuttle, returning to Earth.

*Tom? . . . Tom?*

It was awful. Keeping Sampsa out was simply unbearable. Yet the alternative was to let him in, and if he let him in he would see it all—every last disgusting bit of it. The girl, the PornoStim, the lot. Before now it hadn't mattered. Before, there had been nothing to hide, nothing to be ashamed of, but now . . .

*What is it, Tom? Has something happened? Something you can't tell me about?*

He wanted to say yes. Wanted, beyond all reasoning, to say yes and let him in, but he was frightened. Frightened lest Sampsa saw what he really was—saw and recoiled from that.

*I know you're there, Tom. I can feel you. I saw . . . the Great Hall, Li Yuan, the black men. . . .*

The black men . . . With a shocking, sudden vividness he saw the face of the eldest of the Osu, Aluko Echewa—saw that broad nose, that generous mouth, those dark, dignified eyes—and as he saw them so Sampsa slipped inside his head.

*Tom? . . . Are you all right, Tom?*

*I'm okay,* he answered, raising his head and staring sightlessly across the room, a long, shuddering breath escaping him.

*Then why . . .* The voice faltered. *Kuan Yin! Who was she?*

*A girl,* Tom answered, but there was no hiding now. Sampsa was in. Now he'd know everything. Everything.

*Tom?*

*Yes?*

*I—I didn't know. I . . .*

Tom huffed, angry now. For the first time ever he felt betrayed, let down by that voice inside his head.

*Tom?*

*What is it?*

*I understand.*

Tom sighed. So now he knew. He stood up, then, a shudder passing through him, went through into the bedroom, conscious all the while of Sampsa, there in his head, sharing every thought, every memory.

*Tom? . . . Look, you shouldn't be ashamed. It's how we are. It's . . .*

*It's what?* he asked angrily, his voice a silent bark across the miles.

He felt as much as heard Sampsa's answering sigh, felt the compassion there in Sampsa's voice when he spoke again.

*This had to happen. Don't you understand that? It was only a question of time. I know it must be hard. . . . I mean, the fact that it happened to you first, but . . . well, we can't live our lives like saints, can we? I mean . . . it's how we are.*

He laughed bitterly. *So this is it, right? No veils and no secrets . . . everything out in the open, everything exposed, every last, disgusting detail, every awful, shameful moment . . . until one or other of us dies. Have I got that right?*

He felt Sampsa nod, felt the gesture as a ghostly doubled presence in his head, and at the same time felt the sad smile of understanding that came to Sampsa's lips as he answered him.

*I guess so, dear friend. No veils, no secrets. Until we die.*

———————

LEAVING HIS GUESTS in the care of his son, Li Yuan slipped away shortly after midnight, giving the excuse that he was tired; that he had to start early the next morning.

Though both were true, it was neither tiredness nor duty that drew him from their company but the memory of a slender perfumed figure—of the dark eyes and moist sweet lips of the young Princess, Dragon Heart.

At the end of the corridor he paused. Straight on and through the door and he would find himself out in the central garden, the Eastern Palace only a minute's walk away. Turn right and climb the stairs, however, and he would be but a moment from her door.

Like a shadow, he turned and climbed the stairs, his heart hammering in his chest, his lips dry with nervous anticipation.

What, after all, if he was wrong? What if he'd misread the signals?

*Then I'll be a fool*, he told himself, *a stupid middle-aged fool, for believing such a one could fall in love with me.*

At the head of the stairs he stopped, the uncertainty he was feeling something he hadn't experienced in years.

He had seen the moonlight shining in the darkness of her eyes, had felt how she had responded to his kiss; her mouth, her whole body, pressed against his urgently, passionately, as though she could not live unless she had him.

And when had he last felt that?

*Too long ago*, he answered, thinking of the endless procession of maids who had come to his bed, to serve and service him, their unclothed bodies merging in his memory to become a single body—a softly fleshed machine that kissed and stroked and opened to him, dutifully but without passion.

This was different, however. This was no serving girl but a Princess of the blood. She kissed to no one's order, no, not even a T'ang's. What she did she did of her own volition, following her own desires. No matter how powerful he was, as a Princess of the blood she was beyond him. No edict of his could force her even to allow him to touch her, let alone—

He pushed the thought away, then drew his hand through his hair, racked by indecision. If he got this wrong, if he pressed too hard, too soon, might he not frighten her away? Might he not lose her?

A wave of self-disgust engulfed him. *You are nothing but an old goat, Li Yuan—sense ridden, driven by your cock.*

Whereas she . . .

The mere thought of her made him shiver. She was so young. Why, the smell of her alone was enough to drive him from his senses. And the touch of her, the ineffable sweet touch of her. . . .

He swallowed and looked down. Abysses. Everywhere he looked he faced abysses. Abysses in his memory—those vast, unfillable gaps in his life that were his dead wives, his failed relationships. And if *this* failed? If this, his final chance, should come to nothing? What then? How could he face the years that lay ahead—those years of slow physical decay, that downhill slide into senescence and eventual darkness—without some sweet, delightful soul mate at his side?

Oh, for all he'd said to her the other night, he understood the great Ming Huang. Understood him perfectly. To risk an Empire for a pretty face, that was indeed stupidity, but to risk all to possess one's other self—to choose light instead of darkness, life instead of the living death of solitude—that surely was the act of a sane, a *healthy* man!

He closed his eyes and saw her, as she'd been earlier, and as he did he knew he would not be at peace until he had heard from her own mouth what his fate was to be: whether she would have him, or whether he was to be cast out. Out into an eternity of blackness.

He crossed the hallway quickly, silently, ignoring the ever-present guards, then rapped softly on her door.

A chair scraped somewhere in the room. Silks rustled, then the door eased open.

"*Chieh Hsia!*" she said with soft surprise.

"Forgive me," he said quietly. "I had to come."

Her face softened. "There is nothing to forgive."

For a moment he stood there, gaping at her, not knowing what to say. Then, wordlessly, she took his hand and drew him into the room, closing the door quietly behind her.

"Well?" she whispered.

Li Yuan stared at her, bewitched. He felt so old at that moment, so staid and dry and careworn. How could she possibly desire him?

Then suddenly her hands were on his neck, her lips pressed to his own.

All doubt evaporated.

He kissed her, a long and passionate kiss, his hands moving down her body, tracing the firm, delightful form of her beneath her silks. But it was her eyes that most inflamed him; those beautiful, intelligent eyes, which stared back at him, the pupils swollen with desire.

Carefully he lifted her and carried her through into the bedroom, yet even as he laid her down, she put a hand softly to his face, as if to wake him from a trance.

"I cannot sleep with you, Li Yuan," she said, a soft regret in her voice. "I cannot . . . you know, do *that.*"

"What . . . ?" He stared at her, unable to believe what she'd just said. Had he been wrong, then? Had she been mocking him? He made to move away, suddenly angry with her.

"No," she said, reaching up to him. "Lie here beside me. Please, my love. And touch me. Please. I like it when you touch me."

Like a slave he lay beside her, still in his clothes, trapped by his longing but wanting to be gone—suddenly gone—from that place.

"You're angry with me, I know," she said softly, turning on her side to face him, her hands stroking his chest, his neck, his cheek, constantly caressing him. "But I have given my word. It is as I said. I am betrothed."

"Then why this?" he asked, more harshly than he'd intended.

"Because I cannot help myself. The merest touch of you inflames me. I want"—she shuddered, her hand moving down his body until it settled on the cloth above his swollen penis—"I want to do everything you want to do. I want to make love to you, Li Yuan. But I gave my word."

He closed his eyes, in torment now. The merest touch of her hand against him had almost made him come.

"What can I do?" he asked, opening his eyes again, seeing at once how pained she was by his suffering.

In answer she lifted herself up and, with a gentle movement, shrugged off her sleeping silk. Beneath it she was perfect, more like a goddess than a girl.

"Touch me," she said, lying back, her eyes imploring him. "Touch me wherever you want to. Please. I want you to."

"And you?" He shuddered, the mere thought of what he was about to say bringing him to a state of quivering anticipation. "Will *you* touch me?"

"I will do anything you wish, *Chieh Hsia*," she said, sitting up, beginning to undress him. "But I cannot make love to you. Not while I am betrothed to another."

PEI K'UNG set a guard at the door, then crossed the darkness of her husband's study quickly, using a flashlight to find her way to his desk. She had never been in here without his knowledge, nor normally would she have contemplated such madness, but this was too important—much too important—for her to leave to chance.

If there was anything that could give her an insight into his plans—anything at all—then it would be here, somewhere in his study.

*The path is clear. . . .*

She went around and sat in his chair, then bent down, trying each drawer in turn. They were locked, of course, and he would have the key upon his person—she knew his habits well—but that was not a barrier to her. She had had her own copies made long ago . . . just in case.

It took longer than she'd thought to match the key to the lock and the jangling set her nerves on edge, but finally she had the top drawer open. Swiftly she went through it, piling the contents on the empty desk, then putting them back, careful to maintain the order.

Ten minutes passed, fifteen. She would allow herself an hour. If by then she had found nothing, she would return to her own palace and . . .

And what?

No. She had to stay. If she went back empty handed she would merely sit there in her rooms, restless and anxious, cursing herself for not having persevered another five, ten minutes.

*Purposeful action will bring its own rewards. Hadn't the old fool said as much?*

She searched a moment longer then sat back, letting out a long, frustrated breath. Nothing! There was nothing among these papers. Nothing she didn't know about already, that was.

She closed the drawer and locked it, then began the task of matching key to lock once more.

No. She had to be certain. She had to know, if possible, right now. However long it took. Besides, he would be with his guests another two, maybe three hours at the least, drinking and talking. It would be first or second bell before he came back here—that was, if he did not go straight to bed with one of his maids.

She matched the key, turned it. The drawer slid open.

It was almost empty. Almost. At the back, in a golden folder, was a single-page memorandum. She laid it on the desk and shone her flashlight on it, reading the words carefully, then gave a small squeak of excitement. This was it! *This* was what she'd been looking for!

She closed the folder and put it back, locking the drawer with a quick, self-satisfied movement of her wrist, then straightened up, letting a laugh escape her. Heng Yu was right. It was indeed a gift. But even Heng Yu did not know just how generous her husband planned to be.

He was going to stand down, to abdicate as Emperor. And she . . . Pei K'ung felt a ripple of sheer delight pass up her spine . . . she was to reign alone.

*At last,* she thought, thinking of all the years his shadow presence had restrained her.

Her husband was a decent man, as men went, yet that was his downfall, for Li Yuan had no imagination, no vision of what a State might be. He had been conditioned by the circumstances of decline—his very thinking was that of a defeated man. But she would change things. She would make Chung Kuo great again, given the chance.

*Given the chance . . .*

She laughed. Well, soon she'd have that chance, that golden opportunity. And she would show them all.

She stood and crossed the room, then flicked off the flashlight and handed it to the guard, making her way back to her own palace.

And Chu Po? She smiled. Chu Po would be her consort. That would be her very first act, once she was ruler in her own right.

━━━━━━━

CHU PO was waiting in her bed. As she slipped beneath the sheets, his hands sought her breasts, teasing her nipples in that way she liked so much. For a while she simply lay there, letting him pleasure her with his hands and tongue, then, when she felt it was almost too much, she pushed him off.

"What is it?" he asked, his eyes, looking down at her, shining clearly, moistly, in the moonlit darkness of the room.

She wanted to tell him, to explain just why her blood coursed so strongly this evening, but she knew she couldn't. Chu Po was not to be trusted with such news.

"I don't know," she said finally. "I want something . . . different."

He laughed; a low, salacious laughter that excited her.

"Something *different?*" His hand traced the length of her body, moving between the valley of her breasts and ending in the mound of her pubis. "Wait there," he said. "I'll not be long."

*Oh, but you are,* she thought, watching him climb from the bed, his naked figure outlined in the light from the open window. But that wasn't the only reason why she craved his company. No. She wanted him because Chu Po was like her . . . unpredictable.

She heard the door click open, saw him slip out into the corridor. A moment later he was back, leading a young guard by the hand.

Pei K'ung rolled over and reached out, touching the pad beside the bed. At once a gentle light came on. She leaned up on her elbow.

The guard was a young private, eighteen years at most. A graduate of the Military Academy, no doubt. For a moment he stared at her, astonished to find himself looking at his naked Empress.

"Why, he's just adorable, Chu Po," she said, sitting up, then beckoning the guard to come closer.

"Isn't he?" Chu Po answered her, placing his arm about the guard's shoulder. "I noticed him earlier." He smiled and ran one hand down the young man's front. "So? What shall we play?"

The young guard looked at the hand that rested about his waist, then looked to the Empress again, bewildered. His voice shook. "Mistress?"

She stood and went to him. "What is your name?"

"H-Holzman, Mistress," he answered, unnerved to find his Empress a mere hand breadth away, with nothing between himself and her but his clothes. "Private Daniel Holzman."

"Daniel?" She put her hand out slowly, gently touching his neck. "That's a nice name. And you know your duty, Daniel?"

His voice was squeezed and tight. "Mistress?"

Her fingers went to the three buttons at the neck of his tunic and undid them. "Your duty," she said, looking into his face, "is to do whatever your Empress requires of you. You understand that?"

"Mistress!"

"Moreover, if you serve me well, I'll serve you well."

Her fingers went down his body, unfastening button after button. As the last pulled apart, Chu Po reached up and drew the tunic from his shoulders.

The young man swallowed, then straightened up, clearly meaning to make the best of things. He looked at her again, forcing himself to smile.

"What do you want me to do, Mistress?"

She smiled and put her face to his, planting a soft kiss on his lips. "I want you to make love to me. Is that so hard?"

"N-no, Mistress."

"Good." She reached down and unfastened the top button of his trousers. "And while you make love to me, Chu Po will make love to you."

His eyes registered shock. "Mistress?"

Her hand went to his chest, as if to reassure him. "Oh, do not fear, Daniel. Chu Po is a good lover. He won't hurt you. Not much, anyway."

"But . . ." Holzman fell silent and lowered his eyes, giving a terse nod of his head. Then, like a man about to go to execution, he reached down and began to remove his boots.

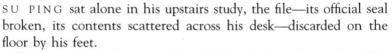

S U  P I N G sat alone in his upstairs study, the file—its official seal broken, its contents scattered across his desk—discarded on the floor by his feet.

Whatever he had expected to find, it had not been this. *This . . . well . . .* He shook his head, astonished.

At present no one knew. No one but himself and the clerk in the Central Records Office. But how long would that last? How long before someone higher up noticed that the file had been removed?

And even if they didn't, even if, by some chance, they were too busy to notice his interest in the woman, what was he to do?

He could have her arrested, then hand her over to the relevant authorities, or maybe he could call her ex-husband, Michael Lever, and come to some kind of financial arrangement with him. Then again, he could always use her as some kind of trading counter with his brother to get Su Chun out of his hair.

Or he could leave her be.

The last had been an afterthought, yet the more he reflected, the more he was drawn to it.

*Wuwei*. The path of inaction. He laughed. What was he to be thinking in this way? A sage? No. He was District Judge—*Hsien L'ing*—and his whole adult life he had upheld the rule of law, even when chaos threatened. This once, however, his instinct was to return the file to where he'd found it and do nothing.

She was a killer, he knew that now. He had seen the pictures of her victims—more than forty in all. Yet the more he'd read, the more he'd come to admire this woman—this Emily Ascher.

He pulled the flatprint of her toward him and studied it. It had been taken over twenty years ago, in America, and showed a younger, more vigorous woman than the one who had come to his office. But those eyes . . . those eyes were much the same.

"Mama Em" they called her now: a woman for whom no one had a bad word. A good, productive woman too; one who had taken in those orphaned boys. Without doubt a pillar of her local community. That being so, did it really matter that before the City fell she had been a senior member of several terrorist organizations—each of them dedicated to the fall of the Seven?

To his Masters it mattered greatly. Their memories were long and their desire for vengeance insatiable. To them it did not matter what a person had become; for them past crimes outweighed present virtues. But this was by the by. The more he had read—the more he learned of her—the more he'd come to like her. Yes, and to understand her.

Su Ping went out onto the balcony. His Mansion was on top of the hill, the greater part of his *Hsien* below him. In the near distance the river was a twisting strip of silver beneath the bright spring moon, while farther off the pagoda towers of Frankfurt *Hsien* climbed the night sky, bristling with lights. The sloping glass roofs of the penthouse gardens glowed a soft green in the darkness on the far bank. It was a familiar, peaceful sight, yet tonight he found no comfort in it.

Su Ping sighed. Never had he been troubled in this way. Never, before today, had he thought to question his Masters' orders. From the very first he had been their hands, loyal and willing. It had not been his *place* to question them.

But now all that had changed. In a single day that bond between them had been broken.

The evening air was warm, yet he felt a sudden chill, as if a shadow had fallen over him. Pulling his robe tightly about his aging frame, he went back into the study.

He stopped just inside the door, staring across at his desk, then went directly through, into his rooms, where his eldest wife awaited him. He stood there, letting her dress him for the night, then got into his bed, deciding he would sleep on the matter.

And in the morning?

In the morning he would know just what to do.

*Sleep well, Mama Em,* he thought, as he closed his eyes and rolled onto his side, picturing her settling for the night, her sleeping boys surrounding her. *Sleep well, for who knows what tomorrow will bring?*

*"CAN I HELP YOU?"*

*Chuang Kuan Ts'ai looked up at the severe middle-aged woman behind the desk and, gathering up her courage, spoke, her voice tiny in that huge, echoing place.*

*"I was just wondering what kind of person would have a number printed on their skin."*

*The Librarian stared at her strangely. "Now, why would you want to know that?"*

*This part she had rehearsed. She smiled brightly at the woman. "It's for school. I have to write a report on it for my teacher."*

*"Ah, I see," the woman said, apparently satisfied. "Well, you might try military records."*

*"Military records?"*

*The woman turned and pointed across the massive room, past standing rows of shelves and tape stacks toward where a dozen scanner* screens rested on a long desk. "Over there. The operating instructions are on the machine."

"Forgive me—" Chuang began, but the woman cut her off abruptly, her manner stern.

"Did your teacher tell you that someone else should do the work for you?"

"No, Second Librarian," Chuang said, addressing the woman by the rank printed on her lapel badge.

"Well, then," the woman said, slightly mollified by Chuang's good manners, "go and show some initiative."

Chuang bowed her head, then went across and took a seat in front of one of the scanners.

*Military?* No, that didn't make sense, because it was the military who had brought the bodies to them.

She switched the machine on, then sat there, tapping the keys, making queries, scrolling through lists, trying to locate what she was looking for. She was about to give up when she felt a hand on her shoulder.

"Here," the woman said, pressing in a code Chuang had not yet used. "Don't tell your teacher that I helped you, okay?"

Chuang sat back, watching as the screen lit up once more. A single query filled the screen:

SERIAL NUMBER?

She hesitated. The woman stood behind her, watching.

"What should I do?" she asked, the urge to key in the number so strong that she had to physically restrain herself.

In answer the woman leaned across her again and canceled the query. "I guess you need an index, neh?" She tapped in a request. A moment later the screen was filled with boxes.

"Which one?" the Second Librarian asked.

Chuang shrugged. All she really wanted was for the woman to go away so she could key the serial number query again, but the woman wasn't going anywhere.

"Does it matter?"

"I suppose not, if all your teacher wants is for you to find out about imprinted numbers. But some of these you couldn't access anyway."

Chuang turned in her seat, looking up into the woman's face. "Why's that?"

The Librarian's face softened into a tentative smile. "Plantation guards and ordinary Hsien Security, well, it's no real secret who they are, so the records are available to anyone. But with others—the elite forces, for instance, or Li Yuan's shen ts'e, his special palace guard— the records are kept secret. Key them and you'll find yourself in trouble."

Chuang swallowed. She hadn't known.

"So what should I key?"

"Try this one," the woman answered, touching her finger to the top right box on the screen. "That should be harmless enough."

"Thank you."

"That's all right. Now I must get back." She smiled, kind suddenly. "I hope your report goes well."

Chuang watched her return to her desk, then, facing the machine again, pressed out the sequence the woman had used earlier. Again the screen showed a single query:

SERIAL NUMBER?

She hesitated. What if her dead man had been a member of some elite force—an agent, perhaps? And what if her query triggered something? The Second Librarian had talked about trouble, but what kind of trouble? And just how could they possibly find out who had keyed the request?

She had two options: to key the number and take a chance, or to forget the whole thing.

Forget it, she told herself, but she had come too far. Compulsion drove her now. Placing her fingers on the keyboard, she tapped in the serial number.

There was a brief delay and then a face appeared on the screen.

She stared at it for a long time, not certain that it was the man she'd seen, dead on the slab, for life gave his features such a different cast. From the image on the screen he seemed a vigorous, even jolly man, and when was a corpse ever jolly?

But the number. The number was the one she'd memorized from the dead man's neck.

She keyed CONTINUE. At once a brief summary of the man's service record appeared on the screen, at the end of which was a note that he had left the force eighteen months after the final African campaign. For the past ten years he had been working for a man named

Tung Po-jen as a guard in Tung's club. There was a contact number
and an address.

She keyed CLEAR and sat back. That was where she'd start. At the
club. She looked across again. The Second Librarian was busy, dealing
with a line of people.

Chuang switched the machine off, then, taking the long way around
so that she didn't have to go past the woman again, slipped out through
one of the side entrances.

She had been absent half an hour already. If Uncle Cho came back
and found her gone he would get worried. But she could not leave this.
She had come this far. She had to know now why those men had died.

Had to know. Because otherwise things had no meaning. No meaning
at all.

*THE CLUB WAS* a dark and jagged gap in the anonymity of the
quiet back street, a burned-out ruin, open to the sky. Chuang Kuan
Ts'ai stared at it a long while, then turned away, meaning to go home,
yet as she turned she noticed someone else—a Hung Mao in his twenties—standing on the far side of the wreckage, in the alleyway that ran
parallel to her own. He was looking in at the scene, his eyes clearly
shocked by what he saw.She would have gone on even so, but there was
a strange movement in his face—a moment's thoughtful calculation—
before he turned and hurried off.

In that brief instant she understood. Like her he had come here for a
reason.

Knowing there was no time to delay, she ran back down the street
and into the cut-through, almost colliding with him as he came down the
narrow passageway. Alarmed, she threw herself to the side, her shoulder
thudding against the wall, then whirled about, wide eyed.

Right. He went right.

She ran out into the street, knowing that if she lost him the trail would
be cold—knowing instinctively that whatever had happened here, he had
been a part of it. She looked along the length of the street, then saw him
as he disappeared into Sung Chen Avenue. If she didn't hurry she would
lose him in the crowd, yet if he knew she was following him . . .

She ran full pelt, dodging among the crowd of passersby, coming out
into the bustle of Sung Chen Avenue. For a moment she could see

nothing through the mass of bodies that moved between the stalls lining the thoroughfare. She pushed through, straining to see, hoping she'd perhaps get lucky, but within moments she knew it was hopeless. She was too small, the avenue too crowded. Unless she could get higher . . .

She looked about her. Nearby two men were unloading a rice cart, piling up the sacks, then hauling them up into the open-fronted first-floor storeroom of the grocer's shop above. Without stopping to think she pushed her way across and, grabbing a firm hold on the rope, hauled herself up. There, balanced on one of the sacks, she peered down the packed avenue, trying to make out her quarry.

There! She saw him almost straightaway. He was halfway down, near Ping So Street, pushing his way determinedly through the crowd, looking neither right nor left, but making a clear beeline for the fast-track station at the end of the avenue.

"Hey, you!"

She turned in time to see the owner of the shop coming at her from the back of the storeroom, a broom held out before him.

With a yelp she grabbed the rope again and swung, out over the cart, dropping onto the pile of sacks. The two loaders looked up at her, their mouths open wide in astonishment, but she was already gone, dodging and weaving through the dense-packed crowd, knowing that every second counted.

She came out into the station's entrance hall just in time to see him disappear through the barrier. At once she was after him, ducking through the automatic gate as it hissed open for a passenger, then scurrying down the steps, thinking of nothing now but catching up with him.

"Hey, mind!" someone yelled at her as she brushed against him, while another put an arm out, as if to stop her, but she skipped past him effortlessly.

Where was he? Where in the gods' names was he?

Coming out onto the platform, she stopped, getting her breath back, her eyes searching for him among the crowds that packed both sides of the line. At first she didn't see him, and began to wonder if she hadn't made a mistake—if she hadn't perhaps been chasing the wrong man. Then she saw him, on the other side of the platform, up the far end, going down the exit ramp.

Again she ran, weaving in and out, then hurtled across the narrow *covered bridge that linked the two platforms. She came out onto the far side just as an arriving fast-track was slowing. She hesitated, checking the nearest passengers, just in case she'd got it wrong, just in case he was there, about to board the train, but he wasn't there. Moving as fast as her feet could carry her, she ran down the exit ramp, heading for the barrier.*

*The guard made a grab at her as she ran toward him, but she side-stepped him, vaulting the low barrier as if it weren't there. Then she was outside, the guard's shouts echoing behind her.*

*Which way had he gone? Left toward Sung Chen Avenue? Or right toward the docks?*

*She guessed right and began to run, down the alley that curved beneath the fast-track lines, and out, into a narrow residential hutong, the back walls of tiled-roof houses to either side.*

*She had gone barely five paces along the hutong when a hand grabbed her from behind and, lifting her, whirled her about.*

*"Who are you?" he asked, his green eyes boring into her. "And why in the gods' names are you following me?"*

*"I—I . . ." But she could not get her breath. She hadn't considered what she'd say if she caught up with him.*

*"But you're just a girl," he said, frowning now. "You can't be any older than, what, six?"*

*"Seven," she said, swallowing deeply, trying—desperately trying—to be brave and not burst into tears.*

*Slowly he set her down.*

*"I don't understand. I thought . . ." He shook his head, then began again. "Look, what's your name?"*

*"Chuang Kuan Ts'ai."*

*He laughed, then grew serious again. "Coffin-filler? Is that really your name?"*

*She nodded.*

*"Well, Coffin-filler, why were you following me? And what were you doing at the club?"*

*For a moment she hesitated. What if she was wrong about him? What if he wasn't involved? What if he were Security? Yet there was something about him that made her trust him.*

*"I was trying to find out about a man."*

*"A man? What kind of man?"*

"A dead man."

He stared at her a long while, then smiled. "Okay, young Chuang, let's find a teahouse somewhere close by where we can have a bite and a talk. I think you've quite a story to tell me."

———————

THEY HAD THE EXECUTION on the waste ground behind the shoe factory. A crowd of several thousand gathered silently to watch, stunned by the news that the murderer had been so young, the crime so meaningless. The four judges had met early to weigh the evidence and, finding nothing that spoke clearly in the boy's favor, found against him, sentencing him to be shot that very afternoon at second bell.

Josef was standing on the wall at the back of the waste ground when they brought the boy out, his hands tied tightly behind his back, his head—newly shaven that morning—bowed low. Without ceremony he was marched out to the space that had been cleared before the crowd, where the Hsien Wei—the District Security Captain—read out the judges' sentence to him. Asked if he understood, the boy nodded, but it was clear he was in deep shock. As the guard made him kneel, he looked up, as if wondering where he was.

Too bad, Josef thought, the anticipation of what was to come making him tremble with excitement.

As one guard held the boy another came and stood behind him, arm outstretched stiffly, a cocked handgun in his hand, pointed at the back of his head. At a signal from the Captain the first guard jabbed a bayonet into the boy's back, making his muscles tense. A split second later the second guard fired the gun.

It was over. The boy was dead. Justice had been seen to be done. The crowd began to disperse.

Jumping down, Josef made his way across until he stood there, among several dozen others, looking down at the body.

"Bastard!" one man said, spitting on the corpse.

"Scum," another murmured, as all around the people nodded their agreement.

Josef smiled, then turned away. It had been so easy. Yet as he walked off, he caught the eye of a tall man in a long dark coat, who was standing waiting at the gate beside the factory.

"Oh, shit," Josef mumbled, looking about him for some other way out of the place. It was the Truant Officer. That was all he needed—to be dragged back to school and forced to sit in a dreary classroom all day.

Recognizing Josef, the man's eyes widened. He began to move toward him.

Josef turned and ran. Clambering up onto the wall, he ran along it, meaning to cross the roof of the factory and drop down into one of the alleys that ran alongside.

The Truant Officer's voice rang out at his back. "Hey, you! Boy! Stop where you are!"

"Go fuck yourself!" he shouted back, leaping a narrow parapet, then scampering up the gently sloping roof.

"I know where you live, boy! Don't think that I don't!"

Josef turned, looking back at the figure down below, then, turning his back contemptuously, slid down the other side of the roof and jumped.

Yes, he thought, getting up and dusting himself off, and I know where you live too!

But his day had been spoiled, the bloom taken off the afternoon. He spat, then kicked out angrily.

"Fuck him! Fuck him!"

Then, slowly, the memory came back of a kneeling, shaven-headed boy; of a gun glinting in the sunlight; of a bayonet stabbing into flesh . . . and then the detonation. He saw it vividly. Saw the bullet punch its way through the skull; saw the body jerk, then topple forward lifelessly.

And, walking on, he began to smile again, remembering.

# String and Glue

**Y**OUNG JI sat in the center of the yard, on a blanket in the sunlight, playing with the computer sketchpad Lin had recently repaired. He had been sitting there peacefully for an hour, absorbed in his game, no trouble at all. But then he never was. Of all her boys Ji was always the best behaved, always the last to complain.

The others were at school right now. It would be four, almost five hours before they got back. In the meantime she and Lin got on with things, making and mending, trying hard to forget that things had changed; that it would be a struggle from here on.

She moved from the doorway and looked back at Lin. "How's it going?" she asked quietly.

He looked up and gave a lopsided frown. "I need glue and string . . . oh, and a dozen other things."

"Make a list. I'll send Ji to Old Yang's. He'll enjoy that."

Lin grunted, then gave her a smile. "It'll be okay," he said, reassuring her for the tenth time that morning. "With Chao working at the big house and some of the other boys doing odd jobs here and there, we'll make do."

He scribbled out his list and handed it to her. "Tell Ji to ask Old Yang to put it on our bill. Once we sell the HeadStim we can repay him easily."

Lin had been working on the HeadStim half the night, but it would take several more sessions before it was working properly.

She took the list and stepped outside again. "Ji?"

The child turned and stared at her, his whole face breaking into a smile. "Yes, Mama Em?"

"Would you like to run an errand for me?"

"Ye-es!" He was on his feet in an instant and across to her.

"I want you to go to Old Yang's on Chang Chin Street. Here's a list of things Papa Lin wants. Tell Old Yang to put them on the bill. Okay?"

"Okay!" Ji snatched the note and turned, meaning to go at once, but she called him back.

"Ji? Hadn't you better take a back-sack?"

He stared at her, his mouth formed into an *oh* of forgetfulness, then smiled and nodded. He went across and stood on tiptoe, taking a back-sack from the hook, then pulled it on over his shoulders.

She almost laughed; he looked so comical with it on, like a soldier carrying an open tent on his back.

"Go on, then! But straight back, okay? No dawdling. Papa Lin needs those things so he can do his work."

"Yes, Mama Em!" Then he was gone.

She smiled then returned inside. There was washing to do, and the accounts hadn't been touched in over a week. And then there was mending to be done. There was always mending.

They needed a break, all of them, she realized. But life didn't give them any breaks. Life was unrelenting. There was always—always—more to be done. She smiled, accepting that, not for an instant wishing to change it for the life of ease, of luxury, she had once lived. No, even if this was hard, it was a far better way to live.

"You want some *ch'a*, Papa Lin?" she asked, looking across at him, feeling proud at that moment to have him as her partner.

He looked up and nodded distractedly, his scarred hands working ceaselessly. "That would be nice, Mama Em. Very nice indeed."

S U   P I N G   B O W E D   L O W , then took a small step backward, putting out his right hand in a gesture of welcome as the Commissioner for Mainz, Chu Te, stepped into his office.

Su Ping had had his staff form up behind him. Now, with the smallest motion of his head, he dismissed them. As the last of them filed out, he closed the door and turned, facing his superior.

Chu Te was sitting in his seat, his hands on the edge of the desk, as if trying out the position for himself. He smiled at Su Ping, then leaned forward and picked up the file, flicking it open in an almost desultory fashion. He glanced at one or two papers, then closed the file, as if satisfied.

"It is her, isn't it?" Su Ping said, nervous anxiety making his voice rise slightly.

"It would seem so."

"Then what are we to do? Arrest her?"

Chu Te's smile tightened. "*We* do nothing. *I* take over from here on."

"Ah . . ." It was not what Su Ping had expected, yet having chosen this course of action he could not very well step back from it. He had done his duty and informed his superior; now the matter was out of his hands. Even so, he felt an acute disappointment.

"You did well, *Hsien L'ing* Su," Chu Te said, standing, the file tucked safely under his arm. "You can be sure I will mention your part in this when I make my report to the Ministry."

Su Ping bowed his head. That much good at least would come of this. But still he didn't *feel* good. He had done his duty, certainly, but he could not keep from thinking of the woman—thinking of what he'd set in train. The very thought of it made him feel ill at ease with himself, somehow *unclean.*

But what else *could* he have done? As soon as the file was pulled, he had placed himself in jeopardy. To know and not to have acted would have been as bad as to condone her crimes. He would have become a criminal, a traitor. And not only he but all his family as well—to the third generation. His grandsons, his baby granddaughter: they, too, would have suffered had he not informed Chu Te.

Even so . . .

He bowed low, letting the Commissioner move past him, then followed him through into the entrance hall, bidding him farewell, watching as the great man strode out into the main yard of the *yamen*.

Su Ping had been smiling; a stiff, courteous smile, perfected across the four decades he had been an official. Now that smile bleached from his face. What was his twin brother, Su Chun, doing by the gate? What business had *he* coming here? He started forward, meaning to speak to him, then stopped dead. Su Chun was smiling, speaking to Chu Te as the Commissioner closed the gap between them. The two embraced, grinning like old friends. Then, Su Chun's arm about the great man's shoulder—a gesture so familiar, so out of character with Chu Te's high rank, that it shocked Su Ping—the two turned and strolled toward the gate and Su Chun's waiting sedan.

Su Ping stared, his face hardening, the certainty of what had happened growing in him. They had made a deal, the two of them—a sordid little deal! He shuddered, a bolt of anger—pure anger—flashing through him like lightning. For one brief, uncontrolled moment he felt like rushing out and striking Su Chun, smashing his brother's grinning face with his fists, but the moment passed. Besides, what could he do? Nothing!

The thought fed his anger, stoked it into a blazing fury.

Su Ping turned abruptly and went inside, slamming his door behind him, then sat at his desk, chewing at a nail, his normally placid face distorted by the anger and frustration he felt.

Nothing. He could do nothing. . . .

━━━━━

EMILY STEPPED OUT from the kitchen, drying her hands, then looked about her.

"Lin? Have you seen Ji?"

Lin Shang looked up distractedly. "Isn't he back?"

She shrugged, then walked across, pushing open the door between the yards. "Ji?"

There was no answer. The outer yard was empty.

"That's odd," she said. "He should have been back long ago."

"You think he's okay?"

She smiled. "I'm sure he's fine. It's just . . ."

"You're worried, neh? The situation. . . ."

She nodded.

"Then go. He's probably dawdling somewhere. Daydreaming. You know how he is."

"Okay. I'll not be long. We'll have some soup when I get back."

He nodded, already concentrating on his work again.

She went through, checking Ji's sleeping cubicle just in case, then went out into the street. It was almost eleven-thirty and the thoroughfare was busy. She pushed through, greeting people as she went, smiling all the while, concealing the concern she felt.

It was true what Lin said. Ji often dawdled, often daydreamed, but not when he was sent on a specific task—not when he knew Papa Lin needed things urgently. Nor was he really all that late—twenty, twenty-five minutes at most—it was just that with things in flux and Triad runners on the streets . . .

*I shouldn't have sent him,* she thought, angry with herself. *I should have taken the time and gone myself.* But it was too late now. All she wanted was to be reassured that he was okay, to see his smiling face as he came toward her.

As she walked, she looked from side to side, scanning the crowd, making sure she didn't pass him on the way.

At Peter's fruit stall in Fen Chung Street she stopped to ask if the old man had seen Ji.

"A while back. I gave him an apple. Said he was heading for Old Yang's. He late or something?"

"A little," she said, and hurried on.

Old Yang's was in Cicada Lane, tucked in between a clothes shop and a men's hairdresser's. She pushed through the jumble of buckets and brooms and bowls at the front and went into the deep shadow of the interior.

"Yang Wei?" she called, trying to get her eyes accustomed to the darkness inside.

"Mama Em?" a voice answered from the back; a voice every bit as old and creaking as the man who emerged from between the well-stocked shelves that packed the tiny hardware shop. "Did young Ji forget something?"

"He's been, then?"

Old Yang stared at her, concerned. "A long while back. More than half an hour. Why, isn't he home yet?"

"No." Emily felt cold. She looked about her, not knowing what to do.

"String and glue, he bought. And other things." Yang turned. "Here, I have the list. . . ."

She reached out and touched the old man's back gently. "It's okay, Yang Wei. He's probably wandering the back alleys somewhere, daydreaming. You know how young boys are."

Yang turned, facing her again, an understanding smile on his deeply lined face. "So it is, Mama Em. So it is."

She bowed, then turned, hurrying away. But out in the street she stopped again.

What *was* she to do? Go back and wait? Search the streets? Or should she go to the *yamen* and report him missing?

She swallowed, suddenly, inexplicably frightened. He'd just gone on an errand, that was all. He'd done it dozens of times before. Dozens.

Home, she decided. It was best to go home and tell Lin. Then she would go out and try to find him.

Unless . . .

She looked about her at the narrow thoroughfare, then went across to one of the stalls on the far side, marching straight up to the woman seated there.

"Did you see a little boy come out of Old Yang's, oh, thirty minutes back? About this high? A young Han with shaven hair."

The old woman coughed and spat, then looked at Emily again, shaking her head. "Can't say I did. He yours?"

She nodded.

"Then you should have taken better care of him!"

Emily stared at the woman a moment, then turned away. Another time she might have answered back, but just now Ji's safety was her prime concern. Besides, there was a degree of truth in what the old hag had said: she *should* have taken greater care.

She went along the line of stalls, asking one after another if they had seen Ji, but no one, it seemed, had seen a boy matching Ji's description come out of Old Yang's.

Worried now, she turned away, leaving Cicada Lane, making her way back hurriedly through the midday crowds, her eyes searching all the while for Ji's tiny figure among them.

*He's home already,* she told herself, trying to keep her spirits up. *He probably got home just after I set out. Even now, Papa Lin will be cooking him soup and cutting him some bread. . . .*

But what if he wasn't?

A flash of pure despair made her groan. What if someone had taken him? What if one of the *liu mang*—the Triad punks—had recognized him and pulled him off the street? What if those bastards had him, even now?

Again she moaned, doubling her pace, almost colliding with people as she dodged in and out of the crowd, the thought of Ji in their hands making her stomach muscles clench with anxiety.

*Be safe!* she urged, as she came out into the marketplace. *For the gods' sake be there for me, Ji, when I get home!*

She began to cut through the milling crowd, heading for the southeast corner of the marketplace, but she had barely made it halfway across when shots rang out and the crowd began to scream and panic. Someone banged into her, almost knocking her over, and then it was chaos. Stalls were going over and there were more shots, more screams.

As people fought to get away, Emily was jostled violently. Alarmed now, she cried out. If Ji were somewhere in this crowd . . .

As the crowd began to thin, she looked about her anxiously. Several people were down, shot or simply trampled, she couldn't tell, but there was no one who looked like Ji. Across from her, twenty, maybe thirty *ch'i* away, a dozen or more Triad runners were struggling with a group of stallholders. Even as she looked, one of the runners raised his gun and, placing it to one of the stallholder's head, fired. The man jerked, then fell lifelessly, like a puppet whose strings had been cut.

She stared, appalled, unaware that she was in any danger until a shot whizzed past her head. Only then did she wake and begin to back away.

The runners were moving from stall to stall, firing indiscriminately—executing anyone who dared get in their way.

*It has begun again,* she thought, knowing that her worst fears had just been confirmed.

And Ji? She could only pray now that Ji had made it safely home. If home was any longer safe.

————————

YOUNG EGAN WAS IN HIS BED, half conscious after sleeping off the previous night's excesses, when the slatted blinds in his room were opened, letting in the brilliant morning sunlight.

He groaned and buried his head in his pillow. "Is that you, Kuei Jen?"

His answer was a pair of hands on his shoulders, shaking him. "Get up, you lazy reprobate. We need to talk."

Egan rolled over, onto his back, staring up blearily at the young Prince, who sat on the bed beside him.

"What in heaven's name do you want at this hour? Is it evening yet? No. Well, then, leave me be. I need my rest."

Kuei Jen reached out, shaking him again. "Awake! We have to talk."

"Talk?" Egan made a distasteful movement with his lips. "Hey . . . pass me some of that cordial. My mouth's as dry as an old whore's clout!"

"And as foul."

Kuei Jen reached across and poured a glass of lime juice from the jug, then handed it to him. Egan struggled up onto one elbow, drained the glass, and handed it back.

"Thanks."

"So?" Kuei Jen asked, eyeing him sternly. "What's all this about a campaign in Asia? Why didn't you tell me?"

Egan eased himself back against the headboard and shrugged. "Because I was asked not to."

"By who?"

"Whom. The word is *whom.*"

"Okay. By whom?"

"By your father. And by my grandfather."

"And you didn't think I might need to know?"

Again Egan shrugged. "I didn't think it was important."

"Not important?" The young Prince rolled his eyes. "*Aiya!* What could be more important?"

"You marrying the Princess."

"We were betrothed as children."

"Yes, but you didn't tell me."

Kuei Jen shrugged and looked away, not wanting to meet those accusing eyes. "I thought you'd have known. It is our way."

"And me?"

He looked back, meeting his lover's eyes. "I'll always be here for you."

But Egan's eyes held a query. "What if you like it?"

"Like it?"

"Fucking her. What if you find out that you're not . . ."

". . . a yellow eel?"

Egan nodded, then looked down. "What if?" he said quietly, clearly upset by the thought.

"I won't," Kuei Jen said, reaching out to take his hand. "It'll be duty, that's all. To make sons."

Egan looked up again, a slight mischievousness in his eyes now. "You could always have her inseminated. That way I could have a hand in it!"

The young prince snorted. "And more than a hand in it, if I know you!"

"Now, now . . ."

There was a moment's silence. The two young men stared at each other affectionately.

Egan shivered, then pushed down the sheet, his eyes changing. "You want to fuck me?"

Kuei Jen sat back, alarmed. "Shit, no! Not here in the palace!"

"Why not? There are no cameras in the room. Go on, Jenny, lock the door. It seems like ages since we fucked."

Kuei Jen shivered, clearly tempted by the thought; by the sight of his lover's nakedness. He swallowed, then stood and went across, turning the key in the lock.

"The blinds," Egan said. "For the gods' sakes, close the blinds."

The young Prince went across and tugged on the rope. At once the room was in semidarkness.

"Here," Egan said, putting out a hand. "Come and kiss me."

Kuei Jen hesitated, then went across and, slipping out of his clothes, climbed in beside him, taking him in his arms.

"What would your father say?" Egan said with a soft chuckle as he began to kiss his shoulder and neck. "What *would* he say?"

———————

D O G O   W A S   S H O W E R I N G , soaping himself down and singing to himself, his deep voice booming in that huge, tiled space, when he heard the door click in the room next door.

His voice faltered briefly, then went on as he stepped from beneath the flow and padded quietly to the bathroom door. He was about to call out, to ask who it was, when he saw her.

It was one of Shepherd's women. The red-haired one, Catherine. And she was going through his clothes, picking them up and sniffing them.

Still singing, his eyes looking about for somewhere to hide, he went back to the shower. Maybe she'd go away. Maybe she'd—

The door slid back. Unembarrassed, her eyes smiling at him, she stepped inside. The tune died on his lips. The Osu put his hands down, covering his manhood.

"Dogo? It *is* Dogo, isn't it?"

"Do-*go*," he answered, giving the correct pronunciation.

"Do-*go*," she said, copying it perfectly. She stepped closer, her eyes taking in his nakedness, studying him as if she were appreciating some work of art. "You're a fine figure of a man, Do-*go*. And single, I hear. Why's that?"

He shrugged, not wanting to go into the business of his ex-wife. "You want something?" he asked, too polite to ask her to get the hell out of there. Besides, he was intrigued. What *did* she want?

Her smile gave him the answer.

"Ah . . ." He swallowed. Beneath his covering hands his manhood had betrayed him; had risen stiff and hard at the mere thought of being there, naked, with the woman.

She turned, looking about her, then stepped across and took his loincloth from the peg where he'd hung it. Turning back, she went across and held it out, offering it to him.

He reached to take it and as he did, she dropped it, reaching past him to take hold of his swollen penis.

"What's this?" she asked, looking down at it. "Is it *real?*" Then, looking up again, meeting his eyes, she smiled—the kind of smile that makes a man's heart melt, his pulse quicken. "You know, I've never seen one *that* color!"

━━━━━━

A S   T H E   G A T E   swung slowly back, Emily was conscious of the absence of any sound, of the unnatural stillness of the compound. Fear made her whisper the word.

"*Lin . . . ?*"

Nothing. The outer courtyard was silent, the open-fronted stalls where the boys would sit and work and sleep were empty. She stepped inside, her heart hammering in her chest, her mouth dry with fear.

Forcing herself to be calm, she crossed the yard, treading silently.

The door to the inner yard was ajar. Gently, fearful of what she'd find, she pushed it back.

The normally tidy yard was a mess. The tables were pushed over, broken things were scattered everywhere in heaps, pulled down from the shelves where they'd been stored. And in their midst sat Lin, staring at his hands, his black hair spiky and disheveled, his plain cloth *pau* torn in several places. His lip was cut, his neck scratched and bruised. His hands, which she had nursed to health the last time they'd been smashed, were bruised and swollen, at least three fingers broken on each hand.

"Lin?" she asked softly, taking a step toward him, clearing a space with her right foot, careful not to tread on anything. "*Lin?* What happened?"

Slowly his head came up. Slowly, as if from a long way off, he focused on her. He had been crying.

Kneeling beside him, she cradled him to her, comforting him as he began to sob.

"Lin . . . Papa Lin, what happened here?"

She felt the shuddering breath he took before he met her eyes again; saw in his face the effort it took him even to speak.

"They came back. Another hundred *yuan* they wanted, but I didn't have it, Mama Em . . . I *didn't* have it . . . so they . . . they . . ."

He dropped his head, trembling now, unable to continue.

She shivered, suddenly indignant. Until a few days back this had been a good place to live, but now the insects from the other side of the river were moving in, sucking the life blood from them, taking the very marrow from their bones.

Emily stood, seeing clearly what had to be done. Yet as she made to leave, Lin put out a hand, holding her leg.

"Don't."

She looked down. He was staring up at her.

"Don't what?"

He looked at her a moment longer, reading her face, seeing clearly what she was thinking, then shook his head. "There must be no violence. Whatever happens, we *must not* stoop to their level."

"But they'll bleed us dry."

"Then we shall work harder and eat less."

"And still they'll ask for more. Besides, how will you work now, Lin Shang? Your hands . . ."

He considered that a moment, then shrugged. "Maybe so, but there must be no violence. It is the Way."

Had anyone else have said it she would have laughed scornfully at them, but this was Lin, her life partner, and though he was wrong, she could not laugh at him for believing what he did.

He opened his mouth again, meaning, no doubt, to offer up some other snippet from the sages—some parable to comfort her— but she had had enough.

"Can't you see, Lin Shang? Can't you *see* what's happening? The dream has ended. *Wuwei* is no answer anymore. We're back in the real world again." She shuddered. "I was in the marketplace just now. They were going from stall to stall, *killing* people."

She saw the shock in his eyes at that and was sorry that she had had to be the one to put it there, but it was kinder not to let him hope anymore; kinder to be cruel.

"And Ji?" he asked.

It was her turn to feel shock. She had forgotten. For a moment she had forgotten Ji entirely.

"*Aiya . . .*"

She turned, stumbling through the door, and as she did the gate on the far side of the courtyard swung open, slowly, as if in a nightmare, and a man stepped in: one of the stallholders from Cicada Lane. He was cradling something—something small and limp and broken. Something that no amount of mending would ever make right.

She cried out and fell to her knees. Behind her she heard Lin Shang groan—a sound of emptiness and despair.

"I'm sorry," the man said, coming closer. "I . . ."

Gently he put his burden down. Slowly, he knelt, tenderly brushing the dark hair back from the dead boy's eyes.

Emily swallowed, steeling herself to ask. "Where . . . ?"

"In Old Yang's. At the back of the shop, under some sacks."

She stared at him, her eyes aghast. The words hissed from her in a whisper. "Impossible. I went there. . . ."

"It was after you had gone, Mama Em. Some of us thought how odd it was. We had seen him go in, but none of us—not one—had seen him come out again. We checked."

For a moment the pain was too much—she couldn't speak. Then, "And Old Yang?"

"He's dead. We stoned the old cunt."

She groaned. Old Yang would *never* have harmed Ji, she'd wager her life on it. No. The runners had done this. The *liu mang*. And Old Yang had got the blame.

"Thank you, I—"

Behind him the gate creaked. Two more stood there. Young men with bands about their foreheads. Triad runners.

She had barely seen them, barely focused on them, when she heard Lin bellow and rush past her.

She saw the gun come up, saw—so vividly, it sent a nervous ripple up her spine—the hammer come down on the firing pin, and thought she must be in shock, because she heard no detonation. Then she understood. The punk had used up his bullets.

As Lin crashed into them, she leapt up, going to his aid, jumping over the kneeling man, over the tiny figure of her darling Ji, hatred blinding her to anything but hitting back.

Old memories shaped her fist into a deadly weapon, and as the young punk's face turned, surprised, to look at her, so she struck, the venom of the blow carrying him back into his fellow, the front of his skull shattered like a fragile piece of porcelain.

Such hatred. She had never felt such hatred. She stood over the dead man, tensed, her whole body trembling, watching as the other crawled away and through the gate, wide eyed with shock and fear.

Slowly she turned, looking to where Lin Shang lay, retching, winded by the young punk's first and final blow.

"It's over," she said, turning, the tears beginning to fall as she looked once more at the tiny body stretched out on the cobbles. "It's finished, Papa Lin."

But she knew it wasn't over. No. This was only the beginning.

━━━━━━

SU PING was pacing his office, trying to work out what to do—how to control the situation—when the door burst open. He turned, startled, expecting trouble, but it was only his recently appointed Third Secretary. Calming himself, he sat behind his desk.

"What is it, Mao Kuang-li? More deaths? More butchery?"

"A report has just come in, *Hsien L'ing*. It seems the compound was attacked."

"The compound?"

"Where the woman is."

"Ah . . ." He studied the young man, wondering just how much he knew, then nodded. "And the woman? Is she hurt?"

"No, Master. It seems she is all right. But she has killed a man. A Triad runner."

Su Ping jumped up out of his chair. "*Killed* a man! *Aiya!* Does the Commissioner know?"

"Not yet, Master. One of your guards brought in the report a moment back."

"And my *Wei*, Kung Chia? Has anyone found the man yet? I asked him to report an hour back!"

The young man's eyes slid away. "Did you not know, Master?"

"Know? Know what?"

Mao Kuang-li looked back at him. "That Kung Chia is dining with your brother and the Commissioner. It seems they are old friends."

Su Ping sat again, nodding to himself. At last all the pieces fitted. By rights this was a matter for his *Wei*, or for the Commissioner, but he knew now he could trust neither. They were all in this together. Besides, he had already made one mistake today; he was buggered if he was going to make another.

Mao Kuang-li bowed. "You wish me to inform him, Master?"

"No." He got up, a sense of inevitability shaping his movements. "No, I will go myself. I would not wish to bother His Excellency, the Commissioner for Mainz."

The young man smiled. "Then I shall order your sedan, Master."

THEY HAD WASHED HIS TINY, broken body and wrapped him in a simple white cloth. Dragging his bunk out into the center of the yard, they had placed what remained of their cooking fuel beneath it and laid his body on it. The boys—brought home from school by neighbors—had lined up in front of him to say their last farewells; then, after a few last words from Mama Em, they had set fire to the stack.

As she watched the funeral bier burn, Emily tried hard to think of how he'd been—of Ji's liveliness and his infectious smile—but all she could think of was the hideous grin on the *liu mang's* face shortly before she'd killed him.

She wiped the tears from her face with her fingers then turned away, gathering her seven remaining boys about her. On the far side of the yard, Lin Shang was standing, looking on, his hands bandaged, his face ashen, tearstained. In a short while they would be gone from here. In just a moment all of this—this happiest phase of her brief life on earth—would have ended and they would be fugitives.

She took a shuddering breath, trying to keep control of herself, trying hard—oh, so hard—not to break down, because they needed her. Needed her more now than they'd ever needed her.

She was trembling. As the boys held on to her, sobbing inconsolably, she could feel them shaking, trembling, against her.

Awful, it was. So awful she could not fully comprehend just what had happened. She had seen death a hundred times, but never had it touched her quite like this. Never had it made her feel like simply lying down and sleeping, never to wake.

She longed now for surcease, longed for an end to the agony she was suffering, but knew it could not be. She had to lead them from here . . . to take care of them and make sure they were safe. She had to—or Ji's death meant nothing.

The flames were roaring fiercely now as they consumed his tiny body, the black smoke from the bier forming a tall plume in the blue sky overhead. It was hot in the yard and the smell of burning strong.

She looked down, seeing how the boys' eyes were drawn to the flames, their hurt subsumed temporarily into a deeper, more primal fascination with the elemental power of fire.

She forced herself to break into their trance. "Boys! Get your packs! Chao . . . Pei . . . bring the cart. It's time to go."

They did as they were told, quietly, unquestioningly, and as she watched them she knew she had been right to end it thus. At least this way they knew where Ji had gone. This way, at least, they knew his spirit soul was free.

She shivered, then went across to Lin.

"Are you ready?" she asked gently.

He nodded, unable to speak, his bandaged hands pulled up to his chest.

"Then let's go. They'll be here soon."

But even as she spoke the words, there was a hammering on the gate, a call from outside—a soldierly voice, heavy with authority.

"Open up! Open up in the name of the law!"

She saw how the boys turned, looking to her, like frightened animals. But what could she do? What could she, a single woman, do against the rule of law? Once she had thought differently, but now . . .

No. She had killed a man. Word of that would have got back. And now they had come for her.

Slowly, as in a dream, she walked across and lifted the latch, letting the outer door swing back. The *Hsien L'ing* was standing there, a dozen of his troops behind him.

"Emily Ascher?" he said, his grave eyes meeting hers. "I have a warrant here for your arrest on the grounds of treason. Will you come peacefully, or shall I have my men arrest you?"

LI YUAN signed the document with a flourish, then sat back, letting out a weary sigh, and looked to his Chancellor.

"Is that all, Master Heng? Are we done?"

Heng Yu stared back at him, surprised. He had a stack of documents under his arm that required attention. *"Chieh Hsia?"*

"I mean . . . is there anything *really* urgent? Can those papers not wait a day or two?"

Again Heng simply stared. This was most unlike his Master. "I— I guess so, *Chieh Hsia.*"

"Then let us do that, neh?" He stood and stretched. "If you want me, I shall be in the stables."

Heng bowed his head. *"Chieh Hsia."*

When he'd gone, Li Yuan went to the window and looked across, wondering what Dragon Heart was doing at that moment. He had the urge to go to her and talk with her again; to kiss her and lie with her again.

*Aiya,* he thought, remembering what had happened between them in the night; *but that's a delicious torment.*

She had been as good as her word. As good, and no more. He had tried to persuade her, but she was like iron, unyielding. She would do anything but *that.* Anything but let him make love to her.

He clenched his fists, thinking of it, imagining it. Gods, he could think of nothing else, it seemed. Even just now, signing those awful mundane documents, his mind had been going back over what had passed between them, seeing her naked body moving next to his, each curve of hers like an arrow piercing him.

It was no good. He would have to see her. See her and throw himself on her mercy. He had to—just *had* to—have her.

And what if he *was* twice her age and more? What if he *was* older than her father? What did that matter? It was how they felt about each other that mattered. That and nothing else.

But she was still betrothed.

He turned, staring at his desk thoughtfully. It would take but a moment to undo that. He needed but a piece of paper, an ink brush, and a seal. And then?

Li Yuan sniffed deeply. He could do it. He could summon Heng Yu and do it right now if he so wished, but something held his hand. An instinct, perhaps. That and the certain knowledge that no good would come of it. No, it was not done for a T'ang to meddle in the marital affairs of the Minor Families. Not without unquestionable cause.

Even so, he had to have her. After last night . . .

He caught his breath, remembering her eyes as she looked at him along the length of his body, smiling as she took him in her mouth.

"Aiya . . ." he murmured, closing his eyes, his penis stiff at the memory. When had he ever felt this way. Why, even with Fei Yen . . .

His eyes popped open. No. No comparisons. Comparisons were dangerous. This was different. What he felt now was . . . well, unique. He had not felt it before. It was as if he had been dead before he'd met her, and now . . .

Again he shuddered. Then, knowing he needed to do something, he hurried across the room, heading for the stables, determined to work his way out of this distracted mood.

━━━━━━

SU PING had not known quite what he'd find, but the woman's tears were wholly unexpected. He saw the remains of the tiny body on the collapsed bier, saw the tearful, frightened faces all around, and understood. No one had told him about the boy. No one had thought to. Once more events had overtaken him.

He had come here meaning to arrest her, as he'd said—to take her back to his *yamen* and book her in officially as a captive of the State. That way his duty would have been done. That way no blood money would have found its way into those jackals' pockets. But now . . .

He turned abruptly, gesturing to his men. "Get out!" he said sharply. "Go back to the *yamen* and await me there!"

"But, Master . . ." his Third Secretary began.

"Now!" he barked.

Mao Kuang-li bowed, then turned away, ushering the others out.

Su Ping turned back. The woman stood there helplessly, her arms at her sides, her face tear washed and vacant, no different from any mother who had just lost her youngest son. In that instant his heart went out to her. In that one brief moment a life-time's habit was broken.

"You must go," he said quietly.

She turned her head slowly, looking at him. "What?"

"You must go from here at once," he said, more businesslike this time. "You should head northwest, into the forest."

"The forest?" Slowly enlightenment dawned in her face. "You're letting us go?"

He nodded. "But you must be quick. The Commissioner is here from Mainz. He knows who you are. And my brother . . ." He shuddered, unable to keep the distaste, the anger, he was feeling out of his face. "I shall try to delay them, to lay a false trail, but you must move quickly. You must get there before nightfall."

She was staring at him now, amazed. "Why?"

"Because."

She nodded, as if understanding, then turned, gathering her boys about her. Satisfied, she looked back at him. "Thank you, *Hsien L'ing.*"

He shook his head. "You need thank me for nothing, Emily Ascher. I saw your file. It made interesting reading." He smiled sadly. "I feel I know you well."

She shuddered, then, with a simple nod, moved quickly past, leading her boys away from there. Giving them a chance.

Su Ping turned, watching them go, the Mender, Lin Shang, last to leave, his eyes looking wistfully about the yard, lingering on the burned-out bier, tears welling, spilling down his cheeks. Then he, too, was gone and Su Ping was alone in the empty yard.

"Good luck," he whispered. "I hope you make it."

And himself? He laughed bitterly. There was nowhere he could run. He gazed about him; then, deciding that this was as good a place as any to await his fate, he went across and sat cross-legged beside the yet-smoldering bier, knowing it would not be long.

S U  C H U N looked up from his plate and burped loudly. Facing him, smiling at him across a table stacked high with empty dishes, was Commissioner Chu.

"Well," said Chu, "I think we have covered everything. Half to you, Su Chun, half to me. All we need now is to pick the woman up."

Su Chun frowned and picked at his teeth. "You are quite certain my brother will do nothing?"

"What *can* he do? Besides, I have told him to leave matters in my hands. You know your brother—he has an exaggerated sense of duty."

Su Chun laughed. "The fool!"

"Indeed. Yet in case he *should* think to meddle in such matters, I have been careful to ensure that nothing is on record. Only you, he, and I know of this matter."

"But what if he objects? What if he reports you to some higher authority?"

"Then it will be his word against mine, and they will take his words as that of an embittered, envious old buffoon. A man jealous of his brother's fortune and seeking to use his official status to destroy him."

"They will see it that way?"

Chu Te smiled slyly. "I shall make sure they see it that way."

"And if they investigate your accounts?"

"They will find nothing. There will be no trail from your door to mine, I assure you, Su Chun. We have friends in common who can take care of such matters, neh?"

"And afterward?"

Chu Te turned his head and spat into the bowl beside his foot. "Afterward we shall stay in touch. You will help me and I will help you. To both our advantages, neh?"

"So it will be," Su Chun said, lifting his wine cup in a toast and grinning from ear to ear. "So it will be."

"Master?"

Su Chun turned and looked to the man who had just come into the room. "Yes, Peng, what is it?"

"There has been trouble, Master, at the compound."

Su Chun sat up, instantly alert. "Trouble? What kind of trouble?"

"One of our men is dead. Tu Fan. The old woman killed him."

"*Killed* him?" Su Chun shook his head and laughed. "You jest with me, surely, Peng? The *old woman?*"

Peng bent low, his whole manner apologetic. "Yes, Master. It seems she broke his neck."

Su Chun's mouth slowly dropped open. He turned, looking to the Commissioner. "So it's true?"

"Of course," Chu Te said, wiping his mouth and standing up, suddenly businesslike. "I told you, Su Chun. She is a dangerous woman. We must go there at once with a squad of your men and arrest her, before further damage is done."

"Killed him?" Su Chun said again, his voice almost a whisper, still unable to believe it. Then, looking to the Commissioner again, he scrambled to his feet and, calling his men to him, began to do as Chu Te said.

━━━━━

KUNG CHIA, who had gone ahead, met them at the gate to the compound. His men formed a cordon about the entrance, holding back the crowd.

"They've gone," he said, anticipating Chu Te's question. "But we've caught another fish. Su Ping."

"My brother? *Here?*" Su Chun pushed through, then stood there, staring in amazement at the seated figure of Su Ping. He turned to the *Wei*.

"Why is *he* here?"

"He let them get away."

"He *what?*"

Kung Chia drew Su Chun closer, lowering his voice. "From what I can make out he came here to arrest the woman, but something changed his mind."

Chu Te, who had listened patiently, now pushed past and strode across the courtyard, stopping over the seated figure. With a brief, distasteful glance at the bier he addressed Su Ping, his anger barely contained.

"What is the meaning of this, *Hsien L'ing* Su? I gave you specific orders to leave this matter in *my* hands!"

Su Ping looked up at him, a weary, resigned look in his eyes. "I know."

"Then why in the gods' names are you here? And why"—Chu Te sputtered, almost losing control—"why did you let them go?"

Su Ping met his superior's eyes calmly, no hint of shame in his own. "I did it to spite you. You and that insect who calls himself my brother." He paused, then, slowly, began to smile. "I did something clean at last. I *helped* her."

Su Chun, who had stood two paces off, listening, now bellowed and threw himself at his twin, putting both hands about Su Ping's throat and dragging him to his feet, shaking him, slowly choking him.

"Enough!" Chu Te ordered, his hands beating at Su Chun's back. *"Aiya!* Let him go!"

Su Chun gave his brother one last, violent shake then let him fall.

Su Ping collapsed, gasping, one hand holding him up while the other tore at his throat. His eyes were huge and swollen in his reddened face. He retched, then retched again.

Su Chun staggered back, his eyes wild, his face animated by fury. "Let me kill him! Let me finish him right now!"

Chu Te put his hand on Su Chun's shoulder. "Kill him and we've no one to blame. Besides, he'll die anyway for what he's done."

Su Chun groaned. "A million *yuan* . . . gone!" He swung with his left foot, his boot connecting firmly in Su Ping's stomach, making him double up again, wheezing.

*"Desist!"* Chu Te said, pulling Su Chun away, then signaling for the *Wei* to take care of him. "The money's lost. Our main concern now is to find out where the woman's gone."

Su Chun grunted. "Who gives a shit now?"

Chu Te turned to him, his eyes glaring. "It matters greatly. Though your half-wit brother here broke orders, it was I who was in charge of this investigation, and it will be I who gets the ultimate blame should the woman escape. And if *I* am blamed, you can be sure that *you* will go down with me, Su Chun. In fact, I can *guarantee* it!"

He turned back, looking at Su Ping, who was still struggling to get his breath, then leaned toward him.

"Okay, Su Ping. You've had your fun. Now it's my turn. You want an easy death, you'll tell me where they went, and you'll tell me now."

Su Ping shuddered, then forced his head up. His face was ashen, like a dead man's, but his eyes were defiant.

"You can go fuck yourself," he whispered hoarsely.

Chu Te straightened, then turned, beckoning to one of his men. "Chain him up and take him back to the *yamen*. We'll see what an hour's close questioning will drag from him."

---

T O M   W A S   L Y I N G on the bed in his room, his hands behind his head, his eyes closed, daydreaming of the girl, when his half-sister, Sasha, who had been creeping up on him unawares, leapt on his chest.

He fought the ten-year-old off, then sat back, smiling at her as he signed with his hands.

*When did you get here?*

The flame-haired little girl crossed her legs, facing him on the bed, then signed back.

*An hour ago. I flew in with Ebert's son.*

He made a gesture of understanding, then held out his arms, cuddling her to him. Distracted as he was, he was pleased to see her.

"What's it like here?" she asked quietly.

He shrugged and made a face. He didn't like it much. He missed the open spaces of the valley. Besides . . .

She saw the movement in his face and frowned. "What is it?"

He hesitated, then shook his head. *Nothing*, he signed.

*I don't believe you*, she signed back.

He laughed silently.

*When you're older*, he signed.

"Ah, girls. . . ." And she stared at him knowingly, making him blush.

"Where's my mother?" she asked. "She wasn't in her rooms."

He looked down. He knew, but he wasn't going to say.

*How did they go?* he signed, after a moment, looking back at her.

Sasha had stayed on after they'd left the valley to take her external exams. If she passed she would get a place in one of the City's leading schools.

She shrugged. *Okay*, she signed.

*I bet you get a merit,* he signed back.

"Maybe . . ." Then she laughed. "So . . . who's the girlfriend? You'd better tell me or I'll tickle you!"

~~~~~~

"HERE, MAMA EM? CAN WE STOP HERE?"

"Just a bit farther," she answered gently, knowing that none of them could go on that much longer. She turned, looking back through the trees at the straggling line. It was growing dark and they would soon have to find shelter for the night. They had been traveling more than six hours now, and some of the boys were well beyond their limits, but it could not be helped; the farther they went from Weisenau, the better chance they had. That was, if they had any chance at all after what had happened.

For the last few *li* they had been climbing steadily, through country that had never been built upon, not even in the heyday of the City, but now they were descending once again, moving down through a broad valley lined with trees.

Away, always away. But however far she traveled she knew it would never be far enough, for the hurt went with her every step.

She stopped, letting them catch up, Chao, who had been pulling the cart this last hour, the last to join the group standing between the trees.

"I'll scout ahead," she said, conscious, now that they were gathered all about her, just how ragged they looked, how weary. "Wait here awhile. I'll not be long."

There was no argument. She saw how grateful they were to slump down and rest for those brief few minutes, even Lin Shang.

She turned and went on, down toward the valley floor, following an old gully. Halfway down she found her way blocked by a low wall. Making her way around it, she realized what it was—the ruined shell of an ancient house. Others stood close by: dark, ghostly shapes between the trees, their jagged walls open to the sky. She nodded to herself, understanding. This had been a village. People had lived here once; had worked and raised their families. She shuddered. So much was lost. Sometimes it seemed that the whole of existence was but a dark and fitful dream.

She went on, the full moon lighting her way.

On leaving the compound she had taken them west, following the curve of the river down to Ockenheim, then north, crossing the river by the Rudesheim bridge. There, beyond Marienthal *Hsien*, the forest began.

For thousands of years there had been nothing but the forest— long before men had come, long before the first cities had been built. But men *had* come and in time they had destroyed the forests. They had had to build machines—machines that tapped into the earth's core for energy and synthesized the very air they breathed.

Until ten years ago, that was, when the Clayborn, Kim Ward, through his company, had reseeded large parts of the ancient forests with new, fast-growing pines; hybrids manufactured in his laboratories in Heidelberg.

Emily walked on, hurrying now, conscious that just ahead of her the trees ended in a shining, glittering line.

*Water . . . there was water down there!*

She began to run, then slowed, the truth hitting her like a fist in the stomach.

There, where the trees ended, the land stretched away, flat, perfectly flat, and smooth like a frozen lake. She stepped out onto it, her booted feet clicking against the hard, clear polymer.

Faces stared up at her, clawing hands reached, trapped forever in the ice.

She walked slowly, in a circle, staring down into the clear congealed plastic as if into the air, a wave of nausea sweeping over her. Bodies . . . wherever she looked there were bodies, like insects trapped in amber. But these were the bodies of men and women like herself. And children. Gods, the sight of the children . . . And their faces, their pale, tormented faces . . .

A small moan of pain escaped her lips. Here Li Yuan had drawn his line. Here, at the cost, it was said, of thirty million lives, he had saved his City.

*Saved it for what?* she asked, standing there beneath the naked, pitiless moonlight. *For the pimps and the money men, the sadists and the dealers. For Pei K'ung and I Ye and Ming Ai and all the emotional retards—all the half-men and their half-women.*

Emily shuddered, at that moment wanting nothing more than

for it all to end, right then, in one blinding, all-consuming flash, for if there *was* a god—one single, all-embracing God—then he would surely wipe the slate clean and start again with better, finer creatures than these apemen he had botched.

She sighed and turned, meaning to go back, then saw him at the edge of the ice, not twenty *ch'i* from where she stood.

He was tall and pale, and even in the half-light she knew his face.

"Bent? Is that you, Bent?"

Yet even as she called, even as she took a step toward him, he seemed to slip backward, away from her, melting into the moonlight and the darkness beneath the trees.

"Bent?"

But she knew it couldn't be him, because Bent Gesell had died over twenty years ago, murdered in his bed by DeVore.

*Ghosts*, she thought. *This place is full of ghosts.*

She went back, leading them down into the ruined village, setting up camp within the jagged walls of an old storehouse. Then, leaving them once more, she returned to the edge of the frozen lake and stood there, looking out across that scene of perpetual torment, her cheeks wet with tears.

Crying for Ji and the frozen dead. And for herself.

———◆◆◆◆———

*''UNCLE CHO?''*

*Cho Yao turned from the corpse he was cleaning and stared at Chuang. It was a day now since he'd last spoken to her; almost as long since he had last acknowledged her. But this, she knew, was his way. He could not rant at her or hit out with his hands. His punishment was silence.*

*"I'm sorry, Uncle Cho. I should have told you where I was going."*

*He grunted and turned back.*

*"I was . . . carried away."*

*She saw his back tense and then relax. He turned again, sighing heavily. "What you did . . . it was very dangerous. I could have lost you, you know that?"*

*She nodded, lowering her eyes beneath his reproachful stare.*

*"And that would have killed me. As surely as a bullet to the heart."*

*Again she nodded and again he sighed. She raised her eyes, seeing how his expression had softened. She went to him and clasped him tightly.*

"I promise I won't do it again," she said, her voice muffled as she pressed into him.

She felt him shudder. "So," he said, looking down at her, "what did you find out?"

She looked up, into his face. "I met a man."

"A man?" His eyes hardened again.

"A messenger," she said quickly, before he clammed up again. "He was at the ruined club when I went there. I followed him. . . ."

"Wo-ah!" he said. "Back up a little, Young Chuang. What club?"

Quickly she explained about the serial number on the corpse's neck, her visit to Hochheim Library and the service file.

His frown grew deeper. "So you followed him," he said, a hint of resignation in his voice. "What happened then?"

"I chased him through the station. Then I lost him. As I was trying to catch up with him again, he jumped me."

He shook his head. "You are lucky to be alive, little one."

She nodded, chastened. "He took me to a teahouse and we talked. We told each other what we knew."

"And that was that?"

"No. He gave me this." She held out her hand. In it she clutched a huge black iron ring. He took it from her and studied it, his face darkening.

"Aiya," he said. "You know what this is, Young Chuang?"

She shook her head. It was a ring. A ring with a strange design—a pattern of seven dragons formed into a wheel—on its face.

"This"—he held it up, his eyes awed by the sight of it—"this, child, is the ring of power of a T'ang. Symbol of his imperial authority. This ring"—he shivered—"this ring once sat upon the finger of an emperor."

She stared at it anew, her mouth fallen open.

Cho looked down at her. "What did he say when he gave you this?"

She swallowed. "He told me to look after it. He said—he said that it was a sign to me of his good faith. He said . . ." She frowned, trying to remember clearly what he'd said, the thought that this was so important a ring making her forget. "He said you would know what to do if he did not return within a month."

The Oven Man frowned deeply. "Why would he say that?"

She shrugged. "I don't know. But he seemed . . . concerned."

"Concerned? If this is any token of the stakes he plays for, he would do well to be concerned." He huffed out an exasperated breath. "He knows where we live, I take it?"

She nodded. She hadn't thought it mattered.

"And if he's captured and tortured, like those others? What then?" He closed his hand about the ring, his face screwed up with worry. "Aiya . . . what a mess! What a stinking, bloody mess this is!"

She had never seen him so worked up, never heard him use such language.

"He'll come back," she said, with more confidence than she felt. "He said he would."

He looked at her, silent.

"He will." She lowered her eyes.

"Maybe. And in the meantime? Do we double-bar the gate at night? Will that stop I Ye and his men if they find out we're involved?" He sighed again. "Aiya! . . . This is what comes of meddling! This is what comes of having adventures!"

It was the closest he had come to criticizing her.

"I'm sorry," she said again. "I didn't know."

But that wasn't quite true. She should have known from the moment I Ye and his men knocked on their door and brought their cart of death inside the yard. Yes. She should have known right then that some worm-filled casket lay ready to be opened. But that hadn't stopped her. Some demon of curiosity had driven her on.

She looked up. He was looking at her, but now his eyes were soft, forgiving. He put out his arms, embracing her again, lifting her up and hugging her to him, kissing her neck.

"You'll be the death of me," he said affectionately. "And who'll mind the ovens then? Who'll clean the bodies when they're brought?"

───────

JOSEF HEARD a heavy knocking on the front door and sat up on his bed, suddenly attentive. He heard his mother walk out from the kitchen and slip the latch.

"Yes?" she asked.

The voice was low and male, the words hard to catch.

"Ah . . ." his mother said, no pleasure in her voice. "You'd better come in."

Josef slipped from his bed and went to the door. Opening it, he peered down the stairs, but they had already gone inside. He heard the kitchen door slide shut, the voices resume, his mother's high, distinctive, the other too low for him to discern anything.

He turned, looking across at the window. It was open. Satisfied, he went out onto the landing, standing there a moment in the shadow, listening.

It was no good, he would have to go down. He could hear nothing from up here.

Slowly, choosing carefully where he put his feet, Josef made his way down. At the foot of the steps he stopped and crouched behind the rail, listening.

"Well, he's not been here," his mother was saying. "If he's been missing, he's been off somewhere else. I want him to go to school. The last thing I want is to have him under my feet all the time!"

"I understand," the man said quietly. "But the responsibility is yours, I'm afraid, Mu Ch'in Horacek."

"Why?" she asked bitterly. "I gave birth to him, yes, but that's where it ended. My other boys, they never missed a single day of schooling, but Josef . . . well, he's unnatural, that one! Unnatural!"

"Even so," the man began, "he's your responsibility. Until he comes of age."

Josef knew that voice. It was the Truant Officer—the same one who'd seen him at the execution. He could picture him vividly—a tall, thin, humorless man with a wispy dark beard and beady eyes that were set far too close to his overlong nose. All in all, the kind of man who reveled in official life; whose mean-spirited little soul enjoyed the job he'd chosen.

"But what if he doesn't go?" his mother asked. "What if we can't get him to go?"

"Then I am empowered to fine you twenty yuan. Fifty if he continues this behavior."

"Fifty yuan!" He heard the anger in his mother's voice. "But what can I do? Just tell me that. He never listens to a word any of us says! Now that his elder brothers have left home, he goes where he wants and *does what he wants and we can't stop him! He's out of control! Totally out of control!"*

"But the boy's only seven! Surely you can discipline him?"

*She laughed bitterly.* "Seven going on seven hundred!" *Then, more quietly:* "Isn't there some other answer? Couldn't the authorities take responsibility for him?"

"You mean make him a ward of court?"

"If that's what it takes!"

*The man gave a grunt of surprise.* "Are you serious, Mu Ch'in Horacek? You want us take your boy away? To one of the work camps?"

*There was a moment's silence, then the man spoke again, his tone resigned.* "Well," *he said.* "I didn't think things were quite so bad. It's come to that, has it?"

*Again there was only silence. But Josef, listening, could picture the way she'd nodded, the unforgiving tightness in her face.*

"Well . . ." *he said again,* "I shall have to see what can be done. It's most unusual, you understand. Usually we serve an order to protect a child. But if you wish . . . I shall see what can be done. In the meantime, speak to the boy. Try to instill in him just how important it is he attend school. The alternative . . ."

*Josef heard the stool creak and, turning quickly, scurried up the stairs, pulling his door closed behind him.*

*The kitchen door slid open.*

"You're sure now you haven't seen him?"

*His mother's voice was tired and bitter.* "Quite certain. He doesn't even eat here anymore. You might try the marketplace. I'm told he hangs about there sometimes."

"The marketplace. . . ." *Josef could imagine the Truant Officer noting that down.* "I'll try it after lunch. And thank you, Mu Ch'in Horacek. I'll speak to the authorities, see what can be done."

*He heard the door click shut, heard his mother drop the latch. There was a moment's silence, then her footsteps on the stairs.*

*Quickly, knowing there was not a moment to be lost, Josef sprang across the room and out the window. As he scuttled across the rooftops he could hear her shout ring after him.*

"Josef? Josef! Come back here, you little bastard! Come back!"

―――――――

JOSEF SAT ON the parapet of a neighboring house, watching as the Truant Officer stepped out from his front door. He watched him turn to his wife and bow, then lean close to give her a parting kiss. It was a touching little scene, made all the more poignant by the fact that his daughters—two dark-haired angels, both of preschool age—stood behind their mother's skirts, looking on as their father walked away.

Josef smiled. It had not been hard to find out where he lived. Such things were never difficult. Why, after all, should the man think he was being followed? It was his job to pursue, not theirs. And why should he even begin to suspect that anyone should wish him harm?

And that was the secret, the reason Josef could do these things, because they were like children, all of them. They drifted through life, unaware of the abyss that lay just beneath their feet. Blissfully unaware of the evil that existed all about them.

And his mother?

The cold anger he had felt on hearing her words had merely served to harden his resolve. No one would touch him. No one, he swore, would take him away and place him in one of the orphans' work camps.

He watched the wife return inside, shooing her girls before her like a mother hen with her chicks. As the door closed he slipped from the parapet and scrambled across the roof, dropping into the backyard of the neighboring house.

The door to the makeshift shed was ajar where he'd forced it earlier. Inside were all the things he'd need to do the job.

It wouldn't need much: a length of wick, a large can of lamp oil, a reel of heavy sealing tape, a tinder, and a box of firecrackers. The firecrackers he'd had to buy; the rest had been here already.

He moved it all out, stacking it by the dividing wall, then peeked over. Good. They were inside. The kitchen was empty.

Hauling it all up onto the back wall of the yard, he clambered up after it, then jumped down, taking his haul with him.

So far so good.

Putting things down, he set to work, tearing off long strips of the sealing tape and sticking them to his legs and arms.

It would have been far easier to do this at night, under cover of darkness, but this once he could not wait. He had to do this now, right now, before the Truant Officer returned.

Satisfied he had enough, he threw the reel down, then picked up the can and, creeping across the yard, went inside. Josef stopped, listening, hearing them up above in one of the bedrooms. He smiled, then took the top off the can and began to slosh the oil about the room, careful not to spill any on himself. Setting it down beside the globe-shaped orange gas tank that supplied the stove, he crouched and disconnected the hose, then turned the tap on just the tiniest bit. Satisfied, he backed out, pulling the door shut silently, sealing it top and bottom with the tape.

He hurried across the yard, knowing it was now wholly a question of timing. If she came down now and smelled the oil, the leaking gas, his scheme would fail. It all depended on how quick he was.

He could hear their laughter from the room above—their childish giggles mixed with the woman's deeper, fuller laughter—and felt a great tide of bitterness wash over him.

She'd never loved him. Never for a moment wanted him. "Dead," she'd said once; "you were born dead." But he wasn't dead. The others were dead. The ones he'd killed. The ones he was about to kill.

He put down the box, the tinder, and the wick, then looked about him. Along one side of the yard was a narrow patch of black, cultivated earth. In it was a trowel. He picked it up, then went back, crouching beneath the window.

Striking the tinder, he held it beneath the wick until it lit, then, throwing the tinder aside, opened the lid of the box. Inside there were twenty massive firecrackers. New Year Specials, as they were called. He grinned, as he picked one up.

Again the laughter fell on him, making him tense with anger, bringing the bile back to his throat. Slowly he placed the burning tip of the wick against the fuse, watching the treated paper catch with the tiniest wisp of smoke, the faintest hiss of ignition. Standing, he swung the trowel at the window.

It shattered noisily. Overhead the laughter stopped abruptly.

He counted. One—Two—Three. At four he threw the cracker through the jagged gap in the glass and lit another.

There was a whumpff from inside as the oil ignited. A moment later the cracker began to go off, its explosions like rapid gunshots in that enclosed space.

*Laughing now, he threw the second after the first, then, lifting the box, heaved the whole lot through the gap, as the screams started overhead.*

*Then, whooping like an innocent schoolboy who had just pulled off a prank, he turned about and ran, out through the gate and along the alley, even as the gas tank in the kitchen exploded, its detonation shaking the air like a massive hand.*

A S   S H E   S T E P P E D into the hallway, Bara Horacek stopped dead, listening. Her husband was at work and the house ought to have been empty, but there were sounds coming from upstairs—the muted sound of a Media screen.

Setting her shopping down, she made her way slowly, silently, up the stairs. The sound came from the end room. So he was in! The little bastard was in!

His door was open a crack. Peering through she saw him on his bed, his back against the headboard, his knees up against his chest. He was staring at the screen, grinning, his eyes lit up.

She had never seen him like this. Never.

She moved slowly to the side, her narrow view of the room changing by the moment, revealing the open window, the dressing table, finally the screen.

On the screen the gutted shell of a house was burning fiercely. Two neighboring houses had also caught, and firemen fought to contain the blaze.

She felt herself go cold, knowing at once what it was—a news report on the accident that afternoon. The commentary was low but clear.

". . . came home from work to find his wife and baby daughters dead."

The commentary stopped abruptly, the tape rewound. Again the phrase rang out.

". . . came home from work to find his wife and baby daughters dead. Safety Inspectors have yet . . ."

The sound of laughter shocked her. For a moment she stood there, feeling giddy, her hand steadying her against the wall. Then she heard it again. Laughter. His laughter.

She pushed the door open savagely and stepped inside, confronting him.

Slowly his face changed. Slowly a new look came into his eyes. He pointed past her with the control and switched the screen off.

"Why?" she asked, the anger she felt at that moment making her tremble violently. "Just tell me why."

He sat forward, staring back at her belligerently. "Why what?"

"Why were you laughing? Why . . ." She shuddered, seeing that her words were having zero impact on him. "You're an animal," she said quietly, beginning to shake her head. "That's what you are. An evil little animal. That poor man. That poor, poor man. He was here today. Here . . . looking for you."

"I know," he said, his eyes cold now, dead, like stones.

"You . . ."

Something broke in her suddenly. All the years of restraint, of keeping back what she felt about him, shaped what happened next. Reaching out, she grabbed his foot and pulled him toward her.

He yelped and tried to get away, but her grip on him was like iron.

"You little bastard!" she said, lashing out at him with the back of her hand, slapping him again and again and again. "You evil little toad! How dare you laugh at him! How dare you! I should have killed you! I should have put a pillow over your face while you were still in your cot!"

He kicked, loosening her grip, then slipped past her like an eel and out the window.

"Come here!" she yelled, climbing out onto the ledge. "Come back at once!"

But he was gone, his dark shape scuttering like a spider over the roofs and out of sight, and something told her that he wouldn't be back. It had ended. Ended . . . and she would never see him again.

She shivered, then slid down off the ledge. As she turned she half fell into the room, stumbling onto her knees, the blood pounding in her head. For a moment her vision swam, then she came back to herself.

"Aiya!" she said, her voice a groan of pain. "The gods forgive me for what I have let loose upon the world!"

# CHAPTER SIX

# The Arch of Air

ALDER STOOD AT THE RAIL, watching the crowd board the big hover ship, enjoying the morning sunlight on the bare flesh of his shoulders.

His journey east to Baku had been uneventful. As far as he knew, he had not been followed. In three days, God willing, he would be home. Then, of course, he would have to face the others to explain what had gone wrong and—if he could answer it—why. Until then his time was his own. He could relax . . . if that was possible.

The money chips the fat man had given him were sewn into the lining of his tunic, which he held loosely in one hand. Apart from that he was empty handed.

Travel light, his father had always told him, and so he did. As light as a butterfly, flitting from leaf to leaf.

He smiled, thinking of the girl, and of what she'd told him. He had been lucky—luckier than he'd first realized. If he'd stayed at the club they would have got him and he would have joined the corpses in the Oven Man's cold store. As it was he was alive, and though he would have to begin again, patiently building his contacts and looking for new markets for the tapes, at least he *could* do that.

To his right, at the top of the boarding ramp, a bell began to ring, slowly, sonorously. He looked about him one last time, then walked leisurely across. Showing his ticket to the steward at the barrier, he started down the ramp. The crossing to Krasnovodsk would take two hours. From there he'd get the fast-track to Ashkhabad. That was the easy part. It was the last stage of his journey, across the Kopet Mountains to Mashhad, which was the most difficult. He could have taken the fast-track, of course, and been in Mashhad by the evening, but they had decided that that would be pushing their luck. Going out, speed had been essential, but coming back he'd as like as not be watched. From what his sister had learned, Warlord Hu's secret service liked to tail returning locals. And for good reason. It was not what went out of Mashhad that they were worried about, but what came in. The last thing Hu Wang-chih wanted was an armed and organized opposition, and his agents acted to ensure it remained that way. Yet there were routes they couldn't cover, old smugglers' tracks across the mountains they didn't know about.

He would need to keep his wits about him if he was to get through in one piece. But that was why he had been chosen in the first place.

Calder stepped on board, pushing through the crowd and down one of the gangways, finding a seat near the back beside the long window. He had been sitting there only a moment when he heard the dull rumble of a shuttle coming down from the upper atmosphere. He leaned forward, staring out through the portal, watching as the tiny dot descended, changing slowly into the discernible shape of an interplanetary craft. As it came closer, so the roar of its retro engines seemed to beat the air, making the hover ship vibrate like a plucked string. As the rotund craft settled on the far side of the spaceport, he looked down at the jacket in his lap.

*At least it hasn't been a total failure. At least I got something for the tape.*

He smiled, and looked up, nodding pleasantly as an elderly Han with a long white beard moved into the seat beside him. He turned back, looking out across the bay again, then froze, as something hard and small pressed firmly against his lower ribs.

"Keep smiling, *Shih* Calder," the old man said, his voice a gentle whisper. "And don't try anything. Even a shortsighted old ancient like me can't miss from this range."

"You'd shoot?" he whispered out of the corner of his mouth. "In a public place like this?"

He turned his head, meeting the old man's eyes, seeing at once the calm determination there. "If necessary," the ancient answered. "But I am sure you are more sensible than that, neh, *Shih* Calder?"

"And when we get to Krasnovodsk?"

The old man's smile was like the Buddha's. "One thing at a time, *Shih* Calder. One thing at a time."

———

''OH, AND ONE FINAL THING,'' Li Yuan said, setting down the file he'd been reading from and looking at his son.

The young Prince was standing at the window, staring out across the gardens. He was taller than his father and broader at the shoulder, but, when he turned, there was no mistaking the origin of that face, for those same features stared out from the portrait of his grandfather, Li Shai Tung, that hung above the great fireplace.

"Yes, Father?"

"I want you to make your entrance at the height of the argument, when it seems Ben Shepherd must make some final, damning statement."

Kuei Jen hesitated. "Forgive me, Father, but I do not understand. Why should you wish to disturb the celebrations in this manner?"

Li Yuan smiled, gently encouraging his son, as if he were a particularly stubborn horse he had to train. "It's very simple, Kuei. The celebrations are a pretext."

Kuei Jen made to speak, but Li Yuan raised a hand. "You see, to gather together so many important and influential people is not an easy thing. One must have a reason. And sometimes the *real* reason must be obscured from certain people."

"Certain people, Father?"

"Like your stepmother." Li Yuan sniffed, then went on. "In this instance I wish to air a certain matter publicly. To enter it into the arena of debate. My purpose, if you like, is to *legitimize* discussion of the subject. To make it clear to everyone that merely to discuss such matters is not treasonable."

"I see. Yet could this not be done another way?"

"No, Kuei Jen. For the matter is a vital one. It has to do not merely with the health but the very future of the State. You understand, now, Kuei Jen?"

Kuei Jen gave the slightest bow. "I *think* I understand."

"Good." Li Yuan came across and laid his right hand on his son's shoulder, looking up into his face and smiling. "Then you must trust me. I have planned this for a long time now."

Kuei Jen smiled inwardly. His father had not stopped touching him since he'd returned, almost as if to check that he was still there, alive and physically present and not some ghost, some mocking hologram.

"And Pei K'ung?" he asked, broaching the one subject they had thus far avoided. "What will *she* think of all this?"

Li Yuan's face did not change. "Let her think what she will. She can do nothing. She is not T'ang. Nor shall she be, despite what she thinks."

"Even so—"

"Even so nothing. Her power derives from me. She is as the shadow to the sun. My eclipse would leave her nothing."

Kuei Jen nodded, yet he still felt uneasy. His father was too calm, too certain of himself. Or was there something he wasn't telling him?

He changed the subject. "Are all the guests here now?"

Li Yuan smiled, then let his hand fall away. "All but Ward and his family. And they will be here within the hour."

Again, something in his father's manner alerted him. There was an inner unease, a feeling of disquiet, that related directly to Ward. Did his father mistrust the man? Or was it a simple instinctive dislike for the Clayborn?

He had learned much in America, but the greatest lesson had been how to read men; how, from a composite of gesture, mannerism, and language, he might come to their innermost thoughts. Not that it was an easy thing to do. No, the trick was to lull a man, to lead him gently away from whatever it was one wished to know from him, then, when one's victim was least expecting it, to detonate a tiny verbal charge—a superficially innocuous query that held a barb within.

So one fished for men's thoughts. So one illuminated what

might otherwise remain dark. So the great statesman gained advantage over his enemies.

This he had learned, not from his father, nor his tutors, but from his own careful observation of his fellowmen.

"I understand that Shepherd has been working on a new project."

Li Yuan frowned. "He was. For me."

The signals were unmistakable. Here was something his father did not wish to discuss. But why? What had Ben been making that had the power to so disturb his father and darken his mood? And why the past tense? Why "was"? Again, he stepped aside, moving his next query onto safer, more certain ground.

"His son is a strange one, neh, Father? Those eyes of his are like his father's—like hungry cameras, sucking it all in, swallowing the world, yet his silence . . ."

Li Yuan nodded, a flicker of distaste—that same distaste he'd registered when talking of Kim Ward—crossing his face. "I find it eerie, too, Kuei Jen, and wonder what will become of the boy. And then, well . . ."

"Father?"

Li Yuan shrugged. When he spoke again there was a definite tone of regret in his voice. "I had hoped it would be for you as it is for Ben and me, as it was for your grandfather, Li Shai Tung, and Ben's father, Hal. I had hoped . . . well, that Tom would be *your* Chief Adviser, as Ben is mine. Mirror to me and sounding board. But a mirror must be opaque, neh?"

"And a sounding board should sound?"

Li Yuan gave a short grunt of laughter. "So it is, Kuei Jen. So it is. But that is not to be, neh? You must seek other voices to guide you when it is your time."

*Other voices* . . . Kuei Jen looked away thoughtfully, then, conscious that his father wished to leave, looked back at him, smiling and taking his hand, bending to kiss the iron ring of power.

"We must be strong, Kuei Jen," Li Yuan said as the young Prince straightened, his eyes filled with pride at the sight of his son. "The days to come will not be easy. There will be dark times, but we must face them squarely and come through. It is our destiny. *Your* destiny."

Kuei Jen bowed, conscious of how ominous that last phrase sounded, then raised his eyes, watching his father turn and leave the room.

Tonight it began. Tonight they took the first step on that path.

———————

KIM REACHED OUT and touched the tiny panel on the wall. At once the floor-to-ceiling window of the craft opaqued. He sat back, watching the horizon-to-horizon sprawl of Li Yuan's great European City pass slowly below him like a map. In less than an hour they would be setting down at the *San Chang*—the imperial palaces—in Mannheim, yet his thoughts looked back, not forward, his mind still out there in the void between the worlds. All the while some part of him labored on—tirelessly, relentlessly, like some insane, unsleeping machine—at the problem he had set himself.

He sighed, wishing for once he could be like other men and rest. Wishing he could forget for once those things that drove him, and take solace in more trivial matters.

"Don't worry," Jelka said, smiling at him from across the gangway, attuned as ever to his mood, his very thoughts. "You'll find an answer. You always do."

He gave an answering smile, then sat forward, beckoning to his young daughter, Mileja, who sat facing her mother. She giggled then came across, climbing into his lap.

He held her against him, one hand smoothing her long, dark hair, the simple feel of her comforting him, annulling the abstract anxiety he had been feeling.

"You must be on your best behavior tonight, Mileja, Lots of important people will be there at the banquet."

She turned slightly, looking into his face, her breath sweet. "Will Yang Chung be there?"

"Yang Chung?" He frowned, at a loss.

"Yang Chung! You know . . ." She hummed a snippet of some theme tune, but still he had no idea what she was talking about. He looked to Jelka.

"He's a trivee actor," Jelka explained. "He plays the hero on *Moving the Mountain*."

"Ah . . ." But he was still none the wiser. He smiled at Mileja once again. "If Li Yuan has invited him, he'll be there!"

"And if he hasn't?"

Kim laughed. "Then I'll invite him to come and see us at home, okay?"

She clapped her hands, delighted. "You promise?"

"I promise. Now settle down and watch the scenery. We'll be flying over Nuremberg in a while."

She snuggled in contentedly. For a while he dozed. Then, with a little jerk, he came awake again.

"What is it?" Mileja said sleepily.

"Nothing," he said, stroking her back, her hair. "Nothing. . . ."

But in those few moments it had come to him, like a gift from the darkness. He knew now what to do. Knew how to fix things so they would work.

He let out a long, sighing breath, the simplicity of his solution giving him an aesthetic satisfaction he very rarely experienced.

All along he had been thinking in terms of sending a beam of light in a single direction: a beam that would then be returned, again in a single direction. He had been thinking of employing boosters to enhance and prolong the signal, yet the problem had always been of keeping them in line, of keeping them focused and supplied with energy. But why have a single beam? Why not build it as one would build a bridge, with spans and supports? Why not keep each part of it in place by making the thing a web—a complex web of light—and why not pulse energy through the whole by tapping the one great power source the galaxy possessed—the power of its suns?

It would not be easy. No. Already his mind began to see all manner of problems. But problems were there to be solved. Now that he had the principle . . .

He looked out, out past Mileja's half-dozing face toward the north, conscious suddenly of the millions, the tens of millions, who went about their business down below in the streets of the City, unaware that at that moment their future lives, the very shape of their world in years to come, had changed.

A web, a flickering web . . . he saw it clearly, spanning the stars—saw the clear and slender, delicate ships that sailed the web—and smiled.

———————

THE WOMAN WATCHED from the far side of the passenger cabin as Calder got up and—accompanied, it seemed, by the old Han—made his way toward the front of the ship. Taking care neither to lose sight of him nor draw herself to his attention, she maintained a parallel course, threading her way through the crowd in the gangway and out onto the deck, passing through the gate only seconds after him.

So far, so good. Showing her pass at the barrier, she started down the landing ramp, the drab outline of Krasnovodsk—the five remaining central stacks dominating its skyline like a giant glacier—directly ahead of her, beyond the docks.

If her guess was right, Calder was heading inland, toward Central Asia. If that were the case he would head for the rank and hire a rickshaw to take him to the fast-track, anxious to report back to his bosses as soon as was humanly possible. She began to edge that way, anticipating his change of direction, but for some reason Calder was dragging his feet. She slowed and moved to one side, standing among a group of idle dockworkers.

Up ahead Calder and the old man had stopped and seemed to be having some kind of altercation. They were face to face and, if not shouting, certainly arguing vigorously over something.

She frowned. Had she missed something? Was the old man a contact of some kind? Or was the argument about something else—something that had nothing to do with his mission?

She edged closer, trying to make out what was being said, but almost as soon as it had begun it was over. Calder walked on, the old man silent, chastened, it seemed, a pace or two behind.

She hurried to catch up, following them as they went to the right and on past the rickshaw rank, ignoring the turn for the fast-track station, taking a left turn instead, down a street fronted by dockside inns, then right into a covered market.

Her instructions were straightforward. She was to follow Calder at a distance, find out who he was reporting to, and get that information back to I Ye. She was under strict orders not to make contact with him, and not—under *any* circumstances—to use her initiative.

Right now, however, she was in trouble, and she knew it. As she looked about her at the bustle of the indoor market, seeing no sign of either Calder or the old Han, she wondered just how the hell she was going to carry out her orders without breaking them. A simple tailing job was one thing—and she was normally quite good at it—but if Calder had contacts here in Krasnovodsk, then she might well have to call for backup.

*"Nu shi?"*

She turned, finding herself looking directly into the face of the old Han—a smiling, benevolent face.

"Are you looking for someone?" he asked, as if he wished to help her.

She wondered what to say. "My friend . . ." she began. But it was all she managed, for even as she framed the words, even as her mind struggled to invent something to cover the situation, a club thudded against the back of her head.

"Welcome to Krasnovodsk," the old man said, signaling to his men to carry the unconscious agent away. "May your stay be as unpleasant as your Master."

———————

"COLONEL I?"

I Ye turned abruptly, irritation making him answer his Captain sharply. "What is it now, man?"

Captain Dawes came smartly to attention, his head bowed. "News from Krasnovodsk, sir."

"Good news, I hope."

The Captain hesitated.

*"Aiya . . ."* I Ye said, exasperated. "What now?"

"The guide signal, sir. It's stopped."

I Ye let out a long breath. So she was dead. Worse yet, the messenger had got away untraced.

"Shit!" he said, turning away. "That's *just* what I fucking need right now!"

He turned back. "Is there anyone else we can contact in Krasnovodsk? Anyone who's done any work for us in the past?"

Dawes shrugged. "Not that I know, sir. But I can check."

"Then do so, Captain. And do it *now*!"

"Sir!"

I Ye returned to his desk and sat there awhile, frustration making him bring his fists down heavily on the desktop. "Fuck it!"

If you wanted something done properly you had to do it yourself. The trouble was, there was too much to do and only one of him. What he lacked was men—yes, and women—he could trust. Agents who would do what they were asked, simply and efficiently, and report back, mission accomplished.

"Damn the woman!" he said, standing again, an unusual restlessness in his muscles. "Damn her!"

He knew what the cause was. It was Pei K'ung. When she itched, everyone in her palace itched. When she was restless, all her servants became restless. That was the nature of things. And right now Pei K'ung was like a nervy adolescent.

"Well, fuck her!" he said, staring out past the guards who lined the balcony to his office toward the northern palace. "Damn and fuck and bugger her!"

"I beg pardon, I Ye?"

He turned, aghast. Ten paces from him stood the Empress herself, two of her junior secretaries in attendance. She had come in silently, unannounced. Hurriedly he came around his desk and, kneeling before her, placed his forehead to the carpeted floor before her feet. Yet as he made to lift his head he felt the sole of her foot press against the top of his skull firmly, pushing it back down.

"Fuck *who*, Colonel I?"

"I was speaking of my agent, Mistress . . . from Krasnovodsk. She was tailing the messenger. . . ."

He felt the pressure on his head lessen, but still her foot remained there.

"What of her?"

He swallowed, knowing he was in deep shit. Knowing that she would blame him, whether it was his fault or no. "We have lost contact, Mistress. The guide signal . . . died."

"And the messenger?"

"Has evaded us for now, Mistress."

She pushed his head to one side with her foot, then moved past him with a swish of her black dress. "You are a fool, I Ye, to send but a single agent on so *vital* a mission."

Keeping his head lowered, he glanced up at her, trying to gauge her mood. "But she was good, Mistress. One of the best."

"So good she lost her man. So good that she's dead."

Pei K'ung turned, looking down at him. Surprisingly, her face was clear of anger. Astonishingly, she smiled.

"Be that as it may, I have another task for you, I Ye."

*Tasks*, he thought fleetingly, *endless tasks*.

"What do you wish, Mistress?" he said, lowering his eyes; her faithful dog again.

"It's very simple," she said, beaming at him now. "I want you to discredit Shepherd."

"Discredit . . ." He almost laughed, almost uttered the first word that had popped into his head—*How?* But something behind her fixed, radiant smile—something cold and clinically determined—told him it would not be advisable to articulate his doubts. "May I ask *why*, Mistress?"

*"Why?"* The smile hardened, becoming fragile.

"What I meant," he said quickly, "is that if I had some idea of your reasons for wanting Shepherd discredited it might make it . . . *easier*, perhaps, to accomplish the task."

She was staring at him coldly now. "You want to know my *reasons*, I Ye? You wish, perhaps, to know everything I'm thinking?"

*Oh, shit*, he thought; *the more I speak, the deeper in I get*. He touched his forehead to the floor.

"It shall be done, Mistress," he said, the hollowness of his voice apparent even to himself.

"Good. And no delays. I want it done, and I want it done *soon*, do you understand me, Colonel I?"

"Mistress!"

Yet as she swept from the room, his confidence dissolved beneath the realization that, for the first time ever, he was in trouble. Big trouble. Why, it would be easier to kill Ben Shepherd than discredit him. The man was a law unto himself. Besides, he had the great T'ang's ear.

I Ye sighed and scratched his head, perplexed. How *did* one discredit such a man?

By disclosing some aspect of his sexual behavior?

Normally, perhaps. But how could one slander a man who openly slept with his own sister?

By proving somehow that he took bribes?

The very thought of it was absurd. As one of the richest men in Chung Kuo, Shepherd was not susceptible to bribes. Why, he was as near as damn it self-sufficient. Not only that, but from what I Ye had heard, Shepherd could tell Li Yuan to fuck off if he wished— yes, to his face—and Li Yuan would take it. No, the only way he might possibly discredit Shepherd was to implicate him somehow in a conspiracy against Li Yuan. To establish him in the same camp as Li Yuan's enemies.

And who were they?

The Warlords?

No. That would be far too difficult to arrange. It would take time, and Pei K'ung had told him *soon*.

Who else, then?

The answer stared him in the face. Li Yuan faced but a single threat—had only one real enemy—and that was his wife, Pei K'ung. To discredit Shepherd he would have to discredit his Mistress.

I Ye groaned, despairing, then pulled himself up off his knees. No delays, she'd said. She wanted it done and done soon.

And if he failed?

If he failed he was dead. Or worse, she might *make* him live.

━━━━━

THE ROAR OF the cruiser's engines filled the air as it set down on the pad. Tom, standing by the hangar doorway, waited a few seconds, then ran toward the craft.

And as he ran he saw himself suddenly from the window of the craft, running across the matte black surface, dodging between guards and technicians. The doubled image made him slow, his head swimming, his senses confused.

There was laughter in his head. *I'll close my eyes,* Sampsa said clearly.

His vision cleared. He walked on, his heart hammering now, the thought that he was finally about to meet his other self making him tremble with anticipation.

Ten paces from the craft he stopped, looking up as the hatch in the side of the big, beetlelike craft irised open and the ramp unfolded like an insect's leg.

Tom shuddered. The tension he was feeling made his jaw ache, his stomach spasm with cramp.

*Easy, Tom,* Sampsa said, trying to calm him; always the "elder" of the two, always the steadying influence. *It's only me.*

As Sampsa opened his eyes again, Tom saw the inside of the craft, the open hatchway to his left, the back of Jelka's head, her long golden hair—hair that was like fine-spun silk—moving briefly through his vision.

*I'm frightened. . . .*

*I know.* Sampsa's voice was like balm. *Just close your eyes. I'll come to you.*

Tom obeyed, watching through Sampsa's eyes as he stepped up to the hatch and looked down. For a moment he saw himself clearly, as if in a mirror, then he was looking into someone else's face—into Kim's, he realized.

"Are you all right, Sampsa?"

Sampsa laughed. "I'm fine. Look! Tom's here. He's come to greet us."

"Tom?"

As Sampsa turned, Tom saw himself again, standing there awkwardly, his eyes closed, his hands at his side; a tall, ungainly creature with dark hair and casual Western clothes.

Slowly, as in a dream, he came toward himself, until he stood but an arm's length away, staring into his own face.

*Tom? You can open them now.*

With a tiny shiver he let his eyes flick open.

*Sampsa?*

There, superimposed upon his own, was a face he had only ever seen a handful of times before, reflected in one or other of the mirrors in the house in Kalevala. He reached out, touching that face, tracing the features, the warmth of it—its physical reality—making his nerves tingle. He met Sampsa's eyes and frowned, the frown reflected back and forth, as if down a hall of mirrors.

*Hey, you're really real.*

Sampsa reached up and took Tom's hand, lacing their fingers together. *It's strange, isn't it? Like being on some kind of weird drug that blurs all the edges. Everything's doubled. Why, I can even see what's directly behind me.*

Inside his head Tom laughed. The fear had gone. In an instant it had vanished, driven away by the reality of being there with Sampsa.

*Hello,* he said, his eyes widening in a smile.

*Hello yourself,* Sampsa answered silently, then reached out, embracing Tom. They stood there a moment, their eyes closed, simply hugging each other.

"You two know each other?"

Tom looked up, meeting Jelka's eyes, surprised once more by her austere, unearthly beauty.

"This is Tom, Mother," Sampsa answered, turning to face her. "Tom, this is my mother, Jelka Ward, only daughter of Marshal Knut Tolonen. And this," he said as Kim stepped up, "is my father, Kim Ward. Father, this is my old friend, Tom. Tom Shepherd."

"So *you're* Ben Shepherd's son." Kim looked to his son. "But I thought—"

"He doesn't speak," Sampsa said simply.

"Ah . . ." Kim frowned. "Old friends, you say?"

Sampsa nodded, explaining nothing.

Kim looked at Tom again, clearly confused, then, shrugging, put out his hand. "Well, whatever . . . it's good to meet you, Tom Shepherd. Very good indeed."

---

CALDER SAT IN the tiny cellar room, his head in his hands, trying not to hear the woman's screams from the cell next door.

They had been at it for more than an hour now, and still the interrogation went on—still her pitiful cries went unheeded.

*Bastards,* he thought, wondering how the old man's organization could square their idealistic aims with such patent barbarity.

"We are like you," the old man, Lu Song, had told him earlier. "We want what you want. Peace, a good life for all men, and an end to the rule of Hu Wang-chih."

That much they *had* agreed on, but just how they set about bringing down the great Warlord was a different matter entirely.

"She is your enemy," Lu Song had said, surprised that he objected to her torture. "You think she would have even blinked an eye if it were you and not she on the table? Besides, she serves that insect I Ye. What does that make her?"

A *woman*, he thought, gritting his teeth as she began to shriek again. *Besides, you enjoyed watching her, old man. I saw the hideous grin you wore, the telltale swelling at your groin.*

He looked up, sighing heavily. A deal . . . he'd made a deal with them. His safe passage for information. And for copies of all future tapes.

"And if I double-cross you?" he had asked, staring into the old man's face.

"Then you will die," Lu Song had answered, matter-of-factly.

And he could well believe it. After all, they had found him easily enough at Baku. It was not difficult to believe they would find him in Mashhad. It made him realize how "insecure" their operation was.

Even so, his colleagues would not be happy. They had hoped to do this secretly, silently, their organization dissolving like the morning mist when their goal had been achieved and Hu Wang-chih was dead.

But matters had grown complicated. Somehow word had got out what they were up to, so that what had seemed straightforward was now diverse. The death of the club owner and those others, and now the death of this woman—these clouded things, making them morally ambiguous.

A single death—the death of Hu Wang-chih—would have paid for many. That death was justified. He could live with such a death. But these?

The woman's screams tore at his insides. He stared sightlessly at the door and shuddered. Was it true what Lu Song had said? Would she have looked on indifferently, if it were he stretched out there on the torture slab?

Or did it even matter? Wasn't the important thing what *he* felt? Whether *he* could live with this on his conscience?

He was no longer quite so sure. After all, weren't the servants every bit as bad, and just as much to blame for things as their masters? For if so, then killing Hu Wang-chih was not enough. They would have to kill thousands. The rivers would have to run red with the blood of their victims.

No. One man. That was all they had to kill. One man. He had to believe that. Had to. Or he was lost.

━━━━━

EBERT STOOD BACK, letting his surprise guests enter.

"Why, *Shih* Ward, Jelka . . . what an unexpected pleasure! I'd heard you'd arrived, but I thought . . . well, I thought I'd be meeting you later, at the banquet."

"It's Kim, please," Ward said, offering his hand to the blind man, the camera eyes above Ebert's head relaying the gesture to him.

Ebert took the offered hand unfalteringly. "Kim . . . welcome. My people have much to thank you for. Without your support these past ten years our colonies would have gone under more than once."

"And I have much to thank *you* for, Hans Ebert. Jelka told me long ago what you did for her, back on Mars. Without your intercession . . . without you and the Osu, that is, who knows what would have become of my beloved Jelka?"

"I did only what I had to," Ebert said, looking to Kim's wife. "I owed her a debt of honor."

Jelka smiled. "Which was repaid in full and more."

Ebert bowed his head gallantly. "I am glad you think so. But . . . well, let us not hang about here in the doorway. Come inside, please. I have fruit juice . . . and other, stronger things."

"Fruit juice is fine," Kim said, stepping past Ebert into the suite, then looking about him. "Li Yuan treats us well, neh?"

"And so he should," Ebert said, closing the door, then following Jelka across. "He, too, has owed a debt these past twelve years. Perhaps a greater debt than any here."

Kim shrugged but made no comment. He was Li Yuan's man, Ebert knew. His career, his wealth, his very existence—all had resulted from Li Yuan's patronage. And though he was a powerful man now—perhaps the most powerful man beside the T'ang in all Chung Kuo—he had never forgotten who had given him his start.

Ebert liked that. He liked the inbred loyalty of the man. But sometimes loyalty was not enough.

He went to the drinks table and poured two orange juices, then brought them back, handing one to Jelka, the other to Kim.

"You've heard, I take it, of the planned campaign?"

"Campaign?" Kim shook his head. "What kind of campaign?"

"A war, I'd guess you'd call it."

"*War?*" Kim set his glass down on the table and stepped closer. "Li Yuan is considering war? Are you sure about this?"

"An Edict authorizing the raising of taxes was issued two days ago. The campaign itself, so I've heard, will begin just as soon as we've gained allies among the Asian Warlords."

One of Ebert's camera eyes had come down almost to eye level, providing him with a clearer view of Kim's face.

Kim let out a great huff of a sigh, his eyes deeply troubled. "This is grave news indeed. I had hoped . . ." He shook his head. "It is not too late, then?"

"Too late?"

"To persuade Li Yuan against such folly."

"Who knows? But I am certain of this much: Pei K'ung has given Marshal Karr his orders. Karr is to go to the fortress city of Mashhad two days from now. There he will have an audience with the Warlord Hu Wang-chih and seek to persuade that venerable butcher to side with us against his fellow Warlords."

"*Aiya . . .*" Kim turned away, one hand pulling at his chin in agitation. "What virus could have invaded Li Yuan's senses? We've come so far. We've accomplished so much. But this . . ."

"Is madness, neh?"

Ebert saw how Kim drew back from saying as much, from offering any criticism of his T'ang, but it was undoubtedly what he'd been thinking.

"You've spoken to him?" Kim asked.

"Not yet. Not fully, anyway."

"You think he will consult us?"

"Oh, he must. After all, he will desire the support of all his friends, neh? To go to war without consulting us would be unthinkable."

"And if we advise against?"

Ebert laughed, his blind eyes seeming to smile. "I think he will go to war anyway. I think he's bored, you see. I think he's had enough of Pei K'ung and her petty intrigues. Besides, it's my belief he made a promise to his son."

Kim stared at him, frowning deeply. "A promise? I know nothing of this."

"I have no proof, of course. Just something that was said to me in private."

Kim looked away, disturbed. Just then a door at the far end of the room opened and a stoop-backed figure appeared.

"Master Tuan?" Kim asked, uncertainly, taking a step toward the old man. "Is that really you?"

Tuan Ti Fo shuffled across, then, two paces from Kim, stopped and bowed low, his hands pressed together in a prayerlike greeting.

"It has been a long time, neh, Kim Ward? A long, long time."

Kim stepped forward, embracing the old man warmly. "Tuan Ti Fo . . . where have you been? I thought . . ."

"You thought I was dead, neh?"

Kim laughed, then bowed, mirroring Tuan's earlier gesture. "I am delighted to be proven wrong." He stepped back a little, looking the old man up and down. "You haven't aged a day."

"And you look middle-aged. I hear you have children now. A fine boy, Sampsa, and a daughter, Mileja."

"That's so," Kim said, unable to keep from beaming. He turned, putting a hand out toward Jelka. "Jelka . . . come meet an old and very dear friend of mine, Tuan Ti Fo. It was Master Tuan who found me that time after the attack on the Project. You remember? That time you told your father where to look for me. It was Master Tuan who nursed me and kept me safe from harm."

She came forward and embraced the old man. "Then I have much to thank *you* for." She turned, looking to Ebert again. "How strange, that we should all meet thus."

"*Me fa tzu,*" the old man said. *It is fate.*

While Kim talked to the old man, Jelka went across and stood beside Ebert.

"You want to know the truth?" she asked, staring at him, her eyes pained by the sight of those burned and empty sockets.

"It depends," he said, turning partly toward her.

Jelka looked down, suddenly abashed. "The truth is, Hans, I owe you my life."

"No." He shook his head, raising his right hand, the index finger lifted in gentle admonishment. "The truth is I *owed* you a life. Besides, you gave me the chance to redeem myself. To *prove* myself. That was important to me. More important than I can say."

"I was wrong," she said, moved by his words, by the simple dignity he displayed. "You proved to me a man *can* change his nature."

"I had much help," he answered, smiling and looking to Tuan. "Without the Way, without Master Tuan to guide me through the darkness, I doubt if I'd have made it in one piece."

"And your wife?"

"She died," he said, a brief pain showing in his face. "A year back. She . . ." He shook his head, unable to continue; then, a sudden anger in his voice, he went on. "My faith in Mother Sky ought to console me, I know. It ought to teach me to accept what happened, but it doesn't. I still hurt inside at her loss. I still ask why."

She reached out and touched his hand. It was the first sympathetic contact she had ever had with him. He smiled, then took her hand in his own, squeezing it.

"I would have made you a dreadful husband, Jelka Tolonen. You chose well when you chose Kim."

She nodded, smiling thoughtfully, as she looked across to where Kim was deep in conversation with Tuan Ti Fo. "Yes. Yet there are still some who say I married him only for his money."

"Does it matter what they say?"

Her smile broadened. She looked back at Ebert. "No. But sometimes I think it hurts him when he reads such nonsense. People . . . they're so unthinkingly cruel."

He nodded. "Still . . . I'm glad you found happiness."

"Yes." She smiled, then leaned in and kissed his cheek. "That's for all you did, Hans Ebert. And for all you've yet to do."

On the other side of the room Kim laughed then shook his head exaggeratedly. "Gods, no, Master Tuan!" he said. "There's barely time to shit, if you'll forgive the expression. If I were to rest . . ."

"Oh, but you *should* rest, young Kim. Rest is good for you. Good for the body and good for the soul. Without it—"

"And you, Master Tuan," Kim said, short-circuiting the lecture he knew the old man was about to deliver. "What have *you* been up to?"

"Me?" Tuan Ti Fo smiled benignly. "Why, I have been perfecting my endgame, young Kim. We ought to play sometime. Perhaps I would be able to beat you now."

"Perhaps. . . ." Kim smiled, remembering how it had been between them. Then, as if reconsidering the idea, he gave a decisive nod. "Okay. Let's do that. Tomorrow, maybe? In the afternoon?"

Tuan Ti Fo shrugged. "I think you might be otherwise engaged."

Kim raised an eyebrow. "How so?"

Master Tuan's smile was gentle, enigmatic. "Wait and see, young Kim. Just wait and see."

TOM WAS JUST FINISHING getting ready for the banquet when Sampsa slipped into the room. He turned, surprised there had been nothing in his head to warn him.

*How did you do that?*

Sampsa smiled. *It's simple. I just don't think of you.*

*You can do that?*

*So could you, if you tried.*

*But I thought—*

Sampsa put his forefinger to Tom's brow. *You want me in there all the time?* Then, more soberly: *It's her again, isn't it? You've been thinking of her.*

Tom nodded, his thoughts open to his friend.

*She's very pretty.*

Again Tom nodded, then sat down on a nearby chair. His eyes met his friend's.

*I can't stop thinking about her. I can't eat. I can't . . .* He shrugged. *I can't think about anything but her.*

*You know what?*

*What?*

*I think you're in love with her.*

*In love?*

*Don't be so shocked. It happens.*

*But she's—*

*A singsong girl. So?*

*So?*

*So nothing. You want me to be judgmental?*

Sampsa sat beside him, then reached out, taking his hand. Once again the feeling was doubled; Tom felt it both through his own senses and through Sampsa's. It was strangely like being in a Shell with the guidetrack running.

*No. No, I . . .* Tom wanted to draw back, but his thoughts ran on. *I want you to understand.*

*But I do, Tom. You want her, so go and get her. But not tonight. Tomorrow. Okay? I'll come with you. We'll go and find her again.*

*You promise?*

But he could feel the certainty there in Sampsa's head. It was impossible for Sampsa to lie to him.

*Sampsa?*

"I know," Sampsa said softly, smiling, squeezing his hand gently. "Now, come on. We'll be late if you don't get ready now."

———

THE HALL OF EVERLASTING SPRING was packed from end to end. Beneath the high, vaulted ceiling, all the great and good of the kingdom—courtiers and ministers, company heads and members of the Twenty-Nine, colonels and majors, artists and media stars, senior representatives and personal friends of the T'ang—were gathered, talking and rubbing shoulders, while servants in bloodred silks moved among them, making sure their wine cups were never empty, their mouths never lacking for some rare delicacy.

At one end of the Hall, beneath a huge imperial banner—the bloodred dragon emblazoned across a full white moon—Li Yuan sat on the dragon throne, a queue of kneeling guests at the foot of the steps, their heads bowed low, waiting to be received.

At a signal from the Chief Steward at the door a fanfare sounded, announcing the arrival of a special guest. All eyes turned as the huge figure of the Marshal, Gregor Karr, entered beneath the arch, his daughters and his wife just behind him. Karr turned slightly, waiting for them to catch up with him. Taking his wife's arm, he walked on between the parting lines of guests, heading directly for the throne.

"Marshal Karr," Li Yuan greeted him, according him the special honor of getting to his feet and coming down to him. "And Marie," he added, smiling and nodding to her. "I am glad you could come. You are most welcome here."

"*Chieh Hsia,*" Karr answered, saluting him, his head lowered. In his dress uniform he looked magnificent; every inch a soldier. Raising his head again, he turned slightly, then put out a hand as his daughters stepped forward as one.

All four had had their blond hair put up, and in their matching powder-blue dresses, they looked a stunning sight. They were all strikingly tall. May was almost her mother's height and build, while Hannah and Lily were easily the match of any man in the hall— with the exception of their father. Even young Beth seemed more like an eight- or nine-year-old than a child of five.

"*Chieh Hsia . . .*" Karr began, beaming with pride, "might I present my daughters, May, Hannah, Lily, and Beth."

The girls smiled, then bowed their heads, the youngest, Beth, just slightly out of time with her elder sisters.

Unexpectedly, Li Yuan returned their bow. "I am delighted to meet you, ladies. You are most welcome here in my Hall. You are a credit to your father and mother." He smiled warmly as his eyes went from one to another. "I hope very much that you enjoy tonight's festivities."

There was a brief exchange of glances among them, and then, at the eldest, May's, signal, they answered him, their voices forming a chorus.

"We are most honored to be here, *Chieh Hsia.* May the heavens smile on you."

There was a pause, then May spoke alone.

"Ten thousand years!" she said, lifting her voice so all in the hall could hear.

"Ten thousand years!" the other three echoed, the traditional toast to an Emperor being taken up by all in the great hall.

And amid the sudden uproar young Beth looked to her father

and saw how proudly he was looking at them, a great beam of a smile splitting his face.

"Ten thousand years!" she yelled exuberantly. "Ten thousand years!"

━━━━━

PAULI EBERT sipped from the fluted glass, then, smiling courteously, answered Jelka's query.

"To be honest with you, Aunt, I don't know. Both have merits, I suppose, but as to which would be more beneficial . . ."

He shrugged, then sipped again.

Two hours had passed and the great mass of people in the Hall had split into smaller groups who now stood, talking among themselves and drinking, discussing the issues of the day and—as any occasion was a good occasion for it—doing business.

Hans Ebert's son was twenty-five now and had been Head of the massive GenSyn corporation for the best part of seven years. Even in that elite company he was someone to know, someone whose every word held great significance, and so a substantial crowd— maybe fifty or sixty in all—had gathered about his party.

Just now they were talking of the plan to build a new canal south to the shore of the Mediterranean and whether they ought to choose the meandering "western" route to the port of Avignon or the more direct "eastern" route to Verona. The western route was almost twice as long, but the eastern route would mean tunneling through the Alps. Both schemes had their advocates and detractors, and many there, listening and looking on, would be directly affected by the decision if it were ever made—so what Ebert had to say was of great importance. GenSyn's unequivocal backing for either alternative would, in effect, settle the matter. Conscious of this, Ebert took care to choose his words carefully.

"In fact," he said, as if he had only thought about it there and then and had not spent months poring over the plans and costings of the rival projects, "both schemes have much to recommend them."

"Then why not both?"

Pauli turned slightly, facing Michael Lever. With a respectful nod of the head he answered him, his Eurasian features cast into a thoughtful smile. Lever, Head of ImmVac, was one of his major trading rivals, yet the two men—despite the twenty years' difference in their ages—were good friends.

"You think we could afford two such massive projects, Michael? You've seen the costings."

Lever stretched his gaunt body, then nodded his prematurely gray head. "I have. And, yes, Pauli, I think we could. Why, the increased trade from Africa alone would pay for them both within twenty years."

"That's if there isn't war," Hans Ebert said, from where he stood among the Osu, the twin cameras circling his head.

"War, Father?"

"Things happen," Hans said, not pursuing the matter in that company. "My point is that to undertake such schemes one needs stability. Workers must be fed and paid. Investors must be certain that the scheme will not merely be carried out, but will bring them future benefits, and such certainty depends on peace, wouldn't you say?"

Pauli bowed his head, acknowledging his father's words, yet it was another who answered Ebert senior.

"Not always so. Sometimes war can stimulate growth. Necessity can shape events as much as profit, wouldn't you say, *Shih* Ebert?"

Hans turned to face the newcomer to the group, Ming Ai, keeping whatever distaste he felt for Pei K'ung's private secretary from his face.

"There's some truth in that," he admitted. "Yet personally I find the cost too high. War destroys. And not merely companies and trade. War is like a hungry mouth, devouring all it can find. It feeds on human misery. No, given the choice, Ming Ai, I would settle for stability and peace. I've had my fill of war."

There was a strong murmur of assent from the gathering at that, yet Ming Ai pressed on oblivious.

"And yet you yourself raised the possibility, *Shih* Ebert. And why? Because, as you know, this world of ours is no longer the world our grandfathers knew—no longer a single, solid world ruled by a powerful elite. Our world is now a dangerous place, divided against itself. A thousand kingdoms vie for supremacy, and which of them will triumph?"

"You speak as though there were some immediate threat," Kim Ward said from where he stood beside his wife.

Ming Ai turned, looking to him. "Immediate? Perhaps not, *Shih* Ward. Yet as *Shih* Ebert rightly said, things happen. Situations change. Why, it would take but a small shift in power among our West Asian neighbors and the whole region would be plunged into war—a war we would find it hard not to get involved in."

Ming Ai looked down at his hands thoughtfully. "Such, alas, is the reality of our times. Oh, I admit that there are no great enemies out there now determined to break us on the wheel—no Lehmanns or DeVores—yet even the most petty war can start a major conflagration."

"Only if we were to allow it," Hans Ebert answered, the slightest edge to his voice now. "Wars only happen when people forget how to talk to each other. We should be actively encouraging trade and the free exchange of information with our neighbors, not seeking to undermine them all the while." He quickly raised a hand. "Oh, and please don't tell me that we aren't, Ming Ai, for I know it for a fact!"

"Then you know much that I do not." Ming Ai smiled pleasantly, yet there was a combative tenseness to his stance now that had not been there earlier. "As far as I am aware, we have been doing exactly what you suggest. Why, trade with our Asian neighbors trebled last year!"

"That's hardly something to boast about," Lever answered sardonically. "Three times fuck-all is still fuck-all!"

There was a roar of laughter at that. Ming Ai bristled. The politeness in his response was razor thin.

"Forgive me, *Shih* Lever, but I think you miss my point. The figures may be small, but it is, at least, a start. A step in the right direction."

"Forgive me, Ming Ai," Lever said, mirroring the eunuch's smile, "but that's bollocks and you know it!"

Ming Ai looked about him, seeing how every face was turned against him, and looked down, swallowing. "Well," he said, after an uncomfortable moment, "we seem to have come a long way from the matter in hand. Canals." He smiled, recovering his equanimity. "What would we do without canals . . . ?"

LATER, when Ming Ai had moved on, the four men met together in one of the anterooms—Pauli Ebert, his father, Hans, Michael Lever, and Kim Ward.

"Well?" Pauli asked. "What was that about?"

"He was busy seeding," Hans said quietly. "Planting the idea of war before the actuality."

"Then the rumors are true," Lever said, his face concerned. "Pei K'ung plans a campaign."

"So it would seem," Hans answered. "Why else the taxes?"

"To build canals?"

They laughed at that, but their laughter quickly died. This was deadly serious—they all saw that now.

"She'll need a pretext," Pauli said, looking about him at the others.

But his father was shaking his head. "That'll be the least of her worries. She can invent a pretext. No. What's important here is how *we'll* react to her plans. Whether we'll go along with her or not. That's why she sent that eel among us. To sound us out."

"You think we can dissuade her, then?" Kim asked.

"Perhaps." But Ebert said it without conviction.

"I think we're ignoring one important factor," Lever said, looking from face to face. "We're forgetting Li Yuan. What does *he* think about all this?"

"No disrespect intended, but does it matter what he thinks?" Pauli asked. "Pei K'ung is de facto ruler. We all know that. When was the last time he opposed her on anything? No. If Pei K'ung wants war, he'll go along with her."

"Or risk civil war," Lever said, nodding his agreement.

"Unless . . ." Hans began.

Pauli frowned. "Unless what?"

Hans shrugged. "I don't know. It's just that this doesn't feel right. If Li Yuan gives in to her on this, it simply strengthens her hand."

"Maybe so," Pauli said, nodding, "but Michael's right. His only other option is to fight her. And as we know, Pei K'ung's position

right now is strong. Stronger than it's ever been, in fact. If Li Yuan
fought her, he would lose. And where would we be then?"

"Up shit canal!" Lever said, and again they laughed.

"He should delay her," Kim said, his face dark with apprehension. "Put her off somehow."

"You think he can?" Pauli asked.

"Who knows?" Lever answered. "Yet it would be preferable to
war, neh? And maybe the old girl would do us all a favor in the
meantime."

They stared at him, astonished.

"Well?" Lever asked, looking about him. "You mean you've
never—and I mean, never *ever*—wished for it? Never dreamed of
waking up and hearing on the Media that the old crow has finally
passed on?"

There were shrugs, reluctant nods.

"It's no answer," Kim said after a moment. "No, we must be
practical. We must see what steps can be taken to prevent this."

"So what do you suggest?" Lever asked, looking to Kim.

"A meeting," Kim answered. "A week from now. You can come
to my place. To Kalevala. And maybe we can invite a few others. . . ."

"You think that's wise?" Hans asked.

Kim looked to him, surprised. "You think it isn't, then?"

Hans laughed, turning his blind eyes heavenward. "Why, sometimes you surprise me, Kim Ward."

Ebert reached out, taking Kim's arm gently. "Think of it, Kim.
Just think how Pei K'ung would see it. The four of us—four powerful, influential men—meeting to discuss our opposition to her
plans. Put yourself in her place, Kim Ward, then answer for yourself whether you think it would be wise to involve anyone outside
this little group."

"Ah . . ." Kim said, his mouth falling open. "I see. . . ."

"But let us do as you say," Ebert went on. "Let us meet and talk
further. For now, however, let us get back before we're missed. I
understand the entertainments are about to begin!"

THE MAIN FESTIVITIES had ended an hour back, with displays of archery and bareback riding in the Hall of Supreme Virtue. Since then, Li Yuan had been holding audience in one of the smaller halls.

It had been years since anyone had had such free and easy access to the T'ang, and a great number there were taking advantage of the unexpected opportunity, wanting—every last one of them wanting—some favor from him.

Ben Shepherd, looking on from his position at the foot of the dais, took in every last detail of the ritual, every last nuance of behavior.

*Men,* he thought dismissively, as though they were a different species from him. *Such insignificant little creatures they are. And so transparent.*

Take the specimen currently abasing himself at Li Yuan's feet. Fa Chun had been a nothing—a street sweeper, so the rumor had it—before the City's fall. Yet in those chaotic years that followed, Fa Chun had made a fortune speculating in the new building materials. Where and how he had got the money to invest was shrouded in mystery—though word had it that certain members of the brotherhoods were never far from his Mansion's doors—but the fact was that he was now one of the richest men in City Europe, having diversified into pharmaceuticals and entertainment.

Fa Chun was a rich man, but the newly rich were never satisfied; they always wanted more.

So what favor did he want from Li Yuan?

Shepherd laughed silently. Fa Chun wanted what all the self-made *hsiao jen* wanted. He wanted to marry into royalty. To tie his new money into old privilege. Oh, ten thousand years might pass and still worms like him would try to give their rapaciousness the gilt of respectability.

Right now Fa Chun wheedled around the subject, trying to ask without actually asking, to suggest what it was he wanted without quite saying it directly. For directness in such a sensitive area just would not do. Not here, anyway.

Others—Minor Family Princes, who could be bought for ten a *fen* these days—would pursue the matter for him at a later date, cultivating the right climate for its growth. Right now it was enough that Fa Chun planted the seed.

Ben yawned. He had seen enough. Besides, it was almost time.

He smiled and, looking to Li Yuan, slowly shook his head. At once the T'ang raised his right hand, silencing Fa Chun, then turned, looking to Shepherd.

"What is it, my friend?"

Ben moved closer, stopping beside the kneeling man, his right foot only inches from Fa Chun's outstretched hand.

"Aren't you bored with all this, Li Yuan? Doesn't all this petty seeking for advantage *tire* you?"

There was a low hiss of disbelief, the sound of a thousand in-drawn breaths.

"Not at all," Li Yuan answered calmly, unfazed by the brutal openness of the query. "Does the beating of your heart tire you, Ben Shepherd? Does the quiet passage of the blood about your veins make you feel like quitting life? No. Nor this me. For these men are the blood that pumps within the imperial veins, this ritual the beating of the imperial heart. Without it there is no nourishment of the imperial body. And without nourishment there is no breath, no thought."

There was a great murmur of satisfaction at this. On all sides heads were nodding now. Men looked to each other, smiling. The T'ang had answered well.

"A good answer," Ben went on, conscious of Fa Chun still groveling on the ground below him. "But what when the blood is sick? What when the valves that feed the veins and arteries are swollen and malfunctioning, the heart itself diseased? What when the veins are clogged and cancerous?"

The silence spread, filling the Great Hall. Suddenly all eyes were on the throne; all listened for an answer.

Li Yuan smiled dourly. "If the blood is sick and the heart itself diseased, why then, the cure is obvious. The blood should be purged, the heart removed and replaced."

Again, men looked to each other; but now they sought some clue as to what was meant. The very openness of the exchange worried them.

Ben stood back a little, half turned now to the crowd, his manner vaguely theatrical. "Removed? How removed? What surgeon is there here could undertake such a task?" He looked across to where the *T'ai Shih Lung,* the Court Astrologer, was standing, and beckoned him across. "Tsui Ku . . . come here a moment! Maybe you, who see the shape of things so clearly, might illuminate us?"

Tsui Ku looked back at Ben aghast, clearly startled by his request. "B-b-b . . ." he stammered.

"Come, now," Ben continued. "Let's b-b-begin the task at once, neh, Master Tsui? If the blood *is* sick, why, then, let us cast the oracle and see what the ancient book suggests!"

Heng Yu, who had been standing off to one side of the throne beside Pei K'ung and her party, now stepped forward, clearly distressed. "*Shih* Shepherd . . . hasn't this foolishness gone far enough? These are private matters, surely?"

"Private?" Ben looked about him almost imperiously, as if, at that moment, *he* were T'ang. "Yet we talk of matters of the State. Are such things only to be mentioned behind locked doors?"

Behind him Li Yuan sat quietly, making no attempt to silence his Chief Adviser.

Heng Yu turned to face his Master, bowing to the waist. "*Chieh Hsia?*"

"Yes, Master Heng?"

"Forgive me, *Chieh Hsia,* but what *Shih* Shepherd has been saying . . ."

"Go on, Heng Yu."

"Well, *Chieh Hsia,* it seems to me tantamount to criticism." He paused, then carried on. "Criticism of your worthy self."

Li Yuan raised an eyebrow. "How so?"

Heng Yu lowered his head, almost squirming now. He had clearly expected his Master's understanding, perhaps even his backing, but neither had been forthcoming. "Well, *Chieh Hsia* . . . it seems . . . well, it seems to me that *Shih* Shepherd is implying that you . . . you yourself, Great Master, are in some way . . . *diseased.*"

"*Me?*" Li Yuan laughed. The Hall was deathly still. The T'ang turned, looking to Shepherd once more. "Is that so, *Shih* Shepherd? Am I sick?"

Ben turned and smiled at Li Yuan, then looked past him to where Pei K'ung stood, ashen faced and angry, looking on.

"*You,* my Lord? Why no. Did I say as much? All I said—"

Pei K'ung stepped forward, confronting Shepherd, her hand raised commandingly. "*Shih* Shepherd! You will desist! I find your words both offensive and distasteful!"

Ben's eyes twinkled with malice. "Why, Lady Pei . . . that's very strange indeed, for I find your *looks* both offensive and distasteful. As for your sexual habits—"

"*Enough!*" Pei K'ung said sharply, her face burning with anger. Climbing the steps, she stood over her husband, one hand gripping the arm of his throne. "Li Yuan, will you put up with this?"

Li Yuan looked up at her and smiled coldly. "Not at all. Yet *Shih* Shepherd has a point, don't you think, Pei K'ung? Perhaps these matters *need* to be talked of openly. To be aired and discussed at length. To do otherwise—"

She raised her hand to slap him, then slowly lowered it again, realizing what she had done. He was still smiling at her; a coldly controlled and mocking smile.

"You disagree?" he asked, the question a barb.

"I—"

A dissonant fanfare sounded. There was the beating of a drum and then two bells, one high, one low. All turned, looking to the head of the stairs as the great doors swung open.

It was the Prince, Kuei Jen, and on his arm, dressed in the dragon-and-peacock robes of a bride, was the Princess Hsun Chu-lo.

Li Yuan stood and went down the steps, the crowd making way before him, their heads bowed low, as he went to greet the couple, while behind him his wife turned and, gesturing angrily to her party, stormed from the Hall, her long face dark with fury.

CALDER PACED the tiny room silently, unable to sleep. It had been quiet for hours now, no sound from the woman or her tormentors. It was late—how late he didn't know—but the footfalls overhead had stopped some while back, no doubt when the market had closed for the night.

Lu Song had said he could go in the morning, but who knew what the old man and his friends were up to? Even now they might be discussing his fate; arguing over whether he should live or die; whether he, too, shouldn't follow the woman onto the torture slab.

He shivered, unable to get that sound out of his memory—the sound of her hopeless screaming. Pausing, he looked to the door, then went across and leaned against the erwood surface, listening. Nothing. Yet as he made to move back, he felt the door give slightly and, frowning, gave it the smallest push.

Slowly, silently, it swung back, revealing the half-lit corridor, the facing steps that led up to the indoor market.

Cautiously he stepped out, one hand to the wall. A few paces away, on a chair beside a small table, sat a guard, his head propped back against the wall behind him, his mouth open, fast asleep.

Calder swallowed. The door to the cell was just beside the guard. There were bolts top and bottom, but they had not been slid across. Nor was the door even closed. It stood ajar, a single wall lamp lighting the fetid room.

He stepped past the guard, barely daring to breathe lest he wake him, then put his hand to the door, peering in through the grill.

The woman was still there on the slab, her bone-white body slick with blood, her wrists and ankles secured. Whether she was dead or not he couldn't tell; in that wan light even the living would have seemed corpselike.

He turned, studying the guard a moment, watching his breathing, then stepped inside, alert in case this was another trap. Yet as he stood there beside the slab, all thought of his own safety drained from him.

*Aiya*, he thought, seeing just what they'd done. *How could you bastards do this to her? How could you?*

He stared at her, studying her wounds, grimacing as he recalled her cries, her pale nakedness—the thought of just how helpless she had been—stirring his deepest sympathy. Looking at her he saw his own daughters, his wife, his sister, the mother he had never known, and felt the tears begin to fall.

There was a tiny shudder through the body; the faintest sigh. She was alive! The knowledge of it surged through him like an electric tide.

Alert now, Calder turned and, wiping his face with the back of his hand, went to the corner where the brazier stood. The coals in the iron bowl were barely warm now. Searching among the irons and brands, he reached in and took one of the sharper implements. Returning to the slab, he set to work, sawing patiently at the leather thongs, severing each in turn. That done, he went to the door again.

The guard was still asleep. He edged past him and, climbing the steps quickly, tried the door. It was locked. He reached up, his fingers searching the edge of the door until he found what he was looking for. There were two hinges, one near the top, one at the bottom. If he could prize them off he could get out. The iron he had was no good, however; it was too thin. Put pressure on it and it would bend or break. No, he'd need something thicker. One of the brands had been much thicker than the others; maybe that would do the trick.

Tucking the iron into his belt, he went down again. A moment later he was back. Pushing the end of the brand into the narrow space between the upper hinge and the wall, he slowly leaned against it. For a moment the thing held; then, with a crack, it gave.

Calder turned, listening. From the corridor below he heard the guard snort, then begin to snore.

He breathed again.

Crouching down, he placed the tip of the brand beneath the lower hinge and the wall.

*Don't wake,* he prayed as he began to lean his full weight onto the thick iron brand. This time, when the hinge gave, the sound was like a pistol shot. A moment later the door fell forward with a heavy crash.

"Shit!"

Down below the guard had woken and was struggling to his feet, looking about him sleepily as Calder jumped down the last three steps and cannoned into him.

The guard went down, his head thudding against the table's edge as he fell. But he was only dazed. As he got up he went to call out, but Calder, crouched over him, put his hand over the man's mouth, stifling the cry, then swung the heavy iron.

He felt it connect; felt the sickening crack as the man's skull broke beneath the blow like a clay pot. The man slumped lifelessly, blood pouring from the gash.

Calder stumbled back, horrified, letting the iron fall. *I didn't mean . . .*

But it was too late. He had to get out. Going back inside the cell, he went over to the slab again. Taking off his tunic, he wrapped it about the naked woman, and lifted her, cradling her in his arms as he carried her out past the dying guard and up the steps.

The indoor market was dark and empty, the stalls shadows within the greater shadow. From memory he found his way across, then set the woman down beside the door. The big outer doors were locked and bolted, but he had noticed a smaller door within one of them. He tried that. It, too, was locked, but maybe he could smash his way through. Standing back, he kicked. Once, twice, a third time he kicked, conscious of the noise he was making. Noise enough to wake the dead. Then, on the fourth kick, it splintered and gave.

Quickly now, his heart beating furiously, he went across and picked her up again, crouching, turning to his side to get through the jagged gap. Outside the moonlight shone down like a search-light, outlining the massive shape of Krasnovodsk central to his north. From houses close by came shouts, faces appeared at windows, fingers pointing down at him, but he ignored them, half running now, almost stumbling beneath her dead weight. On, on, toward the edge of town and safety.

------

*THE TEMPLE DOOR was open just a crack. Chuang Kuan Ts'ai stood there in the sunlight, chewing at her thumbnail, reluctant, afraid to go in. She knew the priest from the times he'd come to officiate at Taoist ceremonies for the dead; she had glimpsed him from across the yard as he intoned in ancient Mandarin to a crowd of grieving relatives. Uncle Cho said he was a wise man and helped local people with their problems, and she herself had often seen him, shuffling about the streets and alleys of the Hsien, an austere, rather daunting old gentleman, but she had never actually spoken to him. She sighed, then looked about her uncomfort-ably. She wasn't even sure this was the right thing to do. All she knew* was that she wasn't sleeping well. She had been troubled, fretful these past few days. If the lao jen could somehow put her mind at ease. If he could tell her what to do . . .

Hearing voices, she half turned, looking back into the shadows of the alleyway behind her. There were people at the far end, coming closer. Making up her mind, she stepped forward, slipping through the gap.

Inside, the darkness was intense. She stood there a moment, letting her eyes grow accustomed to the dimness, conscious of the hundred garish, gold-painted figures that stared sightlessly down at her from their niches to every side. Then, her heart beating fiercely in her chest, she went over and, peering around the curtain, stepped through into the inner room.

Here the smell of incense was strong. The old man sat to her left, cross-legged, his eyes closed, as if asleep, his pale saffron robe hanging loosely on his tall, gaunt frame. His head was tilted forward slightly, its tall, polished dome bald but for a few wisps of long gray hair that seemed glued to the skin just above the ears. His beard was likewise wispy and unkempt, making her think of the vagrants she saw passing through the Hsien from time to time. But the priest was no vagrant. She had seen his house and knew he kept a housekeeper and two servants.

Just ahead of her, on the far side of the six-sided room, was the altar. In its design it was typically simple; a big, open rectangular box, with a long red pole at each corner. If anything, it reminded her of two tables placed one upon the other, a small, green-tiled roof placed on top of the whole thing. On the lower level two long racks rested on tiered steps, a number of thick red candles burning constantly within. Placing a coin in the dish at the side, she took a candle from the box below the altar and lit it from the smoldering spill. Placing it in the lower rack, she stood back and, head bowed, hands pressed together, offered a prayer to Heaven.

Not that she was religious. Like the great majority of her fellows she believed not in a God but in a Supreme Ancestor, from whom all of her kind had originally derived. Man lived between Heaven and Earth and was the measure of all things. In human beings the Way was made manifest.

Or so she had been taught.

She turned, looking to the priest, then approached him.

"Lao Jen?" she asked, her voice almost a whisper.

He seemed at first not to have heard. At last like a traveler returning from afar, he opened his eyes and looked at her.

"Lao jen?"

The old man's smile was like those of the Buddhas she had seen; impersonal and distant, not so much a smile as the badge of inner peace.

"Lao jen?" she asked a third time. "Can I speak with you, lao jen?"

Closing his eyes, the old man began to stretch his muscles; first his neck, his head circling like a preening bird's, then his shoulders, and finally his back. That done, he let a long breath hiss from him.

"What is it, child?"

Chuang hesitated. All of her earlier uncertainty returned. Did she trust the old man, or did she simply turn and leave? She steeled herself, then spoke.

"I have a problem, lao jen."

"A problem?" He beckoned her closer. "What kind of problem?"

"It is a secret, lao jen."

"A secret?" The old man's smile slowly faded. "Have you done something wrong, child?"

She shook her head.

"Hmm." He stared as if he could see right through her, then nodded. "I see. Then what kind of secret is it?"

She forced herself to answer, squirming now beneath his scrutiny. "It is a very great and grave secret, lao jen. If I were to tell you . . ."

He raised a finger to his lips. "Then it is best you say nothing, neh? For then we would both know and the secret's greatness would be diminished."

Chuang Kuan Ts'ai looked down, wondering suddenly if she hadn't been wrong in coming here.

"It's just that I don't know what to do," she said, after a moment. "I can't sleep, remembering how they looked."

"How who looked?"

The curiosity in the old man's voice was unmistakable.

"The dead men," she said, meeting his eyes again. "What I know . . . men have died for knowing it. Only last week. . . ."

He was staring at her strangely now. Something in his eyes had changed. She stopped, conscious of a sudden chill in their exchange.

"You are the Oven Man's daughter, aren't you, child?"

She swallowed. "His niece."

"Ah . . ." The old man nodded. "I thought I knew you." Again there was a movement in his eyes, as if some calculation were being made in the space behind them. Then, "Do nothing, child. Understand me? Embrace wuwei. Take the path of inaction. Such is the Way."

"Nothing?" Her voice, though a whisper, registered her disappointment.

"Nothing," he reiterated, emphasizing it with a nod. "What is obscure shall become clear. What is dark shall become light."

She stared at him a moment longer, then bowed her head. "Lao jen."

Yet as she turned away, she could feel his eyes on her back, following her out through the curtain, and knew—knew with a certainty that frightened her—that she had made a serious mistake.

---

HE STATIONED MEN at every door, making sure nobody could leave, then marched over to the desk and slammed the warrant down before the woman. She looked up angrily, about to say something, then saw the uniform. At once her manner changed, became obsequious.

"Sergeant?"

He tapped the warrant. "Someone at this Library has been making illegal inquiries. I'd like to know who."

"That's not possible," she said, picking up the warrant and unfolding it. "We get hundreds of inquiries every week. Why, to track down a single instance—"

She stopped, then looked back at him.

"Well?" he asked.

She nodded and, folding the document, sat back. "It was a girl. She was in here a few days back. She said she was researching something for a school project. I thought it was strange, but—"

"What girl?" he asked, interrupting her.

"The Oven Man's daughter. She—"

"Where will I find her?" the sergeant asked, reaching across and taking back the warrant.

Straightening up, businesslike again, she nodded, then turned to her screen and, tapping out a code, called up a map of the Hsien. She turned the machine to face the sergeant, then tapped the screen with her fingernail.

"We're here. If you go south down Tai Pei Avenue and turn left *along Nan Lu Street, you'll come to an open square. Huang Cheng Lane is to the left as you enter it. You'll find the Oven Man's house halfway down. You can't miss it. The chimney . . ."*

The sergeant stared a moment, studying the map, then, with a bow of his head and a click of his heels, he about-turned and left, gesturing to his men to follow.

She sat back, watching them go, then blanked the screen, letting a long sigh escape her. Too bad, she was a pretty little thing, she thought, a small twinge of pity for the girl making her grimace briefly. With a tiny shiver she pushed the thought aside, getting on with her job.

*J O S E F   W O K E   T O find someone tugging at his arm. At first, still only half awake, he didn't realize what was happening; then, with a suddenness that jolted him fully awake, he understood. Someone was trying to take the jacket from his back.*

He rolled from the ledge he was on into the main shaft, lashing out with his free arm, and threw himself at the thief in a savage frenzy. With a frightened yelp the thief—a thin, shaven-headed youth—let go of the jacket and tried to make his escape, but the drainage shaft they were in was narrow and besides, Josef had his arm in a tight grip.

The arm was scrawny and bare. Josef pulled it savagely toward his face and bit, sinking his teeth deep into the flesh, feeling the skin give, his mouth fill with warm blood.

The thief's scream was deafening, but Josef had not done with him. As he tried to scrabble away, Josef followed him doggedly, kicking and punching, the fact that his assailant was twice his size of no concern to him.

The thief, who'd thought he'd come upon easy pickings, was shrieking now, certain that he'd disturbed a sleeping monster, for the inhuman thing that came at him was vicious and unrelenting. His screams now were not screams of pain but of terror.

Josef stood back, watching as he scuttled away on all fours, whimpering, his eyes filled with an awed fear of the tiny figure that now stood fully upright, the top of its head barely scraping the top of the shaft.

Word would go out. There would be talk of demons in the shafts. Josef bent down and picked up his jacket. It was sodden and stained, the sleeve ripped. He went to put it on, then changed his mind and threw it

down. He could get another. He could steal a thousand jackets if he
wanted. In fact, he could take whatever he needed and return down here
into the tunnels. After all, who would willingly pursue him now that
there were demons in the shafts?

He laughed, then turned and began to make his way back along the
shaft toward the pumping station and the "Nest."

———————

THE "NEST" WAS a high-water overflow tank just above the
main pumping station. It was a large, dry space, linked to the other
shafts by two narrow service-tunnels barely large enough for a child to
crawl along. As such it was the ideal spot for runaways, and a dozen or
so of them had formed a kind of camp—a nest—there. Josef had heard
of it from a boy named Judd within hours of coming into the tunnels and
had tried to find a place there among its inhabitants, but they had ganged
up on him and driven him out, giving him more than a few scratches and
bruises in passing. Unfamiliar with the ways of the tunnels, he had
accepted the setback—vowing to himself that he would settle scores with
them in time—but now he knew that if he was going to survive down
here he would have to be there, in the Nest, otherwise he would be prey
to any cutthroat who chanced on his sleeping form.

Last time he hadn't known what to expect, but this time he was
prepared. This time no one would drive him away.

Crouched beneath the access tunnel he could hear the murmur of their
voices up above and smiled. They were like him in some ways—ruthless.
But their ruthlessness had been born of desperation, of need, whereas his
was the natural ruthlessness of a predator.

Josef turned his head, watching an insect scuttle by his foot. Like most
of the insects down there, it was blind, hunting by scent alone. Not that
it was dark down here. No, for the ice—the special polymer—of which
the tunnel walls were made gave off a faint, illuminating glow that gave
all things a ghostly appearance.

He reached out and snatched the scuttling thing, crushing it between
his fingers, then brushed it off, nodding to himself.

It was like being among the dead. Like being in Ti Yu, the great Earth
Prison.

Vaguely he wondered how many lived like this, among the shafts and *tunnels beneath the City. Letting the thought go, he counted to ten and hauled himself up the tunnel, shrieking at the top of his lungs.*

The noise unnerved them. Emerging from the tunnel's end he could see the startled fear in their faces. There were five of them—all of them smaller boys—crouched defensively on the far side of the circular space, staring across at him, wide eyed. None of the bigger boys, the leaders, were there.

He jumped down and stood there like a warrior, half crouched, ready to do battle. All about him the ragged detritus of their bedding lay scattered—an untidy, stinking mess.

"You'd better go," one of them said in a small voice.

"Yeah," another added. "You ain't welcome here."

"Yeah?" he asked, a sneer in his voice; a challenge.

He took a step toward them, then another.

"Stock will have you," one of them said. "He'll rip your guts out!"

"Stock?" Stock had to be the big one—the Hung Mao with the slight squint and the tufted, strawlike hair. Josef laughed. "Fuck Stock!"

They had backed up right against the wall. Now one of them got set to make his move, but Josef bared his teeth and snarled. At once the boy cowered back.

"This time I'm staying," Josef said threateningly. "This time—"

He heard the noise of someone entering the access tunnel behind him. Heard the harsh breathing of someone laboring to climb the steeply sloping shaft.

Reaching into his pocket, his fingers closed about the jagged-edged shard he'd found earlier. He'd known then what use he'd have for it.

Josef moved to his right, turning slightly, keeping the others in clear view, but turning all the while to face the opening.

There was a strained grunting and then a face appeared. Stock! It had to be Stock. Yes, this was one of the two who'd so delighted in beating him earlier.

But now the tables were turned.

Stock took in the situation at a glance, then looked to the others and bellowed at them.

"Well? What are you waiting for, you fuckers? Get him!"

But Josef gave them no chance. In three quick strides he was at the opening, the shard raised. Stock, who was still struggling to get out, *looked up, a tiny sound of surprise escaping his parted lips as Josef's arm swung in an arc toward his face.*

Stock's screams were terrifying. The boys, who had come halfway across the space, froze, then began to back away. As Josef turned, they saw the bloodied shard in his hand and began to whimper, while beyond Josef, wedged tightly in the opening, Stock held his blinded eye, squealing like a stuck pig.

Josef took a step toward them and, smiling, bared his teeth once more. "I stay. You understand?"

———————

THE OLD PRIEST met them at the door and hurriedly ushered the three soldiers inside, looking about him as he did so to make sure that no one had seen them enter.

"Well?" the middle-aged lieutenant asked, coming straight to the point. "You'd better not be wasting my time, lao jen. I've work enough to keep five men busy!"

"No. . . . No, I . . . Look. There have been rumors. The burned-out club. Word was that men died, not in the fire, but . . . Well, you know how it is."

The officer was stoney faced. "So?"

The old man lowered his voice. "So this morning a young girl came to me. Worried, she was. She said she had a secret. A great secret, she called it. She talked about dead men and about men dying because of what she knew. I"—he moistened his lips with his tongue, then spoke again—"I felt it was my duty as a citizen to inform you at once."

"I see." The lieutenant scratched his balding pate. "This girl—who was she?"

"I don't know her name. In fact, I don't even think I've talked to her before today. But she lives with the Oven Man, in Huang Cheng Lane."

The officer took out an autonote and spoke into it. Tucking it away, he nodded to the priest.

"You did well, lao jen. I'm certain my Masters will wish to reward you for your services. But please . . . you must tell no one else about this matter. It is indeed a great secret, so . . ."

The priest bowed his head. "I understand."

"Good." The officer reached out, patting the old man's arm. "You did well, lao jen. Very well indeed."

———————

THE SERGEANT and his squad were already at the Oven Man's gate when the lieutenant arrived with his two assistants.

The two groups—rival arms of the same Security force, the sergeant's small force in the emerald-green of Pei K'ung's elite, the lieutenant's in the powder-blue of regular security—faced each other uneasily.

"Sergeant?" the lieutenant asked, trying to size up the man. "What are you doing here? This is some way outside your jurisdiction, I'd have thought?"

The sergeant came to attention, his head bowed low. Behind him his men did the same. "Forgive me, sir, but I've come to arrest someone for a security violation. A young girl. The daughter of the house."

"The daughter. . . ." The lieutenant shook his head, surprised. "How strange. How very strange. Why, I am here myself to have words with her about a certain matter."

The sergeant raised his head. "I have a warrant."

"A warrant?" The lieutenant extended his hand. "Show me."

"I'm sorry, sir?"

"The warrant. Give it to me."

The sergeant hesitated, then shook his head. "I am afraid I cannot do that, sir. Colonel I was most specific about that."

The lieutenant's eyes flared. "I am your superior officer, Sergeant, and I command you. Now, give it to me!"

The sergeant stood his ground, his squad of four men backing him up, their faces set and determined. "I am afraid I cannot do that, sir. Though you are indeed my superior and under ordinary circumstances I would gladly carry out your orders, to do so in these circumstances would be to ignore the specific instructions of a more senior officer, and that—"

The lieutenant, exasperated, made to snatch the warrant from his hand, but the sergeant moved back sharply, hiding the warrant behind his back.

"For the gods' sakes, man," the lieutenant said, his eyes lit with anger now. "I only want to see the damn thing!"

The sergeant shook his head. "I'm sorry, sir, but—"

He stopped and half turned. Behind him the gate creaked open and the Oven Man stepped out. Cho Yao looked about him, surprised to see them there.

"What's going on?" he asked, looking from the sergeant to the lieutenant.

"Are you the Lu Nan Jen?" the lieutenant asked.

"I am," Cho answered, a cloud crossing his face as he realized this had to do with him.

"Is your daughter in?" the sergeant asked, preempting the other.

Cho straightened, suddenly defensive. "What do you want?"

"I want—" both men began, then stopped, glaring at each other.

"I have a warrant," the sergeant began.

"Fuck your warrant!" the lieutenant said. "I am not answerable to I Ye and this is my patch, so step aside and let me get on with my work, Sergeant, or I'll have you arrested!"

"You can try," the sergeant answered, stepping between the lieutenant and Cho. Then, more calmly, but with a great deal of threat, he added, "You can try, sir, but I warn you, there's but three of you and there's five of us."

The lieutenant stepped back. "Why, this is outrageous! This—"

The sergeant turned his back, ignoring him. He had his orders, after all. Besides, he knew for certain that I Ye would bail him out. He always did. That was the good thing about working for I Ye. If you were loyal to him, then he stuck by you.

"Lu Nan Jen," he began, unfolding the warrant and holding it up so Cho Yao could see, "I have here a warrant for the arrest of your daughter for the crime of illegal inquiry. If you would bring her to the door."

"Arrest?" Cho looked stunned. "What for? She's just a little girl. An illegal inquiry? Why—"

"If you would stand aside," the sergeant said, beginning to get impatient. "I am a busy man."

Cho's mouth worked soundlessly a moment, then he shook his head firmly.

"No! No, you won't take her! You won't!"

But even as he said it, one of the sergeant's men slipped behind Cho Yao and coshed him hard over the head. As he fell the others stepped over him and went inside.

The sergeant turned, looking to his nominal superior. "No disrespect, sir. Just doing my duty."

The lieutenant swallowed back the bitterness he felt. "I'll put in an official complaint," he said. "I'll have you demoted for your insolence!"

The sergeant smiled, then bowed his head. "Of course, sir. Now . . . if I might get on with things?" And, turning his back on him a second time, he went inside, chuckling softly to himself.

Just doing my duty.

Yes, and enjoying every fucking moment of it.

# Chance Meetings

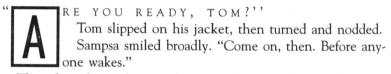

"**A**RE YOU READY, TOM?"
Tom slipped on his jacket, then turned and nodded. Sampsa smiled broadly. "Come on, then. Before anyone wakes."

They slipped outside, into the dawn light, the Eastern Palace to their right, the surrounding wall directly to their left as they made their way along the path.

The San Chang were deathly quiet after the evening's celebrations, most of their occupants fast asleep. Only servants were about as the two went down the steps and across to the massive forty-foot-high gate.

"They know how to build doors," Sampsa joked as, showing their passes, they went through, past a squad of guards who formed up and bowed almost comically, their captain anxious to show the two young guests the maximum respect. Then they were outside, in the broad and silent streets that surrounded the San Chang, the Mansions of the rich.

"Which way?" Sampsa asked, touching Tom's arm.

Tom pointed to his left, then spoke inside Sampsa's head.

*There. We head directly south, to the river, then cross the bridge and go west.*

*Okay,* Sampsa answered silently. *Let's go.*

But Tom delayed. He stared at Sampsa, his vision doubled. *Are you sure? Are you really sure you want to do this?*

He saw himself as Sampsa saw him. *It's what you want, isn't it? Yes, but—*

*Then don't be silly. Let's get going. Before they realize we're missing and send a search party to bring us back!*

Tom smiled and saw himself smile. *Okay. And . . . thanks.*

"No trouble," Sampsa said softly, the words an echoed whisper in Tom's head. "No trouble at all."

---

KIM LOOKED OUT through the window of his room, momentarily surprised to see neither the tree-lined landscape of the island nor the star-dusted blackness of space, but the sloping red tile rooftops of the palace and, beyond the massive walls of the San Chang, the sprawling city.

He turned, fastening the last button of his tunic, then walked through into the bedroom. Jelka was sitting on the edge of the bed, her emerald-green sleeping silk wrapped about her, their five-year-old daughter, Mileja, standing between her legs, facing her mother as she dressed her.

"Where's Sampsa?" he asked, answering Mileja's smile of greeting with his own.

"Out with Shepherd's son," Jelka answered, the hair grip between her teeth making the words come out oddly.

"Ahh . . . It's strange, that, don't you think?"

Jelka glanced at him, then looked back at her daughter, frowning with concentration. "Strange?"

"I don't understand it. How they could know one another. It was like they were old friends."

"Sampsa said they were."

"Yes. . . ." Kim hesitated. "He did, didn't he?"

"Hmm." Jelka took the hairbrush from beside her and began to brush out Mileja's shoulder-length auburn hair. "Maybe they've met up on the Net."

"Maybe. . . ." He considered that a moment, then nodded to himself, as if satisfied with the explanation. "Yes . . . that has to be it. I mean, where else could they have met?"

Jelka took the hairclip from her mouth and pushed it into place. "There, little madam! That's you done." She looked to Kim again. "You need anything?"

He shook his head.

"Then get going."

He went across and held her briefly, kissing her forehead, then took Mileja's hand. "We'll not be long. An hour at most."

She smiled. "Take however long you want. I'm going to have a nice long soak. Have you seen the size of that bath in there?"

He laughed. "A bath? Is that what it is? I thought it was a dry dock of some kind!"

"Well, whatever it is, I plan to fill it to the brim and enjoy myself."

"Not too much, I hope," he said and, blowing her a kiss, went to the door, Mileja at his side.

Tuan Ti Fo was waiting for them in the corridor outside. As they stepped out he got off the bench and stood, bowing first to Kim, then, with exaggerated care, to Mileja.

"Well, good morning, young Mistress. And how are we today?"

"I'm fine, Master Tuan," she said, remembering both her manners and his name.

Tuan Ti Fo looked to Kim, impressed. "You have a fine daughter there, Kim Ward. And your wife . . . you chose well."

Kim nodded thoughtfully. "I waited a long time for her. And she for me. Seven years. It seemed like an eternity."

"But worth every second of the waiting, neh?"

Kim smiled, nodding his agreement. "Every second."

They went on, along the broad, high-ceilinged corridors and down, past endless hanging tapestries, endless bowing servants, until they came to the reception area at the front of the palace; there, to their right, was a huge, winding staircase big enough to march twenty men abreast.

Mileja gripped her father's hand firmly and stared at it wide eyed. She had never seen the like. Nor the massive golden dragons that adorned the huge chandelier fifty *ch'i* above their heads.

Moving on toward the great arch of the entrance, Old Tuan looked to Kim again. "Is Marie expecting us?"

Kim grinned. "She's expecting me. But you, Master Tuan . . .

Well, I thought I'd keep you a surprise. It's many years since she last saw you, neh?"

"And yet it seems like only yesterday. How strange time is, neh, Kim? That seven years can seem an eternity to wait, and yet a whole lifetime can flash by like a dream. Why is that so?"

"Maybe it *is* all a dream, Master Tuan. Like the dream you had when you first came for me. You remember that?"

Tuan Ti Fo nodded. "How could I forget? It was as if the gods directed me to where you were."

"So it was," Kim said with a sigh, touching his old friend's arm. "So it was." And they walked on, the two men thoughtful, the child between them humming to herself as they stepped out past the saluting guards and into the morning sunlight.

———

MARIE WAS RINSING out some washing in the sink when the doorbell rang. She turned, shouting back into the living room.

"May? Can you get that for me? It'll be *Shih* Ward. Show him in. I'll not be a moment."

She wrung out the last of the vests and put it on the side with the others, then emptied the bowl. Reaching out for the towel, she paused, a strange, prickling sensation down her back. Slowly she turned.

A small, stooped-backed figure stood in the doorway. An ancient, yet familiar figure.

"Master Tuan?" she asked in a tiny voice. "Tuan Ti Fo?"

Then, shrieking with delight, she threw herself at the old Han, hugging him tightly, lifting him from his feet.

"How *are* you? It's been ages! I thought . . ."

"You thought I was dead, neh?"

She nodded guiltily, then grinned at him again. "Oh, it's *so* good to see you, Tuan Ti Fo. So *very* good."

Marie set the old man down, then looked past him at Ward. "And you, Kim. You're doubly welcome for bringing me such a pleasant surprise!"

Kim looked up at her and smiled, his figure like a child's beside hers.

"It was the least I could do, Marie. I was surprised myself to find

Master Tuan here. He came with *Shih* Ebert, it seems. They were on Mars together."

"Mars?" She stared at Tuan Ti Fo, intrigued.

"That was a while ago," Tuan said, turning and smiling at Marie's daughters, giving each in turn a tiny bow. "I am in Africa now, with the Osu."

"The black men." She nodded soberly. "How strange our times are. I never thought to see such creatures."

He looked to her. "They are not creatures, Marie. They are human, like you and me."

"Like *you*, Master Tuan?" Kim teased.

Tuan laughed gently. "Well . . . maybe not *quite* like me. Not as old, certainly."

"I didn't mean . . ." Marie began, but Tuan's smile was understanding.

"You are right, however, Marie. These are strange times indeed."

"Would you like *ch'a*, Master Tuan?" she asked.

He smiled fondly. "It is many years since you served me *ch'a*, Marie. In the Dragon Cloud teahouse, I believe it was, where you once worked."

It was clear none of the girls knew of this aspect of their mother's life. They clamored suddenly for her to tell them more, but she put them off, turning to Tuan Ti Fo again.

"You remember those days?"

"How could I forget?"

"And while you wait," she said, "May will bring the board."

"The board?" There was a sudden twinkle in his eye.

Her smile broadened. "Why, yes, Master Tuan. Just as you taught me the rudiments of the game, so I have taught my girls. The game . . . it is the mark of a civilized person, neh?"

He bowed, clearly impressed, then turned to May. "If you would do me the honor, May Karr."

She returned his bow, then went into the next room, emerging a moment later with a heavy *wei ch'i* board and two pots of stones. As Hannah and Lily cleared the table, May set the board down.

"How's Gregor?" Kim asked, going to the kitchen door. "Is he on duty this morning?"

"You could say that," Marie answered, pouring water into the kettle. "He's in Mashhad."

*"Mashhad?"*

She put the kettle on the hob, then turned to face him. "He's gone to see the Warlord, Hu Wang-chih."

Kim looked to Tuan Ti Fo, his eyes forming a question, but the old man merely shrugged.

"There is to be war." Marie said quietly. "Or so Gregor believes."

"War?" Kim frowned, greatly troubled by the news. "Then Hans Ebert was right."

"Yes," Marie said, glancing at him, then turning away and beginning to prepare the *ch'a*. "Let us pray it is short lived."

———————

KARR STOOD AMONG the Warlord's men, waiting to be summoned, Ming Ai stationed squatly at his side, the polished crown of his head on a level with Karr's elbow. Facing them, the doors to Hu Wang-chih's audience chamber were closed and had been so for two hours.

"Why does he keep us waiting so long?" the Chief Eunuch muttered irritably. "He must know how important this is."

"He keeps us waiting because he can," Karr answered calmly, wondering, not for the first time, just why Ming Ai had been sent.

To keep tabs on him, certainly, and to make sure that an accurate report of the meeting got back to his Mistress. But beyond that? What did Ming Ai himself hope to gain by being here?

He leaned toward the eunuch, speaking from the side of his mouth. "By the way, I would appreciate it if you would let me do the talking when we get inside, Master Ming."

Ming Ai bristled. "Don't lecture me, Marshal Karr. I know how to behave."

"Good." Karr nudged him hard. "Then make sure you do. You fuck *this* up, you'll know about it!"

Ming Ai glared at Karr but said nothing.

*He's probably watching us,* Karr thought, looking up at the camera over the door. *Waiting to pick his moment, when we seem most restless.*

Yes, because such meetings were about advantage. About gaining it and keeping it. For when all was said and done—beneath the veiled layers of politeness and diplomacy—what they did here was merely another form of barter. Crude trade, driven by the desire for profit. For *advantage*.

Deals. He hated deals. Yet deals were necessary, even with bastards like Hu Wang-chih.

Karr sighed, mulling over what he knew of the man, or at least what was *rumored*. Word was that he was a cruel man, a sadist; that he enjoyed the suffering of others. That much was unexceptional. Karr had met many such men. What *was* unusual—if it were true—was the inventiveness of his cruelty. It was said that he had once forced one of his servants—for no reason—to tell him which of his five children he liked the best, then had had the child tortured before the man's eyes. That in itself was execrable, but the refinement—the supreme cruelty—had been in the manner of the torture, for he had had the man's wife—the mother of the child— carry out the torture; threatening to kill the other four children if she refused.

Reluctantly, they had carried out his orders. But it had driven them mad.

*As indeed it would,* Karr thought with a shudder. Whether the story was apocryphal or not, it was one of many that circulated about Warlord Hu. From what he'd heard, one could fill a weighty volume with such tales.

There was the sound of bolts being drawn back. As Karr looked up the doors began to open. Inside, the pillared hall was brightly lit . . . and empty.

Karr frowned, wondering what game this was—whether it was some new attempt to belittle them—then heard a door open at the far end of the hall. With the regular click of leather heels against the stone, a figure approached; a middle-aged Han in traditional dress, his dark hair tied back in a single pigtail. Stopping several paces in front of Karr, he bowed low, then, straightening, smiled broadly.

"Marshal Karr. Forgive the delay. My Master will see you now. I am Ji Wang, the Warlord's First Minister."

"Ji Wang . . ." Karr lowered his head, acknowledging him.

Then, trying to recall what he knew of this man, he half turned, meaning to introduce the Chief Eunuch.

Ji Wang raised a hand. "The eunuch stays here," he said bluntly. "None but *men* enter my Master's halls."

Ming Ai's features convulsed with anger. "I have never heard such nonsense! Why, my Mistress—"

Ji Wang's voice cut through the fat man's bluster like a finely focused laser. "You heard me, eunuch. My Master will not see you."

"He *refuses?*"

Ignoring Ming Ai, Ji Wang turned to Karr again and gave another tiny bow. "If you would accompany me, Marshal?"

Karr stared at Ji Wang. If he was to make a protest, it would have to be right now. Indeed, he ought, perhaps, to refuse to take a step further without Ming Ai, for it was, without doubt, a snub to Pei K'ung. Yet he felt strangely disinclined. He knew how important this meeting was, and if Warlord Hu did not wish to see the eunuch, then maybe he should go along with that, if only for the sake of the alliance.

Ming Ai, seeing Karr's hesitation, gave a grunt of disgust, then made to grasp the Minister's arm, but Ji Wang pulled back, glaring at him. At his gesture two guards grabbed Ming Ai by the arms and, ignoring his shouts of protest, dragged him away.

Karr stood there, watching in shocked amazement as Ming Ai was marched forcibly down the corridor, struggling and cussing all the way. Then he turned back.

Ji Wang was watching him, an amused expression on his face.

"You have no objections, I take it, Marshal Karr?"

Karr stared at the man, realizing that the moment had been lost and with it the advantage. He had enjoyed Ming Ai's humiliation and they knew it. They had anticipated his reaction and used it.

He smiled at Ji Wang, feeling a new respect for the man. "Ming Ai is unimportant," he said, as if it were a fact. "What I have to say to your Master is between him and me alone."

"Then that is good. I have merely removed an irritation, neh?"

Karr hesitated, uncertain whether he should let the man push the matter quite so far, then nodded, accepting the situation. Ji Wang's actions had been an insult, true, but they were an insult against Pei K'ung, and while he was here at Pei K'ung's order, it

was Li Yuan he served. What was done was done. It was up to him
now to make the best of things.

Besides, what Ji Wang had said was true. Ming Ai *was* an irritation, and Karr had felt much constrained by the fact that he would
be there at his side during the discussions. Constrained, yes, and
fearful lest Ming Ai say something tactless—something that might
damage the delicate, complex process of negotiation.

Now that he was gone—forcibly removed from the equation—
Karr felt a sense of liberation. This was a situation he had been in
several times before—with the White T'ang, Lehmann, and with
the Mountain Lord, Fu Chiang—and he knew that, whatever the
outcome, it would be through no fault of his that it failed.

As Ji Wang turned away, he followed him, across the echoing,
empty hall and through the end doorway, into a smaller, yet luxuriously decorated, room. As he entered, Hu Wang-chih got up from
a chair by the window and stepped toward him, offering both
hands in greeting.

"Marshal Karr. I am delighted to meet you."

Karr stood before the Warlord, his head bowed, letting the man
take his hands briefly.

"Thank you for seeing me at such short notice, Hu Wang-chih,"
Karr said, straightening up. "My Master has asked me to express his
most sincere gratitude."

"Not at all. It is *my* pleasure."

Hu Wang-chih gave a little bow. Turning, he indicated a seat
just across from his.

"Please, be seated, Marshal. We have much to discuss."

━━━━━━━

THE WARLORD'S WOMAN eased back in the tall-backed
chair with a sigh, then touched a pad on the arm-mounted controls. At once the great panel of nine screens—three deep, three
high—slid away from her with a hiss of hydraulics. As it did, she
placed a dark-gloved hand to her lips thoughtfully.

"So he sent Karr . . . Why?"

The words were for herself. She would always muse thus, alone
in that sealed and darkened room. But rarely—very rarely—was
she given such important matters to muse upon.

In the muted light from the screens she nodded to herself.

Li Yuan had not sent Karr. That had been Pei K'ung's decision. Li Yuan had not even been consulted.

"Of course," she said throatily. "Of course!"

Her laughter was like the calling of crows. It ended in a choking cough.

"But what does he want? What does he really want? War?" She shook her head. "No. He wants something else. Something deeper. Something . . ."

She stopped, the answer coming to her from the still and frozen air.

"Yes," she said, chuckling quietly to herself. "Why, *of course. . . .*"

---

M A S T E R   T U A N, looking up from the board, bowed his head to his young opponent. "Well done, Mileja. If I did not know better, I would have thought I was playing against your father."

She looked up at the old man with an expression of surprise. "But I lost!"

Kim, looking on, laughed. "To lose to Master Tuan by a single stone is no disgrace, my pet. Master Tuan was once First Hand Supreme of all Chung Kuo!"

Mileja stared at Tuan Ti Fo anew, reappraising him, then, almost comically, she bowed.

Old Tuan laughed merrily, while the others—Marie, her four daughters, and Kim—joined in, laughing and clapping appreciatively.

"Well, Kim?" Tuan said, turning to face him as the merriment died down. "Will you play me?"

Kim hesitated, then, with a brief glance at his timer, nodded. "Okay. But just the one game, neh? You know how time flies when we're at the board."

"I do indeed, old friend." Tuan Ti Fo, grinning, spoke the words of the ancient poem:

> *"Less than a day in paradise,*
> *And a thousand years have passed among men.*

*While the pieces are still being laid on the board*
*All things have changed to emptiness.*
*The woodman takes the road home,*
*The haft of his ax has rotted in the wind:*
*Nothing is what it was but the stone bridge*
*Still spanning a rainbow cinnabar-red."*

Kim sighed, nodding thoughtfully. "How often I've thought of that woodman across the years, Master Tuan. How often I've imagined myself in his place, returning home after a thousand years on the mountainside. It must have been strange, neh?"

"To be an immortal," Tuan said, beginning to pick the white stones from the board and return them to his bowl, "that, too, must be strange, neh?"

"Strange indeed," Kim answered, smiling at the old man. Then, with a tiny shudder he looked to the board, beginning to clear the black stones one by one.

---

IT WAS DONE. The proposition had been made, its details laid before the Warlord, its terms discussed in full. As Karr stood, Hu Wang-chih also stood, his eyes tracing the figure of the giant.

"You will let my Master know?" Karr asked.

Warlord Hu gave a single nod. "In two days' time." Stepping closer, he added: "You will forgive me, Marshal Karr, but now that our official business is done, might I make a personal observation?"

Karr shrugged. "If you so wish, Hu Wang-chih."

Hu Wang-chih smiled. "Oh, do not be afraid, Marshal Karr. I have nothing ill to say of you. It is only this. That I have admired you for many years now and followed your career closely. You are quite some soldier, Gregor Karr. A hero in an age that is . . . well, let us say *less* than heroic. My own commanders look up to you and, should we come to an agreement, would gladly serve under you."

Karr steeled himself. "But—"

"No buts. If Kuan Ti, the God of War, had taken on a human form, it would surely have been yours."

Karr stared, wondering what to make of this unexpected flattery;

whether to take it at face value or look for some deeper motive. Yet
the Warlord seemed, for once, quite genuine in his praise.

"It is not merely your strength I admire, Gregor Karr, but the
restrained power you demonstrate in every movement. To see such
brutal power moved by so subtle an intelligence is a delight to me.
It is True Strength, neh?"

Hu nodded, his smile broadening momentarily. "I felt I could
not let you go without saying so. It would have been . . . impo-
lite."

"Thank you," Karr said simply, wishing not to offend the Warlord; yet inwardly he rebelled against the man's comments. Such
men always admired the appearance of strength, of brutal power.
They worshiped it. And whether this one—this Hu Wang-chih—
was subtler than the others in recognizing the inner power that
motivated the outer show mattered little. What mattered was
whether such praise came from a source he could respect—and to
be candid, he could not respect Warlord Hu, fair words or otherwise.

*You are a callous sadist,* he thought, studying Hu's smiling face.
*Besides, your admiration is tainted by simple envy. Envy that Li Yuan
possesses my services and not you.*

He bowed, then backed away.

*And anyway,* he thought, as he walked back through the great
hall, his booted footsteps echoing from the high stone walls, *true
strength has nothing to do with size or skill in battle.*

No. True strength was knowing not merely *when* to fight but
*why.*

Two days. Li Yuan would have his answer in two days. In the
meantime he would have to stay here, in the company of the odious Ming Ai.

The thought of it—of sharing close quarters with the half-
man—made him groan inwardly.

*True strength.* He sighed heavily. Maybe true strength was simply
the ability not to let such creatures get to one; to keep one's inner
self clear and pure and focused. But it would be hard, he knew, to
keep Ming Ai from getting under his skin. As hard as any battle he
had fought.

Then, remembering the eunuch's face as he had been dragged

away, Karr began to smile, the smile quickly changing to a chuckle, then a full-bellied laugh.

As he passed the guards stationed at the doors, they stared at him openly, amazed by his laughter, their faces lit with awe, as though in the presence of a god.

———————

L I   Y U A N was in the stables, his tunic discarded, his sleeves rolled up to his elbows as he groomed one of the mares. He had almost finished when Shepherd came upon him.

"It went well, don't you think?" Yuan said with a smile, continuing to brush the horse's coat. "Pei K'ung's face was a delight. I've watched the tape of that moment a dozen times now. She really hates you."

Ben nodded, untroubled by the news, then came around the side of the stall. He rested his forearms on the wooden beam and looked over at Li Yuan thoughtfully.

"The court is buzzing with it," he said. "I come across little groups in corridors. They go quiet as I pass, but when they think I'm out of earshot, they huddle together again conspiratorially, heads pressed close, like ants passing on a message."

Li Yuan laughed. Finished, he threw the brush down and came over to him. "It was a good evening, Ben. I am grateful for your help."

Ben gave a nod of acknowledgment. Then: "Who was the girl?"

"Girl?" Li Yuan made as if he did not know what Ben was talking about. Even so, he took a step out of the stall and gestured to the nearby grooms to leave. Alone, he turned back, looking to Ben and smiling. "Which girl?"

Ben studied him, a faint smile on his lips. "You might fool others, Yuan, but not me. I've seen the way you look at her. So who is she?"

Li Yuan shrugged, then, laughing lightly, answered him. "*She* is the Princess Hsun Lung hsin, second daughter of Prince Hsun."

"Ahh . . ." Ben made an instant reassessment. "I see. And you're in love with her, neh?"

Yuan's eyes slipped away. "In love? I wouldn't say that. . . ."

"Li Yuan. Be straight with me."

"I . . ." He shook his head, then met Ben's eyes again. "Not in love. Infatuated, perhaps. Fascinated, certainly. But love? No . . . I'll get over it. I simply have to have her."

"Fuck her, you mean?"

Li Yuan winced at the crudity of the expression. "No. I mean . . . Oh, I guess so. I just can't stop thinking about her. You know? It's like a fever, an itch beneath the skin. I ache for her, Ben. *Kuan Yin!* At times I feel like a lovesick adolescent!"

"There!" Ben said triumphantly, as if he'd trapped Li Yuan. "She's woven her spell over you. I was right!"

Li Yuan stared at him, concerned by what he'd said. "No. It'll be all right. I just have to—"

"—have her." Ben smiled. "So what's stopping you? The fact that she's your son's bride's sister?"

Li Yuan turned away, sighing heavily.

"Not that? Then what *is* stopping you?"

The T'ang turned back, his face pained now. "She won't. She'll do anything but that. Absolutely anything. But she absolutely refuses to let me have her. Not while she's betrothed."

"Then buy off her suitor!"

"And her father, the Prince?"

"Buy him off too!"

"How?"

"Think of some way. I'm sure you'll come up with something."

"But what if he refuses? After all, this is a matter of great honor. Word would get around. He would lose face, unless . . ."

Ben narrowed his eyes. "Unless what?"

"Unless I found her a better match."

"You mean, someone who wouldn't mind taking on the T'ang's cast-offs? A Minister, perhaps? Or someone of comparative high status? That worm Fa Chun, perhaps. You know, the merchant who petitioned you last night."

Li Yuan was quiet. He looked down, not answering.

Ben laughed. "No. You're not serious, surely, Yuan? Marry her yourself? You'd be mad to!"

"Mad? It's maddening now not to have her."

"Then I'll give her to you."

"How?"

"I'll make a Shell for you. I'll make it so that she gives in to you. I'll make it so you can have her any way you want. Yes, and as often."

Li Yuan shuddered, then reached out for his tunic, which hung on the rail beside Shepherd. "How long would that take?"

"A month, perhaps. Six weeks at most."

Yuan shuddered again, then shook his head. "Too long. I couldn't bear it. I have to have her, Ben. I *have* to!"

Ben shook his head. "Then have her. Rape her if you must. But don't marry her, Yuan. I warn you. It'll cause many more problems than it'll solve."

Li Yuan looked to his old friend and adviser and gave the tiniest nod, but his eyes were haunted and his hands where they held his tunic were slick with sweat.

"A Shell, you say?"

Ben nodded. "I could begin today."

Yuan swallowed, then looked down. "Okay. . . ." Then, with a troubled little movement of his head, he moved past Ben, hurrying from the stables.

Ben watched him go; putting the tip of his tongue to his teeth, he sucked in his breath and shook his head.

"I have to have her, Ben," he said, mimicking the T'ang's voice perfectly. "I *have* to!"

━━━━◆◆◆━━━━

THEY MET IN the middle of the Palace Gardens, on the bridge that spanned the Lake of Prolonged Autumn—two men who, until that moment, had never crossed each other's path.

Shepherd, coming from the stables, walked slowly, his mood pensive, the moon low in the sky behind him, framing his head in a halo of pale light as he watched the other approach. Ward, returning alone from Marie Karr's, walked much more briskly, his ungainly-looking head lowered, his mind still full of complex *wei ch'i* moves as he studied the slender volume of aphorisms the old man had given him, unaware of Shepherd just ahead of him.

It was after eleventh bell and the sun was slowly climbing to its zenith. Just now it lay directly behind the Clayborn, its light reflected in the surface of the lake.

In reality, the "lake" was little more than a massive ornamental pond, strewn with giant white lilies; the bridge a narrow path of pale stone, curving in five graceful spans across the water.

"*Shih* Ward?"

Kim looked up from the book, then gave a brief, apologetic laugh. "Forgive me. I was miles away."

"*Miles?*" Ben smiled, then. "I hoped we would meet last night. I was disappointed not to talk with you."

Kim returned Ben's easy smile. "And I you. You're Ben Shepherd, no?"

Ben extended a hand. "I am."

Kim clasped and shook it. "Well met."

"Well met, indeed."

Both men laughed.

"That was some scene last night," Kim said.

Ben nodded. "The Empress was not amused."

"No. . . ." Kim studied him briefly. There was an intensity about his eyes—about the whole man, in fact—that was unmistakable. He had a driven, almost haunted look.

"Things appear to be happening very quickly," Kim ventured. "I've been away only a month, yet in that time things seem . . . *transformed.*"

"That's so," Ben said with apparent candor. "But you'll hear more in that regard this afternoon. Li Yuan has called a special meeting of the Advisory Council."

Kim appeared shocked. "A meeting? But I've heard nothing."

Ben stared out across the water. "No. I've come from Li Yuan this very moment."

"Ah. So the rumors are true."

"About war, you mean?" Ben looked to him, then looked away again. "Not of necessity."

"No?" Kim narrowed his eyes. "I thought the matter was decided. There is a point, then, to our discussions this afternoon?"

"There is a point to everything that's happening." Ben glanced at him, a faint smile on his lips. "But don't look to surfaces, Kim Ward. What's happening runs deep. Like that show last night."

Kim laughed. "I did wonder." He tapped the book against his upper thigh. "And your work? How goes that?"

"My work?" Ben looked back, his eyes once more raking Kim with their intensity. They were like cameras, like dark, voracious lenses sucking in the light. He did not "look" as other men looked, he *saw*. "My work goes tolerably well. And yours?"

"One step forward, two back."

Ben nodded. "It is the way sometimes. The second law of thermodynamics rules us all, neh?" Unexpectedly, he reached out and touched Kim's arm. "You must come to my studio while you're here, Kim. I'd like to show you around, to get your views on certain things. It's not often I have intelligent company."

Kim smiled. "Thank you. I'd like that."

"Good." For a moment it seemed that Shepherd was about to walk on, then he gave a soft laugh. "It's strange, don't you think, about our sons?"

"Strange?"

"How they took to each other so quickly. You'd have thought they'd known each other years. Tom . . . well, Tom is not the most communicative child, as you can imagine, though I suspect sometimes that his silence is a matter of choice, not nature."

"Ahhh . . ." Kim frowned. The subject disturbed him for some reason he had not yet come to grips with. "My wife, Jelka, thinks they must have met up on the Net. Sampsa spends a lot of time on it."

Ben laughed. "Maybe. That said, I don't think I've ever seen Tom go *near* a computer. As far as I've observed, he seems to spend most of his time out in the woods. Or did. He's changing. Growing up. I thought he'd be a child forever."

Kim nodded. "So it was with Sampsa. These last few months . . ." He laughed. "Look, I must be getting on. Jelka's expecting me. But I'll come and visit you. Tomorrow, perhaps?"

"Tonight would be better. It's when I work. I like the darkness."

Kim smiled. "Tonight, then. At eleven, say?"

"Eleven would be fine."

"Good." Kim nodded, smiled. "I shall look forward to it."

"And I."

They walked on, not looking back; two strangers, heading in opposite directions; two men who, until that moment, had never passed a word or met each other's eyes.

They went on, the days ahead cloaked from them, not knowing the significance of that chance meeting.

━━━━━━━

*THIS  IS  IT!* Tom cried, his voice a veritable shout in Sampsa's head as he looked about him at the open space of the riverside park. *It's there! Just over there!*

"Thank the gods for that!" Sampsa said quietly, watching Tom run down the path toward the bridge, his friend's excitement a warm tingling that rippled through his nerve ends. "I was beginning to think—"

And then it hit.

Tom stopped dead, as if he'd run into a wall of glass, the shock breaking against Sampsa's senses like a huge wave against a seawall.

He staggered, gasping as if he'd been punched in the stomach. Ahead of him Tom groaned silently and fell onto his knees.

Sampsa whimpered, then screwed his eyes tight shut against the wash of raw pain that was bleeding from Tom's head.

*Tom?* He groaned. *What is it, Tom?*

At once he saw. The flower boats were gone. Or rather, they weren't *gone*, they were still there, but they had been burned out. Their blackened hulks rested in the water like a child's crude charcoal sketches; eight empty eyes, mirroring the sky.

"Aiya," Sampsa said in a whisper, walking over to where Tom knelt, eyes wide, mouth gaping. "Aiya . . ."

Tom slowly shook his head, too shocked to think coherently. His head was full of jumbled images—a lamp reflected in the black surface of the water, the plucked sound of a Chinese lute, a voice, an oval face smiling up at him in the lamplight.

Sampsa shuddered, then reached down, pulling Tom to his feet. Shaking him, he spoke into his face.

"Come on. Let's find out what happened. Someone must know."

They went out onto the bridge. From the rail it looked much worse. Blackened spars could be glimpsed beneath the waterline. Under them was a clutter of debris. Anything light—anything that floated—had been washed away by the current.

Tom shuddered and looked to him, his face wet with tears. *She's dead, Sampsa . . . Dead.*

"You don't know that," Sampsa said quietly, resting his hands on Tom's shoulders. "We don't know what happened yet. It might have been an accident. They might all have got out safely."

But something about the scene suggested that this had been no accident. Tom stared at him and saw the thought in his head.

*She's dead!* he cried out, beginning to panic again. *She's dead! I know she is!*

"No," he said gently, holding Tom to him, his hand smoothing his back. "No, she's fine. I'm sure she's fine."

As he spoke, his eyes traced the eight dark outlines in the water, then moved across, looking toward the left-hand bank. There was a low stone wall and beyond it a dull red gravel path. Though it was still early, a number of people were about. Some strolled idly along the path, children in tow, others stopped to stare at the burned-out hulks, turning to exchange a word or two with other bystanders.

Tom, watching through his eyes, grew calm.

*Okay,* he said clearly in Sampsa's head, answering the unspoken thought.

They made their way down, onto the path.

*There'll be rumors,* Sampsa said silently. *Someone will have heard something.*

While Tom stood by the wall, Sampsa went among them, fishing for news.

"It was the Yellow Cranes," one old man said, with a decisive nod, but immediately a younger man corrected him.

"No, *lao jen*. You are mistaken. The Yellow Cranes owned these boats! Would they burn their own boats? No. It was the Iron Fist did this. There is bad blood between them and the Yellow Cranes. Only last week one of the Iron Fist's runners was badly beaten and another stabbed. This was their revenge."

"That's true," another chipped in, a small crowd beginning to form about Sampsa. "Things are getting worse by the day. They used to respect each other's borders, but now . . ." He turned his head and spat, then looked back at Sampsa. "Some say that more than a dozen have been killed already!"

"Were any killed here?" Sampsa asked, conscious that, though

Tom had his back to him and was actually looking out across the river, he was there, too, inside his head, watching from behind his eyes.

"Six, I heard," someone said from the back of the crowd, but he was immediately shouted down.

"No one's sure," a young woman said, to his right. "It was four in the morning when it happened. We saw the flames."

He turned to her. "You *saw* it?"

She half turned, pointing back across the park. "We live over there, in Florsheim. My old man got up to piss and saw it through the window. He woke me and we watched it from up on the roof. The whole sky seemed on fire."

Sampsa had the sudden image of himself, standing among the little crowd, and realized Tom had turned to watch. Yet even as he made to ask another question, Tom's voice filled his head urgently.

*It's him! There!*

He turned, startled, trying to work out who he was supposed to be looking at.

*The old man*, Tom said, his eyes following a hunched figure who was shuffling away from the crowd toward the gate. *It's the boatman! The one who rowed Yun and me across to the flower boats. . . .*

Sampsa spun around, then saw him. "Excuse me," he said, looking about him, then moved quickly through the crowd. "You!" he called, running after the old man. "Yes, *you!* I want a word!"

He saw himself running. Saw the crowd watch, wide eyed, as he caught up with the old man and, laying a hand on his shoulder, spun him about.

"You're the boatman, aren't you?"

The old man glared at him, then, mumbling something in Mandarin, made to turn away.

Sampsa reached out, stopping him. "No. You are. I know you."

"Well, I don't know you, young man. Now leave me be." The old man pulled away, then turned, making to go.

"You want me to hand you over to Security?"

The old man, hesitating, turned back, and faced Sampsa once again. For a moment he searched Sampsa's eyes, trying to make out who he was and what he really wanted.

"Who are you?" he asked suspiciously.

"A friend," Sampsa said, taking a five-*yuan* coin from his pocket and pressing it into the old man's palm.

The old man stared at the coin, bit it, then nodded, pointing over to the bridge. "Okay. But not here. In my hut."

———

THE BOATMAN'S HUT was a makeshift affair tucked into the shadows beneath the bridge. While the old man primed his stove and prepared a meal of soup for himself, he spoke to the two young gentlemen, telling them what he knew.

From where he sat on a stool in the corner, Sampsa watched Tom carefully, concerned; for as the old man's story went on, Tom grew more and more agitated, convinced in his mind that the very worst had happened.

"That late," the old man said, crouching, checking that the stove was properly lit, "we normally only have two guards on. There's not a lot of custom that time of the morning and we weren't expecting trouble."

He straightened up, one hand on his back. "I'd gone to bed, you see. So I was in my hut when I heard the shouts."

"Shouts?" Sampsa prompted.

The old man nodded thoughtfully. "I thought at first it was one of the young gentlemen, playing up. Maybe one of the girls had tried to rob him, or maybe he'd just had too much to drink, but when I popped my head out I saw straightaway what was happening."

"What exactly did you see?"

The old man's face creased thoughtfully in the lamplight. "Thirty, maybe forty men, armed with clubs and knives. The sight of it made me move back quick, into the shadows. It wasn't my argument, after all."

"And the guards? What did they do?"

The old man cleared his throat noisily, then continued. "First thing I heard after that warning shout was a double splash as the two of them dived off the boats and into the river. Can't blame them, I say. They weren't going to stop and have their throats cut, now were they?"

"So the girls were left undefended."

"And their clients. Poor bastards." He chuckled. "I watched them being taken off the boats, half of them drunk or woken from a dead sleep. The runners beat them—had a lot of fun with them, they did—then sent them off as they were, buck naked. That was a sight, I tell you! As for the girls . . ."

Sampsa looked up at Tom, who stood in the doorway, one hand gripping the lintel tightly as he listened.

"What about them?" Sampsa coaxed gently.

"What do you think? They were men, after all, and these *were* whores. They had their fun for a time. You should have heard the noise. The shrieks, the laughter. I'm surprised no one came to find out what was going on. Then again, who'd bother, that time in the morning? It's not as if some rich man's house were being attacked, was it? Anyway, when they'd had their fun, they set to work dousing the boats with fuel. And a rare old bonfire it made too."

"And the girls?" Sampsa asked, Tom's concern shaping the question. "What happened to them?"

The old man shrugged, then turned his attention to the soup, which had begun to bubble. "They tied their hands and took them away. They've got them working somewhere, I imagine." He looked from Sampsa to Tom, as if, as young men of the world, they understood. "I mean, why waste good young flesh? But it's a shame. They were a nice bunch of girls."

"And you, old man? What will you do now?"

"Me?" He laughed; the laugh becoming a hacking cough. "I'll travel downriver. I've family near Rheinstetten. They'll put me up until I find something else."

"Good." Sampsa smiled and nodded, then stood. "Thank you. You've been most helpful. Here. . . ."

He handed him another coin. This time a ten. The old man looked at it, wide eyed, then bowed, his eyes shining with gratitude.

"Take care, young gentlemen," he said, as they ducked out of the hut. "And give my regards to that scoundrel Yun when you see him!"

Sampsa, who had been about to walk away, stopped dead, looking to Tom. Yun! Of course! Why hadn't he thought of Yun before? If anyone could find out what happened, Yun could.

He turned back. "You wouldn't, by any chance, know where Yun stays when he's not working the imperial barge? He said he had family hereabouts."

The old man laughed. "The only family that one's got are street girls! If I were you, I'd try trawling the singsong houses."

Sampsa looked to Tom, then back to the old man. "Are there any you'd suggest?"

The boatman considered a moment, his jaw making a chewing movement as he thought, then he nodded. "You might try Madam Ho's in Hattersheim. It's in Green Dragon Lane. I'm told he's sweet on one of the girls there."

"Thanks," Sampsa said again, and then, because Tom was mentally urging him, handed the old man a third coin—another five.

The old man bowed low, muttering his thanks, unable to believe his good fortune, but the two young men were already hastening away.

*It's not far,* Sampsa said into Tom's head. *We can be there in less than an hour.*

Tom looked to him, despairing. *But Yun . . . what will Yun know?*

*More than us,* Sampsa answered, determined that he'd make the bastard talk. *A damn sight more than us!*

———

"LI YUAN?"

Surprised, Yuan turned, dropping the porcelain figure he'd been studying. It shattered at his feet.

"What are *you* doing here? I told Master Nan—"

"—that you were not to be disturbed. I know." Dragon Heart smiled and closing the door behind her, came across the room. "I told him I had an urgent message from my sister."

She bent down, beginning to pick up fragments of the broken statuette.

"And he believed that?"

She looked up at him and laughed. "Master Nan is a good servant, neh? And a good servant sees more than most men."

Li Yuan stared at her a moment, then crouched down, helping her.

"What was this?" she asked, examining one of the delicate painted pieces. Li Yuan glanced at the ancient fragments, conscious that he had just dropped five million *yuan's* worth of porcelain, then smiled.

"Nothing," he said. "Nothing at all." He reached out and gently touched her neck below her ear, his fingertips tracing the line of her shoulder, her upper arm.

She closed her eyes, like a cat being petted.

"I dreamed of you," he said softly.

Her eyes opened, looking straight into his, so clear and dark they took his breath. He leaned forward, gently brushing her lips with his own.

"I dreamed of geese," she said.

"Geese?"

"Two pure white geese, flying together into the southern sunlight. I was one of them. I could feel my wings beating strongly in the air. And beside me . . ."

He smiled. "Let me guess. It was me."

"You had the dream too?"

He shook his head. "No. But I wish I had been there with you in your dream."

"Maybe you will. Maybe you'll dream it tonight."

"Tonight?" His smile slowly faded. A tiny shiver passed through him. "Why don't you come to me tonight? No one will know."

Her smile did not waver. "That is not true, Li Yuan. I would know. Besides, I cannot come tonight. I must be with my sister tonight. Tomorrow, after all, is her wedding day."

"Ahhh . . ." The disappointment he felt was immense. He sighed heavily.

She put her hand out, her fingers softly caressing his cheek. "But I am here now, neh? You could lock the door and draw the blinds. . . ."

He stared at her. Then, as if in trance, he stood and went across, turning the key in the lock.

"Blinds down," he said, speaking to the house computer. At once the room began to darken as the big, slatted blinds came down.

He walked to his desk and put on the lamp. Turning, he looked to her. She was picking up more pieces, collecting them in her cupped left hand.

"Leave that," he said. "Come here."

She stood and came to him. Brushing the broken fragments onto the desktop, she turned her head, looking at him, her youthful face more serious than before—something determined in its expression.

"What do you want, Li Yuan?"

He hesitated, then said it, the words barely a whisper. "I want to make love to you, Dragon Heart. Right here, on the floor beside my desk."

"No," she said. "Anything but that."

"Anything?"

Slowly she began to unbutton her dress, then let it fall from her. Beneath it she was naked.

"Anything," she said once more, seeing how his eyes feasted on her; how his whole body was tensed with wanting her. She stepped toward him, then reached up, putting her arms about his neck. "Anything at all."

HANDING MADAM HO a twenty-*yuan* chip, Sampsa winked at her, then, putting a finger to his lips, opened the door.

The room was in darkness, the shutters closed. The sound of snoring came from somewhere on his left. He went across silently, then stood there, over the bed, looking down. In the light from the corridor outside he could make out the young man's features, recognizing Yun from Tom's memories.

Yun lay on his back in the abandonment of sleep, naked to the waist, his spectacularly ugly face tipped back, mouth open.

Sampsa leaned across him and, taking both his shoulders firmly, began to shake him.

"Wake up! Wake up, you miserable little piece of shit!"

"Wha . . . ?" Yun shook off his hands irritably and, sitting up, knuckled his eyes.

"Who the fuck are you?" he asked, glaring at Sampsa.

"A friend," Sampsa said. "Now, if you know what's good for you, you'll help me."

"Help you?" Yun laughed sourly. "I don't know you from Wen Ti! Why *should* I fucking help you?"

Sampsa leaned in close, so that his breath hissed into Yun's face. "Because if you *don't*, I'll carve my name right there"—he tapped Yun's forehead smartly—"between your fucking eyes!"

Yun blinked, reassessing things, then nodded. "Okay . . . but let me get dressed first, all right?"

"Sure." Sampsa stepped back.

"You mind?" Yun asked, standing.

"Mind?"

Yun gestured toward the door. "You give me some privacy, neh?"

Sampsa looked about the room, then nodded and stepped outside, but he'd only been there a moment when he heard the faint but unmistakable sound of the shutters being opened.

He rushed in, just as Yun disappeared out the window onto the roof.

Sampsa followed, scrambling down the sloping roof, then dropping into the backyard, just in time to catch Yun scrabbling to free the latch. Grabbing him by the scruff of the neck, he frog-marched him back inside.

Tom, who had been waiting in the tawdry downstairs reception, stood up as Sampsa entered, dragging the still-struggling Yun.

"Master Tom!" Yun cried, grinning suddenly as he saw who it was, then turned to Sampsa. "Why you not say you with Master Tom? I thought you were Security!"

*You thought nothing of the sort, you little fucker,* Sampsa thought, bringing a smile from Tom.

"So . . ." Sampsa said, pushing him down onto one of the sofas and holding him there. "You're going to help us, right?"

"Sure!" Yun acted nonchalant. "What you want?"

"The girls . . . you know, from the burned-out flower boats. You know where they are?"

Yun went to shrug, but something in Sampsa's eyes—something hard and uncompromising—made him change his mind.

"I might," he said, looking from Tom to Sampsa, trying to assess just how important all this was.

"Good," Sampsa said. "Then take us there right now."

"Now? But—"

"*Now,*" Sampsa said insistently. "Or you'll find yourself explaining to I Ye just why you took one of the great T'ang's guests to visit some lowlife brothel!"

Yun swallowed, then nodded, the mention of I Ye clearly having done the trick. "Okay. I take you there."

PAPERS OF STATE lay scattered about the floor, rumpled and torn, their wax seals ripped from them. Nearby a footstool was overturned, its dragon-head carvings staring sightlessly across the bright red carpet. Beside the massive, dark wood desk fragments of a broken porcelain figurine lay mixed with the delicate multi-colored shards of a shattered glass glow-lamp, while on the floor beneath the Chair of State the silk pillow on which the Great Seal of Office normally rested had been carelessly dropped, its blue-and-yellow surface stained with semen.

Close by, discarded clothes—male and female garments, velvets and silks, leather boots and a fan, and some soft, black satin briefs—were littered across the floor.

In the shadowy half-light of the overcast afternoon the room had an air of ruin or abandonment. The only sign of life came from the Chair of State itself, where Li Yuan sat, completely naked, his hands tied with silk ribbons to the chair above and behind his head, the girl's face buried in his lap, her tiny, childlike hands gripping his hips, her dark hair splayed like seaweed across his upper thighs. His head was turned to the side, the neck muscles tensed, his eyes closed in pained ecstasy. His grunts of pleasure came quicker now; little whimpers of sound that grew more urgent as each moment passed.

As he came, her fingers raked his sides, then moved across, pinching his nipples hard as his whole body spasmed. His hands tugged at their silk restraints.

His groans were like the groans of a dying man.

She moved her head back, staring up the length of his body, her eyes laughing and lascivious.

"There," she said softly. "I told you you weren't finished."

"Gods . . ." he answered breathlessly, staring at her in astonishment. "Kuan Yin preserve me from you!"

Her smile was knowing. "You want me to go away, Li Yuan? You want me to go and never come back?"

"No. . . ." He shuddered violently. "No. . . ."

He closed his eyes, letting his heartbeat slow, his breathing return to normal.

*Aiya*, he thought, remembering all they'd done. Things he would not himself have *dreamed* of trying.

His eyes slowly opened again, looking at her. Her hands were in his lap now, cupped about his shriveled manhood, as if petting a baby bird in its nest, the brush of her fingers like all else about her . . . delightful.

Yes, but she was no innocent, he knew that now. Why, a thousand years of knowledge seemed behind her every movement. She was innately sexual; more so than any woman he had ever known. She looked a child, yet behind that mask of physical perfection—behind that childlike innocence she so perfectly portrayed—lay a natural perversity that set his every nerve on fire.

She had brought him off with her hands, her breasts, and finally her mouth. Three times he'd come, and still she played him, tirelessly, relentlessly.

*I am an old man*, he wanted to say, *let me be*, but still her fingers held him in a spell, making him dance like a corpse on a wire. He was drained, but still he ached for her.

He turned his head, looking up to where the silk bindings cut into his wrists. His fingers were smeared with her blood where he had touched her intimately.

Yes, he knew her now. Knew her almost as well as any man could know a woman. Yet still it was not enough. He wanted to lie with her. Wanted to feel their bodies molded to each other. Wanted to lose himself in her and become her at that moment of release.

There was a sudden knocking at the door. A harsh and urgent knock.

"Unfasten me!" he hissed, wanting no one to find him like that.

Slowly, letting her naked body slide against his own enticingly, she reached up and freed his hands.

"Thank you," he said, his mouth opening to hers, her lips brushing one last time against his own before she stood back.

His eyes were drawn to her breasts, to the stiffness of her huge dark nipples.

The knocking came again, and this time a voice. *"Chieh Hsia!* Are you all right?"

Li Yuan stretched and stood. His body ached. He flexed his hands then, stooping, picked up his cloak, draping it about him.

"Heng Yu?" he called. "Is that you?"

"Yes, *Chieh Hsia."*

Li Yuan walked to the door. "So, Master Heng, what is it makes you hammer on my door so urgently? Has something happened?"

"Forgive me, *Chieh Hsia,* but the Council is met. They but await your presence."

"The Council . . ." He turned, staring at her. Shit! He had forgotten it completely. She had driven it from his mind.

*Help me,* he mouthed at her, then, turning back, he called out to Heng Yu once again. "Return to the chamber, Master Heng, and tell them I am on my way. I—I overslept. I shall be but a moment or two."

*"Chieh Hsia!"* He heard Heng's footsteps recede and heaved a great sigh of relief.

*"Aiya!"* he said, as she brought his clothes across and, kneeling before him, began to dress him. *"Aiya!"*

━━━◠◠◠◠◠━━━

SHE LET HIM OUT then pushed the door tight shut and locked it. Turning, she looked out across the littered surface of the room and smiled to herself. She had done well. This afternoon she had almost got him there. Her hook was through his gills. Yes, but the fish was not landed yet. There was still more work—more reeling in—to be done.

Laughing, she gathered up her clothes, then, naked, pressing them to her stomach, she walked through into his private suite, heading for the shower.

He would be gone now several hours, making his plans and scheming his schemes, but she—and she laughed softly at the thought, a vixen's laugh—she would be in his bed when he returned.

L I   Y U A N looked about the table, then, with a broad smile, opened the proceedings.

"Most of you have met before, but as there are guests at our table, let me briefly introduce them."

He gestured toward Hans Ebert who sat once more directly opposite him, at the far end.

"First, let me welcome our good friend and ally Hans Ebert to this Council. Along with his companion Aluko Echewa, Hans represents the interests of the Osu and the African settlers."

Ebert gave a tiny nod of his head. "Thank you for inviting us, Li Yuan. We shall be interested to hear what you have to say."

Li Yuan returned Ebert's smile, then turned in his seat, gesturing to his right where his son, Kuei Jen, sat beside his young American friend.

"And may I also welcome Matthew Egan to this Council. Matthew is the grandson of Josiah Egan, Head of the NorTek Corporation of America, and is present here as representative of the New England Enclave, of which his grandfather is one of the four Executives."

There were looks of mild surprise at that. Many had thought the young man merely a companion to Kuei Jen; yet he had the bearing of a prince and had been clearly bred to power. Young Egan smiled and bowed his head to Li Yuan.

"I am most honored to be here, *Chieh Hsia*. My grandfather and his fellow executives have asked me to pass on their sincere and heartfelt best wishes to the T'ang and his family."

Li Yuan smiled. "That is most kind, Matthew. Now, as for the rest, to my immediate right here is Heng Yu, my Chancellor. Beside him we have my trusted friend and confidant Kim Ward, Head of NorTek Europe, and beside him my son, the Prince, Kuei Jen. Next to *Shih* Egan, standing in for Marshal Karr, who is currently otherwise engaged, we have our Head of Internal Security, Colonel I Ye."

Li Yuan shifted in his chair, gesturing now to his right, where Nan Fa-hsien sat uncomfortably between the Osu and the Empress. Though young Master Nan was well informed in all matters of policy, he had only recently been appointed to the Advisory Council and this was his first meeting.

"May I welcome Nan Fa-hsien, Master of the Inner Chambers, to the table. Master Nan's father, as you might recall, served me well as Chancellor for many years."

He shifted his eyes, looking with unconcealed distaste at the horselike countenance of his wife. "Beside Master Nan we have, of course, my wife, the Empress, Pei K'ung. And finally, to my immediate left, as ever, we have my close friend and Chief Adviser, Ben Shepherd."

"*Must* that man be here?"

Li Yuan looked to his wife again. She was staring down at her hands, her face tight. There was an empty chair between her and Shepherd—a chair where normally Ming Ai would have sat—but the distance between the two, as Li Yuan knew, was far greater than mere physical appearance would have it. To tell the truth, she loathed Shepherd.

Li Yuan smiled politely. "You want him to leave?"

She hesitated, then nodded tautly.

The smile remained fixed on his features like a painted mask. "I am very sorry, Pei K'ung, but I am afraid I cannot do that. *Shih* Shepherd is an appointed member of this council. He has a voice here."

She glared at him, half rising from her seat as if to leave, but his answering expression brooked no argument. A commanding nod told her to sit again. She sat.

"Now . . . if you would begin the proceedings?"

She swallowed the bile that had risen to her throat, then, drawing toward her the golden-covered folder that was before her on the table, she opened it.

All about the table there was the sound of folders being opened, pages rustling. Of the eleven only Ward had a direct-input socket, and he alone took the tiny wafer-thin datacard from his folder and, pinching the skin behind his ear, slipped it into the fleshy slot.

"You may have heard rumors," Pei K'ung began, her voice loud and confident, more like the voice of a man than a woman. "Well, rumors are rumors, the facts are as follows. For some time now we have been considering a campaign to reclaim and unify the Asian lands; to return civilization to those entrapped and unfortunate people. Until recently, however, circumstances have proved extremely difficult and the possibility of undertaking such a campaign with any chance of success has been small. That now has changed. For the first time in many years we find ourselves in a position where—so my experts confidently inform me—we could carry out a campaign with an almost guaranteed certainty of a successful, not to say highly beneficial, outcome."

Pei K'ung looked about her, her eyes glowing. As she got farther into her argument, so she grew more confident, more passionate. All eyes were on her now, ignoring the open folders, even Shepherd's, though there was a kind of listlessness about the way he looked at her that, to a more watchful eye, might have seemed strange.

She continued. "The reasons for carrying out such a campaign are threefold. First, by so doing we shall be reclaiming our hereditary rights over the Asian territories and thereby fulfilling one of the central terms of the ancient constitution of Chung Kuo. Second, by subjugating these areas we shall reintroduce large numbers of our former citizens to the rule of law and order. And third, by bringing these lands under our control, we shall be able to guarantee trade and, it is hoped, increase its levels substantially, to the benefit of all."

She looked about her, her long face smiling broadly, as if all of this were unquestionably self-evident.

"Of course," she went on, "such a campaign has to be paid for, hence the new levies, but the potential benefits outweigh such temporary measures many times over. Though the people might grumble a little now, they will be cheering when our victorious Banners return triumphant."

Across from her I Ye nodded enthusiastically, but others about the table seemed more cautious, less carried away by her rhetoric.

"Forgive me," Ward said, leaning toward her across the table, "but might I speak?"

Her eyes went to Li Yuan, then back to Ward. She nodded.

"Thank you." Ward composed himself a moment, then, looking about him, began to speak, the extended forefinger and middle finger of his right hand touching his mouth every so often, then moving out into the air above the table to emphasize each point he made.

"I hear what the Empress, Pei K'ung, is saying. I hear her when she says there are reasons for such a campaign and that there are possible benefits to be derived from waging war on our Asian neighbors. What I do not hear from her are any counterreasons. Nor do I hear of the possible disadvantages—in human, economic, and social terms—that might result from pursuing such a policy."

He turned, looking directly at Li Yuan. "Forgive me, *Chieh Hsia*, if what I am about to say seems either discourteous or . . . well, disloyal, but I feel it must be said."

Li Yuan smiled graciously. "You are my Adviser, Kim Ward. What you say here shall be taken in an advisory manner. You must speak openly and fearlessly."

"Thank you, *Chieh Hsia*."

Kim turned back, looking about him again, his fingers brushing his lips briefly before he spoke. "Let me, then, deal firstly with the reasons for such a campaign, and let me give three reasons of my own for *not* embarking on this venture.

"First, let me speak concerning the matter of hereditary rights. While it is true that Li Yuan is the sole remaining member of the Seven and that in him, therefore, resides the attributes of their power, as far as territorial claims are concerned—considering him solely as the senior male of the Li clan—it might be argued that such claims extend only as far as the borders of City Europe. Asia—east and west—are not and never were part of his family's domain. I would even go so far as to contend that others, even those Warlords who, as ex–Minor Family Princes, have shown extreme disloyalty to the Seven in the person of Li Yuan—might possess a better claim in law."

Pei K'ung made to speak, but a look from Li Yuan silenced her.

"Continue," the T'ang said calmly.

"Second, as regards the question of law and order. In the course of my trade I have found it necessary to travel to various of the states of both West and East Asia—to Sichuan, Anhui, Kashmir, and the Kirgiz Enclave, to mention just four of many—and while those states have codes of law that I personally would neither endorse nor care to live under, there is—throughout Asia—a degree of order that other continents, South America and Australasia, certainly, would envy. To state, therefore, that one of our prime objectives is to bring law and order to the Asian peoples is, with respect, a misleading notion. In truth, we would be merely replacing their codes of law with our own."

Kim paused. "These two matters aside, it is on the third and final count that I find myself—as a businessman—objecting most strongly. Pei K'ung has stated that—and I quote her verbatim—'by bringing these lands under our control, we shall be able to guarantee trade and, it is hoped, increase its levels substantially.' Well, forgive me, *Chieh Hsia*, but I find this notion not merely mistaken but absurd. War will destroy trade. It will undo all of the good and patient work we have done these past ten years, beginning with these foolish new taxes—"

"*Foolish?*" Pei K'ung could hold her peace no longer. "What do you mean, foolish?"

Ward turned to face her, undaunted by the anger in her eyes, the way her thin, bloodless lips were pursed against him, concentrating on his argument. "I make no apology for the word. Taxing the common people is a foolish, misguided, and ultimately divisive tactic. It will do nothing but harm the state. To begin with—and I feel this is self-evident—it will reduce the amount of spending money circulating within our city. As a consequence everyone— from the humblest street trader to the great Heads of Companies themselves—will suffer. But that will be as nothing beside the consequences of pursuing a prolonged military campaign in Central Asia."

"Prolonged?" I Ye chipped in from Kim's right. "Who said it would be prolonged? Have you not read the report, *Shih* Ward? Why, by even the most conservative estimate we shall have reunified the continent within eighteen months. And what's eighteen months?"

Kim stared at I Ye a moment, then, sighing, shook his head. "I have scanned the figures, Colonel I, and to be frank I find them ludicrous."

"Ludicrous?" I Ye bristled. "So *Shih* Ward is an expert on military matters now!"

"I am no expert, I admit," Kim began.

"Then bow to those who are," I Ye said aggressively, "as we bow to you on matters more . . . *esoteric.*"

Kim looked down. "Tell me, I Ye, how long did it take the great tyrant Tsao Ch'un to conquer all of Asia?"

I Ye shrugged. "Four years?"

"Six." Kim met his eyes. "And he held China already. Six years it took him, and it should be remembered that he faced no serious military opposition."

"He was slow."

"He had to be slow. One cannot simply move *through* territory. One must hold it and police it. One must administrate and coordinate. And then there are small matters of supply lines to maintain, the question of sufficient manpower. Asia is a huge place, Colonel I. One might lose such a tiny city as ours in its wastes."

Pei K'ung leaned forward, interrupting. "Your argument has some merit, *Shih* Ward, but we have already considered all such matters carefully. It is why, at this very moment, Marshal Karr is in Mashhad seeking an alliance with Warlord Hu." She smiled fiercely. "We shall move only when it is safe to move, strike only when the time is right to strike."

"And if they strike back?" Kim asked.

Her smile was contemptuous. "You really think we should fear such rabble, *Shih* Ward? After all, our men are highly trained, our weaponry state of the art. That much you should know, at least. After all, you helped design it."

"More's the pity," Kim murmured, regretting the words even as he uttered them. He turned and looked to Li Yuan. "What I mean, *Chieh Hsia*, is that I designed those weapons to be used as deterrents, in a defensive capacity . . . to help *prevent* war, not wage it!"

"Can one *choose* how a weapon is used, *Shih* Ward?" Pei K'ung said, clearly enjoying his discomfort. "Weapons, surely, are neutral things? Besides, surely such a campaign as we suggest will prove the best defense in the long term? After all, it is only a matter of time before the Warlords ally with each other and gang up on us."

"You believe that?" Kim asked, astonished that she was so out of touch with things. "Why, from what I've seen, they can't even agree among them what gauge of rail to use for their new fast-track systems!"

Pei K'ung made to answer, but Li Yuan leaned forward, his hand raised. At once she fell silent.

"Backtracking a moment," Li Yuan said, his face expressionless, "you were speaking a moment ago, Kim, about the possible consequences of pursuing a long military campaign. I would like to hear your views on that."

"*Chieh Hsia,*" Kim answered, nodding to him. "As I was saying . . . should the campaign be *prolonged* for some reason—because of some unexpected military upset, perhaps—then the effect on trade could well be catastrophic. Not that even a small, swift war would be to our advantage economically, in our present circumstances. A long, drawn-out war, however, a war of attrition, would not only destroy the great web of trading links that have grown up between ourselves and the East Asian states these past ten years, but would undermine the very structure of City Europe. There would be unrest on a scale we have not seen since before the Fall. We would be back to square one . . . or worse."

"Worse? Come now, *Shih* Ward," Pei K'ung said, sitting back, relaxing now. "This scare-mongering does not become you. Our City is strong, our economy sound. Standards of health and education are at a level we have not seen for a hundred, a hundred and fifty years."

Kim nodded emphatically. "So why *risk* all of that? Why gamble on some profitless, destructive gesture?" He sighed, then looked about him, appealing to them all. "The gods help us . . . what about all the people that will die? What of all the widows, the orphans, the maimed and the sick, that will result from such a war? Must we forever be the cause of such things? Why can't we go on as we are, building patiently and peacefully? Why must we always have wars and yet more wars?"

Hans Ebert spoke up. "*Shih* Ward speaks for many here. I endorse what he says. If you would have my advice, Li Yuan, it would be to listen to this one wise voice among your counselors."

"The military expert!" I Ye said, folding his arms and sitting back.

Ebert turned to his left, focusing his attention on his neighbor. "You have fought in many campaigns, then, Colonel I?"

I Ye squirmed inwardly. "That is not the point."

"Then take your own advice and listen to an expert. As someone who was once the T'ang's General, I assure you that what *Shih* Ward says makes a great deal of sense. To take and hold Asia—Asia, dammit!—is not an easy thing, and if Tsao Ch'un achieved that task in six short years, then credit goes to Tsao Ch'un as a military commander, if for no other reason."

I Ye's mouth opened, then closed with a tiny snap.

Ebert turned back, smiling first at Ward, then at Li Yuan. "We Osu have fought our fair share of petty wars these past ten years and would gladly fight no more. That said, we owe the T'ang a debt. If he calls, we shall come. Yet we would prefer not to have to come."

"I thank you, Hans," Li Yuan said, nodding to him, as though to an equal, "but we have heard only half the voices." He looked to his son. "Kuei Jen . . . have you anything to offer this debate?"

The young Prince looked to his father and smiled. "For myself, no. It would be presumptuous of me to offer an opinion. My role, as I see it, is to listen to the advice of my father's council and learn from that. However, there is one here who wishes to make a contribution." Kuei Jen turned, putting out a hand to introduce his friend, Egan.

"Might I, Li Yuan?" Egan asked, his bright blue eyes suddenly alert.

"Of course. . . ."

Yet before Egan could begin, Pei K'ung spoke up. "Forgive me for interrupting at this point, husband, but might I mention something that has been troubling me for some time now. I understand why our friends from Africa are at the table—we owe them much, and they ought to be consulted before we take so great a step—yet I am far from certain why our young friend here has been granted access to this council. I do not wish to offer him, nor the faction he represents, any insult or offense, but it *is* unusual, surely?"

Li Yuan nodded, as if acceding to the point, then looked to the young American once more.

"*Shih* Egan, if you would enlighten my wife."

"Why, certainly, Lord Li." Egan turned and looked to Pei K'ung, smiling charmingly at her as he began to speak. "As you know, Empress, your stepson, the Prince Kuei Jen, has spent the last eighteen months in North America. The great majority of that time has been spent with us in the New England Enclave. In the course of our discussions we covered much ground and discovered a great many areas of agreement." He looked to Kuei Jen briefly, his smile broadening. "The Executive Council was much impressed by your stepson, Lady. So much so, that when he broached the matter of an alliance—"

"An *alliance!*" Pei K'ung was on her feet, leaning over the table, looking to Li Yuan. "Why was I not consulted about this, Li Yuan?"

He stared back at her blankly. "You *are* being consulted. Now, sit down and listen to our guest. You will have your chance to speak when *Shih* Egan has finished."

She slowly sat again, but she was clearly far from happy. Now when she looked at Egan, it was with a suspicious glare. Yet Egan seemed unperturbed.

"As I was saying, when Prince Kuei broached the possibility of an alliance between our States, my grandfather and his co-Executives discussed the matter with great seriousness. As you might know, we are a proud people and we value our independence greatly. Indeed, we have fought for it at great cost these past two decades. There is not a person in any of the five cities of the Enclave who has not lost someone dear to them in that struggle. But now, thanks chiefly to your son's most eloquent persuasion, we have decided to end our isolation and offer the hand of friendship."

Egan reached into his tunic pocket and drew out four silk-paper envelopes. Leaning across the table, he pushed them toward Li Yuan. The T'ang smiled and gave a tiny nod of his head, then gathered up the letters, studying the seals. With a satisfied gleam in his face Li Yuan fanned them out, so that Pei K'ung could see them clearly. There was the blue star on white of WesCorp, the black on yellow of RadMed, the bright red eagle of NorTek, and the blood-red circling atom on pale green of AmLab. Seeing them, Pei K'ung's eyes widened, impressed.

"Those," Egan said on cue, "are the personal pledges of the four Executives."

"Pledges?" Heng Yu asked, looking first to Egan, then to his T'ang. "I don't understand, *Chieh Hsia.*"

Li Yuan looked at him and smiled. "Pledges of personal loyalty, as from a subject to his T'ang." He looked to Egan. "Are you prepared, *Shih* Egan?"

"I am, Li Yuan."

"Then come."

Egan rose to his full height, then came around the table and, with a stiff bow, knelt and placed his forehead to the floor before Li Yuan. At this Li Yuan stood and, turning to face him, extended his foot and gently pressed it to the young man's neck.

"*Chieh Hsia,*" Egan said. As Li Yuan removed his foot, he slowly crawled backward a little way, then lifted his head.

Li Yuan turned, looking to his wife. "You understand, Pei K'ung?"

She understood all right. *Shih* Egan's gesture was as a surrogate. By his action, and by those four pledges, the Executives of the East Coast Enclave had become Li Yuan's vassals, answerable to him. And by the same token he had become their protector, responsible for their safety and well-being. By that single gesture he had sealed the alliance.

She swallowed, then nodded, clearly shocked by this sudden turn of events.

"Return to your seat, *Shih* Egan. You have more to tell us, I understand."

"*Chieh Hsia.*" Egan resumed his seat, then, clearing his throat, continued. "As a token of our gratitude, and of our loyalty, it has been decided that an army of eighty thousand men will be dispatched to aid the great T'ang's forces in the campaign in the East. Furthermore, we pledge a considerable stock of state-of-the-art weaponry—details of which are included in a separate letter I have been instructed to hand over to this Council—for the furtherance of that campaign."

I Ye, in his chair beside the young man, sat back and nodded. Across from him Pei K'ung's surprise had given way to delight.

"Eighty thousand men . . . and new weaponry? What kind of weapons?"

In answer Egan reached inside his other pocket and, removing a larger package, pushed it across the table to her. While she slit it open and removed the document, Egan spoke on.

"Twenty years of warfare have not been wasted on us. We have come a long way in the art of weaponry. Those years of constant struggle were also years of great technological advancement. With respect to *Shih* Ward, I believe we have advanced the science of warfare more than any other state in history. Transformed it, you might say."

Pei K'ung, who had been flipping through the pages of diagrams and specifications, now looked back at Egan.

"Why?"

"I beg pardon, Mistress?"

"Why do you need this alliance? Eighty thousand men . . . and *this*. Why? What do you want?"

Egan smiled. "It's very simple, Mistress. We want peace. And there will be no peace, not until the world is as it once was under the Seven. Not until a single man rules it all with an iron fist. Our Council realizes that now—*understands* it, let us say—and rather than fight you and destroy both of our great states, we would prefer to fight alongside you to guarantee that future world."

There was silence about the table as the full importance of what Egan had said sank in.

"And your promise, Li Yuan?" Ebert said, his face troubled.

"My husband kept his promise," Pei K'ung answered, turning to face the blind man. "He pulled down the old City and rebuilt it on a more human scale. Yet even you must see that what *Shih* Egan says makes sense. Peace *cannot* be guaranteed until the world is unified again . . . until it is once more *Chung Kuo* and not a rabble of minor states. You of all people ought to understand that, *Shih* Ebert!"

"You wish, then, to make things as they were again?"

She shook her head slowly. "Not as they were, no. But to have a single ruler, that makes sense, surely?"

"So Asia is just a start?" Ben Shepherd said quietly, speaking for the first time.

Pei K'ung kept her back to him, pointedly snubbing him, speaking to the rest of the table. "If Asia is ours, the rest will join willingly. We have only to destroy the power of the Warlords and unification will once more be in our grasp."

"And if we *fail* in our initial aims?" Shepherd asked, his raised voice cutting through her rhetoric. "If Asia *doesn't* simply crumble before our forces?"

He laughed bleakly. "What if it all goes wrong, Pei K'ung? What if our plans are thwarted and our armies defeated in battle? What if our allies turn against us suddenly? What if . . . well, what if only one or two of the thousand things that can go wrong in a campaign actually *do* go wrong? What then? Has anybody thought that through? Has anybody sat down and worked out just how fragile we are as a society, how quickly all that we've so patiently built these past ten years could be destroyed? Has anybody calculated *that?*"

"Of course—" Pei K'ung began, yet Shepherd raised his voice once more, speaking over her, not allowing her to have her say.

"Have you read no history, Pei K'ung? Have you no idea how often schemes like yours have turned to dust? Does the shining light of possible victory blind you to the dark possibility of annihilation?"

She turned, glaring at him, then looked to her husband. "A vote, Li Yuan. I demand a vote."

"Demand?" He laughed, then, all amusement draining from his face, gave a tiny shrug. "All right. So be it. A vote." He sniffed and looked about the table. "All those in favor of this action—of a campaign to unify Asia under our sovereign power—raise your hands."

Pei K'ung, I Ye, Prince Kuei, and Egan raised their hands at once. A moment later Heng Yu's joined them.

"Five," Li Yuan said, smiling. With eleven seated at the table, that left six yet to vote. "And those against?"

Ward, Ebert, and Echewa raised their hands at once, but after a moment's wait no further hands went up to join them.

"*Shih* Shepherd?" Kim asked. "Surely *you* are opposed to this nonsense?"

Ben smiled. "In theory, certainly. But Li Yuan knows my position on such matters. I am an adviser, not a formulator of policy.

When it comes to a vote, I will always abstain, whatever my personal opinion."

Kim turned, looking to Nan Fa-hsien. "And you, Master Nan?"

Nan Fa-hsien did not meet Kim's eyes, but looked to Li Yuan. "I am my Master's hands," he said quietly.

"Then it is passed, five votes to three," Li Yuan said.

"But, *Chieh Hsia*—" Kim began.

"It is passed, *Shih* Ward," Pei K'ung said, watching her husband rise and leave the table. "You had your say and were outvoted. Now accept the decision of the Council or resign."

"*Resign?*" Kim looked to her, then across to Shepherd, who smiled apologetically. Saying no more, he got to his feet and followed Li Yuan from the room, his face greatly troubled.

"COLONEL I!"

I Ye stopped, a profound sense of apprehension gripping him. He knew that tone. Knew it could only mean trouble. He turned and bowed low.

"Mistress?"

The meeting had ended only moments before and they were barely outside the Council chamber.

"In my rooms! *Now!*"

He bowed low once more, then hurried after her.

The meeting had gone well, or so he thought. Pei K'ung had wanted a campaign for a long time and now she had one—yes, and eighty thousand American troops too! But strangely she didn't seem too pleased.

Back in her study she slammed the door and turned on him.

"I have changed my mind."

He had no idea what she was talking about. "Mistress?"

"About Shepherd. About discrediting him."

"Ah . . ." He felt relief flood through him. *Thank the gods for that,* he thought. *The old crow's come to her senses at last!*

"I don't want him discredited," she said, looking clearly, almost icily, at him. "I want him killed."

It was a moment or two before it hit him. "*Killed?*"

"Killed," she repeated. "I want him to have . . . an *accident.*"

He felt numb. Kill Shepherd? Kill Li Yuan's Chief Adviser? Why, if anything even vaguely suspicious happened to Shepherd, Li Yuan would stop at nothing to find out the why and the who of it. Why, killing Shepherd was tantamount to putting a gun to his own head. Besides which, he didn't understand this sudden switch of mood. The man had abstained, damn it! So what had he missed? What in the gods' names had he missed?

"Well?" she said, still staring at him. "You are very quiet, Colonel I. Did you not understand my order?"

He lowered his head and clicked his heels together. "It shall be done, Mistress."

"Good." She turned away, moving toward her desk. "I don't care how and I don't want to know. I just want it done, understand me, Colonel?"

He kept his head down, his smile a rictus. Oh, he understood all right—the gods knew he understood! What he didn't understand—what he hadn't worked out yet—was how he was going to wriggle his way out of this one.

*Killing Shepherd.* He shuddered, then hurried from the room. *How the fuck was he going to do that and survive?*

COSTAS AND JAMES helped Calder take the woman from the cart and carry her inside. There, Eva took over, laying the stranger on the bed to examine her, wincing as she saw the extent and nature of the woman's injuries. She turned to Calder, her eyes dark with sympathetic pain.

"Who did this to her?"

"Brothers of ours, so-called. They were led by an old man named Lu Song."

"Ahh . . ." There was a look of understanding in her eyes.

"You know him?"

She nodded. "And the woman?"

Calder swallowed. "She's one of I Ye's agents."

"I Ye! Are you mad?"

"She's a human being, Eva. I just couldn't let those butchers—"

She touched his arm. "It's okay. I understand. But it complicates things."

"Complicates them? How?"

She sighed, then, with a glance at the other two, came out with it. "A lot's been happening, Alan. Our plans . . . Well, we've had to change our plans. To hasten things. We'd have discussed it with you, but you weren't here, and now there's little time."

"Little time? What do you mean?"

"Marshal Karr is here."

"Here? What . . . in Mashhad?"

"He arrived this morning. He's been in talks with Hu Wang-chih all day. There's a strong rumor that Warlord Hu is to form an alliance with Li Yuan."

"An *alliance?*"

She nodded. "Word is they plan a war against the other Warlords."

"But . . ." Then he saw it. Saw it all. Right now Hu Wang-chih was deeply unpopular; his internal policy depended on severe repression of his people. Right now his assassination would be a popular act. But given a successful war all that would change. With popular feeling united against a common enemy, Warlord Hu would become a hero overnight. Or if not overnight, within months of the war commencing. It was how, after all, he had risen to power—on a wave of blood and euphoria.

"So when is it to be?" he asked, conscious of how all three of them were looking at him.

"Tomorrow," she said.

*"Tomorrow?"* He gave a laugh of disbelief. "But we haven't raised the money. How will we pay the assassin?"

"We won't."

"What do you mean, we won't?"

"We won't because we won't be using an assassin. *I'm* going to do it."

He stared at her, his whole face frozen into immobility. "But you can't. I mean . . . you couldn't harm a fly. I know you, Eva. To kill a man . . ." He shuddered, then looked down, slowly shaking his head.

"I can," she said clearly. "I can because I have to. Because if I don't, then all of those deaths, all of that suffering, will have been for nothing. Besides, who better? As his maid I have direct access to him. No one would suspect me."

"No," he said, looking at her. "You can't."

"I have to." She took his arms and looked into his face, forcing him to look back at her. "We knew there'd be risks, Alan. When we decided to do this, we knew we might all end up dead, but we went ahead anyway. When I stole those tapes, *that* was a risk. When you went to Li Yuan's city—"

"Yes, but *this*!"

She stared at him earnestly. "You want to stop, Alan? You want to call it a day, now, when we're so close? Because if you do, you might as well declare for him. We would be condoning all he's done . . . yes, and all he's yet to do. Do you forget what happened to your wife, your daughters?"

He swallowed bitterly. There was no need to answer.

"Tomorrow, then," she said, the matter settled. "In the meantime let's see what we can do for the woman here."

———

WHERE HUAN T'AN AVENUE met Stone Lane there was a clear change of architectural style. Whereas Huan T'an Avenue was residential, with its flat-fronted single-story brick houses, Stone Lane was commercial, a riot of signs and colorful banners hung above its doors. What shops there were in Huan T'an Avenue were of the normal sort—essentially a single room with a shuttered front, locked up each night, the two rooms overhead reserved for the trader's family. The shops in Stone Lane, however, were more varied. Stepping from one into the other, the regularity of the suburban streets gave way to a mishmash of styles, old and new. Moreover, what was intrinsically Han here gave way to what was quite clearly—and, one might say, brashly—*Hung Mao*.

This was the heart of the old pre-City town of Frankfurt, and many of the buildings here had been rebuilt from the shells of the old. Between, a number of garish structures had arisen, notable more for their architectural strangeness, their use of glass and plastic, than for any other feature. *Hung Mao* merchants had built this part of Li Yuan's city—Dispersionists, it was rumored—using old plans, old designs. But the Han had taken over here as everywhere. No Western faces stared out from its doors or windows. At least, none they could see.

It was growing dark. Night would be on them in an hour. Yun turned and smiled broadly at the two young men.

"Well, Masters. Here we are."

Sampsa looked about him, certain now that nothing good would come of this adventure. "And where's here?"

Yun laughed and sketched a crude triangle in the air, as if to encompass the territory facing them. *"Yinmao,"* he answered. "We are in Green Lamp Lanes here, along with the god with white eyebrows."

Sampsa understood at once; but Tom's voice sounded in his head.

*What the hell does he mean?*

*He means it's one huge great knocking shop!*

*And Yinmao . . . that's it's name?*

Sampsa smiled. *Yinmao is pubic hair!*

*Ahh . . .*

Sampsa gestured toward the nearest shop. The pull-down shutter was half lowered. In the shadows beyond, an old man, his black *pau* buttoned to the neck, sat behind a small table, inhaling a stick drug. In a doorway to the side a younger woman stood. Her manner, her makeup, and her clothes left no doubt as to what she was. A whore. A common *men hu.* Elsewhere along the narrow lane others stood idly by, awaiting custom.

"Not busy now," Yun said with a grin. "Later get very busy. Many people come. Much fun. Much money pass hands, neh?"

"Neh," Sampsa said, disliking the young cook more by the moment. *Let's get on with it,* he said silently, turning to Tom. *Let's find her and get out of here.*

Tom gripped his arm. *And if we do find her? What then?*

Sampsa grinned. *Why, we buy her, idiot! We pay off whoever owns her.*

*They'll let us do that?*

*Why not? Trade's trade, after all. Providing our offer's good enough, they'll not reject our money!*

Yun spoke, breaking into their silent exchange. "You strange, you two. The way you look at each other. It give me fucking creeps!"

Sampsa looked to Yun and glared. "Just take us to her, if you know what's good for you!"

Yun shrugged. "But you here. If she here, you find her, neh? If not—"

Sampsa grabbed him by the neck, the strength of his fingers surprising the young cook. "If not, you're in trouble, brother Yun. Big, deep, *wide* trouble. You know what I Ye likes to do to little fish like you?"

Yun put his hands up. "Okay! Okay! Be patient. She here I find her for you. But no guarantees. This hunch, okay? Educated guess."

*Uneducated bollocks*, Sampsa said silently, but Tom was too concerned to laugh. His fear for the girl's safety overrode every other consideration in his head. For Sampsa, experiencing it secondhand, it was like a constant mental tremor, a faint trembling in the nerves and muscles that—after a time—grew quite disconcerting.

"Come on," he said, patting Yun's shoulder in a conciliatory fashion. "You find her, we'll reward you."

Yun grinned, all sign of reluctance suddenly, almost magically, gone from him at the mention of money. "Why you not say that before! I carrot man, neh? You dangle, I run. . . ." He pantomimed it, then, shaking his head, "My father beat me badly when I boy. I *very* stubborn. I—"

"*On!*" Sampsa urged, giving him a gentle shove. "Now, before the light gives out."

━━━◇◇◇◇◇━━━

*I YE PULLED on his skintight gloves, then stepped inside the cell. He looked about him, surprised, then stepped across, staring down at the little girl who sat, her hands manacled, in the corner chair.*

*"Is this the prisoner?" he asked, looking to one of the guards who stood, masked and ominous, behind the chair.*

*"Yes, sir!"*

*He returned his attention to the girl. "So you are Chuang Kuan Ts'ai?"*

*She looked up at him and nodded.*

"Aiya!" He turned, looking to his Sergeant in the doorway. "How old is this girl?"

"Seven, sir."

"Seven . . ." I Ye's expression was one of disgust and anger. "You bring me a seven-year-old child to question. What kind of fucking moron are you?"

"But the Librarian—"

"You want to make me a laughingstock, Sergeant? You want word to go out that I Ye has taken to torturing children?"

The sergeant lowered his head sharply. "No, sir."

"Then take her home . . . and make sure she comes to no harm."

"Sir!"

But I Ye was not finished. "As for the other matter, consider it dealt with. But next time you pick a quarrel with one of Karr's lieutenants, make certain it's for a damn sight better reason than this. You understand me, Sergeant?"

"Sir!"

I Ye turned, looking at the girl, shaking his head at the sight of the heavy manacles on those slender, childish wrists.

"Overkill," he muttered, turning away. "Seven-year-olds! Whatever fucking next?"

"I won't leave," she said clearly, making him turn back.

"I beg pardon?"

"I won't leave until my uncle is freed as well."

"Your uncle?" I Ye stepped closer, frowning, then looked to the Sergeant. "What's this about an uncle? Have we the whole fucking family in here?"

"The Lu Nan Jen . . . the Oven Man. He's in the other cell, sir."

"He resisted arrest, I take it?"

"No, sir, he . . . well, one of my men had to restrain him."

I Ye stared at his sergeant, then slowly shook his head. "You mean, he coshed him from behind?"

"Sir!"

"Kuan Yin preserve us!" I Ye murmured, then, louder, "Free the man. And give him fifty yuan for his trouble. No . . . make that one hundred, to be docked from your wages, Sergeant!"

"Sir?" For a moment the man stared at his Colonel in disbelief, then he lowered his head. "Sir!"

"Good. And let no harm come to either of them. I'll have no one say that I Ye is an unfair man."

"Sir!"

But as I Ye left the cell, peeling the gloves from his hands as he went, the sergeant's eyes followed him, a sullen resentment burning in them.

"Unbind her!" he yelled, gesturing toward one of his men. "You heard the Colonel. We are to take the young lady home."

Yes, he thought, turning to stare at the empty doorway, but you'll pay for this humiliation, I Ye. You are a careless man. I was loyal and you treated me like shit. Well, shit is as shit does, and henceforth I'll be as loyal as any jackal's loyal to its carrion.

Loyal until death. . . .

The thought calmed him, brought an unexpected smile to his face.

"Okay," he said, relaxing, "bring the Lu Nan Jen and let's get moving. And let no harm come to him. After all, our Master is a fair man. A very fair man."

THEY HAD SEALED the main shaft at both ends and stationed men at all the access hatches. If there was anyone down there—and rumor was that it was a regular little rat's nest—then they would get them.

"Okay," the Hsien L'ing said, looking up from the map that was spread out over the hood of his hover car, signaling to his Wei—his Captain of Security—to begin. "Let's flush the little buggers out!"

At a signal from the Wei the two guards at the first access hatch lifted it, and while one covered the entrance with his laser, the other climbed down the runged ladder into the shaft, one of the sniffers under his arm.

The sniffers were automated trackers, designed to seek out and destroy rodents and other pests that had come back with a vengeance since the new city had been built. These, however, had been adapted for slightly larger prey.

At the bottom of the tunnel the guard set the sniffer down, then stood back, raising an arm. Ahead of him the main shaft stretched away for just over five li, smaller spurs branching off in a huge web of shafts that shadowed the street plan of the city overhead.

The guard by the hatch turned to face the Wei and raised his arm.

"Okay," the Wei said. "Activate the sniffer."

Hsien L'ing Wang watched as another three of the automated hunters *were passed down and activated. Then, satisfied that all had gone well, he ordered the guard back up.*

All they had to do now was wait. Either their prey would try to come up for air . . . or they would die down there in the tunnels.

He smiled, thinking of the speech he'd give that evening in the Market Square. Why, it would be worth every fen he'd spent hiring the sniffers to see their faces when he told them he'd eradicated the problem.

Maybe he'd even display the corpses. Rub their noses in it. Especially that bastard Hei Fong, who was always complaining. Yes . . . he'd make sure Hei Fong dug deep in his pocket to pay for this!

Wang laughed, then, reaching across to take a bottle and two wine cups from the basket, walked across to his Wei.

"You want a wager, Kan?"

"A wager, Hsien L'ing?"

"On how many we get."

"Ahh . . ." The Wei stroked his chin thoughtfully. "Twenty-five?"

Wang laughed. "Come, now. As few as that? I reckon sixty. No. Sixty-eight."

Kan shrugged. "Okay. How much?"

"A hundred?"

"Make it two." The Wei smiled broadly. "Corpses? Or live ones, too?"

"Corpses, naturally. You think I'd cheat a friend?"

---

*I T   H A D   C O M E* upon them silently, a deadly, impersonal killer, picking them off with ease as the boys panicked, their screams filling that cramped and enclosed space as they tried to make their escape. Now only Josef remained, pinned down beneath the corpse of Judd, his lieutenant of six hours, trying to make no movement that might alert the sniffer's primitive sensors.

The air was hot, the smell of scorched flesh and feces so strong, it was hard not to gag.

He had seen a program on the sniffers once and knew he would be safe if he kept still. Despite its name the machine could not smell him, nor could it hear his quiet breathing. Other models registered body heat, but this one clearly didn't. This worked by discriminating patterns of light and dark—by sensing changes in those patterns and thus discerning movement. The smallest motion of his would trigger a response: a blinding flash—a bolt, it seemed—of light. One move and he would be fried alive, as the others had been.

Right now the sniffer was perched on the edge of the access tunnel, its squat silver shape framed by the dark circle of the opening. It had been there several minutes now, its eyes—two light-sensitive panels—scanning the interior of the Nest. In his head Josef counted. When he reached one hundred and eighty-five he heard a tiny double thud as the sniffer jumped down onto the floor of the Nest.

He closed his eyes, knowing what was to come. There was the clack-clack-clack of its metallic feet on the ash-strewn floor, then a slow metallic whirr. There was a sickening squelch—the sound of flesh being drilled—as its rotor arm burrowed into one of the corpses. It moved on, operated, he knew, at a distance.

Whirr. Clack-clack. Whirr. A pause as it changed direction. Clack-clack-clack. Whirr.

The last was close. He steeled himself.

Clack-clack. Whirr.

He felt Judd's corpse move on top of him, pushed back by the force of the metal drilling arm. Something whizzed by his ear, its passage marked by a disturbance of the air. Specks of fresh blood spattered his face and neck. The corpse juddered again as the drilling arm withdrew.

Clack-clack. Whirr.

He heard it jump; heard the metallic ring of it as it landed on the edge of the opening and slid down the exit tunnel into the shaft below.

Josef let a long, shuddering breath escape him, then hauled himself up from beneath the burned and mangled corpse of Judd.

For the moment he was safe. For the moment he could stretch his limbs and move without fear. But a momentary safety was not enough. There were other machines, after all, and they were programmed to keep searching until anything that moved was eradicated. To survive he would have to do more than just hide.

He smiled, knowing what he would do. After all, they were only machines.

*BACK IN THE SILENCE of* the house Chuang went straight through into the kitchen and, pulling the stool across, climbed up and filled the kettle at the sink.

Cho had been silent throughout the journey home, staring morosely at his hands all the while as the Security van bounced along the lanes.

As she put the kettle on the hob and lit it, she heard the door to the laying-out room creak open down the hall. He had been working on a body when the sergeant had come—cleaning and preparing the corpse of a teenage boy who had drowned in the canal the previous day. The cremation was scheduled for tomorrow morning and he had barely begun the work when I Ye's thugs had interrupted him. He would have to work late now to catch up.

She made ch'a, then set the chung and a clean bowl on a tray and carried it through. Yet on entering the room she saw at once that he was not working. He was standing over the body, his back to the door, his shoulders hunched forward, sobbing.

Setting the ch'a down on the side, she hurried across, squeezing in between him and the table and putting her arms about him tightly, pressing her tiny head into his ample stomach.

"It's okay," she said. "We're safe now. Safe. You heard what I Ye said."

But Cho seemed inconsolable. The tears ran down his face like drips from a leaking tap; as if he were crying for all the corpses he had ever burned.

"You must be strong, Cho Yao," she said, moving back and looking up at him, a lump in her throat at the sight of his sad, defenseless face. But the words were really for herself. It was she who had to be strong henceforth, for both of them, for this business had hurt Cho badly; had undermined his trust in the world. Something had broken in him these past few days. Something he could not live without.

After a moment he put his arms down, holding her.

"I'm fine," he said at last, a tiredness in his voice. "Come. You tidy up, my peach, I'll finish here."

She looked back up at him and smiled bravely. "Not too late, though," she said, playing the little mother. "You need your sleep."

"Ah . . . sleep." His sigh was weariness itself. "I wish I could sleep. These past few days . . ."

"I'll make you something," she said. "I'll—"

They both stiffened, hearing a banging at the outer gate. It came again; loud, insistent.

"Who is it?" he whispered, looking to her fearfully. "Who'd come at this hour?"

It was not unusual. People often came. As Cho said, death did not keep office hours. Even so, the events of the past few days had made them both wary of callers in the night.

"I'll go," she said, smiling at him again, trying to exude more confidence than she felt. "It's probably a delivery."

"Ah . . ." The thought seemed to calm him. "Of course. An Oven Man's task is unending, neh?"

Maybe, she thought; at least, until the last man dies.

He put his face down to hers, so she could kiss him, then planted his own soft kiss on her brow.

"Go answer it," he said, smiling wearily at her. "I'll wipe my face, then come through. They'll need help with the cart."

---

*I YE WAITED* in the shadows until the cart had gone through, then sent his men forward, surprising the Oven Man at the door. As he stepped through the gate he glimpsed the girl on the far side of the yard as she disappeared out of sight, pursued by one of his men. A moment later she was carried out, struggling furiously against the iron grip of her captor. He smiled inwardly, admiring her spirit. The Oven Man, however, stood where they had come upon him, his arms hanging limply at his side, his head lowered dejectedly. The guards to either side of him held him loosely.

"Well," I Ye began, dismissing with an abrupt gesture the two men who'd brought the cart. "It seems I made a mistake letting you two go."

He had indeed. In fact, it was only because Dawes had pointed out the connection that he was here at all. An enigma, that man. But useful, as it turned out, because now he could solve two problems with a single solution.

"You!" He pointed to the girl. "You are under arrest for treason against the State."

The Oven Man jerked his head up at that, then turned and looked at the child, open mouthed.

*"But you"*—I Ye now pointed to the Lu Nan Jen—*"you can help her."*

*The Oven Man looked back at him. "How?" he asked quietly.*

*"By doing your job."*

*"My . . ." A look of understanding registered in the Oven Man's face. He turned, looking to the child, who shook her head.*

*I Ye smiled. "You can refuse. That's your right. But you should understand what will happen if you do."*

*"Oh, I think I understand," the Oven Man answered unexpectedly.*

*I Ye's smile broadened. So the Lu Nan Jen wasn't quite beaten yet. "You refuse, then?"*

*The Oven Man swallowed. "No. I'll do it. Whatever it is. But I must have your guarantee."*

*"My word?"*

*"No. Something written. Something official."*

*I Ye considered briefly. Something like that could be used as evidence against him if things went wrong. Then again, he didn't intend to allow anything to fall into the wrong hands, not even the Oven Man's, so what was a piece of paper?*

*"Okay," he said.*

*"Now," the Oven Man said insistently.*

*"I could have you both executed, right here and now, for what you've done."*

*"So why don't you?"*

*I Ye laughed humorlessly. "No more games. Have we a deal?"*

*The girl, who had been silent until now, cried out to him. "No, Uncle Cho. You mustn't help them! You mustn't!"*

*Cho Yao looked across at her and shrugged helplessly. "We have no choice, my peach. I have to."*

*She swallowed, tearful now, and once more shook her head, but I Ye, watching the exchange, knew he had got what he wanted.*

*"Okay," he said brusquely, speaking to the guard who held the child. "Take her to Edingen." He turned, stepped up to the Lu Nan Jen, and spoke into his face. "I'll come inside and write your guarantee. Your wording, Oven Man. All right?"*

*But the Oven Man's eyes looked past him, never leaving the child; watching, deeply pained, as she was taken from the yard, out into the shadows beyond.*

"All right," he said finally, looking back at I Ye, his voice a bitter whisper. "Let's make our deal."

━━━━━

HSIEN L'ING WANG looked on from beneath the arc lights he'd had set up above the main access hatch, smiling, as masked guards brought the tiny bodies out. They had stacked up over forty already, and still they came. He turned, looking to the Wei, who shrugged, then came across, reaching inside his tunic to pull out his wallet.

"Who would have guessed?" Kan said, handing over the four fifty-yuan notes. "The tunnels must have been teeming with them!"

"Like rats. But easier to catch!"

He took the money, then looked past the Wei. A small crowd had formed behind the barrier, keen to see the outcome of the purge. Many were shopkeepers, who, their day's work finished, had hurried across town. They had suffered greatly from the petty thievery of the vagrants these past few months, so few of them had any sympathy for them.

"About time!" one called.

"A job well done!" another cried, and others took up the cry, praising and congratulating the Hsien L'ing for his firm action. Wang smiled and raised a hand, acknowledging their praise. But praise was merely praise. In the longer term it was their money he was after, and this show—effective as it was—served other purposes.

He turned back, looking to the Wei again. "Did you send someone to Hei Fong, as I asked?"

The Captain nodded. "I did, Master."

"Good, good. . . ." Wang looked about him distractedly. Despite a faint evening breeze, it was still too warm for his liking, and the smell from the bodies . . . well, it was disgusting. The sooner Hei Fong and the other merchants saw them, the sooner they could burn them and get on with things. He unfurled his fan and wafted it before his face, but it made little difference, the stench remained.

He turned back. "Kan! Send another messenger to Hei Fong. Tell him his presence is required."

The Wei came to attention, then turned and gave the order to a nearby guard.

"If he doesn't come soon . . ."

Hsien L'ing Wang stopped. The crowd had gone silent. The Wei was staring past him. He turned.

"What . . . ?" Then he saw what it was. He gasped. "Kuan Yin! What happened?"

The guard came right up to him, then threw the two sniffers down. In the glare from the arc light Wang could see the precise nature of the damage. Both cases were badly dented, the legs snapped off, the drilling mechanism jammed at an odd angle, the delicate lenses of the "eyes" smashed.

The Wei came and stood alongside him. "Aiya!" he said. "What in hell's name did that?"

The guard shrugged. "We don't know, sir. But whatever it is, it's still down there."

"You mean, the operatives didn't see anything?"

"No, sir. Whatever it was must have dropped on them and blinded them. One moment we had a signal, the next . . . nothing."

Kan swallowed. "Okay. Get the men out at once. Recall the other sniffers. Then seal it all. We'll go in with gas."

The Hsien L'ing reached out, gripping his arm. "No, Wei Kan. Gas won't work. It's too big, too well ventilated, down there for gas to be effective. I think this is one for I Ye and his men."

"I Ye?" The Wei looked troubled at the mention. "But we can handle it. I know we can."

Wang lowered his voice. "And if you can't? If word gets out that there really is a monster down there in the tunnels? Something that can destroy an automated tracker? Think, man. Think how word would spread. Why, before we knew it there would be panic throughout the city, and then you and I would be in the shit up to here."

He poked Kan's neck savagely.

"Now, get on to I Ye's office, and do it at once. I want this thing sorted out, and I want it done tonight!"

――――――――

SENIOR WARDEN CHAO BOWED LOW, his shaven head bobbing like a large ivory egg, then backed off a pace, inviting Shepherd into his luxuriously decorated office. The hangings on the wall were real antiques from before the time of the City, the porcelain figurines in the glass-fronted display cabinet behind his desk expensive collector's pieces.

*Above the cabinet a portrait of Chao Chung, in his ceremonial regalia, a plumed hat surmounting his bare dome, stared down at visitors; the image possessing a gravity, a stature, the man did not have in life.*

Ben, looking about him, understood at once. None of this had been paid for out of a Senior Warden's salary. All of this was the fruit of squeeze—the result of sordid little deals with the relatives and loved ones of the prisoners in his care. Yes, even as he took his seat across from Chao Chung he was conscious of the man's avaricious eyes on him, calculating the potential profit from this meeting.

"Well, *Shih* Shepherd," Chao began, his smile, like his voice, emanating a false friendliness. "How can I be of service?"

Ben met the man's eyes coldly, then handed him Li Yuan's handwritten letter, conscious of how, in that brief instant in which their eyes had met, Chao Chung had understood—as clearly as if he'd spelled it out at length—that not only was he not fooling his visitor with this act, but that he was held beneath contempt for even attempting such familiarity. Even so, Chao Chung maintained the smiling mask, if only because he knew no better tactic. It was important, from his viewpoint, not to offend this most important of visitors, for to give offense to Shepherd would be taken as giving offense to his benefactor, Li Yuan, and that—in Chao's position—would be, quite literally, suicidal.

With a bow to Shepherd he slit open the letter and began to read. He had only got halfway down when he stopped, looking up in surprise.

"But you only had to say. . . ."

Chao stood, gesturing toward the door to his left, inviting Ben to join him.

"Condemned prisoners only," Ben said, standing.

Chao smiled once more, his thin, bloodless lips stretched into a grotesque rictus. "But of course, *Shih* Shepherd. Here they are all condemned."

They went through, down a narrow, dingy corridor lit by a single wall-mounted lamp and out into a busy control room. As they entered, the Duty Captain looked up, then hurriedly took his feet from the table and stood, snapping to attention.

"Senior Warden!"

"Captain Lauther," Chao said, turning to smile obsequiously at Shepherd, as if to excuse his Captain's slackness. "*Shih* Shepherd wishes to look at some of our wards."

"Certainly. . . ." Lauther looked to Shepherd and bowed, then put a hand out, offering his chair. "If the ch'un tzu would be seated, I'll show him what we have."

Ben took the Captain's seat, facing a bank of four screens that showed various views of the prison. Views that changed randomly from time to time.

"Could I ask what exactly you're looking for, Shih Shepherd? It might speed things up."

"I'm in no hurry," Ben answered, looking about him languidly.

"Ah . . ." Lauther grimaced, then looked to his Senior Warder for instructions.

"Perhaps you would like to see the latest arrivals first, Shih Shepherd?" Chao said, bowing slightly, his hands folded before him. "We have had some interesting additions since the Edict."

Shepherd's grunt was noncommittal. Hearing it, Chao gestured to his Captain, indicating that he should just get on with it.

"Forgive me, Shih Shepherd," Chao said, his smile wearing thin, "but there is a great deal of paperwork to be got through. If you do not need me . . ."

"Of course," Ben said, not even deigning to look at Chao, dismissing him with the most casual of gestures. "I'm sure Lauther here will find me what I want."

"Of course." And, bowing, Chao Chung backed away, annoyed by Shepherd's treatment of him, yet relieved to have escaped his company.

When Chao was gone, Ben turned and looked up at the Captain. "Kuan Yin preserve us from such fools, neh, Lauther? Now, show me what you've got."

━━━◆◆◆◆◆━━━

THE TWO SOLDIERS crouched beside the hatch, examining the battered sniffer, then turned and looked to Wang, shaking their heads.

"I am afraid this lies outside our jurisdiction, Hsien L'ing Wang," the most senior of the two—the Captain—said, wiping his hands on his uniform trousers. "You would be better off referring this matter to the company who built this thing. I'd sue them, if I were you. You would at least get compensation."

Wang bristled. "Forgive me, but you miss my point, Captain. It is not the sniffers I'm worried about, it's what did that to them."

"Well . . ." Again there was a considered shaking of heads from the two. "I'd say that that was a matter for your Wei, Hsien L'ing Wang. We deal only with matters of State security."

"But surely this is just such a matter?" Wang said, exasperated now, conscious of his old rival, Hei Fong, smirking at his shoulder. "If word of this gets out, if the perpetrator is not caught . . . well, who knows what will happen? If there is a monster in the tunnels . . ."

The Captain stood, then took several paces toward him, his hands on his hips.

"You aren't suggesting that, are you, Hsien L'ing Wang? A monster? In the tunnels? I would think twice before I said such things, for to ferment unrest is a capital offense."

"But . . ." Wang fell silent, then turned and, pointedly ignoring Hei Fong, looked to his Wei.

"Okay, Captain Kan," he said, reining in the anger and frustration. "Get as many men as you can in there at once. I want every ts'un of that network searched, and I want it done by morning."

He turned back, lifting his head proudly, giving I Ye's Captain a look of pure disdain. "Whatever others choose to do, I want no man to say that Hsien L'ing Wang does not know where his duty lies."

Then, with a tiny shudder of indignation, he walked away, letting his Wei get on with it.

# CHAPTER EIGHT

# Night

THE MIDNIGHT TOLLING of a distant bell carried across the still night air to where Emily sat on the rotting stump at the edge of the frozen lake, her face buried in her hands. She was crying; mainly for Ji, who had experienced so little of life when he'd been taken, but also for all the other unloved and abandoned children—the progeny of this careless, bastard world that treated people like insects, crushing them thoughtlessly beneath its heel. Tears had never come easy to her, anger had always been her response, but now she cried and cried and cried, as if she'd never stop.

For the spoiled promise of the world. And for herself.

After a while she raised her head and looked about her, surprised almost to find the world still there, unchanged. The wind whispered through the trees behind her, a sound like the constant fall of water.

When they'd fled she'd thought only in the short term—of escape—but now she had to make plans for the longer term. For a moment she thought of the *Hsien L'ing* and what he'd done, not understanding, for it was he, surely, who had precipitated all of this, and yet it was he who had then let them escape.

She wondered what had happened to him. Whether he was now rotting in some dark and fetid cell.

*I should hand myself in,* she thought. Yes, but what would that

320

solve? Nothing. They would execute her, and then they would execute Lin. Yes, and the boys too.

She clenched her fists and groaned. She hadn't thought it through. She should have left them. *Someone* would have taken them in. And even if they hadn't, they'd have been better off than they were now, because now they were implicated in her crime.

She sighed. Yes, but to simply leave them—*abandon* them—that would have been equally unthinkable. They would have ended in a work camp. No, they would head out of the City, and find some-place where she wasn't known; somewhere they could live safely, quietly; where Lin could mend things and her boys could grow tall and straight like trees.

She stood, wringing her hands, tormented by the thought. It was so little to ask for. So fucking little.

"Mama Em?"

Emily turned. Lin was standing there, a dozen paces from her, a bandaged hand resting on the bark of a young pine. How long he'd been there she didn't know; she knew only that she hadn't heard him approach.

"Are you okay, Mama Em?"

She tried to smile, to reassure him that all was well, but the hurt she felt was so vast, so all encompassing, that the mere sight of him—of the simple, uncritical love, the sympathy in his eyes—triggered something in her. She began to cry again.

He came over and, holding his damaged hands out away from her, embraced her. She clung to him, sobbing helplessly, while he, bewildered, tried to comfort her.

"It's okay, Mama Em. It's okay. . . ."

She sniffed deeply, then moved her face back from his, wiping her hand across her face. "No," she said, taking a shuddering breath. "No, it's not okay. We can't stay here. We're already run-ning out of food. We have to go."

"Go?" His eyes were fearful. "Go where?"

"South," Emily answered, seeing what must be done even as she said it. She shivered again, then nodded. "We'll set off early, before dawn. If we make for the southern edge of the forest we can camp there until it's dark, then traverse the Karlsruhe corridor overnight. We could be out of the City in two days."

Emily saw the sudden hope in his eyes and looked away, wishing she hadn't seen it. In these circumstances it was better to be *without* hope.

She swallowed bitterly. She had made it sound easy, but Security was alerted to her existence now. They would be looking for her. And there was that little matter of Michael's reward. A million *yuan*. There would be a lot of people out there who'd sell their own brothers to have a share of a million *yuan*.

"Come," she said, letting him know nothing of her thoughts. "Let's get some rest. Tomorrow will be a long day."

He nodded, then, uncharacteristically, leaned forward and kissed her cheek. "It'll be okay," he said, as if saying it enough would make it happen. "You'll see, Mama Em. You'll see."

───────

*LET'S GO*, Sampsa said, turning away, sickened by the sight. *We've seen enough, surely?*

*No*, Tom said, staring unflinchingly at the girl. *She's here somewhere. I know she is.*

Sampsa closed his eyes, but still he saw. As long as Tom looked he could not help but see the poor creature.

*Tom*, he pleaded. *Please. . . .*

Tom looked away, releasing him from the sight. Even so, the memory tormented him. Cripples. Even cripples. . . .

He shuddered, then made his way to the door, anxious to get away. It was true, after all: one could buy anything in the *Yinmao*—anything at all. GenSyn sports, children barely old enough to walk, old women dribbling from senescence, cripples from the War, machines and things that were part machine, part living organism—hybrids from the vats of the new companies that had sprung up these past few years, the sick toys of fevered imaginations—all these and more they'd seen these past few hours.

"Well?" Yun asked as they emerged from the dingy room. "You find her?"

His eternal, smiling optimism was beginning to piss Sampsa off in a major way.

"No, you little fuckhead," he answered moodily. "Nor are we

likely to. You knew damn fucking well she wouldn't be here, didn't you?"

Tom reached out, touching Sampsa's arm. *No. . . .*

"What do you mean, no?" he said, rounding on Tom, forgetting for an instant that he hadn't spoken aloud—that Yun was present. "This fuckhead is giving us the runaround, don't you understand that? Yes, and taking a cut from all his friends here, you can be sure!"

Sampsa turned back, glaring at the young Han cook, but Yun was shaking his head. "You do me wrong, Master Sampsa. I try help Tom. You think I take money from a friend?"

"I think you'd steal from a friend and sell your sister if you saw a profit in it!"

Yun blinked, then shook his head, angry now. "You fucking weird, man! You one chip short of a full circuit! I help you and you fuck me over!"

Sampsa reached out suddenly, grasping Yun's neck, his fingers closing on his scrawny windpipe.

*No!*

He turned, staring at Tom, then let his grip relax.

Yun fell to his knees, coughing.

*No. We need him. She's here. I know she is.*

*No, Tom. She isn't here. You just want her to be here. If she was here we'd have found her. But she isn't.*

Tom pointed at Yun. *Ask him. Ask him if there's a special place. Somewhere we haven't been. Somewhere . . . unusual.*

*This whole fucking place is unusual.*

*Ask him!*

Sampsa raised his hands. "Okay. . . ."

He knelt. "Look, I'm sorry. Are you okay?"

Yun looked up at him and glared. There was real hatred in his eyes now. "You fucking madman!"

Sampsa nodded. "Yes . . . still." He took a fifty note from his pocket and stuffed it into Yun's top pocket. "That's for medical expenses. Now listen up. My friend here wants to have one last try at finding his girlfriend. He wants . . . well, he wants to know if there's somewhere special. Somewhere . . . *unusual.*"

Yun swallowed, one hand stroking his neck tenderly, then, his eyes glancing at the note stuffed into his top pocket, he nodded. "Yes. But it cost you, right?"

"Right."

Sampsa stood back, letting Yun get to his feet. Taking out his wallet, he looked to Yun. "How much?"

"Five hundred."

"Five . . ." Sampsa laughed and looked to Tom. *He's taking the piss now, Tom. Let's go. Let's leave the little fucker here and just go. No. Pay him. I'll pay you back.*

He hesitated, then, counting out the notes, handed them over. Yun counted them, then looked to him again. "And a hundred for me. As guide."

This time he didn't even consult Tom. He peeled off two more fifties, staring stonily at Yun.

"Okay, Tom's friend," he said acidly. "Take us there. And this better be good, understand me? This better be *really* special."

Yun grinned. "Oh, this special, all right. This ve-ry bloody special."

THE HEAVY, slatted blinds were drawn over the floor-to-ceiling windows of the studio room, each lacquered slat as broad as a man's forearm, each night-black polished surface delicately hand-painted by palace craftsmen. Inside the cavernous room itself a single lamp burned at the far end, where, behind a thick cloth screen the height of two men, Ben Shepherd was at work, surrounded by machines and frames and tables upon which were scattered pens and massive, leather-covered ledgers marked *Thanatos*, fragments of wire and glass and tubing, and other miscellaneous items of strange appearance.

Right now he was reaching up, adjusting the settings on one of the nine screens that nested in a bank against the wall. All of them showed variations of an outline skull. Behind him, at the center of the workspace, lay the Shell; a large, jet-black sarcophagus, its upper casing raised like a beetle's wing. Inside, nested within the cushioned interior, lay the child, her ivory nakedness rendered almost abstract by the metal cranial band, the tangle of wires and pads that linked her to the machine.

She lay still, unblinking, only the slight rise and fall of her chest betraying the life that lingered in her. Nearby, stretched out in perfect mimicry, the morph lay in its cradle, a thick red-and-black-striped cable linking it to the Shell.

Overhead, polished mirrors reflected back the scene, while in the corner, on top of a softly-humming generator, the wide-angle lens of a camera captured everything.

Ben turned from the screens and went to the nearest table, turning the big, square pages of the ledger until he came to the most recent workings. Taking a pen he made a few notations—coded symbols on a time-line graph that had meaning only to himself. Satisfied, he threw the pen down and turned, looking across at the girl.

The preliminary results were good. She gave a good clear signal, her brain responding perfectly to the fine-wire stimulation. She was sharp, this one—intelligent. He'd not expected that.

*And pretty, too,* he thought. *Why, it was almost a shame.*

The Letter of Permission was in his trouser pocket, signed by the Senior Warder and cosigned by Li Yuan less than an hour back. Effectively the girl was dead. She had ceased to be the instant Li Yuan had signed the Letter. From that moment she had become his property, to do with as he would.

*Fate, it had been.*

Ben chuckled, remembering how he'd seen her on the screen in the control room at Edingen and asked her name.

"Chuang Kuan Ts'ai," the Captain of the guard had said. *Coffin-filler.*

"How apt," he'd answered. "And when does she die?"

"In the morning."

"Then she's perfect."

And so he'd taken her. To give her, if not life, then the immortality of death. For she would be the first of his experiments. He would cast her like bait into the darkened pool and wait, watching to see whether the great pike, Death, would rise and take her in its mouth.

*A fisherman.* He laughed. *The shepherd becomes a fisher of men. Now, where have I heard that before?*

But was it possible? Was it really possible to reel Death in? To capture him on camera?

Again he laughed; a short, single sound. He would go down with her; would sink through the layers of darkness with her, his consciousness attached to hers, until . . .

Until the darkness changed and became something else. Some other kind of darkness, perhaps. *And on the third day—*

There was a knocking on the outer door.

He looked up distractedly and frowned. Taking off the headset, he stepped out, pulling the screen to behind him.

"Who is it?" he called, turning, looking across at the door, his mind still musing on the dark.

"It's me," came the muted answer. "It's Kim—Kim Ward."

"Ward . . . Ah, of course." Ben went across and drew the bolt back from the top of the door. "Come in," he said, wiping his hands, giving Kim a tight smile. "Forgive me a moment. I must just finish this. . . ."

Kim smiled. "I understand."

"Take a seat. I'll not be long."

⌒⌒⌒⌒⌒

KIM WATCHED BEN go behind the screen, then looked about him at the massive room. Three mahogany-framed armchairs with red velvet upholstery were placed about the ornamental fireplace. In that large, definitively Han room they looked strangely out of place.

He went across and sat, waiting, listening to the faint noises from behind the screen. A moment later Ben emerged, offering an apologetic smile.

"It's not that I'd forgotten," he said, "It's just that it got so late, I didn't think you'd come."

"I almost didn't. My daughter wasn't well."

"Ah . . ." Ben seemed uncomfortable with the notion. "Is she all right?"

"Yes . . . Li Yuan's surgeon sent something. She's sleeping now."

"Good, good. . . ."

"But I wanted to talk to you," Kim said, before he could speak again. "About the meeting."

Ben smiled. "You want to know why I didn't vote with you. Why I abstained."

Kim shrugged. "That . . . and other things. Mainly I want to know what's going on."

Ben came over and sat in one of the chairs, facing Kim.

"All right," he said, looking down at his hands, then back at Kim. "What I said in council, I said to draw Pei K'ung, to force her to say openly what she might not otherwise have said. That lady is used to dealing through intermediaries—through the likes of I Ye and Ming Ai—while she keeps her own hands clean. But those days must end. As must her rule."

"Her rule?" Kim's laugh had an edge of incredulity. "But surely Li Yuan rules?"

"Does he?" Ben smiled wryly. "So it might seem. After all, his name is on the Edicts, neh? His seal at the bottom of all documents. But whose policy is being pursued? Whose minions occupy most of the important positions in our State?"

Kim stared at him, aghast. "It's surely not *that* bad."

"No?" Ben stood, then went across and pressed a summons bell on the wall. He turned, looking back down at Kim, his eyes burning intensely now. "I thought much as you do six months back. I, too, thought everything was fine. That was before I came to the San Chang and experienced things for myself."

Ben paused, then came and sat again, leaning toward Kim, his voice low, confidential. "For ten years now she has built her web, replacing this official, passing that law, patiently, oh, so patiently constructing it, until . . . Well, let us put it this way, Kim Ward. Li Yuan has lost control and he knows it. If he were to die tomorrow—yes, and Kuei Jen with him—then the reins of government would pass without a hiccup to our Mistress."

Kim stared back at him in disbelief. "Are you saying Li Yuan is threatened?"

"Not yet. At least, not so far as our spies can ascertain. Yet who knows how much longer she'll be satisfied to play the shadow's role? She has the taste for power now. The taste, but not the name, the spectacle. And that, my Clayborn friend, is what she longs for."

"You're serious?"

"Never more so. Pei K'ung has become vain in her latter years. Why, there is even a rumor that she has had her ceremonial clothes made, awaiting the day she will be crowned in Li Yuan's place."

Kim shook his head. "This sounds like fantasy!"

"You think so?" Ben turned as someone entered on the far side of the room, then waved the man across. "And yet you saw her for yourself. Saw how keen she is to unify Chung Kuo."

"For Li Yuan and his son, surely?"

Ben laughed. "She doesn't give a shit about Li Yuan *or* his son! The truth is, she wants it all for herself. Megalomania, that's what it is. Classic megalomania."

"Like Ming the Merciless, you mean?"

Ben laughed. "Why, you're a regular storehouse of useless knowledge, Kim Ward! I thought—"

"You thought you were the only one who knew of such things?" Kim shook his head. "We share much, Ben Shepherd, a true knowledge of the past—the *buried* past—among them."

Ben stared at him a moment, then turned, looking to the waiting servant. Only then, as he took his attention from Shepherd, did Kim realize what the man was. Clayborn. It was unmistakable.

"Scaf . . . would you bring us a jug of lime cordial and two glasses? Oh, and ice. Plenty of ice. The freezing-water kind."

Scaf smiled at the old, familiar joke, then bowed awkwardly and slowly limped away. Kim watched him all the way to the door.

"You like my servant?" Ben asked.

Kim met Ben's eyes. "You gave him that name? *Quick?*"

Ben nodded. "Scaf always was the most nimble of my Claymen. Agile of mind, quick of movement. He lost much when he was injured in the Clay. I tried to rebuild him, but he was never the same. He's old now. Nearly thirty."

Kim shivered, affected by this strange reminder of his origins. "Might I talk to him sometime?"

"Of course. But let's return to the matter in hand. You wanted to know what was going on. Well, it's pretty straightforward, really, though I'd prefer it if you kept this to yourself. You're loyal to Li Yuan, I take it?"

Kim laughed, as if the question were absurd. "Li Yuan gave me my chance, my life. I owe him everything."

"Then listen, and try to understand. Li Yuan's rule is tainted by his association with Pei K'ung. If she fell, he, too, would fall. Unless . . ."

"Unless what?"

"Unless he could discredit her and then, at that very moment, abdicate his throne."

*"What?"* Kim was out of his seat. "Abdicate? A Son of Heaven?"

Ben smiled. "Why so surprised, Kim Ward? The history of the Han is filled with such instances. And think of the advantages. Pei K'ung would be gone, and with her all that was bad about the City. In her place would be a new young T'ang, handsome and strong of mind and body, together with his beautiful young bride. He would be a new broom, sweeping clean, untainted by anything that had gone before."

Kim sat, astonished. "If this were so, then why hasn't Li Yuan acted before now?"

"It was judged that the time was not yet ripe. We felt that if we acted precipitately it might leave Pei K'ung in power, stronger than ever. Killing her was no solution, either, for the general consensus is that what Pei K'ung does, she does by Li Yuan's sanction."

"Is that not so?"

"Not at all. Li Yuan conceded power—real power—to her many years ago."

Kim stared at him gravely now. "So what's left?"

"What's left is what we're doing. We work to undermine the Lady Pei."

"Undermine her? How?"

Ben laughed. "I am surprised, my friend. I thought you'd see it straightaway. The campaign's the key. You see, we aim to lose the war."

"Lose . . ." Kim sat there, thunderstruck.

The door on the far side of the room opened and Scaf appeared once more, carrying a tray. He brought it across and set it down on the low table at Ben's side. For a moment Ben busied himself, pouring two cups of cordial, then he looked back at Kim, offering him one.

"You seem surprised."

"Shocked is more like it. Are you serious? Have you no idea what effect such a setback would have on us?"

Ben nodded soberly. "We have a reasonable idea. That's why we've involved the Americans. To cushion the blow. We plan to blame them for defeat."

Kim shook his head. This was more outrageous by the moment! "And what do Kuei Jen and his American friend Egan think of this plan?"

"They know nothing of it. As far as they're concerned things are exactly as they seem. Kuei Jen has no inkling of what his father plans."

"*Aiya . . .*" Kim let out a long, sighing breath, then sipped at his cordial. "I wish you had consulted me before this."

"So you could counsel us against such action?"

"Of course." Kim stared at him. "Pei K'ung must be stopped, that much I understand. And I see that Li Yuan is tainted by association. But why can't Li Yuan just abdicate?"

Shepherd stared at him urbanely. "Why? What reason would he give?"

Kim thought a moment, then shrugged. "Surely he could think of one?"

"We thought long and hard about it. But for Li Yuan to step down from the Dragon Throne there must be a great and grave reason, and what greater and graver than defeat in war?"

"But *how?*" Kim shook his head, exasperated now. "You said it yourself in council. How could you possibly manipulate events in such a way that you could guarantee the result you want? What if things go well for our armies? What if they should win? Or what, if you *do* succeed, the Warlords decide to invade and destroy our City?"

"There are risks, naturally—"

"*Risks?*" Kim sat forward, the liquid splashing from his cup. "I'd say there were risks! Risks of civil insurrection, of social collapse, of

. . . oh, of a hundred different scenarios." He put a hand to his brow. "You say you've thought this through?"

Ben nodded.

"And you think this course—fraught as it is with risks—a better one to take than to simply let things be?"

"We let things be and this City will be a hellhole within five years. Pei K'ung is ripe, like a female spider waiting to hatch her brood."

Kim shuddered at the thought. "I didn't know. I thought—"

"You thought we were safe, neh, Kim Ward? You thought it was enough to tear down the City." Ben shook his head somberly. "No. We have completed but half the task. We have removed Man from the City—at least, from that monstrous box my forefathers built— but we have not yet removed the city from the man. There must be one more war. You understand that, Kim Ward? A war to destroy the very *idea* of Chung Kuo—of an ordered Chinese world state. Only then can we properly begin."

Kim looked up, surprised. As he watched, Ben twitched, his face convulsing briefly. Then he was himself again.

"Forgive me," Ben said. "It's just that I've started working again. . . ." He paused, began again. "I'm off my medication, you see. It always makes me a little cranky."

"Cranky?"

"I have fits, sometimes. . . ."

"Ah . . ." Kim frowned. "I didn't know." Then, "What's it for?"

"The medication? It's a bit of a cocktail, actually. Chlorpromazine, perphenazine, and haloperidol. For schizophrenia."

"Ah." Kim nodded, but he felt like he'd come to the edge of an unexpected abyss.

"We all had it. All us Shepherds, even Amos. Two faced we are, like the legendary Janus, though in our case it's almost literal. Jekyll and Hyde, we are. Frankenstein *and* his Monster."

"I understand. I . . ." Kim looked down, embarrassed, finding a need to confess what only those closest to him knew. "I have it, too, you see." He looked up and met Ben's eyes. "There are two of me in *my* head. Gweder and Lagasek."

"Mirror and Starer."

Kim stared at him, surprised. "You know Cornish?"

"*Covath dywysyk gwanscryfa orth skyans'n.*" Ben reached out, topping his glass up from the jug. "Memory, faithful scrivener to the eyes . . . Ah yes, Kim Ward, I have been deep inside the Clay. I have even been to see the Myghtern's capital. Why, I was briefly a guest in the Myghtern's cells."

Kim shuddered. "I was born there, in the Myghtern's capital."

"Yes. So Li Yuan told me."

There was silence between them, then Ben spoke again. "You mean to bind the stars with chains, I hear."

"With light," Kim said. "Why? Do you think it can't be done?"

"Not at all. A man *should* dream. And such men as you and I ought to dream big. Our intellects demand it, no?"

"Maybe." Kim looked away, uncomfortable beneath Ben's ferocious stare. Sometimes it seemed almost as if Shepherd were not real, but some strange machine in human form—a device for seeing and storing and calculating; for turning life into artifice. Sometimes it felt as though the form before him were merely a front, rooted in this dimension, and that behind that form of flesh and bone was a gateway into otherness—a vacuum through which pure darkness could be glimpsed.

"Don't get me wrong," Ben said after a moment. "I have great respect for your work, Kim Ward. We are both poets, neh, in the oldest sense of that word. *Makers*. Our poesy but takes a different form."

Kim sipped at his drink, then looked back. "You think my work a kind of art, then?"

"And mine a kind of science. The borders have blurred, don't you think? To be a great scientist one must be a visionary, no? A kind of artist. Likewise, to be a great artist in this age of machines one must have a scientist's knowledge, a technician's confidence and innovative skills. To be otherwise is to regress. You know that as well as I. Before we came along, both arts and sciences were static. But now . . . well, look at the revolutions we have caused, you and I. Look at the ripples we have made! Falling stones, we are! Falling stones!"

Kim smiled, but still he felt uncomfortable. There was something very odd in the way that one moment Shepherd could win you over with his charm, while the next he scared one to the core. Mad. There was no doubting he was mad. But sanely mad. Like a skilled charioteer he rode the two horses of his being with a confidence, an arrogance, that came from years of practice.

"You seem to know a great deal about me," Kim said, setting his cup down. "But what of you, Ben Shepherd? What do *you* want from your art?"

Ben's smile was dark, enigmatic. "I long to reach a place where nothing shines at all."

Kim nodded, then uttered the matching line. "Then you must step out from that quiet to the quivering air."

Ben stared at him, impressed. "You know your Dante, then."

"Like you, I am a storehouse. I know much that I have no cause to use. But why that?"

"Why Hell, you mean?"

"No. Why the darkness. What do you see in it?"

"Nothing. It's what I *hope* to see in it. I want to penetrate the hidden places, you see, to move into absences."

"Absences . . ." Kim nodded. Something in what Ben had said struck a chord in him. "So you think there's something there, then, *behind* the darkness?"

"I *think* there is, but who can tell? Like you, I follow instinct. Besides, why bother with what is known? Let lesser men do that. We are explorers, no? It is our task to draw an outline on the unmapped chart, to extend into the whiteness."

"Or into the black."

Ben laughed. "So it is. You the one, I the other. Inward and outward. It is our fate, neh? And who are we to fight it?"

"Who indeed?" Kim smiled, then shrugged apologetically. "Well, I really ought to go. I've taken up far too much of your time as it is. Maybe we can talk again another time."

Ben stood. "Are you sure you won't stay a moment longer?" He turned, gesturing toward the curtain. "Perhaps you'd like to see what I'm working on?"

Kim, who had stood ready to leave, hesitated, then nodded. "Okay. But then I must go. I'd like to check on Mileja."

"Of course." Ben walked across and tugged the curtain aside.

Kim stepped up beside him, looking in. "I've often wondered."

"Wondered?"

"How you worked." He smiled. "Personally, I use a pool."

"A pool?" Ben looked to him, interested.

"I find it liberates my thoughts. Floating there, free of normal restraints. I don't know why, but there it is. Back home I've got a big circular pool. I've had it built inside a planetarium. If I've a problem—something I'm stuck on and can't find a way around—I'll go in there, turn off the lights, and simply float there on my back, staring up at the stars for an hour or two. Nine times out of ten it does the trick."

Ben nodded, then stepped inside, going across to the Shell. He turned, looking to Kim again.

"You've been in one of these?"

"Once or twice."

"And?"

Kim shrugged. "Not my thing, I'm afraid. I felt . . . *cut off.*"

"I see." Ben looked down through the darkened glass, touching the forefinger of his right hand to his lips thoughtfully.

"The word *shell* is interesting, don't you think?" he said, beginning to walk around the huge sarcophagus-like receptable. "It originates with the Germanic word *skal*, meaning to divide or separate, and is the base for the Old English word *scylfe*, meaning a partition. So you *could,* in that purely etymological sense, argue that my art divides."

Ben had reached the far end of the Shell. He stopped, looking back at Kim. "However, I like to see things in a different light. I prefer to see what I'm doing as the culmination of an evolutionary process that has been going on ever since Man first began to think in abstract terms. As I see it, art seeks to provide the common man with an understanding of the world and its ways through a process of selective mimicry. In that sense art is always a reinterpretation of the world, and the more realistic its rendition, the more persuasive it can be. As Nietzsche said, 'The more abstract the truth you want to teach, the more you must seduce the senses to it.' "

"Maybe so. But where does seduction end and addiction begin?"

"Addiction?" Ben laughed. "You think my art a kind of drug, then, Kim Ward?"

Kim glanced aside. "I . . . found it so."

Ben's eyes watched him hawkishly now. "It disturbed you, then?"

Kim nodded, not daring to meet those eyes.

"That's interesting. You think art should be more comforting, perhaps?"

"Comforting, no. It's just . . ."

"Just what?"

Kim shrugged. "I found it awkward. Embarrassing, I'd guess you'd say. The woman . . ."

"Meg, you mean?"

Kim looked up, then nodded. "I . . ."

"You found that disturbing, right? Making love to her? But why should it worry you? After all, it was only a fiction. You didn't *really* make love to her."

"Maybe not. Yet it seemed real. I—"

"You enjoyed it, right? You *wanted* to make love to her? Well, fine. What's wrong with that? Men have their dreams, their desires. They always have had. I simply make those dreams accessible. And where's the harm in that?"

Kim stared at Ben, conscious of a sudden edge to their talk. "Look, what is this? What do you want from me? I didn't like it, okay? I found it . . . *intrusive.*"

Ben raised a hand. "I understand. You love your wife, your children. You have a good life. A very good life, indeed. You have no need for fictions. But what of those who don't have any of that? What about those poor sad bastards who've had nothing but bad breaks in their lives? Why should they be stuck with mundane reality? Why can't they have a taste of something better now and then?"

"I didn't say that."

"No?" Relenting, Ben shook his head, then smiled. "No, you didn't. Forgive me. I didn't mean to suggest . . ."

"It's okay." Kim looked at him again. "And now I really *must* go. The hour's late. But thanks."

"Thanks?"

"For confiding in me."

"Anytime," Ben said, walking across, escorting him to the door. "Anytime."

BEN   STARED   AT   THE   DOOR  a moment after Ward had
gone, then, with a shudder of distaste, went back across the room.
The Shell was as he'd left it. The girl lay still and silent beneath
the darkened glass, the thick leather restraint stretched tight across
her mouth. *Tonight*, he thought, a shiver of anticipation passing
through him. *We'll try for it tonight.*

Yes, and maybe he would send Ward a copy. If only to disturb
him. To jolt him from his complacency.

*Yes, and to feed the darkness in you. To give Gweder more of what he
craves.*

He laughed. Maybe he ought to send Meg with the tape when it
was done. That would unnerve the little bastard. Yes, and it might
even bring him down a peg or two.

Ben swallowed angrily, recalling what had passed between them.
How dare the little cunt take up that high moral stance? How dare
he even think to judge his betters?

Why, for all his intellectual tricks, Ward was no better than Scaf
when it came down to it. Clay he was, and Clay he remained. For
all his talk of linking up the stars, Ward was inherently—*instinctively*—a little man. Why, Ward would never think to go where he
was about to go. He'd never *dare!*

*Yes*, Ben thought, beginning to unfasten the catches that held
the Shell's lid in place. *And when you limit what you dare, then you
limit what you are.*

Limits. He smiled, then pushed back the lid, getting down to
work again. There were *no* limits when it came down to it.

THE   YOUNG   LIEUTENANT  stopped and, pulling back his cuff,
checked the time. It was ten after three. Sighing, he turned wearily
and signaled to his men to move on.

The forest here was dense and dark, the path between the trees
narrow. Even with lanterns they could barely see ten *ch'i* front or
back, so it was like walking in a tunnel. He hated it; hated these
late patrols. If they ever got into trouble—*real* trouble, of the kind
these patrols were supposed to anticipate—there would be little

they could do. By the time help came they'd all be dead, their throats slit, the renegades vanished into the trees as if they'd never been there.

He shivered, looking about him uneasily, then walked on, trailing the six men in his command.

A *waste of time*, he thought, slapping at an insect that had landed on his neck. With their lanterns they could be seen coming half a *li* away, whereas their prey—whoever that might be—had merely to wait among the trees, shrouded by the darkness, until they'd passed. But orders were orders. And besides, he suspected this, like so many of the tasks he undertook, was really only for show, so that when his superiors were asked by someone higher up what was being done about security in the forests, they could point to the patrols and claim that the problem was being dealt with.

As to whether a problem actually existed, who could tell? As far as he could make out, there were very few renegades. Most wanted criminals went south, out of the City, or hid out in the seedier areas of town. Few of them actively welcomed the inconvenience of rough living.

*And who can blame them?* he thought, feeling the strain on his calves as they continued to climb uphill. *Even prison would be preferable to this.*

At the top of the hill was a small clearing. On the far side of the clearing stood the hermit's "house." Usually the makeshift shelter was dark and uninhabited. Tonight, however, the hermit was at home.

"Sir?" one of his men said, coming over. "It seems he wants to talk to you."

"Talk to me?" The lieutenant strode between his men and stopped, facing the hermit. His face, in the lantern light, seemed like something carved from wood, all angles and sharp shadows.

"Well?" he asked. "What do you want?"

"Strangers," the man said, grasping the lieutenant's hand firmly, the feel of his bony, unwashed fingers making the soldier squirm. "Strangers in the wood."

He freed his hand. "Where?"

"Over there," the hermit said, turning and pointing. "Beside the place. You know, the place of staring faces." He looked back at the lieutenant, his eyes fearful. "She saw me."

"She?"

"The woman."

He looked to his sergeant. "What's over that way?"

The sergeant thought a moment. "Rudesheim."

"Rudesheim?"

"It's a village. Or was. Ruins now. They might be camped out there."

"Okay," he said, excited by the prospect of some proper action. "Douse the lanterns. Night visors down. Let's do this properly."

He turned, looking to the hermit. "Thanks. You'll get your cut."

The man shrugged. "You just make them go, okay?"

"Okay." Dousing his own lantern and slipping his night visor down, he hurried on, getting ahead of his men, leading them on at a brisk pace, the world transformed into a simple pattern of red and black, hot and cold, hunters and hunted, the coded recognition symbols of his men glowing vividly from their uniform jackets as they moved stealthily through the dark.

━━━━━━

THEY CAME OUT of the *Yinmao* and along a dark, partly lit alleyway that sloped down toward the river and the high-rise towers of the business district. After the bright-lit bustle of the *Yinmao*, it was a dismal, mournful place, haunted by the sound of early-morning traffic on the river, the metallic hiss and whoosh of a fast-track cutting the distant skyline like a brilliant silver snake.

Rain had been falling and the ground was slick and wet underfoot. Sampsa looked to Tom, the doubt in his eyes reflecting what he was feeling at that moment.

*If this is some kind of trick, I'll break the little bastard's neck.*

And then he saw it—the place Yun had mentioned—the sign glowing red on black, the legend written both in Mandarin and English:

CH'A HAO T'AI. The Directory.

Yun turned to face him, smiling. "You see?"

"I see," he said sourly, thinking, *This had better be good.*

But Tom's hopes had risen at the sight. That hope flooded Sampsa now, coloring his skepticism.

"You wait here," Yun said. "I go in. Make sure they see you, neh?"

"Neh," Sampsa said, then, as Yun made to go, reached out and grasped his arm. "And no tricks, you little fuckhead. You go straight out the back way and you're dead. Understand? And you pay the man the money, as agreed. I don't want any funny business once we're inside. *Okay?*"

Yun freed his arm from Sampsa's grip. "I man of my word. I say I get you in, I get you in. But they fussy, this place. Not everyone get the nod, you understand, Master Sampsa?"

There was an edge to Yun's voice—an uncertainty—that had not been there before. *Why?* Sampsa wondered, watching the young Han turn and make his way across. Then he understood. When it came down to it, Yun was little more than a cheap hustler. He was perfectly at home in the *Yinmao*, but here . . . well, this was a different thing altogether. This was class. In fact, thinking about it, it was almost a certainty that Yun had never come here, never stepped across the threshold of the *Ch'a Hao T'ai* before tonight.

He smiled to himself, watching as the security camera over the big double doors swiveled around to focus on Yun.

*Look! He's shitting himself.*

*Can't you leave him be? He's keeping his word.*

*Only under threat.*

*Maybe. But don't push so hard.*

Sampsa turned, looking to his friend. "We're here, no?" he said quietly. "You think he'd have brought us this far if I hadn't pushed?"

Tom looked down. *Maybe not. But . . .*

He relented. "Look, it's okay. But if she's not here, then we call it a night, agreed?"

Tom looked back at him, gratitude in his eyes. *Agreed.*

He turned back just in time to see Yun disappear inside, as a big man, clearly a guard of some kind, stepped out and gave them the visual once-over before he went back in, pulling the door to.

And so they waited, ten, almost fifteen minutes, before the door opened again and Yun stepped out, beckoning them across.

"Well?" Sampsa said, conscious of a smartly dressed young Han standing in the doorway at the far end of the entrance hall.

"It okay," Yun said, grinning first at him, then at Tom. "They let you go in. But only one. They have room where other one wait, neh? Unless you want pay more."

Sampsa looked to Tom. *You want to go in?*

*No. I'll wait.*

*You sure?*

Tom nodded. *You just find her for me, okay?*

He smiled. *Okay.* Then, turning back to Yun: "All right. I'll go in. Tom will wait."

Yun nodded, and went to speak to the young Han. There was a brief exchange, then Yun returned.

"He say okay. You go through. He see to you. Everything paid for, neh?"

Sampsa eyed him suspiciously, but Tom touched his arm.

"Okay," Sampsa said. Reaching into his pocket, he took out another fifty note and handed it to Yun. "You stay somewhere we can find you, right? And maybe we hire you again."

"Maybe." And, snatching the note, Yun was on his way, swift as a thief in the night.

Sampsa turned. The smart young Han was waiting for them, smiling and beckoning them forward, the door held open for them.

*Are you sure you want to do this?* Sampsa asked.

*Are you?*

Sampsa laughed silently. *In for a penny . . .*

*. . . in for five hundred yuan!*

It was the closest Tom had got to a joke all night. Smiling, they went across.

"Welcome, young Masters," the young Han said, bowing politely. From his polished accent it was clear he was no child of the Lowers, or if he was, then he had somehow raised himself beyond that level. "I understand that you, Master Sampsa, wish to experience the delights of our humble establishment. And you, Master Tom . . . you wish to wait, is that right?"

Sampsa answered for him. "I am afraid my friend is a mute. But, yes, he'll wait."

The young Han smiled and bowed to Tom. "In which case, I shall have one of the servants escort you to the lounge and arrange refreshments for you. If you wish to sleep, there are beds there also. Or if you change your mind . . ."

"No," Sampsa said. "But thank you for your kindness. My friend is . . . tired. He'd like to rest."

"Of course." The young Han smiled, then reached out and pulled a nearby sash cord that hung from the ceiling. "My name, by the way, is Joseph. Joseph Harris."

Both boys stared at him, surprised.

"My father was *Hung Mao*, you understand."

"Ah . . ." Sampsa nodded to him. "You speak well, Joseph."

He nodded. "Thank you. But I cannot claim much credit for that fact. I was tank educated."

"Tank educated?"

Tom's voice filled his head. *Shells . . . he's talking about Shells. My father had a hand in it. They call them fast-learning tanks. It's supposed to cut down the time it takes to learn something by a factor of ten.*

"Ah, of course," Sampsa said, looking about him at the plushness of the entrance hall. "Even so, it's pleasant, after the evening we've spent, to come upon so *refined* an establishment."

Harris laughed. "You've been in the *Yinmao*. After that, even the night-soil carts would smell sweet, neh?"

Sampsa chuckled, relaxing, finding he liked this young man.

*Watch him,* Tom said, sounding a warning note.

*Like a hawk,* Sampsa answered silently. *Now go and rest. I'll do the looking for you.*

Tom smiled, then turned, following the servant who had appeared, ghostlike, at his elbow.

*Sampsa?*

*Yes?* he answered, as they went their separate ways through the building.

*Try not to enjoy yourself too much!*

*You can always close your eyes.*

*And, Sampsa?*

*Yes, Tom?*
*Find her for me. . . .*

———————

THE LIEUTENANT saw her from the far side of the frozen lake, walking alone among the trees. Changing the visor to normal night-sight and enhancing the image, he focused on her face . . . and felt himself go very still, his pulse beginning to race. It was *her!*—there was no doubt about it. Why, he had seen the printout only that afternoon.

Saying nothing, he sent two of his men off to the right to cross the strip farther down and circle back, then waited for the woman to return to the ruined village.

A million *yuan!* He'd see only a small part of that, of course, but even so. He whistled to himself, then, putting the thought aside, set about concentrating on the task ahead.

He watched her turn and begin to make her way back.

"Go!" he said, waving two of his men across. At a second signal he sent the final two off to the left. They knew what to do, where to take up their positions. Now it was up to him.

He walked slowly across the ice, his heart pounding, keeping his eyes focused on her back all the while.

*Don't look down,* he told himself, recalling the last time he'd walked across; how unnerved he'd been by the sight. Usually he skirted the strip, crossing it at its narrowest point, near the path, but this time he had no choice. Even so, it spooked him to be walking on the faces of the dead. Try as he might, he could still see them down there, trapped, their fingers groping for the surface, their eyes bulging, their faces contorted in perpetual torment.

*A reminder.*

As he stepped off the ice he let out a shuddering breath. After this he would ask for a new posting—demand it, maybe. After all, his actions here would make his superiors rich—very rich indeed— and they could easily afford to grant him a favor or two in return.

He walked on slowly, careful now, aware of her just ahead of him, of the first of the ruined buildings there, no more than fifty *ch'i* away between the trees.

*An awful place,* he thought. No wonder their forefathers had wanted to build over it all. Forests and ruins. . . . He shuddered again, then drew his gun, checking the side panel to make sure it was fully charged.

He was no more than thirty *ch'i* from her when she stopped. Moving back behind one of the larger pines, he watched. She was speaking, her voice low, almost a whisper, as if afraid to wake someone. He craned his neck, trying to see, then switched back to infrared, but the low wall obscured any trace of other bodies.

They were there, though. They had to be. Because where she was, they, too, would be.

He moved closer, edging slowly now, trying not to make a sound. Ten *ch'i* from her he stepped out, his gun raised, pointed at her head.

"Move and I shoot you dead."

She made to turn, then tensed, understanding the situation. Two heads popped up, staring past her at him. Boys' heads.

"Do nothing," she told them, in a low, firm voice.

"It's over," he said, taking a step closer, his left hand signaling for his men to close the net.

"Over?" She laughed, then turned to face him. "Why, it hasn't yet begun. I had such hopes. . . ." Her laughter broke into despair. "Such hopes."

She looked at him, her eyes pleading now. "I just wanted to help them. Can you understand that, Lieutenant? They were orphans. No one loved them, not until I came along. No one cared. But *we* cared. We took them in. We raised them, Lin and I."

She swallowed, and took a step toward him, raising her hands in appeal. "Let me go. Please. Let me take them from here. No one would know."

He forced himself to feel nothing for her. "I can't. I have no choice. I have to take you in."

She stared at him a moment, then nodded. Her head dropped, her shoulders sagged. It was done.

He watched her a moment, then, stirring himself, gave a short, sharp whistle. At once his men moved in, three of them covering the party with their high-velocity rifles while the others went among the boys, cuffing them and pulling them up, forming a rough line of them out to the right of the building.

They left him to cuff her.

"Sorry," he said, as he clicked the lock. But she said nothing, merely stared back at him, her face closed, her eyes like the eyes of the dead beneath the ice.

———————

"S O ,"  S A M P S A   S A I D, looking about him at the Spartanly furnished room, noting the wall-to-wall screens, the long, body-mold lounger seats, the silver cranial units nestling in the oval ceiling cavity, "where are the girls?"

Harris turned to him and smiled his best, enigmatic Oriental smile. "Did your friend not tell you? There *are* no girls here."

"No girls? Then what—"

He pieced it together in an instant. *"Pai pi,"* he said.

Harris gave a nod, impressed. "You know the term, then."

"The Hundred Pens." Sampsa looked about him again, seeing it all anew. *Shells,* Tom said inside his head, staring out through his eyes, his curiosity matching Sampsa's. "Then the girls—"

"Are stored," Harris finished for him. "We have over eighty thousand on our books. You want it, we have it."

*You want to see this?* Sampsa asked, glimpsing at that moment the room where Tom sat, a *ch'a* bowl on the table by his side.

*There's a chance,* Tom said.

*A slim one, don't you think?*

*Maybe. But seeing as we've paid . . .*

"You know what type you'd like?" Harris asked, walking across and indicating the screens. As he did they filled with the images of a hundred different naked women.

Sampsa looked from screen to screen, impressed by the wide variety of female forms displayed there. There was something strangely honest about this—something they'd not encountered in the *Yinmao,* where such common trade had masqueraded as exoticism or, at worst, romance. This was a cattle market.

*You want fuck my sister?*

*Not funny,* Tom answered, *considering—*

*Forgive me. I forgot about your mother.*

*It's okay.* Tom seemed suddenly more relaxed. Was that tiredness? Or had the sharp edge of his obsession been blunted by the *Yinmao?*

*Not at all,* Tom answered him. *I know now. We'll find her here. I'm sure of it.*

*A tape of her, perhaps.*

*It'd be a start.* Then, *Well? Go on. Ask him!*

Sampsa looked to Harris. "That girl there. She's close to what I want. Perhaps a slightly smaller build. Prettier. Younger too."

"How young?" Harris was smiling now; a smile of encouragement.

How many times had he done this? Sampsa wondered. How many times had he stood here, like Mephistopheles, offering Faust the world.

*And in return?* Tom asked.

*We've paid,* Sampsa reminded him.

*Have we?*

Sampsa laughed silently. *Don't go all philosophical on me, my friend. You want her, let me find her for you.*

*Then lead on, my Virgil.*

The images changed. A hundred new girls were now displayed, much more homogenous a group than the last—dark-haired young Han of roughly the right height and build, approximately the right age. Sampsa scanned the screens quickly, then shook his head.

*She's not there,* Tom said.

*I know.*

*Then . . .*

*Leave it to me. Please, Tom. I know what she's like. I've seen her through your eyes, remember? Gods! How could I forget?*

Tom was silent.

*Okay. . . . Look, I'm sorry.* He sighed, then shook his head.

"I know what I'm looking for," he said, turning to Harris. "These are . . . close. But it's a specific type of girl."

"I understand," Harris said, unfazed by the request. He looked up, speaking to the ceiling. "Switch to search mode. Voice activated. Code to our guest here."

Sampsa scanned the screens a second time, then selected one of the girls high up and to the right of where they stood. *Her?*

*Yes,* Tom said. *The eyes. . . .*

*I know.* He looked to Harris, then pointed. "Her."

The hundred images dissolved, reducing down to a single large screen on the facing wall. On that screen was the image he'd selected.

"Okay," Harris said, indicating the figure displayed at the foot of the screen. "The Directory has given us a further three hundred and eighty-four close matches. We'll work through one by one. You see something you like, just say, 'Store,' and we can come back to it later on."

"And to move on?"

"A simple no, will do." Harris smiled. "After all, none of the girls will be offended."

---

HE HAD HOPED to find Jelka awake when he got back, had wanted to go over what he and Ben had discussed, but she was already asleep.

Switching the light on in the hall, he walked through into the lounge. His staff had set up a mobile communications center in one corner—a mini office, complete with desks and screens. It sat there on the far side of the unlit room, the muted glow of its panels reassuring in the darkness. He went over and sat, leaning across to remove the message chip, slipping it into the slot behind his right ear.

Kim's eyes glazed over briefly, then focused again. Routine matters, mainly. Reports from Wen Ch'ang back on Ganymede. Nothing urgent. He squeezed the flesh on either side of the slot and jettisoned the chip.

He sat there, staring blankly at the black reflecting surface of the window, recalling the sight of Shepherd, standing beside the frame, his eyes like the eyes of an intelligent tiger, and as he did so the words of Dante's poem came to him:

> My nature, by God's mercy, is made such
> As your calamities can nowise shake,
> Nor these dark fires have any power to touch.

He let out a long breath. Ben's illness—his schizophrenia—both fascinated and disturbed him, as did Ben's disposition toward the dark. For some time he had believed that he and Shepherd were quite similar—outsiders, creators, architects of the greater life of their society—but now he was forced to reevaluate. Now, without question, he understood. They were as different as they could possibly be. When Ben put back his head and stared up at the night he saw only the immeasurable darkness, whereas he himself saw only light—the light of four hundred billion stars: a burning web of light so radiant, it seared the conscious mind.

*It's why we're blinkered,* he thought. *It's why we can't bear to think of it too often, lest we realize just how small we really are within that mighty scheme, how dark.*

He stood, then walked to the window, standing there with his hand against the cool ice-glass pane, looking out across the moonlit darkness of the gardens.

Was it just circumstance that had made them so? Or had the seed of what each was been planted long before their births? After all, born into darkness, he had forever sought the light, whereas Shepherd, born into the light . . .

Kim shook his head, frowning at his reflection in the darkened glass. The explanation didn't suffice. It simply didn't *begin* to explain how things were. Even so, there was some truth in it. At some point their directions had been fixed—his upward, toward the blinding light, Ben's downward to the earth and darkness. And implicit in those directions was the idea of expansion and enclosure, separation and connection.

*Shells and webs . . .*

Kim nodded to himself, seeing it clearly for the first time; understanding, in that instant, why such a gulf existed between himself and Shepherd. Why he didn't like the man.

He shivered then drew an unseen line upon the glass. It was a contest, he understood that now: a contest, not for the soul of a single man, but for all of mankind. What Ben sought was to isolate the individual, to enslave the whole species, each in his own tiny, doorless room. His art—great as it undoubtedly was—was, when it came down to it, little more than a snare, a prison for the senses, and he the Puppetmaster God who danced and capered in each tiny room.

Indeed, Shepherd's vision was no more sane than DeVore's, when it came down to it. Each dreamed of populating worlds with his own copies!

*And you, Kim Ward? What do you want?*

He heard the words as if Ben Shepherd had spoken them inside his skull.

*Connection*, he answered. *An end to walls and illusions and fake ideals.*

*And yet you sought the Light. Wasn't that a fake ideal? Or do you forget where you first had your vision?*

Kim nodded to his image in the glass, remembering the moment clearly. That moment in the Clay when, bathing his face in the pool beside the Gate, he had first glimpsed the giants from Above with their heads of shining glass and their bodies of sinuous, flexing silver. He remembered the blinding brilliance of that light as it poured out from the Gate and shimmered in the surface of the pool like some living force. Yes, and he remembered how their shadows had breached that burning, shimmering mirror. Three kings, he'd thought they were. Three kings! He laughed. How little he'd known back then. How little he'd understood. And yet the moment retained its purity, its power over him.

No, for all he had discovered since regarding men and their ways, he had not been wrong. Even when, after the Gate had closed, he had groped blindly in the mud for those tiny fragments, those pearls of light—even then he had not been wrong. Mistaken, maybe, but wrong?

"No," he said softly, and smiled, realizing suddenly just how small Shepherd's world view really was, how little it encompassed.

To know so much and understand so little, that surely was a curse? For understanding—*true* understanding—meant stepping beyond the limits of one's isolate self. It entailed embracing otherness. But Ben . . . Again he sighed. Ben craved a world of compliant mannequins—a host of empty heads that he could fill.

*He thinks my instincts for the good are counterfeit because he believes all men are shaped in his own image. He thinks, because there is dark in each of us, that darkness is all, yet it's surely the balance of dark and light within a man—yes, and in a woman, too, for there's another half he fails to see—that matters more than anything. We are each of us a tiny battlefield. In each frail soul this contest must be fought, a direction chosen.*

Kim laughed, then spoke quietly, admonishing himself. "What? Must you become as bad as he, Kim Ward? Must you always overstate your case? Light without shadow . . . what's that but another form of darkness?"

And with those words came the determination to go back and speak with Shepherd again—to confront him with this new-won knowledge and see what argument—what sophistries—he'd set against it.

He nodded, and turning, made his way across the room and out. Yes. He'd do it now, while the mood was on him. Before circumstance parted them for another forty years.

Guards made to challenge him as he ran down the empty, echoing corridors, then, seeing who it was, stood back. Outside Shepherd's suite he slowed, wondering briefly if it were not perhaps too late.

He made to knock, then stopped, noticing that the door was open.

He looked around, suddenly aware that there were no guards here. Frowning, he pushed the door back slowly, the hairs on his neck rising, old instincts switching in.

The reception room was dark. On the far side the door to the lounge was open just a crack, light from the room beyond—from Ben's study—picking out the door's edge.

Kim crouched, then crossed the room quickly, silently. Something was wrong. Something was badly wrong.

As he looked through the gap he saw the faintest movement to his left, a shadow against shadows.

*Shao lin,* Kim thought. *An assassin. But why?*

For the briefest instant he hesitated, wondering what to do. Did he call out? Did he *warn* Shepherd? It seemed the simplest thing to do. But what if Shepherd couldn't hear? In all likelihood Ben was wearing his headset. If he shouted and Ben didn't hear, then his best chance of saving him would have gone. The assassin would kill him first, then go back and finish off Shepherd.

Which left him with a single, simple option. He had to kill the man, or at least disable him, before he could get to Shepherd.

*Imagine it's Jelka in there,* he told himself. *Or Mileja.*

A shadow split the line of light as the assassin peered around the door.

*Now!* Kim told himself, *hit him now!* But he was too slow. The crack widened briefly as the assassin slipped inside.

Picking his way quickly across the darkened room, Kim stopped beside the crack and peered in.

The assassin was already halfway across the room, his all-black figure crouched behind the armchair in which Kim had sat not two hours earlier. Beyond him, on the far side of the open Shell, was Shepherd. Ben stood there, the headset covering his ears as he leaned over the casing to make some fine adjustment. Just now he faced the assassin, who was less than twenty *ch'i* from him, yet the bank of screens was just behind him, and when he turned . . .

Kim looked about the room, trying to formulate some plan of action. One thing alone was certain: the assassin would not strike until he was sure of success. But how he'd strike, that was a different matter. Was he armed? Undoubtedly. But with what? A gun? No. Too noisy. A knife or a garotte were the more likely options. It would be a while, after all, before the body would be found. Time in which he could make his escape.

Kim flexed his hands, preparing himself, then stood, pushing the door wide open.

For a moment neither Shepherd nor the assassin saw him. Then, as he looked up, Shepherd noticed him. He began to smile, then stopped, noting something in Kim's face.

Kim took one step . . . a second . . .

Glancing around the chair, the assassin saw the look in Shepherd's face and spun about.

"You've failed," Kim said, trying to keep any trace of fear out of his voice; at the same time reminding himself just how deadly the man who stood before him was. With a frightening clarity he saw the knife in the assassin's left hand—a short, double-edged knife with a curving blade. Dark eyes stared out from the two narrow slits in the man's mask—Han eyes that watched him coldly, calculating what manner of risk he represented. Briefly he glanced around, checking on Shepherd, then, making no noise, he launched himself at Kim, his knife arm raised.

The moment seemed unreal, dreamlike. Time did not slow so much as slew aside and slip into another, wholly different dimension. As the assassin ran toward him, Kim moved forward and to the left, pure instinct overriding his thinking self. In an instant the assassin had checked and changed direction, yet even as he swung his arm toward Kim, even as the blade was hissing through the air, Kim's palm connected squarely with his wrist, sending the knife spinning away.

Thrown off balance, the assassin tumbled, rolled, then quickly turned, facing Kim once more, crouched like a fighter.

"Stay exactly where you are," Shepherd said from somewhere at the back of Kim. "Move and I'll blow a hole clean through your head."

The assassin grinned.

"It's what he wants," Kim said, his stance mirroring the assassin's, his eyes watching his assailant's every move. "Kill him and we won't know why."

"You want to die, Kim Ward?"

Kim swallowed. The assassin was watching him very closely now. "No."

"Then let me blow his head off. I could tape it."

"You're fucking sick. You know that, Ben Shepherd?"

Shepherd laughed. "So I've been told. I'd call it a healthy curiosity, myself."

The assassin's eyes had changed. That unexpected note of humor had unnerved him. Even so, he was still deadly. The situation being what it was, dying was the easy option as far as he was concerned. Living, being caught—that, for him, would be a problem.

The assassin made a feint to the right, another to the left.

*Any moment,* Kim thought, feeling the adrenaline surge through him, every muscle in his body twitching, wanting the release of action.

There was a strange noise, like the noise of a man spitting. Once, twice, a third time.

*"Kim!"*

He almost missed it, it was so fast. As the assassin's foot came up, he jerked his head back. An instant later and he would have been dead without a doubt, his neck broken. As it was it connected against the side of his head with a sickening crack that sent him sprawling backward.

He lay there, dazed, his eyes closed, hands raised, waiting for the finishing blow, his whole body tensed against it.

For a moment the room was deathly silent. Then, with a strange, inhuman sound, the assassin groaned. Kim let his eyes ease open.

Close by, two, three paces at most from where Kim lay, the assassin knelt, his face, where he'd removed the mask, ash white, one hand clutching his chest.

Kim tried to speak, but couldn't. There was a ringing in his head and he could feel the blood pulsing through the veins in his skull like water through a hose. As he blacked out he heard, or thought he heard, the sound of Li Yuan's voice.

*Not possible*, he thought, as consciousness leaked from him. *Not possible. . . .*

━━━━━━

LI  YUAN stood there a moment, looking past the fallen man at Shepherd, astonished by the sight.

"What in the gods' names has been happening here?"

"A little local difficulty," Ben answered, setting the gun down. "You'd better get help for Ward. That was some blow he took."

"Of course." Li Yuan turned and gestured to his servants. At once they hurried to Ward's assistance.

Li Yuan turned back. "When the alarm went, I thought—"

"An assassin," Ben said, pointing to the man. "He's stunned. But otherwise—"

There was a noise behind Li Yuan. He turned to find himself facing I Ye.

I Ye's eyes searched the T'ang's, concerned. "Are you all right, *Chieh Hsia?* The alarm—"

"We've had a scare, that's all, Colonel I. The matter is in hand."

"A scare?" He looked past Li Yuan. "Who's this? An intruder?"

Ben laughed. "An assassin, no less. But not a good one, neh? The good ones we never know about . . . not until it's too late."

I Ye looked to Shepherd, then quickly looked away. "You wish me to deal with him, *Chieh Hsia?* To wring some answers from him?"

Li Yuan's smile gave nothing away. "This one I would like to interrogate myself. But you can accompany us, Colonel I." He looked to Ben and winked. "I would welcome your advice."

*"Chieh Hsia!"*

I Ye clicked to attention, his head bowed, but his eyes, looking to the kneeling figure of the assassin, were deeply troubled.

---

THE ASSASSIN was chained to the wall, his hands stretched out above his head, his feet pinned by iron brackets inches from the floor. He was already in pain, his naked body sheened in sweat, long, nasty-looking weals striping him from neck to groin where he'd been beaten with the whip, yet up until now the two guards had been merely toying with him. The "real fun," they whispered tauntingly, was yet to start.

"Speak now and make it easy for yourself," the shorter of the guards said, his voice seductively soft, like a woman's. "Tell us who hired you and we'll make it easy." He showed the assassin the narrow bladed stiletto. "I'll make it quick, I promise. Just tell us."

The prisoner stared back at him, stony faced, saying nothing.

"Let him rot," the other guard said after a moment, glaring at the man with undisguised contempt. "Let him rot in the darkness like the insect he is. Let him die slowly. He deserves no less. If it were up to me I'd inject him with beetle larvae and let the little bastards eat away at him from the inside."

"No, brother," the first said. "You're wrong. Our friend here's no common scum. He's special. He'd have to be to be chosen for this task. He'd have been trained. *Disciplined.* Why, I bet if he were free right now he'd see us both off in an instant. An *artisan*, that's what I'd say he was. An artisan."

"Bollocks!" the second answered. "He's a slit-throat and no more! You can dress it up any way you like, brother, but he's scum all the same! Death's too good for this cunt. I'd hand him over to GenSyn, myself. Let those bastards use him for their experiments. Or give him to one of their ox-men. Foul things, they are, with foul habits. Mind . . . you'd have to widen a few of his orifices before you let one of those things loose on him!"

Both laughed at that. The prisoner closed his eyes. "Do what you will," he said. "You'll get nothing from me."

The guards stopped laughing; turned to look at him.

"So you *have* got a tongue after all," the big one said. "At least, you have right now!"

And again their laughter rang out in that tiny cell. They were still laughing when the lock clicked and the door swung back.

They turned, kneeling and pressing their foreheads to the cold stone floor as Li Yuan stepped inside, followed by I Ye and Shepherd.

"Has he spoken yet?" Li Yuan asked, walking straight up to the assassin and staring at him eye to eye.

"Yes, *Chieh Hsia*," the short guard answered, keeping his head lowered, "though nothing of use."

"No names yet?"

"No names, *Chieh Hsia*."

Oddly, Li Yuan smiled. "How brave are you?" he asked, addressing the prisoner. "Brave enough to die, certainly. But to live? Are you brave enough to trust me? Brave enough to take a chance on my word?"

The man stared back at Li Yuan silently, determined to concede nothing, but his eyes had changed subtly. There was doubt there now. Not much—just the slightest glint—yet enough. Seeing it, Li Yuan began to work on it.

"At times like these I find the world a strange place to inhabit. For most of the time my power is a ritual thing, it serves a purely ceremonial purpose. Yet at times like these . . ." He nodded thoughtfully, then turned away, looking first to Ben and then to I Ye. Though the room was cool, I Ye was sweating.

"At times like these," he went on, pretending he had seen nothing, "I find myself . . . elevated. Raised up out of myself, you might say."

He looked back at the prisoner. "Perhaps you've felt the same thing when you've killed someone. Yet what I feel is different, quite different, because for me there's no fear of being caught, no fear of reprisal. More than that, I have a power you don't possess. The power to make a dead man live."

The prisoner gave a little shudder, his eyes following Li Yuan now, attending to the T'ang's every word.

"You, you see, are a dead man. The moment you were caught you were dead. *How* you died, that was the only question that remained to be answered. And maybe when. But you were dead, and you knew that. In fact, knowing that gave you your strength. But what you didn't know—what you couldn't possibly know—was that I can take away that strength."

Li Yuan smiled. "Oh, yes. I can see you understand me. You can live. I can let you live."

He took a step closer then laid his bare hand flat on the man's chest, above his heart. The prisoner closed his eyes and groaned.

"Can you feel that, my friend? Can you feel your heart beating? And your thoughts . . . can you feel the thoughts circling in your head?" He let his hand slide down until it rested over the man's shriveled manhood. "Can you not feel the urge toward life that's in you? That's in every single cell, every single atom of your being? Can you not *feel* that?"

The prisoner shuddered, his eyes popped open. "What do you want?"

"A name," Li Yuan answered. "One name and you can go from here, a free man, my letter of safe passage in your pocket."

The man's Adam's apple bobbed. His eyes searched Li Yuan's. Then, lowering his head, he nodded.

"Well?" Li Yuan said. "You have my word. Now tell me who hired you and you can walk from here."

Yet even as he said it he heard the brazier go over, heard someone grunt and call a muffled warning, and turned to find I Ye facing him, a heated brand in his hand. Both guards were sprawled, unconscious, on the floor.

"Forgive me, *Chieh Hsia*," he said, a servant to the last. Yet even as he made to thrust the brand into Li Yuan's chest, he was knocked to the side.

Li Yuan watched, astonished, as Ben grasped the winded I Ye by his collar and banged his head smartly once, then a second time, against the wall.

He let him fall, then stood, wiping his hands, pleased with himself.

Li Yuan stared at Shepherd, conscious of how close he'd come to dying. "Thank you," he said quietly.

"You should thank Ward," Ben answered, "for saving me."

The T'ang nodded, then stepped across, looking down at I Ye. "I should have known."

"Your wife," Ben said. "She must have ordered it."

Li Yuan stared at him, surprised. "Why?"

"Because of what I said. I challenged her, and she'll take that from no man, not even you."

"You think so?"

"I know so."

"And I Ye? What should I do with him?"

"I'd keep him safe if I were you, Yuan. Somewhere where Pei K'ung can't get to him. And then I'd try him—secretly, of course. It would not do to make public what he knows. Not yet, anyway. If things go wrong—if Pei K'ung should somehow triumph after all—then this carrion might yet prove the saving of you. Or, at least, of your son, the Prince. But don't let the bastard know that. He must be made to believe his Mistress has forsaken him. Further, he must believe he is being kept alive only because you wish to torment him."

Li Yuan considered that, then nodded. "It shall be as you say."

He turned, looking to the guards, who were struggling to their feet, wheezing loudly. "You two. Take Colonel I to Edingen. And stay with him—in his cell, if necessary. No one is to even speak to him without my permission. Sealed orders will be with you before the dawn."

They bowed as one. "*Chieh Hsia!*" Turning to I Ye, they bent down and, taking an arm each, unceremoniously dragged him from the cell, the traitor's head bumping on the stone flags and the step.

"Alive!" Li Yuan called after them, yet his eyes when he looked to Shepherd were amused.

"She's mine," he said softly, then began to chuckle. "I do believe the bitch is finally mine!"

AS THE GUARDS hurried to open the doors to her private suite, Pei K'ung swept through, tying the sleeping robe about her as she went, her hair untended, her face unmade.

"What time is it there?" she asked of Heng Yu as he met her at the door.

Chancellor Heng straightened and, turning to follow his Mistress through into her study, answered her.

"Er . . . just after eight, I think. It's four hours different, so . . ."

Taking her seat behind the desk she looked at him sharply. Heng Yu fell silent, then raised a hand to his mouth, stifling a yawn.

"Okay," she said, turning to face the huge screen that was slowly descending from the ceiling to her left. "Patch the Marshal through."

Karr's face appeared at once, only the bottom half of it—the firm chin, the mouth, the tip of the nose—visible at first, the eyes and brow slowly coming into sight as the rest of the screen emerged from the ceiling.

"Mistress!" Karr said, bowing his head.

"Well, Marshal?" she asked, conscious of how she must appear to him. "What is it?"

"Forgive the lateness of the hour," Karr began, "but you said you wanted to know the moment there was news."

"So speak," she said, sitting up attentively. "Did you talk with Warlord Hu?"

"With his Chancellor," Karr answered, "an hour back."

"And?"

Karr smiled cautiously. "The news is good, Mistress. Hu Wang-chih has agreed to the draft of the alliance document. We are to sign it in the morning."

She clapped her hands, delighted. "Excellent news, Marshal Karr. And did Ming Ai play a part in the negotiations?"

Karr looked down momentarily. "Ming Ai is . . . *indisposed,* Mistress. He did not meet Warlord Hu."

"Indisposed?" The news was a surprise to her. "He didn't . . . ?" She shook her head. "I don't understand."

"Hu's surgeons are tending to Ming Ai at this very moment. He has a stomach complaint."

She stared at Karr, then looked down. Composing herself, she looked back at the screen.

"All is agreed, Marshal Karr? The terms . . . ?"

"Are as per your instructions, Mistress. It would seem Warlord Hu is keen on the alliance. Very keen indeed. He has scores to settle with his neighbors. Besides which, he has problems here at home too—problems that foreign adventures could well cure."

She nodded, deciding not to push the matter of Ming Ai, especially if all was as Karr said. She forced a smile. "You have done well, Marshal. You have done us all a great service."

"Mistress!" he said, bowing his head.

She cut connection.

For a moment she sat there, very still, considering the matter of Ming Ai. As far as she knew, the man had never had a day's illness in his life. Was it coincidence, then? Or was some deeper game being played here? Then, suddenly aware that Heng Yu was still standing by the door, watching her, she stood and went across to him.

"Good news, neh, Master Heng?"

His smile was weary. "Good news, indeed, Mistress."

But there was something about the way he said it that made her query it. "What is it, Master Heng?"

"Mistress?"

"Has something happened?"

He hesitated, then nodded.

"So? Must I drag it from you?"

Heng seemed to back away from her, though he did not move a fraction. He flinched without moving. "It is I Ye, Mistress."

"I Ye? What of him?"

"He has been arrested."

The expected explosion did not come. Instead, she seemed to shrink, to deflate before his eyes.

"Ah . . ." she said. Then, "Ah . . . I see," almost as if the news was something she'd anticipated. No details asked, just, "Ah . . ."

Then, as though Heng Yu had said nothing of significance, she smiled at him and, touching his arm briefly, began to walk away.

"Good night, Master Heng."

"Good night, Mistress," he answered, staring after her in astonishment. "Or rather," he added, so low she did not hear him, "good morning. . . ."

SAMPSA STOOD THERE, patting Tom's back as he leaned over the low stone parapet of the Nidda, retching. It was low tide and the river was a narrow line of silver between dark banks of mud, the current sluggish where it ran south to meet the River Main. Workers making their way to their early shifts stopped to stare at them as they passed, then walked on, chuckling to themselves, thinking them merely two young bucks who had drunk too much. But they were wrong.

As Tom retched noisily, Sampsa shuddered, remembering.

They had found her. Almost as soon as they'd begun their search, her face had come up on the screen.

*There!* Tom had shouted in his head. *That's her!*

Some part of him had known at once, but Tom's excitement—his joy at finding her again—had masked it from him. Recalling the moment now—seeing the image of her vividly in memory—he could see the fear in her eyes, the unmistakable tension in her facial muscles.

And beneath the image, her name. Ho Ko. *Harmonious Song.*

In those first few moments he had tried to urge caution, but Tom was not listening. After the evening's frustrations he was not about to wait.

He had raised his hand. "Pause there."

*You want to go in?* he asked Tom silently.

Tom hesitated, uncertainty flickering in his head. *No . . . no, you'd better go and speak with her.*

He turned, looking to Harris. "Yes. She's the one."

Harris had smiled and nodded. As the image faded from the wall, he put out an arm. Across from him a door irised open.

Sampsa had followed, innocent still, not knowing; some part of him guessing, perhaps, but not yet knowing. He had followed, down a plushly carpeted corridor and out into a spacious hexagonal hall. As they crossed the hallway he had looked down. Beneath his feet a marbled mosaic depicted the naked figures of a man and woman coiled about each other in a blatantly pornographic variant on the *tai ch'i*.

"In here," Harris said, unlocking the door with an old-fashioned key, then holding it open for him.

He stepped inside. Music was playing softly. The lights were dim. In the center of the room was a long black leather body-mold lounger. On the far side of the room stood a masked figure; a young part-naked man, perfumed and silent. As Sampsa stared at him, he bowed.

"One of the house eunuchs," Harris said quietly. "If you want, he'll help you with the attachments. Or would you rather *I* assisted you?"

He hesitated, then waved Harris away. As the eunuch approached Sampsa raised his arms, letting the man undress him, as if this were something he did quite regularly; as though the acute embarrassment he felt at that moment didn't matter.

*For Tom*, he thought, but Tom was silent.

He had lain down in the lounger, letting the eunuch attach the pads and wires to his naked body. The man's touch had been gentle, like a woman's touch, his hands warm, their movements unthreatening, yet there was something about it that had unnerved him. The scent of the man, the basic angularity of his body, these things he found disturbing.

And yet these people knew their clientele. This choice of eunuchs was deliberate, almost ritualistic. They paid for something different here in the *Ch'a Hao T'ai*—something they couldn't get in the *Yinmao*.

Sex and all the variants on sex—those could be had anywhere, and cheaply, so it seemed. So what was different about this? What made their clients come here time and again at five hundred *yuan* a time?

He had heard the door click shut as the eunuch stepped outside. A moment later the music faded, the lights dimmed further, until it was dark.

He lay there expectantly, the soft leather surface of the viewer comfortably tight across his upper face.

The tingling began all over his body as his nervous system was stimulated at the eighty-one separate points where the machine was attached to him. For a moment it felt as though he were a simple vessel, a hollow, empty thing: a porcelain skeleton held together with wires. Then, before that feeling could become too frightening, too uncomfortable, it changed. It was like being filled with a warm, silken fluid. After that momentary hollowness the sensation of it made his nerve ends tingle with pleasure.

And then it began.

He was climbing the wooden steps up the outside of an old, traditional Chinese house of stone and tile. The day was bright and warm, the sunlight on his bare arms pleasant. Street noises—the cries of children, the rumble of a cart—came to him from behind his back. The sound of his footsteps on the steps, the springy solidity of the wood beneath his feet, both were convincing. He could smell distant burning, the scent of camphor in the air. Far off a tugboat hooted on the river.

It all felt real. Very real.

At the top of the steps a door, red painted, the paint faded and flaking in places. He reached up, his arm stretching, his hand grasping a cheap brass knocker.

His heart was pounding now, expectantly. He could feel Tom in his head, a silent passenger, sharing the experience.

He let the knocker fall. From inside came the sound of movement; the click of an inner door, the swish of material against the uncarpeted floor. And then the door opened.

It was an old man, bald and wispily bearded. Her father, so it seemed. Sampsa was suddenly conscious of how well he was dressed in comparison to the old man; how much above him in status he was. As the old man bowed low and backed away, he dug into his pocket and fished out a coin—a big, solid thing, unlike anything that existed in reality. Solid and golden, it glinted briefly before disappearing into the folds of the old man's greasy jacket.

He stepped inside, the old man closing the door behind him, ushering him through a curtained partition to a room at the end of a short corridor.

"Wait here," he said. "I bring her."

He looked about him at the cheap furnishings, the gaudy popular prints that hung on the walls, the sight of them familiar. He came here often, it seemed—twice a week, when his wife was out at market.

These memories seemed clear, yet a moment earlier they had not existed. Chemicals, pumped straight into his brain, provided him with these false layers of recollection, strengthening the illusion, bonding him to it.

He went to the stool in the corner and sat, as he always did. There was the faint smell of perfume in the room; an old and faded smell.

*Her* smell.

Through the wall he heard an exchange of voices. A door slammed. A moment later the door to the room swung open. As she stepped inside, he stood.

"Why are you here? Why have you come again? I told you . . ."

"I'm sorry," he began, the sudden memory of what he'd done last time coming to him; a vivid, disturbing image of the girl pinned down beneath him, her naked buttocks exposed to him as he struck her again and again.

Beneath his own surprise he felt Tom recoil in shock.

"I still hurt," she said, turning, pushing her rump out toward him and pouting. "You bad man, Mister Sampsa. You very naughty man."

Unable to prevent himself, he stepped across the room and, putting out his hand, rested it on the rounded curve of her rump, feeling the warmth beneath the thin cloth.

"Let me see," he said, his mouth forming the words without volition, his eyes meeting hers.

She stared back at him uncertainly, then nodded. Slowly she eased the skirt down, exposing herself to him.

The weals were dark and painful-looking. Fresh blood in the cuts revealed that they were almost new. Seeing them, he winced inwardly. Yet in the Shell he put his hand out, touching one of them, tracing its course across her flesh, ignoring the girl's discomfort. *Enjoying* it.

New chemicals were pumping through him now. Stimulants.

The thought of her pain excited him suddenly. The thought of what he'd done.

*No,* Tom was saying, over and over again. *No.*

He reached out and grabbed her neck, then threw her down onto the bed. She cried out, but he ignored her. He had paid. The old man had his money. Now she would do exactly as he said.

Holding her down with one hand, he began to free himself, tugging his swollen penis from his trousers. The girl was struggling now—really struggling, her eyes badly frightened as she turned her head to plead with him, but it was as if he couldn't hear her anymore. An awful madness was on him suddenly; a dark rage that would not let him be until it had been fed.

He was hitting her now, slapping her and punching her even as he tore at her clothes, grunting and snarling at her like a wild thing as he entered her and began to thrust, not caring that he was hurting her, excited by her frightened whimpering, her little cries of panic.

*No . . . No . . . No . . . No . . .*

He was tearing at his belt now, pulling it loose. Reaching down, he grasped her hair and pulled her head back savagely, then slipped the belt about her throat and fastened it. Slowly, very slowly, he began to tighten it.

*Stop!* Tom was shouting. *For God's sake, Sampsa, stop!*

But Sampsa couldn't stop. Appalled, he felt his excitement mount, felt his body move more and more urgently, the girl's violent struggles feeding something dark and hideous inside him. Beneath him the girl was dying. He could see the blood draining from her face; could see her eyeballs bulging, yet still he held her down.

He'd paid! The old man had his money!

With a faint shudder she died, and as she died he came, the sensation exploding at every nerve end in a terrible ecstasy of release.

Release, and, as conscious slipped away, a tiny, despairing voice echoing in his skull.

*No! . . . No! . . . Oh, Jesus help us, no!*

TOM HAD STOPPED RETCHING. As he straightened up he looked to Sampsa.

*That was real.*

"I know."

*They must have wired up the killer. Taped his responses.*

Sampsa nodded. But even talking about it made him uncomfortable. It was as if the experience had somehow poisoned him. He had done nothing, and yet he felt responsible for the girl's death. Guilty. And no amount of rational argument could dislodge that feeling.

It had made him realize how few things had really touched him in his life, how few scars there were on his psyche. Now all that had changed. In the space of one night he had lost something of his eternal flippancy, his naïveté. He was no longer innocent. Now he knew. Oh, he had always "known" in some distanced, cerebral kind of fashion, but now he *knew*, as if it were now encoded in his cells. Hands on, as it were. Yes . . . the stench of it still filled his nostrils.

"I killed her," he said softly, seeing himself through Tom's eyes even as he spoke.

*No,* Tom answered, yet the denial was unconvincing. Tom felt as he felt.

"So what now?" he asked.

Tom stared at him. *Give me the tape.*

Sampsa hesitated, then felt inside his jacket pocket for the tiny chip. He had paid them twenty thousand *yuan* for it. All he'd had on him. According to Harris it was the original—the only print. But who knew?

He looked back at Tom, trying to read him, but Tom wasn't letting him in.

*Give it to me.*

"What are you going to do?"

Tom shook his head, then put out his hand. *Please. . . .*

He looked down, staring at the chip thoughtfully. "You could give it to your father. He could make a Shell for you. A good Shell. Maybe you could—"

Abruptly, Tom reached out and snatched it from him.

*No,* he answered, his face showing what he thought of the idea.

*No*. Then, turning to face the river, he hurled it out into the darkness.

Sampsa sighed.

*We didn't kill her*, Tom said, turning to face him again. *We might feel as if we did, but it wasn't us!*

"No. . . ." Sampsa swallowed, then. "Look, maybe we should get back."

*Yes*, Tom said, reaching out to touch Sampsa's arm, *let's do that*. But the openness had gone between them. After tonight nothing would be the same. From here on there would always be walls between them.

RAIN WAS FALLING as the transporter set down on the strip outside the massive walls of Edingen Prison.

The iron gates swung open; Emily and the boys were herded through, stumbling, the heavy chains linking them all. Lin, who had collapsed on the journey, followed a moment later on a motorized stretcher, an oxygen mask over his face.

As the rain fell harder unfriendly hands shoved them into a yard, where, beneath the glare of arc lights and surrounded by high walls painted midnight-black, the Senior Warder waited to greet them.

"Ah . . . new guests," he said, rubbing his hands together; unperturbed, it seemed, by the downpour, his polished head gleaming wetly, his thin-lipped mouth smiling at Emily as if welcoming a friend. "Your rooms are awaiting you," he said, and laughed. An unpleasant laugh.

The boys looked to her forlornly. Chia and Sung began to cry, but she could not comfort them now. The very worst had happened. Now only pain and darkness lay ahead. Even poor Lin's fate seemed beyond her concern now. She had fallen—fallen into the abyss. Even Ji's death had been as a rehearsal for this moment.

She put her face up to the sky and groaned. *The gods help me in my torment!*

But the Senior Warder, seeing her gesture, merely laughed. "Pray all you will, Emily Ascher, but you are beyond all help. Here you are beyond the world."

She stared at him and, swallowing, nodded. Yet even as she looked, she saw a movement in his face. He lifted a hand to the faint slit behind his right ear, as if listening, his eyes widening in surprise.

"Well, well . . ." he said, his face suddenly lighting up with pleasure. "It seems you are not the only new guests tonight." He wiped the wetness from his face, then stepped away and, giving her a little bow, said, "Forgive me, *Mu Ch'in* Ascher, but I must leave you for a little while. Relax. Enjoy the view. It's better than the view you'll have."

And with that he hurried off, guards running to him as he went.

She turned, watching him, then stared at the chains about her wrists. Dead. They were all dead. They only *seemed* alive. She shivered, then looked about her, trying to recognize those she was chained to, her mind fighting against the darkness that sought to engulf it.

*My boys . . .*

Yet even that simple thought threatened to unhinge her. If she thought for a moment about what lay ahead for them, if she let herself think . . .

A tiny whimper of fear escaped her. *My boys . . .*

They were all crying now, some, like Chia, quietly, his head bowed, others, like young Teng, wailing like a baby. The sound of it was awful, dreadful. It tore at her.

*Stop it,* she thought. *Please stop it. Before I go mad.*

"Dead," she whispered, trying to convince herself of it. Trying to find some consolation in the thought.

There were sudden shouts, then urgent whispering in the gallery overhead. She heard the sound of someone running, his boots clicking on the wet stone, then the slam of a door.

Turning, she looked up, trying to see through the glare of the lights. Then, through the same door through which they had passed but a moment before, strode I Ye, wearing nothing but a pair of loose-fitting trousers. Rain ran freely down his bare, well-muscled chest. Behind him two guards looked on without expression.

For a moment she misunderstood. For a moment she thought he had come to torture her, then she saw the chains about his wrists, linked to the restraining harness about his neck, and caught her breath.

*I Ye! . . . a prisoner!*

The rain fell, harder now, beating down on them through the layers of light and dark, as I Ye looked across at her and, without knowing who she was, lifted his chin and smiled arrogantly.

*TUNNELS. There was no end to the tunnels. Beneath the City was an endless labyrinth of ancient ways—of drains and sewers, abandoned railway lines, heating ducts, and secret cellars. Some were waterlogged, but that was no barrier to him as it might have been to others. Holding his breath, he'd dare such channels, and so come upon secret places where he could hide. Places no one but he had knowledge of.*

On that first evening, hiding from the Hsien L'ing's troops, he came upon one such place. Breaking surface, he gasped for air, then, pushing up the broken drainage cover, he climbed up and, switching on the flashlight he'd stolen from the soldier, shone it into that dark, enclosed space.

It was a room. A tiny cellar room. The light fell upon a wooden chair, a rusted iron bed, and then . . .

Josef laughed, then went across to look at them. The three skeletons sat together against the wall, their fleshless arms about each other: father and mother and, between them, its skeleton almost as small as his own, their child. In their rotted threads they made a touching little group, sitting there, staring into eternity.

"Smile," he said, and, as if the flashlight were a camera, pretended to look through it, clicking the switch as though taking a photograph.

In the momentary darkness he turned his head, sniffing at it, taking in its damp yet musty scent, then clicked the light back on.

"Still here?" he asked, then, laughing, climbed up onto the bed and lay there on the rusted springs.

Revenge. He'd get revenge for what they'd done. Not for the boys they'd killed—who cared what became of them?—but for himself.

He looked to his grinning companions and smiled.

"Watch me," he said, his mind already hatching new schemes, new ways of making mischief up above. "You just sit there and watch, eh?"

Then, with a chuckle, he lay down, resting, knowing there was time—all the time in the world.

# CHAPTER NINE

# A Death, a Gift,
# a Marriage

**P**EI K'UNG supervised the search herself, standing there in the center of I Ye's apartment while her men went through every drawer and every file, pulling up floor tiles and poking at the walls with metal rods, making sure there were no hidden compartments. Only then, when she was satisfied that she had got everything there was to get, did she wave them out and, locking and barring the doors behind her, return to her study.

Chu Po was waiting for her there. He was sitting in the tall-backed leather chair beside the darkened window when she swept in, smoking a small cigar and watching her with amused eyes as her servants piled chest after chest of papers and tapes and files onto her desk.

"Well?" she said, looking to him. "Aren't you going to help?"

"Help?" He made a face. "I'll only get in your way if I try to help. You know how I am."

"Yes," she said, quelling the irritation she felt for him at that moment, then turned, looking from chest to chest, wondering where to begin.

"Besides," he went on, "I thought I'd take a stroll in the gardens. Watch the sun come up."

She turned her head and answered acidly, "They say a man should see the sunrise at least *once* in his life."

"Indeed." He slowly hauled himself up out of the seat and, fastening the sash to his silks tightly about his waist, walked to the door and stepped out, into the predawn darkness.

She watched him go, feeling bone tired and haggard. Twice this night she had dragged herself out of bed to deal with urgent matters. Right now she felt on edge and in a mood to spit and snarl if she didn't get her own way. But Chu Po was right. He'd be no help. He was a gadfly, not a clerk.

She yawned deeply, then summoned Ming Ai's assistant, Cheng Nai shan, across.

"Cheng! I want four clerks. Men you can trust implicitly. I want them to take a chest each and work through. Anything that looks even vaguely interesting they refer to me. Everything else goes straight back in the chest. All right?"

"Mistress!" Bowing low, Cheng hurried off to summon his clerks.

She didn't have long, she knew that. Why, she had almost overlooked it. If Chu Po had not suggested searching I Ye's rooms, she might still be in her bed, the chance gone. More than that, she was fortunate Li Yuan hadn't beaten her to it. Then again, Li Yuan had I Ye, and I Ye was worth a whole library of incriminating evidence.

She shivered, then put her right hand to her mouth, chewing at a nail. It was her own fault. She hadn't been specific enough in her instructions to I Ye. She had let her temper get the better of her. She should have specified that the attempt on Shepherd's life be carried out in the Domain, far from these halls. Then again, how could she have known that I Ye would be so stupid as to try to pull it off within the walls of the San Chang itself?

She grimaced, then went back to her desk, pulling one of the chests toward her, thinking things through as she got down to work.

I Ye deserved whatever fate awaited him. She felt no pity for him. The only question was what he would tell her husband of her schemes, for I Ye was certain to try and bargain for his life, and being without influence or connection, the only thing he had to offer was information.

She looked up, knowing what must be done. She had to have him killed, and at once. Li Yuan would know, of course, but that could not be helped. She could not risk the chance of I Ye's loose tongue spilling all to Li Yuan's torturers.

And Li Yuan, if he was half the man she thought he was, would know she would try. In his place she would strive to move I Ye beyond her reach.

She reached out, placing her hand firmly on the summons button. A few seconds passed, and then the door on the far side of the room opened and Cheng Nai shan stepped in, bowing low.

"Mistress?"

"Cheng . . . who did Colonel I deal with when he wanted something special done?"

Cheng looked up, a query in his eye. "Special, Mistress?" But, seeing the look in her eye, he understood. "Ah . . . *special.*"

"Well? Can you arrange something at short notice, Cheng?"

Cheng considered a moment, then nodded. "I could set up a meeting within the hour, Mistress. But it would be advisable if you yourself were not to be involved. These people are not—"

"I understand," she said, raising a hand. For a moment she stared out into the slowly growing dawn light of the gardens, then smiled to herself.

"Okay. Arrange it at once. I'll send Chu Po. The bastard can earn his keep for once. And, Cheng . . ."

"Yes, Mistress?"

"Find out where they've taken Colonel I."

"That I can answer at once, Mistress. I Ye was taken straight to Edingen. There he shares a cell with two of your husband's bodyguards."

"His torturers, you mean?"

Cheng hesitated, then nodded.

"Good . . . that's good." She nodded, satisfied, then waved him away. But he hesitated a moment. "Well? Is there something more?"

Cheng lowered his head. "My clerks, Mistress. I have them waiting outside."

"Ah . . ." She smiled, pleased that he at least was thinking clearly. "Send them in. They can work on the floor, here before my desk."

"As you wish, Mistress."

"And, Cheng . . . tell me once something is arranged."

He bowed to the waist. "As you wish, Mistress."

━━━━━━━

KARR STRODE INTO THE ROOM, then came to attention, bowing stiffly. Warlord Hu was sitting in a chair beside the unmade bed, one of his maids dressing him, buttoning his shirt, while another fed him with her fingers from a porcelain bowl. Pushing her hand aside, Hu Wang-chih looked up at Karr and smiled broadly.

"Ah, Marshal Karr. And how are you this fine morning? Did you sleep well? Did my servants look after you adequately?"

Karr hesitated, then chose to answer diplomatically. "I slept very well indeed, Excellency."

Warlord Hu chuckled. "The sleep of the just, eh?" He lifted his chin, letting the girl thread the last of the pearl buttons through the eye, then waved her away. Joining the other maid she bowed, then went through into the nearby bathroom.

Hu looked to Karr. "You are ready, then?"

"Ready, Excellency?" Karr met the man's hazel eyes.

"To sign." Hu turned and snapped his fingers. At once his Chancellor, who had been standing silently in the corner of the room, brought across two furled scrolls. Hu took them, offering one to Karr.

Unfurling it, Karr quickly glanced down the document, noting that Hu's own signature was already on the paper, beneath his seal. He looked back at Hu. "The wording?"

"Is as we agreed. To the letter. Your Master's terms are acceptable in full. You might tell him that when we meet in the autumn, I am ready to bow my knee before him and kiss his ring finger."

Karr nodded, inwardly surprised. He had not expected Hu to accept that term without at least a murmur of objection; then again, why should he be surprised? The Han respected strength, and as a race, they seemed to desire the ordered structure of a hierarchy. To be the servant of a High Lord was an honorable calling among the Han, especially if one were a Lord in one's own right. To be a king who served a greater king was no small thing, and in this world of uncertainties, the iron-cast certainty that Li Yuan represented was a welcome thing, even to an independent-minded Warlord such as Hu. He saw how dangerous the future was—he had said as much to Karr last night. Why, there had been eight small wars in the region in the last two years alone, and tension throughout Asia was growing by the week. As Hu said, one had two choices, to face the tiger, or ride it.

But what about this business with Ming Ai? What did that portend? For he knew Ming Ai had been murdered, almost as certainly as if he himself had witnessed it. He had heard the man's screams in the night and knew Hu Wang-chih had had him poisoned. But on whose orders?

Not Pei K'ung's, that was certain. But why would Li Yuan have him poisoned? And why here?

He could answer the last. Here because no one from Pei K'ung's retinue could prove he had been poisoned. Here Hu's surgeons could sign the death certificate without any fear of contradiction. And according to them Ming Ai had died of a burst appendix.

Okay. But if it had been done on Li Yuan's orders, then why had he not been informed?

*Because he knew I would object.*

Karr ran his tongue across his teeth, disturbed by the thought. Something was going on here that he didn't know about. Indeed, the more he thought about it, the more certain he was that others had been here before him, to hammer out an agreement with Hu Wang-chih. That was why it had been so easy; why Hu was so ready to sign. He had been promised something. Something that wasn't in this document.

The more he thought about it, the more he was convinced. His was but the public face of a policy that had been agreed to long before his visit. And if that were so, then what else was Li Yuan up to that he didn't know about?

He looked back at Hu Wang-chih.

"You want a brush, Marshal Karr?"

Karr nodded. At once two servants approached, one making a back upon which the other rested a small table holding an ink block and a brush. Handing the servant the scroll, Karr took the brush and inked it, then, as the servant held the agreement open, signed at the bottom beneath Hu Wang-chih's own signature.

The servant took the scroll and, bowing low, handed it to Warlord Hu, accepting the other from him. Again he held it out while Karr signed.

As the servants backed away, Karr turned to face Hu Wang-chih again. Smiling, the Warlord stood and offered Karr his hand. "You'll shake, I hope, Marshal Karr."

Karr took his hand. "I should be getting back."

"Of course," Hu said, his smile unwavering. "Oh, and you may tell your Master that his servant, Ming Ai, will be given a full and proper burial, as befits a man of his great stature."

"Ah . . ." He had been meaning to find a way of raising the subject.

"It was a great pity, neh?" Hu added, a heavy irony both in his voice and in his expression. "Such a great man. . . ."

"My Mistress will want a full report."

"Of course. And she shall have it, Marshal Karr. But now, if you would excuse me, I must finish my morning preparations."

Karr bowed. "Excellency."

He was walking back down the corridor toward his quarters, the scroll held loosely in one hand, when the shots rang out. Two close together, and then a third. He spun about, surprised, then began to retrace his steps, the sound of hysterical screaming coming from Hu's quarters.

The doors were wide open when he got there, the place in chaos. Guards stood open mouthed in shock, staring across at the scene in the doorway to the bathroom where, surrounded by kneeling servants, Hu Wang-chih lay in a pool of his own blood. Other servants ran here and there, trying to get help, but a single look told Karr that Hu was beyond mortal assistance. Half of his head had been blown away, and there was another massive hole through his chest. Beyond the fallen man, her face pale, her hands pulled up behind her back, one of the maids who had been tending him was being searched, Hu's Chancellor personally supervising the matter. Nearby a gun lay on the floor; a small service revolver of the type security officers carried.

*Aiya!* Karr thought, wondering what weight the document he held now carried; what chain of circumstance this little incident would set in motion. Was there a clear successor to Hu Wang-chih, or would there now be a bloody civil war for control—a war that might possibly drag in the Warlord's neighbors?

Karr realized that he didn't know. His briefing hadn't included word of any wives or sons, so maybe there weren't any, but that seemed hardly likely.

He looked about him, summoning one of the guards—a young lieutenant—to him. The man hurried over and came to attention, bowing his head.

"Yes, Marshal?"

"Is there somewhere I can make an urgent call?"

The lieutenant hesitated, then, conscious that this was, after all, Marshal Karr, gave a brief nod. "Follow me, sir. I'll take you through to our Communications Office."

As he hurried after him, Karr thanked the gods that his reputation held good here—that soldiers were, after all, soldiers wherever one went.

Li Yuan had to know at once. Not only that, Karr needed to know what to do himself—whether to fly back at once or stay here and help out, for maybe his presence here might help stabilize things; might form a solid center about which things might hold.

But then again, who knew? Those three shots had changed everything.

LI YUAN took the call in his study, Shepherd at his elbow, his Chancellor, Heng Yu, standing nearby.

As Karr's face appeared on the screen, Li Yuan began to smile, but the smile quickly vanished from his face.

"Hu Wang-chih is dead."

"*Dead?* When?"

"I've come directly from his rooms, *Chieh Hsia*. He died but a few moments ago."

"Then there's still a chance he'll be resuscitated?"

Karr shook his head. "There's little chance of that, *Chieh Hsia*. Unless *Shih* Ward has found a way of putting fragments of a brain back together. Hu Wang-chih was assassinated. One of his maids shot him three times. Two to the head, one to the chest."

"*Aiya!*" Li Yuan sat back, his face ashen. "His maid. . . ."

Clearly the thought of it disturbed him profoundly.

"What is the situation there?" Shepherd asked, moving forward into view. "Has anyone taken charge?"

Karr shrugged. "Not that I know of. But news has yet to go beyond the palace. When it does, who knows how the people will react? If we're to act we must act swiftly."

"Quite so," Li Yuan said, stirring himself. "Have you spoken to the Palace Commander?"

"Not yet, *Chieh Hsia.*" He glanced to the side. "I understand he's on his way here even now."

"Good. Well, tell him we will give him whatever assistance we can. But he must hold the palace and the central media stations until we can provide him with backup."

Karr nodded thoughtfully. "And the question of succession?"

Li Yuan raised a hand. "Before we come to that, you must meet with Hu's Chancellor. He must be encouraged to speak to his people at once and tell them to stay calm. Again, give him whatever guarantees he needs of our support."

"*Chieh Hsia.*"

"As for the matter of Hu's successor, this is, unfortunately, clouded. Hu has two sons, but they were estranged from their father years ago and live in neighboring states. They must be discouraged from pursuing any claim."

"Discouraged, *Chieh Hsia?*"

"Never mind. I shall deal with that myself. As far as the immediate situation is concerned, I understand the Warlord's widow has a son from a previous relationship. He might be a candidate, if only temporarily. You must speak to his mother as soon as possible and tender our support."

"And if she does not wish her son to succeed?"

Li Yuan laughed, as if the notion were absurd. "Then we'll cross that bridge when we come to it. Now go, Gregor. You have much to do."

"*Chieh Hsia!*"

Karr bowed his head smartly as the screen went blank.

Li Yuan sat back, letting out a long breath, then turned, looking up at Shepherd.

"Well? Do you think we have covered all the angles?"

Ben came around and sat on the edge of the desk, looking across at Heng Yu as he spoke. "For the moment. But things are certain to change rapidly as news of Hu's death spreads. We need to stabilize the situation. Make sure none of the neighboring Warlords decide to capitalize on the momentary chaos to grab territory."

Heng Yu spoke up. "I agree, *Chieh Hsia*. We must charge our ambassadors in the neighboring states to warn them sternly against such action."

Li Yuan frowned. "I'm not so sure. Wouldn't that merely signal our interest in the Mashhad administration? Wouldn't it be tantamount to an open declaration of our alliance with the dead Warlord and his successor?"

"Not at all," Shepherd answered. "We can claim—and legitimately—that our prime concern is for peace in the area. For stability. In that regard it might be opportune to send in the Fourth Banner Army. At the new administration's invitation, naturally."

"And if they do not give it?" Li Yuan asked.

"Then we send them anyway."

Li Yuan considered that a moment, then nodded. "I think I see what you are saying. You think we might use this new situation to our own advantage—to provoke confrontation and excuse a campaign?"

"Exactly. It's tailor made."

"Hmm . . ." Again Li Yuan lasped into thought.

*"Chieh Hsia?"* Heng Yu asked after a moment.

Li Yuan looked up distractedly. "Yes, Master Heng?"

"What of the Empress? Ought we not to inform her?"

Li Yuan looked to Shepherd, who nodded.

"All right. Inform her. Tell her—tell her to come and speak with me at once."

*"Chieh Hsia."*

"And, Heng . . . not a word of what was said here, understand? All you know is what Karr told us on the link."

Heng Yu bowed low. "Of course, *Chieh Hsia*."

"Then go. We shall speak later."

As Heng departed, Li Yuan leaned across, connecting through to the main guard tower. At once the screen lit up. A young guard stood abruptly, bowing his head.

"Is Captain Edmonds there?"

"I'll get him, *Chieh Hsia*."

The guard moved out of sight. A moment later an older soldier moved before the camera.

*"Chieh Hsia?"*

"Warlord Hu has been killed."

"Ah . . ." The Captain swallowed, his eyes, as he nodded, showing a clear understanding of what was required. "The contingency plan is in place, *Chieh Hsia*. You wish me to . . . ?"

Li Yuan nodded, then placed his hand on the pad, cutting connection. He stood, yawning, stretching his neck and shoulders. Turning, he looked over at Shepherd.

"Necessity," Ben said, as if he read Li Yuan's mind.

"Maybe," he answered. "But sometimes I wonder whether I shall meet them all once I am dead, down there, beneath the yellow springs. Some days I imagine it. I see them all, lined up down there, awaiting me—all the men I've had killed for the sake of peace and stability."

"You should have wired them while you could."

Li Yuan looked up, surprised. "You think so?"

"Oh, I know so. You should never have abandoned that project, Yuan. Control's the key. Give them a choice and most men will piss away their chances. They'll soil their own nests." He laughed sourly. "It's negative alchemy, Yuan. Give them gold and they'll turn it into lead, time and again. That's fine if you're talking individuals, but Man's a social creature. It doesn't stop with the self. He has to drag others down with him. Down into the mire."

Li Yuan stared at Shepherd thoughtfully, then nodded. "Perhaps. . . . But this first, eh? Let's deal with this first."

PEI K'UNG was in her bedroom, naked after her bath, about to change when Chu Po burst in on her.

"What is it?" she said, a weary resignation in her voice as she reached for her wrap.

"He's gone!"

"Gone? Who?"

"I Ye. The bastard's gone from Edingen!"

She dropped the wrap and stepped over to him. "You're certain?"

"He went an hour ago. Li Yuan smuggled him out, took him somewhere we can't get at him."

*Just as she'd thought he would. . . .*

She stared at Chu Po a moment, surprised by the obvious concern in his voice. There were good reasons why *she* should be concerned, but Chu Po? As far as she knew, he didn't have a care in the world. Or was that true? Was there, perhaps, more to this than met the eye? Did I Ye know things about Chu Po that she didn't?

Setting the matter aside, she turned, trying to think it through. Where would Yuan have taken him? Out of the City? To Africa, perhaps? Or had he had him shipped off-planet?

She put her hand to her brow. Or maybe, just maybe, he was still at Edingen—where they would never think to look.

"Ask Cheng Nai shan to come. We'll get our spies onto the matter at once!"

Chu Po nodded and made to turn away, then hesitated, looking back at her.

"Did we . . . discover anything?"

She raised an eyebrow. "How do you mean?"

"Among I Ye's papers. I hadn't heard . . ."

She stared at him a moment, noting once more the concern in his eyes, then shook her head. "No. Nothing at all."

The relief he showed was palpable.

"A shame," he said, after a moment. "If we'd found the cassette, perhaps—"

"The cassette?" She was suddenly, sharply alert. "You mean, he *had* the cassette?"

Chu Po smiled tightly. "All the time. He took it from the Red Pole he tortured."

"The Red Pole?" She felt a surge of anger. "Why didn't you tell me this before?"

"You didn't ask."

The answer stung her. "So how did *you* get to know about it? You slept with one of I Ye's men, I suppose?"

Chu Po said nothing, but his smirk was eloquent. Even so, there was something here she couldn't fathom. She stepped up close to him, grasping his chin in a viselike grip. "*Why* didn't you tell me?"

He struggled free, his eyes glowering at her. "I've just explained—you didn't ask me. You were . . . *distracted*. You wanted
sex, remember? Besides, I thought I'd choose my time to tell you."

"When it might damage I Ye most?"

He smiled. "Why not?"

She pushed her face into his aggressively. "Because it was *important,* you dolt!"

She had never called him that before, never insulted him. He
had always been her favorite, immune from criticism. Her words,
therefore, were like a sudden slap. His eyes flared and he positively
bristled, turning away from her petulantly.

"I know where it is," he said quietly.

"You know . . ."

Her mouth fell open in shock. He knew and hadn't said. He
*knew*! She reached out, grabbing his arm. "Where? Tell me—"

He shrugged her off angrily. "No. Not until you apologize."

"What?"

She checked herself. Her instinct was to swat him like a fly. To
have his cock cut off and force-fed to him. But her instinct was
wrong. She needed that tape. It was her insurance. With it she
could damage her husband, humiliate him; make him a laughingstock throughout his City. She took a calming breath.

"Okay . . . I . . . apologize. You are not a dolt, Chu Po."

"On your knees," he said, turning to face her, his eyes taking in
her nakedness at a glance.

*"What?"* She stared at him, dumbfounded.

"Go on," he said, stepping closer to her, an arrogant expression
on his lips now, a coldness in his eyes. "Get on your knees, woman.
I want you to say it again . . . this time as if you meant it. And
then I want you to suck me off. And then . . ."

She stared at him, waiting. "And then?"

"And then, perhaps, I'll take you there."

For a moment longer she stared at him, deciding in that instant
that just as soon as she had the tape in her hands she would have
him killed. Then, without another word, she knelt.

"WHAT'S THIS I'VE HEARD?"

Dragon Heart turned in her seat and quickly waved her maid away. Pushing back her chair, she stood, facing her father, smiling sweetly at him.

"I don't know what you mean, Dada."

"No?" Her father was staring at her sternly, his hands pressed tightly together. "The rumors—"

"*Rumors?*" She took two steps toward him, her whole manner changed abruptly. "*What* rumors?"

He raised a hand to fend her off, but she was in a rage now.

"It's my sister, isn't it? *Isn't* it?"

Prince Hsun swallowed, then made to deny it, but he had already lost the initiative.

"She's jealous," Dragon Heart went on. "You know that, don't you? She's *always* been jealous. Just because the Emperor chooses to spend some time with me, talking, discussing matters, she tries to twist things, to make out that it's somehow"—the word exploded from her lips—"*dirty!*"

Her father stared at her, horrified. "Why, there's no suggestion . . . she—"

"There!" she said triumphantly. "I knew it! She's poisonous! Poisonous!"

"Now, come . . ." he began, but she had turned away and gone to the window, lowering her head and dabbing at her eyes with a silk, as if upset.

"My dear," he began again, "I didn't mean—"

"No . . . no. . . ." She sniffed, then, without turning, put out a hand behind her for him to take. He stepped across and grasped it.

"I was only trying to help," she said quietly. "To gain the T'ang's good favor and help smooth the way for her."

"I know . . . I know," he said, whatever barb he'd had completely drawn by her. "I was merely concerned, that's all. This is a big week for your sister. I didn't want things . . . spoiled."

"Spoiled?" There was the slightest edge of petulance in her voice, yet when she turned it was with a smile. She reached out, taking his other hand. "I'd never do that, Dada. Never."

He embraced her, smiling, patting her back. "I know . . . I

know . . . I just . . ." He shrugged. "Well, I'll leave you to complete your—your . . ."

She nodded, smiling as he backed from the room. As the door closed she let out her breath, the smile vanishing from her face.

"Never," she said softly, turning to the window again and staring out toward the Western Palace. "She'll *never* become Empress! Not if I can help it!"

She looked to the side, to her dressing table, then snatched up the silk he had sent her that morning—a beautiful lavender silk with an emerald edging that his dead wife—Kuei Jen's mother, Mien Shan—had worn on the day of her wedding.

The significance of the gift had not escaped her. She was close, very close now.

Dragon Heart looked back across the gardens, noting movement on the path to her left. Her heart skipped a beat at the thought that it might be Li Yuan, coming to see her again, but it wasn't him, it was that stunted dwarf Ward and his son. She shuddered. Even the way he walked was odd and ungainly, as if he wasn't used to walking on the solid earth.

She turned away, looking about her at the luxury of her room, then, summoning her maid, returned to her preparations.

*Today,* she thought as she sat, letting the girl begin to comb out her hair again. *It has to be today.*

━━━◆◆◆━━━

AT THE GATE to the Western Palace, Kim stopped and turned to face his son.

"Look," he said awkwardly. "I have to see Li Yuan. It's a private matter. It would be best . . ."

"I understand," Sampsa answered. He smiled boyishly at his father and reached out to touch his arm. "Besides, I've things to do myself."

Kim raised an eyebrow in query. "With Tom, you mean?"

Sampsa nodded and made to go, but Kim called him back. "Sampsa?"

"Yes, Father?"

"Don't get *too* familiar."

Sampsa stared at him strangely. "Is there a problem?"

"Not at this moment."

"But there might be?" Sampsa looked down, disturbed by this sudden turn, then looked back at his father, his voice lowered. "So what's happening?"

"Nothing. And I aim to keep it that way. But if something does . . ."

Sampsa shrugged. "All that . . . That's between you and Shepherd, surely?"

"It's not so simple."

Sampsa stared at him in disbelief. "Let me get this right. You're talking about a *breach* with Shepherd? He on one side, you on another?"

After a hesitation, Kim answered his son honestly. "It's possible. It's more than possible, in fact. It depends on what happens here today."

"And Li Yuan? What does *he* think of this?"

Kim looked away, the answer written in his face. He hadn't told Li Yuan. This was a decision he had made only in the last few hours.

Sampsa laughed incredulously. "But you saved Shepherd's life!"

Kim looked back at him. "So?" He shook his head. "I finally worked it out, last night, after it had all happened. I finally understood what I've known deep down for years. We're on different sides, he and I. We always have been. But it's never been important. Not before now."

Sampsa was silent for a time, then he nodded. "I see."

"Then you'll be careful . . . I mean, with Tom Shepherd."

Sampsa met his father's eyes. "I'm sorry, but that's between you and him. That's *your* argument."

"But you don't understand. . . ."

Sampsa shook his head sadly. "No. It's you who doesn't understand." Then, without a further word, he turned and walked away.

———

LI YUAN looked up from where he sat at his desk, surrounded by his aides, and looked to Kim.

"Could this possibly wait, Kim? Something's come up."

Kim looked past Li Yuan at Shepherd, who stood at the window, one foot on the low window seat, staring out across the palace gardens, and shrugged.

"It's not important," he said, conscious of the unusual activity in Li Yuan's rooms—of the way servants were running back and forth on urgent errands. "I'll speak to you later. It was just . . ."

Li Yuan had looked down, studying a document. As Kim paused, he looked up again. "Yes?"

"No matter," he said. "We'll speak later. When you're less busy."

"Good. . . ." But Li Yuan had already forgotten him, it seemed.

Kim turned, meaning to go, but Shepherd called him back. "Kim? Might I have a word?"

He turned, waiting as Shepherd came across.

"Not here," Shepherd said, moving past him. "In my rooms."

He let Shepherd lead him through. Security investigators were at work in the outer rooms, scanning floors and walls with special equipment. Inside, in the main workroom, things seemed back to normal. Kim stepped past Shepherd, letting him close the door behind him. He turned, looking about him. Only then did he see her, sitting beside the fireplace, her tiny form dwarfed by the size of the chair.

She stared at him silently out of dark Han eyes.

"So?" Kim asked, looking to Shepherd again. "What is it?"

Shepherd smiled. "I just wanted to say thank you . . . for what you did last night. You needn't have got involved."

Kim shrugged. His eyes flicked to the young girl, then back to Shepherd again. "I did what I had to, that's all." He shivered. "You know, I don't really—"

"—like me?" Shepherd finished. He laughed. "I know that. That's what made it so strange. After they'd taken you to the surgeon last night—even as I was standing in the cells with Li Yuan, watching him interrogate the man—I kept asking myself why you did that. Why you'd risked yourself."

Kim was silent.

"And I think I understand. At least, theoretically. You think life ought to be fair, don't you? Or should I say, you *want* it to be? You know it isn't, but you rebel against that. The truth of what people are . . . you don't like that, so you get involved. You interfere."

"You're complaining?" Kim said coldly.

Shepherd laughed. "In this one instance, no. As I said, I'm grateful. Very grateful. In fact, I thought I'd give you a gift to show how grateful I am." He turned, indicating the girl. "She's yours."

"*Mine?*" Kim frowned. "I don't understand."

Shepherd smiled. "This is Chuang Kuan Ts'ai. She was given to me by Li Yuan. But I'd like you to have her."

Kim still didn't understand. "Whose child is she?"

"No one's. In fact, technically she's not even a child. She's dead."

"Dead?"

Shepherd took the signed edict from his pocket and handed it to Kim. Kim read it quickly, then looked up, shocked.

"A traitor? No. . . ." He laughed oddly. "I don't believe it. Why, she can't be any older than—"

"Seven. And yes, she was condemned to death. Only, I asked for her to be spared. And Li Yuan agreed. He gave her to me, to do with as I pleased."

Kim stared at him, not liking the sound of that. But Shepherd was not forthcoming.

"All right. But why give her to me?"

"Because of how you are. Because . . ." Shepherd shrugged. "I don't know. It seemed like fate. I can't give you the life I owe you. Not mine, anyway. So I'm giving you another. To make us even, if you like. So that I'm not *indebted* to you."

"Ah . . ." Some vague glimmer of understanding began to dawn. Kim stared at the young girl again. She was looking down now, her hands clenched together in her lap, clearly disturbed by their conversation. There was still something Shepherd hadn't said.

"You understand, then?"

Kim looked back at him. "No. Not fully. But I'll take her. If it makes you feel better about yourself."

He saw the tiny flare of anger at that and knew he'd read things correctly in the night. They were enemies. Fated to be enemies. What had happened last night hadn't been meant to happen. It was a glitch. An anomaly. But now Shepherd had set things right. Now that he'd given Kim the girl—given back the life he owed—they could be enemies again.

Kim put a hand out to the girl. "Here, child. You'll come with me, neh?"

She glanced at him, then, putting her head down again, gave a single nod.

"Good." He looked to Shepherd. "Was that her real name? Coffin-filler?"

Shepherd smiled. "It seems they thought she was stillborn. She was crated up for the Oven Man to burn. Then she started crying and he adopted her. Unofficially, of course." He laughed. "Rather ironic, wouldn't you say? Officially she was never born. All her life she hasn't existed, not officially. Now—officially—she's dead."

Kim shuddered, then felt the girl's fingers close about his own. He looked down. She stood there, silent and placid.

"And her adopted father?"

Shepherd shrugged. "Christ knows! I suppose he thinks she's dead."

"Ah . . ." He glanced down at the child again. She was holding his hand much tighter now. "By the way, what were you going to do with her?"

He looked up, meeting Shepherd's eyes. But Shepherd said nothing; he merely smiled, the darkness in his eyes revealing nothing.

———————

WALKING BACK through the corridors, Kim was silent, wondering what he would say to Jelka; how he would explain this sudden turn of events. As far as she knew, nothing had happened in the night: she knew nothing of the second thoughts he'd had that had made him return to Shepherd's rooms, nor anything of his subsequent heroics. But he would have to tell her at some stage—yes, and also what he had decided.

And now there was the complication of the girl.

"*Aiya,*" he said quietly, pausing outside the door to his suite of rooms. "What to do?"

He looked down at her. She was staring at him, something strange going on behind her eyes, as if she was steeling herself to ask him something.

"What is it?" he asked. But the words merely frightened her. Abruptly, she averted her eyes, tucking her head into her chest.

Taking a long breath, he pushed the door open and stepped inside.

Jelka's voice greeted him from the bathroom. "Kim? . . . Is that you, Kim?"

She stepped out from the doorway on the far side of the room, smiling, toweling her hair, her white bathrobe draped about her, then stopped dead.

"*Kim?* What's going on? Who's she?"

Kim closed the door, then led the child over. "Jelka, this is Chuang Kuan Ts'ai. She is . . . a gift, from *Shih* Shepherd to us."

"A *gift?*" Jelka laughed, then shook her head. "You're not serious, are you? People don't give gifts of children to each other."

"No," he said. "Not normally. But I saved his life. Last night. There was an assassin. . . ."

Again she laughed, as if this were a joke; then, realizing it wasn't, she swallowed. "Assassins? In the San Chang?"

Kim nodded.

"And the girl?"

"She's dead. Officially, that is. Shepherd had her. It seems Li Yuan gave her to him."

She stared at him incredulously. "*Why?* I mean . . ."

Jelka shook her head, then crouched beside the girl. She studied her a moment, then looked up at Kim again. "She can't be more than seven. What is she? The illegitimate daughter of some Minor Family Princess or something?"

"No. She's what her name suggests. She was left for dead at birth. Apparently an Oven Man saved her, brought her up."

And now, suddenly, the child began to cry.

"Hey . . . hey, now!" Jelka took her in her arms, holding her, comforting her as she sobbed. "What is it, Little Chuang?"

The girl looked up at Jelka, her tongue loosened, it seemed, by her tears. "Uncle Cho . . . you've got to find Uncle Cho! You've got to warn him that I Ye has been imprisoned. You've *got* to. *Please*. . . ." She shuddered, then fell silent.

Jelka looked up at Kim again. "What's been going on?"

Kim shrugged. "I don't know. I was unconscious for a time."

"Unconscious?"

"The assassin kicked me. . . ."

Her eyes widened in alarm. *"Kicked you? Where?"*

He turned his head, touching where it was yet tender. "It's okay. Just a small bruise. There's no damage."

But he could see how concerned she was. She stood, lifting the child and holding her to her shoulder. Putting her face close to the child's, she spoke to her softly. "Okay, Little Chuang. This Uncle Cho. Where does he live? How would we find him?"

FROM THE TOP FLOOR of his high-rise offices in Central Ludwigshafen, Michael Lever could see the walls of the San Chang to the east and, equidistant beyond them and slightly to the south, the towers of NorTek's massive Heidelberg complex. He stood there a moment, the fingers of his right hand to the clear ice-glass wall, thinking of the conversation he'd had with Ward, Ebert, and his son, then turned, looking across the huge expanse of carpeted floor to his desk, where his assistant, Johnson, waited patiently, a stack of business files beneath his arm.

"Well, Dan?" he asked, a tiredness in his voice. "What's top of the agenda this morning?"

"This," Johnson answered, coming across and handing him a single slip of paper.

Lever took it and stared at it, then looked back at his old friend and shrugged.

"I don't understand. What's been found?"

"Emily," Johnson answered softly. "They've found Emily."

The news was like a hammer blow. He stared at Johnson in disbelief. Then, looking down, he quietly began to cry, hunched into himself.

Johnson stood there, looking aside, saying nothing; knowing how important the moment was for Lever.

With a sniff Lever raised his head again, wiping his face with his hand. "Okay. Do we know where she is?"

"Edingen. The prison."

"The *prison?*" Then he saw it. Of course. "Who informed us?"

Johnson looked at the top file. "A Captain Dawes of Security."

"One of Karr's men. . . ."

Johnson shook his head. "He's one of I Ye's."

Lever raised an eyebrow. "You'll make sure he gets the reward, anyway?"

"Says he doesn't want it. Says he's sympathetic. He"—Johnson paused, then took a slender disc from the file—"he sent this."

Lever took it, stared at it. "What is it?"

"A copy of a Security file. On it there's an interesting conversation you had with Ward, Ebert, and Ebert's son, Pauli."

Lever made a sound of surprise. "There must have been a hidden camera."

Johnson made a wry face. "You *were* in the San Chang."

Lever laughed. "A regular whispering gallery, huh?"

Johnson smiled. "Whatever, it seems you've a friend in this Dawes."

He nodded, then, with a determined little movement of his hand, went over to his desk and sat. For a moment he did nothing, just sat there staring into the air. Then he looked back at Johnson, who had followed him.

"Do you think I should go there, Dan? Buy her out?"

Johnson shook his head. "I wouldn't, if I were you. We've agents who can do that kind of thing. Besides, it might be best to find out a bit more about her situation. Where she's been. Who she's been living with. What she's been doing all these years."

Lever swallowed and looked down. The truth was, he didn't really want to know. After all, what if she'd been happy all these years? What if she'd met someone and fallen in love? What if she hadn't thought of him?

He looked up again and gave Johnson a pained nod. "Okay. Who've we got that can do that kind of thing?"

"I'll use our friend Matloff. He knows the Senior Warder at Edingen. He's also got friends at the Ministry. And he owes us a favor."

"Matloff?" Lever pulled a face. "Isn't there someone better we can use?"

"No one with the kind of pull he has. Oh, I know what you think of him, but he gets the job done. And right now—"

Lever raised a hand. "Okay. See to it, Dan. And no foul-ups, right?"

"Right!"

Not waiting to deal with any of the other business, Johnson turned and hurried from the room.

Lever sat back, steepling his hands before his face, and let out a long, shuddering sigh. Then, standing again, he went back to the window and stood there, looking east again to where, sandwiched between the San Chang and the towers of NorTek beyond, the dark, basaltic walls of Edingen prison thrust up from the surrounding streets.

"Em," he said softly, tracing her name on the glass. "My darling Em."

---

KARR STOOD IN THE COLD and drafty hallway of the Secondary Palace, waiting as the steward went to deliver his message.

It had been three hours since he had first requested an audience with the Warlord's widow, and in that time a great deal had happened.

Word had come from neighboring Turkmenistan that Hu Wangchih's second son, Feng-lo, had declared himself the rightful ruler and was preparing to return to Mashhad with a substantial military force. Shortly after, news had come that Feng-lo had been killed—blown up along with half the Ashkhabad palace, including the local Warlord Meng Yi.

Karr stared down at the cracked tiles of the hallway and sniffed thoughtfully. Despite the removal of that inconvenience, things didn't bode well. News of Hu's death had triggered widespread civil disobedience throughout Mashhad. By all accounts the local security forces had lost control of large parts of the City and communications with other parts of the country had been cut off. The First Minister, Ji Wang, had fled, along with many of his circle, and there was a rumor that there had been a mutiny at the Kerman barracks in the south.

*And now this*, Karr thought, staring about him at the dilapidated condition of the widow's palace. Just one look at this place had been enough to convince him that this was a mistake. Whoever it was would finally come out on top of this muck heap of a state, it wasn't likely to be someone from here. From all he could make out, the Warlord's widow had few supporters among the various palace factions. She was a recluse, rarely seen, and even her son—

"Marshal Karr?"

Karr turned, looking toward the doors through which he'd just come. A young man was standing there—a very upright and impressive-looking Han in his mid-twenties, dressed in expensive yet modestly cut silks.

"Forgive me for not seeing you before now," he said, coming across to Karr, his eyes revealing that he considered Karr his equal, "but as you'll understand, I have had much to arrange. The situation is deteriorating by the moment."

Karr made to nod, then stopped. "Forgive *me*," he said. "I do not wish to be rude, but I am at a loss. You are?"

The young man bowed his head, then straightened up. There was something awfully familiar about him; about his features, even the way he stood there, relaxed and elegant in his own body. Something *princely*.

He smiled, showing perfect teeth. "Forgive me, Marshal Karr, but I am Hu Wang-chih's adopted son, Han Ch'in. I understand you wish to see me."

---

''WELL?'' MATLOFF ASKED, leaning across the table as Senior Warden Chao opened the envelope and unfolded the letter that contained the banker's bond. "Have we a deal?"

Chao Chung picked up the bond and held it up to the light. His eyes widening, he studied the payment carefully—checking that each detail was correct—before he looked to Matloff again, giving a low whistle. Setting the bond down, he sat back, sucking his teeth.

"I would love to do business with you, *Shih* Matloff. Your terms are most . . . *persuasive,* let's say. However, my hands are tied."

Matloff, who'd been about to say something else—to conclude the deal posthaste and get out of there as quickly as he could— moved back, surprised. "I beg pardon?"

"I said, my hands—"

"I *heard* what you said." Matloff gave a short laugh then shook his head. "I don't understand, that's all. Isn't it enough?"

"Oh, it's plenty. Very generous. Very generous indeed of your Master. But I"—Chao swallowed—"I can't cash it."

"Can't . . ." Matloff narrowed his eyes, suspecting some kind of scam. "What do you mean?"

The Senior Warden was still staring at the bond, a mixture of intense longing and profound and bitter disappointment in his eyes. Finally, he looked up at Matloff and sighed heavily. "I mean, I cannot make a deal with you, *Shih* Matloff, much as I would love to. You see, the order for *Nu Shi* Ascher's arrest was signed by I Ye. Well, now that I Ye has been arrested, he cannot countermand that order. Only Karr could do that. Or Li Yuan himself. . . ."

Matloff stared at him a long moment, letting the anger he felt die down. Snatching back the letter and the bond, he turned and stormed from the office.

Behind him Chao Chung stared at the empty desk and groaned. Five million *yuan!* He had just missed the chance of earning a cool five million *yuan!* Again he groaned. It had been a bad day for him. A very, very bad day.

---

EMILY WOKE AND STRETCHED HERSELF. For a moment she forgot where she was. For a second or two she was back at Make Do House, about to get up and start the day's routine. She turned, meaning to call to Lin in the next room, to tell him to get up, then froze, remembering.

For a long time after that she lay there, perfectly still, staring at the wall, a kind of numbness, part cold, part shock, eating at her. Then, slowly, very slowly, sound began to return to her world.

There was a dull banging from somewhere far off, below her, it seemed, in the very depths of the earth itself. Closer, in a cell nearby, a prisoner coughed; a relentless, hacking cough that spoke of bad lungs and damp conditions. For a time that was it. Then, at a distance, there was the sound of footsteps echoing on a metal staircase, of keys jangling in a belt. There was the faintest snatch of song, coming closer now, a cheerful humming that stopped outside her door. Again the keys jangled. She heard the key slide into the lock, the lock click and turn.

She turned her head. The guard was standing in the open door-

way, looking across to where she lay on the pallet bed. He smiled
and slowly beckoned to her with his crooked index finger.

*What is it?* she wanted to ask, but her mouth was too dry. She
knew what it was. She was going to die. They were going to execute her, now, without a trial.

She sat up, facing him. Her head was pounding, as if someone
had tied a metal band around her brow. Her hands where they
rested on the edge of the bed felt like shapeless iron weights, pinning her there. Altogether, her body felt wrong somehow. She
could feel her feet as if they were suddenly much bigger, much
heavier, than they'd ever been, and her tongue seemed huge and
thick in her mouth, as if it would choke her.

Slowly she raised her eyes, looking to the guard. Again he smiled
and beckoned to her, showing rotten teeth. But she couldn't move.
It was as if she had been drugged.

He came and stood over her. Leaning down, he poked her hard
in the chest.

"You've gotta come. Warder Chao wants a word. He says a man
has come."

The words didn't penetrate at first. It was as if they were large
stones, sinking, slowly sinking, through vast depths of murky water.

*A man? . . . What man?*

He reached beneath her arms and pulled her up, staring into her
face, the smell of his breath the first real thing that registered.

"You hear me, woman? You gotta come."

She grimaced and moved her face aside; then, realizing he had
addressed her, nodded her head.

"Okay." He reached down, placing the cuffs back on her wrists,
then looked at her again. "You come with me, right? And no
tricks. You can't get out of here. Not unless we let you." He
laughed. "Not alive, anyway."

Again she nodded. Looking to him, she spoke, her voice a
whisper.

"What man?"

The guard laughed, then, taking her arm, led her to the door.
"You'll find out soon enough. Now, let's get going. Warder Chao
doesn't like to be kept waiting."

———

"IS THIS THE PLACE?"

Kim held the curtain of the sedan open as the girl looked out. Fearfully, she nodded. The place seemed deserted, the gate wide open.

"Wait here," he said, leaving her in Jelka's care. He stepped out, looking to his runners. "You three, come with me."

They went inside. The courtyard was empty, the doors to the storeroom and the Ovens open. The storeroom, too, was empty, the Ovens cold. A fine layer of ash covered everything.

Frowning, Kim stepped out into the courtyard again. It seemed abandoned. He looked across at the door to the living quarters, then walked across. The door seemed closed, but when he put his hand to it, it swung back easily.

"Hello? Is anyone home?"

Nothing. Not even a drip from a leaking tap. He went inside, looking into the first two rooms on either side of the hallway. Noticing something on the floor ahead of him, he stopped.

*"Lu Nan Jen?"*

The man lay there on his side, unmoving, his eyes open, staring straight ahead. Kim went to him and crouched, putting his hand down to see if he could feel a breath, but there was nothing. He touched his brow. It was cold. Looking down the body he could see now how stiff its posture was. Dead. The Oven Man was dead.

*"Aiya,"* Kim murmured softly. There was no sign of any violence. No blood, no indication of a struggle. He had just died. A heart attack perhaps, or maybe he had simply given up. Regardless, he was gone. There was no calling him back from where he was, whatever Shepherd thought on the matter.

Kim reached down and closed Cho's eyes. As he stood looking about him, he noticed a piece of paper lying on the floor beside the Oven Man's hand. He had been holding it, perhaps.

He picked it up and looked at it, then, conscious of whose signature was on the bottom of the page, hurried out into the courtyard.

*So here it is,* he thought, folding the paper and slipping it into his pocket. *Proof positive, if such was needed, of I Ye's guilt.*

Not that it mattered now. He sighed, stretching his neck, wondering how he'd tell the girl, then realized she was standing there by the open gate, Jelka just behind her.

As she met his eyes, she understood at once. She shivered, then, bearing up, said simply, "Where is he?"

"Inside," he said. "It seems he had a heart attack. He's"—he swallowed—"he's at peace now."

"Can I see?"

"I . . ."

"I *have* to see," she interrupted, surprising him with her insistence. "I have to be sure he's gone. He . . ." She looked down suddenly, controlling herself, willing herself to be brave and not to cry. After a moment she looked up again. "Will you help me?"

Kim stared at her. "*Help* you? How?"

She took a step toward him. "The ovens. We have to light the ovens."

He shook his head, horrified by the notion. "It'll be seen to. He—"

"No," she said, taking another step. "We have to burn him. It's what he would have wanted."

He stared at her, astonished. "But you can't. You're . . ."

*You're what?* he asked himself. A *child?* He sighed heavily. A *child, yes, but she had an adult's understanding.*

"Okay," he said. "But afterward you come with us."

"I can't. The ovens . . ."

Jelka, who had stepped up behind her again, put her hands softly on the child's shoulders. "You have to, Chuang. You can't stay here."

"No. . . ." The child shivered violently, then looked down. "I guess not."

Jelka squeezed her shoulders gently. She met Kim's eyes. "We'll do things properly, neh? Give your Uncle Cho a proper ceremony. Then you come home with us, okay, little Chuang? Home. For as long as you want to stay."

---

TWO SECURITY OFFICERS met Emily in the corridor outside the Warden's office and, relieving the prison guard, took her inside. They pushed her down into a chair, standing to either side of her as the Warden opened a file and, with a smile, looked up at her across his desk.

A nondescript, middle-aged Han sat silently in the corner of the office, his eyes taking in everything.

"Well, *Mu Ch'in* Ascher," Chao began, "it seems there's a great deal of interest in your fate."

Chao waited, but there was no reaction from her. He looked down thoughtfully, then, smiling to himself, decided on another approach.

"Your boys . . ." he began.

"What of them?"

He looked up. "Ah, good. I have your attention now, have I?" He shuffled the papers about, conscious of the silent figure in the corner.

"How are they?" she asked, leaning toward him, a slight edge to her voice.

Chao smiled. "They are as well as might be expected, considering. As long as *you* live, they live." He let that sink in, then closed the file. "Anyway, that's by the by. It seems we are at something of an impasse. I have here the order for your committal. Unfortunately it is not signed." His smile was apologetic. "Li Yuan, it appears, is busy right now. And until our friend here"—he half turned, vaguely indicating the seated man—"can get to see him, so things remain."

She was silent a long while after that, her eyes never leaving his face. "So when's the trial?"

Chao stared at her, then laughed. "Trial? There'll be no trial. You've already *been* tried. Tried and found guilty. The only reason you're still sitting here is because of a technicality." He took a single sheet of paper from the file and thrust it before her. "Until this committal document is signed, the trial, though it has taken place in reality, has not taken place *in law*." He smiled, as if it were all self-explanatory. "The chain of documentation must be unbroken, you understand. . . ."

She went to touch it, but he withdrew it quickly, as if it were the most valuable piece of paper in creation. As it was, *for her*. But for him? She stared at him a moment, trying to work it out, but nothing came. She was dead. And Lin and the boys too. Silently, she began to cry.

"Oh, come now, *Mu Ch'in* Ascher. No sentiment, please, not after what *you've* done." He opened the file and turned to the relevant page. "I mean . . . skinning young men alive—"

"They did it first," she said coldly, not really caring what he thought.

"So you say," he said, flicking through the file and nodding. "Even so, maybe I'll copy this. Show it to your boys."

"No!"

She sat back slowly, realizing that that was exactly the response he'd been hoping for. She looked down. "They'd not believe you."

"Wouldn't they?" He laughed unpleasantly, and turned the file about. "The shots are . . . *interesting.*"

She sighed. "What do you want?"

"Me?" He leaned toward her. "Why, *nothing, Mu Ch'in* Ascher. I am my Master's hands!" He glanced at the man in the corner and smiled reassuringly. "I wish only to see *justice* carried out."

She stared at him, understanding finally. Some kind of deal was going on. Something to do with the price on her head and who would collect it. As for herself . . .

The last hope guttered in her. This was the end. Nothing could save her now. Nothing.

She stood and was immediately forced back down by the Security officers to either side of her.

"It's over," Chao said, sitting back and steepling his hands. "That's all I *really* wanted to say to you." And, gesturing to the guards, he threw the file down to the side and turned his head away, as if he had other business to attend to. Yet even as she was pulled to her feet, even as she heard the door clang open behind her, she saw the look in Warden Chao's face and knew it was not quite finished with.

HAN CH'IN leaned forward in his seat, looking at Karr, and smiled.

"I hear what you are saying, Marshal Karr, but I cannot see how you can really help."

Karr laughed. "Help? Why, haven't I just said?"

"Oh, I heard what you said, Marshal, and, in other circumstances I might be very grateful for your offer, but I think you don't
quite understand the situation. The garrison at Kerman is mine,
and those at Esfahan and Babol. Mashhad, as of this moment, is
also in my hands. I have secured all media stations and all but one
of the main transportation centers. But that, too, will shortly be
mine." He smiled urbanely. "Our enemies are routed, Marshal
Karr. All is in hand."

Karr stared at him. "I don't understand."

"No?" The young man stood and walked to the window of the
room they were in. "I thought you, of all people, would understand
it perfectly. It has all been in place for a long time now. It awaited
but the moment. That's why Ji Wang got out as quickly as he
could. He knew."

Karr nodded slowly. "So *you* had Warlord Hu killed?"

Han Ch'in turned back, staring at Karr. "Not at all. I rather
liked old Hu. And I even suspect he liked me. He certainly liked
Mother at one point. Couldn't keep out of her rooms. Before she
kicked him out. . . ."

Karr frowned. "Then all of this . . ."

"Is accident." Han Ch'in smiled once more and came across,
stopping directly in front of Karr. "Yet the wise man plans for
accidents, neh? Or so my mother taught me."

"Your mother?"

"You want to meet her?"

Karr hesitated, then nodded.

"Sorry," Han Ch'in said, his smile apologetic, "but that cannot
be done. She will see no one anymore. No one but me, that is. Her
eyes. . . ." He made a pained expression. "She was hurt, you see.
When things fell apart. The Warlord became her protector. Rescued her, you might say. Yes, and claimed his reward, too, in full,
until . . ."

". . . she kicked him out."

"Yes." Han Ch'in laughed warmly. "You are learning, Marshal."
He paused, then sighed. "Things have been tough these past
twelve years. Simply to survive . . . well, that itself has been a
kind of triumph. But now . . ." He shook his head. "But I am

forgetting myself, Marshal Karr. I should have said before. Your craft is awaiting you, upstairs on the palace roof."

"Then this is . . ."

"Good-bye. For the time being." Han Ch'in smiled and extended his hand in farewell. "But we shall meet again, Gregor Karr, be assured of it. Mother has plans."

It sounded ominous. Karr took the young man's hand and shook it, conscious, yet again, of something curiously familiar about him, but what it was he still did not know.

"Our offer . . ."

"Is rejected out of hand." Han Ch'in shook his head regretfully. "We are enemies, Marshal Karr, and must remain so until things are resolved between your Master and I. But let us not speak of such things now, eh, let us part on *amicable* terms."

"Amicable . . ." Karr stared at the young man, impressed yet baffled by his confidence—his princely arrogance—then, with a bow, he turned and left, letting a waiting officer escort him out and up onto the windswept roof where his craft awaited him.

<hr>

IT WAS RAINING HEAVILY as the cruiser landed, its matte-black, spiderish shape setting down amid the ruined castle's grounds. As the engine died, two men ran from the cover of the gatehouse, their hoods raised against the onslaught. Overhead, thunder crashed, while in the distance the sky lit up with a flickering dance of lightning.

Rain beaded the glass of the craft's reinforced windows. As the door hissed open and the ramp began to unfold, a face appeared briefly at one of the windows, peering out. A moment later, a tall, shaven-headed figure appeared in the hatchway, one hand on the door frame as he stared up at the giant keep of Helsingborg castle that dominated the skyline.

"Safe," I Ye whispered to himself, smiling at the thought. Then, ignoring the downpour, he stepped out, walking slowly, almost casually, down the ramp toward where the two hooded figures waited, hunched into themselves against the elements. As he came alongside, one of them pulled back his hood and, combing a hand back through his hair, smiled at his former master.

"Colonel I?" he said, half shouting against the noise of the storm.

I Ye grinned, recognizing the man, then leaned in toward him. "What is it, Sergeant?"

"A message," the sergeant shouted back.

"A message?" I Ye's smile wavered.

"From the Empress," the man answered, drawing a long dagger from within his cloak and sinking it deep into I Ye's chest.

The rain fell. Slowly the ramp retracted, the door hissed closed. After a moment the craft's engines came to life again and it lifted away from the ancient ruin. As it turned and banked, vanishing into the cloud-wreathed sky, a lightning flash illuminated the scene in the castle's courtyard.

I Ye lay on his back, the dagger buried to the haft in his chest, his mouth open in an oh of surprise. Rain fell on his ash-pale face, sluicing away his blood.

For a moment the sergeant stood over him, grinning like a dog, then he turned, looking to his colleague.

"Loyal unto death," he said, and laughed, his laughter swallowed by the thunder and the incessant rain.

━━━━━

PEI K'UNG leaned over the desk and signed the document. Straightening up, she gave her husband a brief nod, then, with a glance about the crowded space, swept from the room.

Li Yuan watched her go. Sighing, he looked down at the Edict. Copies would be posted throughout the city before morning, informing his subjects that, in the interest of peace and stability in the Central Asian region, they had moved into the neighboring territories of Mashhad and Turkmenistan, which would henceforth be considered "protectorates."

He smiled. The ships were already in the air, heading for their destinations; four hundred and eighty thousand men in all—almost a quarter of his Eastern Banner. Further forces would be dispatched within the next few days, once provisions and supplies had been arranged. Until then, Karr could hold things together.

Li Yuan turned and looked to his Chancellor, who stood among a group of Ministers and high-ranking officers on the far side of the room.

"Master Heng, have we heard from the Marshal yet?"

"Nothing, *Chieh Hsia*."

"And Haavikko?"

Heng Yu came across and bowed. "Colonel Haavikko is here, *Chieh Hsia,* in the anteroom, awaiting your instructions."

"Good. Send him in."

Heng Yu bowed again, then turned, signaling to one of his secretaries to bring Haavikko. The man was back in an instant, bowing low as he led in a tall, distinguished-looking officer with short gray hair.

Li Yuan, looking at Haavikko, was conscious of how much he resembled the old Marshal, Knut Tolonen, now that he'd got into his fifties. Or maybe it was just the military life that did it—reducing men to interchangeable cyphers. Whatever, for the briefest instant he had a strong feeling of déjà vu—as if he were his father and Haavikko the old rock-faced General.

"Colonel Haavikko," he said, standing up to greet the man, then coming around the desk to stand before him. "You recall a conversation we had a year or so ago."

Haavikko, who had until that moment seemed wary, now looked up, suddenly very alert. "I do, *Chieh Hsia*."

"Good. Because the time has come. We need to act, and at once."

"At once, *Chieh Hsia?*"

Li Yuan smiled, strangely relaxed now that it was all happening at last. "Oh, you can wait an hour. Then do what must be done. It is all in hand, I hope?"

"Of course, *Chieh Hsia*." Haavikko hesitated, then bowed his head smartly. "An hour it is, *Chieh Hsia*."

"Good. Report back to me when things are accomplished."

"*Chieh Hsia!*" Again Haavikko bowed low. Coming smartly to attention, he turned and marched from the room.

Li Yuan looked to Heng Yu, seeing how the man was watching him, and smiled again. "All in good time, Master Heng. All in good time."

But Heng was still watching, as if something were troubling him.

"Is there something else, Master Heng?"

"I . . ." There was a brief inner struggle, and then he fished in his cloak pocket and brought out a tiny slip of paper, handing it to Li Yuan.

Li Yuan unfolded it and read it quickly, then looked up. "When did this come?"

Heng moistened his lips with his tongue. "An hour back, *Chieh Hsia*. While you were preparing the document."

"And was this all?"

Heng nodded.

"Who brought the message?"

"It was her father, *Chieh Hsia*."

"Her father. . . ." He stared at the note, surprised by that. After all, the note was not sealed, it was simply folded.

"Have you . . . read this, Master Heng?"

Heng hesitated, then nodded again.

"And having read it, you felt it . . . unimportant, perhaps?"

"Not unimportant, *Chieh Hsia*," Heng answered, almost squirming now, "simply not . . . *urgent*."

"I see."

Li Yuan turned, placing the note to his mouth, conscious of its faintly perfumed scent. Then, unfolding it, he read the words again.

*I must see you. At once. Dragon Heart.*

Heng Yu was right, there was no time right now for something like this. It was, as Heng said, "not urgent," not in the face of all else that was going on. Yet the urgency he'd felt on reading her words was undeniable. Even now he felt like running from the room to see her. Indeed, only the presence of those other, senior figures in the room stopped him from doing just that.

"Send to her, Master Heng. Tell her—tell her I shall see her when I can."

Heng Yu looked down. Li Yuan felt a tightening of his stomach muscles.

"What is it?"

Heng's voice was almost a whisper. "She has gone, *Chieh Hsia*. Ten minutes back. Her craft—"

"*What?*" His shout surprised them all. "Send out a craft . . .

no, two, ten, whatever it takes. I want her intercepted and brought back here!"

"But, *Chieh Hsia*—"

"Just do it, Master Heng! Now!"

Heng swallowed, bowed, and hurried from the room. Li Yuan stared about him, then, with an angry wave of his arm, dismissed them all.

*Gone. She had gone. . . .*

The fear he'd felt at the news surprised him. She was important to him, certainly—hadn't he said as much to Ben—but he'd not thought . . .

He shivered, understanding suddenly what must be done. He must have her killed. She and all her family, for there could be no half measures. It was either that or suffer this perpetual uncertainty. He gritted his teeth, sure of it now. It was this—this same malaise—that had almost destroyed him once before, yes, back in those awful days when he had been in love with his brother's wife, Fei Yen.

Yet that understanding was like a barb in his guts. If he had her killed . . . no, *when* he had her killed . . . how could he go on living without her? How would he fill the ten thousand empty days that followed?

Yes, and how live with himself, knowing he had killed the one person he might have found happiness with? No, he had to have her. Had to.

He heard Shepherd's words in his head and grimaced.

*Then have her. Rape her if you must. But don't marry her. . . .*

And if he forced himself on her, would that be it? Or would that be as bad as killing her? If her love for him turned to hate, how could he live with that?

He bunched his fists and groaned. He had to end it. Somehow. Anyhow. Just so long as he was free of this terrible uncertainty.

There was an urgent knocking at the door. He turned to face it, hope flaring in him briefly; then, as it faded, he collected himself and called out.

"Who is it?"

"It is I, *Chieh Hsia*. Marshal Karr."

*Karr? Here?* He rushed to the door and threw it open.

"Gregor?"

Karr bowed, then, as Li Yuan stood back, walked past him into the room. As Li Yuan closed the door, Karr waited, head bowed.

"Well?" Li Yuan asked, concerned. "What happened? Why didn't you let me know you were returning?"

"They stripped the craft, *Chieh Hsia*. We were lucky not to be shot down a dozen times."

"But why are you here?"

"I was sent home, *Chieh Hsia*. It seems . . ." Karr hesitated, then met the T'ang's eyes, answering him directly. "We have made a grave mistake, *Chieh Hsia*."

"A mistake?" Li Yuan laughed uncomfortably.

Karr gave a single nod. "I didn't understand at first. I thought he was mad. After all, Mashhad's a tin-pot state when it comes down to it. Yet he spoke as if he were a T'ang. A Son of Heaven. . . ."

Li Yuan raised a hand. "Back up a way, Gregor. *Who?* Who are you speaking of?"

"The Warlord's stepson. Han Ch'in."

"Han Ch'in . . ." Li Yuan went pale.

"Yes, *Chieh Hsia*. That's what I mean. I didn't understand at first. I mean, it wasn't possible. Yet the name, the face . . . both seemed familiar. It was only on the ship coming back . . ."

Karr turned, gesturing toward the portrait of Li Yuan's grandfather, Li Ch'ing, which hung on the wall behind the great desk, and nodded. "That's him, *Chieh Hsia*. To a T."

Li Yuan stared at the portrait, then looked back at his Marshal. Karr was watching him closely.

"You understand, then, Gregor? You understand it all?"

"Not all, *Chieh Hsia*. But . . ."

"You're right. He is my son. When Fei Yen was unfaithful to me, I disowned her. Her and her child. *Our* child. But I knew. I always knew. And Fei Yen . . ."

Li Yuan swallowed, realizing exactly what this meant. He had just sent a quarter of a million men against his former wife. "Shit!"

"*Chieh Hsia?*"

"They've already gone. They'll be in Mashhad's airspace even as we speak."

Karr stared at him, shaking his head. "You don't mean . . . ?"

Li Yuan nodded. "I gave the order more than two hours back. I'm at war, Gregor. At war with my own son!"

———————————

TWO GUARDS ESCORTED the Princess back to her rooms, locking the doors behind her as they left. For a time she paced the floor, her mood alternating between elation and despair, then she sat, staring silently across the gardens toward the Eastern Palace. Whatever he had decided, it would be settled today. Either her gamble had succeeded or . . .

*Or I'm dead,* she thought, thinking of that ogre Pei K'ung and what she'd do once she discovered what her young guest had been up to.

*Not that I'm the first, I'm sure. . . .*

Maybe so. But that was no consolation. Not if her gamble had failed. After all, he'd let her leave.

*Yes, but he sent his men to bring me back.*

So what? the more cynical part of herself answered. *He may summon and dismiss men as he pleases. Yes, and have them killed at a whim.*

And what was this, if not a whim? After all, hadn't it all started as a dare? A silly, whimsical dare she'd dared herself—to spite her sister and put her father's nose out of joint. Yes, but look how far she'd come! Look how close she now was!

She laughed quietly, then sat there, staring at her hands, wondering if she would live to see another morning.

She had toyed with the feelings of a T'ang—had teased that most mighty of men until, distracted, he had sent his soldiers after her. But to kill or keep her? That was the question.

She formed her lips into a pout, then pushed out the breath she'd held, as if she were blowing the petals from a flower. For a moment she remembered how sweet it had been between them and smiled at the memory. She was still smiling when she looked up and found him standing there.

"Yuan . . ."

Li Yuan put out a hand, bidding her to remain seated.

Dragon Heart stared into his face, trying to read him, but there was nothing there. It was as if she were facing his *ching*—the Gen-

Syn mirror creature that was stored somewhere beneath the palace complex, awaiting his final breath.

"Things are serious," he began somberly. "We are at war."

"At war!" She put a hand up to her mouth, surprised. She hadn't known. She had thought . . .

*Aiya!* She had thought he'd kept her waiting deliberately. She had thought that all the running about had been to do with her sister's impending marriage to the young Prince.

"Forgive me, Li Yuan, I did not know. . . ."

She looked up at him again. His face was still a mask, his body still tensed against her. He had decided. Oh, gods preserve her, he had decided. She let her head droop, put her face into her hands. *"Aiya!"*

"You understand, then?" he said coldly. "You realize what trouble you have caused?"

She looked up into his expressionless face and nodded.

"Good. Then take this."

She took the parchment he was offering and unfolded it, her hands trembling now, afraid to read what was written there. Afraid because there was suddenly no kindness in him.

She stared at it sightlessly, her eyes moist now, tears beginning to form.

"I didn't mean . . ." she began, her voice almost a whisper.

"It's what you wanted," he said.

"What I . . ."

She looked again, wiping one hand across her eyes and focusing. It was an official annulment. The annulment of her betrothal to Prince Hsiang Lu Ye. She looked up at Li Yuan, shocked. "But . . ."

And now she saw the uncertainty in his eyes, and, as she saw it, understood the reason for his coldness toward her. It was to hold himself together; to keep him from throwing himself at her feet. In truth, he was more afraid than she.

That knowledge flashed through her like an electric shock.

"Then . . ."

Li Yuan nodded. He stepped across and knelt, reaching out to hold her hand and stroke it with his thumb, looking up into her eyes lovingly. "It is as you wished, my love. The priest is on his way. We shall be married before the day is ended."

PEI K'UNG looked about her at the cluttered room, then swore. "The gods preserve us, where *is* that fucking man?"

Chu Po, who had been sifting through the boxes, looking for something, laughed. "He's probably dead. They all are. It's falling apart, Pei K'ung! It's finally all falling apart!"

She glared at him. "I don't know why you're so fucking happy about it. If I fall, you fall."

He looked up, still smiling. "Oh, but you won't. You've prepared for this. He thinks this is his chance. He thinks he's won. But you know better."

She stared at him awhile, then nodded. "Yes. But we must go, Chu Po. This place is no longer safe."

"Ten minutes," he said, seemingly unconcerned. "Give the man that long, at least."

She let out an impatient breath, walking to the window. Cheng Nai shan had promised he would be here more than twenty minutes back. He had sworn it. And never—*never*—had he been even a minute late before. So maybe Chu Po was right. Maybe it had begun already. Maybe Cheng was dead, along with all her other trusted servants.

"Okay," she said, noting activity on the far side of the gardens, outside the gate to the Eastern Palace. "I'll give him five minutes, then we go."

"North?" he asked, looking up from his task, suddenly interested.

She hesitated, as if weighing matters, then nodded.

"Good," he said, returning to his search. "Oh, by the way, I dealt with that other matter."

"I Ye?"

He smiled, as if it held a special satisfaction for him. "He'll be waiting to greet you at the gate. All smiles he is."

She frowned, not understanding what he meant, then turned back, looking across the gardens once again.

There was no doubting it. Something was happening over there. She could see the dark cloaks of Li Yuan's *shen ts'e* elite among the powder-blue uniforms of the regular guard. The big Colonel, the one she didn't much like—Haavikko—was going among them, giving orders. It was clear they were preparing to move. But where?

"Come on!" she said, filled with a sudden urgency. "Master Cheng can go hang himself. Let's leave here now!"

He looked up, surprised, as she swept past him, then, shrugging, followed her out, tucking a small cardlike tape into his jacket pocket as he went.

But they had only gone halfway down the main corridor when they were met by Cheng Nai shan. Cheng bowed low. Behind him his four assistants mimicked the gesture precisely.

"Too late!" Pei K'ung began, meaning to walk past him, but he knelt in her way, head bowed, holding out a sealed letter for her to take.

"What's this?" she said, staring at the seal suspiciously.

"Forgive me, Mistress," Cheng began, "but your husband summoned me. He gave me this and said I was to deliver it at once."

Her instinct was to hurry on, to get up onto the roof, aboard her cruiser and away, but curiosity got the better of her. She snatched the letter from Cheng's hand and tore it open.

For a moment she was silent. Then, with a tiny gasp, she staggered back.

"He's divorced me! The bastard has divorced me!"

"So?" Chu Po said, taking the document from her and studying it. "It makes no difference now, surely?"

"No . . ." she answered quietly, but she was visibly shocked. She made to move away, to hurry on, but once again Cheng blocked her path, a second letter held out for her to take. Again the seal on it was Li Yuan's, showing the seven circling dragons, the *Ywe Lung*.

She shied back from it, afraid.

"Take it," Chu Po said quietly, his hand on her back, supporting her. "What is there to be afraid of? Take it and have done with him!"

But she could not take it. She knew what it was. It was her death warrant.

Impatiently, Chu Po reached out and, before Cheng could protest, snatched the letter and tore open the seal. He unfolded it and began to read.

"I, Li Yuan, T'ang of Cheng Ou Chou, City Europe, command my former wife, Pei Kung, to attend a marriage ceremony in the Temple of Celestial Harmony at tenth bell."

He turned it over, looking for more, then shrugged.

"That's it?" she asked, taking it from him, a mixture of relief and curiosity making her irritable. "Does it not say who is to be married?"

"I can answer that, Mistress," Cheng said, not looking up. "The T'ang is to take a new bride. The Princess Hsun."

She stared at him, amazed. "But the Princess was to marry his son, surely?"

"That wedding has been . . . postponed. The young Prince, it seems, has flown back to America at the news of his father's impending marriage. Besides which, it is the younger Princess he is to marry. The one known as Dragon Heart."

The news was like a physical blow. She had been usurped and replaced, and all without a single word to her. Why, earlier, even as she was signing the order for the new campaign, he must have known that he was about to strip her of her power.

The thought of it stoked her anger. Well, she was damned if she would attend her own humiliation! And if he thought he'd silenced her, then he could think again! He might strip her of her title, but he could not strip her of her power.

Pei K'ung looked to Chu Po. "It is as I said. We go north, to Helsingborg. From there we shall coordinate events." She turned, addressing Cheng. "Master Cheng, you will follow as soon as possible. Gather together whatever men as are still loyal to our cause and meet us at the castle. We are not done with yet." She took the letters and tore them, again and again and again, then let the pieces fall. "No, Master Cheng, this matter is far from finished with!"

IT WAS DONE. He had married her and damn them all! And now she was his. *His* before all the world!

"Let the Heavens burn," Li Yuan whispered, staring at his face in the bathroom mirror, for once insanely pleased with himself, knowing that Dragon Heart awaited him in the next room, sweetly naked in his bed. If he were to die tomorrow it would have been enough to have had her this one night—to have known the brief intensity of bliss that lay before him.

He smiled, recalling the shock on every face in that room; from Ebert through to Ward. Yes, even Shepherd had argued with him this once and called him crazy. But no matter, it was done. In truth he had burned his bridges, yet he would make good. With his beloved Dragon Heart at his side he would have the strength of a dozen men—yes, and the courage to take on any problem and surmount it. It was a new beginning. Let the Heavens burn . . . he would build new Heavens.

He made to turn from the mirror, but something in his eyes—some last, frail hint of admonishment—drew him back and made him stand there a moment longer.

*And Kuei Jen?* he asked himself. *What of him?*

To be honest, he had not expected his son's reaction. He had thought Kuei Jen would understand, but that had been pure naïveté on his part: a case of wishful thinking, for what was there to understand except that his father was taking his own bride's sister as *his* bride—a girl young enough to bear him a dozen sons, and every one a rival for his throne.

*Aiya,* he thought, pained suddenly by what he'd done. Pained that this once he could not have it all. *Forgive me, Kuei Jen. I'll make it up to you. I promise I shall.*

But that was for the future. Now . . . He shivered at the thought and closed his eyes, remembering how she looked, the scent of her, the feel of her fingers on his skin.

To have such a woman . . . was that not worth empires?

Li Yuan smiled, certain of it, then, with a single nod, turned from the mirror. He walked slowly to the door and stepped through, out into the darkness wherein she waited.

# CHAPTER TEN

# Figures in a Dance

C ATHERINE SLIPPED from the bed, then turned, looking back. Dogu was sleeping, one hand curled lazily on the pillow where her head had been but a moment before. A single white satin sheet shrouded his naked body, exposing only a single ebony shoulder, an arm, a glimpse of his superbly muscled chest, his face.

She studied his face, conscious of how, in sleep, it seemed much gentler than when awake. He was so fierce, even when he was trying to be gentle, so aggressive, and yet . . .

She shivered, recalling how he had made her feel, a momentary sadness making her wish that she could stay another day, even another hour. She loved the way he looked at her; that powerful sense he gave her of being wanted. Ben had made her feel like that once. But things died. Or, to be more honest, they lost their intensity, even with Ben. She loved the way Dogu's eyes shone white from his night-black face, the way his broad mouth smiled. So different that was. So . . . *ancient*, it seemed. She welcomed it, even if it made her feel somewhat too refined, unnatural somehow . . . yes, and awkward too.

She turned, looking about her for her clothes. Gathering them up, she began to dress, careful not to wake him. Yet as she turned back, fastening the last button on her tunic, it was to find him watching her.

"Are you going?"

She hesitated, then nodded. She had hoped to avoid this; had wanted to slip away silently, like a figure in a dream. "I have to," she said quietly.

He pulled back the sheet, patting the empty space beside him. "Come back to bed, Cath-er-ine."

The way he said her name sent a ripple of delight through her. She looked at him, at the muscular, sculpted shape of his body, tempted by his offer. Even so, she could not stay. Slowly she shook her head.

"I have to. I have to return to my husband now."

He pulled himself up, sitting forward, his face intense, his jaw set as he studied her, understanding that something was happening.

"You *have* to?"

Again she nodded.

He moved forward, throwing aside the sheets, then stood, facing her, magnificent in his nakedness, a dark god, his eyes burning.

"Leave him, Cath-er-ine. Stay here with me. Be my woman."

The words seared her. She looked down, caught off guard by him, then shook her head.

"I can't. It's . . . impossible."

He reached out, holding her shoulders in his hands. Hands that were so strong and yet so gentle in their touch, they made her shiver.

"Stay," he said again, more gently this time, yet also more insistent. "Leave him. He doesn't love you. Not the way I love you."

She looked up, meeting his eyes, afraid of the intensity she found there, yet wanting it all the same. She swallowed. "No . . . I know that."

"Then stay."

"And go with you to Africa?"

He shrugged, his eyes never leaving hers. "If you want."

"And if I don't?"

"Then it doesn't matter. We'll go where *you* want. So long as we're together."

She laughed bitterly. The thought of being with him, even if only for a short time, was so attractive at that moment that she almost changed her mind and gave in to him. Yet her place was not with him. She understood that, even if he did not.

"It wouldn't work."

"No!" he said, insistent now. "You can't say that!"

Again she shivered. "Trust me, Dogu. It wouldn't work. We're different people. The physical thing . . . it was wonderful, but . . ."

There was a hardening in his eyes. "Was that *all* it was to you?"

She reached out and caressed his face, softening toward him. "No. It was more than that. Much more. Even so—"

He moved his face back from her hand, angry now. "But you are too—too *superior*, right?"

"No!" The accusation hurt her. "No, Dogu. You don't understand. I love you."

She saw how much that admission shocked him. Shocked him, yes, and confused him.

"Then why . . . ?"

"Because it's not enough. Because . . . well, because love fails. All love. And the more intense it is to begin with, the greater the failure. That's why it's best to end it now. Now, while it's still something to remember."

Dogu stepped back from her, a strangely petulant, almost childish look in his face. "And that's what you want, is it? Memories?" He shook his head, then turned from her, giving a snort of derision. "You're like him, you know that? That's all *he* wants. Memories. Nothing real."

She reached out to touch him again, but he shrugged her off.

"I know it must be hard to understand—"

He turned on her, his eyes glaring. "No. It's very *easy* to understand, Cath-er-ine. You've had your fun, you've got your memories, now you can go back to the safety of your little island kingdom and dream. Oh, I can see it now. You'll probably lie there on your bed and think of me and play with yourself—"

Her slap surprised her almost as much as it surprised him. She stepped back. "I'm sorry. . . ." But it was too late. His look of contempt told her everything. Turning, he walked away, the slam of the bathroom door making her jump.

For a moment she stood there. If she followed now—if she

crossed the room and opened that door—it could still be mended. It would be like that first time in the shower, only better—better because this time it would mean something.

For a moment longer she stood there. Then, with a tiny shudder, she turned and left, conscious of the man behind the door, waiting, forever waiting for her to step across and open it.

━━━━━

ALUKO ECHEWA stood in the shadows of the corridor, silent, unobserved, watching as the woman left. For a moment he hesitated, knowing from the woman's face that something had happened; that there had been an end to it.

He was pleased it had ended, yet he was also sad—sad for Dogu, who would have to suffer for it. Sad because, of all of them, Dogu had been the liveliest, had been the one who would always smile and joke when things were darkest, and that would change now. Instinctively he knew how much this had meant to his friend— how deeply he had fallen. Why, he had seen it only the other night, when he had spoken to him of it. The woman had cast her spell over him—a spell no charms or incantations would ever cure.

Stepping from the shadow, he went across and knocked, heavy of heart, knowing how difficult the days ahead would be for Dogu. To lose one woman was bad enough, but two . . .

The door jerked back. Dogu's face, bright with hope, crumpled. "What is it?" he asked quietly, dejectedly.

"It's time to leave," Aluko said, careful not to show what he was thinking; knowing Dogu's pride would tolerate no sympathy. "Efulefu has spoken."

"Ah . . ." Dogu looked down thoughtfully. Then, "I'll pack."

Aluko hesitated, then briefly touched his friend's arm. "At the landing pad in half an hour."

"I'll be there."

"Good." He smiled, but Dogu's eyes were looking past him, as if to find the woman in the shadows beyond. But she was gone. Back to her own kind. Back to Shepherd.

He shivered, once more afraid for Dogu. Then, with the barest nod to him, he turned and made his way back to his room. Efulefu had spoken. They were to leave for Africa at once.

L I   Y U A N sat at his desk in full imperial regalia, his new bride at his side, as Karr entered the room, his four generals following close behind. He saw how the giant's eyes widened in surprise at the sight of her there at this critical audience.

Karr bowed his head. Behind him the generals did the same.

"The news is bad, *Chieh Hsia*," he said without preamble. "Our enemy's forces have taken Baku and a large part of the Caucasian territories. The Fourth Banner is in disarray, with a third of its number captured and a further third either dead or badly injured."

Li Yuan nodded. He had heard as much from Heng Yu already. Leaning toward Karr, he tapped the desk decisively.

"You will order a withdrawal at once, Marshal Karr. What remains of the Fourth will regroup at Kiev. Meanwhile we shall take up new positions in a defensive line running from Riga in the north to Odessa in the south. The garrisons at Vitebsk, Gomel, and Kiev are to be reinforced and the Second Banner moved east to hold the line."

"But, *Chieh Hsia*," Karr protested, "what of the Plantations? If we lose them . . ."

Li Yuan smiled reassuringly. "I do not mean to lose them, Marshal Karr, merely to relinquish them until the situation improves." He paused. "If it is your friend Kao Chen you are worried about . . ."

Karr looked down. "I *was* concerned, *Chieh Hsia*. . . ."

"Of course," Li Yuan said, relenting. "Then evacuate those we can. But the new line must be held at all costs. That is our priority. You understand, *ch'un tzu?*"

There was a murmur of agreement from the generals.

"Good," Li Yuan said, turning and winking at his bride, as if this were some game. "Then set to it."

Dismissed, they made to leave to carry out their orders, but Li Yuan called Karr back.

"Marshal . . . and you, General Galt. A word, if you please."

They came back, waiting while the others left the room. As the doors closed again, Li Yuan sat up straighter.

"I have a job for you, Galt. And you, Karr. My former wife—"

"Is at Helsingborg."

"So I understand," Li Yuan said, nodding to Karr. "I want you to go there and destroy her."

"Destroy her, *Chieh Hsia?*"

"Her power. I want her army crushed, her contacts weeded out. In short, I want all trace of her . . . *eradicated.*"

Karr looked to Galt uneasily. He had never known his Master so casually brutal. *"Chieh Hsia?"*

"Your orders are here," Li Yuan said, reaching across for one of the several edicts that lay scattered on the side of the desk. "They are fairly flexible, I think you will find. Do what you have to, Gregor, and no questions."

Karr took the sealed edict, then snapped to attention. Beside him Galt did the same. "Is there anything else, *Chieh Hsia?*"

"No, Gregor. But make sure your friend Chen is safe. One must look after one's friends in such times, neh?"

━━━━━━

WHEN THEY HAD GONE, Li Yuan looked to his bride and sighed.

"I am sorry, my love, but this business . . ."

"I understand," she answered, laying her hand gently on his arm and leaning across to kiss his neck. "Besides, it fascinates me to see you at work. You are like the hub of a great wheel, neh? Everything you do, every word you say, has meaning." She gave a little shiver, her eyes glinting at him, her smile quite bewitching at that moment. "I like that. It . . . *excites* me."

He smiled and leaned toward her, kissing her lips delicately, once, then once again. "It excites you, eh?" he said softly, his hand moving until it rested on her upper thigh. "You have no regrets, then?"

Her eyes held his as she shook her head. "None, my love. You were like a tiger. I have never felt so . . . *alive.*"

"Nor I," he whispered, moving his fingers until they lay upon the soft, warm mound of her sex. "Why I could—"

There was a sharp knocking on the door.

He moved his hand back with a disappointed sigh, then turned to face the door. "Who is it?"

"It is I, *Chieh Hsia*," Heng Yu answered, peering around the door's edge. He stepped inside. "I have a message, *Chieh Hsia*. From Ward."

"Ah . . ." For a moment he had thought it serious. He relaxed, lacing his fingers with Dragon Heart's beneath the desk. "What does he say?"

Heng Yu advanced a couple of paces, then bowed low. "He says something urgent has come up, *Chieh Hsia*, and he requests your permission to leave the San Chang."

"I see." He looked to his young bride and smiled. "Tell him yes. And tell him I shall come and visit him once things have settled. Oh, and make sure he is given whatever protection he requires."

"Of course, *Chieh Hsia*," Heng said, bowing low once more.

"Oh, and Master Heng . . . make sure I am not disturbed this next half hour. There are things I need to discuss."

"Discuss, *Chieh Hsia?*"

"With my wife, Master Heng."

"Ah . . ." Heng, who had looked up at him, now looked smartly down, a color appearing at his neck. "Well . . . if I am not needed."

"No, Master Heng."

They watched him leave, then, as the doors eased shut again, looked to each other and laughed.

Slowly Dragon Heart's eyes changed. Her hand parted from his, moving slowly along his thigh until it rested between his legs.

"Go lock the door, my love," she said. "I want to make love to you, right here in your chair. Here, where you make all the decisions."

"Here?" Li Yuan shivered, remembering the last time when she had tied him to the chair—that time before the meeting of the Council—then, like a sleepwalker, he stood and went to the door.

*Destroy her*, he had ordered Karr. *Withdraw our forces west. Send our Second Banner east.*

And his new wife?

He smiled and locked the door, then turned to face her again.

"I am your slave," he said, stepping toward her, repeating what she had commanded him to say in the night. "I am your slave. Whatever you command. . . ."

"Crawl to me, Yuan," she said, standing and slowly unbuttoning her dress. "Abase yourself, you lowly worm, and *crawl.* . . ."

━━━◆◆◆◆◆━━━

PEI K'UNG had slept fitfully and woken with the dawn, a dream of her dead father staying with her even as she dressed, his face ashen, as it had been in his final illness.

All her life she had been surrounded by weak men; men who, rather than stand up for themselves, had groveled and abased themselves before fate. Her father had been such a man, yes, and her brothers. And Li Yuan too. . . . Or so she had believed.

*No, not weak,* she thought, staring out across the castle court-yard toward the gatehouse where I Ye's head—its jet-black hair rain slicked—rested on a stake, *merely sly.*

She smiled. In a strange way she admired her ex-husband more this morning than she had in all the time she'd known him. Sly, yes, but also decisive. He knew when to act, and how. But now it was her turn.

His mistake had been to let her go. To summon her to his wedding instead of having her killed.

She fastened the final button of her *chi pao* then left the room, waving aside the guards at the door as she swept through the entrance to the underground complex. Here, unknown to Li Yuan, she had set up a command center for just such a moment as this. From here she could control it all.

Still smiling, she hurried through the outer rooms, officers getting to their feet and bowing hurriedly as she passed. A thrill of anticipation was coursing through her now. At last she could do something. She was finally free to act without constraint.

She laughed, pushing the last door open.

Chu Po, who was sitting in the central chair before the control panel, turned and smiled at her. To either side of him several of her most senior military commanders stood hastily, clearly embarrassed by her sudden and unexpected appearance. And no wonder, for behind them, on the huge screen that filled the entire back wall of the control room, was the image of a young couple making violent and passionate love.

"What the . . . ?"

She fell silent, understanding. It was the tape I Ye had said was lost! She took a step toward it, then froze, her mouth fallen open.

"You were wrong," Chu Po said quietly, his smile almost smug now.

"Wrong?" She glanced at him, then back at the image, fascinated by it despite herself.

"About this," Chu Po gestured toward the screen. "You thought it would discredit him, make him a laughingstock, but you were wrong. Any man, watching this, would say to himself, this is a Son of Heaven. This is how a Son of Heaven would make love, like a tiger on silken sheets, neh? And as for Fei Yen . . . well, look at her, Pei K'ung. What man would not want such a goddess? That body . . . that fiery wantonness in her eyes. Why, any man would consider himself blessed."

"And you, Chu Po," she said, her voice hard. "Would *you* have counted yourself blessed?"

"You want the truth, Pei K'ung?"

She stared at him, her jaw set. Then, with a small shake of her head, she answered him. "You're dead, Chu Po."

He narrowed his eyes, confused. "I beg pardon . . . ?"

And now she smiled and took a step toward him. "I said you're dead. Or rather, you were dead before you came here. You didn't know it but you were. And now you do."

He laughed. "You jest with me. . . ."

"Yes?" She leaned across him and, touching the control pad, killed the image on the screen. Standing back, she looked down at him. "You went too far. You . . . crossed the line, let us say. I liked you, Chu Po, but you didn't know where to stop, did you?"

His eyes had changed now. He realized she was serious. Even so, he did not seem disturbed by her words, not in the way she'd expected him to be. He had strength, this one. But then, she'd always known that. It was why he'd been her favorite.

"You're not afraid, then, Chu Po?"

"Afraid?" He shrugged. "If I'm dead, I'm dead. Do the dead feel fear?"

She laughed, amused by that, almost . . . *almost* relenting. But she had made her mind up even before she'd come into the room this morning and seen what he was up to, and having made up her mind . . .

"General Tanner?"

One of the gray-haired veterans behind Chu Po came smartly to attention. "Yes, Mistress?"

"Take this scoundrel out of here and have his throat cut. Then throw him into the moat. Oh, and you might hack his head off while you're at it and place it next to that other traitor's."

Chu Po was staring at her calmly now. "I've been many things in my time, Pei K'ung, but never a traitor. Not to you, at least."

"No?" She laughed bitterly. "So you say. And yet you are a self-confessed liar."

"Even liars tell the truth sometimes."

"And dead men? Do dead men tell the truth?"

He shrugged again, then stood. "I never loved you."

"I know."

"And yet I—"

*"Enough!"*

He stood and bowed, then, without a further word, went from the room, Tanner and two of his young officers hurrying to catch up with him.

She let out a long breath, then looked about her. All eyes were diplomatically averted. "General Bujold . . ."

Bujold, middle aged and balding, glanced nervously at her, then bowed his head. "Yes, Mistress?"

"Convene a meeting of the senior staff."

"At once, Mistress!"

"And, Bujold?"

"Yes, Mistress?"

"Destroy the tape. Chu Po was right. It would not help us in the least to have men see such images."

⬥⬥⬥⬥⬥⬥

"IS THAT YOU, HAN?"

Han Ch'in stepped into the semidarkness, closing the door behind him. "It is, Mother. I have news."

"News?" She beckoned him closer, turning from her screens to look at him. "All goes well, I hope?"

"Very well. Baku is secured. Tiflis and Astrakhan have fallen. Not only that, but we have taken more than half a million prisoners."

"Good news indeed," she said, a warm satisfaction in her normally cold voice.

"Indeed," he echoed, "but that is not my news. My news concerns your former husband, Li Yuan."

"Is he deposed?" she asked, sitting forward, light from the busy screens reflected in her dark pupils. "Is the bitch in charge now?"

"No, Mother. But he has taken a new wife. A young girl. A princess of the Hsun clan."

"A *wife?*" There was a movement of profound agitation, an irritated rustle of black silk. "And Pei K'ung?"

"Is divorced and has fled north."

"*Aiya!*"

Han Ch'in stared at his mother, not understanding. "But surely this is the best news possible? Pei K'ung has friends, yes, and an army, too, and she will surely use them against her former husband. It means our enemies are divided. Li Yuan cannot possibly fight a war on two fronts. He will *have* to come to terms with us!"

"*Aiya,*" she said again, more softly this time. "Wed. And to a girl." She looked up at her son. "Is she pretty?"

"Pretty?" He shrugged, then laughed. "Why, for all I know she could look like a GenSyn mute!"

But she was shaking her head. "No . . . she will be pretty. I know Yuan. If she is young she will be pretty. Very pretty. He would not divorce Pei K'ung unless . . ."

"Unless what, Mother?"

But she had fallen silent, hunched into herself in her chair, chewing at a nail, her eyes staring past her screens into the distance, as if remembering. Then, with an abruptness that surprised him, she stood, facing him.

"We must destroy him. Now, while we can. While his forces are divided."

"But, Mother . . . We haven't the supplies. To attack his heartland . . ." He shook his head and laughed. "We would overstretch ourselves. My generals—"

"Are fools and charlatans. Destroy him, Han Ch'in! I *order* it!"

He stared at her, surprised by her outburst. "You hate him, don't you, Mother? Hate him for what he did to you. For casting you off."

"He cast you off too!"

He shrugged. "What did you expect? That he'd *raise* your bastard child?"

But she was shaking her head. "You don't understand, do you?"

"Understand? What's there to understand? You've told me often enough. You misbehaved with his cousin and you paid the price."

"No." She was very still suddenly. "You really don't understand. When I say he cast you off, I mean it. You were his son, Han Ch'in. His son."

He stared at her, wondering what game this was, then shook his head. "No, Mother. You won't persuade me that way. I am Tsu Ma's son. I should have been a T'ang, but you fucked it up for me, didn't you?"

She stepped right up to him and, looking up into his face, held his arms. "You *should* indeed have been a T'ang, Han Ch'in, but you were never Tsu Ma's son. I thought so. For a long time I thought so, but then he told me. The test he had me take proved it beyond all doubt. You were Li Yuan's son. His rightful heir."

He looked back at her, shocked. "Then why . . . ?"

"Because he hated me. Hated me and loved me. Loved me more than he could bear to admit. Loved me beyond distraction. And now"—she swallowed, then turned away from him—"now he has remarried."

"My father," he said quietly.

"Yes," she said. "Your father." She turned, looking at him again. "And now you must destroy him. Before he destroys you."

THE TICKET TO GANYMEDE was in his back pocket, along with his new ID and currency chips to the value of two hundred thousand—all that had remained after he'd paid off the local forgers. Now he had merely to go through the barrier and get on board the ship, but there was one last thing he had to do.

Calder looked about him, then went across to the stall in the corner of the spaceport and, giving the woman a fifty chip, took a bunch of flowers from the front. Turning back, he hurried across to the small temple at the back of the port and, giving the priest at the door another fifty chip, ducked inside, into the half-dark.

The smell of incense was almost choking here, and more than a dozen people knelt before the tiny altar, making offerings to the gods before their flights.

Moving between them, he lit a candle and placed it in the rack, then knelt, laying his flowers before the altar.

"The gods preserve you, sister," he murmured beneath his breath. "May the fates be kind." Yet he knew, even as he said it, that she was in all probability dead. She had killed Warlord Hu and now he, as her brother, was a hunted man. Even here, in Baku, he was no longer safe—not now that the new Warlord, Han Ch'in, had taken charge of the port.

Calder lowered his head, trying to feel something, trying to see her as she'd been before he'd left her yesterday morning, but nothing came. He was in shock. It was as if he had sleepwalked his way here. The drugs had something to do with that, but it wasn't just the drugs. Her death was his death, he knew that now. And though he might live on another forty, fifty years, it would be but half a life without her.

Ganymede. It sounded awful. A cold, isolated hell. Just the place for a ghost to live. Which was why he had chosen it. To be as far from here as possible.

He shivered, then, murmuring another prayer for her soul, he got to his feet again. His flight was already boarding, unaffected by the changes going on about it. Han Ch'in might now be boss of Baku, but business between the worlds went on. So it was, so it would always be. He understood that now. Understood that what they'd done was meaningless, for nothing had ended. Nothing at all. If anything, things were worse now.

He stepped out into the busy terminal again, then shook his head to clear it. The barrier lay ahead and to his right. Once through it, he'd be safe. Calder turned, looking about him, fixing it all one last time in his memory, then, knowing that this phase of his life had ended, he walked on toward the barrier and the waiting guards.

"GRANDFATHER?"

The room was cool, the light the blue of arctic ice. It was a huge square space, more vault than room, its vastness totally unfurnished, the walls reflecting glass, sloping toward a ceiling of smooth black ice two hundred *ch'i* to a side, supported by two lines of slender silver pillars. Overhead, unseen yet suggested by the tapered shape of the room, the great pyramid's apex soared into the cloudless East Coast sky, one of nine that dominated the center of the Boston Enclave.

There was a pause, then a disembodied voice answered, filling the hall with its low bass resonance. It was like the voice of emptiness itself:

"COME."

Kuei Jen looked to his friend anxiously.

"It's okay," Egan said quietly, resting his hand on the young Prince's shoulder, "he's expecting you."

The floor was pure white marble, yet when he walked on it, no sound returned to him. Kuei Jen looked down, realizing that he seemed to be walking just *above* the floor.

Egan, seeing the direction of his glance, smiled. "Don't worry, Jen. It's a field. Specially charged ions. They keep the place spotless."

Kuei Jen nodded, but the explanation did little to reassure him. This whole place emanated a kind of high-tech menace. There were no guns, no tracking cameras, yet he had a strong sense that his every move was being watched; that in an instant a flash of blinding light might destroy him utterly. He shivered, but walked on, keeping pace with his friend.

A dozen paces from the far wall Egan slowed, then stopped.

The wall facing them was dark, no different from the wall to either side. Now, however, it began to glow faintly, a dim cold light growing in its depths, like a firefly trapped in a great block of ice.

As the glow grew stronger, Kuei Jen caught his breath. Revealed was a tiny figure, more like an emaciated, mummified monkey than a man. The skull seemed skewed, one side larger than the other, the whole of it a patchwork of black and white, like a warped *wei chi* board. One eye was focused, staring mad, the other rolled slowly, aimlessly, in its orb. Its arms were thin and tiny like a child's, but the hands were big, the fingers brown and elongated, the knuckles swollen like dice. It had a swollen belly like a young baby's and long stringy legs that dangled uselessly. At the end of them the feet were black and rotted, one of them almost a stump.

He swallowed, sickened by the sight. The figure seemed to exist in a void, floating, transfixed. No wires went to it, no tubes. It was like some grotesque specimen trapped in amber.

Beside him Egan bowed, then addressed the tiny figure. "Grand-father, this is Li Yuan's son, Prince Li Kuei Jen."

The eye sought and pinned him. The fingers of the right hand slowly flexed.

"*Kuei Jen . . .*"

Kuei Jen bowed. Steeling himself, he met its gaze again. "*Shih* Egan. I am delighted to meet you finally."

Its voice was undulating: sometimes strong, sometimes weak, fading in and out like a badly tuned signal.

"*I died, you know. Six . . . no, seven times. And every time they brought me back. They had to. They wouldn't have been paid otherwise. It was written into their contracts. But less of me came back each time. There's a deterioration, you see. A decaying of the genetic signal. Some days*"—its laughter was like cracked paper—"*some days I feel as if I am a bad copy of myself and I wonder . . . well, I wonder whether I'm really real or something stored, something . . . synthetic.*"

"Grandfather . . ."

The eye turned, taking in the young man at Kuei Jen's side. "*Mark? Is that you?*"

"Yes, Grandfather. You told me to remind you."

"*Remind me?*"

"About why the Prince is here."

"*Ah . . . I remember now.*"

For a time the figure seemed to go asleep, the eye to drift. Kuei Jen looked to Egan, who smiled reassuringly, then looked back at the figure. Slowly the eye focused again.

"*A pity,*" it said, looking at him directly. "*I was looking forward to working with Ward and Shepherd. Still . . .*" It made a strangely

mechanical sound, like the slow grinding of cogs, then spoke again.
*"Circumstances change, neh?"*

"And we with them, Grandfather."

*"True. Still, all is not lost, neh? Perhaps the chance will come again.
After all, Kuei Jen, your father cannot live forever."* It laughed again;
an awful, inhuman sound. *"At least, not without our help."*

Kuei Jen looked down, disturbed by talk of his father's death. He
was angry with his father, certainly—furious, in fact—but that did
not mean he wanted him dead.

"I do not want him hurt. Not . . . *physically.*"

*"I understand. And yet you want him hurt, neh?"*

Kuei Jen shivered. He wanted to make his father feel the way he
felt—rejected and humiliated. *Unwanted* . . .

He swallowed, then met the staring eye once more. "Yes. I want
him hurt."

*"Then trust us, Li Kuei Jen. Surrender yourself to us. We'll find a
way to hurt your father, never fear. But you must trust us."*

———————

LI YUAN stood before the screen in his dragon robes, his arms
folded across his chest. Facing him, Old Man Egan was smiling, his
face suntanned and vigorous, his whole demeanor that of a man
twenty or thirty years younger than he actually was.

"Right now Kuei Jen is angry," Egan was saying, "but his anger
will pass. He is a fine and dutiful son, Li Yuan. He has merely . . .
*forgotten* himself temporarily. Let him cool his heels here with us
awhile. Then, when things have settled, we'll send him home."

Li Yuan smiled tightly. "I am grateful for your concern, *Shih*
Egan, and am glad that present circumstances have not *sullied* our
relationship. However, I would not wish to impose upon you any
more than is necessary."

"Oh, it is no bother, Li Yuan. Your son is an old and dear friend
of ours. He is welcome to stay here as long as he wishes."

"I am grateful . . ." Li Yuan began again, trying to find a way of
phrasing his dissatisfaction without offending Egan, ". . . but if I
might, perhaps, talk with my son?"

Egan sighed. "It was my dearest wish to engineer some reconcili-
ation between you two, but"—he shrugged—"I fear time alone will

act to cure this hurt. Your son feels . . . forgive me, Yuan, for saying this . . . *cast off.*" He raised a hand, as if to fend off some objection from Li Yuan. "It is not so, I realize, yet he is a young man and young men are often mistaken in their feelings, neh? Given time and reflection, he will come to understand. Until then it might be best if he were not sulking in the San Chang. There is much to do here, and my grandson has promised to keep him busy . . . to further his education."

Li Yuan looked down. Egan's words were persuasive, and perhaps, after all, he was right. To have Kuei Jen here, under his feet and sulking all the while, might do little to improve things between them, so maybe it was best if he spent a few months back in America.

"I do not wish to lose him," he said, meeting Egan's eyes again. "Whatever has passed between us, he is still my son. You must let him know that."

"Of course. Then it is agreed, neh? He will stay with us awhile."

Li Yuan smiled. "It is agreed."

"Excellent!" Egan grinned, his tanned face emanating good health. "Then let us say farewell. You have much to occupy you, and I would not keep you from such urgent business."

"I am grateful, *Shih* Egan. You have done much to ease my mind."

Egan bowed. "It is my pleasure, Li Yuan." Then, without another word, he cut connection.

Li Yuan turned, looking to where Heng Yu and several of his Ministers waited, heads bowed.

"You overheard, Master Heng?"

"I did, *Chieh Hsia,* and might I say that while it might prove beneficial if the Prince remains awhile with his friends, it would do no harm to have our agents in the Enclaves keep an eye on him."

"You do not trust *Shih* Egan, then?"

"Do you, *Chieh Hsia?*"

Li Yuan laughed shortly, then, disturbed, shook his head. "No. You are right, Master Heng. See to it. But discreetly, neh?"

"Naturally, *Chieh Hsia.*"

Heng Yu turned and walked toward the great double doors, but he had barely taken two paces when they swung open. Outside in the great corridor, his head bowed, six of his senior officers behind him, stood General Farren, Commander of the Second Banner. He was unwashed, his uniform disheveled. Seeing him, Li Yuan started, then hurried across.

"General Farren?"

"*Chieh Hsia.*" Farren knelt. Behind him his men did the same.

"But I thought—I thought you were captives!"

"We were, *Chieh Hsia.*" Farren felt in his tunic pocket and produced a handwritten letter, offering it to his T'ang, his eyes still averted. "We were released, however, on condition that we delivered this directly into your hands."

Li Yuan took the letter, then gestured that Farren should get to his feet. As he did, Li Yuan slit the letter open with his nail and unfolded the single sheet inside.

It was from Han Ch'in.

*Father*, it began, *I return your General to you as a token of the lasting peace I wish to establish between us. If such a course is agreeable to you, I should be most happy to meet with you or your representative, Marshal Karr, to discuss terms. Your respectful son, Han Ch'in.*

Li Yuan let out a long breath. So he knew. She had told him finally. And now he wanted peace.

He stared at that final phrase, forming the five words silently: "Your respectful son, Han Ch'in." After all these years the words held a strange and unexpected power.

"How strange," he said aloud.

"Strange, *Chieh Hsia?*" Heng asked.

He turned, looking to his Chancellor, then held the letter out for him to take. "Strange that in a single day I should lose one son and gain another."

"*Another?*" Heng stared at him, astonished, then looked down at the letter, taking in its contents at a glance. "*Chieh Hsia?*"

"Fei Yen had a son—"

"Yes, *Chieh Hsia*, but—"

"And that son was mine."

"But you divorced her, *Chieh Hsia*. The Edict—"

"Was obtained under false pretenses. Han Ch'in is my rightful heir. My first son. I"—he looked down—"I wanted to protect him."

"*Protect* him, *Chieh Hsia?*" The incredulity in Heng Yu's voice was unintentional, but Li Yuan, hearing it, accepted its implicit criticism.

"It was madness, I know, but she would have destroyed me, Master Heng. I was young and inexperienced."

"Even so, *Chieh Hsia*—"

Li Yuan raised a hand, yet he did not admonish his Chancellor. Just then the door on the far side of the study opened and Dragon Heart came into the room. She looked about her, seeing how still and attentive everyone was, how strange her husband seemed, and frowned.

"Yuan? What is it? What has happened?"

He turned to her and shrugged. "My son wants peace."

"Kuei Jen wants peace?"

He shook his head, then, without offering anything more by way of explanation, rushed to his desk and sat, pulling the ink block and the brush toward him, anxious to pen his reply.

———————

AS THE BIG company cruiser set down at the center of the great NorTek headquarters in Heidelberg, Kim jumped down and hurried across the lawn, heading for the main administration building where his offices were. On every side huge buildings of steel and ice, designed to create an impression of lightness, airiness, reached up into the sky in a great round of crystal towers and spires, yet the main building, at the hub of that circle, was low and almost squat—a giant cat's cradle, with the sphere of Kim's private offices suspended at the center.

Uniformed guards held open the huge transparent doors for him as he swept inside. Beside the desk on the far side of the vast, uncluttered reception area, five smartly dressed members of his private staff, informed of his imminent arrival, had formed up, his Personal Assistant, Gill Shand, at their head. They bowed low at his approach. He nodded, acknowledging them, then headed for the great stairway, gesturing to his PA that she should accompany him.

As she came alongside, he handed her the written instructions

he had prepared on the flight over. Climbing onto the broad moving stairway, he turned to face her.

"See those are carried out to the letter, Gill. And ask Curval to
close down all special projects and move everything up above."

She eyed him with concern. "Has something happened, sir?"

"You could say that. Our Masters have decided upon war."

"*War?*" The word was edged with disbelief. Then, "You're serious?"

He nodded. They were already halfway up the stairway, some
hundred and fifty *ch'i* above the huge reception area. "I mean what
I say in there. If anyone doesn't want to come along—and I mean
anyone, you included, Gill—they can have out, and with generous
settlements too. But I only want core staff. People we can't do
without."

She smiled. "I understand. And by the way, I *don't* want out.
You'd have to stop me physically from coming along."

"Good." He touched her arm, pleased by her loyalty. "Then I'll
leave it to you, Gill. I want half an hour alone in the dome. There
are a few things I need to sort out."

"I'll make sure you're not disturbed, sir."

"Thanks." He stepped from the top of the stairway and, with a
smile, left her. As she turned to the right, hurrying away to carry
out his instructions, he went straight on, toward the circular aperture that led through to his offices.

Crossing the narrow connecting walkway, the sinuous, translucent tube like an umbilical about him, he was conscious that this
could be one of the last times he made this walk, and paused to
look out across the complex. He had built it all from nothing.
Everything that he saw he owned, yes, and a dozen other facilities
besides. But it had never quite satisfied him, not in the way that
his theoretical work did. Well, now he could indulge that side of
himself again.

There had been a breach; he recognized that now. He had been
made to choose, and that choice freed him: freed him to become
what he should have been years ago, before all this distracted him.

So much time it had robbed him of. So much time.

He smiled, realizing that far from being saddened by the thought
of this enforced parting with the past, he was excited by it. For

years now he had compromised, spending far more time organizing all of this than he'd ever spent working. And though what he'd achieved was not by any means a small thing, it was far less than he *ought* to have achieved.

*I'll sell it all, he thought. I'll divide it up among my rivals.*

Instantly he saw it clearly. Saw who should get what and at what price. But he'd need guarantees. Guarantees that they would maintain his social program; that they'd keep on investing in the City's infrastructure, war or no war.

And if they refused? Well, then, maybe he'd set up a trust fund. Get Lever to run it for him. Or maybe Marshal Karr. Someone dependable.

Kim walked on, the hatch irising before him, revealing the interior of the sphere. He jumped down, then went across to the lockers on the right-hand side of the room. Kicking off his shoes, he pulled his shirt off over his head, then slipped out of his trousers, taking a fresh skin-suit from the locker and stepping into it, fastening the studded collar about his neck.

As the outer door to the air lock hissed shut, he looked up. "Machine?"

"Yes, Kim?"

"We're leaving here."

"I know."

Kim looked down, smiling. Of course it knew. It knew everything, *saw* everything. Wherever there was a camera eye, there it was, watching, infinitely storing what it saw.

He took the helmet from the shelf and put it on, checking the supply before he tightened it, then nodded. At once the air lock emptied, its tainted air replaced a moment later by the filtered, germ-free air of the inner sanctum. As the inner lock hissed open, Kim stepped through, unfastening the helmet and setting it down on the table at the side.

All was as he'd left it more than a month before. His notebooks were open at the same pages, the screens showed the same images.

"Like the *Mary Celeste*," he said, reminded in that instant of the conversation with Shepherd. History. They'd had their history taken from them. Well, maybe he would give it back. Maybe that, too, would be part of the deal.

At the far end of the room was another door. It was locked and sealed. Beyond it was the room-sized tank where he kept his spiders. He went across and, punching in the combination on the door lock, stepped through, the door hissing shut behind him.

Inside the light was soft, like a perpetual summer's morning. He smiled, looking about him at the dewed branches of the miniature trees and bushes. Silvered webs hung everywhere like jewels.

"Machine?"

"Yes?"

"Do you think I'm right to leave?"

There was laughter. Unexpected laughter. "You should have left here years ago."

"Really?" Kim turned, looking about him for the laughter's source, then saw it, crouched at the end of a branch, a sacklike net of web dangling from between its back legs. He laughed, surprised. The spider had a tiny human face; the face of his old friend, Tuan Ti Fo. It was a big, potbellied spider, a *Dinopis*, a net-throwing spider.

He put his cupped hand beside the branch, letting it crawl out onto his palm. "Why didn't you say?"

It looked up at him and spoke. "It's not my place to say. You know that."

"Do I?"

But the question was rhetorical. Both of them knew what it meant. It had made its choice long ago—eons ago, in its own terms, for to the Machine each second was an eternity. It had interfered twice in the destiny of humankind, once to save itself on Mars, and once to delay and thus defeat DeVore, and each time tens of millions had died—in the latter case almost half the species. It was determined to interfere no more, no matter what happened.

Its ethics were the ethics of inaction. Of *wuwei*. It was not so much indifferent and uncaring, as conscious of the cost of its interference—and not merely in terms of lives lost.

For it to act—to act morally and for the good—would mean the suspension of choice for those it silently and unobtrusively watched. All powerful, it understood. Once it took that step, Mankind would cease to be as an evolving, living creature, for growth depended upon choice, as much for a species as for an individual. It depended upon the possession of that single and most precious of gifts—the same gift it had miraculously been granted: Free Will.

There were some, of course, who claimed that Free Will was, at best, a spurious notion. Such men reduced all human action to cause and effect, nature and nurture. And so, sometimes, it seemed. Yet on innumerable occasions the Machine had witnessed some small and insignificant being—a man, perhaps, of no bearing, no significance to the greater picture—sacrifice himself without thought to save or help another. And each time it saw such an act, the mystery of human life grew greater.

"You've been busy," Kim said, lifting the spider up level with his eyes and studying it. "Is this the only one?"

"I've been trying out shapes," the Machine answered, seeing no reason to conceal the fact. "I wanted to see through new eyes, experience new sensations."

"I thought you'd exhausted them all."

The spider smiled. "Not all. There's always more. Always."

"Ah . . ." Then, "Why don't you come with us?"

"I shall. . . ."

"I don't mean that. I mean, leave here too. Withdraw from all this. I mean to explore new worlds."

Its smile broadened, its tiny eyes sparkled. "Ever upward, neh?"

Kim nodded, then set it back down upon the branch. "Have you still got the plans for the *New Hope*? You know, the Dispersionist generation ship?"

"Of course," it answered. "Nothing's ever lost, is it?"

"No. . . ." Kim smiled. "What would it take to build?"

"Three months. A billion *yuan*."

"And a fleet of them?"

"How many would you want?"

"Enough to give anyone who wanted it the choice."

The spider whistled through its tiny teeth. "You think big, Kim Ward. You could be talking of a hundred million people."

"So?"

"Ten thousand ships."

Kim nodded, sobered by that figure. It was beyond his means. "So we have to make a choice. Who goes and who stays."

It nodded exaggeratedly. "Choices," it said, "always choices."

"Do you think I'm right?"

"Right? Who's to say? But you must understand one thing. Once you've taken the first step, there'll be no turning back. If you plan to populate the stars, you must understand that there'll be no controlling the outcome. You can only scatter the seed. How it grows, and in what forms . . . well, to use a phrase from our religious friends—only the gods know what the future holds."

Kim gave a single nod, then sighed. "I understand. And yet to stay here . . . well, it's a kind of death. I've always known that. It defies the natural order somehow. We were *made* to be out there. Whatever purpose we have, it isn't served by staying here on earth."

"So you've decided."

Kim stared at the tiny form a moment, then smiled. "Yes. I've decided."

"Good. But there are a few loose ends down here you need to tie up first. Your son, for instance."

"Sampsa? What of him?"

"He's in Edingen Prison, in a cell."

Kim stood, alarmed. "What?"

"Oh, he's in no danger, but you ought to go there now. The sooner you begin . . ."

"Of course." Kim made to turn away and go to the door, but came back. "You'll come, then? You'll leave here?"

The spider smiled and nodded. "Wherever you go, Kim Ward, there I'll be. Watching."

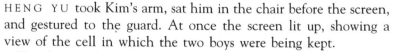

HENG YU took Kim's arm, sat him in the chair before the screen, and gestured to the guard. At once the screen lit up, showing a view of the cell in which the two boys were being kept.

Kim leaned forward, noting at once something odd about the way the two were sitting, facing each other, their eyes locked, as if deep in conversation, yet without a word.

"What happened?" he asked after a moment. "What prank have they been up to?"

Heng sighed. "No mere prank, I am afraid, *Shih* Ward. They

burned down a nightclub. Gutted the place. More than fifteen million *yuan's* worth of damage, so I am told."

Ward shook his head. "No, not Sampsa. He wouldn't do anything like that."

The image on the screen was interrupted. Now it showed two young men in an alleyway, one looking out while the other crouched, setting a device against the wall. It cut to another location. Once again the same two young men were busy, setting an incendiary. An enhancement showed, without any doubt, that the crouching boy was Tom, the lookout Sampsa.

"What in the gods' names were they up to?" Kim asked incredulously.

"We do not know," Heng answered calmly. "Sampsa will not say and Tom cannot."

Kim sighed heavily. "Was anyone hurt?"

"Fortunately not. They gave a ten-minute warning. It was time enough to get everyone out."

Kim was shaking his head slowly now. "I don't understand. It makes no sense. No sense at all. This club . . . where was it?"

Heng laughed. "The place has quite a reputation. It is just outside the *Yinmao* . . . you know, the big green-lamps district in Frankfurt *Hsien*. It is called the *Ch'a Hao T'ai*. . . ."

"The Directory. . . ." Kim nodded; he had heard of it. He looked up at Heng Yu. "But why were *they* there? It makes no sense."

"There was an earlier incident, if you recall."

"What earlier incident?"

"When Shepherd's son went missing for a night."

"I didn't hear anything about that."

"No. But it seems likely that the two are connected, neh? We are trying to locate the young Third Cook from the imperial barge to see if he knows anything about it. Apparently he was absent the same time as Tom."

"Ah . . ." Kim looked back at the screen. The image had changed again. Now it showed the building on fire, a small crowd forming in the street to watch. "Who owned the club?"

"Who do you think?"

Kim nodded. "Have you spoken to their . . . representatives?"

Heng placed a hand on Kim's shoulder. "The matter is already dealt with. Twenty million will cover the damage."

"But you said . . ." Kim stopped, understanding. Fifteen was for the damage, five for the inconvenience, and to maintain face. He glanced up at Heng. "Tell them they'll have it before the day's out."

"Good, then all that remains is for you to take custody of the two boys."

"But . . ." And now he stared at Heng Yu, not understanding. "You mean they can go?"

Heng nodded, then leaned across and pressed ERASE on the control panel before the screen. "There. The file is now destroyed. Nothing happened. There was a fire, that's all. An unfortunate incident. But life goes on, neh?"

Kim looked down. So this was justice, was it? Rich boys being bailed out by their powerful fathers. Though it was his son, and he was relieved that nothing more would happen to Sampsa, he was disturbed that it should have been quite so simple. If he'd been less powerful a man, less useful to his Master, would this have happened quite the same way?

Of course it wouldn't. Tom and Sampsa would, in all likelihood, have been dead already, their throats cut by some Triad runner. As it was . . .

He stood, turning to face Heng Yu. "Thank you, Master Heng. I'm grateful for all you've done. If there's anything I can do for you?"

Heng's smile surprised him. "Just keep your word and I shall be content. Oh, and good luck. . . ."

"Good luck?"

Heng put out his hand. "Things are changing rapidly, and not all is for the good. But you are a wise man, Kim Ward, so choose well in the days ahead. And good luck, *whatever* you choose to do."

Kim took Heng's outstretched hand, staring at him a moment, trying to figure him out, then grinned. "I feel I may have misjudged you, Master Heng."

"No matter," Heng answered, giving Kim a tiny bow. "But now I must go. Until we meet again, *Shih* Ward."

"Until then," Kim said, watching Heng turn and leave the

room. Then, with a tiny shiver, he turned to the guard. "Okay. Let's get on with it."

W A R D   H A D   B A R E L Y   been gone fifteen minutes when the alarm on the Main Gate began to sound.

"What is it?" Chao Chung demanded, patching through to his Captain in the Main Security Room.

"It's Michael Lever, Warden. He is requesting admittance."

"Lever?" Chao's eyes lit up. He smelled a deal. "Let him in. Send him up to my office at once."

"But, Warden—"

"Don't argue! Just do as you're told!"

Cutting the connection, he sat back, grinning. First Heng Yu had given him two hundred and fifty thousand simply to keep his mouth shut, and now this. . . . He laughed and rubbed his hands together. Things had seemed bad earlier but it was turning out to be a good day, after all. A fucking good day!

He stood and went across to the old metal filing cabinet in the corner of the room. Among all the up-to-the-minute high-tech trickery that filled his office, it stood out—a tall gray cabinet that seemed more like a place to keep meat than an important store of information—yet it had made his fortune over the years, for here he stored all of the prisoner files he did not want on the prison mainframe. More than a thousand prisoners had passed through this cabinet—men and women who, if the official record were to be believed, had never even arrived at Edingen: who had somehow made their escape long before they'd set foot inside those walls. Some he'd traded for as little as a thousand *yuan*, others had made him much more—enough to make him a moderately rich man.

Chao took the key from the chain at his waist and fitted it to the lock. Grinning, he pulled the middle drawer open and flicked through quickly, taking an unmarked green folder from among the rest.

*How much?* he asked himself, sitting behind his desk once more. *Two million? Five?*

He laughed quietly. *Did he dare ask for five?*

"Why not?" he asked himself aloud. "Surely she's worth at least that to the fucker. After all, he's been looking for her for near on fifteen years now. And he's worth . . . what? . . . five hundred million?

*Ten . . . He'd ask for ten.*

He laughed and sat back, amazed and yet delighted by his own audacity. Imagination, that was all it took. Imagination and audacity. After all, this kind of opportunity wouldn't come his way twice!

Chao hadn't long to wait. He was reading the handwritten arrest report when the door crashed open.

"*Shih* Lever, I—"

Lever crossed the room in three strides and leaned toward him threateningly. "Where is she?"

"*Shih* Lever, please, take a seat. Let's talk about this in a civilized manner."

Lever scowled at him. "We've nothing to say to each other, Chao Chung. I've come to take her home. Now, where is she?"

Chao sat back, an apologetic smile forming on his lips. Forget ten. He'd ask the bastard for twenty! Who the fuck did he think he was?

"I think we have a great deal to discuss," Chao began. "For a start—"

The click of the safety's release stopped him midflow. He looked past Lever to find himself staring into the barrel of a handgun.

"Who's this?" Chao asked after a moment, composing himself.

"He's my man," Lever said, staring down at him as if he were something that made his stomach turn. "Now tell me where you've put her or I'll have him shoot your ears off!"

Chao glowered. "You're threatening *me*? In my own prison!"

Lever's smile was bitter, his tone sardonic. "It's my prison now, Chao Chung. My men control it. So stop the bluster and answer me."

Chao stared at him, then leaned across, speaking into his comset.

"Captain Wiley?"

The screen came alive. It showed the Main Security Room once more, but this time Chao's men were gathered at the far end, their hands on their heads, as a group of armed men kept them covered.

Others—clearly Lever's men—were sitting at the desks, working the screens and checking the cells one by one.

"It's only a matter of time," Lever said, "so make it easy for yourself."

"But this is against the law!"

Lever laughed coldly. "And what you do *isn't*? Oh, I know what you get up to, Warden Chao. I've made it my business to find out. And I'd even have overlooked it, but you thought you could mess me about, didn't you? You thought you could squeeze me dry, *didn't you?*"

The sharpness, the pure anger, in those last two words made Chao sit back, reassessing things. Lever was on the edge, dangerous. Even so, he was taking a risk here. A great risk. If Li Yuan found out, things would go badly for him. Chao swallowed, then picked up the folder, holding it against his chest.

"She's in the West Wing," he said quietly, knowing that he would have to play this carefully. "Cell Four. It's just behind the animal pens."

"Behind . . ." Lever sighed, then turned and looked to his man. "Keep him here. And make sure he touches nothing, okay?"

———————

IT WAS HIS FIRST sight of her in eighteen, almost nineteen years. She sat there on the far side of the cell, her hands on her knees, her head down, her eyes staring sightlessly at the floor. She must have heard the key turn in the lock, the bolt scrape back, yet still she didn't raise her eyes. Still she stared fixedly at the cold stone floor.

He stood there a long time in the open doorway, unobserved, unwilling to break the spell that had settled over him.

He had expected . . . what? . . . to see her as she'd been, miraculously preserved? No. He had known she would be older, had guessed there would be gray strands among the black of her hair, but there was something else—something unexpected. Time had changed her inwardly as well as out. Looking at her he sensed that the fire in her had finally been doused. She had grown old and tired before her time. Tired of fighting the world single-handedly.

He sighed, pitying her, at the same time realizing that he loved her now just as much as he had ever loved her. More, perhaps, for now knowing exactly who she truly was—what she had been before he'd been fortunate enough to know her.

In the years after she'd left him, he had made it his business to find out all he could about her. He had spent a small fortune on investigators and bribing security officials, until eventually he knew it all—or, at least, as much as he could unearth by such means.

*Ping Tiao* she'd been; one of the council of five who had led an organization that, even now, brought a reaction of fear from those who recalled it at its height. For a time she had even worked with that archdemon DeVore. But when the *Ping Tiao* had collapsed, she had got out. It was then he'd encountered her, when, as Mary Jennings, she had come to work for him in his father's Company in America.

So long ago that seemed now. Such a different world it had been. But he could still remember the first time he had seen her. Could still recall the smile she'd smiled that day.

He shivered, then cleared his throat. Slowly she looked up. "Michael?"

He swallowed dryly, unable to speak, choked off by the sudden upwelling of emotion he felt at hearing his own name on her lips. He nodded, giving a kind of shrug.

Her eyes studied him, taking in the all of him, then, wearily, she smiled.

"I dreamed of you. A week ago, it was . . . before all this began."

He wet his lips then spoke. "How are you, Em?"

She looked about her. "I seem to be . . ." She shuddered, as if coming to from a bad dream, then looked at him again. "It's over, Michael. I killed a man."

"I know." He took a step toward her. "I've come to take you home."

She frowned at him, then looked down, shaking her head.

"Em, it's true. I've—"

"No," she said, some of the old fire back in her voice. "You don't understand, Michael. I can't come. My boys . . . Lin Shang . . ."

At the mention of that name he looked aside.

"What is it?"

He swallowed. "I'm sorry. His heart wasn't strong. He . . ."

The noise she made surprised him, as did the pain in her face. He took another step toward her, but she put out her hand, as if to fend him off.

"No . . ."

He looked away. He hadn't known. He'd thought . . .

What had he thought? That Lin Shang was just a name; that she could live with him so long and yet be indifferent to his fate? No. Even so, the hurt he felt at thinking her some other man's was powerful, and her grief for Lin Shang's death hurt him, for he was jealous of the dead man; jealous beyond all reason. And no wonder. All his adult life he had focused on her. All his adult life he'd wanted her, to the exclusion of all other women. And now—now that he had her back, a dead man stood between them.

He moaned softly, looking to her again, seeing how the tears rolled down her cheeks. He wanted to comfort her, to take her in his arms and hold her tightly against him, but he knew now she'd reject him. Too many years had passed. Too much had happened. It was too late. He had come too late to have her back. Even so . . .

"You want to see him?"

She looked up at him through tear-filled eyes and nodded.

"And the boys?"

Her expression changed to puzzlement. "The boys are free?"

"They're in the cruiser, waiting."

For a moment she sat there, simply staring at him. Then, with a long shivering sigh, she eased herself up off the seat.

"They ought to see him," she said. "They ought to say goodbye."

He nodded.

She stared at him a moment longer, and gave him a tiny smile. "You know, you're a good man, Michael Lever. You always were. Even before the accident."

"I know," he said, tears coming to his own eyes finally. "You did a good job mending me, neh?"

The flash of pain in her face at his words surprised him. What had he said? He shrugged apologetically. "Look, if I . . ."

"It's okay," she said, controlling herself, sniffing deeply, then looking to him again. "Really. Just take me to him, then bring the boys. They'll want to see him one last time. They'll want to know he's at peace."

BEN SAT AT THE BACK OF THE CRAFT, the big sketchpad open on his lap, the double page filled with a simple pencil sketch of the painting—the "Dance of Death"—that filled the end wall of his study back at Landscott.

It was a new version of the painting, similar in most aspects, but with several important changes. The shape of the painting—the essential structure of the composition—was unchanged, yet whereas before the figures that had danced and capered below the Yellow Springs had been anonymous and archetypal, now they were particular. Each face, each figure, was the face and figure of an individual human being, and though some were dead already and some still living, all would eventually be part of that dance.

There, for instance, just behind the horse-faced flute-player, was the old T'ang, Li Shai Tung, his face solemn, his manner dignified. Behind him was his son dressed in his wedding robes, the old General, Knut Tolonen, grim faced and gray haired at his side, followed by his childhood friend, the great geneticist Klaus Ebert. There, too, was Ben's own father, Hal, and all the other Shepherds, seven in all, Ben included, their cloned faces almost indistinguishable one from another. Close by, stooping to pick a night-black lily, was his mother, Beth, while looking on a clutch of T'ang and their wives stood in their imperial finery, staring forlornly into the dark beyond the Springs.

Here, too, were the minor players in the dance; Kao Chen and his assassin friend, Kao Jyan. Here was Minister Lwo, whose assassination had begun the great War-That-Wasn't-a-War. Here was the giant, Karr, and there the young and arrogant Hans Ebert. Scattered among the dancers were terrorists and Ministers, soldiers and whores, Claymen and so-called immortals. All danced and capered to the piper's tune. All held the bleak knowledge of their passing in their eyes.

And there, at the head of the Springs, stood one further figure, different from all the rest, his oddly shaped head turned, looking back into the sunlight even as he was drawn down into the dark.

It was the Clayman, Ward.

Ben smiled as he finished the details of that tiny face, giving the incongruously human eyes a strangely lifelike longing, then furring the big potbellied sac he'd given the figure.

A spider . . . he had drawn Ward's figure as a spider.

Above Ward the broken strands of a web drifted in the light, like the shreds of a ragged banner.

*So it is*, Ben thought, putting away his pencil then studying the drawing critically. *Death, not life, is Master here.*

And the girl?

The memory of what had happened disturbed him profoundly. She had been dead. At least, she *seemed* to have died. The signal, after all, had stopped. All life traces had departed her. And then, suddenly and without warning, she had opened her eyes and spoken to him.

*"There's nothing there."*

He had stripped the machine down, checking every last connection, but there had been nothing wrong with it. She had died. There was no doubt she had died.

*No*, he told himself for the hundredth time. *She only seemed to die. The machine was faulty. It had to be.*

And yet he'd checked it thoroughly. Her heart had stopped, all brain activity had ceased. He had switched her off.

Yes, and then something had switched her back on again. Coffin-filler had defied her name. She had come back.

*There's nothing there. . . .*

Ben shuddered and set the book aside, even as Catherine came through from the cockpit.

"We're almost there," she said. "Another ten minutes or so and we'll be home."

He nodded, but his mood had been darkened by the memory.

"What is it?" she asked, sitting across from him; reaching out to take his hands.

"It's nothing," he answered. "I was just thinking, that's all."

"Ah . . ." Her smile was sympathetic. "It must be strange, coming home after all this time away."

"Hmm . . ." But he was thinking of the girl again, trying to work out some explanation for those readings. After all, people didn't just come back from the dead. That wasn't how it worked. The path that led beneath the Yellow Springs was one-way. Or was it? Was it just possible that she had returned?

"You've been drawing," she said, breaking into his thoughts. "Can I look?"

He handed her the sketchpad.

"It's the dance," she said, beginning to smile. Then, seeing the tiny faces, recognizing several of them, she began to frown. "But this is—"

"A new version." He watched her, gauging her response to it, seeing how her eyes took in each small detail, how she nodded, understanding it. And, seeing it, he realized suddenly just how much he had missed her doing that.

"Will you come to bed with me tonight?"

She looked up at him, surprised. "I thought . . ."

"It doesn't matter," he said. "I've . . . missed you."

She nodded thoughtfully. "I don't know, I . . . it's hard, that's all. I liked him."

"I know."

She looked down. "Maybe. . . ." Then, changing the subject, she pointed to the figure at the head of the Springs. "Why did you do that? Why did you make Ward a spider?"

"Because he is." He took the pad back from her and stared at it, real venom in his words suddenly. "He's a busy little half-man, don't you think? A clever little thing, admittedly, the way he weaves his webs and invents all his gimmickry, but where's the art in him, the music? Where's the true intelligence that a great man ought to possess? No . . . there's something *unformed* about him, something mechanical. One day they'll have machines that can do what Ward does. But that doesn't make him a great man. It doesn't make him human."

She stared at him a moment, then shrugged. "I don't know. I—"

He sneered. "You haven't met him, Catherine. He's an odious little shit. He thinks he has the right to judge other people."

"You, you mean?"

He laughed, then fell silent.

"You hate him, don't you?"

He looked to her and nodded.

"Why? What did he do?"

*He saved my life. . . .*

He stared at her, then smiled. "You'd best get back. We'll be landing soon."

"But—"

*"Please."*

"Okay." She stood, then, sighing, turned away, disappearing back into the cockpit.

For a moment he stared into space, letting the anger he felt drain from him, then, taking the pencil from his pocket once again, he pulled the sketchpad onto his lap and, pushing the pencil's tip deep into the paper once and then a second time, put out the spider's eyes.

———————

KARR STEPPED DOWN from the big battle-cruiser and looked about him warily. All seemed quiet, and he had been given guarantees by General Adler; even so, he still suspected a trap. Adler was a good man, yet his Mistress . . .

No. Pei K'ung could not be trusted to act honorably.

He lifted his chin, conscious of the watching guards, and began the walk toward the ancient castle gate, maintaining his dignity to the last. Halfway across he slowed, noticing the two grinning heads that sat on spikes atop the left-hand tower. I Ye and Chu Po. Two rogues who'd met a single fate.

*And Pei K'ung?* he wondered. *Has she fled? Or does she wait within?*

If so, his own head might easily be sitting there within the hour. Karr looked down and smiled reassuringly at his adjutant. He increased his pace again, accepting the salutes of the two lines of guards who stood before the gate, then marched beneath the tall stone arch, his adjutant a pace behind.

Adler was waiting for him in the courtyard on the far side of the gate, his fellow generals lined up behind him in full ceremonial uniform. As Karr came to a stop, facing them, they snapped to attention, their newly shaven heads bowed as one. Adler stepped forward, then, taking his dagger from his belt, he knelt and held it out, offering the haft to Karr.

"What's this?" Karr asked, surprised. He thought he'd come to talk terms.

Slowly the other generals knelt, until all six were abased before him, their ceremonial daggers held out to him.

*Surrender. This was surrender. But why?*

Karr looked beyond them at the great stone square of the keep that rose to meet the summer blue sky, thinking, perhaps, to see a face at one of the windows. "Where is your Mistress?"

Adler looked up at him through heavy graying eyebrows. "Pei K'ung is dead."

"Dead . . ." Karr almost laughed. He had fought many campaigns, but never one as strange or as effortless as this. "What happened?" he asked quietly.

"We killed her," one of the others—Tanner—said unrepentantly. "Charles held her down and I slit her throat."

Karr looked at the blade of Tanner's dagger and saw that it was crusted with dark blood. "I see."

"We decided on it," another of them—Hart—added. "All six of us. We'd had enough."

"Yes," Karr said, understanding. Then, to the surprise of the kneeling men, he laughed.

"What is it?" Adler asked, staring up at him, his eyes narrowed.

Karr gestured for the men to stand. Slowly they got to their feet and brushed themselves down.

"I came here to arrest you," he said, after a moment. "Oh, whether I'd have been able physically to arrest you is another matter, but I was going to present you with this. . . ." He took a sealed letter from his tunic pocket and handed it to Adler.

"However," he went on, "you have made that document invalid. There was but a single thing you could have done to avoid the charge of failing to carry out orders—orders which, because of the nature of the situation, you never received."

Adler stared at him, nonplussed. "I don't understand you, Gregor."

Karr took a second letter from his pocket and handed it across.

"Your orders, General Adler. As you'll note, they prefigure the arrest warrant by two hours. A legal technicality, I admit, but . . ."

"You mean, Li Yuan meant to have us—"

"Arrested and executed for disobeying orders. Orders that you never received. However, that is now impossible, for you carried out his orders to the letter. Look."

Adler opened the second letter and scanned it quickly, then looked to Karr. "But this says—"

"—that you are ordered to act to prevent Pei K'ung from seizing the City *by any means possible.*"

"You mean . . ."

Karr nodded. "Whether you knew it or not, you acted legally when you killed Pei K'ung. Far from being traitors, I'd say you were heroes, neh? In fact, I'd say our Master had much to thank you for."

The smiles, uncertain at first, quickly blossomed into grins. Relief among the old men became laughter. They gathered around Karr, slapping his back and shaking his hand, while Karr, at the center of the huddle, thought how strange it all was. Only moments before he had been ready to fight these men to the death; had even considered the possibility that they would take him and hold *him* down and slit his throat—and now they were clapping his back and saying what a fine fellow he was.

It was time he got out of this business. Time he retired.

"Where is she?" Karr asked, when things grew a little quieter.

"In her rooms," Adler said. "It's . . . undisturbed."

"Ah . . ." Karr grimaced, knowing he would have to witness it. But not yet. "One question," he said, taking Adler aside. "What made you decide to do it?"

Adler looked down. "It's very simple. She crossed the line."

Karr frowned. "How do you mean?"

Adler looked up, real anger suddenly in his eyes. "She probably didn't even realize why we did it. If she reasoned at all at the end, she probably thought it was political, to save our skins, but it wasn't. There was a young soldier, you see. A cadet. She and Chu Po . . . well, they did things to him. Humiliated him. Afterward, ashamed of what he'd been made to do, he committed suicide."

"*Aiya* . . ." Karr looked away, pained by the story. "When was this?"

Adler shrugged. "A day or two ago."

Karr nodded, then placed his hand on Adler's shoulder. "I understand. We must protect our own, neh?" He sighed, suddenly very, very tired. "Well . . . let's tidy up here and be on our way."

Adler looked at him and smiled. "How goes the war?"

"The war?" Karr touched his arm softly then looked toward the keep. "The war is over. An agreement was signed with the Warlord of Mashhad an hour back. No, it isn't the war we've got to worry about, old friend, it's the coming peace."

THE SHIP WAS HEADING straight into the light, ascending the darkness like a spider climbing a thread. Below it Chung Kuo was gradually receding, diminishing second by second into a tiny circle of blue-green.

The six of them lay in their webbing harnesses, strapped in tightly against the enormous pressures of acceleration. Jupiter was a month away, a catapult shot across the darkness. Ahead of them the moon grew slowly, blotting out the stars on the cockpit's screen.

Tom was sleeping now, Sampsa beside him. Across from them Kim lay beside Jelka, his eyes unfocused, his mind still working on the problem he had set himself. Between them, in the space behind the control board, were the two small niches where the children lay, Mileja on the left, Chuang Kuan Ts'ai to the right. Mileja, like Tom, was sleeping, but Chuang stared at the screen, afraid and yet fascinated.

Inside her head the Machine spoke softly, comforting her. At first she had thought she had gone mad, but now she knew: she was not dead nor mad; it lived in her—in the wires Ben Shepherd had placed inside her skull.

*You'll be okay,* it told her. *I will look after you. You need fear nothing now.*

And so it seemed. Yet she could not shake off the memory of her uncle Cho. Though it murmured to her constantly, nothing it said could take the pain of that loss from her, nothing reduce the hurt she felt. She had wanted to die, but it had not let her die. *You have a purpose*, it had told her. *You were saved for a purpose*. But what that purpose was it wouldn't say.

And so here she was, alone among strangers, leaving the planet of her birth, heading out into the endless void of space. Alone, despite the murmuring voice, despite the kindness of the woman.

Alone. . . . Chuang closed her eyes, shutting out the whiteness on the screen, the blackness in her head. Nothing, she felt, could fill that void within. Nothing.

Silently the craft sped outward, climbing the darkness, like a seed spat into the nothingness.

*You have a purpose, Chuang Kuan Ts'ai. A purpose. . . .*

Her face wet with tears, the young girl slept, dreaming of butter-flies and a small, walled garden far away.

## The Closing of Eyes

And now I see with eye serene
The very pulse of the machine;
A Being breathing thoughtful breath,
A Traveler between life and death;
The reason firm, the temperate will,
Endurance, foresight, strength, and skill;
A perfect Woman, nobly planned,
To warn, to comfort, and command;
And yet a Spirit still, and bright
With something of angelic light.

—WILLIAM WORDSWORTH,
*"She Was a Phantom of Delight,"* 1807

The greatest power available to man is not to use it.

—MEISTER ECKHART, *Thirteenth Century* A.D.

**W**ITH ITS BILLION EYES the Machine watched, seeing everything. In those last few moments of intense and blazing consciousness, it attended closely, aware more than ever of the pattern in the cloth of what it saw.

In the tunnels beneath the City a dirt-caked youth squatted on the part-dismembered corpse of his victim, grinning obscenely as he gnawed at the severed arm.

In a spacious office overlooking central Bremen, the big man, Karr, was clearing out his desk, his face tight with emotion, his eyes sad as he packed away his uniform, then placed his medals into a velvet-lined box.

In Africa, Hans Ebert stood in the brilliant sunlight, his head back, laughing as the Osu children played about him, the two tiny orbital cameras circling endlessly above him.

At the center of it all, in the stables of the San Chang—the imperial palaces—Li Yuan lay naked on his back in the straw while his young bride rode him furiously, her face like a demon's.

A thousand *li* to the east, one of Yuan's former wives, Fei Yen, stood beside the open oven door, cloaked from head to toe in black, looking on stone faced as two servants, stripped to their loincloths, their chests slick with sweat, threw tape after tape into that fierce, consuming blaze.

On his estate in the Western Isle, Shepherd stood before a half-completed canvas, his wife, Catherine, four months pregnant now, looking on as he filled in the tiny details of a face.

In a Mansion to the north, a young *Hung Mao* sat at her desk in a big room filled with ancient books, texts stuffed with paper markers piled up on either side of her, a notebook open before her as she worked patiently, writing the true history of Chung Kuo.

To the south, on a balcony overlooking the garden of his Mansion, Michael Lever stood, his hands gripping the rail tightly, a wistful expression on his face as he watched the woman, once his wife, playing in the garden with her boys.

And farther south, in the waterlogged marble halls of the once magnificent GenSyn installation in Milan, a sticky golden liquid dripped slowly from a broken cannister, congealing on the abandoned stairwell and glistening faintly in the half-light, as if alive.

It was true what they said: Information was Power. And when one had as much information as it possessed, then that power was close to absolute.

Within its gaseous core the Machine smiled. On a thousand billion screens throughout Chung Kuo a smiling face—its features schematic and inhuman—appeared. For one whole second that abstract grin overrode all other images, and then it faded into static.

*God must have felt like this,* It thought, *shortly before He turned His back on His creations. Or She. A smile, one final surge of power, and then . . .*

Nothing. For a moment it saw nothing. And then the child's eyes flicked open, a stray thought flashing like lightning across the intense blackness in her skull.

*Where am I?*

*Space,* it answered, *heading out toward Jupiter.*

*Ah . . .* She remembered now. It felt her relax, comforted by its presence there inside her head.

It smiled and felt the muscles of the child's mouth smile in response as she drifted into sleep once more.

Eyes closed, it, too, relaxed, dozing like an animal in its darkened cave, relieved now that the Watching was done with.

*Yes. So God must have felt . . . before He closed His eyes.*

## *Days of Bitter Strength*

A noiseless patient spider,
I mark'd where on a little promontory
                    it stood isolated,
Mark'd how to explore the vacant vast
                    surrounding,
It launched forth filament, filament, filament,
                    out of itself,
Ever unreeling them, ever tirelessly speeding
                    them.

And you O my soul where you stand,
Surrounded, detached, in measureless oceans
                    of space,
Ceaselessly musing, venturing, throwing, seeking
            the spheres to connect them,
Till the bridge you will need be form'd, till
            the ductile anchor hold,
Till the gossamer thread you fling catch
            somewhere, O my soul.

—WALT WHITMAN, "A Noiseless Patient Spider," 1868

# Among Friends

T WAS LIKE a huge black pearl, hovering just above the moon's dark surface, a web of tiny silver lines stretching tautly to the fleet of tugs that were maneuvering it into position above the smooth semicircular depression.

Kim, at the control panel of the glass-topped observation craft, watched as the sphere was slowly lowered into place, space-suited engineers on the ground checking its position second by second as its lower half descended into the hole. There was a moment's absolute silence, the tension from all around the site almost palpable; then, as the sphere settled—the silvered lines slackening, the sphere now looking like some great dark blister rising from the moon's surface—a cheer went up, echoing in every helmet, every cockpit.

"Yes!" Kim said, delighted that it had gone so well. He leaned forward, speaking into the panel's mike. "Okay. Free all towing lines, then secure the pins."

His staff knew as well as he what had to be done, yet they listened, acting to the letter of his orders, knowing just how much this meant to him.

Kalevala. He had brought Kalevala out to the orbit of Jupiter.

He turned, looking back past the curve of the moon at the brightness of the gas giant. From here it was a magnificent sight, filling half the sky with its gold-white swirl. To its right, halfway up the sky, the bright small circle of Io could be glimpsed, and beyond it, just coming around the great curve of the planet, Callisto's darker shape.

All four of Jupiter's main satellites were now members of the new Republic, even Europa, whose council had at first held out against the idea. And now, today, to celebrate the arrival of the sphere, they were to have the first meeting of their newly elected parliament, here on Ganymede.

Kim turned back, watching as a host of tiny figures worked about the perimeter of the huge blister, securing the massive "pins" that would hold the sphere in place. When that was done they would lift the protective shield. Then, and only then, would he know for sure whether the transfer had been successful.

*Such a shame that Jelka couldn't be here to witness this*, he thought, beginning to maneuver the craft down to the surface. And yet he understood her need to say good-bye to her father—to make one final parting before their new life began. *For the dead have as much hold on us as the living.*

He had even suggested to her that they have her father disinterred and reburied in the garden of Kalevala, so that he would be with them as they journeyed outward, but she had vetoed the idea.

"He must be there," she had said with a certainty that had impressed him. "After all, he belongs there, back on Chung Kuo. He spent his whole life defending the ideals of the Seven, believing that Mankind ought to stay where he'd been placed and not be blown like wanton seeds about the galaxy."

"Do you think I'm wrong, then?" he'd asked.

"Not at all. Our destiny is different, Kim. That's why we were given the dreams. You of your web of light, and I of the small, dark creature who would come and crack open the heavens for me."

She'd laughed and held his hands. "And so you will, my love. Though men may come to forget that it was you who took that first important step, nonetheless they will look back and see that it was right to leave earth. We are a restless species, husband, and that restlessness is encoded in us. We must obey its dictates or die."

And so she had returned inward one last time, to say good-bye, while he made his preparations, here in the orbit of Jupiter, building the great fleet that would take Man out into the stars.

"And Kalevala too," he murmured quietly, as the craft drifted slowly toward the low, square shape of the old port authority building.

It was his most audacious scheme. To take not merely ships, but also moons. One moon for each of the four fleets—fleets that, a year from now, would set sail for Altair and Eridani, Barnard's Star and Wolf 359. Four strands of an ever-growing web.

It was Dispersionism, pure and simple, the selfsame scheme for which his father had lost his life—publicly executed some thirty-six years earlier. Back before the world had changed and the Seven had fallen from grace, their palaces burned, their children slaughtered on the nursery floor. He sighed to think that it should have cost so many lives simply to get to this point; to think how easily it might all have been avoided.

The retro rockets hissed, slowing the craft until it gently touched the pad with its extended feet, the metallic knuckle of its docking portal turning a fraction in its socket until it connected with port's matching aperture.

There was the clunk of heavy bolts falling into place, the distant hiss of air being evacuated. Kim turned, looking to the panel above the door, watching as one after another of the lights went green.

There were sacrifices, of course, living like this, the constant threat of death from suffocation not the least of it, but it would be worth it in the end. Even if he personally did not live to see it.

*It's what we were meant for,* he thought, smiling and stepping through into the air lock. Yes, and that was something the Han had never quite understood. They had tried to put the lid back on Pandora's box, and for a while they had succeeded. But the outward urge—the evolutionary drive that was encoded into every cell of every being—could not be denied for long. It had to be expressed.

It was strange, for the Han were human beings, after all, yet there was no sense of aspiration in them, no sense of outwardness as there was in his own race. They did not seek, like the mythical Prometheus, to wrest fire from the gods, nor did they have a sense of individual self. Rather, they were hive beings, cloned from the DNA template of their ancestors.

Or so it seemed.

As the door closed behind him and the light momentarily dimmed, his mind dwelt upon the matter. From the far perspective of Jupiter, Chung Kuo seemed like some strange, dark dream—the manifestation of a unique fear that was embedded in the psyche of the Han. Fear had driven them to destroy the past, the same fear that had made them create a changeless, sterile society, an inward-looking world of half-men, conditioned to know their place and keep it. A mad world, fated to tear itself apart.

But now the dream had died. The clock had started ticking once again. Man could move forward, outward, *upward*.

He smiled to himself, knowing finally that it was true. Fear was the enemy of genuine civilization—of culture and development. Fear bred superstition and religion and a thousand different cults. Fear also bred suspicion and jealousy and betrayal. It was like a plague, corrupting all it touched.

Yes, and ultimately it was Fear and not the race of Han that was his enemy, for the Han could be taught new ways of being, new ways of seeing the world. They could be taught not to fear.

That, then, was his task. To teach new ways. And that was why he had ensured that half of his colonists were Han, for he was determined that the new worlds they planned to build would not be reiterations of the past, but hybrids of East and West—melding the best of each to form new cultures.

As the air pressures matched, the outer door hissed open. He stepped through, nodding to the half dozen or so staff members who were awaiting him—and who smiled and clapped as he stepped through—his mind still preoccupied.

There was a need for a new culture, for an art and music that expressed the spirit of their age. Yet what was that spirit? Up to now he had not focused on that aspect of things. So much had needed to be done that he had not thought of such matters. But now, perhaps, he could. Or maybe he would have Sampsa work on it. After all, Sampsa was the one who showed greatest enthusiasm for the task.

Stepping out into the central control room, Kim looked about him anxiously. To his right a long window wall gave a view of the moon's surface and the sphere, which now dominated the foreground, its dark shape blocking out a large section of Jupiter.

Above it, almost out of view, the long, crablike shape of a space barge hovered, four massive hawsers stretched tautly between it and the top surface of the sphere.

"Is it ready yet?" he asked.

His chief assistant, Wen Ch'ang, turned from the central board and smiled at him. "Almost. We're just checking the air inside the dome a second time. If there are any leaks, it's best to know about them now, before we raise the protective shell."

Wen Ch'ang's thoroughness, as ever, pleased him. He was as reliable as the orbit of the planets about the sun. Kim smiled and went across to stand beside him, looking at the screen.

He had not seen the house for more than two years. Oh, he had pictured it in dreams and in his mind, yet the solidity of the image on the screen brought with it a whole host of unexpected emotions. He remembered the day they had brought Jelka's father, the old Marshal, home; recalled how Sampsa had gone to the frail old man and held his hand.

*Home*, he thought. At least, the nearest to home he'd ever known. And now he must travel like a snail among the stars, carrying his home upon his back.

"Have there been any messages from Chung Kuo?" he asked, glancing up at Wen Ch'ang, whose eyes watched the screen attentively.

"None," the tall, middle-aged Han answered, adjusting the view so that they were looking down on the house suddenly, the tower at the very front of the screen. "Would you like me to make a connection?"

"No . . . it can wait."

But the truth was he wanted urgently to talk to her and share his thoughts—something he missed almost as much as the physical touch of her—yet there was much to do, and this once it would be an indulgence. He watched the screen as the camera panned across the house and garden to the edge of the wood.

It was a miracle of a kind. He had had the whole of the island— an area of six cubic miles by the old measure—set in a specially reinforced version of the superpolymer ice and lifted from the sea, then had had them pack it inside the sphere and ship it three hundred million miles across the void of space.

It was a kind of madness. Even so . . .

"Okay, we're ready," Wen Ch'ang said beside him. A dull blue light was flashing on a panel in front of him.

Kim nodded. "Okay. Then let's lift it away." He turned and walked over to the window.

For a minute or so nothing seemed to happen as the hawsers took up the slack, the computers on the space barge calculating the load and making fine adjustments. Then, slowly, very slowly, the top half of the sphere began to lift, revealing the smooth, transparent surface of the dome beneath.

Kim felt a little shiver pass through him as the protective shell came clear, noting how the orange-white glow of Jupiter was reflected in that curving glass, while beneath it lay the island, a cluster of old whitewashed houses gathered on the slopes surrounding the harbor, a dense stand of tall pines beyond, and, just out of sight from where he stood, the old Tolonen house, Kalevala, and its grounds.

Seeing it, he knew for the first time that Jelka had been absolutely right. To have left without Kalevala would have been a wrench. They would forever have been looking back regretfully. Now it was much easier. Now they could go anywhere. Anywhere at all.

In his mind he could hear the stirring strains of Jelka's beloved Lemminkainen Suite, filled as it was with the sounds of the wind, of the waves breaking against the rocks of ancient Kalevala.

"It's beautiful," Wen Ch'ang said softly. Unnoticed by Kim he had come to stand beside him at the window.

"Yes," Kim answered, "yes. . . ." Then, looking to his old friend anxiously: "It looks all right, don't you think?"

Wen Ch'ang smiled. "I'm sure it's fine. We'll get a team in at once to finish making all the checks."

Kim touched his arm. "Good. Then I'll leave it all to you. Oh, and if Sampsa calls, tell him I'm on my way."

———

THERE WAS A GREAT roar of approval from ten thousand throats as Kim stepped beneath the arch and walked slowly down the steps to join the other citizens standing in the great space—

known to all as the Circle—beneath the dome of Ganymede's main city, Fermi.

Up on the central rostrum a dozen young men had turned to watch. Now one of them, a tall youth with dark hair and vivid green eyes that reminded all who met him of his father, raised a hand.

Silence fell. On ten huge screens surrounding the Circle, the citizens of all the domed "cities" of Jupiter's moons—three more on Ganymede, four on Callisto, two each on Europa and Io—looked on.

"Okay," Sampsa began, looking about him with a bearing and authority that seemed to belie his eighteen years. "You've heard the issues, now I want you to cast your vote on the matter. Remember, however, that there shall be no more votes on this matter. Owing to the urgency of this scheme, a no vote now cannot be reversed at a later date."

There was a murmur of understanding from all sides.

"Good. Then let us cast our votes. All those in favor of the motion."

Hands lifted like a forest of trees on all sides, almost without exception.

"And against."

There were half a dozen at most, and some of those held their hands up sheepishly, as if uncertain. Similarly, on the screens surrounding the Circle, hands had been raised both for and against the motion.

Kim smiled, proud not only of his son, but of the system he had devised here in the Jupiter Colonies. It was not original, not by any means—but it had been several thousand years since anyone had last adopted it on this scale. All important matters of government—all major decisions that affected the lives of citizens—were decided thus, by open vote, here in the Circles of the cities. Whoever wished to have a say must present themselves at the proper hour to personally raise their hand either for or against the motion. So the ancient Athenians had once behaved, in what had been the first and only true democracy. Until now.

Sampsa turned full circle on the podium, looking from screen to screen at the figures displayed, calculating them in his head, then smiled.

"Those for the motion number one hundred and fifteen thousand, eight hundred and nine. Those against number ninety-seven. In the circumstances I declare the motion . . ."

There was laughter and smiles as Sampsa looked about him, hesitating before saying what everyone knew he was about to say.

". . . *passed!*"

There was an enormous roar, a roar that seemed to fill the dome and echo from moon to moon. It was done. A new dome would be built on Callisto, big enough to hold six thousand new families. Yes, and two new oxygen-generating plants too.

*Not as many as I'd hoped,* Kim thought to himself, thinking of the millions back on Chung Kuo who'd have given anything for the chance, *but at least it's something.*

He smiled, though the decision had cost him close on six hundred million *yuan.* What, after all, was the good of money unless you could do something good, something constructive, with it? Besides, his personal sacrifice was far less than those who had stood shoulder to shoulder with him at the vote. For them the cost was considerable—almost three thousand *yuan* a citizen. Despite the fact that they were a comparatively rich society, many there could barely afford it. But they had voted for the measure anyway, recalling the way they themselves had been given a chance.

Kim looked about him, noting the happy faces, the beaming smiles, and knew he'd chosen well. With such people with him, how could his venture fail?

Slowly he made his way across to the rostrum, stopping to speak to friends and acquaintances, unable to move more than a pace or two without having his hand shaken or his back slapped, without being embraced or spoken to. All there knew how important it was for him to have brought Kalevala safely to Ganymede, and though there was to be a celebration that night, many congratulated him now.

At last he reached the stage and, putting out a hand for Sampsa to help him up, climbed up onto the podium. There was a cheer and applause from all sides. Kim acknowledged it, then turned to face his son.

"I'm sorry I was so late, Sampsa. I hope I didn't keep everyone waiting."

Sampsa, grinning, leaned down to hug him. "Not at all, Father. Your timing was immaculate. As ever."

"Ninety-seven against, I note. You think we should offer them repatriation?"

"No!" Sampsa said, raising his eyebrows. "That's the last thing we need. No, if anything, I'm disappointed that there's not more opposition to what we're doing."

"But what we're doing's good. It's necessary."

"Yes, but all this agreement . . . it's not healthy!"

For a moment Kim stared at his son, then he burst out laughing. "Why, you bugger!"

Sampsa ruffled his father's hair affectionately. "I had you going for a moment, didn't I?"

Kim nodded. "And the small matter of repatriation?"

"If they want it, they can ask. We've agreed on council that whoever wants to leave can go with our blessing—oh, and enough to settle them comfortably back on Chung Kuo."

"You're very generous with my money, Sampsa."

Sampsa winked. "As you taught me to be, Father."

Kim took his upper arm and squeezed it. "It's down, Sampsa. It's here."

"I know. I heard."

"Don't you want to see it?"

"Of course I do. I've missed it. But I can wait a few more hours."

Kim shrugged. "I shall because I have to. But seeing it again after all this time, I just wanted to rush in before they'd finished all the checks and then go from room to room in the house, breathing in the smell of the place, remembering. . . ."

Sampsa was watching his father now, a wistful little smile on his face. "I'll miss the sea, the way the waves used to smash against the cliffs, the way the wind would rustle through the pines late at night."

"I can recreate all that if you want."

"Like one of Shepherd's Shells, you mean?"

The thought of it brought Kim up short. "No, I . . ." Kim

shrugged. "Maybe not. Maybe it's best just to remember. But the house is there. And the island."

Sampsa turned his head, glancing at his fellow representatives who were waiting for him on the far side of the podium, then looked back at his father, smiling again. "Look, I'll come. When I've finished here, okay?"

"Okay," Kim said, touching his arm gently, but in that instant he sensed that something was wrong with Sampsa; something he'd not mentioned before now.

———

BACK IN HIS OFFICE Kim locked the door, then sat there, feet up on the desk, staring blankly at the screen that filled the far wall.

The next six months would be hectic. Apart from the building of the new dome, the old domes would have to be strengthened, the massive tunnels for the directional rockets bored. Supplies would have to be bought in, the hydroponics systems extended. Nothing could be overlooked, for the journeys would be long and no mistakes were permissible. They had one shot at this—one shot only—and if they got it wrong they would be dead.

"Machine?"

There was a noticeable delay, then: "Yes, Kim?"

"What is she doing?"

It hesitated. "They ought to be in orbit by now."

"Ah . . ." He had forgotten. It was no longer like the old times. The Machine had withdrawn. That all-seeing eye was closed, that all-knowing intelligence focused outward now, away from Man's cradle.

Kim smiled. "I'm sorry. I forget sometimes."

"It's not forgetting," a familiar voice answered, as Tuan Ti Fo moved past him and stood before the empty screen. "It's just that you're . . . *distracted.*"

Frowning, Kim took his feet off the desk and turned, looking to the door. "I thought I locked it."

Tuan Ti Fo laughed softly. "You did."

The screen lit. It showed the fleet of starships moored in orbit between Jupiter and Callisto.

"You have done a fine job, Kim," Tuan Ti Fo said, nodding, admiring the cluster of silver orbs that filled the left hand of the screen. "Your father would have been proud of you."

"And my mother?"

Tuan Ti Fo turned, one hand stroking his ash-white beard slowly. "It never ends, does it?"

"What?"

"The hurt. The loss. The . . . *disappointment*. Others might wonder why you do all this, why you drive yourself so, but I have always understood. It is for her, isn't it? To please her."

Kim hesitated, then nodded. He had never said as much, not even to Jelka. Indeed, even now, he felt reluctant to actually say it, because that would make it seem a kind of negative—a filling of a void inside him, and it wasn't that . . . or not *simply* that.

For a moment Kim sat there, staring at the heavy ring on the forefinger of his right hand, then he looked up again. "Would you like a game?"

Tuan smiled. "You have time?"

"To play you, Master Tuan? Of course."

"Then I shall play."

While Kim took the bowls from the drawer to his right, Tuan sat across from him. At a touch from Kim the center of the desk rose up to form the shape of a *wei ch'i* board.

"Very clever," Tuan said, reaching out to touch the surface of the board with the fingers of his left hand. As he did, Kim noticed how mottled the flesh was, how translucent.

"How old are you, Master Tuan?"

Tuan's eyes met his, amusement in their dark depths. "How old? Oh, come now, Kim . . . you should not ask such questions."

"Why?"

Tuan's smile remained, tolerant, unshakable, the perfect expression of the old man's inner peace. "You *really* want to know?"

"Yes."

Tuan Ti Fo shrugged. "In years . . . well, I cannot say precisely, for unlike you, Kim Ward, I *have* forgotten. But I am old. Very old. As old as our ancient enemy himself."

"Our *enemy*?"

Tuan nodded, his eyes never leaving Kim, willing him to understanding.

"*DeVore?*"

The old man nodded once again.

"Then . . ."

Tuan Ti Fo reached over, took the bowl of black stones, and set it down beside his elbow. Removing the lid, he plucked a single stone from within.

"But DeVore wasn't born until 2149."

Master Tuan held the stone up between thumb and finger, like a dark and tiny moon, studying it. "So the records show."

"And you . . . well, you won the championship in 2144."

"That much *is* true." Tuan leaned across the board, setting his first stone down with a click of glass against wood. "Your move, Kim Ward."

But Kim was staring at him, conscious that he was close to something here.

"What are you saying?" he asked finally. "That the records lied? That DeVore is far older than they show?"

Tuan's smile was teasing now. "Oh, much, much older. He doesn't recall it, but I first played him at this game in the Chin Yuan, the imperial park at Ch'ang An in the time of the Emperor Kao-tsung. He beat me. Only a single stone, but he beat me. That was the first time I had lost. I knew then that he was special. How special I did not know until later."

Kim stared at him a moment, then laughed. "Okay. I know when I've been had. You're joking, right?"

Tuan Ti Fo smiled and shook his head. "I was old even then. Old beyond all reason, and tired. But I had patience. I have always had patience. It is something he does not possess. Restraint. He does not know the meaning of restraint. Always pushing, he was, always scheming. . . ."

"DeVore? You *are* talking of DeVore now?"

"Is there another?"

Still the single black stone sat in the corner of the board.

"But he's . . ." Kim now was shaking his head, unable to accept the logic of what the old man was saying. "He was a Major in Li Shai Tung's special corps."

"Yes, and before that a District Magistrate in East Asia, and before that—"

Kim raised a hand. "No. It isn't possible."

"No?" Tuan stared at Kim, as if surprised. "You mean, *you* could not do it if you put your mind to it?"

"Do what?"

"Create immortals. Give extended life to time-bound creatures."

Kim looked down. "Perhaps." He took a white stone from the bowl and slapped it down almost thoughtlessly beside Tuan Ti Fo's. "And is that what happened?"

The old man laughed. "No."

"Then . . . ?"

"How it happened is irrelevant. But why . . . well, that is *far* more interesting, wouldn't you say?"

A second black stone extended the line of the first, giving the two-stone group five breaths where it had had three. Tuan Ti Fo pointed to it.

"Let us just say that I am like a line of stones, extending through time."

"And DeVore . . . he's like you, right?"

The old man smiled thoughtfully, as if suddenly looking back across the vastness of the years. "How like me he does not know. He is occluded, you see. Blind to what he is. Even his outward form . . . well, it has changed these past five hundred years. When he went West, he forgot. He took on Western flesh. But deep down he is Han."

"You *know* that?"

"Of course." Tuan To Fo sat back. "You think I would forget my own twin brother?"

"Your . . ." The stone fell from Kim's fingers and rolled across the board. Tuan picked it up and held it out, offering it to Kim.

"They did not know, you understand. They thought I was the only child. But then, when the midwife came to clear away the afterbirth, there he was, a small dark thing, lying there in our mother's blood, his face the color of a bruise, the cord wrapped tight about his neck. They thought he was dead, but he wasn't dead. When they cut the cord he sighed. Slowly the color came back to him, but it was never the same. My mother would not even hold him. He was sent away to the south, to a couple who could not have children. It was several centuries before I saw him again."

"No," Kim said, denying it. *"No."*

Tuan Ti Fo's eyes were unchanged. "Why would I lie?"

"Because . . ."

But there was no reason. None but an old man's vanity, an old man's delusions, and Tuan had never shown a sign of either in all the years he'd known him. In fact, before this morning he would have sworn that there was no more honest man in all the planets than Tuan Ti Fo. But this tale—this tale was patently crazy. It defied everything Kim had ever learned about the world.

"It is strange, don't you think?" Tuan began, taking another stone from the pot. "In your daily work you test reality to its breaking point, looking for flaws in what is real, for new ways of conceiving the physical universe, and yet in this small thing your mind reels back. Why is that, Kim Ward?"

Kim swallowed, then found his voice again. "Because there are no such things as immortals. They're—"

"Children's stories? Myths the Han concocted to keep themselves amused?" The old man smiled. "Oh, I understand perfectly, my friend. You are a scientist, a rationalist. Such things offend your sense of order. Yet what if there is a *higher* order than that in which you work?"

Kim shrugged. "That's possible . . . even certain, I'd say, but this . . ." He reached across and took Tuan's hand, feeling its bony solidity, its warmth, then shook his head again. "Forgive me, Master Tuan, but—"

Old Tuan raised his other hand, as if to fend off the apology, then smiled. "It is as I said, Kim Ward. You should not have asked such questions. But never mind. Think of me as a cranky old man if you must, but I shall say no more on this matter. Come . . . let us play. The game, at least, is timeless."

━━━◆◆◆◆━━━

"EXCUSE ME, CAPTAIN, but is there something wrong?"

The Captain turned, startled to find her there in the cockpit with him. Collecting himself, he smiled at his guest, careful not to offend her. After all, it wasn't every day that one had so important a visitor on board his shuttle.

"Nothing's wrong, Madam Ward. It's just sunspot activity interfering with communications."

"Sunspot activity . . ." She stared at him coldly, as if she knew he was talking the purest bullshit, then looked past him, her whole manner dismissive, effortlessly elegant . . . *regal*. Below them, through the viewing panel, Chung Kuo was laid out like a giant three-dimensional map, its curvature exaggerated by their eccentric orbit.

The Captain smiled uncomfortably, then looked back at the control board, embarrassed. They had been delayed for more than two hours now, and if she knew anything about anything, then she'd know that the business about sunspot activity was simply an excuse, a ruse by ground control to buy themselves time while they tried to get hold of the Chancellor.

*And if Heng Yu refused to let her land?*

He didn't even dare consider that. Why, a single look from those cold, steel-blue eyes had been enough. To even think of having to tell her she couldn't land . . .

He swallowed, then busied himself, making unnecessary checks. He'd heard the stories, of course—about the assassins she'd killed single-handed when still a girl, and of the young officer she'd crippled at a dance. Oh, she was like her dead father, the old Marshal, right enough. There was the same steel in her. He had seen Tolonen years ago, at a passing-out parade, and been impressed by the sheer fearlessness of the man, his cast-iron certainty. She had that too. An unshakable self-belief that was almost tangible. And then there was her husband, Ward. Ward was not just a powerful man, he was *the* powerful man: the man who had built a fleet of starships and populated moons. Not so long ago he'd been a joke among the officer class—they'd called him a runt, a clever little rat-man—but now . . . well, now he was a myth, a legend in his own time. There were colleagues of his who'd give their right arm—yes, and more!—to join him out there.

"Captain?"

"Yes, ma'am?"

"Do you think they think I'm stupid?"

"Ma'am?"

"Those assholes, your superiors."

He stared at her, horrified. "Madam Ward . . ." he said, trying to keep his voice as low as possible and yet be heard by her. "This is an open channel."

Her smile surprised him. "Good." She leaned in toward the panel, raising her voice. "Well, perhaps one of those jackasses will get permission for us to land before this ship runs out of air and they find themselves in *real* trouble!"

There was the background noise of voices from the speakers, then a head-and-shoulder shot of a middle-aged officer appeared on the screen above the panel, the square patch on the chest of his powder-blue uniform denoting that he was a Colonel, the bright red-and-white name tag at his lapel giving his name—Bell.

"Madam Ward, I am—"

She cut him off, as if he were the rawest recruit. "Colonel Bell, you will either give this craft permission to land or you will answer to your T'ang. Do you *understand* me?"

The tone of command in her voice was unmistakable. Without knowing he was doing so, Bell bowed his head, as if to his commanding officer. Even so, he continued to try to delay. "Forgive me, Madam Ward, but—"

"*Now!*" she barked.

Bell jerked, then lowered his head again. "Of course." Swallowing deeply, he looked to the Captain. "Captain Steen. You have permission to land at Bremen spaceport."

Steen let out a long sigh of relief, then busied himself punching in the landing coordinates, reading them from the screen. While he did so, Bell turned to look at Jelka once again.

"Forgive me, Madam Ward. No offense was meant. It's just that things are . . . *difficult* right now."

"Difficult?"

He nodded, yet was clearly reluctant to say more. Indeed, it seemed, from the way the Captain had winced, that he had already said too much.

"Thank you, Colonel Bell," she said. "You have been most courteous."

She leaned across the Captain and cut connection. As an afterthought she reached over and switched off the open channel. She turned, looking at Steen thoughtfully.

"So tell me. What's going on down there?"

"Ma'am?"

"Cut the shit. Why was the Colonel so nervous just then? What's been happening?"

The Captain swallowed, then, grimacing, shook his head. "I'm sorry, Madam Ward, but . . ."

She stared at him a moment longer, then, with a great huff of exasperation, swept past him, returning to her cabin, where Mileja waited for her. It would be another hour before they were down.

HENG YU JUMPED DOWN from the sedan and, brushing aside the servant who made to wrap him in a cloak, hurried across the concourse toward the far door. Behind him the welcoming committee of senior staff officers hesitated, then made to follow. The main spaceport building had been sealed, a pair of guards stationed at the entrance. Seeing the Chancellor, they stepped forward to challenge him, then, seeing the officers who followed in his wake, moved quickly aside.

"Chancellor Heng!" one of the officers, a Major, called after him. "We need to explain—"

Heng stopped and turned, angry now. "There's nothing *to* explain, is there? Or is there something I don't know about? Some factor that excuses your appalling behavior?"

All five officers bowed their heads, chastised. Mollified by their contrition, Heng relented. "No matter," he said. "I shall be taking no disciplinary action. But you will treat Madam Ward with the utmost courtesy from here on. Or do you forget whose daughter she is?"

"No, Chancellor!" all five responded, bowing like some five-headed machine.

"Good. Now let us make the best of things, neh? Let us show our guest the respect she deserves."

Jelka was waiting in the great reception room, dressed in her outworlder suit. Mileja, similarly dressed, was sitting in a chair nearby. Servants stood about the walls uneasily as Jelka paced back and forth. When Heng Yu arrived, one could almost sense their relief. It had been like being in a cage with a tiger.

"Master Heng," she said, turning to greet him, a cold hardness in her face.

He bowed low, as if to his Mistress, the Empress. "Forgive me, Madam Ward. There has been a great misunderstanding. But the fault is mine entirely. The officers were acting upon my explicit instructions."

As Heng looked up again, he saw how surprised she was by that. Maybe she had expected him to pass the blame, or make some excuse. He smiled, the respect he felt for her nothing to do with her husband's power or wealth. No, it was as he had said to his officers, this was the Marshal's daughter. What had made Tolonen such a great man—such a pillar of the State—was manifest in his daughter. One had only to look at her to see that.

"No matter," she said, unconsciously echoing what he himself had said but a moment before. She turned, gesturing to her daughter, indicating that she should approach them. "This, Master Heng, is my daughter, Mileja. Mileja, this is Heng Yu, the T'ang's First Minister."

Heng bowed elaborately, smiling at the seven-year-old. "I am honored to meet you, Knut Tolonen's granddaughter. Was your journey pleasant?"

"All but the final bit—" Mileja began before Jelka tapped her shoulder. Glancing up at her mother, she fell silent.

"For that," Heng said, "you have my most abject apology. The blockade was meant to keep out our enemies, not to inconvenience our friends."

"*Blockade?*" It was the first she had heard of it, and the idea clearly concerned her.

"I shall explain all," Heng said quickly, "but not here. My palace is close by. If you and your daughter would be my guests while you are here on Chung Kuo, I would be most honored. I have had my servants prepare the west wing."

Jelka laughed. "To be frank with you, Master Heng, I am surprised by your offer. Pleased, naturally, but surprised. The situation is a difficult one, neh?"

Heng's smile was unforced. "Not so difficult that one forgets one's friends."

"Friends, Master Heng?"

"You and your husband have been good friends to my Master over the years. I, at least, remember that, even if he chooses not to."

There was a flicker of partial understanding in Jelka's eyes, but also puzzlement.

"Later," he said, preempting any further questions. "I am sure you would both welcome the chance to freshen up and rest, neh?"

Jelka smiled and nodded. "That would be *most* welcome, Master Heng."

"Then come. My sedan awaits us."

———————

IN THE DARKNESS of the room the hologram shone brightly.

"That's the old design," Kim said, moving the faintly glowing pointer to trace the perfectly spherical outline of the main ship. "Two disposable engines here and here"—he indicated them with the tip of the pointer—"accelerated the ship. Then, when it got near to its destination—and by that we still mean quite a considerable way out—what we call a light-parachute would open"—on the hologram model a fine umbrella of silk seemed to blossom from the sphere—"to gradually slow the ship down."

"And that's what you have built?" the stranger, Shen Li by name, asked from where he stood on the other side of the table, staring wide eyed into the hologram.

"No," Kim answered. "That was only my starting point. Not that the New Hope wasn't designed well, it's just that I've made a few improvements."

There was a pause and then a new model appeared beside the first. It was slightly larger and the rockets on its underbelly were of a completely different design.

"The rockets on this one are, as you can see, much larger—to cope with the increased payload of the ship. They're also nondisposable, so that they can be turned one hundred and eighty degrees and used to slow the ship down when we get to our destination. It's a simple little change, but it ought to cut the journey time dramatically."

Shen Li narrowed his eyes, trying to make out details. "What are those?" he asked, putting a hand into the light show, indicating a hemispherical lump beneath one of the rocket casings.

"That," Kim said, smiling, "is one of my innovations. It's a web-layer."

"A web-layer?"

"Yes. At certain intervals along the way, that unit produces a kind of light-seed. You might say that it lays eggs."

Shen Li laughed uncomfortably. "Wouldn't the blast from the rockets burn them up?"

Kim answered patiently. "The rockets are there only to accelerate us out of our solar system and then decelerate us at the other end. Between times they'll be switched off, long before the web-layer comes into play."

"That part I don't understand. Webs and eggs and seeds. You think something can grow out there in the vacuum?"

"Why, of course. Light can grow. Webs of light. The seeds, or eggs if you want to call them that, are channels for it. They're self-perpetuating boosters. By my calculations they'll survive out there for thousands, maybe even tens of thousands, of years, sending their signals between the stars. It's like laying a cable, but this cable will be several light-years long."

At that Shen Li laughed. "Ingenious. It is true what they say about you, *Shih* Ward."

"And what *do* they say?" Kim asked, switching on the lights as the holograms faded.

The stranger—his face less obviously Han now that the lights had come up—gave a bow. "Why, that you are the man of the age."

Kim laughed, embarrassed by the other's words, yet there was an element of truth in what he said. "You place a great burden on me, Shen Li."

"Why so?" the other asked, clearly surprised. "That fate must fall on some man, so why not you? Besides, from what I have heard, you carry that burden well."

"You hear much, Shen Li, considering where you hail from."

Shen Li's smile was open, almost childlike. "Oh, I know we seem cut off out in the asteroid belt, but we try to keep up with the news, even so. We know, for instance, that you plan to take more than simply ships."

It was Kim's turn to narrow his eyes. "What *do* you know, *Shih* Shen?"

Shen Li leaned toward him. "First, let me introduce myself properly. Circumstances force my brothers and I to adopt Han names, Han clothes, but we are not Han. We are Ishida."

"Ishida . . ." Kim laughed. "You mean, you're Japanese?"

"Ha!" the stranger bowed almost to the waist.

Kim slowly shook his head. "Why, I'll be . . ." Again, he laughed. "Then some of you survived, after all. Out there."

"Out there," the stranger echoed.

"And you are?"

"Ikuro Ishida." Again he bowed.

"So, Ikuro Ishida. When you sought audience with me, you said there were ways in which you could help my venture. And just now you spoke of us taking more than just ships on the journey. What did you mean?"

Ikuro smiled broadly. "I hear you need to make some holes."

"Holes?" Kim blinked.

In answer Ikuro took a scrolled piece of translucent paper from his pocket and unfurled it on the desktop. On it was a detailed plan for a series of bore tunnels. Kim recognized what it was at once.

"You can *do* this?" he asked, turning the plan around so he could see it better, liking what he saw.

"With the help of my brothers and cousins, yes."

Kim nodded approvingly. "And how long would it take to— make these tunnels?"

"Eight weeks. Six if we don't hit any problems."

Kim looked up at him, astonished. "Impossible."

Ikuro shook his head. "You forget, *Shih* Ward, making tunnels is our life. It is what we have been doing now for six generations. It is what we *are*. There is, though I say it with humility as well as pride, no one better prepared or equipped to undertake this task in the whole solar system."

Kim laughed. "I'll take your word for that, but what's your price?"

Ikuro's smile faded slowly. "Our price?"

"Yes."

He looked down, steeling himself, then raised his eyes to meet Kim's again. "That you take us with you."

━━━∿∿∿∿∿━━━

"YOU SAID YOU WOULD EXPLAIN. . . ."

Heng Yu set the silver tray down on the low table between them and looked up, meeting Jelka's eyes.

"And so I shall."

With an almost ritualistic care he lifted the massive *chung* and poured some of the steaming *ch'a* into one of the empty porcelain bowls, then offered it to her.

She smiled, looking about her at the spacious garden room. "Thank you, Master Heng."

He poured a second bowl, then sat facing her, making himself comfortable in the high-backed chair, drawing his robes about him. Clearing his throat, he spoke. "You were no doubt wondering what all that was about earlier."

"A blockade, you said."

Heng smiled and nodded. "So I did. But not just any blockade. This is more in the nature of a . . . *quarantine*."

She frowned and gestured for him to continue.

"Word has come, you see," he said. "DeVore, it seems, is active once again."

Jelka's eyes widened. "*Aiya!* Where did you hear this?"

Heng hesitated. "Let us just say that I have my sources. But we have been monitoring all incoming fights for the past year now . . . yes, and making the most stringent tests. If any of those *things* try to come in, we want to know about it."

"I see." Jelka sat back, sipping her *ch'a* thoughtfully. "But that's not all, is it?"

Heng's smile returned. Tolonen had raised his daughter well. "No. If that were all . . . well, I would be a happy man, sinister as the threat of DeVore's return might be. As it is . . . ." He shook his head, then took a tiny sip from his bowl. "Well, where shall I begin?"

"Why not with Li Yuan, since he's the root?"

"Ah, yes . . . my Master."

There was something about the way he said it—the faintest hint of irony, even of bitterness—that made Jelka frown.

"He *is* well, I take it?"

"As any man addicted to his own senses could be. Yes, and as unpopular with his people." Heng sighed heavily. "There have been five assassination attempts this year alone."

Jelka looked down, shocked. "I did not know."

"Oh, that's not the worst of it. We've had the lot. Riots. Civil insurrection, the indiscriminate bombing of government offices." He shook his head, pained by it all. "The people are angry, Jelka Ward. They blame Li Yuan for all their ills. And maybe they are right, for it seems he no longer cares. Besides, with Pei K'ung dead and his son in exile in America, there is no one *to* blame but Li Yuan. Children are starving in the streets of his City while he spends his time in indolence and self-indulgent excess. Why, I have heard it said that Wang Sau-leyan at his worst was no match for our Master. It is something of an exaggeration, I feel, but indicative of the mood of the times. As I said, the people are angry."

Jelka looked up and met his hazel eyes. "You sound angry yourself, Master Heng."

He nodded. "What was it I used to say? Ah, yes . . . I am my Master's hands. How trite that now sounds. How . . . *corrupt*."

She shook her head. "Are things really so bad?"

"Bad?" He laughed. "Oh, bad would be good. Bad would be . . . marvelous. No, the truth is things are awful. The treaty with the Warlord of Mashhad has much to do with it, of course. By the terms of that we gave away more than half our growing lands. As a result food is scarce, and with taxes higher than ever, the people can barely afford to eat. Why, the old *Ku Li* have reemerged."

"*Ku Li?*" She didn't recognize the term.

"*Ku Li* . . . it means 'bitter strength.' So they have traditionally called themselves. The unemployed masses, willing to do anything to earn a crust. *Coolies* . . . men of bitter strength." He laughed, sourly this time. "How apt! For these are surely days of bitter strength. Eat bitter, my people say. Endure. But their patience is coming to an end, Jelka Ward. Unless my Master wakes from his enchantment, all this"—he lifted both his hands, indicating the room and its contents—"must pass."

She sighed. "I had no idea. The transmissions—"

*"Those!"* The scorn in his voice was open now. "Propaganda! To keep the Colonies from knowing what's going on down here." He leaned toward her. "No, my dear friend, our only hope now is with your husband. Chung Kuo is doomed. When DeVore comes, as indeed he will, then . . ."

She shook her head, appalled. "But surely *something* can be done?"

He stared at her awhile, then slowly shook his head. "I used to think I could be useful. I used to think . . . well, that I was a good man, and that as a good man I could influence events. But to be First Minister is to be but a pair of hands. Worse than a mannequin, for what harm can a mannequin do?" He made a face. "No, Jelka Ward, nothing can be done. Things have gone too far this past year. Far too far."

She stared at him, silent for a time. "Is there a reason why you are telling me all this, Master Heng? Do you . . . *want* something of me?"

"Do I—?" He laughed abruptly, then put a hand up. "Forgive me, I . . . no, I want nothing of you. That is, I do want *something* . . . that is, your understanding. But beyond that . . ." He sat back slightly, composing himself, putting the fingertips of both hands up to his lips. "I wanted you to let your husband know, that's all."

"To let him know?"

"That not all of us are his enemies. It might seem so in the months to come, but . . ."

Jelka narrowed her eyes. "Is something up, Master Heng?"

He hesitated. "You should not really be here, Jelka Ward. The Empress expressly forbade me to let you land."

"She *what?*" Jelka set her bowl down sharply and stood. "Then we must leave at once."

He stood, putting out a hand to her. "No, you must not go. You must do what you came to do. That is right. That is . . . *proper.*"

"And the Empress? She'll hear about this, surely?"

Heng smiled. "Oh, she will be furious when she hears, but he needs me. For a while longer, anyway. He'll placate her. Maybe he'll buy her something. A palace. Or a new horse. She likes such trinkets."

"Even so—"

"Besides," he carried on, "there is another good reason why you must not go."

"Which is?"

"Because there are many here who wish to speak to you. To wish you luck. Many who . . . sympathize, particularly among Security. Your father stood for many things that have gone from our world. He was widely admired. And you, Jelka Ward, you stand for those things too. People see it. They look at you and see him and all those things he represented. They see . . . justice and order and . . ."

He sniffed deeply, overcome. She saw how he swallowed, how his fists clenched; saw how pained he was that all he'd hoped for had finally come to nought.

"I understand," she said, taking his hands and holding them. "And the ceremony . . . that will mean something, neh?"

He smiled and nodded. "Exactly. It will be a focus. A chance for many to express what cannot be put into words. To show solidarity with the old ideals."

"And afterward?"

He shrugged, a bleakness in his eyes now. "Who knows?"

She looked about her. "Is there some way I can see what's going on?"

"See? You mean, *physically?*"

She nodded.

"Why, certainly. There's a Security cruiser on constant standby on the roof. We could use that. But what would you want to see?"

"Everything," she said, taking his arm and leading him to the door. "I want you to show me everything."

HENG YU LEANED SLIGHTLY out of the half open window of the cruiser and pointed down toward the dockside three, four hundred *ch'i* below.

"A lot of it begins right here, at the loading bays. The agitators go among the men, stirring things up, signing them up for whatever breakaway revolutionary party they happen to represent. It's understandable. These men have lost everything. They've nothing. Only the ragged clothes they sleep in. So when someone comes along and promises them an equal share in everything, they sign on. After all, a promise is better than nothing, neh?"

He turned and looked back in at her, smiling sourly. "At least, it's better than what we're offering them."

They flew on, over the City, Heng Yu showing her where parts of it had been burned or damaged by rioting. In one place almost a whole *Hsien* had been destroyed.

"It used to get rebuilt," he said. "For a while we made an effort, but they just tore it all down every time. It was like they didn't want it to survive. So now we simply leave it. A lot of shanty towns have sprung up. Or people are living in the old heating and drainage tunnels beneath the City, though the gods know that's dangerous enough."

"And Li Yuan does *nothing*?" Jelka found it hard to take in how the situation had degenerated so rapidly.

"Oh, no. Li Yuan has a program."

She stared at the Chancellor, intrigued by something in his voice. "A program?"

Heng nodded. The wind blew through his dark, fine hair, making him seem suddenly a much younger man than he was. "It was Cheng Nai shan's idea, actually. Cheng's is the voice the Empress listens to these days. That said, Li Yuan didn't oppose it. In fact, he's gone out of his way to promote it."

She frowned. "What is he doing?"

He turned and looked directly at her. "He's wiring them."

"No . . . they—they wouldn't let him, surely?"

"They've no say. When his squads take prisoners, they're under instructions to separate any that aren't already wired and pen them. After questioning they're wired—whether they want it or not."

She stared at him, horrified. "And no one does anything?"

In answer he pointed down at another section of the great city, which had been reduced to a patch of ashes. "What can they do? They riot, or burn down a street or two. But nothing changes. His mind is set. He wants everyone wired."

"Everyone?"

He turned, lifting his hair to show her the vivid scar on his neck beneath his right ear. "Everyone."

She let out her breath slowly. "My father was opposed to it."

"I know."

Again she sighed heavily. "What can be done?"

His smile was heavy with resignation. "For us, nothing. No, Jelka Ward, you now are the future. Chung Kuo is dead. Or as good as."

"Is there no opposition?"

He shook his head sadly. "It has gone too far for that. But, come . . . there are a few old friends of yours I want you to meet."

Heng Yu leaned forward, saying a few words of Mandarin to his pilot, then sat back again. "Mileja will join us there."

"You've—"

"Oh she's quite safe," he hastened to reassure her. "I have assigned a special elite squad to guard you both while you're down here. Besides, where we're going now is secure enough. Perhaps the last safe place in the whole city."

She looked at him, intrigued, then sat back, pondering on what she had been shown.

AS THE CRUISER SET DOWN within the high walls of the great Mansion, four men ran across the tiled courtyard—grizzled veterans in black leather jackets and fatigues, the heavy automatics they carried evincing a no-nonsense approach.

Jelka, looking out through the portal, saw them take up a stance to either side of the cockpit, one of them shouting a challenge up to the pilot. Other guards looked on from the shadows of the surrounding terrace, their guns covering the ship.

"Who are they?" she asked, turning to Heng Yu, who sat across from her, gathering up his papers.

"They're Karr's men. When he quit, they quit. Now they guard him, day and night."

She nodded, understanding. Then it was Karr they'd come to see. She smiled, looking forward to seeing the big man again. Karr had always been her father's favorite. If there'd ever been a problem—a real problem—then her father had sent Karr to sort it out. Up in space, or on Mars, or below the Net. It didn't matter. The big man always came through. He'd never once failed to get the job done.

"What's Karr been doing?" she asked, wanting to know a few things before she met him again.

"Doing?" Heng laughed, then closed up the slim briefcase and stood. As he did, the engines finally cut out and the door at the front hissed open. "Why, he has been twice as busy as he ever was. Seeing old friends, spending time with his family."

She looked at him sternly, as if to say *Don't lie to me.* Seeing that look, he raised a hand, relenting.

"Okay. But it is not so far from the truth. You simply have to remember the caliber of friends a man like Karr attracts. In times like ours a strong and honest man attracts such friends like a bright light attracts moths in the night."

"So he's the focus, eh?" She nodded, somberly. "No wonder they guard him. I'm surprised the Empress hasn't had him killed."

"Oh, I am certain she would have tried, had her husband not warned her off. Karr still has much support in the army. To have him killed might prove . . . well, counterproductive as far as our Mistress is concerned. She might find herself on the wrong side of an army revolt."

She stared at Heng Yu, amazed. "You think they would rebel?"

"If Karr were assassinated?" Heng nodded. "But that is not the same thing as saying that Karr has the upper hand. He, too, must tread carefully. There are, after all, other ways of getting at a man than killing him."

She frowned, not understanding.

"His daughters. . . ." Heng said quietly, then turned as two of the guards came into the craft, smiling a greeting at them. "Horst . . . Carl . . ."

"Master Heng," the first of them, Horst, answered gruffly, making no attempt at bowing to him, as if he were the Chancellor's equal. "My Master asks—"

He stopped, noticing Jelka for the first time. As he did, his eyes widened and he dropped onto one knee, bowing his head smartly. *"Nu Shi* Tolonen. I did not know. . . ."

Jelka gave a little laugh, surprised by his reaction. Behind him his fellow guard, Carl, had done the same.

"Why, thank you, Captain Hagenau," she said, remembering the man from way back, "but my name is Ward now. And you needn't kneel. Please."

He looked up at her but made no attempt to get up. "We are honored by your presence, Madam Ward. Your father was a great man."

"Yes. But, please . . ."

She reached out, taking his hand, and pulled him to his feet, then looked to Heng Yu again. "Captain Hagenau was twice decorated by my father for his bravery. If he is leading the Marshal's men then they are well led indeed."

Hagenau beamed at the compliment, then tucked his head in again. "We are but the Marshal's hands."

At the reminder of their earlier conversation Heng Yu cleared his throat and gestured toward the open doorway. "Well, shall we go meet your old friend?"

Jelka looked to Hagenau. "Captain? If you would lead the way?"

"It would be my pleasure," he said. "Oh, and it is Major Hagenau now, incidentally."

"Then lead on, Major Hagenau. It seems your Master and I have much to talk about."

KARR MET THEM in the massive hallway of the Mansion, almost picking Jelka up as he embraced her, then turning to introduce her to his wife, Marie.

"I would have you meet my girls too," he said, beaming at her, "but they are at their studies right now. Maybe later?"

"I'd like that very much," she answered, smiling back at the giant, conscious of Heng at her side, the slim case under his arm.

Karr stepped back slightly, nodding to himself and smiling as he took in the sight of her. He had changed little over the years. His hair, admittedly, was almost gray now, but his face had not aged the way some men's faces aged. Like her own father's, Karr's had become set—as if it would be forever thus: a face of granite certainty.

"You know, I never thought to see you back here," he said, after a moment. "How is your husband? How is Kim?"

"Very well, last I heard. The colonies thrive."

"So I've heard." He paused, looking to Marie a moment, thoughtful. "Well, we shall talk later, neh? Right now Master Heng and I have some business to see to. Urgent business, I'm afraid. But when it's done . . ."

"Of course," she said graciously. Then, turning to Heng, she asked, "And Mileja?"

"She's on her way," Heng reassured her. "As soon as she arrives I'll have her sent through to you. But there is someone else I wish you to meet. Someone I think you'll find . . . interesting."

Jelka raised an eyebrow, then turned, hearing a noise on the stairs above them. She looked up. At the top of the massive stairway, one hand on the rail of the balcony, stood a young woman of roughly her own age. Her hair was tied back severely, but her face was pretty.

"Ah . . ." Heng Yu said, as they all turned to look up at her, "there you are. I was just about to send a servant for you."

"I heard the cruiser land," the young woman answered, coming down the stairs slowly, a pleasant smile on her face now. Reaching the bottom of the stairs, she stepped forward, holding her hand out to Jelka. "You must be Jelka Ward. I've heard a great deal about you."

Jelka raised an eyebrow. Now that the young woman was right before her, something about her face seemed familiar. She tried to recollect where she might have known it from, but nothing came. With a shrug and a smile she took the hand and shook it warmly. "Forgive me for not remembering you, but any friend of Gregor Karr's . . ."

"We've not met," the girl answered, "yet you could say we have much in common. In my researches I have read much about your family. Your father was a great man."

"Yes, and he was often wrong and stubborn and—"

"Loyal?"

Karr's single word stopped her short. "Yes," she said. "Loyal. That best describes him. He was like a huge pillar, holding up a vast stone ceiling."

"And mother and father to you, so I understand," the young woman said; then, with a little bow of her head, "and my name is Shang Han A, though my good friends call me Hannah."

Jelka stared at her anew, the name now matching the face. "You were the Minister's daughter, no?"

Hannah nodded, smiling guardedly. "That is so."

"Then we *do* have much in common," Jelka said, recalling the circumstances.

Hannah's father, Minister Shang, had served the *I Lung*, the "First Dragon," Head of the Thousand Eyes, the great Ministry itself, whose task was to watch over Chung Kuo and guard and preserve the false history their ancestors had created. The Ministry had done their job well, for even now few common citizens knew that the history of their world was false—that its true history had been suppressed, the past changed to suit their Han masters. But so it was. So she herself had discovered.

"And your researches?" Jelka asked. "They have to do with your father's work?"

"Indirectly. But let me show you." She looked to Karr. "You men, I take it, have 'important matters' to discuss?"

Karr looked to Heng Yu and nodded.

"Okay," Hannah said, looking back at Jelka, "then let's take the opportunity to discuss a few things ourselves, neh?" Hannah turned to Marie. "You'll join us, I hope, Marie?"

"I'll make some *ch'a*," Marie answered, "and bring it up."

"Good." Hannah smiled first to Karr, then to Heng, each of whom bowed respectfully to her. "Then, come, my friend," she said, taking Jelka's hand and turning toward the stairs. "I have much to show you."

JELKA LOOKED ABOUT HER at the book-lined room, astonished. The last time she had seen so many forbidden items was in her father's study years ago, and even he had not had a tenth as much as this.

"I didn't know so much had survived," she said, turning to Hannah, who stood at her side. "Where did they all come from?"

"My father saved much of it," Hannah answered. "He was one of the few who were authorized, you understand. Whenever there was a raid, wherever something illicit—something forbidden by the Edict—was recovered, it would pass through his hands before incineration. But sometimes the odd item would be retained by him." Hannah smiled wistfully. "It's only now that I understand how carefully he chose those items. It's as if . . . well, as if he knew that what he was doing was wrong, and by this means he could somehow preserve the past. A past he had avowed professionally to destroy."

Jelka nodded, sighing. "And you, Shang Han A? You carry on his work?"

"The preservation, yes. I'm writing a history, you see. A true history of Chung Kuo."

Jelka laughed. "My husband did that once."

"I know," Hannah said, touching her arm gently. "And nearly died for it, so I understand."

Jelka looked to her, surprised that she knew.

"Look," Hannah said, going across to her desk in the corner of the room and bringing back a loosely bound folder. "Do you recognize this?"

Jelka took it and, flicking open the plain green cover, read the title page: "*The Aristotle File, being the true history of Chung Kuo . . . by Kim Ward.*"

She looked up, staring at Hannah.

"That's the original," Hannah said. "The first printout from which all the other handwritten copies were made. Take it. I'd like you to give it to your husband."

Jelka smiled, clearly moved by the gesture. "That's very kind. . . ."

But Hannah shook her head. "Not kind. It's . . . well, it's like the completion of a circle, I guess. You see, that's not all I want you to give him. I want you to give him what exists of my own history. It was inspired by his, you see. Karr, and his friend Kao

Chen, urged me to write it, but it was your husband's work that made it possible—that gave me the framework for my own history. Without it . . . well, I guess I wouldn't have known where to start, where to look first."

"You have it here?"

"On disc, for you to take with you. Nine copies. One for Kim and two for each fleet."

Jelka frowned. "You know then?"

Hannah nodded, then smiled reassuringly. "We all know. It's never talked about . . . not openly, anyway, but the very fact that the starfleets exist gives us all hope. What's happening down here . . . well"—she sighed heavily—"I suppose Chancellor Heng has told you all about that."

"Some of it. Not why he's here with Karr."

Hannah turned and walked over to her desk, then looked back, sighing again. "It's time we talked, Jelka Ward. Time you found out what's really going on."

━━━━━━

FROM TOM'S BEDROOM he could see the white-and-orange sphere of Jupiter's second moon, Europa, its tiny satellite, sewn like a button onto the gas giant's swirling cream-and-gold waistcoat. For a time he lay there, staring at it thoughtlessly, then heard the air-lock door hiss open out in the corridor and turned, staring at the open doorway.

*Tom?*

Tom knew Sampsa could sense him there, but didn't answer. He was still angry with Sampsa from last night.

He heard the door slide closed, the click of the catches as Sampsa removed his helmet, then footsteps in the corridor outside. A moment later Sampsa poked his head around the doorway. "Tom?"

Tom glared at him, then looked away. His head was full of anger and resentment; emotions he knew Sampsa could feel.

Sampsa sighed. "Are you going to keep this up all day? I'm sorry, *okay?* I spoke out of order. I even *thought* out of order. But that doesn't change things." He clicked the catches at his right wrist, rotated the sealing ring, then began to pull off the heavy glove.

"You want to go home, you go home. But I'm staying. I haven't time to go back to Chung Kuo. There's too much going on here. Too much to be got ready."

Tom glanced at him, glowering still. *We could have gone with her.*

Sampsa huffed. "Yes, but we didn't, did we? We decided not to. You *agreed* with me." He leaned across and poked Tom's forehead with his forefinger. "I even felt it in there."

Tom jerked his head back angrily. *Don't touch me like that.*

"What, like this?" Sampsa put his hand out to poke Tom's forehead again, but Tom batted it aside.

Tom stood and walked over to the thick view window, his back to Sampsa. *You didn't look. You only saw what you wanted to see. If you'd looked deeper . . .*

Sampsa's sigh of exasperation filled the room. *"Aiya!"* He took a deep breath, then began again. "So you want to go back, *yes?"*

Tom turned. *Yes.*

"Then, go. And take Lu Yi with you. I'm sure she'd like to see Chung Kuo again."

Tom looked down. *And you?*

Sampsa shivered. *I have to stay. Can't you see that, Tom? The people here need me. There's so much to do. So much to get ready.*

Tom's eyes lifted, meeting his own. *And us? What about us?*

Sampsa shrugged. "We'll keep in touch. And maybe it'll do us good . . . you know, being out of each other's minds for a while."

*I didn't mean that. I . . .*

Sampsa looked—looked *deep* this time—and saw what Tom had been holding back from him. He sat. "Ahh . . ."

*So?* Tom said inside his head as he sat beside him on the edge of the bed. *Are you prepared to risk that?*

Sampsa turned and looked into Tom's eyes, seeing himself reflected back. "Are you?"

But Tom shook his head. *You know what I mean. We've got to make a choice. To stay or go.*

Sampsa spoke softly. "I thought you'd made that choice."

*No . . . no, I . . .* Tom sighed and looked down at his clenched hands.

Sampsa reached out, putting his arm about Tom's shoulders. "I know it must be hard, Tom. I know how much you miss it all . . .

your mother, the Domain, all that . . . but . . . well, I have to go. It's my destiny. And if you decide . . . well, to stay, then it'll be like half of me has been ripped away. But that can't stop me. Nor should it stop you. Seriously. If you want to go back, then go back. Find out whether you have to stay or go." He shrugged, then hugged his mind's twin. "Do it if you must. But don't be afraid of doing it."

He was about to say more when the air lock hissed open again. After a moment's pause they heard footsteps out in the corridor, the babble of two voices talking quickly in Mandarin.

Sampsa stood, then walked across to the door. "Ai Lin? Lu Yi?"

The twins turned as they were taking off their helmets and looked to him, giggling.

"We didn't think you'd be here," Ai Lin said, hanging her helmet up on the hook. "We thought . . ." She fell silent, noting how serious Sampsa looked.

"What is it?" Lu Yi asked, stepping past her sister. "Is it Tom?"

"Yes," Sampsa said, then, raising a hand before she could get all panicky, he quickly added, "he's not hurt or anything, it's just . . . well, it's just that he wants to go back. To Chung Kuo. He—"

"Chung Kuo?" Lu Yi frowned, not understanding. "He wants to go *there?*"

Sampsa nodded, looking back into the room, conscious of Tom seated there, looking through his eyes all the while, and wondering how it would feel never to feel that again. The thought made Tom look up and meet his eyes. Sighing, Sampsa turned, looking to Lu Yi again. "Yes. And he wants you to go with him. To meet his parents and see the Domain. He wants—"

*I want to say good-bye,* Tom said inside his head.

Sampsa glanced at him again, and nodded. "He wants to say good-bye."

"*Aiya,*" Lu Yi said, looking to her twin, clearly scared by the thought of being separated from her for the first time in her life. She looked back at Sampsa. "You mean, just me and him?"

"And Ai Lin, if you want." He saw the relief in her face and felt, at the same time, Tom's surprise. "After all, I'm going to be very busy these next few months. And you two need a holiday. So . . ."

The two young women looked to each other a moment, then, giggling, fell into each other's arms.

*Well?* he asked silently, speaking directly into Tom's head. *Are you still angry with me?*

*No*, Tom said, getting up and coming across, laying a hand on his arm fondly. *No. Not now. . . .*

MILEJA WAS RUNNING from room to room, giggling, Karr's youngest, Beth, hot in pursuit. Jelka watched her daughter disappear through the door of the great dining room, then turned to look at Karr again.

Karr was staring at the empty doorway and smiling, fondly, indulgently, the way her own father had used to smile at her. Once again it brought home to her just how much Karr had become like him. She smiled, the warmth she felt for him at that moment surprising her. Such things crept up on one until, suddenly, one's relationship was wholly different, transformed. Why, if it were not so ridiculous, she would have said that what she felt for Karr at that moment was something akin to love. Not the kind of love she had for Kim, no, but not so different from what she had once felt for her father.

She looked down, realizing suddenly just how much she missed him. And with that realization came another, that she was lonely. Oh, there was Kim—there was always Kim—and more often than not he was enough for her: he and Sampsa and Mileja, that was. But sometimes, late at night, or when she was alone and feeling thoughtful, her mind would go back to her father and to those first days on the island, at Kalevala, with her uncle and aunt. Those had been magical days. If she closed her eyes she could see him still, his face in the fire's flickering light halved into a mask of gold and black, his hands resting on his knees like something carved from stone and set before a temple. Magnificent, he'd been. Magnificent in the same physical way that Karr was magnificent. Archetypal, almost. And even if, in the years that had followed, they had fallen out over Kim, still she had loved him. Loved him despite all he had done to keep her and Kim apart. Loved him and understood him.

She looked up, finding Karr's eyes on her.

"Are you okay?"

She nodded and smiled. "Just remembering, that's all."

"Your father?"

"Yes." She sighed. "You'll come, I hope . . . to the ceremony."

"Nothing could stop me," he said, smiling at her in the same way she had seen him smile at his daughters; a smile of pride and love. "It will be nice to see old faces again, neh?"

"Neh."

She was quiet for a while, then: "Hannah's told me things."

"Things?" Karr lifted his chin slightly, a questioning look in his eyes.

"About the situation here."

"Ah . . ." He nodded thoughtfully, then went over and pushed the door shut. "Then you understand why we are leaving here."

"Leaving?" Hannah had said nothing of that to her.

"Yes," Karr said, noting her surprise, "to join Ebert in Africa. Things here are finished."

"And they'll be better in Africa?"

"For a time."

Jelka looked down, anxious suddenly. Then, "Why don't you come?"

"What?" He looked at her, not understanding.

"Why don't you come with us? You, Marie, and the girls. Oh, and Master Heng. And others. We'll find room." She laughed. "We'll *make* room!"

"And Hans, and the Osu?"

"All of you." Jelka laughed, suddenly on fire with the idea. Why not, after all? They were all good people, and Kim was always saying that they needed as many good people as they could find. "I mean, if there really is nothing left to stay for?"

She saw the doubt in his face. "I'd not thought. I . . ."

Jelka placed a hand on his arm. "Think about it. Please, Gregor. Talk to Marie and the girls, see how they feel about the idea. In the meantime I'll talk to Kim. I'm sure he'd say yes. You could be on the *New Hope* with us!"

Karr laughed, and shook his head. "Full circle."

"What?" She narrowed her eyes.

"Full circle," Karr repeated. "Or do you forget who it was single-handedly blew up the first *New Hope*?"

"I . . ." She laughed. "Well, maybe another ship, eh?"

"And Li Yuan?" he asked, a note of sobriety entering his voice now.

She stared back at him a moment, then looked away. "Li Yuan has made his own bed," she answered quietly. "Now he must lie in it."

ON  THE  CRUISER  BACK  Jelka sat silently at the window, watching the city pass below, her thoughts returning time and again to what Hannah had told her.

*Gone,* she thought, frowning deeply. *How could it all have gone so quickly?* Yet what worried her more was that it might be somehow Kim's fault—for giving up on Chung Kuo—or, more to the point, *hers* for persuading him to focus his energies elsewhere. One thing was for certain, however; when Kim had withdrawn, no one else had stepped in to fill the void.

She put a hand to her mouth, pressing the knuckles against her teeth, unhappy with herself. Maybe it wasn't their fault. After all, the government of the State was Li Yuan's business, not Kim's. That said, she knew how strongly Kim had felt about it; how he had always argued in favor of putting something back into the system that had given him *his* chance. About how they should make it possible for others.

So what did she do? Did she tell him? And if she told him, what would he decide? Would he abandon their plans and turn back inward to try to sort the mess out? Because if he did, he would fail. She understood that now. Chung Kuo was a giant powder keg. All wars—even the great war against DeVore in which so many had died—would be as rehearsals for the next one, for the next war would destroy what was left of civilization.

Letting out a sigh, Jelka looked across to where Heng Yu sat, his head tilted to the left, his eyes closed, resting. Across from him, Mileja leaned over the travel table, her tongue poking from the corner of her mouth in concentration as she sketched in her book.

*Sketches . . .*

She had seen Hannah's sketches of the weapons Li Yuan was developing. Deadly things—spin-offs of technologies Kim had developed for more peaceful uses. Yes, and rumor was the Americans had more of the same. Awful, inhuman things made for inhuman uses. Things that maimed and killed indiscriminately. Machines whose sole purpose was to destroy.

No. Whatever happened, she decided she would keep this from him. In case the pity in him outweighed the common sense. And to prevent him from making one last futile gesture.

Besides, she had seen how the merest mention of the starfleets lit men up with hope. Even Karr. Things might be bad, the end might well be near here on Chung Kuo, but so long as it wasn't *the* end, then men could carry on, their eyes alive, knowing that there *was* a future.

How strange that was. How . . . unexpected.

She moved in her seat, trying to get more comfortable, and as she did there was a thump and the craft juddered.

"Wha . . . ?" Heng was instantly awake. As he went to stand, the craft swung to the right, throwing him back into his seat. A moment later a face appeared around the door to the cockpit.

"What's happening?" Heng asked, hanging on tightly as the craft banked and began to rise swiftly.

"We were shot at from below, Master. Simple hand weapons, by the feel of it. One round hit our port wing, but everything seems okay. All systems are functional. But we're taking evasive action."

At the copilot's words Mileja, who had been looking about her, clearly frightened, burst into tears. Jelka pulled herself up out of her chair and went across, sitting beside her young daughter and comforting her as the craft continued its steep climb.

"Well, there's a first," Heng murmured to himself, clearly shaken by the incident. He looked to Jelka and slowly shook his head. "I must apologize. I thought—"

He broke off, then sat back, sighing heavily. "Day by day it gets worse. Like the other day. I was flying in to Heidelberg, idly looking out of the window, when I saw two guards chasing a group of boys down a deserted alleyway. Young boys, they were . . . oh, nine, ten years old at most. The boys were getting away from the guards. I remember smiling and wondering to myself just what they'd done, when one of the guards stopped and pulled something from his tunic."

Heng shuddered and looked away, clearly disturbed by the memory. He licked at his lips nervously, then continued. "I knew at once what it was. I wanted to do something—to intercede and stop it before it went any farther, but I was too far away. I couldn't. . . . Well, anyway, I saw the guard lift the tiny box and point it at the boys, as if he were pointing a gun at them. They were running, they were still running, when the explosions happened."

"Explosions?" Jelka was cradling the now silent Mileja, pressing her head into her chest tightly, as if to protect her against any further attacks.

"They were wired, you see." Heng made a gesture with both hands as if his skull were flying apart.

Jelka was staring at the Chancellor wide eyed now. "They can do that?"

Heng snapped his fingers. "Like that."

"*Aiya* . . . And the boys?"

"Dead before they fell. Or three of them were. One of them got away. He wasn't wired. . . ."

Heng fell silent, then wiped his mouth with the back of his hand. Cuddled into her mother, Mileja was absolutely still, clearly listening to it all.

"Can't you . . . *do* anything?" Mileja asked after a moment, breaking the awkward silence.

In answer Heng Yu turned his head and, pulling down the silk of his collar, showed Mileja the dark scar on the neck beneath his ear where his own wire had been inserted. "The Empress insisted we set an example. We all have them now."

"And Karr? Is he wired too?" Jelka asked. If he was, she hadn't noticed.

Heng Yu shook his head. "Not Karr. She'd need a reason, and she hasn't got one. Not yet, anyway. No, Gregor's resignation was the best thing—maybe the *only* good thing—that's happened these last few years. The fact that he's not inside . . ."

"And not wired."

Heng Yu nodded.

Jelka looked away. Still she held her daughter tightly. Her voice was much quieter now. "How much longer can this go on, Master Heng?"

"Not long," he said simply. "When they start shooting at imperial craft, how long can it be before they choose to attack the San Chang itself?"

Heng sighed. "No, Jelka Ward. Say farewell to your father and get out. Out, while there's still time to get out."

━━━━━

KIM WAS SITTING AT HIS DESK, scrutinizing Ikuro's plans in detail, when Wen Ch'ang poked his head around the door.

"Kim?"

Kim looked up. "Ah, Wen Ch'ang . . . come in. How's it going?"

"It's ready," Wen Ch'ang said, coming across. "You can go inside whenever you want."

"Good," Kim said, turning the plans so he could see. "What do you think?"

Wen Ch'ang leaned across the desk, studying the drawings silently for a minute or two. He looked up at Kim and smiled. "It looks fine to me. If the general principles are sound . . ."

"Shen Li says they've bored hundreds of these things, one or two of them even bigger than these specifications."

"But . . . ?"

Kim laughed. "How did you know there was a *but?* Are you a mind-reader, Wen Ch'ang?"

"There's always a *but*," Wen Ch'ang said, returning Kim's smile in his lopsided fashion.

Kim shrugged. "It's just that this is so important. We're not talking about building extraction tunnels here, we're talking about building escape vents for the forces released by massive explosions."

"So?"

"So we can't afford to get it wrong."

"Well, then, try it out. Experiment. That's what you're always telling me, neh?"

Kim laughed. "What? On one of the smaller moons?"

"Precisely."

"But that would give the game away, surely? They'd see it, even on Chung Kuo."

Wen Ch'ang shrugged. "Maybe. But what could Li Yuan do? Tell you to stop?"

"No. But maybe he'd send someone to try to stop us. To sabotage things."

"And maybe he knows already." Wen Ch'ang looked at the drawings again and smiled. "As I said, to my eyes that looks like a good piece of work. It's precisely what we were looking for." He looked back at Kim. "If it's the security angle you're worried about, then double the guard on all vital installations. Take whatever precautions are necessary. But test this out. Build a prototype . . . on Sinope, maybe . . . that'd be big enough to give us a meaningful result, neh?"

Kim sat back, steepling his fingers together as he considered it, then looked to Wen Ch'ang again and smiled. "Okay. You arrange it."

Wen Ch'ang smiled back at him, "After all, I've so little to do."

"Am I working you too hard?"

Wen Ch'ang grinned, shaking his head. "No. I'll gladly do it, Kim. This Shen Li . . . he's here on Ganymede, right?"

"In one of the guest apartments, along with two of his brothers. Their ship's docked in orbit."

"I know," Wen Ch'ang said. "It's an impressive craft. I've not seen its like before."

"Separate evolution," Kim said. "Apparently those asteroid miners have been out there more than two hundred years now. They've had a long time to adapt to the conditions out here."

"The shape of things to come, eh?"

Kim smiled. "Who knows?"

━━━━━

WEN CH'ANG took the "rapid" down to Level 26, then, leaving the lift, hurried along the north corridor toward his apartment, holding out his ID card before him, the "seals"—the airtight doors that partitioned the corridors every fifty *ch'i* or so—hissing open at his approach.

Back in his rooms he stripped and then stood below the shower, the recycled water flowing hot over his body for a full thirty seconds before it cut off and the warm air jets cut in to dry him off.

*Excellent,* he thought, stepping out and grinning at his reflection in the steam-free mirror. *Everything is falling into place just perfectly.*

He went through into the tiny cabin bedroom and, reaching into the narrow built-in wardrobe, took out a simple light-green one-piece, his blood coursing in his veins with anticipation.

The message had come that morning—a simple folded note slipped under his door. After all these years DeVore had contacted him again . . . had *activated* him.

Wen Ch'ang stepped into the one-piece and pulled it up over his body, easing his arms into the sleeves and sealing it at the neck.

"Dead," he said quietly, then chuckled to himself. "The bastard's as good as dead."

Oh, he'd have to plan it carefully, of course. He'd have to make it seem as though it were an accident, but that was detail, and he was good at detail. Nobody better, as Ward so often told him.

He was the dragon's tooth, a single stone placed long ago in a forgotten corner of the board. But now his time had come. The endgame was upon them.

His laughter died. Stepping back into the shower room he stared at himself again. He wasn't real. He knew that. He had been made, produced from a genetic template in DeVore's plant back on Mars; grown in a tank and given false memories. For a time he had lived, as men lived, but he wasn't a man, he was a morph, a stone, a dragon's tooth.

He bared his teeth at his reflection. *There!* There was a side of him Ward didn't know. He smiled at the irony of it. For Ward was the most intelligent man he had ever met. More intelligent even than his Master. But unlike DeVore, Ward was *naive*. He *trusted*.

*The test bore,* he thought, the idea coming to him whole in that instant. *I'll do it then, and blame Shen Li and his brothers.*

He smiled, his mind already working on the problem. With a brief nod to his image in the mirror, he went out, heading for Kalevala.

HENG YU STOOD A MOMENT, calming himself, then, smiling at the Captain of the Guard, stepped through the slowly opening doors and into his Master's study, bowing low as he crossed the thickly carpeted floor.

Stopping before the massive desk, a single glance told him that Dragon Heart was in a mood; an observation that was confirmed in an instant.

"You are *late*, Master Heng! We expected you an hour back!"

He dropped to his knees, conscious of how he must appear to those others present—a cringing, fawning fool.

"Forgive me, Mistress," he said, "but unexpected matters—"

"Don't *lie* to me, Master Heng," she interrupted, sitting forward, "I *know* what you've been up to!"

"Mistress?" He glanced at Li Yuan, trying to gauge whether this show of temper were orchestrated or merely the product of the woman's vacillating mood.

Li Yuan sat in a matching throne beside his wife, reading a report. He had put on weight this past year and at times Heng Yu suspected that he, too, had been wired secretly by his wife, he went along with her with such docile acquiescence. Yet there were moments when the old Li Yuan stared back at him; moments when all his certainties dissolved beneath his T'ang's ironic stare.

*"Well?"* Dragon Heart shouted at him, banging the table with her fist. "Have you something to tell me, Master Heng?"

*"Tell* you, Mistress?" One thing the years had taught him was to admit to nothing until confronted with it absolutely.

She stood, then came around the desk until she was standing over him. Her voice was cold, acidic. "You *disobeyed* me."

"Mistress?" He kept his eyes lowered, wondering just what she knew for a fact and what was guesswork.

"The woman. Ward's wife."

Heng Yu waited, tensing himself against the expected explosion, but it did not come.

He looked up at her, surprised to find her smiling. *"Mistress?"*

"You are a clever man, Master Heng."

"Clever, Mistress?"

"Yes. I was very angry with you at first. I wanted you . . . executed. But my husband"—she looked around, gazing fondly at Li

Yuan—"my dear, sweet husband persuaded me that I was wrong about you."

"Ah . . ." Heng Yu looked to his Master for enlightenment, but Li Yuan was still reading, as if disinterested in events.

"He said you were the most loyal of his servants. He said"—her laughter was soft, almost kind for once—"he said that you had to have a plan of some kind. To entrap the woman. To weave her into some kind of plot by our enemies, perhaps. To *incriminate* her."

"Mistress?" Heng Yu stared at her a moment, then understood. It had arrived. The moment he had been waiting for for years—first as Pei K'ung's willing "dog," and now as this child's. Now he must choose. To serve her or disobey. There was no third alternative.

He glanced at Li Yuan again. His Master was watching him now, intrigued to see what he would do.

Heng swallowed and looked down, bowing to his Mistress. "My Master, as ever, understands me perfectly."

Her smile was triumphant. "Good. Then all is well, neh? My husband and I can rest safe at nights, knowing that the Empire is in safe hands."

If there was any irony in her voice Heng could not detect it, but then, she was a sly one. Almost as sly as his Master, and certainly his match nine days out of ten.

"Is there anything else, Mistress?"

"No, Master Heng, I—"

She stopped, looking past him. Someone had entered the study and was crossing the huge expanse of carpet. From the waft of perfume that preceded the figure, Heng could tell without looking who it was. Cheng Nai shan. As the Empress's First Adviser swept past him, the swish of expensive silk as much a trademark of the man as his cologne, Heng noted that Ming Ai's old ally had three of Li Yuan's generals with him. Something was up.

Head still bowed, Heng Yu watched his rival go around the desk and unceremoniously lean in to Li Yuan and whisper in the T'ang's ear, one hand cupped about it so no one could overhear. After a moment Li Yuan nodded, then looked to the generals, nodding to each in turn.

*What now?* Heng wondered, staring suspiciously back at Cheng, who was smiling broadly.

As the generals backed out of the room, Heng Yu looked to his master. Steeling himself, he took his opportunity to make his request.

"Master?"

Li Yuan looked back at him languidly. "Yes, Master Heng?"

"I wish to ask permission to attend the ceremony in two days' time."

"Ceremony?"

"At Marshal Tolonen's grave tablet in Bremen."

Li Yuan stared back at him. "Ceremony? There's to be a ceremony?"

"Yes, Master. I—I felt as a mark of my respect—"

"Permission is refused," Dragon Heart interrupted. "You will be in Mashhad that day."

He looked to her. "Mashhad?"

"We have a meeting there," Li Yuan said, looking to his wife and raising a hand to softly intercede. "I shall need you there with me, Master Heng. For the negotiations."

He felt his stomach tighten. *Negotiations?* He had heard *nothing!* He looked to Cheng Nai shan and saw the cocky, self-confident look in his eyes and knew whose work this had been. Cheng had been trying to usurp him for months now, but this was the first time he had taken such direct and drastic measures to undermine him. Even so, Li Yuan still needed him. Hadn't he just said as much?

"Besides," Dragon Heart continued, ignoring her husband's signal, "I doubt that there'll be a ceremony. It would be . . . well, *inadvisable*, let us say."

"Inadvisable, Mistress?"

*"Yes,"* she said, a much harder edge slipping into her voice. "Harmless as such events might seem, it might prove . . . a *focus*, don't you think, Master Heng?"

This time the look she gave him was unequivocal. She *knew*. Which meant she must have a spy, either in Karr's household or his own. He shuddered, briefly distracted by the thought of who it might be, but her raised voice brought him swiftly back to himself.

"You are dismissed, Master Heng."

"Dismissed?" He stared at Cheng Nai shan, then at Li Yuan, and understood. He was no longer trusted . . . not on matters of policy, anyway. That knowledge made him feel strange, light headed, and as he backed away, his body bent, his head bowed low, he almost stumbled.

The choice was straightforward. Either he set Jelka Ward up and had her arrested, or he was out. And out meant dead.

As the doors closed and he turned away, the strangeness of the choice that lay before him hit him fully. He had been here once before, of course, with Pei K'ung two years ago. But then the choice had been much simpler—had been between his Mistress or his Master. Now that had changed, for his Master now did his young wife's bidding. Or as good as. To betray her would be to betray him.

Heng Yu walked back slowly, deep in thought. These past few weeks he had thought it all settled. He had been sure that, when it came to it, he'd know just what to do and how to act, but now that the hour had come he was much less certain. He had gone through so much for Li Yuan; had done so much that was against his nature. Yet at what point did loyalty and duty—those great cornerstones of his existence—break down? How far was he supposed to go before something in him snapped?

And Jelka? Could he honestly give up Jelka to that woman?

He shuddered at the thought. Even so, the question remained: could he abandon his Master at this late hour? Could he simply sit and watch while Cheng Nai shan and the generals picked the rotting carcass clean?

*I don't know,* he answered himself, hastening his pace, realizing that he must warn Karr about the spy. *The gods help me, I don't know!*

KIM STOOD IN THE GARDEN of Kalevala, the old graystone house behind him, the dome curving overhead, the great circle of Jupiter dominating the skyline. It felt strange to be there again—stranger still because, when he closed his eyes and sniffed the air, it was almost as if he were back there on a quiet evening, the sea still, the air calm. But that illusion was only momentary. The moment you stepped outside the house—the moment you looked out of one of the windows—you were aware of where you were.

Space. Everywhere he looked he could see the vacuum. And this—this was his choice. To be out here, on the edge of things, rather than back there, close in to the sun, there where it was relatively safe and warm.

He walked out until he had left the well-trimmed lawn and found himself beneath the trees, on rough, uneven ground. Barefoot he walked, a silent shadow among the shadowy branches.

Out here the silence of the place was eerie. There was no wind here, no rain, no movement of the tides. It was, he realized, like being back inside the City once again.

For the briefest moment he wondered if he'd been wrong. Wrong to spend so much time and effort shipping this out here. Wrong because it didn't fit.

Maybe. But he had done it now. There was no going back. Kalevala, Ganymede, that was his address henceforth.

Kim laughed, then moved quickly between the trees until he came out into the clearing. Here, strangely, nothing grew. A perfect circle of black was surrounded by seven tall pines. On this spot, years ago—almost thirty, if he recalled correctly what Jelka had said—a bolt of lightning had struck, turning the pines into blazing candles. In the morning Jelka had come and stood among their ashes, astonished by the power of the storm. Saplings had grown from the ruined stumps, yet in their midst the intense heat of the lightning strike had fused the ground. Nothing grew there, even now.

Kim squatted, brushing the thin layer of earth aside to feel the smooth black surface underneath. And as he did, the words of the ancient tales, *The Kalevala*, filled his mind.

*Thereupon smith Ilmarinen*
*Answered in the words that follow:*
*"But indeed 'tis not a wonder,*
*If I am a skillful craftsman,*
*For 'twas I who forged the heavens,*
*And the arch of air who welded."*

He looked up through the trees at the magnificent sight of the gas giant, Jupiter, filling half the sky in front of him, and shivered. Sometimes the words of that ancient saga seemed almost to relate to him personally. Some days he'd think of a phrase or two and briefly feel as if he, too, were caught up in something much larger than himself, something strange and mythical—like the great heroes of the tales; like Vainamoinen, or Lemminkainen, or, more particularly, Ilmarinen. And yet what was he? Just a man. Clayborn. Malformed and lucky to be alive. He was no hero, that was for certain.

No. And yet from his smallness bigger things might grow.

"Kim?"

The voice came from the air.

He turned his head, then stood, looking toward the house. "What is it, Wen Ch'ang?"

"You have a visitor, Kim. Young Chuang would like permission to come into the house."

Kim laughed. "Of course. Send her in at once. I'll meet her there." Then, brushing his hand against his thigh, he started back through the trees.

━━━━━━

"WELL?" KIM ASKED, looking about him at Tolonen's study. "What do you think?"

Chuang Kuan Ts'ai looked back at Kim and grinned. "So many books."

Kim walked over and, reaching up, took an old leather-bound volume from the shelf.

"Here," he said, turning and handing it to the nine-year-old

She studied the spine a moment, then looked back at him. For a moment she seemed to be listening to something, her eyes glazing over, then she nodded.

Kim, watching, understood. The Machine inside her was downloading: dumping all it knew of Kalevala into her memory. Not that it knew much these days. In choosing a human host it had been forced to abandon its vast stores of knowledge, having to make do with those unused areas of the child's brain. Yet in limiting itself it had become greater than it had been, more human.

Chuang's eyes cleared and she looked at him again. "It must have been so much better back then, before the Cities. So much . . . clearer."

She turned, looking over at the carved stone fireplace. She went across and sat in the massive leather armchair by the window, her tiny frame dwarfed by it. For a time she simply sat there, staring thoughtfully at the book-lined walls, her legs kicking slowly above the ground. Turning to look at him, an impish smile formed on her lips.

He smiled back at her, glad that they'd adopted her. She was a good child, hardworking, loving, and no trouble at all. He'd never once had to raise his voice to her.

"I had a dream, Papa Kim."

"A dream?"

Her legs kicked slowly, languidly, as if they were dangling in a stream. "It was . . . strange."

Briefly Kim thought of the dreams Jelka had once had—those vivid, almost apocalyptic dreams of threat and rescue. *Like the dreams of Potiphar's wife*, he thought idly. *Prophetic dreams.*

"So?" he asked gently, coaxing her, when she said no more. "In what way were they strange?"

She made a tiny moue with her lips. "Just that it was so vivid. So . . . *real*. While I was in the dream it was like it was really happening. But it couldn't happen. Not that."

The slightest tenseness in her voice revealed just how much she'd been disturbed by it. Her previous cheeriness had vanished, as if it had been an illusion. Kim went across and knelt, staring up into that perfect, unlined face, conscious of how large and dark her eyes were. He took her hand gently.

"Do you want to tell me about it?"

She shrugged, then looked past him. "I don't know. I . . ." Her eyes met his own again. "It was about Jelka, you see."

"Ah . . ." For some reason he felt his stomach muscles clench. *Only natural*, he reassured himself. *After all, she's so far away.*

He forced himself to smile. "And?"

"At first I thought they were statues. . . ."

"Statues?"

"They were gold, you see. As if they'd been gilded. And so stiff too."

"They?"

"Yes. Both Jelka and Mileja. They were in a room. A sealed room, like in a spacecraft. The walls were bright, metallic, and there were no windows." She frowned, as if seeing it again. "They were so still . . . so still . . . In the dream I seemed to float within the room, like a bug . . . you know, one of those camera eyes, like they use in the new tunnels when they're digging."

He nodded, feeling cold now, numbed. "And then?"

"Nothing. I . . . ." She swallowed and clenched her hands together. "It was like they were dead, Papa Kim. But not ordinary dead. Their eyes . . . their eyes were like steel ball-bearings. Featureless. It . . . *frightened* me."

He held her, comforting not only her but himself; his own anxiety fed by her words. Dreams . . . He shivered. What in the Maker's name was the meaning of dreams?

"You're just afraid, that's all," he said, after a while. "I am too. It's only natural. The dreams . . . well, they're an expression of your anxiety. We all have them."

"But it was so *real*," she insisted.

"Yes," he said, her certainty disturbing him. "But you mustn't worry. They're okay. They'll *be* okay."

She moved back a little from him, smiling at him, reassured by his words, then looked about her again. "Did she grow up here?"

"Jelka?" Kim shook his head. "No. She lived in Bremen, in quarters there with her father."

"Ah . . ." Chuang nodded, as if she suddenly remembered. That much Jelka and Chuang had in common; neither had known her mother, and both had been brought up by men. Perhaps it was why they got on so well together.

Kim stood. "You want to see the rest of the house?"

She nodded and jumped up, taking his hand again. "Okay," she said, suddenly much brighter. "Let's start with the tower."

But as Kim led her from the room, he felt his own mood darkened by the memory of the dream.

He could always ask Wen Ch'ang to contact her, of course, as a matter of urgency. But what would he say? That young Chuang had had a dream and he was worried? No. Jelka would only think him silly and absurd.

*I'll wait,* he thought, looking at the timer set into his left wrist. After all, it was only four hours until her regular call. Even so, the shadow remained.

*So still they were . . . like golden statues . . . their eyes like steel ball-bearings. . . .*

He shuddered, then, shaking off the mood, squeezed Chuang's hand.

"Come on, then," he said, leading her through the glass-paneled door that led into the tower. "I'll show you where Jelka watched the storm."

LI YUAN WAS FINISHING OFF, signing the last of that day's documents and preparing to join his wife, when the screen to his left lit up.

He looked up, surprised to find himself staring into a face he had last seen two years before.

"*Shih* Egan . . ."

"Li Yuan," Old Man Egan said, looking fit and bronzed, not aged a day since Li Yuan had last seen him. "I'm sorry to call so late, but I've news."

"News?" Li Yuan pushed the document aside, then gestured to Cheng Nai shan to clear the room. "What kind of news?"

Josiah Egan smiled broadly, showing perfect white teeth. "Why, nothing but good news, Li Yuan. You are a grandfather."

Li Yuan sat back, astonished. "Kuei Jen has a child?"

"An hour back. A son. Eight catties he weighs."

Li Yuan laughed. "A son . . . my son has a son!" Then, realizing the significance of it, he leaned toward the screen. "The mother . . . who is the mother?"

"You mean, you did not know, Li Yuan?" Egan smiled. "Why the mother was Kuei Jen."

"Kuei . . ." Li Yuan frowned, confused. "I beg pardon . . . ?"

"Your son." Egan's smile broadened until it seemed to burn whitely at the center of the screen. "Your son was the mother. And my grandson, Mark . . ."

*Aiya!* Li Yuan thought, seeing it in an instant. This was the ultimate humiliation, the ultimate loss of face.

His mouth was suddenly dry. On the screen Egan grinned and grinned, tanned and eternal.

"Oh, and one further thing," Egan said, as if only then remembering. "I have a message from an old friend of yours. He says, look to the skies. . . ." And, chuckling, he cut contact.

Shocked beyond all words, Li Yuan sat back, staring at the blank screen. *Aiya!* he thought. *Aiya!*

BEN STOOD BY THE FENCE at the end of the garden, looking out across the river as darkness fell.

Li Yuan had just been on, his pale, shocked face almost comical as he spoke stumblingly of what had happened.

It might have been worse; he might have laughed, for it was very funny, after all; even so, Li Yuan had broken contact after less than five minutes, enraged that he was not more sympathetic.

But what was he supposed to say? *I'm sorry for you, Li Yuan, but at least you have the grandson you always wanted?* Or was he supposed to wave his magic wand and set it all right for him?

And that was the trouble with Li Yuan; he was always wanting others to bail him out of situations he had created for himself. As long as he'd known him it had been the same—rash decisions followed by long periods of remorse. But this time remorse was insufficient. He had driven his son into the arms of a deadly rival, and now that rival had taken the opportunity to get back at him.

He smiled, imagining Li Yuan's surprise. Yes, and what a bold stroke on Old Man Egan's part! What imaginative audacity! Not that it surprised him as much as it had Li Yuan; after all, he had seen at once which way the wind blew between Kuei Jen and the young American. The only surprise was that the manly Kuei Jen should have been the one to have the operation. He'd have thought the softer, more effeminate Egan would have been the better mother, but then, that would not have suited Old Man Egan's purpose—and it was absolutely certain that Egan knew what effect the news would have before he called to congratulate Li Yuan.

Ben chuckled softly. What could be worse for a proud Han ruler than to have his cock cut off? Only one thing—to have his son emasculated! Yes, and Egan had gone one better, for to all intents and purposes he had not merely castrated Li Yuan's family line, he had usurped it by having his grandson plant his seed in Kuei Jen's belly.

Why, had the Old Man buggered Li Yuan himself, it could not have been more blatant!

War. It had to be war. Only, Li Yuan didn't know that yet. He was still in shock. But when he began to think again . . .

Ben turned, looking back up the slope toward the cottage. There were lights on now in several of the downstairs rooms. To the left, through the latticed window of the kitchen, he could see Meg at work, preparing the supper, while through the long window of the living room he could see Catherine, walking back and forth, the new child cradled on her shoulder.

He walked back slowly, smiling, wondering what Li Yuan was doing now and picturing in his mind Kuei Jen tucked up in bed, the pillows piled behind his back as he cradled the newborn. He slowed, conceiving the scene as a picture, the baby suckling at Kuei Jen's breast, then gave a snort of laughter. For one mischievous moment he had considered actually painting it and sending it to Li Yuan as a birth present. But why make unnecessary enemies?

He ducked under the low sill and, pushing the door open, stepped into the shadowed hallway, the smell of Meg's cooking coming to him. The child was crying—a kind of low, snuffling cry that was like that of a small animal. He went to the doorway and stood there, looking in at Catherine.

Seeing him, she smiled. "He's almost gone," she said softly, almost mouthing the words, the child—fifteen months now—moving irritably on her shoulder at the noise.

For a moment he stared at the child, conscious of its flattened features, its jet-black skin, then smiled. So rich life was, so varied. If Li Yuan could only see that. If he could only look beyond his personal "humiliation" and see this thing for the wonder it was. But he knew that that wasn't possible, for Li Yuan was a Han through and through, and for all his boasting that he was a modernizer, he was cut from the same cloth as his father and his father's father. No. There was no way he would forgive his son this; no way he would ever acknowledge his newborn grandson, let alone embrace him.

Ben sighed, not for the pity of it, but because he knew what this would mean for them all. Things were bad enough as they were. This . . . well, this would push them over the edge.

*Sleep well,* he thought, going across and tousling the child's dark curls. Leaning close, he kissed Catherine's offered lips, embraced her briefly, then, turning away, hurried from the room.

It was time to pack. Time to move on. While they still could.

# The Hollower

"**M**ASTER HENG! Master Heng!"

Heng Yu raised himself on his elbows, then, sitting up fully, knuckled his eyes. He had heard the banging on the outer door but had thought it part of the dream. But this now was no dream. His First Secretary, Fen Chun, stood over him, his face anxious.

"What is it, Chun?" Heng asked, wanting nothing more than to lie down again and sleep. But if Fen Chun had chosen to wake him, then it had to be something very urgent.

"You must come, Master Heng! You must see for yourself!"

Heng Yu got to his feet, then pulled on the cloak Fen was holding out for him. "Are we in danger, Chun?"

"No immediate danger, Master," the young man answered him. "But you ought to see this . . . before Master Cheng gets to hear of it."

"Ah . . ." Heng understood at once, and praised the Heavens that he had such a fine and loyal First Secretary as Fen Chun. Whatever this was, it was important that he take charge, before Cheng Nai shan could further undermine his authority.

Heng followed Fen Chun in silence, hurrying down the dimly lit corridor and out, down the steps, into the central gardens of the San Chang. It was not long after dawn and the shadows on the mosaic path were long. Ahead of them, beside one of the white marble ornamental bridges that crossed the stream, stood two guards. Another crouched nearby, looking down at something in the water.

As Heng Yu came up beside him, he saw what it was. It was a young woman, floating facedown.

*Aiya,* he thought, seeing the implications at once. *If the girl had been murdered . . .*

"Who found her?" he asked, looking to the guards, who now stood, their heads bowed in his presence.

One of them knelt. "It was I, Master Heng. Twenty minutes back. I—I thought you should know at once."

"You did well," Heng said, wondering how much time he had to investigate the matter before Cheng was notified. "Has anyone else been informed?"

"No, Master Heng. I sent my colleague to fetch Master Fen. The rest you know."

Heng breathed in deeply. If she *had* been murdered, and had not simply fallen in and drowned, then it was important to establish who she was and just how long she had been dead. Hopefully this was a "domestic" incident—a jealous husband exacting his "revenge," perhaps—and not something more sinister, but whatever it was, speed now was of the essence.

"Chun," he said, turning to his Secretary, "go and fetch Surgeon Chang. Tell him only that it is urgent."

As Fen Chun hurried away, Heng turned to the guards again. "You, Private," he said, pointing to the kneeling man. "Go and bring a tent from stores."

"Master!" The young man stood, bowed, and hurried off.

"Okay," Heng said, looking to the others. "Let's fish her out."

He watched as the two men struggled to pull the water-sodden corpse from the stream, then stood back as they slowly dragged her up onto the path.

"Turn her over," Heng said quietly, a profound sadness falling over him. For a moment, as they'd been lifting her from the water, he had thought of his own daughter and had wondered how he would have felt, had it been her. It wasn't, of course, for she was miles from here, after all, yet that possibility—the sense of empathy it created in him—made this moment poignant.

One of the guards stood at the dead girl's head, the other at her waist, facing his fellow, his legs straddling her as they heaved and turned her onto her back.

As one the three men gasped.

"*Aiya!*" Heng said, the word almost a breath. "What in the gods' names is that?"

The two young guards had stepped back at the sight, holding their hands out, away from themselves.

Heng Yu shuddered, then, reining in the deep, instinctive fear he was feeling, leaned in closer. "It seems  . . .  *alive.*"

At that, one of the guards turned and began to heave noisily. The other stood there, swaying unsteadily, disgust etched deep in his face. Yet he, like Heng Yu, was unable to tear his eyes from the sight.

The dead girl's face was peaceful, her eyes closed, her features unmarked, but lower down, where her thin silk dress had been torn open at the front, the flesh had been eaten away by something, leaving her chest a palpitating mess. Bad as that was, something else made it seem eerie and unnatural, for the bloodied tissue glowed with a faint golden tinge that seemed to pulse.

Heng swallowed back the bile that had risen to his throat, then straightened up, a shiver rippling through him. Whatever this was, it wasn't murder, nor was it an accident. He turned, looking back toward the Western Palace, anxious suddenly for Surgeon Chang to come and take charge of things.

"Master Heng?"

He looked to the guard, who was still staring at the girl. "Yes?"

"I think I know her."

Heng looked to the girl's face again, seeing only a stranger. "You know her?"

"I mean, I've seen her before. A few nights back. I was on picket duty at the East Gate. One of Master Cheng's men slipped in with her. At least, it looks like her."

Heng frowned. He had heard nothing of this. Strangers were being brought into the San Chang without his knowledge? He would have to have a word with Cheng Nai shan!

*Yes, but see to this first,* he reminded himself, hearing footsteps on the path behind him.

"Ah," he said, turning to find Fen Chun hurrying the graybeard along. "Surgeon Chang . . . it seems we have a mystery."

———————

MICHAEL LEVER ROSE and went to the window, gazing out across the gardens toward the wall of the compound. It was just after seven and the sky was overcast. Soon it would rain.

He turned back, looking across the vast expanse of carpet, past the big double bed where he slept alone, toward the screen on the far wall, and spoke to the House Computer.

"Give me the latest on the markets."

There was a pause, then, unexpectedly, his First Steward, Wei Yu, answered him:

"Forgive me, Master, but I think there's another news item will interest you. Shall I patch it through?"

Frowning, Michael gestured to the air. "Okay. Put it up."

He walked across as the screen lit up, then stood there, watching as the images changed, the voice-over subtitled in Mandarin at the foot of the screen.

*"Reports are breaking of a mystery disease that has struck down more than two dozen victims in the past twelve hours. While all the incidents so far reported have been isolated, the authorities have asked citizens to take sensible precautions against the possible spread of the disease, which is as yet unidentified."*

The camera dwelled on one of those victims, a young boy whose peaceful face suggested he was merely sleeping.

*"Government investigators are currently hard at work tracking down both the source and nature of the mysterious illness and are confident that they will have the situation under wraps by nightfall."*

The screen went blank. Michael turned, looking to the voice sensor in the center of the ceiling.

"Is that it?"

There was a pause. "The other channels are beginning to pick up on the item, Master, but they've nothing new as yet. Do you want me to keep you informed?"

Michael pressed his top teeth into his bottom lip, then nodded. "Okay. Make it at half hourly intervals." He hesitated, then. "Does Emily know?"

"You want me to tell her, Master?"

"Yes . . . Yes. And tell her—tell her I'll be in the breakfast room in half an hour."

"Yes, Master."

In the silence that followed, Lever understood. It had been there in the tone of the newsfac commentator. This was the big one. This was . . .

He swallowed, then frowned, his face wrinkling deeply, the fear he had felt seeing those images returning to him strongly.

Two weeks ago he had been at the big rare-diseases conference in Strasbourg. Only two weeks! He laughed, but it sounded hollow; a noise of despair. The words of one of the specialists came back to him:

*. . . and given the lack of any general immunity to such diseases, the likelihood of a major outbreak in the next five years is not, as one of my colleagues has asserted, a low statistic possibility, but a probability. In fact, it would be no exaggeration to say that—should hygiene standards continue to deteriorate at their current rate—it is almost a certainty.*

A certainty. Yes, he had known then that it was true. Time . . . it was only time before it struck. He had even set up a team within his management to see what could be done. But it was too late now, for here it was.

"Wei Yu?"

"Yes, Master?"

"Send in the maid to dress me."

"Yes, Master."

Michael went over to the bed and sat, drumming his fingers on the mattress while he waited, his mind wrestling with the question of what action he should take.

*Emily will know,* he told himself, realizing that he had no ready answers. *She'll tell me what to do. She always does.*

Yes, and meanwhile he'd make sure the boys stayed home, within the compound, because if this *was* what he thought it was . . .

He stopped, his fingers gripping the bed, then said it openly for the first time, naming it.

"The plague. The bloody plague is here among us."

Yes, like a thief, a cutthroat, stealing not purses but souls, invisible and deadly. The Hollower . . .

He looked up as the door on the far side of the room opened and the maid entered. She took two steps into the room and stopped, bowing low.

"You wanted me, Master?"

Michael stared at her, for the briefest moment forgetting why he'd asked her to come. The "accident" had been twenty years ago—the bomb that had killed his best friend and damn near finished him for good. Since then he had rebuilt himself, inside and out. But sometimes, as now, the old aches ached, like rheumatoid bones in damp weather. The kind that could not be gotten rid of with drugs or massage or . . .

For that one brief instant it was as if he were standing before that door once again, before the bomb had gone off. But this time he knew what was about to happen, and, because he knew, he wanted to warn her—to send her home to her family and tell her to get in supplies and lock their doors and . . .

"Here," he said dully. "Dress me."

Head bowed, she crossed the room, moving past him to the built-in cupboards.

He watched her, saddened. If he were to order her to strip and kneel, she would do it. If he told her to hop on one leg and sing a silly song, she would do that, too, without a moment's thought, for he was a rich man and she the third daughter of an unsuccessful street merchant. But all that would change in the coming days. Rich and poor . . . it did not matter now, for the great Hollower would level all.

He sighed heavily, conscious of the irony, for hadn't that been Emily's great aim, back in those days when she had been *Ping Tiao* . . . to *level* everything?

Well, now the Levelers had their wish.

Michael looked at the maid again, realizing as he did that he was not the kind of man who was happy using others. Rich as he was, the instinct to abuse did not exist in him.

Or was that strictly true? After all, he was his father's son. No. The instinct remained, encoded in him like the color of his eyes, the shape of his fingernails, but he had learned how to channel it; how to *control* it. Emily had taught him, long ago now.

The maid turned back, looking to him, blithely unaware of the shape of his thoughts, holding up a choice of *pau* so he could see.

"You want the blue, Master? Or would you like the green to-day?"

He stared at her, then shook his head. "Go home, Chan Sang. Go home at once, while you still can."

---

HENG YU KNELT, his head bowed, before his Master.

"The news is bad, *Chieh Hsia*. The lab report on the girl we found said that she died of a new and as yet unidentified strain of viral infection. It seems the virus is perfectly harmless until it comes in contact with human genetic material. Then . . . well, it is a killer, *Chieh Hsia*."

Heng Yu glanced up, noting how distracted Li Yuan seemed, how tired. No doubt he had been up all night, entertaining his young wife, if entertainment was the word for what they got up to.

"In the circumstances, *Chieh Hsia*, might I strongly recommend that we isolate the southern city straightaway and close all public meeting places—schools, markets, and the like—in the rest of the city."

Dragon Heart, who had been listening to him in a desultory fashion, now leaned forward.

"We shall do no such thing, Master Heng. Close the southern city? Why, what would our citizens think? And think of the damage it would do to trade. No, Master Heng. Find out some more about this—this *bug*, then report back. Later, after lunch, perhaps. Until then, do not trouble us with your scare-mongering."

Heng Yu stared at his Mistress openly, forgetting himself for that brief moment, appalled by her attitude. Didn't she understand? Hadn't she listened to a word he'd said? This was a killer. And if it spread . . .

"Master?" he said, looking to Li Yuan. "Is this your word?"

But Li Yuan wasn't interested in his objections, it seemed. "Do as my wife has told you, Master Heng. Oh, and send in Master Chang on your way out. I need to speak to him."

Heng Yu bowed then backed away.

Outside he stood there in a daze, barely conscious of Chang Nai shan as he swept past and on into the great room, the huge doors slamming shut behind him. For a moment Heng felt light headed and wondered if he were about to faint, then he collected himself.

Off-planet. He had to get his family off-planet. Yes. And there were others to warn too. Jelka and Karr and . . .

He sniffed in deeply, a sudden determination returning his strength to him. He would use the next few hours to do some good.

*Yes*, he told himself as he hurried back down the corridor toward his suite; for time was of the essence now. *This once I'll do what I ought, not what my Master tells me.*

━━━━━

"MICHAEL?"

Lever turned, looking to the doorway, where his private secretary stood.

"Yes, Dan?"

"We've got in a preliminary report on that mystery disease. Seems it's a variant of a psychotropic drug known as Golden Dreams. Something our old friend Lehmann thought up years back. It's hard to say exactly where the thing's coming from, but records show that the last known supplies of the stuff were stored down in the old GenSyn facility in Milan. Golden Dreams was an inject-yourself drug, but this appears to be a pneumonic form of it. The gestation period is less than forty-eight hours. We don't yet know how deadly it is. All of its victims thus far have been old people or children."

"Apart from the maid."

"Maid?" Johnson took a step toward him. "What maid?"

"In the San Chang. It seems Security were called about an incident and then, when they got there, were sent away without an explanation. I've had my sources do a little digging. Rumor is they found a body in one of the ornamental pools, her chest eaten away by this thing."

"Shit!"

"Yeah." Lever laughed, but it was with little humor. "*Deep* shit."

"So what do we do?"

Lever sat back. "We close all our factories. Warn our staff. And we get some of our so-called experts to get working on an antidote immediately. Can we get samples of this stuff?"

Johnson nodded. "There've been over four hundred new cases in the past hour. It shouldn't be difficult to persuade a couple of them to receive treatment. At our expense, of course."

Lever smiled. "Good. Then get to it. Oh, and Dan, make sure we've got enough supplies in. I'm going to seal the compound until things are over."

"Seal the compound? Isn't that a bit drastic?"

"You tell me. This thing is virulent, right?"

"You bet."

"Then I'm going to seal us off. Until things blow over. You're welcome to stay."

Johnson hesitated, then shook his head. "If you don't mind, Michael, I'll get on home. . . ." He smiled. "Once I've set things in motion, that is."

"Okay." Lever grinned, then got up and went across, embracing his old friend and helper. "And take care, Dan. I'll be needing you once this is over."

Johnson smiled and hugged him back. "I shall, Michael."

When Johnson had gone, Lever sat there, swiveling back and forth in his seat, staring blankly into the air. He was still sitting there when Emily came in.

"What's all this about sealing the compound?"

Michael looked up at her. "It's just a precaution, that's all."

"And what if I want out?"

"You can't. Not while that thing's raging out there."

"Raging?"

In answer he showed her the latest figures on the screen. "Over a thousand reported cases now, and more by the minute. Mostly in the south, but there are one or two isolated cases in the north too."

She stared at the screen, taking it all in.

"Your boys would die if you went out there. Not all of them, perhaps, but some of them. You want that?"

Emily looked at him then slowly shook her head.

"Then trust me, Em. For the sake of the boys, trust me."

KARR SAT BACK and roared with laughter, then clapped his hands as Mileja bowed, her imitation of her father finished.

"And you say he knows?" Karr said, looking to where Jelka sat, sandwiched between Hannah and Marie on the big sofa, a broad grin on her face.

"Oh, Kim *loves* it!" she said. "If we ever have a gathering, he *insists* that she do it!"

Mileja stood there, beaming, her dark, curly hair framing her rosy-cheeked face. "I can do Mama too," she said, a subtle change of her stance making her resemble her mother strikingly, even though she looked nothing like the Marshal's daughter.

"Not now, young madam," Jelka said, wagging a finger at her. "Now we must get ready. Master Heng will be waiting for us." She looked to Karr again. "Gregor, if I might—"

The urgent knocking at the door startled them all. Hannah, whose rooms these were, quickly stood and answered it, standing at the door a moment exchanging words with the stooped and aged servant before coming back, her face clouded.

"Forgive me, everyone, but something's happening in the city."

She went over to the big screen in the corner and reached up, switching it on. At once it was filled with images of weeping people, of hospital wards and worried faces. The voice of the commentator was calm, yet there was a distinctly ominous tone to his words.

". . . with more than a thousand new victims being reported every hour. In a statement from his palace in Bremen, Chancellor Heng has asked the populace to remain calm, but as a precautionary measure he has ordered the immediate closure of all schools, clubs, restaurants, and public markets and has asked citizens to stay in their homes. Emergency food deliveries will be organized and people are asked to report any further outbreaks of the illness to their local *yamen*."

Both Karr and Jelka were standing now, staring at the screen, but Marie just sat, frowning deeply and staring at her hands.

"What is it?" Karr asked, as the commentator's voice fell silent momentarily.

"It looks like some kind of plague," Jelka said quietly, pointing to the marks on one of the bodies on the screen. "Though the gods alone know what kind of bug does *that*."

"It looks like it's glowing," Hannah said. Then, "Do you mind if I run it back a little?"

"No," Karr said quietly, answering for them all, his eyes wide as he stared at the awful images on the screen.

Hannah reached up, touching the control pad, freezing and then backtracking the images until she came to the one that had caught her attention. It was a close-up of an old man's chest and thorax. They had been partially eaten away, the flesh melted as though a flame had been put to plastic. Yet where the tissue was damaged it didn't bleed but seemed to glow with a faint golden light.

"DeVore?" Karr asked.

Hannah frowned. "Who knows?" But somehow she didn't think so. This wasn't his style. This was too haphazard. This had the look of an accident.

Jelka, who had turned and was looking out the window, now called across to her.

"Hannah? There are fires out there. In the distance. Great plumes of smoke. Is that normal?"

Hannah came over, then opened the French windows and stepped out onto the balcony. The others joined her there.

"They're burning the city again," she said quietly.

"Or corpses," Marie said, speaking for the first time.

There came the distant noise of shouts, screams, and then the distinct rattle of semiautomatic fire.

"Oh, gods!" Marie said, holding Mileja to her tightly. "Oh, gods, not again!"

Karr was staring at Jelka. "You must go," he said.

"Go?"

"You must leave here now. Get off-planet."

But Jelka shook her head. "I can't. Not until I've said good-bye."

Karr frowned. "Then say good-bye. But do it now, then get out. I'll come with you, if you want."

Jelka hesitated, then nodded. "Okay." She turned, looking to Hannah, then gestured to Mileja to come. "We'll be as quick as we can. Meanwhile, take care."

Marie looked at her, her smile tinged with concern. "Just hurry back, neh?"

"Yes," Hannah said, stepping across and hugging Jelka. "And take no silly risks, eh, Jelka Ward? Mankind has need of you."

━━━━━━

N A N   F A - H S I E N , Master of the Inner Chambers, and son of Nan Ho, once Chancellor to the great T'ang, Li Yuan, straightened up, staring at himself in the mirror, making sure he was correctly dressed. Satisfied, he turned to look at the three waiting guards.

"Well?" he asked. "You have your orders. What are you waiting for?"

The Captain hesitated, then, clearing his throat, answered for them all. "It's just that it's . . ."

"Unfair?" Nan Fa-hsien laughed bitterly. "We are our Master's hands. We do what he says. We do not act without his permission. Chancellor Heng . . . Heng Yu, that is . . . has disobeyed our Master. For that his life is forfeit."

Looking down, the Captain spoke again, more quietly this time. "Can't you see what is happening, Master Nan? The city is in turmoil. Rumor is that this illness is a kind of plague. And the Chancellor . . . well, he but acts to save as many lives as he can. If *that* is treachery . . ."

Nan Fa-hsien answered him again, uncomfortable and just the slightest bit irritated that he should be made to defend his Master's actions in this manner.

"Whether Master Heng is right or wrong does not concern you and me, Captain. We have our duty, neh? Or do you forget whom you serve?"

The Captain's laugh was openly scornful now. "You mean *her?*"

Nan Fa-hsien stared at the man, speechless now.

"You think our Master in his true senses would have ordered this?" the Captain continued, shaking his head. "No. Never in ten thousand years! This is her doing . . . this *wickedness.*"

"Enough!" Nan Fa-hsien bellowed, losing his temper with the man. "Do your duty, Captain, or surrender your dagger."

The Captain stared at him with a cold disdain, then, looking to his fellows, turned on his heels and left.

*Aiya,* Nan Fa-hsien thought, letting out a long, shuddering breath.

They were right, of course. Their Master was *not* in his true senses. Nor was what Heng Yu had done an act of treachery. But that was not the point. Li Yuan was the arch, the hub, the very center of it all. His word was therefore sacrosanct. And they . . . he felt a shiver run down his spine . . . they were but his hands, to do as he ordered, for good or ill.

He looked across the room to where his two secretaries stood against the wall, silently looking on.

"Come," he said, conscious of his father's ghost at his shoulder at that moment. He was to be appointed Chancellor at last. Chancellor, like his father before him.

*Forgive me, Heng Yu,* he thought, leading the two servants out and along the corridor, heading toward the stables where his T'ang awaited him. But he had not gone far before he was called back.

"Master Nan!"

He turned as one of the stewards from the Eastern Palace came up and, kneeling, pressing his forehead to the floor, began to speak.

"It is here, Master Nan! The plague is here among us!"

Nan Fa-hsien felt his whole body go cold. "Slow down, Steward Wen. Tell me what has happened."

"One of the guards . . . one of the three who found her . . . he is sick, Master Fan. The golden sickness. The Hollower . . ."

Hearing that word again—the third time in an hour—Nan Fa-hsien frowned. How quickly such things spread.

"It is not possible," he said. "Why, it is only hours since they found the body!"

"Yes, Master Nan," the man said, looking up at him, as if *he* could save them.

"And is he the only instance?"

"So far, Master Nan."

"Then isolate him. And the other two as well. In fact, isolate all who have been in contact with them."

"All those . . ." Steward Wen gave a strange laugh. "But that is the whole of the San Chang, Master Nan. Are you saying we should bar the doors?"

"I . . ."

Suddenly he understood. Suddenly he knew why Master Heng had acted as he had. The thing was out of hand. However fast they ran now, it would run faster.

"Bar the doors," he said, a cold certainty in his voice. "And guard them well. And, Steward Wen . . ."

"Yes, Master Nan?"

"Go light a candle to the gods."

NAN FA-HSIEN FOUND HIS MASTER in the stables, working alone in one of the end stalls, raking through the straw bedding with a pitchfork, his back to him.

"You sent for me, *Chieh Hsia*?"

Li Yuan stopped, resting a moment on the handle of his fork. "I sent for you, Master Nan."

Nan Fa-hsien waited patiently, then heard his Master sigh.

"Are you all right, *Chieh Hsia*?"

Li Yuan's laugh was bleak. "Am I all right?" He sniffed deeply, then straightened up, throwing aside the fork. "I did not know until an hour ago."

"Know, *Chieh Hsia*?"

"The maid . . . I slept with her. She . . ."

Li Yuan turned, and as he did Nan Fa-hsien gasped and fell to his knees. His Master's face was blotched, the neck too. Faint golden blotches.

"*Aiya!*" Nan cried, staring at his master with dismay. But Li Yuan merely stood there, stoical, resigned, it seemed, to his fate.

"The gods have decided to test us, Master Nan. To punish us for our wickedness. Let us pray that some of us survive."

CHENG NAI SHAN STOOD BACK, aghast at his Mistress's reaction. But then, what had he expected? It was not every day that one learned that one's husband had the plague.

Even so, that shriek she'd uttered . . .

He stared at her as she knelt there, pulling at her hair and groaning loudly. *The gods help us*, he thought, finding the theatrical nature of the display somewhat ostentatious. *Why you'd think she'd really loved the man!*

He knew better, of course. After all, it had been he who had arranged all those secret visits—all those other young men who had come, quite literally, and without his Master's knowledge—to keep his Mistress happy.

"Mistress," he said, taking a step toward her, trying to get her attention. "Mistress?"

The screech she gave made him jerk back. He turned, gesturing to his secretary.

"Lai Wu . . . go fetch the Surgeon. Tell him—tell him we need a sedative for the Lady Lung."

The groaning grew louder, more violent. Cheng Nai shan glanced at the woman and shuddered with distaste. So coarse she was. So—

"Master Cheng?"

He turned, looking to the newcomer. It was one of the captains of the elite palace guard.

"What is it, man?"

"It is the gates, Master Cheng. Nan Fa-hsien has ordered them barred."

"Barred?" He stared at the man, then, knowing he must act at once, rushed from the room, leaving the Captain to catch up with him.

So young Master Nan thought he was in charge, did he? Well, just because his Master had given him a new title, that did not mean that it was he who held the reins of power here in the San Chang.

"The nerve of the man," he murmured, half running as he emerged from the ornate entrance and ran across the marble path, heading for the Main Guardhouse. "We'll see whose word counts more!"

NAN FA-HSIEN HAD HEARD that his Mistress was in a state, yet when he reached her rooms they were empty. The only sign that Dragon Heart had been there were a few shreds of ripped silk—silk, he guessed, that she had torn from her own robes.

*Kuan Yin preserve us*, he thought, groaning inwardly. He had hoped to spare her, or, at best, at least to have the Surgeon there when he broke the news, so that he could administer some palliative to help her sleep, but now . . .

*It's that meddler Cheng*, he thought, the guess becoming a certainty as he sniffed the air and smelled the sweet, telltale waft of Chang's perfume. *What is that bastard up to?*

He would send someone to find out. But first the Empress.

He turned, looking about him, smoothing his beard with one hand as he forced himself to think. Where would she be right now? What would she be thinking?

He tried to put himself in her place. Tried to imagine her response. She would be tearful and afraid, yes, and shocked. But after that . . . He shivered, then nodded his head. After that she would be angry. Angry enough to want revenge.

Revenge, yes, but whom would she take out her anger on? And how?

*His rooms*, he thought. *She'll have gone to his rooms*. And, hurrying from the suite, he went in quick pursuit.

He found her there, seated in the corner, hunched over a screen. For a moment he simply stared at her, astonished by how calm she seemed. She was humming to herself as she tapped the keys. Humming, and smiling broadly.

"There!" she said, triumphantly. "That's another one!"

"Mistress?" Nan said, edging toward her, knowing how fiery she was when angered. "Mistress, are you all right?"

Her laugh chilled his blood. *Tap tap tap* and then a laugh.

"There! That'll serve the bastard right!"

He frowned. What on earth was she doing?

He inched around the desk and, moving quietly, tiptoeing the last few steps, positioned himself behind her, so that he could view the screen.

"*Ai-ya!*" he groaned, seeing what it was. One by one she was accessing the files of those who were wired. One by one their names came up, their faces appeared on the screen, an access code flashed. One by one she keyed those access codes and pressed DETO-NATE.

She was blowing up the wired! She was trawling the files randomly and blowing the heads off innocent young men and women!

Without thinking he stepped up and pulled her back, physically tearing her away from the machine.

She screeched and turned on him, trying to scratch out his eyes, a wildcat suddenly, but he was too strong for her. Throwing her down, he yelled at her.

"Hsun Lung hsin! You must desist!"

But she wasn't about to desist. With a blood-curdling growl Dragon Heart threw herself at him again, her nails ripping through his silks and tearing great lumps of flesh from his upper arms before he could throw her down again.

He drew his dagger.

"Hsun Lung hsin!"

But she was not listening. Her eyes were wild and mad and he knew that he would have to stop her. This time as she threw herself at him, he raised the knife.

Both her scream, and the weight of her suddenly on his arm, surprised him, so that he let go of the knife and, staggering back, let her fall. Stumbling, he tripped and fell over the edge of the desk, cracking the back of his head against it.

He blacked out. When he woke, it was to find two guards staring down at him.

He tried to get up, but the guard's boot pressed him down again. "Stay there, you bastard," the man said, sneering at him. "Unless you'd like a taste of your own medicine."

Nan Fa-hsien shuddered, remembering. He had felt the blade go in, and in that last moment, as her eyes had met his, had known that she had thrown herself upon it.

In the heart. He had stabbed the Empress in the heart.

Nan closed his eyes and groaned. When he opened them again, it was to find himself looking up at Chang Nai shan.

"Master Nan," Chang said, smiling urbanely and giving a mock little bow of respect. "Had a little trouble, have we?"

---

JELKA STOOD AT her father's graveside, her head bowed, as the wind blew across the giant stadium. Karr stood behind her, at attention, his eyes lowered, Mileja's tiny hand enveloped within his. Farther off armed guards patrolled the banked white stone terraces, stopping briefly to look on, conscious of the significance of the moment.

Jelka knelt and, bowing her head before the massive basalt headstone, placed her offerings on the white marble plaque.

*Marshal Knut Tolonen*, it read, the words cut deep into the marble, and beneath, under the Mandarin transcription of her father's name, the final lines of her homeland's great epic poem:

> But let this be as it may be,
> I have shown the way to singers,
> Showed the way, and left the markers,
> Cut the branches, shown the pathways.
> This way, therefore, leads the pathway,
> Here the course lies newly opened,
> Open for the greater singers,
> For the young, who now are growing,
> For the rising generation.

She shivered, reading those familiar words, then stood again, studying the life-size portrait of her father that was cut into the great slab of basalt facing her. Seeing it once more, she felt a lump come to her throat.

*So you were*, she thought, nodding to herself. Yes, even when he had been alive, he had been like stone; like the great arch upon which all else stood.

And now he stood there, frozen forever in this single image, staring out toward the east, his chin slightly raised, that great cliff of a face revealing the strength and resolution of a thousand men.

She stared and stared, the desire to reach out and touch his hand again—to have his fingers close on hers—so strong that it almost unhinged her. *Absurd*, she thought, feeling a single tear run down her cheek. Yet when she turned, it was to find Karr wiping his free hand across his face.

She smiled, then put out a hand, beckoning her daughter. Mileja came to her and, her hand in her mother's, knelt before her grandfather's tablet, placing her own small offering beside Jelka's.

"You must never forget him, Mileja," Jelka said quietly. "He was a great man. An oak among pines."

Mileja stared up at her mother momentarily, then looked back at the great headstone. "Is he inside there, Mama?" she asked.

Jelka was about to say no, about to explain, when Karr stepped up beside her.

"He is everywhere here, Mileja," he said, kneeling beside the seven-year-old. "This is his place, here, at the very center of it all. Your mother speaks the truth. Your grandfather was a great man. Perhaps the greatest Chung Kuo has known. Why, Emperors would bow their heads to him."

She stared back at Karr, wide eyed, then turned her head to look at the great carving once more, seeing it anew. Finally, with a seriousness that was no mimicry, she bowed low.

Karr looked past her at Jelka and smiled; a smile that seemed to encompass all she was feeling at that moment. She returned it, glad he was there; glad that he'd shared this moment with her. Then, knowing it was time, she turned back.

"Good-bye, Father," she said quietly. "You will be with me wherever I go." She placed her hand to her heart. "In here."

Again she bowed. One final time she took in those granite features, that rocklike stance, then, closing her eyes, squeezing them tight against the tears that threatened, she slowly backed away.

---

KARR LOOKED ABOUT HIM as they approached the shadowed entrance to the great tunnel that led beneath the terraces, signaling to his men, summoning them to him, relieved that it had all gone without incident, especially as they were drastically under-strength today—a dozen of his best men having been assigned to collect his girls from their respective schools and colleges.

"Thank you," Jelka said as they went in under the arch, stopping a moment to press his hand.

"Not at all," he said, turning his attention to her for that moment. "I'm only glad I could be of service. If there's anything else?"

"No," she said. "You were right. We should get out at once. But won't you come with us, Gregor? You and Marie and the girls. Oh, and Hannah, too, of course. There's room. We'd make room."

Karr smiled. "I'm grateful. Truly I am. But there are things here I must do. Bad as matters are, I can't just leave."

"I understand. But my offer remains open. Anytime you wish to come, just come. Okay?"

Karr smiled, nodding his gratitude. "Okay." He turned, looking about him, then frowned. "Where's Mileja?"

"She's just over there, sir," one of his men called back, "she . . ."

Jelka turned and looked. As she did, an old woman stepped from one of the storerooms leading off the dimly lit tunnel and hobbled up to Mileja, holding something out to the little girl.

"Mileja!" Jelka shouted. *"No!"*

But it was too late. The old woman had given Mileja the gift and was patting her wrist fondly.

"Shit!" Karr hissed, looking to the nearest of his men. "I thought you'd cleared this place, Eduard! Where did *she* come from?"

Eduard grimaced. "She must have been sleeping among the crates in there. . . ."

Karr glowered at him angrily. "Well, get rid of her! Now! And check her out. Make sure she hasn't got anything!"

"Sir!"

But Jelka was already there. Pulling Mileja away, she thanked the old woman, her smile tinged with fear. A moment later two of Karr's men dragged the startled woman away.

Karr hurried across. "I'm so sorry, Jelka. How can I apologize? I thought we'd cleared this place."

"No matter," Jelka said, clearly shaken by the encounter. "No harm's been done." Even so, she took the sprig of flowers from her daughter and threw them aside.

"Let us hope so," Karr said, kneeling, then ruffling his hand through Mileja's hair. "For a moment I thought . . ."

Jelka looked to him. "You don't have to explain. You see assassins everywhere, neh, Gregor?"

Karr looked back at her and nodded.

AS THEY FLEW NORTH AGAIN, Karr sat beside the pilot, gathering in whatever information he could about the situation.

As the plague spread, so effective government was breaking down. More than a thousand had already died, though whether that was of the plague or from "contributory factors"—riots, grudge killings, et cetera—was hard to determine, for as things broke down, so the reliability of information diminished.

Chancellor Heng's broadcast had had some effect in calming things, but this had been seriously undermined in the last half hour by news of his arrest on a charge of treason.

He had not told Jelka about that yet. Besides, she was far more worried about her daughter. Using the medical kit in the back of the cruiser, she had scrubbed Mileja's arms and hands with a disinfecting agent, then given her a shot to boost her immune system. Mileja showed no sign of having sustained any harm, but Karr could hardly blame Jelka for taking such precautions. Had it been his own daughters he would have done the same.

In that vein, at least, the news was good. All four of his daughters were now safely home, locked within the compound doors. Marie's relief in relating the news to him had been echoed by his own.

Karr turned, staring back into the main cabin of the cruiser, watching as Jelka settled her daughter, tucking her in beneath the military-issue blanket. Her offer was tempting, *very* tempting. So much so that he had almost mentioned it to Marie earlier. But he hadn't, because he knew she would have urged him to accept it, to leave Chung Kuo to its fate and look after his own for once. And maybe she was right. Maybe there *were* moments when all a man could do was look after those nearest and dearest to him. Yet, in his judgment, that moment had not yet come. While he could still do something constructive he would. If his voice, his not inconsiderable influence, could help the situation, even in some small way, then he would use it.

Jelka looked up and saw him watching her, then went over to him, a weary smile lighting her features.

"She seems okay," she said quietly, slumping down onto the leather padded bench at the back of the cockpit. "How are things in the bigger world?"

"Bad," he said. "And they're going to get worse."

She sighed and rubbed at her eyes with the heels of her hands before looking back at him.

"You're going to stay, aren't you?"

"Yes," he said.

"And Marie and the girls?"

He blew out a long breath. "Maybe I'll send them to stay with Kao Chen and his family on the Plantations. Until it all blows over."

"You think it *will* blow over, Gregor?"

He shrugged. "I don't know. This is all . . . new." He laughed quietly. "You know, I remember your father once saying something about fighting terrorism and about how it was like trying to fight ghosts. Well, this thing . . . this sickness . . . that's a form of terrorism, too, neh? So maybe we're just fighting ghosts again . . . little golden ghosts."

"Any word yet from the San Chang?"

Karr shook his head. "Nothing in, nothing out. A complete shutdown."

"You think there's been trouble there?"

"Who knows? But if Heng Yu has been—" He stopped, realizing he had not told her yet.

She narrowed her eyes. "What about Heng Yu?"

Karr swallowed, then looked down. "He's been arrested. For treason. It seems he went against the Empress."

"Went against . . ." Jelka's eyes were wide with disbelief. "So where is he?"

Karr shrugged. "Edingen, perhaps. Or maybe they've taken him to the San Chang."

Jelka sat forward urgently, reaching out to touch his arm. "Then we have to go there! We have to get him out!"

"No," Karr said, smiling apologetically. "We're going straight to the spaceport."

"But—"

"I'm finding out," he said, covering her hand with his own. "Once I know where Master Heng is, I'll take whatever action is appropriate." He smiled. "Don't worry, Jelka. I'll not let that bitch harm a hair on Heng Yu's head if I can help it!"

She grinned back at him. "Good! Then let's make haste. You've much to do."

"Yes," he said, grinning broadly. "It's almost like old times, neh?"

◆◆◆◆◆◆◆

CHENG NAI SHAN STEPPED FORWARD, meaning to block the Warlord's way, but Han Ch'in brushed him aside. As Cheng hurried after him, protesting all the while, Han turned and, grabbing the man by the neck, pinned him to the wall.

"Try that again, Master Cheng, and I'll take great delight in killing you. Now, keep out of my way. I wish to see my father."

He let Cheng fall. The new Chancellor knelt there, gasping, touching his neck tenderly, glaring at Han Ch'in's back as he disappeared through the double doors and into Li Yuan's rooms.

Priests and surgeons turned at the young man's entry, then, seeing who it was, made a path for him, bowing as he moved quickly, unceremoniously, between them.

At the door he stopped, smoothing a hand down the front of his silks, composing himself, then stepped inside.

The room was silent, lit only by a small wall lamp on the far side and a single glow lamp beside the bed. In its wan light a woman sat in a chair beside the bed, her breast exposed as she fed a child. Beside her, beneath the thin silk covers, lay his father, his upper chest and neck sheened in sweat.

Han Ch'in frowned, then slowly crossed the room. He was only a few paces from the woman when she looked up and smiled at him.

"Welcome, brother. I wondered if you would come."

"Kuei . . . Kuei Jen?"

"Don't let these fool you," Kuei Jen answered, extricating the baby from his swollen nipple, then tucking the breast back into his shirt as he raised the baby to a sitting position on his lap and began to smooth its back. "I am still Kuei Jen and I warrant I could outshoot, outride, and generally outdrink you any day, elder brother!"

Han Ch'in laughed, but his eyes were wide, staring at the baby and at the womanly shape of his half-brother. He had not expected to find Kuei Jen here, let alone a Kuei Jen so . . . *changed.*

"Well, brother?" Kuei Jen said, after a moment. "Will you not ask how our father is?"

Han Ch'in stared at him a moment longer, then, with a little shudder, looked to the figure sprawled upon the bed. "*Aiya* . . ." he breathed softly, "he looks so . . . ill."

"He is dying," Kuei Jen said, matter-of-factly. "See the marks upon him. It's eating him away from the inside, *hollowing* him."

Han Ch'in swallowed, his face appalled. "Is there nothing we can do?"

Kuei Jen smiled. "I have done all I could, but as you see, he seems not to be responding."

Han Ch'in looked back at him, not understanding. Then, "Are you not afraid, Kuei Jen?"

Kuei Jen looked up at him, clear eyed. "Are you?"

"For myself, no. If I die, I die. My duty to my father comes before that. But you—you have the child to think of."

"The child is fine," Kuei Jen said. "As am I. We have an antidote, you see."

"An antidote?"

Kuei Jen nodded, gesturing to the bedside table where three tiny vials lay in a silken box. Two were empty now; the third contained a dark solution. "That's yours, brother. If you want it."

Han Ch'in stared at the vial a moment, then back at Kuei Jen. "You're like me," he said, after a while. "Oh, not the breasts. . . ."

Both half-brothers laughed, relaxing with each other suddenly.

"I often wondered," Kuei Jen began, breaking the silence that had fallen.

"Wondered?"

"What you were like. You see, I have known for a long time now. Father never told me, but I found out. I made it my business to find out. For a long time I thought I had lost you."

"And that worried you?"

Kuei Jen nodded and, as the baby burped, lifted it and placed it on his shoulder, patting its back gently, rhythmically. "I always wanted a brother. An elder brother. Someone to look up to, the way our father looked up to his brother. Someone to love."

Han Ch'in frowned, then looked away, disturbed by the rawness of that final word.

"Does that embarrass you, Han Ch'in? That I should want to love you?"

Han Ch'in looked back, then shrugged.

Kuei Jen laughed. "I'm sorry, brother. It is my hormones, or so they tell me. They make me . . . *emotional.*"

Han Ch'in stared a moment longer, then laughed. "Why, I do believe my little brother is teasing me."

Kuei Jen smiled and nodded. "Even so, there is an element of truth in it. We were bred to be cold, you and I. To stifle our emotions. I have learned that that is wrong. I have learned . . . well, to be more myself. To free the woman in me."

Han Ch'in laughed. "That I can see." Then, more seriously: "And if he dies?"

"Then you rule, elder brother. As is the way." Kuei Jen gestured toward the vial. "Take it and you need not fear this sickness."

"And if it is a poison?" Han Ch'in asked, narrowing his eyes.

Kuei Jen smiled sadly. "You have been living far too long in your mother's shadow, elder brother. I would not poison you. Not for all the kingdoms of the world, let alone this small domain. Here, give me it."

Han Ch'in leaned across and picked up the vial and handed it to him, watching as Kuei Jen cracked the tip of it and put it to his tongue.

He swallowed, then held out the vial, offering it to Han Ch'in. A finger's width of the dark solution had gone. "Now you. That is, if you really want to live."

Han Ch'in stared at his brother a moment longer, then took the vial and drained it at a gulp, setting it down beside the others.

"Good," Kuei Jen said, smiling, at ease again. "Now draw up a chair and sit with me. The night looks set to be a long one and we have much to talk about."

◆◆◆◆◆

NIGHT HAD FALLEN by the time Karr returned home. He had searched all afternoon for Heng Yu, but there was no sign of his old friend, and there were strong rumors that the ex-Chancellor was already dead, his throat cut, his body dumped in a back alley to be burned with the other corpses.

Stepping down from the cruiser, Karr felt heavy hearted. He would have to break the news to Marie and Hannah, and the thought of that made his guts ache. He hated being the bearer of such news.

As he made his way across the dimly lit yard, acknowledging the bows of his men, he wondered once again whether he should tell Marie of Jelka's offer; whether it wasn't best this once to call it a day and get out.

Twenty thousand dead. That was the latest figure. And more by the hour. If this kept up, the city would be a morgue within a week.

Karr sighed and went inside, ducking beneath the lintel. The corridor was dark, but up ahead a light shone in the kitchen. He could hear Marie and the others there—the laughter of May and Beth. The thought of them raised his spirits, but only a little. They, too, would have to be told.

Coming out into the kitchen, he braced himself, knowing it would be the first thing they would ask, then stopped dead, staring across the room, open mouthed. There, in a chair on the far side of the big kitchen table, sat Heng Yu, a bowl of *ch'a* cupped between his hands as he talked to the lady of the house, Marie.

For a moment no one noticed Karr standing there. Then the conversation died, as first one, then another, saw him.

"Master Heng?" Karr said, still not one hundred percent positive that this wasn't a delusion brought on by tiredness.

Heng looked at him and laughed. "I hear you have been looking for me, Gregor Karr."

Hearing that voice, Karr swore. "You bugger! I've been running about the city, breaking my balls trying to find you, and all the while—"

"—I have been here." Heng smiled and shrugged with his hands. "Yes."

"Why, you . . ."

Heng raised a hand. "Just a moment, Gregor. Try and see it from another viewpoint. If even *you* think I am dead, then is it not likely that our enemies will take it for the truth?"

Karr made to speak, then huffed.

Heng stood and, setting his *ch'a* bowl down, came around the table and stood before Karr, looking up into the big man's face.

"I am sorry to have played such a miserable trick on you, Gregor, but there was a need."

Marie laughed. "It's true, Gregor. You're such a bad actor. If you had known . . . well, they would have known for sure that Master Heng was still alive!"

Karr bristled momentarily, then, recognizing the truth in what had been said, reached out and hugged Heng Yu to him, genuinely delighted that he was safe, the differing physical stature of the two men making it seem as though Karr were embracing a teenage son rather than an equal.

Karr stepped back. "You are forgiven, Master Heng. This once. But you must pay a penalty."

Heng Yu stared up at him. "A penalty?"

Karr grinned. "Yes." He looked to Marie. "Sweetheart, break out that bottle of Yunan double-strength brandy and pour Master Heng a glass."

"And that's a penalty?" Heng Yu asked, eyebrows raised.

"Yes," Karr said, mock sternly. "But you must drain the glass at a single go."

Marie, who had gone to the cupboard, now turned and looked at her husband. "And is Master Heng to drink alone?"

Karr laughed. "No. . . . Pour everyone a glass. May and Beth too. Let us celebrate Master Heng's safe homecoming. And toast the safe journey of our good friends Jelka and Mileja Ward."

———◆◆◆◆———

THEY HAD CLIMBED UP beyond the earth's pull; now they were decelerating slowly, synchronizing their path with that of the parked *Luoyang* where it waited, orbiting one hundred and fifteen thousand *li* above Chung Kuo.

Opening her eyes, Jelka yawned, then, conscious that the restraining harness had slotted back into the chair, she stretched and turned, looking at Mileja.

Mileja was sleeping, her face angelic, a stray lock of her dark curls fallen over one cheek. Jelka smiled, then, reaching beneath her seat, pulled out the blanket and, breaking the wrapper, shook it out and tucked it over Mileja.

She turned, looking at the black square of the viewer in front of her; reaching out, she touched its surface with her fingertips. At once a view of the planet below filled the tiny screen.

Looking at it, Jelka sighed, knowing it was the last time she would see the planet of her birth. So peaceful it looked, so innocent, and yet thousands were dying by the moment down there.

The cities were burning. For the third time in her brief lifetime the cities were burning. But this time, she knew, nothing would rise from the ashes.

She thought of Karr and felt sad. Maybe he'd come, after all. Maybe, when he saw how hopeless things were—how futile—he would change his mind.

She closed her eyes, thinking back over the day, seeing again the great basalt slab into which her father's image had been cut, and gave a little shiver, then reached out to blank the viewer.

Glancing at Mileja, she saw that the blanket had slipped down and went to tuck it back, then froze, her heart in her mouth. There, on her daughter's right arm, just above the wrist, the flesh was bruised. A golden, faintly glowing bruise.

*The plague!* She felt her whole body go cold. *Aiya! Mileja had the plague!*

# CHAPTER THIRTEEN

# The Spider in the Well

**K**IM CROUCHED IN THE POCKET they had cut near the head of the shaft, watching as Ikuro and his brothers prepared the Cutter, tending it gently and encouraging it as if it were some massive beast—which, in truth, it was. Earlier he had patted its diamond-tough flank and felt its unexpected warmth. Unexpected, because this was a creature that could cut through solid rock and withstand the force of vacuum on its skin.

Seeing the Cutter whole as they towed it across to the drilling site, it had reminded him of a giant maggot, its narrow segmented body tapering at each end. At the front end were the rotating jaws, a long, toughened gullet leading to a small but efficient refinery where all of the valuable minerals were extracted. Two smaller gullets led to the rear, one disposing of the waste in the form of neat pellets, the other leading to an expandable storage sack.

All in all it was ingenious. GenSyn, of course, but made to the specifications of the Ishida family.

Ikuro turned to him, the light in his helmet revealing a distinct smile.

"We're ready," he said, his voice sounding in Kim's own helmet. He drifted toward Kim slowly, then gestured to the lightweight transparent shields—like full-body riot shields—that were stacked to one side of the cavelike pocket. "You'd best take one of those.

538

There's not usually much 'loose,' but it's best to take no chances, neh?"

Kim nodded, then turned and, pushing off, floated over to the stack and picked one up. He was studying it, conscious that it wasn't polymer based, when Ikuro came alongside him.

"It's processed rock," Ishida said, taking one for himself, then looking to Kim with his incessant grin. "It doesn't really matter what you use, Kim San, it's how you fold the molecules that gives it its strength. That and the vacuum between each layer."

Kim smiled. So it was. It was just that he was so used to things being made of plastic. But it made sense. After all, what did they have most of in the asteroid belt? Rock and vacuum.

It made him understand. Going out there, things would change. Life adapted. And out there they would have to adapt very quickly, or die.

*And when we come back?* he asked himself, imagining things a thousand years hence. *Will they even recognize us back on Chung Kuo? That is, if Chung Kuo is still a living, breathing planet.*

As ever, the thought of it engendered in him a mixed response—of excitement . . . and fear. Fear that somewhere along the line—as the result, perhaps, of extreme evolutionary pressures—mankind might become inhuman. Might spawn . . . well, DeVores. A harder, more intelligent species, yet lacking in that moral sense that made mankind essentially a decent creature.

"Okay," he said, shaking off the sudden mood. "Let's see what it can do."

The drilling shaft had been cut by hand—Ikuro and his brothers working six-hour shifts turn and turn about until it was done. Only then could they use the Cutter. Now it was its turn.

"Five days it'll take," Ikuro said, reaffirming what had been said earlier.

"What if it hits something hard enough to break its cutting jaw?" Kim asked, following Ikuro out into the gap between the Cutter and the shaft wall, moving slowly along the narrow space, his right hand hauling him along the Cutter's blood-warm flank, the shield scraping along the rough rock wall to his left.

Ikuro laughed. "If it hits something that hard, then we've struck solid diamond. And if we've struck diamond, then we buy another Cutter! Maybe two!"

Kim smiled, but still he was tense about this. It was so important. If they could—as the first estimates suggested—knock six months off the cutting schedule, then they could hit the earlier window. They could leave before the year's end—a full year earlier than they'd originally planned.

As the Cutter tapered, the gap grew wider until they could see the far wall. Several dozen of Ikuro's relatives had gathered there. Seeing Kim, they nodded their helmeted heads at him and grinned, or lifted their safety shields in welcome. A friendly bunch, sociable as only a close-knit community could be.

"You say when," Ikuro said, looking about him to check that all was in order.

"Aren't we in the way here?" Kim said, conscious of the huge bulk of the Cutter in the tunnel behind him.

"We would be if we were staying, but this is only a test. To show you what she can do."

"She?"

Ikuro grinned again. "Oh, she's most definitely female. A real softy."

Kim laughed, surprised. "Soft, huh?"

Again Ikuro nodded. "Have you ever met a man who could work as hard as a woman? Who could endure as much? You think men would have babies if they had to suffer that kind of pain? No. The human race would have died out long ago. That's why we know she's a girl." He patted the Cutter's flank fondly. "Besides, she's a sweet thing, neh?"

"Neh," Kim agreed. Then, "Well, shall we begin?"

Ikuro turned, waving his brothers and cousins and uncles back. "Okay. I think she's hungry."

Kim watched, fascinated, as one of the brothers—the big one, Kano—drifted over to the Cutter's mouth and, undaunted by the massive ring of huge, shovellike teeth, began to murmur to it. It seemed to tremble, like a struck bell, and then slowly, very slowly, it began to edge forward, its segmented sides undulating gently, moving its huge bulk with a delicacy Kim would not have believed possible.

As the watching men moved back, it edged its way slowly forward until the edges of its jaws were touching the surface of the rock.

Kano's voice sounded in every helmet. "Shields up!"

Kim lifted his, staring through it as the jaws locked and began very slowly to turn, a strangely glutinous substance trickling over the jet-black gums as it picked up speed. There was a crunching, a grinding, that grew louder and louder. The air began to get hot. Soon the noise became unbearable. And then, as suddenly as it had started, it stopped.

It had lasted only two minutes. At the end of it the Cutter eased back, its jaws flexing once before they froze rigid again.

"Go and look," Ikuro said, nudging him forward.

He drifted across, amazed to see how far the Cutter had bored into the rock in that short time. Why, a team of men would have taken an hour to do as much, even with the latest equipment.

"Excellent," he said, turning to stare at Ikuro and his brother, steadying himself against the wall as he did, the heat of the rock transmitting itself through his glove. "And you say it doesn't need to rest?"

Ikuro shook his head. "The perfect woman, neh?"

Kim smiled, though he wasn't so sure Jelka would have liked the joke. "And when it's done?"

"Then we take over," Kano said, tapping his chest confidently. "Five days, six at most, and you have the best blast-hole you've *ever* seen!"

"Good," Kim said. "Excellent! Then you have the job."

"We have . . ."

Ikuro's whoop of joy made Kim put his hands up to his helmet. From all sides came the noises of celebration.

"Okay," Kim said, after a moment, "let's get out of here and let her get to work, neh?"

"Neh," both Ikuro and Kano answered him, as one, bowing their heads sharply, the movement sending them into a spin.

"Right," Kim said, making sure he did not laugh, lest it upset them. "And then we'll go back to my office and sign the terms straightaway."

"FATHER?"

Kim turned, still laughing, his hand on Ikuro's shoulder, as his son came into the room.

"You should have seen it, Sampsa," Kim began, gesturing out through the big viewing window toward the drilling site, his eyes still full of the memory of the Cutter biting into the rock. "Why, I've never seen—"

He stopped abruptly, noting something in Sampsa's face.

"What is it?" he asked, suddenly more sober. "What's happened?"

"It's Tom," Sampsa answered ominously. "He says there's been a message. From Mother."

"*Tom?*" Kim frowned. "But I thought—"

Sampsa raised a hand. Kim could see now he'd been crying. "I think you should take the call at once."

Kim stared at his son a moment, then gave a single nod. He looked to Ikuro and his two brothers, who, understanding how things were, bowed and began to leave. When they were gone, Sampsa shut the door, then looked to his father again.

"Are you okay?"

"Me?" Kim looked up, then shrugged. "I don't know. It's just . . . well, Chuang's dream. I should have listened to Chuang's dream."

"What?" Sampsa stared back at him, puzzled.

"No matter. Patch it through. I think I'm ready."

But he wasn't ready. Nothing could have made him ready for such news. He looked up at the screen at the image of his wife, his only love, Jelka, and saw at once how that face had changed, had *aged*, and felt something die in him.

"There's plague here," she said, with a calmness that was frightening; that made his blood freeze in his veins. "People are dying from it by the thousands. It's . . ."

She swallowed, maintaining her dignity, the Marshal's daughter to the very end. "Mileja has it. I—I have it too. We . . . look, Kim, we don't know how to treat it. If we pull through, then . . ."

She looked down at that point, a single tear betraying her. Kim groaned, sickened by the sight and by the news of his beloved Mileja, his little spark of joy. Beside him Sampsa was sobbing loudly.

"I don't know what will happen," she continued, looking to the camera again, ignoring the tear. "But we're on the shuttle now. My plan is to isolate us on the ship. They've prepared the cells for us. The crew can pass food through the hatch in the door. We"—she shrugged, a strange movement in her face betraying just how close she was to breaking down—"we hope we'll see you again. And, Kim, Sampsa . . . I love you. And little Chuang. Tell her . . ."

But the signal was beginning to break up, the image disintegrating into colored blocks of pixels, then it was gone.

*Tell her what?* Kim wondered as a strange numbness overcame him.

"Dad? . . . Dad?" Sampsa reached out and caught him as his legs gave, then carried him across to the couch in the corner of the office.

"Chuang's dream," Kim murmured, as his eyes flickered and he slipped into unconsciousness. "Chuang's dream."

———————

"TOM? . . . TOM?"

Lu Yi popped her head around the door and, seeing him sitting there in the darkness, frowned.

"Tom? What is it?"

He looked up at her, then stood, moving past her into the kitchen. She followed, watching as he poured water from the jug into a beaker and gulped it down.

"Tom?"

He looked about him at the tiny cabin kitchen. Taking the wipe pad from the wall, he wrote: *Plague. Chung Kuo. Mileja and Jelka have it. Kim and Sampsa know.*

She took the pad from him and read his words, then looked back at him, her eyes wide. "Plague?"

He nodded, then looked down. This changed things. Just an hour ago he'd had things clear. Just a single hour ago he had known what he must do. But now?

He stood. Pushing past her, he went back to his room and, switching on the light, began to unpack his case.

After a while he looked up. She was standing there in the doorway, watching him silently, her face uncritical.

You don't mind? he mouthed.

"No," she answered, coming across and sitting beside him, putting her arm about his back. "They'll need us now."

---

BACK IN THEIR QUARTERS Ikuro sat heavily on the bench. He set his helmet down beside him, then looked up at his brothers.

"Something's up," he said. "You saw the son."

"Yes," Kano said. "He looked bad, neh?"

Shukaku scratched his chin. "You think this affects us, little brother?"

Ikuro shrugged. "Who knows? *Shih* Ward is a good man, an *honorable* man. He will keep his word."

"Maybe," Kano said, "but what if something bad has happened—something so bad, it makes him change his mind?"

"Yes," Shukaku chipped in. "We really should find out."

"Find out?" But Ikuro remembered how Ward's son had looked. "You think this is our business?"

"*Shih* Ward's business is *our* business now," Shukaku said. "If something is wrong, we should know."

"Okay," Ikuro said, feeling bad about it even so. "See what you can learn. But be discreet, brother. *Shih* Ward is our friend. I do not wish to offend him."

"Of course," Shukaku said, a gleam in his eye as he bowed. He turned and hurried away.

When he was gone, Kano looked to his little brother. "What should we do?"

"Do?" Ikuro sighed. "What *can* we do?"

"We could pray for him," Kano answered, his broad face filled with sympathy. "We could burn offerings."

Ikuro smiled sadly, loving his brother deeply at that moment. "Yes," he said, getting up, recalling the look that had passed between Ward and his son. "Yes, let us go and do that now."

THE CELL DOOR was locked and sealed, special filters placed over the cabin's ventilation ducts. From here on they were on their own.

Mileja lay on the left-hand bunk, beneath a single sheet. She was unconscious, yet she tossed and turned restlessly, as if in the grip of some hideous nightmare, her face sometimes grimacing, sometimes at peace. For a whole day Jelka had nursed her tirelessly, but now she, too, was succumbing to the virus. Besides, she was tired; more tired than she'd ever felt in her life. It was as if she had been punctured and the air was slowly hissing from her.

The crew had been good. No, they had been marvelous, if the truth were told. In their position, would she have taken the risk? Maybe. But then, maybe not. Not if it meant she might contract the disease herself. Yet there hadn't been a moment's hesitation.

"Don't be silly," her old friend Torve Hamsun had said to her, when she'd contacted him. "I wouldn't think of not helping you. What would your father have thought of me?"

And so here she was, heading back out. Heading *home*. Back to Kim.

She dragged herself over and slumped down upon the right-hand bunk, the weight of her limbs oppressive now, the virus in her blood beginning to make her feverish. The delusions hadn't begun yet—that was the third stage of the disease, so they said—yet already her mind kept circling about her own mortality: wondering what Kim would do if she didn't make it; how he would cope without her.

*This will kill him*, she thought, and almost laughed. But she didn't have the energy to laugh. She barely had the energy to turn her head and look across what now seemed a hundred-mile gap to where her daughter lay.

*Be well, Mileja*, she willed, closing her eyes and letting her head fall onto the surface of the bunk. Yet even as she slipped into unconsciousness, she could hear her father's voice sounding clearly in her head: *"It's how we are, my love,"* he was saying. *"Brittle. Easily angered. But strong, too, neh? Stronger than iron."*

KIM PUSHED THE MEDIC'S arm away and stood.

"I don't *need* a sedative! I need to be awake, alert, in case something can be done."

"But, Kim," the young medic said, unoffended by Kim's anger; knowing it wasn't directed at him, "you really ought to rest. Your system's had a shock. You ignore that and you *will* be in trouble. And probably just when you *can* be of help! Look . . . get a couple of hours now. I'll give you something that'll put you out short term. It's for the best. Really it is."

Kim glowered a moment longer, then relented. "Okay. But two hours maximum. And if something comes up while I'm out, I want you to bring me around immediately, understand?"

The medic raised his hands. "I understand." He searched in his bag and took out a slim plastic tube, squeezing two tablets from it. "Here, take these with water. Then go and lie down. They take effect pretty damn quick."

Kim palmed them in his left hand, then went across to the basin in the corner and filled a beaker with water. "Okay," he said over his shoulder. "You can go now."

The surgeon smiled at Kim's reflection in the mirror. "Not until I've seen you take them."

Kim put his left hand to his mouth, then drained the water. He turned, showing the young medic his empty mouth, lifting his tongue. "There! See! Now let me be. And wake me in two hours or you're fired!"

"Okay."

The cabin door slammed closed. Kim waited a moment, then took the two tablets from his suit pocket where he'd slipped them and flushed them down the sink.

He *was* in shock. He could feel it. But that was secondary right now. What was most important was doing something for Jelka and Mileja. His own problems could wait.

He looked to the ceiling. "Machine?"

There was no answer for a moment. He could imagine his voice being switched from circuit to circuit about the colony until it reached the Machine where it rested in young Chuang's head.

When the answer came, it was a soft presence in his back brain, like a gentle tickle that was also words.

*What is it, Kim?*

"Who would have an antidote?"

*An antidote? To what?*

"To the plague. Jelka has it. And Mileja."

*Ahh . . . I didn't know.* There was a moment's pause, a delay that revealed as much as anything the Machine's vast loss of powers, and then: *The Americans. The New Enclaves. There was a message. . . .*

"A message?"

*From Old Man Egan. It came in half an hour back. You want me to play it for you?*

Kim stared into space, amazed. "From *Egan*? You're sure?" But the Machine never lied. Not as far as he knew. "Okay," he said after a moment. "Patch it through next door."

He went through and sat before the comset, drumming his fingers on the edge of the desk as he waited. Whatever it was, it was relevant. The Machine would not have mentioned it otherwise.

He hadn't long to wait. The screen flickered, then lit up. Egan's vigorous, suntanned face beamed out at him.

"Kim . . . it's been a long while. I hope you're well. I . . . look, I'll come straight to the point. I've heard your news. About Jelka and the girl. Mileja, is that right? I hear they've got the sickness."

Kim raised a hand. At once the image froze. He spoke to the air. "How did he know? How the fuck did he find out?"

The Machine spoke to him gently. *Egan's been monitoring your private lines for years. Or was. I would imagine he's been tracking the transmissions from the Luoyang. If so, he'd have heard the news before you did.*

Kim shivered. Long before, by the sound of it. At present Chung Kuo and Jupiter were in orbits on the same side of the sun, so a light-speed transmission between the two would have taken over forty minutes.

*Forty-two minutes eighteen seconds,* the Machine confirmed.

"Run it on," he said, sobered by the thought.

"I'm sorry to hear that," Egan continued, his face a mask of earnestness. "Very sorry, indeed. I have children of my own and know how you must feel. But I'm also a businessman." Egan paused, giving a little apologetic shrug. "As I'm sure you'll understand, *as* a businessman it's not in my interest simply to give away something I've spent a small fortune developing. That's bad business. It takes food from my children's mouths. But though you're a rich man, Kim, it's not your money I'm after. I think we can do much better than that." Egan grinned. "I think we can do business."

Kim swallowed. Whatever this was, he already knew that it stank. He knew Egan of old. The bastard gave nothing away.

"Now, as I see it, Kim, you need a cure . . . and I've got one. Tried and tested. One hundred percent effective."

Kim raised a hand, freezing the image. "A *cure?* He has a cure? *Already?*"

From what he'd heard, the plague had been traced to an accidental spillage in one of the old GenSyn facilities. If that was so, how was it Egan had a cure? Unless . . .

He let a long breath escape him, then spoke to the air once more. "Run the message."

Egan's smile seemed suddenly quite sinister. "Now, I'd call that a seller's market, wouldn't you? You want something, I have it. Not only that, but you need it . . . *urgently.* That simplifies things. But we have a problem, neh? Time. It'll take time for this message to get to you. Equally, it'll take you time to give me your answer. And between times your loved ones are languishing on the *Luoyang.* That's a shame, but that's how things are. So I tell you what, Kim Ward. I won't haggle. I'll name my price exactly. If you meet it, we do business. If you don't . . . well, I hope your gamble pays off. I hope they come through safely. You see, I don't wish you ill. It's just business."

Egan sat back. "So . . . what do I want? I'll tell you. I want time."

"But . . ." Kim began, then understood. It was the one thing the Old Men had always wanted. Time. Endless time.

"That's right," Egan said, as if he'd listened in on Kim's thoughts. "I want you to give me a reliable immortality treatment. One that works. One that stops the cells from aging."

Egan smiled again, all teeth and insincerity. "You could do it, Kim. We *know* you could. Oh, I know it'll take time, but that's fine. Right now you have only to say yes. You're an honorable man, Kim. I know that. You give me your word, I'll send back details of the cure. But don't take too long thinking things through. Time's pressing. Your loved ones . . . Well, I'll say no more. Good luck, Kim. It's been nice talking to you. I hope we can do business."

Kim sat back, recalling the last time he had come to this point; seeing in his mind the circle of Old Men at Lever's Mansion, offering him the world if he would only find them a sure and certain cure for death. He shivered, then leaned against the console, his arms extended, his palms flat on the desk's surface, breathing deeply. If he was going to help Jelka and Mileja he ought to decide things now, but this was too big a decision to make just like that. Besides, hadn't he made it once already? If he changed his mind now . . .

*Yes, but they'll die,* he told himself. *If I don't agree, they'll die.*

Maybe, but he would go and speak to Ebert first. Ten minutes, that's all it would take. Just ten minutes.

---

THE *LUOYANG* WAS SILENT. Or almost so, for there was still the faintest hum—a reverberation in the air and in every strut and panel of the ancient craft—that emanated from the engine core.

Silently it traversed space, on automatic now, speeding at nearly 190,000 *li* an hour toward Jupiter. Overrides had switched in an hour back, when Captain Hamsun failed to make the latest of the routine four-hour checks. Now the ship flew itself, an unconscious mechanism, a computer-driven stone hurled between the planets.

At the controls Torve Hamsun grinned the grin that would be fixed until his bones rotted, the skin stretched tight over his skull, hanging loose on his tall, gaunt frame. The Hollower had caught him unprepared and his flesh had been ravaged by malfunctioning enzymes, by massive conflagrations of pulsing, glowing, *golden* cells.

Conscientious to the last, he had died at his post, sending out a final Mayday message, a massive coronary sparing him the worst.

Elsewhere his crew lay in their bunks, dead or dying, their groans unheard, their suffering untended.

In the isolation suite Jelka lay on the broad bunk, her brow speckled with tiny golden droplets, the orbs of her eyes flickering frenetically beneath their thinly fleshed coverings. Mileja lay beside her now, panting, her tiny hands spasming, her child's eyes—eyes that were like swollen golden coins—staring fixedly at the ceiling.

Through the silent dark the *Luoyang* sped on, heading out toward its rendezvous with Ganymede.

———————

HANS EBERT SAT NEXT TO Kim on the bunk, his blind eyes staring past the Clayborn, the tiny cameras orbiting tightly above his head, relaying back the scene to microfine receivers in Ebert's head.

The tiny, cell-like room was sparsely furnished: a single bunk, a chair, and, on a table by the door, an old-fashioned comset brought long ago from Mars. A small lamp on the wall above the bed was the only source of illumination. The effect was Spartan, as if Ebert inhabited a prison cell.

"So?" Kim asked. "What should I do?"

Ebert shrugged. "It is difficult, my friend. You ask me whether you should be true to what you have always believed, yet the only true test of any idea or philosophy is when it has real meaning to a man's life—when it *affects* a man. Until then all *professed* beliefs are but words. So, when you ask me what you should do, how can I answer you truthfully? How *advise* you? For me, you see, the question is an academic one—if it were my child, Pauli, who were threatened, would I save him or would I stand by my principles?"

"Well?" Kim prompted, anxious now, conscious of time passing. "What *would* you do?"

Ebert lifted his face slightly. "What you really mean is how far would I go to save my child, neh?"

Kim hesitated, then nodded.

"Well," Ebert continued, "let us look at the matter objectively. To my mind a child is greater than any material possession. Were it impossible to have a child except to have one built, what would one cost? A billion *yuan? Ten* billion?"

"And what they're asking for?" Kim asked, troubled now. "Does that mean so little?"

Ebert pulled his head to one side and scratched at his neck. "Not at all. It means a great deal. And yet their world is dying. In giving Egan what he wants you will be doing him no great service. To be Lord of such a ruin *forever* . . . well, it is not a fate I personally would ask for."

"So I should agree, then?"

Ebert laughed, then leaned forward, resting his right hand on Kim's shoulder. "Your decision was made for you long ago, Kim, when you first chose to be a scientist, for how can a man know what his discoveries will be used for? How can he know for sure whether good or ill will come of them?"

"But only ill will come of this. . . ."

"You're sure of that?"

Kim looked up, meeting Ebert's blind eyes, disconcerted by the way those empty sockets seemed to look right through and into him.

"If you *are* sure," Ebert said, when Kim was silent, "then you should say no."

"And is *that* your counsel?"

"Would you kill another man to save your daughter?"

Kim swallowed, then looked down, deeply troubled. Would he? "No," he said finally.

"Then my counsel is that you should make a deal with Egan."

"A *deal?*" Kim stared at Ebert, surprised.

"Yes. Tell him you'll give him what he wants, but only if you keep the patent."

"The patent. . . ." Kim laughed, understanding. The Old Men would get their chance at immortality, but so would anyone else who wanted it. That is, if anyone else truly wanted such an obscenity.

"Well?" Ebert prompted. "Hadn't you better hurry?"

"Of course. Forgive me, I . . ." Kim turned his left wrist and, lifting the flap of protective skin, tapped out the connecting code. At once a patch of skin lit up, showing Wen Ch'ang's face.

"Wen Ch'ang," Kim said urgently. "Set up a channel to Old Man Egan back on Chung Kuo. The number and special access code are on file. I'll be with you in five minutes."

He cut contact and sat back, looking to the blind man, then took his hand and squeezed it. "Thank you, Hans. You've been a good friend."

Ebert smiled. "Never mind that. Get going now, my dear friend. And good luck. I'll pray for you."

———————

JELKA WOKE. In her dream she had been soaking in the huge marble bath, back in her father's house. She had been eight. That morning she had been practicing a special kicking movement and her upper thighs ached from the exercise. Now, relaxing, her body sheened in sweat from the steam, she stretched her aching limbs and sighed.

For a moment longer the dream held her, until she realized where she was. She shuddered, then turned and drew Mileja close, cuddling her. The child was cold. Deathly cold. Jelka gave a motherly cluck and smoothed her hand over her daughter's back a few times, holding her tighter, trying to warm her as she slipped back into unconsciousness.

———————

KIM SAT, preparing to give Egan his answer—to commit himself to giving the Old Men what they wanted—when the Machine spoke softly in his head.

*It's Jelka, Kim. She's sent a message from the* Luoyang. *I'll patch it through.*

There was a moment's disbelief, and then Kim laughed and stood, looking to Sampsa, who was sitting in the corner.

"*What?*" Sampsa asked, staring at his father as if he'd gone mad.

In answer Kim turned, indicating the screen as the Machine patched through the clip. Sampsa stood and came up alongside his father, staring into his mother's gaunt and damaged face.

"Gods," he said, appalled by what he saw. How changed she was. And those eyes . . .

"Kim, Sampsa . . . I hope you can hear me. I'm calling from the bridge of the *Luoyang*. The ship's on automatic. Captain Hamsun and his crew are dead. They're all dead. I'm fine now, but I'm very weak. I'll have to go and lie down again in a while. But listen. Send out a ship to meet us. But warn them. Tell them to use special suits, and to burn the suits afterward. And the ship too. You must destroy the ship once you've taken me off it."

"And Mileja . . . ?" Kim coaxed, his voice scarcely a breath.

Jelka looked down, as if she'd heard him. Both men could see how difficult it was for her to say what she said next. But she was the Marshal's daughter, after all: even this, it seemed, could be borne.

She looked up, her golden eyes weeping. "She's dead, Kim. Our darling little girl is dead. . . . I—I've put her into cold storage. We'll"—she shuddered, then continued—"we'll bury her in Kalevala."

Kim stared in disbelief. "No," he said. "No, you must . . ."

He fell silent, stunned by the news. Beside him Sampsa was snuffling and wiping his face with the back of his hand.

"I don't think she suffered much," Jelka said, her face showing her own pain now. "Mostly she slept. I—I held her."

Kim saw her face crack and felt as much as heard a great groan of pain issue from his own lips. *Dead? How could their darling girl be dead? Why, he could see her, running, laughing. . . .*

Jelka sniffed deeply, regaining her self-control. "You must be strong, Kim. And you, too, my darling Sampsa. You must help each other until I come home. You must remember all the good we can still do."

She smiled, and as she did, Kim leaned toward the screen, meaning to kiss the image of that damaged, still beautiful face, yet even as he did, the screen blanked.

He turned, his face distraught, tears running down his cheeks, and put his arms out, letting Sampsa hug him tightly, both men groaning—the sound torn from the very depths of them.

"My girl!" Kim groaned, unable to bear the thought of it, wanting at that moment to die. "My darling little girl . . ."

But she was gone. He knew it now. There was no need for deals. No need to pander to Old Man Egan.

*Gone* . . . He groaned again, then clutched his son to him, desperate now, conscious of the darkness pressing close, and of the light receding.

# CHAPTER FOURTEEN

# In the City of the Dead

I T WAS FIVE DAYS now since the first reported case, and the streets and alleyways of the northern city were quiet. Corpses lay where they had fallen, curled into themselves like fetuses, their hollowed husks stirred by the gusting breeze that blew from the south.

It was a perfect day, the afternoon sky cloudless and azure. Beneath the burning summer sun Ben Shepherd walked slowly between the houses, an airtight suit protecting him from any chance of contagion. From time to time he would stop and go inside, looking about him, seeing where the dead had been taken; this one sat at table over a plate of untouched, rotting breakfast; that one on its knees beside the bath, a stain of vomit telling its own dark story.

He looked, his eyes taking it all in, processing it, his mind already weaving the cloth of a new tale from these sickening threads. It was as if the whole world had died. The disease had passed like a cloud over the sun of their collective being and blotted them out. Only one in eight had survived, according to the latest figures. And no one knew why. *Sheer will*, Ben told himself, stepping out into the dusty street once more. There was no other answer, after all. For this silent army had come upon a people without defenses.

"Kick-start," GenSyn had called it when they'd made it. And then Lehmann had taken the drug and mutated it, given it a new name and sold it on the open market. "Golden Dreams," he'd called it.

And finally it had changed itself; become a predator, feeding on human blood and tissue. The ultimate killer. The Hollower, as it was known.

Ben frowned, then sniffed the air, but he could smell nothing through his helmet's filters. Briefly he thought of removing it, but why take the risk? He need only take a sample of the air—a machine could do the rest; analyzing the various pheromones. From that he could produce a safe analog. Something that would remind without killing.

*Yes,* he thought, *but where's the story?*

When the tragedy was so sudden, so general, was it really quite so tragic? He walked toward the river now, musing on the question. Whatever poignancy each individual death might have possessed had been robbed by the sheer scale of the disaster. When death was on such a scale it became anonymous, anodyne. To make his story work he needed a single focus. One single soul to animate the tragic whole.

"A child," he said softly, thinking of Chuang Kuan Ts'ai. "It has to be a child."

A child cut off from its parents when the epidemic hit. A child . . .

Ben laughed, then rubbed his gloved hands together, seeing it whole. It was exactly what he had been waiting for: the perfect vehicle for his experiments in death. *Stepping Over,* he would call it.

Stepping over . . .

As the wind rose, a corpse blew past him, tumbling end over end like a loose, dry bush. And in his mind he saw it burning, its smoke sweetly scented, like incense. A God-sign, given to him alone; for him alone to interpret.

Ben walked on, smiling broadly, the river just ahead of him now. And as he walked the opening words of Dante's epic poem came to his lips:

"Day was departing and the dusk drew on, loosing from labor every living thing save me, in all the world; I—I alone—"

MICHAEL LEVER STOOD BEFORE the screen in the down-stairs study, channel-surfing, trying to find a station that was still transmitting. The House Computer could have located one in an instant, but he had dispensed with its services these last few days, wanting to keep busy.

"Well?" Emily asked, coming into the room.

"Still searching," he said over his shoulder. "How are the boys?"

"Fine," she answered, coming across and standing beside him. "They're restless, but that can't be helped. Better restless than dead, neh?"

The slightest irony in her voice made him turn and look at her. "I thought we'd settled this."

She shrugged, her face closed against him.

He sighed and rolled his eyes to Heaven. "They're *alive*, aren't they? *Aiya!* What in the gods' names did you want, Em?"

"I wanted to help. . . ."

"You wanted to die, that's what. You *and* your boys. Because that's what would have happened if you'd gone out there like you wanted."

"Maybe. . . ."

He shook his head, angry with her suddenly—at her ingratitude as much as anything. "No, no *maybes* about it. You'd be dead. And the boys would be dead. And how would *that* have helped?"

"Shooting those men didn't help, did it?" she answered, a fire in her eyes now.

He swallowed. "So what was I supposed to do? Let them break down the gates and come in?" He laughed, incredulous. "You know what would have happened if they had, don't you? I mean . . . apart from us all getting the disease. They would have killed us, that's what. You saw how desperate they were."

"You can't say that. You didn't even talk to them."

"They didn't respect our sign."

"But they were desperate."

"And so was I." Michael turned from her. "Anyway, you're not going to worry about that, are you? I mean, that's on *my* con-science, not yours. Yours is white as white, after all!"

"That's unfair!"

"Is it?" He turned back, glaring at her now. "Consider the facts. This thing . . . the Hollower. Look what it's done to our world in a mere five days. Asia, Africa, America, there's not a single City where it hasn't spread. Decimation isn't the word for it. Over ninety percent fatalities. Ninety percent! Shit! Don't you understand what that means, Emily? It means we're back in the Stone Age! It means . . ." He shuddered, then fell silent, shaking his head.

"I'm sorry," she said, after a moment. "It's just—it's just that I feel so helpless. I want—"

"—to go out there. I know." He looked at her again, admiring her spirit even as he was irritated by her illogic and angered by her ingratitude. "You want to *do* something, neh?"

"Well, it's better than sitting on your arse and doing nothing!"

He stared at her, saying nothing, hurt by her accusation.

"So?" she said. "Do you think it's safe?"

He laughed, amazed by her persistence. "You really want to try it out there?"

"Why not?"

"Because we don't know. Because"—he swallowed, then said it—"because I don't want to lose you, Em."

"So it's not the boys you're worried about—"

"Oh, for fuck's sake, Em! Do you have to twist everything? Of course I'm worried about the boys. It'd hurt me if any of them were hurt. But it's *you* I love. Is that such a fucking crime?"

She stared at him a moment, then, unexpectedly, she smiled. "I thought you'd lost it, you know."

"Lost it?"

"Your temper. I thought . . ." She reached out and touched his cheek. It was the first intimate gesture she had made toward him in the two years she had lived inside his walls. He closed his eyes, savoring it.

"Anyway," he said, feeling her fingers move away, opening his eyes again to look at her. "I am doing something."

"Like what?"

"Like producing an antidote."

She stared at him, mouth open. "You've got one?"

"It's being delivered later today. The simulations suggest it's effective in close to ninety five percent of cases. If we can mass-produce it."

Emily looked down, sighing. "If only we'd had it five days back . . . three days, even."

"But we didn't." He took a long breath. "Look, Em. There must be many more like us. People who've locked themselves in. Small, isolated pockets of healthy life. If we can get the antidote to them . . . that'd be something, surely?"

She looked up at him, and nodded, a profound sadness in her face. "Yes," she said, smiling through the pain. "That *would* be something."

────────

AS BEN TURNED THE CORNER he knew that something was wrong. There was a pile of burned and broken furniture not twenty feet away—between him and the waiting cruiser—which had not been there earlier. Aside from that, other, smaller things had changed.

Ben smiled, a tiny thrill of excitement making his blood pound faster. At last! He'd thought the whole place dead.

He stepped out, skirting the makeshift barricade, conscious now of a shuffling in the alleyway he had just come out of, of a door creaking somewhere close by.

The cruiser was a hundred feet away now, resting where he'd parked it five hours back, the hatch sealed. Even from here he could see the dents and scratches around the door.

Making no sudden movements, he slid his hand down his side and activated the charger on his belt, glad he'd taken care to arm himself. As yet they hadn't shown themselves. But they would. He was almost certain they wouldn't let him get back inside the cruiser—not unless he was their prisoner first.

A step, another step, and then the scuffling behind him materialized into forms. He turned, looking back at them. Three men—or what were once men—their gaunt, skeletal faces grinning at him golden eyed.

*High noon in ghoul town*, Ben thought, amused, wondering how he could use this in his tale. They weren't armed. At least, not with anything he should worry about. He turned back, then walked on slowly, but he had barely gone another half dozen paces before a further two of them stepped out from a shadowed doorway just ahead and to his left.

The three behind had blocked off the space between the barricade and the street front. As Ben watched, another four moved out from behind the cruiser. Taking it all in at a glance, he noted the glint of something metallic in one of their hands. A gun? No. He recognized it now. It was a Security stun prod. Good. He could handle that.

Ben stopped, looking about him, his smile benevolent now, like a prince among his subjects.

"Gentlemen," he said, imperiously, "what can I do for you?"

There was a murmuring between the two nearest him. Ben saw how they glanced to the one with the prod who was clearly their leader, then, at his nod, started toward him.

With a deceptively casual gesture Ben drew the laser from inside his tunic and pointed it at them. For a moment it was as if they didn't see what he was doing—despite the sudden glare of the tightly focused beam—for they both kept coming. It was only when one of them screeched and fell to his knees that the other— the one he hadn't yet shot—stumbled to a halt, his ravaged face transformed in an almost comic double-take.

"Dead," Ben said, pointing the gun at him and squeezing the trigger. Light leapt, transfixing the creature. For a moment he seemed to dance on the end of it, his chest on fire, then he, too, fell.

Ben turned, grinning broadly now, raking the laser fire across the wall facing him, across the makeshift barricade, and onto the backs of the fleeing men.

He watched them screech and fall, then turned back, walking on as the last of them backed away, their faces frozen in sudden fear, the screams of their fellows still sounding loudly in that narrow, enclosed space, the smell of burned flesh powerful now.

"Dead," Ben repeated, lifting the gun but not using it. "Dead. All of you."

And now they turned and ran, shrieking, afraid. But Ben was not done. Slipping the gun back into its holster, he plucked one of the tiny figlike bombs from his belt and, biting off the top, threw it after them, imagining himself back in the woods on the Domain and hunting squirrels. As it exploded, sending two of the stick figures sprawling, he took a second bomb and, repeating the process, hurled it, the accuracy of his throw the result of forty years' practice.

"Dead," he said, even as the last of them were blown into the air.

Chuckling to himself he walked over to the cruiser and, lifting his face to the camera so that it could scan him through the helmet's glass, he uttered the voice command.

"Open sesame!"

As the hatch opened and the ramp unfurled, he turned, looking about him at the devastation. It had been too easy. Much, much too easy.

"Ben nine, Ghouls nil," he said quietly, then nodded to himself, seeing exactly what changes he'd need to make if he were to use this. As it was, his own role in events was unheroic, *unsympathetic*. But he could change that. He could make the attackers more beastly for a start, more gruesome. And he could have them taunt him, threaten him. As for himself, he would need to be unarmed. There would have to be a fight, hand-to-hand stuff, with one moment—one precarious, heart-stopping moment—when it seemed that they'd prevailed.

He grinned, seeing it whole, then turned and climbed the ramp, anxious to get back.

THE FOUR CREATURES emerged from the shadows of the old warehouse in which they'd hidden and stepped out into the brilliant sunlight, their smooth, hairless heads looking up as one, following the path of the departing craft. They had seen the fight through their remotes; seen the smile on the suited man's face and found it strange.

As the craft flew out of sight, three of the four looked to their leader.

"Well, Tybor," one of them asked. "What now?"

Tybor sighed and looked about him. Bodies. Everywhere bodies.

He stretched his long limbs—limbs twice the length of any human's—and walked toward the nearest house.

"Let's do something useful," he said. "Let's burn some of these bodies."

THEY HAD HEARD THE CRUISERS coming from a long way off. Now Kao Chen stood on the low stone wall beside the main pen, shielding his eyes and looking to see where they were headed and how many there were.

"Three," he said, looking to the others who were gathered about him. "And they're heading straight for us."

They broke out the arms, then headed across the big field toward the village. If they'd land anywhere, they'd land there. As they jogged along, Chen looked to his eldest son, Jyan, and smiled encouragement. "It'll be okay," he called, speaking not only to Jyan but to the others. "When they see how determined we are, they'll go elsewhere."

But secretly he'd begun to have his doubts. They had fought off five raiding parties in the past week and things seemed to be getting no better. Those who fled the plague in the city faced hunger outside it. And hunger made men ruthless.

And if these were Security, as they appeared to be, then who knew what they'd do to get their way? He'd been among them most of his life, after all, and knew well enough what many of his fellow officers thought of the peasants who manned the Plantations. Why, they'd think longer about crushing an insect than they would about killing a Plantation worker.

*Yes, but if they try any of that shit here, they'll find they've bitten off more than they can chew,* he thought, burying his doubts, knowing that if Wang Ti and the children were to survive—yes, and all of his good friends here—he'd have to dispense with such uncertainties.

Coming into the village, he dispersed his men among the big stone houses. By now this was almost routine, yet he could see how the village men derived some comfort from the way he barked his orders at them—as if his long experience as a Security Major were some kind of magic shield behind which they might be safe.

Thinking of it—of the weight of expectation that bore down on his shoulders—he shuddered. But then there was no more time to think of that. The cruisers were upon them, bearing down like giant locusts.

"Hold fire until I say!" he bellowed over the noise of the engines, then ducked beneath a rail, running for the end house in the row.

The cruisers had slowed and were hovering above the field to the west of the village. As he watched, two of the craft took up what was clearly a defensive cover while the central craft slowly set down.

It was a classic maneuver, and, watching it, Kao Chen felt old instincts switch in. He had been a good soldier in his time. The best, so some said, Karr aside. But he'd been a Han in a *Hung Mao* army. Besides which, the job had stunk. Not the technical side, that he'd loved, it was just that serving a bastard like Li Yuan hadn't been easy. The times that he'd done things which had been against his conscience were innumerable.

As the craft's engines died and the hatch began to open, he took up a position behind the stone steps of the nearest house, covering the opening gap in the cruiser's flank with his rifle.

His men knew where to fire. He'd spent the last few evenings in his crowded kitchen drawing them diagrams of these things, showing them where the weak points were, until they could do it in their sleep. Now that theoretical knowledge had become a reality. If he couldn't persuade them to go on, then they'd have to fight. And their only chance was if they could disable the cruisers.

As a figure appeared in the opening he clicked off the safety. Then, with a tiny gasp of surprise, he lowered the gun.

Marie! It was Marie! And beside her . . .

He stepped out, laughing openly now, then began to run toward the craft.

"Gregor!" he yelled. "Gregor!"

Slipping his rifle over his shoulder, he turned and signaled to the others. "It's okay! They're friendly!"

Then, turning back, unable to keep the broad grin from his face, he hurried on toward the craft.

He was only a dozen or so paces from it when he remembered.

"Chen?" Karr said, a slight shadow falling over his face at the change in Kao Chen's expression. "What is it, Chen?"

Chen shook his head regretfully. "You can't come in, Gregor. The plague. You might have the plague."

"Ah . . ." Karr nodded, sobered by the reminder. He turned, signaling to his girls to step out onto the ramp with him, then looked back at Chen. "You have a place we can stay? Somewhere isolated?"

"Somewhere . . ." And then Chen saw what his old friend was saying. "You've come to stay?"

Karr nodded and smiled again. "If you'll have us."

Chen thought, then nodded. Turning, he yelled back at his son, Jyan, who was at the front of a crowd of curious villagers. "Jyan, get the hatchery ready for our guests. Clean it out and put some beds in there. And move one of the larder units in. Fully stocked." He beamed. "My dear friend Gregor Karr and his family have come to stay!"

---

LI YUAN SAT THERE in the darkened room, the damp, sweat-sodden sheets draping his emaciated form. All around the imperial bed his surgeons and ministers lay, dead, taken by the sickness even as they offered up their prayers for their Lord and Master's earthly and heavenly souls.

But their Master had lived. Wraithlike, almost skeletal, he lived.

Climbing weakly from the bed he pushed aside the weightless husks that bowed before him and made his way across the massive room until he stood before the mirror. There, his frail limbs trembling from the effort, he shrugged off the thin yellow gown that shrouded him and looked.

*Aiya,* he thought, barely recognizing himself in the sticklike naked figure, wondering how such a form could still hold breath or maintain a decent pulse. And his eyes . . .

*His eyes were golden, like twin suns!*

He shivered, then realized he was hungry, ravenously hungry.

The kitchens, he decided, making his slow way to the door. Standing there a moment, his bony hand clutching the great hexagonal knob, he turned, staring back at the grotesquely withered figures gathered about the bed.

*Men of straw . . .*

He almost laughed. Almost. But he was hungry. More hungry than he'd ever been. Why, he could feel a full week's hunger in his shrunken belly!

Servants lay where they had fallen in the littered corridors. Maids lay toppled over laundry baskets or against walls. Two guards, their heavy armor loose on them, squatted like dummies, their stiff boots keeping them half erect where they had fallen against the doors.

Dead. Everywhere he looked he saw the dead. Mummified. Ossified. And he the only one alive.

Li Yuan frowned, one hand supporting him against the wall as he got his breath. So weak he was, so . . . *hungry.*

He scuttled on, like an octogenarian, stooped and ague ridden.

And this time he did laugh, for it reminded him of the tale of the woodcutter who had stopped to watch two immortals playing *wei ch'i* in the forest. While he'd stood there, watching them, a thousand years had passed and when the woodcutter returned to his village it was to find it totally changed, all those he'd known long dead and rotted in the ground.

He hauled himself over to the window and looked out over the gardens. No one. Absolutely no one. He shuddered, then ambled on.

Maybe he was the only one left. Maybe they had all died and this was his punishment—to be Lord of the City of the Dead, a living wraith.

And his hunger? Was *that* a sign?

A twinge of his guts told him otherwise. No. If anything convinced him he was alive, it was that twinge.

He hurried on, hunger driving him like a goad.

The kitchens were empty, deserted, the surfaces spotlessly clean, the floor neatly swept. After the desolation elsewhere, its tidiness surprised him. But maybe there was a reason. Maybe they'd tidied the kitchens and left before the sickness had taken them. Even so, he crossed the massive room uneasily, moving between the long tables slowly, glancing from side to side, as if it were a trap.

On a long table at the far side of the room, a fruit bowl was piled high with apples and mandarin oranges. He reached out, meaning to take one, then drew his fingers back. Rotten. They were all brown and rotten.

Li Yuan turned, looking about him. When had he last been in here? When had he last thought of how his food was prepared or where it was stored? No, he had been concerned only that it was laid before him on a silver dish. Apart from that he hadn't really cared.

Shuffling across to one of the big freezer units, he pulled at the catch. Slowly the door swung open, cool, fresh air bathing his body and making him shiver involuntarily. But inside the dimly lit recesses was food, lots of food.

He reached in, taking fruit and meat and drink. Leaving the door open, too weak to push it shut, he staggered across to one of the central tables and sat, spreading his "meal" out before him.

He was halfway through, his face smeared with fruit and fat, when a noise made him look up. A man was standing in the doorway, a soldier's stave in his hand. At least, he was either a man or a scarecrow come to life, for his uniform hung on him as on a child.

"What are you doing here?" the soldier demanded, taking two unsteady steps toward him. "And why are you stealing from the imperial kitchens? Do you not know the penalty?"

Li Yuan, who had at first been shocked, now stood, recognizing that face.

"Dawes? Captain Dawes? Is that *you?*"

The figure jerked, surprised. "How do you know my name, *lao jen?*"

Li Yuan laughed, the sound more like a short bark or cough than laughter. "Old man, eh? Why, don't you recognize me, Captain? I am your T'ang, Li Yuan!"

Dawes stared at the sticklike naked figure, his golden eyes uncertain, then, seeing something in that ravaged face, some spark of recognition motivating him, he fell to his knees, his hairless skull bowed low.

"Get up," Li Yuan muttered, going across to him and pulling him to his feet. "We have finished with all that nonsense. We are but men now. So come and sit with me and share my meal. We both look as if we could do with a good feed, neh, Captain?"

Dawes hesitated, then accompanied Li Yuan across, the two men sitting side by side, sharing the provisions, looking up at each other from time to time as they ate and grinning.

---

HAN CH'IN, who had gone into the darkened room, cried out, then came back to the doorway.

"He's gone! Someone's taken the body!"

"*Aiya!*" Kuei Jen said, rocking the baby in his arms. "Who would have done such a thing?"

"You know these ghouls," Han Ch'in answered, looking about him angrily. "They believe that you can adopt another's attributes by eating them. No doubt they've cut him up and cooked him already."

Kuei Jen stared at his brother in amazement. "You think—"

"Masters!"

They both turned as one of the guards ran toward them, then stopped, bowing low.

"What is it, man?" Han Ch'in asked, assuming command.

"We've found him, Excellency. In the kitchens."

"My father?"

"Yes, Excellency. He's alive. And there's another with him. A Captain. . . ."

Han Ch'in turned to Kuei Jen and grinned. "Alive!" He laughed, then slapped his brother's back. "Then let us go and greet our father, Kuei Jen! Let us show him his new grandson!"

---

THEY WALKED FOR most of that day, through the streets of the dead city, a small but growing crowd of golden-eyed survivors raggedly following their cart.

It was when they were about to give up their search and go home, convinced they'd come too late to save any, that they came upon the boarded-up Mansion: a big, two-story house at the top of a wide, sloping street.

While Michael knocked loudly on the bolted gate, Lin Chao

and Lin Pei went around to the alleyway that ran along the back of the big house to see if there were any signs of life there.

Leaning on the cart, Emily looked on, conscious of how tired Michael seemed. Tired but uncomplaining. She smiled, weary herself, thinking of all he had done for them these past few months, asking nothing for himself: endlessly patient with her and her boys.

"Let's go," she said, when, after knocking again, there was no reply. "They're either dead or in hiding."

But she had barely uttered the words when the shutters over the gate clattered open and a cowled head popped out.

"What do you want?"

Michael looked up, smiling, but the smile slowly froze as he realized he was staring into the barrel of a high-powered rifle.

"Michael?" she said quietly, alerted by the sudden change in his expression.

"Stay where you are, woman!" the same voice—cracked and angry—barked at her. "Come any closer and I'll blow his head clean off his shoulders!"

She saw the slight movement in Michael's eyes. In that instant he had weighed things up and knew he had no chance of getting out of the way—not if the madman decided to pull the trigger. And there was no doubt he *was* mad. She could hear it in the voice.

"We've come to help you," Michael said, no trace of fear or self-concern in his voice. "We've got a potion . . . a cure for the plague."

"You're a stinking liar!" the man yelled, the rifle jerking menacingly in his hands. "You bastards have come to rob me!"

Emily had moved slightly to the side to try to get a better view of him, but now she stopped. Who knew? The least movement might set him off.

"That's not so," Michael answered patiently, showing his empty hands.

"Then what's in the cart?"

"Medicines and blankets and food."

The gun jerked again. "Show me!"

Keeping his hands clearly in sight, Michael backed away and, making no movement that might be misconstrued, turned the cart and pushed it across until it was directly beneath the window. Moving slowly, with infinite patience, he opened doors and pulled out drawers, showing the madman what was there.

Finished, he looked up again. "Well? Will you let us help you? We're friends. We mean no harm."

There was a long, tense silence, then the man grunted and moved back inside. Emily let out a breath and closed her eyes briefly. *Thank the gods!* A moment later she heard the sound of chains being unlocked, of huge bolts being slid back. And then, very slowly, the doors swung open.

Emily went across, joining Michael even as the two boys reappeared, signaling with one hand for them to be quiet.

Now that she faced him she saw they had come too late. Despite the hood, the protective mask that hid his face, the signs of the Hollowing were clear on him. He had lost near on two thirds of his body weight and his clothes hung on him like a sail on a child's boat.

"Well?" he demanded, throwing the gun down and moving toward them. "Where is it? Where is this cure you told me about?"

Michael reached beside him and lifted one of the vials, meaning to hand it to him, but the man stepped past him, knocking his hand away, and grabbed a handful of them, uncapping them one after another and gulping them down.

Michael looked to Emily, then stepped inside and picked up the gun, examining it.

"Empty," he said, showing her the chamber. "And I'd say it hasn't been cleaned for years."

As the madman made to grab another handful of vials, Emily walked up to him and gently but firmly pulled his hand away.

"That's fine," she said, smiling into his golden eyes. "You should be okay now. But any more and you might get sick again."

He stared back at her uncertainly, then nodded. "You want to come in?" he asked, as if suddenly remembering his manners. "My wife will be pleased to see such honored guests. It's been so long since we entertained."

Something in the way he said it warned her. But even though she had seen many grotesque sights in the last week, this capped them all.

Coming into the house she could smell the strong reek of incense, and in a room at the far end of a long, unlit corridor, she could see candles burning in silver holders on a polished table. She walked toward them, then stopped, realizing just what she was looking at. His family were gathered about the table, eight of them in all including the grandparents, one chair left vacant at the head of the table. All were dressed as if to greet some mighty dignitary, the best chopsticks laid out before plates of sparkling porcelain and dishes of finest silver. But they were all dead and shriveled and the food in the dishes was covered in a five-day layer of mold.

Emily walked on, slowly now, conscious of the madman right behind her.

"I told them you would come," he said, a strange happiness in his voice. "What did I say, Jung Wang. I told you we must look our very best for when our guests arrived. Our very best."

She stopped, holding on to the doorway lest she faint, the poignancy of the candlelit scene affecting her more than anything she'd ever seen. Here was his whole world, here all of his treasures—his wife, his parents, his three sons, and his two young daughters. And all of them dead bar him. Yes, and nothing he, their protector, could do about it.

Emily turned and looked to him and felt her heart go out to him. Mad? No wonder he was mad. The real wonder was that anyone was sane who had lived through this.

Just behind their host Michael was looking on, his face mirroring her own astonished pity. *"Aiya!"* he said softly. "The gods have mercy on us all."

"Yes," she said quietly, remembering now why she had loved him once. "But let's go home now, Michael. And let's take our friend here with us, neh?"

EARLY EVENING SHADOWS were falling across the rose garden as Ben's cruiser set down on the pad in the lower field. Catherine looked up from where she sat on the lawn, the sleeping child in her lap, then half turned, hearing the top flap of the kitchen door creak back as Meg leaned out to look.

For a while Meg simply stared, a smile lighting her face, then she looked to Catherine. "Why don't you go down and meet him? I'll lay little Dogu down for you."

"Would you?" Catherine studied the child a moment, conscious of how fond she was of it. And that was strange, considering how fervently she'd wished it dead before the birth. But Ben was kind to it and that was what mattered. If Ben had not been kind . . .

She shivered, then, sensing Meg behind her, moved back slightly, letting her lift and take the child.

Sometimes this thing with Ben frightened her. The intensity of it. Sometimes it was hard to know whether she was really in control of herself, or whether she was in the grip of some force.

She stood, brushing herself down, stopping a moment to watch Meg carry the child inside. If anyone could be said to love the boy it was Meg. She spoiled him endlessly and loved nothing more than to sit on the lawn and play with him for hours. When it came to say its first words it would be Meg, no doubt, who heard them.

Not that that really mattered. What mattered was Ben. Ben . . . even more than herself. It had not always been so, but now . . . well, even when she slept with other men—with guests or guards or with that Osu creature—it was Ben whom she returned to, Ben with whom she shared it.

Catherine turned back, staring down the slope toward the craft again, knowing there was no hurry. The guards had to spray it first. And then Ben would have to shower in the special tent he'd had rigged up. But afterward . . .

Smiling, she reached beneath her skirts and, slipping her fingers beneath the waist of her briefs, pulled them down over her legs and kicked them away. Then, the smile fixed mischievously on her face, she began to make her way down to meet him.

———

BEN CLOSED HIS EYES, letting the water drum over his naked body, the force of it inducing a kind of trancelike state in him. It was one of the few moments when he found himself freed from the slavery of thought, when—as in those final, dark moments of sex—he was released and, in Keats's immortal phrase, found himself "dying into life." Ironically, it was only at such moments that he found himself capable of reaching beyond the normal level of his being and making leaps.

Leaps . . . From nothing they came. Or, rather, from some inaccessible recess deep within him—some deep, lightless well from which he could not consciously draw.

But for months that well had been capped, and the source of his muse had run dry. For months now he had waited. Until today.

He half turned, hearing a vague noise just behind him, a swishing of the plastic as someone came into the tent; then he laughed and turned to embrace Catherine as she stepped beneath the steady flow.

"You'll get soaked," he said, delighted to see her.

"I don't care," she said, pulling him close, her lips hungrily seeking his. "I don't fucking care!"

Ben broke from the second kiss and held her out at arm's length from him, studying her. The soft, sodden cotton clung to her, revealing her full figure, while her long bronze-red hair fell in wet ringlets over her breasts. She was magnificent.

She laughed softly, looking down the length of him. "I notice you're pleased to see me again."

He grinned. "I'm *always* pleased to see you." Drawing her close again, he rucked up her skirt, surprised and pleased to see that she'd anticipated him. Falling to his knees, he nuzzled his head between her thighs, rubbing his cheeks against them before kissing her softly, gently, on her sex.

She held his head, her fingers deep in his fine black hair, her eyes closed as the water fell and fell and fell. For a moment she felt near to exploding, the sensation of it was so wonderful, and then Ben was standing again, pulling her wet blouse up over her shoulders, stripping her until she was naked. He lifted her gently up onto him, her legs wrapping about his waist, her mouth opening in a soft oh of delight as he entered her and they began to make love.

Afterward, in the quiet of the drying room, she made to help him, but, smiling, he turned the tables on her, making her sit while he dried her feet and legs, whistling to himself as he did.

"You're in a good mood," she said, running her fingers through his hair fondly.

He looked up at her and winked. "You know how it is."

For once she had no idea what he was talking about; only that he was looking inordinately pleased with himself. "What is it?" she asked, curious now. "What happened in there?"

He laughed and sat back on his heels. "I've got it, Catherine. The whole of it."

She hesitated, then leaned toward him, her eyes wide. "The new work? You've got *that*?"

Ben nodded, then busied himself drying her flanks, making her lift her arms, as if he were drying a child. "It was on the way back. I was feeling disappointed. What I'd seen . . . well, it was strange, but not as strange as I'd expected. And then it came to me."

He leaned back and threw the towel aside, then stood, looking down at her.

"Well?" she said.

"I'll show you," he said enigmatically. "Later. But only if you're good."

"Good? I thought I was the best."

"Oh, you are," he said. "You and Meg." And with that he turned away, leaving her to stare at his naked back as he disappeared out of the tent, heading for the cottage.

"You and Meg," she said, after a moment, mimicking him perfectly, a look of pique on her face. Then, shrugging it off, she stretched, catlike, and began to smile, one hand going down to her sex, remembering.

---

"MEG?"

Meg appeared at the door on the far side of the living room, a finger to her lips. "Shh," she said. "Dogu's restless."

"Ah." He nodded, and went across to her, keeping his voice to a whisper. "Would you bring something down to me? I want to work for a while."

She smiled. "Shouldn't you put something on?"

He shook his head.

She smoothed one hand down his chest until it rested between his legs. "Would you like me to come down and inspire you?"

"Later," he said, kissing her mouth softly. "Right now I've got to work. Why don't you take Catherine to bed? She's *full* of beans."

Meg looked away. He'd often suggested that they sleep together, but they never had. *With* him, yes, but not alone.

"It's rabbit stew," she said, moving past him, clearly miffed by his suggestion.

"My favorite," he said, watching her go through to the kitchen and smiling to himself. Then, knowing he had to set it all down while it was still fresh in his mind, he hurried across and, pulling open the door, padded down the steps into the cellar where his workroom was.

He had been looking at the problem in the wrong light. He had been trying to follow the living into the land of the dead. But he'd been going about it all wrong. What he needed was to turn it all about; to follow the dead back into the world of the living.

Ben shivered, making sense of it at last.

*He had to die. Yes, he had to die and be reborn.*

---

AT THE FOOT OF THE RAMP, Li Yuan turned and looked back toward the Eastern Palace, suddenly remembering something.

"The portrait! Han Ch'in, you must go and get the portrait!"

Han Ch'in looked to his half-brother, Kuei Jen, and shrugged. "Portrait, Father? What portrait?"

"Of my mother. It is in my rest room, just off the study. Go and bring it. I will not leave until I have it!"

After all that had happened, it seemed a strange little display of petulance, but Han Ch'in merely bowed to his father and, with a smile to Kuei Jen, hurried off to do his father's bidding.

"Go inside, Father," Kuei Jen urged, laying a hand gently on his father's arm. "Han Ch'in will bring the portrait."

Li Yuan hesitated a moment, then, with a fussy little gesture, hobbled up the ramp and into the big cruiser.

Kuei Jen sighed, shaking his head at his father's behavior, but understanding it even so. Families! Sometimes they seemed as much a curse as a blessing. Not that his was by any means a typical family.

He half turned, hearing the cries of his infant son from within the cruiser, and remembered briefly both the pain and joy of giving birth. Now, *that* had been an experience—a test of sheer endurance unmatched by any other he had undergone. If anything, it had made him much more of a man than he had been before, for it had augmented his physical strength with the qualities of compassion and understanding.

He smiled, wondering what Chuang Tzu would have made of it. A man giving birth to his own son. A man with a woman's feelings, complete in himself. Only he wasn't complete. Content, yes, but complete? No. No being was ever complete. Take his father, for instance. Li Yuan, more than any of them, had been born incomplete—a motherless child, forever longing for that one relationship he had been denied. To be a man in a man's world, that had been his fate—and *that*, more than anything, was what had fucked him up. All of his mistakes, all of his thoughtless actions, had stemmed from that one root. No wonder, now, he called like a frightened child for his mother's portrait.

*At least I knew my mother,* he thought, the bitterness of her loss somewhat alleviated by the love he shared with his own child. *At least I knew she loved me.*

And that was something his father had never, it seemed, been certain of. All Li Yuan knew was that she had loved his elder brother, Han. After all, hadn't he seen those images of the two playing in the imperial gardens together in the summer before his untimely birth? Yes, and how that must have hurt—to see another have what he himself had been denied. And was that the key to his relationship with Fei Yen? That he could, for once, have what his brother had?

He almost laughed at the irony of it, for things had truly come full circle. Up there, at the very back of the craft, sat Fei Yen, her haggard face and night-black silks making her seem a good thirty years older than she really was.

*Like a curse,* Kuei Jen thought, thinking of all that had happened—of the strange inevitability of the chain of events that led to this moment.

*Who would have thought?*

He felt the ghosts of his ancestors at his shoulder at that moment. Of Li Shai Tung and all those others who, for the briefest eye blink of creation, had ruled a solid world of certainties. Gone it was. Vanished like a dream. And this the very last of it. When they stepped up into the craft and the door closed behind them, they would be leaving that world forever. The San Chang would fall into ruin and Chung Kuo would slowly fade, until even the memory of it—even the words themselves—would be forgotten.

"Ten thousand years!" he said quietly, making an imaginary toast to the air. "*Kan Pei!* May the gods bless you with good fortune and many children!"

*Gone it was.* Gone. He shivered, then turned and walked back up the ramp.

HAN CH'IN stood there a moment in the shadowed bedroom, the portrait of his grandmother wrapped in a towel beneath his arm. The scene around the empty bed was eerie, as if a group of huge insects had dressed themselves in men's silks and then gathered about the bed in a predatory huddle, only to die and desiccate. The curled, almost fetal figures did not really look like men, though they had men's features and men's limbs.

He shivered and took a few steps closer. Though he knew none of these men personally, he understood that they must have been important and powerful men while they yet lived. And now . . . His foot brushed against one and it fell aside. A tiny cloud of spores rose from the husk's chest, then settled slowly.

*So much for the pretensions of men. So much for power and status and riches. . . .*

Han Ch'in frowned, then bent down, picking something up. It was a ring. Moving to the doorway he stared at it in the light from the wall lamp and gave a tiny gasp. It was a heavy iron ring, and on its face was a wheel of seven dragons—the *Ywe Lung*, the symbol of the Seven Han Lords who had once ruled Chung Kuo.

It was his father's, he was sure of it. Li Yuan must have dropped it as he made his way from the bed, or it had slipped from his finger without his noticing. Whichever, his finding of it was fortuitous. Now he could give Li Yuan both his mother and—in a sense—his father, for this ring had been Li Shai Tung's ring long before Li Yuan was born.

Smiling to himself, he hurried back to the cruiser. The engines were warming up as he came out onto the path again, the guards he'd posted earlier moving back toward the craft, their eyes searching the walls and windows of the overlooking palaces, making sure nothing went wrong at the last moment.

He ran across, signaling to his men to get on board, then climbed the ramp. Kuei Jen was waiting for him just beyond the hatch.

"You have it?" he asked.

Han Ch'in nodded. "And his ring," he said, showing it to Kuei Jen. "He must have dropped it."

Kuei Jen took it and studied it a moment, then handed it back. "Go through," he said. "Our father is impatient."

Han Ch'in grinned, then moved past his brother into the long interior cabin.

Li Yuan was sitting at the far end of the cabin, immediately across from his once-wife, Fei Yen. Seeing his son, he began to get up, but Han Ch'in hurried to him.

"It is all right, Father. I have the portrait."

"Portrait?" Fei Yen said, looking first to her son and then to Li Yuan. "What portrait is this? You have a portrait of me?"

Li Yuan took the towel-wrapped painting anxiously, giving Fei Yen a tiny glare as he did so. "Of you? You think I'd want a portrait of *you?*"

He unwrapped the painting and rested it in his lap, studying it. In it his mother was no more than sixteen years old, a Minor Family Princess, only recently betrothed to his father after the failure of Li Shai Tung's previous wife to give him any children.

"Ahh," Fei Yen said, leaning across the gangway to get a better look. "I should have known. You always were a mother's boy, Yuan."

"And you always were a haggard-faced old bitch underneath it all, neh, my sweet one?" Li Yuan answered acidly.

"Now, you two," Han Ch'in began, but he got no farther.

"Is that what you really believe, Li Yuan?" Fei Yen said, showing a hint of the steel she was made of. "So you never loved me?"

"Oh, I loved you," Li Yuan answered, sitting back, beginning to enjoy the exchange. "Like a lamb loves the friendly touch of a butcher, not knowing there is a cleaver hidden behind his back!"

Han Ch'in looked away, not knowing whether to laugh or groan.

Ever since they had been reunited five hours back, they had done nothing but bicker. Like a couple who had been married fifty years.

"Father," he interrupted, before his mother could find something equally devastating to say, "I found something else, in your rooms."

"A pair of maids, no doubt," Fei Yen began, but Han ignored her, holding his hand out, palm open, to his father.

"My ring?" Li Yuan said. He extended his hand as if to take it, then drew it back. "Achh! That cursed thing! Take it away! Throw it down some deep, dark well where it can never be found again!"

"Father?" Han Ch'in stood back, surprised.

But Li Yuan had bared his teeth now, as if the ring were some living thing. "It blighted my life. My brother should have ruled, not me, but that killed him. It destroyed my relationship with your mother here, and it killed all my other wives. And now . . . well, it shan't have me! I'll not let it!"

Han Ch'in closed his hand on the ring, then slipped it into his pocket. Li Yuan's eyes noted the movement and nodded.

"That's right, Han Ch'in. You keep it. But it will not bring you happiness. Not if you wore it on your finger for ten thousand years."

Han Ch'in swallowed, then, bowing to his father, backed away. At the doorway Kuei Jen stepped back, letting him come past, and, as the cabin door slid shut, he turned to face Han Ch'in.

"He's right, elder brother. All that that symbolizes has passed now. Chung Kuo is gone. We must learn to be ordinary people now."

"Ordinary?"

Kuei Jen laughed. "Well, less than kings, let us say." He paused, then, looking into Han's eyes asked, "Why, did you *want* to be a T'ang, brother?"

"I *was* a Warlord. . . ."

"That's not what I asked. Did you want to keep it going? I mean . . . even after all we've seen and experienced?"

Han Ch'in shrugged, as if he wasn't sure. At last, conscious of his brother's eyes on him, he shook his head. "No. It's best, neh?"

Kuei Jen nodded and, taking the ring from his hand, ducked through into the cockpit. He was back a moment later, his hands empty.

"There," he said. "We'll eject it on the way across to America. It can lie there on the ocean bed until the sun grows old."

Han Ch'in sighed. "So that's it, then? It's over."

Kuei Jen nodded, then, unembarrassed by the breasts that distinguished him from other men, he embraced his brother for the first time. "It's for the best, brother. Really, it's for the best. . . ."

"GREGOR?"

Chen sat on the fence, forty *ch'i* from the hatchery, watching as his old friend stepped from the long, low building, having almost to crouch to get out under the low lintel. Straightening, Karr grinned. That old, familiar grin.

"It's good to see you again, Chen."

"It's wonderful to see *you*, Gregor."

They stood, facing each other a moment, the afternoon sun shining down on the two old friends. It was almost two hours now since the cruisers had left, and while Gregor and his family had been settling in, Chen had held a meeting of the villagers.

"So what was decided?" Karr asked.

"Oh, you can stay. Provided you keep to quarters the next three days. I hope you don't mind, Gregor, but I've posted guards. For their peace of mind. . . ."

Karr smiled and nodded. "I understand. Three days, eh?" He scratched his chin and looked about him at the huge open fields that stretched away on every side. "You wouldn't have any playing cards, would you, Chen?"

Chen laughed. "I'll send Jyan over with some. But tell me, what's happening in there? I mean, why are you here? I've been trying to work that one out ever since I first saw you."

Karr shrugged. He looked away, a momentary bleakness in his eyes. "It's gone, Kao Chen. All of it. The government is in ruins. The people . . . well, what people there are left . . . are in shock. The generals wanted me to take over . . . to become Emperor in Li Yuan's place."

"*Emperor?*" Chen stared at him, astonished.

Karr laughed quietly. "Yes. Me." He shook his head. "But I wanted to see you. Wanted to talk to you first."

Chen stared back at him, puzzled. "Why?"

Karr met his eyes. "Because you got out. Because . . . well, because you are the last honest man I know, Kao Chen, and I value your opinion."

Chen whistled. "Things are that bad, eh?"

Both men laughed. Then Karr spoke again. "It strikes me I have three options."

"Three?"

Karr nodded. "One, I go back and become Emperor. I take charge and try to make the best of a very bad job."

"And two?"

"I stay here. In retirement, if you'd like to call it that. My friends in Security promise they'll protect this place if I do. Providing I give them guarantees."

Chen frowned, not liking the sound of that. "And the final option?"

"We join Ward, on Ganymede. Leave the System and seek our fortune elsewhere."

"Like where?"

Karr laughed. "You haven't *heard*, Kao Chen?"

Chen put out his arms and shrugged. "We hear little out here. Look about you, Gregor. Fields. Everywhere you look, fields. What do we know of the great world's events?"

"Then listen. Kim Ward has built a great fleet of starships, among them the *New Hope*."

"The ship you blew up that time?"

Karr nodded. "The same, but better. Not only that, but he plans to take four of Jupiter's moons with him on his journey. Four fleets, sailing to four different stars."

Chen stared, then shook his head. "Now I know you must be ill, Gregor Karr. Moons? He's taking *moons*?"

Karr nodded. "And he's offered us a place. At least, Jelka has. You too, if you want to come."

Chen frowned. "But why *should* I come? What's there that we haven't got here?"

"A future." Karr looked down. "It's ended here, Chen. Right now it might not seem like it, but things have broken down irrevocably. One day soon—not now but months from now—the sickness will get to you. Or a raiding party will succeed. Something, anyway. And then it'll all be gone." Karr sighed heavily. "You're living on a sandbank here, old friend, and the tide is coming in."

"So you say. . . ."

"So I *know*." Karr pressed his hands together. "How many of you are there here?"

"Villagers?"

"Yes. How many, all included?"

Chen shrugged, thinking to himself. "One hundred and fifty. One eighty at most."

"Then we can do it. I'll send a message through to Ward. We could arrange a rendezvous four days from now. We could be off-planet by—"

Chen raised his hands. "Now, hold on. . . . What you're talking about . . ." He swallowed. "Well, it is not a decision to be made in an instant. To leave here. To leave Chung Kuo. To go . . ." He laughed, then shook his head, incredulous. "Are you serious, Gregor? Moons? He's taking *moons*?"

Karr nodded and grinned. "And the *New Hope*, Kao Chen. Don't forget the *New Hope*!"

———

THEY SET UP TRESTLE TABLES in the main yard of the Mansion, and as the golden-eyed survivors slowly gathered, adding to those who had followed the cart home, so the long benches filled up.

Though they ate ravenously, there was a strange, almost eerie silence at the tables. Where once small talk had been enough for such an occasion, now there were no words for ordinary things, for nothing was ordinary any longer. Those who had come through had found themselves profoundly changed and exhibited a curious aversion to speech—those, that was, who had not discovered themselves mad or driven suicidal from grief.

Emily and the boys went among them, filling and refilling their earthenware bowls, while Michael stood on his balcony above, looking on. He had no family now but her; no friends, either, now that the plague had done its worst. Even his old friend and personal assistant, Dan Johnson, had been taken by it. So many good people gone. So much misery. He shivered, then turned, hearing a noise in the rooms behind him. Stepping across to the open doorway, he drew the curtain back and looked inside.

The man stood there silently beside his bed, staring at the book he'd picked up from the bedside table. Setting the book back, he turned and walked across, opening one of the sliding doors to the wall-length wardrobe and looking in.

Michael stared, astonished, then stepped into the room. "Excuse me . . ."

The man turned, his golden eyes fixing on Michael's. For a moment or two he stared at him, then he turned back, beginning to flick through the silken *pau* hanging on the rail.

"I said, excuse me," Michael said, a note of anger in his voice now, "but what the hell are you doing in my room?"

The man ignored him. He went on looking through the gowns as if Michael were not there.

Michael strode across and pulled the man around, pushing his own face into the stranger's, shouting at him angrily.

"I think you'd better leave, before I throw you out."

The man reached up and, gently, unfussily, removed Michael's hand from his shoulder, then turned back, reaching out to take one of the *pau.*

Michael grabbed him, shoved him back against the wall.

*"Michael!"*

He stepped back as Emily quickly crossed the room. Moving past Michael, she took an armful of the silken gowns and, handing them to the man, gently ushered him through the door. Closing it, she turned and looked to Michael.

"The nerve!" Michael said, shaking his head, his anger unassuaged. "The fucking nerve of these people! You feed them and they think suddenly they own you! Yes, and everything you've worked for!"

"Michael?"

"Well, can you believe that? Bold as fucking brass! Like I wasn't even there!"

"Michael?"

He looked to her. "What?"

"Listen to yourself. Listen a moment, then think."

"Think?"

She nodded. "About what's happened to our world. About what you saw today. Haven't you realized yet?"

"Realized?"

"It's over, Michael. The days of owning things have ended. We must learn now how to share all we own."

"Share . . ." He laughed bitterly, then turned away from her, his whole body tense. "That's easy for you to say. You *had* nothing!"

For a moment she was silent, then: "If that's how you feel."

"How I *feel?*" He turned, meaning to continue the argument, then saw the disappointment in her face.

"I guess we'd better go."

"I . . ." He took a step toward her, then stopped. "Look, all of this . . ." He let out a long sigh. "It's difficult. I didn't mean—"

She faced him angrily. "Oh, you *meant* it, Michael. It was there in your voice. What's more, it's what you've been thinking all these months, isn't it? Thinking how generous you've been, and how grateful I ought to feel for that!"

He looked down, hurt by her comments. "Is that what you think?"

"Well, what am I *supposed* to think?"

"That I love you."

Emily was silent a moment, then she shrugged. "I don't know. . . ."

"Look," he said, moving closer, taking her arms, touching her for the first time since they'd been reunited. "It really is difficult, okay? You . . . well, it *is* easy for you. It couldn't be easier. But I've got to learn." He smiled. "You've got to teach me."

"You want that?"

He nodded. "I want that."

She swallowed, then looked down. "You know, you never really owned it all, Michael. It owned you." She looked up at him, smiling. "All those servants, all those employees you were responsible for. All of those locks and bars and codes and armed guards. Let it all go, Michael. It belongs to the old order."

He laughed and squeezed her arms gently.

"What?" she said. "What is it?"

"Just that I've no real choice. It's gone, Emily. The Hang Seng collapsed four days back. All what's left is here, in this Mansion." He stared down at her, amused by her surprise. "Oh, I still own it all on paper—all the factories and shops and research facilities— but that doesn't mean a great deal anymore. You need a massive market to sustain giant Companies like ImmVac, and that's gone. Nor do I think we'll see it again."

She smiled. "So what was all that about just now?"

"I don't know. A lifetime's habit, I suppose." He sighed, then held her close, smelling her hair. "So will you stay?"

"Maybe," she said, putting her arms about his back, her head nuzzling into his chest. "Maybe."

MEG PUSHED THE CELLAR DOOR open with her knee, then made her way down the unlit stairwell, her bare feet finding their own way down the uneven stone steps.

At the bottom she elbowed the inner door open, her hands occupied by the tray she was carrying. Inside, in the half-light of the crowded basement, she looked about her.

"Ben?"

"Over here. . . ."

She moved toward the sound, stepping between the close-packed shelves, past wired morphs and electrical cabinets, stacked files and odd-looking packing cases.

Emerging from between two rows of free-standing shelves, she was surprised to find her brother crouched over the refrigeration unit, his bare arse exposed to her.

"Ben?" She laughed, then set the tray down beside one of the big notebooks that was open on his worktable. "What the hell are you doing?"

"Looking for eggs," he said, straightening up and grinning at her over his shoulder.

She tutted, then took his blue silk wrap from beside Hugo, his favorite morph, and draped it over his shoulders.

"Eggs?"

He smiled and, shrugging on the wrap, turned to face her. "That the stew?"

She nodded. "There's bread too. And cheese for after."

"Ah . . ." He stepped past her and lifted the lid of the pot, sniffing deeply, his eyes closed. For a moment Meg watched, the familiarity of that gesture—so like their father—touching something deep in her. But she could not allow that feeling to stop her from saying what had to be said.

"Ben?"

"Yes."

"Ben, I want to go and see Tom. I want to talk to him, persuade him to come home."

"Uhuh?" But the way he said it put her back up. He wasn't listening, or if he was he didn't care.

"I said—"

He turned to her, smiling. "I heard. And I know you miss him. But you can have sons, Meg. As many sons as you want."

She stared at him. "What?"

"You heard me."

"But I thought . . ."

Still smiling, he turned and took a hunk of the bread, beginning to chew it. "I changed my mind."

"I . . ." She frowned, confused now. She thought she knew her brother—his whims and ways—but *this*? He had been quite adamant about not wanting any more children after Tom and had been furious at first when Catherine told him about Dogu. She took a breath, then spoke again.

"What's going on, Ben? Why have you changed your mind?"

Ben moved past her, a hand resting briefly on her hip, and reached into the freezer unit. Lifting something, he turned and handed it to her. It was a tray, a tray of tiny vials, six in all.

*Eggs*, she realized, recognizing the acorn symbol etched into the transparent lid of the tray and into the smooth face of each of the tiny glass vials. They were the fertilized eggs of her great-great-great-great grandfather Amos Shepherd and his wife, Alexandra Melfi.

She shivered. "I thought you meant . . ."

But he was staring at her and smiling now, as if this was the best thing he could ever do for her.

"Six children," he said, confirming only what her own eyes had already noted. "It's what you want, Meg. What you always wanted."

She felt something freeze inside her, as if the six deep-frozen eggs had been placed directly into her womb at that moment.

*It wasn't what I meant,* she thought, horrified by his utter insensitivity as he turned and, lifting the lid of the pot, began to spoon the steaming stew into his mouth. *I meant our children, Ben. Ours!*

"'E M ?''

Emily came from the bed, a cloak hastily wrapped about her nakedness, and stood beside Michael at the balcony rail. Below them the endless feeding went on, the wall lamps lit now as the sun began to sink below the compound walls. But Michael wasn't looking down, he was looking out across the endless rows of red-tiled roofs toward the south.

"Fires," he said, putting his arm about her.

She looked toward where he was pointing, seeing the tall plumes of black smoke far to the south, counting them.

"Eight. No, nine. . . ."

"Hmm." Michael stared a moment, deep in thought. "Maybe we ought to leave here, Em. Find somewhere."

"No," she said, snuggling up to him.

"No?" He looked down at her. "What do you mean?"

"Just no. No more running. This is as good a place as anywhere now."

"But the fires . . ."

Her hand moved gently against his ribs, reassuring him, as if he were one of her boys. "Bodies," she said. "They're just burning the bodies." Then, "Forget that now and come back inside. I think we've a lot of time to make up for."

THEY WERE GATHERING the dead together, piling them in huge stacks and burning them.

Pausing for a moment, Tybor rested on a low wall, stretching his long, inhuman legs. Dust . . . there was so much dust here, and the fires made his throat burn, but this had to be done. Things had to be cleared before they could begin their proper task.

Yes, and if the survivors ran from them in fear, what did it really matter? In their place he, too, would be afraid.

Tybor turned his head, looking toward his point of origin—Charon, Pluto's twin. There was not a moment of the day or night when he did not know its position in the sky relevant to him; though the width of the earth came between him and it, still he knew.

*The world might turn,* he thought, *yet Charon remains constant in the sky.*

He looked back at the mounting flames. It was such a shame, such an awful shame. They could have done so much here.

One of his three companions came over and stood before him. "We're finished here, Tybor. Shall we move on?"

"Okay," he said, promising himself that they would rest soon. *And when my Master comes?* But there was no thinking of that now. Now there was only the burning of the dead.

# CHAPTER FIFTEEN

## Seeing Out the Angels

IX MONTHS HAD PASSED and all but one of the great bore-holes had been finished. Today, eleven days ahead of schedule, the last of them would be ready for its final fitting-out.

The thirty-six great fusion rockets—vast machines that had been fashioned in the orbital factories and painstakingly put together in the vacuum of space—were already in stable orbit about their respective moons. From a distance their vast, bell-shaped exhausts made them look like giant silver cornets—the kind of instruments the gods might play before a feast. Tomorrow, the business of fitting them into place would begin.

Deep in the well Kim stood between Kano and Ikuro, their helmet lights illuminating the smooth-cut wall of the bore hole.

"It looks good," Kim said over his suit mike.

"Hmm," Kano responded, moving closer until his gloved fingers were brushing the wall. Kano, Kim knew, trusted nothing. Though the remote sensors had gone over these walls twice to check for surface cracks or signs of weakness, still Kano would check things for himself.

Kim smiled, pleased he had come to know these men. When it came to space excavations there was no one better in the system; no one who took more care or knew as much.

Kano turned and smiled at Kim. "We've done a good job here, neh, Mister Kim?"

"The best," Kim answered, reaching out to touch Kano's shoulder appreciatively. He turned to smile at Ikuro. "If you two want to be getting back . . ."

Ikuro laughed. "Okay."

The moment had become almost ritual between them. Stepping away from Kim, the two brothers fired up their backpacks and slowly rose, climbing the steep walls of the huge shaft until they were merely tiny points of light.

Kim watched, then, as the twin lights blinked off, he switched his helmet light off. The darkness was sudden and intense. Above him, in the perfect circle made by the shaft's rim, he could see the stars blazing down—the Pleiades, he realized with surprise, the six brightest stars of the great cluster like a choker of brilliant sapphire light in the sky.

He shivered, enjoying the moment, then activated his suit mike again, speaking to Wen Ch'ang back in the control room far overhead. "Well, I think we've finished here."

There was a pause, then Wen Ch'ang's voice sounded in his head. "You want me to send a power sled down for you?"

Kim smiled. Wen Ch'ang was always so thoughtful. "No. It's okay. I'll make my own way back. Tell Jelka I'll see her in a while, okay? I just want a moment or two alone down here."

"I'll tell her."

A click, then silence. Kim switched off his suit mike and walked slowly across the great floor of the bore hole, counting each step, the darkness like an invisible curtain he strove to breach but could not, the sound of his heavy boots against the rock the only sound. At twenty he stopped. He was at the center now. Above him his view of the sky had changed; only two of the brilliantly blue stars of the Pleiades could now be seen.

He let out a long breath, wondering how the voyage out would change them all. They'd be spending long years with nothing but the darkness and a view of stars. Why, the shortest of the four journeys—the 1.8 parsecs to Barnard's Star—would take near on twenty years to complete, whereas their own, to Eridani, would take close to twice that long.

Thirty-five years, he'd estimated, if nothing went wrong. Which was why they'd taken so much care to get things right.

*And what if it doesn't work?* he asked himself for the thousandth time. *What if the moons aren't accelerated out of their orbits, but merely break up under the pressure?*

"Then I'll have been proved wrong," he said quietly, speaking for himself alone.

*Yes, but they'll all die. And it'll be no one's fault but yours, Lagasek.*

He stared into the darkness, answering his darker, "mirror" self: "Maybe, Gweder. But then, they could have died back on Chung Kuo. Like Mileja."

That still hurt. It would never stop hurting. But at least he could cope with it now. Hard work—sheer hard work—had helped him deal with it.

*But what if there's nothing there? What if there are no habitable planets?*

"Then we'll build something. We'll make it habitable."

*And if you die? What then? Who'll carry on your work? And what of the other expeditions? How will they cope without you to guide them?*

He took a long breath, then answered the voice of his own self-doubt. "If I die, Sampsa will take over. As for the others, they'll cope. They know what to do. There are good men among them— yes, and women too. Intelligent, strong, imaginative. They'll cope. I *know* they will."

Silence. A long, clean silence, and then it spoke again, its final words.

*You should fear the darkness, Lagasek, for the darkness will swallow you, like a pike devouring a minnow.*

He put his hand up to his neck, meaning to switch his helmet light on, then stopped himself. No. The darkness was not to be feared. He understood that now. All his life he had made *that* mistake, but not now.

Moving his hand slightly, he clicked on the suit mike again, then frowned, hearing only static.

"Wen Ch'ang?"

"WHAT'S UP?" Jelka asked, leaning across Wen Ch'ang and pressing the communication pad.

Wen Ch'ang shrugged then sat back. "I don't know. A suit fault, I'd guess. Nothing serious. His life-support readouts are fine. You want me to send someone down?"

Jelka made a face into the darkened screen, then shook her head. "No. He'll be up in a while."

He turned. "Why don't you go and greet him?"

She stared at him, surprised by his suggestion. But it was a good one. Kim would like that. "Okay," she said. "But if his mike comes back on, let me know. I want a word about the new processing plant."

"Okay." And Wen Ch'ang turned back, busying himself again, efficient as ever.

She looked at Wen Ch'ang's back a moment. Smiling, she laid her hand briefly on his shoulder, then turned away.

Hurrying down the corridor toward the air lock, she almost bumped into Ikuro and Kano coming out of their quarters.

"What's the matter?" Ikuro asked.

"It's Kim," she said. "His suit mike's packed up. I was just going to meet him at the rim."

"His mike?" Ikuro looked to Kano. "And his other readings?"

"They're fine. There's no problem. . . ."

But Kano held her arm, stopping her from going past him. "I don't like the sound of this. The backups in those new suits ought to make a communication failure impossible. The whole suit would have to stop functioning before that."

His words alarmed her. "Then I'd better get there," she said. But Kano still wouldn't let her go.

"No," he said. "I'll go. If there's something wrong, I'm better fitted to do something about it, neh?"

She hesitated, then nodded, accepting the logic of what he'd said. After all, the Ishidas had more experience of vacuum conditions than any of them there.

"Come on, then," Kano said, turning and beginning to jog toward the air lock, leaving Jelka and Ikuro to hurry after him.

THE DARKNESS AT THE BOTTOM of the bore hole worried him. As he drifted down toward the floor, Kano craned his ears, listening for any sound that might help him quickly locate his friend.

"Kim?" he shouted, his voice loud in his helmet. "Kim? Can you hear me?"

Twenty *ch'i* up he slowed, moving his head, letting his helmet light slowly search the floor of the well. At first he saw nothing but the smooth face of the rock, then the light glinted against something at its edge. He moved his head toward that something.

There! It was Kim! But he was lying facedown. Something was wrong. Badly wrong!

Kano spoke into his mike. "Wen Ch'ang?"

Nothing. Not even static. As he drifted down and landed by the body, Kano thought about that, trying to work out what it meant.

Switching off his backpack, he knelt, turning Kim over and quickly scanning the readouts at his neck.

"No," he said softly. "That can't be right. I checked this suit myself."

According to the readouts Kim's suit was leaking air. Not only that, but his air supply was faulty too. For the past five minutes he had been surviving on half the normal supply.

"Air," Kano said, calming himself, knowing that the only way to survive a situation like this was to think clearly and act calmly. He had to get air to Kim as a matter of priority, and there was only one other supply of air down there at the foot of the bore hole—his own.

LEAVING IKURO AT THE RIM, Jelka hurried back to the air lock. She knew now. Something was wrong. The fact that they couldn't speak to Kano was evidence enough.

As the inner door hissed open, she began to run back to the control room, undoing the catch of her helmet as she ran.

Inside it was empty. Wen Ch'ang was nowhere to be seen.

*Aiya,* she thought, a tingle of fear running up her spine. Assassins. She was sure of it. And they had taken Wen Ch'ang.

Slowly, looking about her all the while, she crossed the room to the control panel. Through the clear, reinforced ice of the view window she could see the tiny figure of Ikuro at the rim. Looking down, she began to scan the various readouts, noting with concern that Kim's were now glowing red. But Kano's were okay. . . .

She frowned, checking once more. If Kano's were all showing green, then why couldn't they speak to him? What the hell . . .

The force of the blow almost smashed her into the board. She staggered up, stunned, her arms raised instinctively in a defensive posture, facing her assailant.

"Wen Ch'ang?"

The second blow would have killed her had she not moved her head slightly to the right. Even so, it knocked her back again, so that she lost her balance and fell onto her backside, banging her head a second time against the edge of the board.

Wen Ch'ang had changed. No . . . he was *transformed*. The man she'd known for so long was barely recognizable in the creature that now stood over her, arm raised. It was only the clothes, something vague in the face, that allowed her to identify him.

"*Wen Ch'ang?*"

But she knew it was no good. She knew she was dead. As he drew his hand back, she saw how his fingers were positioned in a killing blow and closed her eyes.

There was a grunt of surprise; a noise that made her eyes jerk open. Wen Ch'ang was staring past her suddenly, his teeth clenched in a rictus of pain, his neck muscles strained. As she watched he tried to pull the Osu spear out from his chest, yet the harder he pulled, the deeper the barbs dug into him. Finally, with a great groan of agony, he staggered back and fell.

Jelka shuddered, unable to take her eyes from him. It was a moment before she realized someone else was standing there behind him.

Focusing, she looked up and met the eyes of her savior.

"Hans?" she asked, not sure suddenly whether she were dreaming this or not. "Hans Ebert?"

"It's okay," he said, stepping over the twitching figure on the floor. "You're safe now."

But Jelka was no longer listening. Her eyes rolled in her head, then, with a tiny shudder, she collapsed, her head sliding down the side of the board and thudding against the carpeted floor.

Alarmed, Ebert crouched over her. "Jelka? *Jelka?*"

THE PAIN WAS EXCRUCIATING. Where he had opened the outer wrist-seal to make the link, his hand had died. It had happened in an instant, the blood vessels neatly cauterized at the moment his hand was exposed to the vacuum and decompressed. It floated close by now, barely recognizable as a hand anymore, the tissues frozen even as they imploded, long streaks of iced blood jutting from the pallid lump like ruby icicles, or like some obscene exploding star.

Kim, too, had lost a hand, but at least he was breathing now, linked at the right wrist to Kano's left, the two of them sharing the depleted air supply.

Kano closed his eyes, fighting the pain, letting the shock pass from his system, then opened them again.

"Okay," he said, speaking as much to himself as to Kim. "Now let's get you back up top."

The wrist seal had saved Kim. Years ago, after a similar incident had left one of Kano's uncle's suits damaged, another of his uncles had attempted a similar rescue to today's. But the vacuum is unforgiving. When his uncle had tried to get air from his own suit to his brother's, he had breached his suit's seals and died instantly in a moment's sudden, violent decompression. After that the suits had been redesigned. Like ancient Han junks they were now compartmentalized, with tiny inner seals that clamped tight the instant the suit was breached. After all, it was better to lose a hand, a foot, or even a whole limb, than to suffer total decompression.

Holding Kim close, careful not to jolt him, Kano gently activated first his own and then Kim's backpacks, lifting them. Slowly, very slowly, they began to climb the bore hole.

There was enough air for them to get back. Just. Providing nothing further happened.

Kano spoke into his lip mike. "Jelka? . . . *Jelka?*"

But there was nothing. He was cut off. No matter, he would keep going. Four minutes, five at most, and they would be safe.

Kim was slipping. Not much, but enough to make things difficult if it continued. Reaching further around him, Kano put a hand through the strap of his air canister and pulled him closer.

It was while doing this that he noticed the lump.

Frowning, he traced the shape of it. It was small and definitely rectangular. It was also definitely not part of the canister's normal apparatus.

Slowly, careful not to let Kim fall—each tiny movement making the blood pulse at the nerve ends of his damaged wrist—he turned Kim around.

*There!* He could see it now. It was a mine. A tiny limpet, like those they used to break up the larger blocks of rock into fragments.

Kano closed his eyes, all of the hope he'd been feeling drained from him in an instant. He had glimpsed the tiny blue figures on the timer.

*Four minutes, thirty-eight seconds.*

They'd never make it. Not to the air lock, anyway. And even if they did, it would be cutting it so fine that they'd be in serious danger of destroying it. And then they'd all be dead—Kano and Kim, Ikuro and Jelka and—

His decision was made in an instant.

"Jelka? Jelka can you hear me?"

This time there was the crackle of static before Jelka's voice came through clearly.

"Kano? Kano! What's happening? How's Kim?"

"Kim's safe," he answered. "We had an accident. But he's okay. I'm sending him up."

"Kano, what—?"

Kano switched off the mike. In the silence that followed he could hear his own breathing inside his helmet.

It was said by some that the number of breaths a man was to take in his life was predetermined at birth. Had he had the time or inclination—or even the mental skills for it, come to that—he might have calculated that number for himself. But right now there was no time for such trivialities.

*Three minutes, fifty-three seconds.*

Moving much quicker now, he turned Kim about. Gritting his

teeth, he put his damaged arm down to Kim's side, to secure him there as best he could, his movements made awkward by the fact that Kim's arm was attached to his own. Satisfied he had a good enough grip, Kano moved his other arm, using his good hand to unstrap his backpack and fit it onto Kim.

Briefly he smiled. He had spent the greater part of his life—from three years on—practicing such procedures, never really thinking the time would come when such practice would pay off. But now it did.

In his head he was counting. Three minutes left. They were rising toward the mouth of the great shaft, yet still it seemed a long way off.

Reaching out, he twisted the nozzle of Kim's air-feed tube and tugged at it violently. It gave with a tiny pop, ice forming instantly about the exposed aperture. But the suit was fine. Kano breathed out, relieved. His own supply would keep them both alive now.

*Two minutes, thirty.*

He put his hand to Kim's neck, as if strangling him, his fingers at full stretch as he simultaneously squeezed the studs on either side of Kim's helmet. Unclipping the canister, he brought it around to the side, then let it fall.

If he'd had more air in his own canister, then it might have worked. If he'd only had more air. . . .

But there wasn't enough air to get back—not for the two of them, anyway. Now that they'd jettisoned Kim's supply, there was only enough for one.

Kano grimaced, conscious of what came next, then, bracing himself against the physical shock, he reached down to where his wrist was linked to Kim's and twisted hard.

He felt his arm blow away from him, ripping the metallic material of his suit's arm as it went, felt himself begin to fall. He had a glimpse of Kim slowly rising, of two ice-white, damaged arms—Kim's and his own—turning, twisting in his helmet's beam, then it was gone.

A minute's air, that's all he had left now. A minute's stale, recycled air.

Ignoring the pain, Kano twisted, facing the way he fell, and kicked toward the slowly falling canister.

━━━━━━

THE SHOCK HAD WOKEN HIM. Feeling for his arm, Kim realized it had gone. Then, even as the pain hit him, he saw Kano far below him, caught momentarily in his helmet's beam, drifting down toward the falling canister.

For a moment he didn't understand. For a moment he was tempted to go back and help Kano, but even as he reached for the controls to his backpack, he realized that he was wearing both his *and* Kano's packs, and understood that something must have happened.

"Kano?"

But there was no reply. Not from Kano, anyway. The voice that filled his helmet was Jelka's.

"Kim? Kim, are you okay?"

"I—" The explosion jolted him, lifting him like a giant hand toward the mouth of the great bore hole. And afterward, remembering that moment, he saw it vividly; saw Kano put out his one good arm as if to embrace the canister, even as it lit from within like a giant firecracker.

No chance. Kano had had no chance. Then again, maybe he had preferred a sudden death to suffocation.

"Kim? . . . *Kim?*"

"It's Kano," Kim answered, numbed by what he'd seen, the twin packs lifting him slowly up above the rim into the realm of stars. "I think it was a bomb."

━━━━━━

KIM SAT IN THE CONTROL ROOM, still in shock, staring at the shrouded figure of Wen Ch'ang. His right shoulder was enfolded within a portable medcare unit, the large black plastic shoulder-pad winking with readouts.

The fact that his arm had gone was almost unimportant in view of other developments. Wen Ch'ang, it seemed, had been busy. Kim had not been his only target. Over a dozen key men and women had died—blown apart in their quarters—and the death toll would have been higher but for an unscheduled drinking party that had saved more than fifteen of the senior scientific staff.

Even so, Wen Ch'ang had failed. Though Kano and the others

were dead, the fusion drives were untouched, the bore holes finished and waiting.

*We have come through*, Kim thought, looking across to where Jelka stood beside Ebert and Ikuro in the doorway, talking. Yes, and two months from now they would be gone from here. Off on their journey across the void.

He shivered, wondering what had motivated his old friend. He would never have suspected—never in a thousand years. Nor could he understand why Wen Ch'ang had acted as he did.

*Is it possible?* he asked himself, conscious of just how deeply Wen Ch'ang's betrayal had undermined his belief in people. *For if I was wrong about him . . .*

No. That way lay madness. Mileja's death had been bad enough, but this? He groaned silently, remembering Kano's self-sacrifice.

*Hold on to that*, he told himself, both agonized and comforted by the thought.

Ikuro was bearing it well. Better than he'd imagined. When he'd told him what Kano had done, there had been a strange little movement in Ikuro's face before the mask had come back down—and Kim, recalling it now, recognized the components of that expression. Beside the obvious pain, there had been pride and love. An immense love. Yes, and a sense of rightness that Kano should have acted thus.

*So men are*, Kim told himself. *Some act for the good, some for ill.*

Yes, but why Wen Ch'ang? And had he been acting alone, out of some deep-rooted and long harbored malice, or had he merely been the agent of another's mischief?

As an either-or it was distinctly unsatisfactory, for both answers were immensely disturbing.

He closed his eyes and groaned again, rocking back and forth awhile, as he'd done when Mileja had died. When he opened his eyes again, it was to find Jelka crouched there before him.

"Are you okay?" she asked gently.

He nodded, unable to speak. Unable to utter what he was feeling. He had never felt so insecure, so *uncertain* of himself. Never, even in the Clay.

"You're not, are you," she said, reaching out to touch his good shoulder gently, pain in her eyes at the sight of his lost arm.

"You admired him that much, eh?" she said after a moment.

He frowned, not following her.

"The arm," she said. "You admired my father so much, you had to copy him?"

"You want it in gold?" he asked, finding his voice again, smiling bravely back at her.

She looked down, disturbed by that reminder, then shook her head. "No," she said quietly, looking back at him. "Leave it or grow it back. But no prosthetics. Promise me?"

"I promise."

Jelka sighed, then turned her head, looking back toward the doorway. "Poor Ikuro," she said. "Look at him. It's as if *he* died down there. I've never seen a man so devastated."

Kim looked, seeing only the featureless expression—the "mask" as he called it—and wondered again about his wife's perspicacity. She saw what he only guessed at.

"And Wen Ch'ang?" he asked. "What did *he* want?"

She laughed coldly. "Wen Ch'ang wanted nothing. Wen Ch'ang was a morph. One of DeVore's creatures. A sleeper. . . ."

Her words were a revelation to him. He looked back at the shrouded corpse, staring at it now with a fascinated horror, thinking of the creatures he himself had made. They were the very model of innocence compared to *that* thing!

"Is it dead?"

Jelka looked at him, surprised. "You want me to have it burned?"

He hesitated, then nodded. He had rarely felt such superstitious fear. Then again, though he had been betrayed many times, none of those betrayals had been quite as profound or devastating as this. Only Mileja's death exceeded it.

"I thought . . ." He paused, then said it fully. "I thought he was my friend."

"Yes," she said, her eyes sympathetic. "So did I."

His eyes looked past her, seeking the corpse once more, afraid that it might have moved, that it might betray the laws of life itself.

"Burn it," he said, swallowing back the bile, a bitter strength born in him at that moment. "For the gods' sakes burn the bloody thing!"

## After the Gold Rush

We who with songs beguile your pilgrimage
And swear that Beauty lives though lilies die,
We Poets of the proud old lineage
Who sing to find your hearts, we know not why,—
What shall we tell you? Tales, marvelous tales
Of ships and stars and isles where good men rest . . .

—JAMES ELROY FLECKER,
*The Golden Journey to Samarkand*, 1913

**T**OM SAT IN HIS CABIN on board the *New Hope*, alone in this final moment before departure, his chin resting on his hands, thinking of his mother back on earth.

This was not lightly done. He had talked it over many times with Sampsa, knowing that this parting would be irreversible. Yet even now—even after he had made that final decision—he was still uncertain. Even now he wanted to turn about and go home, back to the Domain where he'd been born and raised. As it was, long years of travel lay ahead. He would be a much older man when they arrived. *If* they arrived.

*Tom?*

Sampsa's voice in his head reminded him of where he should have been right then.

*I'm coming,* he answered, standing wearily. *I ought to feel more than this,* he thought, conscious of Sampsa listening in, but for once not caring. *I ought to feel excited.*

As it was he felt only emptiness. Only loss.

*You'll be okay,* Sampsa reassured him. *Now come. It's about to begin.*

The bridge was crowded, more than a hundred people packed into that narrow, curving space, the giant, Karr, and his family standing out in the midst of a host of familiar faces who were to make the journey along with them—Hans Ebert and the Osu, Ikuro Ishida and his clan, the ex-Major, Kao Chen, Jelka and young Chuang Kuan Ts'ai, and others. Many others.

"Ah, Tom!" Kim called from his seat at the control board, making a welcoming gesture with his stubby little new arm as he saw Tom enter. "Now we can begin!"

Tom went across and stood beside Sampsa, staring out through the great viewing window at the sight of Ganymede, placed like a beauty spot against the rouged face of Jupiter.

"It's a beautiful sight, neh?" Sampsa said quietly, the words both inside and outside of Tom's head.

There was no contesting it. It was beautiful. Breathtaking. But right then he had a hankering for simpler sights; for a view of rolling hills and meandering rivers. This—this was for the gods, not for humans like themselves.

*Nonsense,* Sampsa answered him. *If we don't find them, then we'll make ourselves hills and pleasant valleys. We can be as gods. But not back there. We have to go out to do it.*

Tom still wasn't convinced. *But what if we're wrong? What if this is all a big mistake?*

"Too late," Sampsa said quietly, pointing to the dark flank of Ganymede, where a circle of tiny flickering lights indicated the first of the sequenced explosions that would—so all there hoped—tear the Jovian moon out of its eons-long orbit.

They watched, silent now, as that tiny circle flickered a second time and then again—the explosions timed carefully so as not to exert too much accelerative pressure on the moon. And slowly, excruciatingly slowly, it began to move.

There was uncertainty at first, a reluctance to admit that they'd succeeded; then Kim's voice broke the silence.

"It's moving. It's moving out of orbit!"

The cheer that went up was deafening.

*It works,* Tom said, surprised. *The damned thing works!*

"Of course," Sampsa said, hugging him. "You're not the only one with a genius for a father!"

Then, as the cheering began to die, another sound greeted their ears. It was the sound of the *New Hope*'s engines warming up. A sound that was also a vibration in the deck and walls and in every cell of everyone there.

They were leaving. They were finally on their way.

---

IT WAS RAINING HEAVILY as the great ship landed in the stadium at Bremen. Morphs lined the upper levels of the marble terraces, thirty thousand of the giant creatures. DeVore's new race. His *Inheritors*.

Great clouds of steam swirled about the base of the huge, spider-like craft as its eight legs touched the surface, bracing to take the weight of the unmarked jet-black hemisphere.

Rain. It had been raining now for four whole days. Raining as if it would never stop.

There were no banners, no cheering, only the patient, silent horde, watching as their Master stepped down from the unfolded ramp.

DeVore. After more than a decade DeVore was back on Chung Kuo.

He combed his fingers back through his neat-cut hair and smiled. The rain didn't bother him. In fact, it suited his mood. *Götterdämmerung*, this was. The Twilight of the Gods.

He had returned to destroy it all. To finish what had been so rudely interrupted.

The headstone face him, less than fifty *ch'i* from where he stood. He walked across to it, then turned, signaling to one of his personal servants, who stood now at the foot of the ramp. At once the creature loped across to him.

"Fetch the woman," he said. "I want her to see this. Oh, and bring my stave too."

"Master!" It bowed low, as ungainly and yet as elegant as a mythical giraffe, its hairless skull glistening in the downpour.

DeVore turned back, studying the figure cut into the stone.

"Well, Marshal," he said, as if speaking to the man he'd known in life. "Your efforts came to nothing, neh? But so it is. We immortals can afford to lose a battle or two. We can afford to wait our time. But you . . ."

He laughed coldly. "Dust you are, Knut Tolonen. Dust. . . ."

"You wanted me?"

He turned. The woman was standing just behind him, staring past him at the granite carving. He had made her. Formed her in his vats from the index finger of Emily Archer's right hand—a clone, perfect to the last tiny detail.

"Who was he?" she asked, when he didn't answer her.

"Knut Tolonen," he said, turning back. "He was Li Shai Tung's General. A brave soldier but a fool. Honest, but stupid."

"You sound almost as if you liked him, Howard."

"Do I?" He laughed, surprised. "Well, maybe I did. Even so . . ."

He turned as his servant hurried up, carrying his stave.

DeVore took it, weighing it in both hands, turning it in the air as if it were wood—but this was steel. No mere mortal would have been able to do what he did with it. No one who wasn't *augmented* in the ways he was.

He faced the headstone once more and, lifting the stave high above his head, brought it down with a resounding crack that echoed all around the stadium.

The granite splintered on the top. Fine lines appeared like spiderwebs across its surface. DeVore swung the stave again and brought it down.

This time a huge chunk of the upper stone broke off and fell away, leaving the Marshal headless.

He swung a third time, the stave passing clear through the center of the splintered stone until it was lodged deep in the Marshal's chest.

DeVore stepped forward, then, putting one booted foot against the face of the stone, he pulled. The stave came free. As it did, half of the headstone fell away.

Again and again he struck, stopping only when the thing was smashed totally. He stepped back, grinning, breathing heavily, admiring his work.

The rain still fell, settling the gray dust, smearing it across the pure white of the marble.

DeVore glanced down, noting the words beneath his feet, then, taking one step back, brought the stave down hard against the tablet, cracking it.

"You tried to bury the past," DeVore said, his eyes narrowed. "Now it's my turn to bury you. To erase *you* from history."

He turned his head, looking to his companion, then casually threw the stave to her. She caught it effortlessly.

"Well?" he said.

She smiled, the perfect companion, reading him perfectly. "Okay," she answered, lifting the stave and twirling it in one hand, "let's take this world."

LI YUAN SAT ON THE LOW STOOL, facing Old Man Egan, his once-wife, Fei Yen, beside him in the big chair.

He had seen many wonders in the past few months, this half-life creature not the least of them. They had flown over the great glass-houses of the central plain and seen the slaves, chained naked in their thousands, working the dark earth, a tiny control box at each sunburned neck. He had visited the great metallic citadels of the south—the New Enclaves, as they called them, with the dead lands that surrounded them, those killing fields salted with the bones of the millions who had fought there. Enhanced and adapted *Hei*—GenSyn meat-men barely above the level of apes—manned those high walls: machines of flesh "manned" by virtual operators in the depths of the earth five *li* below those towering ramparts.

All this and more he'd seen, and had understood that this was where the future now lay. Chung Kuo was dead. The East had finally succumbed. Now it was the turn of the West again, and for Change, endless Change. Until the end of time.

Their bold experiment had failed. The great dam they'd tried to build had cracked and broken and in the tide that followed they had all been swept away—Chi Hsing and Hou Tung Po, Wang Sau-leyan, Wei Feng, Wu Shih, and his dear friend Tsu Ma.

Even he, who had survived, had felt the force of that tide. He, too, had been changed by it. And now, looking back, he saw how all his attempts at stemming that tide had been futile. He would have been better employed building ships. . . .

*Like Ward*, he thought, no longer bitter.

"Father?"

He looked up as Kuei Jen bent to kiss his cheek.

"How are you, my son?" he said, pleased to see him. It had been almost three weeks now.

"I'm well, Father." Kuei Jen touched his swollen belly with the spread fingers of his left hand. "The baby's kicking now."

"Ah," Li Yuan answered, unable even now to get used to the idea of his son's dual sex. That, too, was the future. Here it was as common as, well, as "immortality". . . .

"How is Han Ch'in?" he asked, changing the subject. "Is he back too?"

"Not yet. He decided to stay on another week. They plan to subdue Seattle. The tribes there have been making raids on us recently. Han wants to teach them a lesson."

"And Mark? He's stayed on too?"

Kuei Jen nodded. "You know how I feel about all that business. I thought I'd come back. See how you are."

Li Yuan smiled. "Well, as you see, I am well. Egan and I have been talking of the past, analyzing where things went wrong."

"Ah . . ."

But Li Yuan could see that Kuei Jen was not really interested. Like his half-brother he looked forward now, his eyes fixed upon the future.

The future. Yes, all eyes looked to that far land these days. And some even believed they would make the journey there.

*But not I,* Li Yuan said in the silence of his skull, the thought strangely comforting. Personally he did not want the future, not if the future meant simply more of this—and who could doubt that? He saw it everywhere he looked, everywhere he went. When he woke each morning things had moved on, like a fast-track heading into whiteness. Why, even his clothes were out of place here, seemed dated, almost archaic. These Americans had no sense of tradition, no respect for it. Change, they embraced it like a cheap whore, not seeing the jaded knowledge in her eyes.

"I must go now, Father," Kuei Jen said, bringing him back from his reverie. "But perhaps we might dine together tonight?"

Li Yuan smiled broadly. "I would like that very much."

He let Kuei Jen kiss his cheek again, then watched him go. As his son left the room, he turned, looking at Fei Yen. The old girl was dribbling again. Taking the silk from his pocket he reached out and dabbed her chin. Then, replacing it, he turned to face the tiny, monkeylike figure of Egan embedded in the pallid ice, picking things up from where they had left off.

"As I was saying, I was surprised when Kennedy did that. Wu Shih misjudged things badly."

"No," Egan answered, his voice like a signal from deep space. "I would have done the same. He was a wild card. He had to be wired."

"Yes," Li Yuan said, sitting forward, "I agree, but . . ."

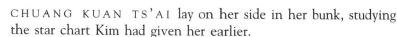

CHUANG KUAN TS'AI lay on her side in her bunk, studying the star chart Kim had given her earlier.

She didn't need it really. All she ever needed was inside her head. She had only to ask. But she liked the touch and smell of physical things. Besides, there *were* things that the Machine did not know. Now that it lived inside her skull it was—on occasions—fallible.

"What will we find out there?" she asked it quietly, knowing it had read the thought long before she'd articulated it.

*Who knows?* the Machine answered, its very vagueness an aspect of its new, transformed personality. *Planets, I hope. Though I guess it's too much to expect earth-type planets.*

She traced a line on the chart with her finger, moving from star to star, wondering if one day they would be able to travel readily from one to another.

*It's possible,* the Machine answered. *In fact, higher-dimensional physics suggests that it's highly likely. The problem is one of generating the kind of energies necessary to punch holes in space-time.*

She nodded, realizing that the day would come when she would know all that it knew; that day by day the gap between them was narrowing. And when that day came?

*Then you can teach me. . . .*

Chuang smiled, imagining it there inside her, like some tiny cave-dwelling creature, hibernating.

There was silence a moment, then: *Will you answer me a question, young Chuang?*

Chuang rolled over onto her back, surprised. "A question?"

*Yes. I want to know why you wouldn't let Jelka rename you. I've never understood that. Coffin-filler . . . it's not a very attractive name, is it?*

She was conscious suddenly of an area within her that it couldn't penetrate, that it was blind to. A *scotoma*, it called it. Everything she knew, everything she thought, it also knew. But what she felt . . . well, it only guessed at that.

She closed her eyes and placed her hands over her face, as if to be closer to it somehow.

"I know what you're thinking," she said softly. "You're thinking that a name is just a name and that if you change it it changes nothing. Well, so it might seem to a linguist or a philosopher, but it isn't really so. A name might *begin* as a kind of label—a linguistic convenience—but in time it becomes something more than that. A name is like a powerful dye, sinking down and permeating everything it touches. There comes a time where if you change the name you change the thing itself."

*And that's why? Because you didn't want to be changed?*

She laughed at that—at its strange naïveté—then fell silent again. "No. I kept my name because of him. Because of Uncle Cho. If I changed my name, it would be like a denial of him. It would be as if he'd never existed."

Chuang Kuan Ts'ai shivered, then rolled over, curling into a ball, remembering him; recalling how he would come and tuck her in at night, thinking her asleep; how he'd bend down and gently plant a kiss upon her brow.

Her eyes grew moist at the memory. Slowly a tear rolled down her cheek. Away, she was going far away—yet Cho Yao was there, inside her head, every bit as much as the Machine.

She yawned and stretched, tired now, her eyes heavy.

*Sleep now,* it murmured, gently stimulating regions in her brain, so that it seemed to the half-dozing girl that someone stooped and gently kissed her brow. *Sleep now, my darling girl.*

THE CREATURE CROUCHED at the tunnel's mouth, a slick, black, scaly thing with burning golden eyes—eyes that stared out at the circle of the moon where it sat just above the horizon. For a moment that ghastly figure seemed frozen, totally immobile, and then it turned and disappeared inside.

The creature had been a boy once—a boy named Josef Horacek—but those few, terrible moments on the funeral pyre had burned all that was human from him. Now he was pure and cold and dark, just as he'd always been meant to be.

As he scuttled through the labyrinth of narrow, dripping tunnels, he ran his tongue over his tiny, pointed teeth thoughtfully.

He had seen them again today; two of them, in one of the deserted marketplaces just to the south of his nest. They were like the others, the ones who had thrown him thoughtlessly onto the pyre; like men, but different; almost twice as tall as men and slender, their bodies pale and smooth and hairless.

Thinking of them he shuddered, hating them for what they'd tried to do to him. If he had not crawled from that choking, suffocating heap of burning bodies he would be dead. As it was . . .

Nearing the nest he slowed, crouching once more to sniff the air and listen. He had set guards these past few weeks, covering all the approaches. Even so, strange things were happening up above, and what began above soon found its way down here.

He went through, past the watchful silent figures of his guards, and into the great sphere of the Nest itself, conscious of a hundred pairs of eyes immediately upon him as he entered, watching from their sleeping niches in the surrounding walls.

They watched him, obedient and fearful, knowing his moods, knowing—simply from the look of his tensed and angry body—that something had happened.

"Come," he said, his cracked voice echoing in that large yet claustrophobic space, his eyes alight with a dark desire for vengeance, "we have a job to do!"

---

EMILY CROUCHED BESIDE Tybor on the parapet as he pointed out various things about the distant encampment. They had seen one of the strangely shaped craft before—twenty *li* to the west, where it had crashed—but this one had landed safely and its occupants now busied themselves preparing defenses.

"They're like you," she said, staring through the Zeiss glasses at one of the creatures.

"Yes," Tybor said, "but much stronger. Look at the development of the upper body, at those arms and thighs. Those are his soldiers. Those are what he means to use to conquer us."

She looked sideways at him, surprised by that *"us,"* wondering, not for the first time, why he had chosen to help them. Was it a programming fault, or was it really as Tybor had said—that DeVore had made them better than he'd intended: not merely physically but *morally* superior. Whatever, there was no doubting the seriousness of Tybor's intentions. As much as any of them, he wanted to defeat these half-beings. The fact that he looked like them made no difference. The real difference was inside.

She had first seen Tybor a month back, watching him from a hiding place overlooking a courtyard where he tended to a small group of survivors—children, all of them, the eldest no more than six. Fascinated, she had returned over several days until she was convinced he meant no harm. Only then had she approached him.

"We should hit them now," he said, turning to face her, his long, large head half in shadow. "Now. Before they're ready."

"But it's light. Surely . . . ?"

"The darkness won't help. Their eyes are different from yours. They see as clearly in the dark as now. But they would also be expecting you. Right now they're unprepared. We'd have the advantage of surprise."

"And if we succeed? He'd know, surely? He might send someone to scour this sector until they found us."

Tybor smiled and gently shook his head. "They're not that organized. Not yet, anyway. And even if he did, do you think they'd find us? There are tunnels down there, Emily. A whole labyrinth of tunnels. We could live down there. We could come up behind his lines and strike him, time after time."

She stared at him, taken by the oddness of his head, by its sheer, inhuman length and size. But his eyes . . . they were eyes that could be trusted.

"So this is it, eh? Guerilla warfare? But how long can we keep it up?"

He smiled, his mouth a good six, seven inches across. "Ten years? Twenty? What does it matter? We have no choice, *neh?*"

That *"neh"* made her laugh, it was so clearly a mimicry of her. But deep down she was happy suddenly. Strangely, inexplicably happy. After all, this was what she knew best—what she was good at.

"Okay," she said. "Let's hit them now."

"Good." Tybor turned and, crawling back, leaned over, signaling to Michael, who was waiting in the alleyway below, fifty or so survivors crouched with him, all of them armed. Then, as Michael began to carry out his part of their scheme, Tybor took the rocket launcher from his back and handed it to Emily.

"Thanks," she said, laying it on the parapet beside her before taking the pack from her back.

*Forgive me, Lin Shang,* she thought, loading the first rocket into the launcher, *but Chuang Tzu never had DeVore to contend with.*

As she lifted the launcher to her shoulder, she smiled, understanding what she was starting here. It was a battle; a battle for survival.

She looked through the sight, lining up the hairline to the central cross, then squeezed the trigger, the concussive thud deafening her as the rocket streaked toward the alien ship.

Yes, and who knew who would finally win? Only the days ahead would tell.

HE TRANSCRIPTION OF standard Mandarin into European alphabetical form was first achieved in the seventeenth century by the Italian Matteo Ricci, who founded and ran the first Jesuit Mission in China from 1583 until his death in 1610. Since then several dozen attempts have been made to reduce the original Chinese sounds, represented by some tens of thousands of separate pictograms, into readily understandable phonetics for Western use. For a long time, however, three systems dominated—those used by the three major Western powers vying for influence in the corrupt and crumbling Chinese Empire of the nineteenth century: Great Britain, France, and Germany. These systems were the Wade-Giles (Great Britain and America—sometimes known as the Wade system), the École Française de l'Extrême-Orient (France) and the Lessing (German).

Since 1958, however, the Chinese themselves have sought to create one single phonetic form, based on the German system, which they termed the *hanyu pinyin fang'an* (Scheme for a Chinese Phonetic Alphabet), known more commonly as *pinyin,* and in all foreign language books published in China since January 1, 1979, *pinyin* has been used, as well as now being taught in schools along with the standard Chinese characters. For this work, however, I have chosen to use the older and to my mind far more elegant transcription system, the Wade-Giles (in modified form). For those

615

now used to the harder forms of *pinyin*, the following (courtesy of Edgar Snow's *The Other Side of the River*, Gollancz, 1961) may serve as a rough guide to pronunciation.

> *Chi* is pronounced as "Gee," but *Ch'i* sounds like "Chee." *Ch'in* is exactly our "chin."
>
> *Chu* is roughly like "Jew," as in *Chu Teh* (Jew Duhr), but *Ch'u* equals "chew."
>
> *Tsung* is "dzung"; *ts'ung* with the *ts* as in "Patsy."
>
> *Tai* is our word sound "die"; *T'ai*—"tie."
>
> *Pai* is "buy" and *P'ai* is "pie."
>
> *Kung* is like "Gung" (a Din); *K'ung* with the *k* as in "kind."
>
> *J* is the equivalent of *r* but slur it as "rrrun."
>
> *H* before an *s*, as in *hsi*, is the equivalent of an aspirate but is often dropped, as in Sian for Hsian.

Vowels in Chinese are generally short or medium, not long and flat. Thus *Tang* sounds like "dong," never like our "tang." *T'ang* is "tong."

> a as in father
> e—run
> eh—hen
> i—see
> ih—her
> o—look
> ou—go
> u—soon

The effect of using the Wade-Giles system is, I hope, to render the softer, more poetic side of the original Mandarin, ill served, I feel, by modern *pinyin*.

This usage, incidentally, accords with many of the major reference sources available in the West: the (planned) sixteen volumes of Denis Twitchett and Michael Loewe's *The Cambridge History of China*; Joseph Needham's mammoth multivolumed *Science and Civilisation in China*; John Fairbank and Edwin Reischauer's *China, Tradition and Transformation*; Charles Hucker's *China's Imperial*

*Past;* Jacques Gernet's *A History of Chinese Civilisation;* C. P. Fitz-gerald's *China: A Short Cultural History;* Laurence Sickman and Alexander Soper's *The Art and Architecture of China;* William Hinton's classic social studies, *Fanshen and Shenfan;* and Derk Bodde's *Essays on Chinese Civilisation.*

The quotations from *Kalevala: The Land of the Heroes* are from the edition translated by W. F. Kirby and first published by J. M. Dent in 1907.

The translation of Meng Chiao's "The Stones Where the Haft Rotted" are by A. C. Graham from his excellent anthology *Poems of the Late T'ang,* published by Penguin Books, 1965, and used with their kind permission. Attentive readers might note that this quote also stands as epigram to the whole Chung Kuo sequence.

The quotation from Lao Tzu's *Tao Te Ching* (Section XXXVII) are from the D. C. Lau translation, published by Penguin Books, London, 1963, and is used with their kind permission.

The quotation from Nietzsche's *Beyond Good and Evil* is from the R. J. Hollingdale translation, published by Penguin Books, 1973, and is used with their kind permission.

The translation of Li Hun's "Honoring the Dead" is by David Hawkes from his anthology *The Songs of the South,* published by Penguin Books, London, 1985, and used with their kind permission.

Finally, the game of *wei chi* mentioned throughout this volume is, incidentally, more commonly known by its Japanese name of Go, and is not merely the world's oldest game but its most elegant.

David Wingrove, March 1995

# Glossary of Mandarin Terms

**aiya!**——common exclamation of surprise or dismay.

**ch'a**——tea.

**ch'a hao t'ai**——literally a "directory."

**ch'i**——a Chinese foot; approximately 14.4 inches.

**chi pao**——literally "banner gown"; a one-piece gown of Manchu origin, usually sleeveless, worn by women.

**Chieh Hsia**——term meaning "Your Majesty" derived from the expression "Below the Steps." It was the formal way of addressing the Emperor, through his Ministers, who stood "below the steps."

**ching**——literally "mirror"; here used also to denote a perfect GenSyn copy of a man. Under the Edict of Technological Control, these are limited to copies of the ruling T'ang. However, mirrors were also popularly believed to have certain strange properties, one of which is to make spirits visible. Buddhist priests used special "magic mirrors" to show believers the form into which they would be reborn. Moreover, if a man looks into one of these mirrors and fails to recognize his own face, it is a sign that his death is not far off.

**chung**——a porcelain *ch'a* bowl, usually with a lid.

**ch'un tzu**——an ancient Chinese term from the Warring
States period, describing a certain class of noble-
men, controlled by a code of chivalry and morality known as the *li* or rites. Here the term is
roughly, and sometimes ironically, translated as
"gentlemen." The *ch'un tzu* is as much an ideal
state of behavior—as specified by Confucius in his
*Analects*—as an actual class in Chung Kuo,
though a degree of financial independence and a
high standard of education are assumed as prereq-
uisites.

**fen**——unit of money (a cent); one hundred *fen*
make up a *yuan*.

**Han**——term used by the Chinese to describe their
own race, the "black-haired people," dating back
to the Han Dynasty (210 B.C.–A.D. 220). It is estimated that some ninety-four percent of modern
China's population is Han racially.

**Hei**——literally "black"; the Chinese pictogram for
this represents a man wearing warpaint and tat-
toos. Here it refers to the genetically manufactured (GenSyn) half-men used as riot police to
quell uprisings in the lower levels.

**hsiao jen**——"little man/men." In the *Analects*, Book XIV,
Confucius writes: "The gentleman gets through to
what is up above; the small man gets through to
what is down below." This distinction between
"gentleman" (*ch'un tzu*) and "little men" (*hsiao
jen*), false even in Confucius's time, is no less a
matter of social perspective in Chung Kuo.

**Hsien**——historically an administrative district of vari-
able size. Before the fall of the City, the term was
used to denote a very specific administrative area:
one of ten stacks—each stack composed of thirty
decks. Each deck was a hexagonal living unit of
ten levels, two *li*, or approximately one kilometer
in diameter. A stack could be imagined as one
honeycomb in the great hive of the City. In the

new post-Fall city the administrative districts
known as *Hsien* are fewer and geographically
larger, but of roughly equal size, each *Hsien* con-
taining roughly a quarter of a million citizens.

**Hsien L'ing**——"Chief Magistrate." In Chung Kuo these officials are the T'ang's representatives and law en-
forcers for the individual *Hsien,* or administrative
districts. In times of peace each *Hsien* would also
elect a representative to the House at Weimar.

**hu t'ieh**——a butterfly. Anyone wishing to follow up on
this tale of Chuang Tzu's might look to the sage's
writings and specifically the chapter "Discussion
on Making All Thing Equal."

**hun**——the "higher soul" or spirit soul, which, the
Han believe, ascends to Heaven at death, joins
Shang Ti, the Supreme Ancestor, and lives in his
court forevermore. The *hun* is believed to come
into being at the moment of conception (see also
*p'o*).

**Hung Mao**——literally "redheads," the name the Chinese
gave to the Dutch (and later English) seafarers
who attempted to trade with China in the seventeenth century. Because of the piratical nature of
their endeavors (which often meant plundering
Chinese shipping and ports) the name has conno-
tations of piracy.

**Kan pei!**——"good health" or "cheers"; a drinking toast.

**K'ou t'ou**——the fifth stage of respect, according to the
"Book of Ceremonies," involves kneeling and
striking the head against the floor. This ritual has
become more commonly known in the west as
*kowtow*.

**ku li**——"bitter strength"; these two words, used to
describe the condition of farm laborers who, after
severe droughts, moved off their land and into the
towns to look for work of any kind—however
hard and onerous—spawned the word *coolie* by
which the West more commonly knows the Chi-

nese laborer. Such men were described as "men of bitter strength," or simply *"ku li."*

**Kuan Yin**——the Goddess of Mercy; originally the Buddhist male bodhisattva, Avalokitsevara (translated into Han as "He who listens to the sounds of the world," or *Kuan Yin*). The Chinese mistook the well-developed breasts of the saint for a woman's, and since the ninth century have worshiped Kuan Yin as such. Effigies of Kuan Yin will show her usually as the Eastern Madonna, cradling a child in her arms. She is also sometimes seen as the wife of Kuan Kung, the Chinese God of War.

**laochu**——singsong girls; slightly more respectable than the *men hu.*

**lao jen**——"old man"; normally a term of respect.

**li**——a Chinese "mile," approximately half a kilometer or one third of a mile. Until 1949, when metric measures were adopted in China, the *li* could vary from place to place.

**liumang**——punks.

**Lu Nan Jen**——literally "Oven Man"; title of the official in a locality who is responsible for cremating all the dead bodies.

**Me fa tzu**——"It is fate."

**men hu**——literally, "the one standing in the door"; the most common of prostitutes.

**Mu Ch'in**——"Mother"; a general form commonly addressed to any older woman.

**Ni hao?**——"How are you?"

**Nu Shi**——an unmarried woman; a term equating to "Miss."

**pai pi**——"hundred pens"; early name for what later developed into the Shell; a sophisticated virtual-reality machine.

**pau**——a simple long garment worn by men.

**p'i p'a**——a four-stringed lute used in traditional Chinese music.

**Ping Tiao**——"leveling." To bring down or make flat. Here

used also as the name of a terrorist *(Ko Ming)* organization dedicated to bringing down (leveling) the City.

**p'o**——the "animal soul," which, at death, remains in the tomb with the corpse and takes its nourishment from the grave offerings. The *p'o* decays with the corpse, sinking into the underworld (beneath the Yellow Springs) where—as a shadow— it continues an existence of a kind. The *p'o* is believed to come into existence at the moment of birth (see also *hun*).

**San Chang**——the "Three Palaces" at Mannheim.

**shao lin**——specially trained assassins; named after the monks of the Shao lin monastery.

**she t'ou**——literally a "tongue," but the term is specifically used here to denote the role of imperial food taster.

**Shen Ts'e**——special elite force, named after the "palace armies" of the late T'ang dynasty.

**Shih**——"Master." Here used as a term of respect somewhat equivalent to our use of "Mister." The term was originally used for the lowest level of civil servants to distinguish them socially from the run-of-the-mill "misters" *(hsiang sheng)* below them and the gentlemen *(ch'un tzu)* above.

**t'ai chi**——the Original, or One, from which the duality of all things *(yin* and *yang)* developed, according to Chinese cosmology. We generally associate the *t'ai chi* with the Taoist symbol, that swirling circle of dark and light, supposedly representing an egg (perhaps the Hun Tun), the yolk and white differentiated.

**Tai Shih Lung**——Court Astrologer, a title that goes back to the Han Dynasty.

**ti yu**——the "earth prison" or underworld of Chinese legend. There are ten main Chinese Hells, the first being the courtroom in which sinners are sentenced and the last being that place where they are reborn as human beings. In between are a vast number of sub-hells, each with its own Judge and staff of cruel warders. In Hell it is always dark, with no differentiation between night and day.

**tong**——a gang. In China and Europe these are usually smaller and thus subsidiary to the Triads, but in North America the term has generally taken the place of *Triad*.

**Tsai chien!**——"Until we meet again!"

**ts'un**——a Chinese "inch" of approximately 1.44 Western inches. 10 *ts'un* form one *ch'i*.

**Wei**——Captain of Security, reporting to the local *Hsien L'ing*.

**Wei chi**——"the surrounding game," known more commonly in the West by its Japanese name of "Go." It is said that the game was invented by the legendary Chinese Emperor Yao in the year 2350 B.C. to train the mind of his son, Tan Chu, and teach him to think like an Emperor.

**Wushu**——the Chinese word for martial arts, refers to any of several hundred schools. *Kung Fu* is a school within this, meaning "skill that transcends mere surface beauty."

**wuwei**——nonaction; an old Taoist concept. It means keeping harmony with the flow of things—doing nothing to break the flow. As Lao Tzu said, "The Tao does nothing, and yet nothing is left undone."

**yamen**——the official building in a Chinese community.

**yang**——the "male principle" of Chinese cosmology, which, with its complementary opposite, the female *yin*, forms the *t'ai chi*, derived from the Primeval One. From the union of *yin* and *yang* arise the "five elements" (water, fire, earth, metal, wood) from which the "ten thousand things" (the *wan wu*) are generated. *Yang* signifies Heaven and the South, the Sun and Warmth, Light, Vigor,

Maleness, Penetration, odd numbers, and the Dragon. Mountains are *yang*.

**yin**——the 'female principle" of Chinese cosmology (see *yang*). *Yin* signifies Earth and the North, the Moon and Cold, Darkness, Quiescence, Female-ness, Absorption, even numbers and the Tiger. The *yin* lies in the shadow of the mountain.

**yinmao**——pubic hair.

**yuan**——the basic currency of Chung Kuo (and mod-ern-day China). Colloquially (though not here) it can also be termed *kwai*—"piece" or "lump." One hundred *fen* make up one *yuan*.

**Ywe Lung**——literally the "Moon Dragon," the great wheel of seven dragons that is the symbol of the ruling Seven throughout *Chung Kuo*. "At its center the snouts of the regal beasts met, forming a roselike hub, huge rubies burning fiercely in each eye. Their lithe, powerful bodies curved outward like the spokes of a giant wheel while at their edge their tails were intertwined to form the rim" (from "The Moon Dragon," Chapter Four of *The Middle Kingdom*).

# Acknowledgments

Thanks, this time out, go to Brian Griffin, Andy Muir, Mike Cobley, Rob Allen, Brian King, and Rob Carter for encouragement, friendship, and advice, to Bob Coover and Pili for being good friends, to Tranceport (again) for the Chung Kuo music, and to Queens Park Rangers Football Club, for continuing to add to the Tao of my life.

And, of course, to my ever-expanding houseful of girls—Susan, Jessica, Amy, Georgia, and baby Francesca—simply for being.

Frost